Y0-BPW-769

Francesca Caccini
at the Medici Court

WOMEN IN CULTURE AND SOCIETY

A series edited by Catharine R. Stimpson

FRANCESCA CACCINI
at the Medici Court

Music and the Circulation of Power

S̲uzanne̲ G. C̲usick̲

With a Foreword by Catharine R. Stimpson

The University of Chicago Press | Chicago and London

SUZANNE G. CUSICK is professor of music at New York University and the author of *Valerio Dorico: Music Printer in Sixteenth-Century Rome.*

The University of Chicago Press, Chicago 60637
The University of Chicago Press, Ltd., London
© 2009 by The University of Chicago
All rights reserved. Published 2009
Printed in the United States of America

18 17 16 15 14 13 12 11 10 09   1 2 3 4 5

ISBN-13: 978-0-226-13212-9   (cloth)
ISBN-10: 0-226-13212-9   (cloth)

This book has received the Weiss/Brown Publication Subvention Award from the Newberry Library. The award supports the publication of outstanding works of scholarship that cover European civilization before 1700 in the areas of music, theater, French or Italian literature, or cultural studies. It is made to commemorate the career of Howard Mayer Brown.

Library of Congress Cataloging-in-Publication Data

Cusick, Suzanne G.
    Francesca Caccini at the Medici court : music and the circulation of power / Suzanne G. Cusick ; with a foreword by Catharine R. Stimpson.
        p. cm. — (Women in culture and society)
    Includes bibliographical references and index.
    ISBN-13: 978-0-226-13212-9 (cloth : alk. paper)
    ISBN-10: 0-226-13212-9 (cloth : alk. paper) 1. Caccini, Francesca, 1587–ca. 1640.
2. Medici, House of. 3. Women composers—Italy—Biography. 4. Feminism and music—Italy. 5. Music—Italy—Florence—16th century—History and criticism. 6. Music—Italy—Florence—17th century—History and criticism. 7. Florence (Italy)—Social life and customs.
I. Title.
    ML410.C19C87 2009
    780.92—dc22
    [B]

                                                                    2008012693

♾ The paper used in this publication meets the minimum requirements of the American National Standard for Information Sciences—Permanence of Paper for Printed Library Materials, ANSI Z39.48-1992.

for Margaret
(chi m'imparadisc'il core)

Contents

Foreword

"Musicians wrestle everywhere," Emily Dickinson once wrote. "All day— among the crowded air / I hear the silver strife." Now Suzanne Cusick has written *Francesca Caccini at the Medici Court: Music and the Circulation of Power* about a woman of immense gifts who wrestled with her time and place. This magnificent book, the first serious study of Caccini, restores her to the crowded air of history.

Caccini was a consummate and prolific craftsman, a "virtuosa," who could unify sounds into meaningful unities. Born in 1587 in Florence, she worked, with courage and cunning and fierce intelligence, to reconcile the tensions of being a virtuous woman and making music. Caccini's family saw to the education of their very bright daughter. Both parents were musicians, her father one of the most influential of his day. He was on the staff of the Medici household, part of the dense network of relations that constituted the "famiglia" of early modern Italian courts. As such, he gave his children advantages and access to powerful people, but he embodied the difficulties, which his daughter would inherit, of being a performer whose entitlements could not keep him from being at the beck and call of noble patrons.

In 1607, Francesca too went into service in the Granducato of Tuscany. Versatile, hardworking, she was to perform by herself and in groups, compose, coach and direct, teach, and play a variety of instruments—and to do all this in churches and chambers and theatrical settings. In that same year, on the orders of the grand duchess, she married Giovanni Battista Signorini, a handsome musician confident and happy enough in his marriage to acknowledge his wife's greater economic success. They had one daughter, Margherita. Their home was Caccini's busy studio and office.

Crucially, Francesca belonged to a women's court, at first presided over by Christine de Lorraine, the wife of Ferdinando I. Christine had been well educated and trained by her grandmother, Catherine de' Medici, a queen of France. She was to be joined by her daughter-in-law Maria Magdalena d'Austria. Cusick is fascinating about the nature, culture, rituals, maneuvers, and obligations of the women's court. In theory Christine and Magdalena were to rule a female universe parallel to but separate from the male universe of urban politics, but they were to become de facto and de jure regents. As such, they exercised real power and authority. Part of Caccini's durability derived from her understanding that sound could be the sophisticated experience of "virtuous female mastery that served her women patrons' artistic and political aims" (p. 61).

By 1626, Caccini, the most prominent woman musician in Europe, was getting foreign commissions. Then Signorini died. Simultaneously, her patrons were preparing their male heir for his public role and for a shift in the public perception of the granducato's powers from a veiled gynocentrism to "unmistakably masculine ones" (p. 252). In 1627, Caccini was dispatched to Lucca to marry a musical minor nobleman, until then a bachelor, Tommaso Rafaelli. He was to die in 1630, leaving her with an infant son, an estate over which she had control, and an elevated social status. She was now a gentildonna.

In 1634, after being quarantined because of the plague, Caccini and her family returned to Tuscany. She reentered Christine's women's community. Although she no longer performed, she and Margherita seem to have participated in its cultural activities and taught the young princesses. Formidable though Cusick's research and scholarship are, and they are formidable, she cannot locate the exact date of Caccini's death, though it was probably in the 1640s. Trained by her mother, Margherita became the third generation of famous Caccini musicians, singing from her convent under the name of Suor Placida Maria.

Little has survived of the hundreds of Francesca Caccini compositions, but among them is a state spectacle, *La liberazione di Ruggiero*. Fortunately, she also left vibrant, subtle letters and a book, *Primo libro delle musiche*, a collection of solo songs and duets in the new Florentine style that is also a teaching manual. It appeared in 1618, just after the Medici began to let their musicians publish under their own names. Cusick analyzes Caccini's music and writing with rigor, clarity, and a contagious delight in Caccini's gifts and achievements.

Francesca Caccini at the Medici Court is a biography of the highest order, but it is more than that. As Francesca adventurously pushed into new terrains for creative women, so Cusick has wrestled with her hope to "stretch and reorient" the conventions of music history (p. xxvi). She uses several tools in addition to her own wit and learning: feminist theory, a framing of Caccini as a "unique existent" (p. xvii) whose life is a series of actions, and a protofeminist work by Cristoforo Bronzini about worthy women written for the elite women of the Medici court. His entry about Caccini has a vision of music as "a medium through which the social energy that sustains relationships and worlds—and that changes them—flowed." Cusick writes simply, "I have tried to be true to that vision" (p. xxi). She has succeeded brilliantly.

Catharine R. Stimpson
New York University

Preface

This book has had many moments of origin: the moment in the late 1960s when the chair of the music department at the women's college I attended told our music history class that women could not create music but could only re-create it as teachers, performers, and patrons; the day my college theory teacher invited us to laugh at the ambitions of "Mrs. Ha Ha Beach" rather than study the voice-leading of augmented sixth chords, on which he would soon test us and find in our failures proof of women's inability to deal with musical abstractions; my smart-alecky vow to cite only women composers' works, and only women musicologists' writings, in my PhD orals, to see if our all-male faculty noticed; the moment years later when a senior musicologist cautioned me that it would be professional suicide to combine the study of early music with feminism; the night a colleague maddeningly played the "kiss motif" from Verdi's *Otello* over and over across the hall from the office where I struggled to prepare a class for his college's first-ever course on women and music; and another vow, sworn at dawn over take-out coffee in New Orleans's Jackson Square, that I would respond to the call for feminist papers at the 1988 meeting of the American Musicological Society, though I had never before considered sharing my ideas about music, gender, and history in a professional community that still seemed to agree with my college teachers' condescension toward musically ambitious women.

But if my work on this book has been sustained in part by the dark energy that fuels what women's historians call "compensatory history," the book itself was conceived in love. The night my colleague played Verdi's "kiss motif" he prevented me from "hearing" the score to one of the few surviving works of musical theater from the era that gave birth to opera, Francesca Caccini's *La liberazione di Ruggiero* (1625). I had no choice but to go to the piano to play and sing through the score if I was to come up with anything intelligent to say about it the next day. I discovered music of astonishing beauty, music that stunned me with bold harmonies beneath rhythmically and melodically subtle musical speech, music with moments as magical and heartbreaking as any moment in a Verdi or Monteverdi score. This music, I thought, could tell us what it was like to be a woman musician in the early modern world—in, that is, the world that gave us opera, the assumption that women could work as singers, and the familiar character types represented in song and on stage that would sustain the emerging sex-gender system of European modernity. This music, and the circumstances that enabled this woman to leave it behind in print, could tell us things we would not otherwise know about how women experienced music and life in a time and place so central to the history of European musical culture that it has taken on the stature of myth. In these thoughts, the idea for this book was born.

Who was Francesca Caccini? A younger contemporary of Galileo, Monteverdi, and Artemisia Gentileschi (all of whom she knew) and of Shakespeare (whom she did not), she served the Medici court in Tuscany as a *musica* (all-around musician) from 1607 to 1627 and again from 1633 to 1641. She was not the only woman musician in her time, but she was unique among them for the value her contemporaries placed on her deep knowledge of that multi-faceted craft and on her work as a composer. In her long service to the Medici, Francesca composed music for at least seventeen theatrical works, all but two staged at court, along with hundreds of shorter vocal works meant for chamber performance. Very little of her music survives—one scene from the 1614 comedy *Il passatempo*, the thirty-six songs and duets published in the *Primo libro delle musiche* of 1618, and the seventy-five-minute *balletto* titled *La liberazione di Ruggiero dall'isola d'Alcina*, first produced in 1625. One of barely a half-dozen wholly sung dramatic works to survive from the first third of the seventeenth century, *La liberazione* earned Francesca posthumous fame as "the first woman composer of opera" and a permanent place in the historiography of her era.[1] Yet neither her music nor her life has been the subject of serious scholarly study until now.

"What was she like? And how did she get away with it?"

Posed by a passionately historicist colleague, these two questions distill some specific desires that a scholarly study of Francesca must satisfy. Many readers want to know what kind of woman could have had a career professionally comparable to Monteverdi's in a time when women musicians were most often imagined (if they were imagined at all) only as *virtuosa* singers likened by dazzled poets to nightingales or sirens. How did Francesca evade containment in tropes that praised female human beings for their resemblance to beautifully vocalizing animals or beautifully seductive monsters? How did she get away with that evasion, that disobedience, that defiance of social norms?

No one knows what Francesca Caccini looked like. Some of her contemporaries referred to her as "la Cecchina," or "little Francesca," suggesting that she may have been a small person. A contemporary who otherwise lavished praise on her noted that she was "little favored by the gifts of nature." [2] Coming less than a page after his praise for her younger sister Settimia for "the harmonious union of her voice's sweetness with the loveliness of her body and soul," his comment helps explain a curious silence in the poems that praise Francesca's music making. [3] None praise her beauty. For that matter, none praise the sound of her voice, as some writers did her sister's and her daughter's, or her contribution as a performer to the success of music composed by others, as some writers praised Vittoria Archilei's. Instead, they praise her synoptic mastery of her craft, a mastery that produced her music's performative power. [4] In her time, there was no higher praise.

Her letters and others' accounts suggest that Francesca could be high-spirited, irreverent, funny, passionately committed to constant study, and especially intrigued by mathematics, philosophy and "the occult"; meticulously deferent in her rhetoric to social hierarchy even as, in her requests, she sought to sidestep convention; beset by anxiety, indecisiveness, even anguish. Capable of sympathy with others' troubles, of advocating for those less powerful than she, of throwing spectacular tantrums when her professional honor was threatened, and of planning revenge on those who crossed her, she was remembered by the same contemporary as having been a person of the "sharpest intelligence . . . friendly . . . charming . . . with sweet and graceful manners toward everyone." [5] He went on to note the power her presence must have had in a room: "whether playing, singing or pleasantly talking, she worked such stunning effects in the minds of her listeners that she changed them from what they had been." [6]

Francesca did not exactly "get away with it." The best evidence suggests that, instead, Francesca's world asked her to be as versatile, inventive, and performatively powerful a musician as possible while being beyond all hint of sexual innuendo or reproach. She had been born at a moment when ensembles of women musicians were the fashion at absolute princes' courts. Francesca's mother sang in one such ensemble under her father's direction, at one of the most artistically ambitious princely courts: that of the Granducato of Tuscany. Ruled by the still-emerging dynasty of the Medici family, the granducato fostered a sense of its public grandeur by spending lavishly on architecture, urban design, humanistic scholarship, theater, spectacle, and music. In Francesca's lifetime, three generations of virtuosa women served the court, including (besides her mother)

Vittoria Concarini ne' Archilei, Settimia Caccini ne' Ghivizzani, Arcangiola Palladini ne' Broumans, Angelica Sciamerone ne' Belli, and Francesca's pupils Maria Botti and Emilia Grazi. Like her sister, Sciamerone, Botti, and Grazi, Francesca was born to her craft, destined to serve as her parents had done.

Francesca's father Giulio helped shape her destiny by training her in that craft, as Tarquinia Molza's and Moderata Fonte's fathers had trained them for literary scholarship and Artemisia Gentileschi's father had trained her for painting. Ambitious for his intellectually gifted daughter, Giulio also gave Francesca a surprisingly broad humanistic education for an artisan girl. As she approached adulthood he created a situation that allowed her to display her composing talent just when Tuscany's French-born grand duchess, Christine de Lorraine, was most inclined to notice. For the next thirty years, Francesca's career unfolded in service to the Medici women's court gathered around Christine. A world of grand duchesses, the princesses who were their in-laws and cousins, the *dame* who served them all and the children they all bore, the women's court functioned as a parallel universe to the Medici court that political (and music) historians have described. It was a universe intended both to protect princely women from the violence of urban political life and to constrain them. Yet from sometime in 1606, when Grand Duke Ferdinando I became too ill to govern, to his widow Christine's death in December 1636, the women's court was widely acknowledged as the de facto seat of Medicean power. Francesca served that court, and the women who presided over it, Christine and her daughter-in-law Maria Magdalena d'Austria, by producing chamber and theatrical music that met their entertainment needs and represented their concerns to the Tuscan elite; by teaching and coaching the performances of the dame who served the Medici women and those of the Medici children; and by being a figure whose deftly managed reputation for excellence and virtue helped sustain both the duchesses' long regency and their shared habit of stretching the limits of conventional womanhood. If Francesca got away with something in history, she did so in tandem with Christine and Magdalena.

※

Writing this book has led me to think deeply about the relation of music to history. Despite its heft, this book is not part of music history's epic tradition. It does not engage very much with the familiar tropes that sustain the mythic Western music history in the United States. Nor does this book advance the claims of particular musical texts, musicians, or "stylistic developments" for a canonicity based on their transhistorical resonances. Neither kind of music history has a place for women musicians *as women*, because neither has a place for any musicians as persons—persons whose stories and artistic work were inevitably rooted in and shaped by historically and culturally specific, gendered, and classed experiences of the material and discursive world. Therefore, in order to formulate answers to my colleague's questions and to develop my own insight that Francesca's music might illuminate elite women's experience of early modern musical culture, I have sidestepped the most traditional concerns of music history and addressed a different set of questions. What were the material and discursive conditions that, interacting with their technical training, shaped musicians' sensibilities in a given time and place? Under what conditions did they live and work? How did their musical labor contribute to the constantly shifting power relations and the circulation of social energy by which their communities understood themselves? How can we read the written traces of musicians' lives—especially, but not exclusively, their scores—as historical documents that illuminate the range of responses that they could have had to their circumstances? More directly, how can knowledge of a musical culture from long ago and far away enrich our notions of how "musicking" can intervene in the relationships that constitute real life? These questions, and the answers I propose in terms of Francesca Caccini, were in part born of my reading in women's history, microhistory, and feminist theory. But neither the questions nor the ways I have addressed them need be limited to women's musical histories: I believe them to be questions about the relation of music to history, to culture, and to the possibilities for human agency that concern us all.

To rethink the relation of music to history is, necessarily, to rethink the ways one will write music history's stories. My ideas about how to tell Francesca's stories have been inspired mainly by Adriana Cavarero's *Relating Narratives*.[7] Reasoning from premises introduced by Hannah Arendt, Cavarero argues that the narrative of a life reveals *who* someone is as "a unique existent," not *what* someone is as a "subject." In her view a life's narrative is always relational, taking into account the uniqueness of the teller and the told and of the relationship between them. Cavarero's insistence on the interrelationships of human existents as the foundation of knowledge has informed many of my choices as a writer, even the choice I have made in this introduction to locate my text in my own relationships with teachers, mentors, and colleagues. More important, I have strived at every turn in this book to tell Francesca's stories as they touch or overlap with those of others—with Christine's and Magdalena's stories, with the stories of other women at court, occasionally with the stories of men such as her father, her frequent collaborator Michelangelo Buonarroti, her two husbands. I have meant thereby to reconstruct the relational world from which Francesca would have made sense of her own experience and from which her contemporaries would have made sense of her. I have meant, too, to make Francesca's gynocentric relational world seem vivid and real, so that readers can both imagine a world very different from their own and imagine their own relationships to these ancestors whose stories they have not known before.

Stories about music and musicians are intrinsic components of any musical culture. One of the most resilient stories of the West's musical culture has been that of modern music's origins in the effort by a group of Florentine scholars and musicians at the turn of the seventeenth century to revive the power of ancient Greek music. Their effort led to the creation of a modern Italian "monody": a kind of accompanied solo song whose characteristic texture and aesthetic principles were to suffuse the music of European elites for centuries, especially in opera. Although long since debunked as only one story among many that can be told about the origins of musical modernity, this story nonetheless remains among the touchstone myths of Eurocentric histories, perhaps because it attributes modern values and sensibilities to classical impulses. The narrative of this book sits aslant that myth. Because I concentrate on Francesca's experience as a woman musician raised in the very house where the new Florentine music was born, I have reconfigured some elements of the myth to show how the story might have seemed from women's perspective.

First, I interpret the self-promoting documents proclaiming the Florentine invention of a new music as having always promoted that music's political utility to its Medici patrons. On the basis of that premise, it is easy to understand that Francesca's women patrons used her musical gifts in ways that were consistent with the artistic policies of their predecessor, Ferdinando I.

Second, my every narrative move is as adamantly gynocentric as the touchstone myths of music history are androcentric. Thus, when I mention two hotly debated musical issues of Francesca's youth—dissonance practice and the relation between words and music—I do so in a way that emphasizes the way the gendered rhetoric of these debates might have been received by women. Thus, too, I read some of her surviving compositions as testaments to that reception and as the witty, sometimes resisting ripostes of a woman whose service included teaching talented girls how to evade the social and sexual dangers of a musical career, as well as how to solve music's technical problems. Further, in my zeal to tell the story of artistic production at the Medici court as Francesca would have experienced it, I have made such self-proclaimed major figures as Jacopo Peri and Marco da Gagliano marginal. Like her older colleague Vittoria Archilei, who moved toward retirement as Francesca entered adulthood, and Francesca's expatriate, apparently estranged sister Settimia, they appear in the narrative only when their activities demonstrably intersected with hers or her patrons'. Yet two powerful men who seem to have been Francesca's lifelong protectors, and who preserved her letters to them, figure more prominently— Michelangelo Buonarroti the younger, great-nephew of the sixteenth-century artist and now best remembered as an important comic poet and playwright of the new Baroque aesthetic, and Andrea Cioli, whose rise through Tuscany's secretariat was eased by his marriage to Christine de Lorraine's *dama d'onore*

Angelica Badii and who served as first secretary of Tuscany from 1626 until his death in 1641.[8]

Third, I have followed the narrative strategy of Francesca's first biographer, the courtier and proto-feminist writer Cristoforo Bronzini, in largely ignoring the "birth of opera" narrative so familiar to musical readers. Indeed, Bronzini's curious failure to mention any Florentine woman's participation in the Medici court's theatrical life led me to reconsider the gendering of genres there and to understand that Francesca's prolific work as a "theatrical" composer was limited to women's genres, staged in women's courtly spaces. It was only because those spaces were important to the state's power for so long that her work among the court's women became part of the public historical record.

The stories this book tells are based on hundreds of documents. Francesca's autograph letters document her interactions with patrons and colleagues from the age of twenty-two to the age of fifty-four. Although some letters are formulaic or businesslike, other seem startlingly frank or artful, revealing a stunning ability to use the conventional tropes of womanhood to communicate what seem like real anxiety, pride, or pain. A manuscript scene from *Il passatempo*, a comedy for which Francesca composed music when she was twenty-seven, and the thirty-six solo and duet *musiche* of her *Primo libro*, published when she was thirty, demonstrate her first maturity as a composer. The score of *La liberazione di Ruggiero*, published when she was thirty-seven, reveals both how her musical thought changed when she was in her thirties and how she conceived and resolved the problems of large-scale musico-dramatic form. Dozens of letters and manuscripts among the papers of Buonarroti refer to Francesca directly or indirectly, as do countless diplomatic reports of musicians' travels or performances and the letters of Medici bureaucrats swapping gossip among themselves. Property, tax, and guardianship records, legal judgments and appeals, payment records, wills, house inventories, convent records, and farmers' contracts give a sense of how Francesca and her two very different husbands lived, how they managed the material conditions of their lives. Taken together, these documents radically deglamorize the world of the court musician, revealing that even those who passed their days among their nation's ruling family were never more than servants in the eyes of their *padroni*. Yet they also portray Francesca as a woman of action who acted as the head of the family when her stepmother, stepsister, or daughter needed an advocate. Finally, because it is impossible to tell Francesca's stories without telling those of the women for and among whom she worked, the letters of Christine de Lorraine and Maria Magdalena d'Austria and of their secretaries have enabled me to decipher the dynamics of the women's court.

Apart from the materials from Francesca's own pen and the letters of her patrons, no document has influenced this book's interpretations more than

Cristoforo Bronzini's massive *Della dignità e nobiltà delle donne.*[9] Bronzini entered the Medici's service in 1615 as the master of ecclesiastical ceremonies for Christine de Lorraine's second son, Cardinal Carlo de' Medici. Sometime in late 1617, probably at Christine's or Magdalena's direction, he began *Della dignità*, which argued that the equality of women and men was an absolute value, necessary to the welfare of the state.[10] Sexual difference, for Bronzini, was irrelevant except insofar as human reproduction required that different body parts be put into play. In a surprising adumbration of late twentieth-century constructionist views, he dismissed the hierarchies of gender as resulting from "the most insolent tyranny of men, usurped unjustly in every sphere of life."[11] Further, Bronzini envisioned an ideal political world in which courageous women would command with *pietà* (mercy, piety, and compliance with social norms for virtue) rather than violence.[12] His arguments were overtly intended to support the de facto and eventually de jure regency that Christine and Magdalena shared.

Bronzini elaborated his ideas about women's and men's equality with biographical sketches of "women worthies" whom he could claim had made important contributions to some human enterprise. These claims usually adjoin a gynocentric exposition of the subject in question, whether it be philosophy, poetry, painting, or politics. Almost always, each woman's excellence is portrayed in terms of a narrowly circumscribed set of womanly virtues. Almost always, a woman somehow linked to the Medici household represents the epitome of female achievement in her science or art. That is how Bronzini positioned his twenty-three-page biographical sketch of Francesca—after much shorter sketches of sixty-three other contemporary women musicians.

Because Bronzini had known Francesca for at least fifteen years when he wrote it, and because his ideal audience—the elite women of the Medici court—knew her person and her story better than he, the sketch is an invaluable biographical source. Yet because Bronzini seems so clearly to have meant to represent the world of women as Christine's and Magdalena's court wanted it seen, his general ideas about music are no less interesting. Three of those have been important to the interpretations in this book. First, in a highly eccentric retelling of the muses' origins, he portrays music as a means by which elite women and their musical servants could collaborate to effect beneficial political change. Second, in several volumes of his manuscript, as well as in the middle of his biography of Francesca, Bronzini asserts the residually Pythagorean view that "nothing in the world is made except of geometry, and music."[13] Third, in several places he cites not Orpheus but Amphion, whose self-accompanied song built the city walls of Thebes, as the ideal musician. And it is to Amphion, not to Orpheus, a siren or a nightingale, that he likens Francesca's musical power. In this world Francesca's music was a medium in which a sharply intelligent artisan-class woman collaborated with princesses to create a desirable community.

Music, that is, was a medium through which the social energy that sustains relationships and worlds—and that changes them—flowed. I have tried to be true to that vision.

※

Eight of this book's chapters tell Francesca Caccini's stories in relation to the discursive and material circumstances that shaped a musica's life in her world. These chapters frame four others that use close readings of her surviving music to probe the possibilities for agency and self-possession that could be imagined by the elite women in that world.

Chapter 1 explores what it meant to Francesca to have been the daughter of early modern Italy's most celebrated singing teacher and one of its most celebrated singers, Giulio Caccini. The Caccini family's intense class ambition, her necessary formation through the institution of womanhood, an engagement from early childhood with the disciplines of her father's craft, and her father's astute insinuation of his family ensemble's usefulness to the Medici court laid the foundation for who and what Francesca would become.

Chapter 2 tells the story of Francesca's eventual placement as a musical servant to the Granducato of Tuscany. Thinking through the ways in which early modern princes used the exchange of musicians to articulate and sustain politically charged kinship ties, I show how Giulio manipulated that system, eventually luring Christine de Lorraine into competition to win Francesca's talents. Francesca's nearly simultaneous marriage to a fellow musician and entry into the granducato's service marked the end of the competition and the beginning of her public career.

Chapter 3 describes the workings of the women's court. Drawing on hundreds of letters and on the ideas of Gayle Rubin and Luce Irigaray, I show how that court's relational world was held together by a traffic in relics, reproductive advice, and women themselves through the grand duchess's management of the marriage arrangements and the monastic placements of Tuscany's elite women. I argue that a world in which women managed the implications of each others' sexualities and advocated for each other in times of trouble would have formed its denizens to expect and to exercise the surprising degree of agency with which they negotiated the constraints of conventional womanhood.

Chapter 4 surveys the ways Francesca's performances and compositions were used by her patrons. Based almost entirely on documents from the court, this chapter focuses on Francesca as these women and their guests, diarists, and apologists might have perceived her—as, that is, little more than an object, little less than an Amphion, to be deployed in the service of their pleasure or their interests. Yet she was also a hard-working woman in the thick of artistic production at court, one able to profit equally from the familiarity her gender gave her with her patrons and from the knowledge of the workings of the courtly world on which collegial relations with the musical men at court depended.

Chapter 5 offers glimpses of the woman who filled the role of musica to the granducato. At her home across town from the palaces, she worked in a whirlwind of composing, copying, teaching, and coaching that was as far as can be imagined from the tranquil isolation of the writer's studio Virginia Woolf envisioned in *A Room of One's Own*. Away from her patrons' presence, Francesca could be protective of her own and her pupils' health, she could be temperamental, and she could conceive exquisitely pointed revenge.

Chapter 6 introduces the principal source for Francesca's music, the *Primo libro delle musiche*, published in 1618. I describe the book's contents, poetic choices, and general style, speculate on her reasons for choosing to publish when she did, and analyze a long letter in which she expressed feelings very close to what Sandra Gilbert and Susan Gubar long ago described as a female authorial complaint: "anxiety of voice."

Chapter 11 traces Francesca's life through the rapid changes wrought by the death of her first husband in December 1626, her quick remarriage in October 1627 to a noble musical amateur from Lucca, his death in June 1630, and her subsequent efforts to return to the Medici's service as the teacher of her talented and therefore desirable daughter Margherita. Thwarted by the plague that swept central Italy in the early 1630s, she returned only in 1634, after enduring three years of quarantine in her late husband's palace. Her lifelong proximity to great power had done nothing to protect her from the cataclysms that marked her entry into widowhood.

Chapter 12 tells the stories of Francesca's life after she returned to her homeland and to a women's court that, while still thriving in its urban center at the Dominican community known as La Crocetta, was no longer the granducato's political center of gravity. A vigorous advocate for her own, her daughter's and other women's concerns, and evidently active in the wholly private musical life of the women's court, Francesca struggled with the constraints imposed by her status as the mother-guardian of a noble son. Shortly after her daughter's future as a nun in the Monastero di San Girolamo sulla costa was secured, ending Francesca's obligations as a mother, she retired from the Medici's service and disappeared from the public record.

Four chapters of this book consist not of storytelling but of critical readings based in my long-standing desire to think about music as a set of actions—as performance—rather than as a set of works. These chapters argue forcefully that Francesca's surviving music shows her to have engaged the conventions of womanhood with intelligence, wit, and a sensibility that clearly shows the influence of the elite women's culture her music was meant to serve. A compact disc of Francesca's music, produced under the artistic direction of Soprano Emily Van Evera, complements my readings.

Chapters 7 and 8 consider Francesca's *Primo libro delle musiche* as a pedagogical text that could systematically teach both musical skills and important lessons in how a musica might solve the perennial problems of women who seek the cultural authority condensed in the word "voice." To develop these readings, I imagined what each song would have taught one of Francesca's court-subsidized pupils to do with her breath, her throat, her hands on an instrument; with technical challenges posed by mode, system, genre and formal conventions; with the cultural imperative to make music that would have power over others while preserving her womanly virtue intact; with the characteristically feminine genre of the lament; and with the competing ideas of love that circulated in lyric poetry modeled either on that of Petrarch or of Chiabrera. I show how the musical acts required of a pupil taught both the physical and mental behaviors necessary to womanly ways of wielding agency and power.

By contrast, in chapters 9 and 10 I have imagined the experiences, and therefore the meanings, available to those who heard and saw the only performance Francesca and her patrons expected *La liberazione di Ruggiero* to have, in February 1625. Chapter 9 locates this work in relation to the political situation of Maria Magdalena d'Austria—her persona, the cultural program by which she sought to manage it, and the particular series of events in which *La liberazione* figured. This chapter proposes meanings that the audience might have gleaned only from the setting, the stage pictures, and the dramatic action implied by the libretto. Chapter 10 focuses solely on Francesca's music. I imagine the historical audience's responses through the vivid recollection of my own responses when I first saw *La liberazione* staged, in Düdingen, Switzerland, in 1999, under the direction of Gabriele Garrido and Ruth Orthmann. I show how Francesca's music both satirized and perfectly realized the aesthetic aims of opera's first theorists, so that her music could have seemed literally to change the power relations among its first audience. More overtly than any other surviving work of early Florentine music-drama, *La liberazione* aspired to and perhaps achieved something like the power of performative speech.

In writing all four of these chapters I have been acutely aware of recent scholarly work that considers music to consist of embodied actions, actions that people do in order to do things to others. My theoretical basis for thinking about the power of Francesca's music to do things in performance hovers above the ground shared, however improbably, by Plato and Judith Butler. At a fundamental level, I have taken seriously—as I believe Francesca and her contemporaries might have done—Plato's notion that making a certain kind of music produces a certain kind of person. I leave implicit the related notion, articulated toward the end of Butler's *Gender Trouble,* that the social categories by which we are known in the world (especially gender and sex) result from our compulsive repetition of the performances that constitute those categories. If one were to accept Butler's argument, one could conclude from my readings of Francesca's *Primo libro delle musiche* that her teaching helped produce a community of elite women who were surprisingly modern in their self-possession, inventiveness, and comfortableness with power. Thus, one could conclude something similar to, but not identical with, Bronzini's claim that Francesca had served the court as its Amphion.

I have tried to describe Francesca's music in the least technical language I could devise, while trying to be faithful to the compositional sensibility I inferred from her work. The result may strike some as an idiosyncratic pastiche of twentieth- and twenty-first-century terminology and sixteenth- and seventeenth-century musical gestures. I try not to pretend that I know how Francesca would have thought about a given sonic gesture as a bit of musical technique, although I try very often to imagine what she might have meant by her gestures. In describing melodic and large-scale tonal structures I have often referred to the system of modes as presented in sixteenth-century theory books; I have done so because I believe Francesca's music shows her thinking to be rooted in that system. Because I began this book very much under the influence of Eric Chafe's *Monteverdi's Tonal Language,* I have used his terminology and his thinking about *mollis* and *durus* as a way to explain Francesca's thinking about harmonic and tonal relations. I refer to her harmonies as major, minor, diminished or augmented chords, and I comment on root movement among harmonies for the sake of intelligibility. I do not pretend to know how she might have thought about chords; I only know that she thought about them very well. She was among the most memorably inventive harmonists of her generation.

⚘

For many years the provisional title of this book was "a romanesca of one's own." I meant to imply by this obvious play on Virginia Woolf's classic essay that the circumstances required for a musical woman to enjoy a fully creative life are different from those for a literary woman.[14] Because music is fundamentally about movement, sociability, and change, women musicians do not so much need rooms of our own, within which we can retreat from the world, as we need ways of being *in* the world that allow us to engage with the often immobilizing and silencing effects of gender norms. But because gender in patriarchal cultures always restricts women's access to some kinds of spaces—usually by defining spatial transgressions as sexual ones—women musicians cannot work without constantly negotiating these interrelated restrictions. Moreover, unlike literature, music is temporal and ephemeral. It is about doing something unrepeatable, about creating experiences that draw attention both to the richness of individual moments that seem to suspend time and to the inevitability of change and death. One way musicians address that inevitability is to shape narrative time and aural space by recourse to temporal and sonic formulas. In the North America of my youth, the most common such formula was the blues. In the central Italy of Francesca's time, the most fashionable of these formulas was the *romanesca*.

The romanesca of the early seventeenth century was an "aria"—literally, a musical way of being, like an air to be put on—that improvising musicians used to perform narrative texts as self-accompanied song.[15] As with any aria, a singer of the romanesca constructed its characteristic way of being from certain melodic and harmonic gestures. These divided a poetic text into couplets consisting of musically antecedent and consequent phrases: the antecedent descended from the fifth degree of a scale to its second degree, provoking anticipation of eventual rest on the first (and also the final) degree; the consequent began again at the fifth degree, and descended all the way to that final, giving closure to the thought. To accompany this extremely general vocal norm, the singer would touch harmonies that, too, produced antecedent and consequent phrases: in the simplest twenty-first century terms, the antecedent phrase would follow the progression B♭–F–g–D, and the consequent would follow the progression B♭–F–g–D–g.

But as the six romanescas Francesca published in 1618 show, to sing a romanesca could be to push constantly, brilliantly, inventively against a framework that was almost endlessly elastic—to see how far you could stretch the relationship between what a cultural norm like the *romanesca* was and what you could make it do while you sang your tale.

A way of being that could not exist independent of the ways of doing things with text and music that produced it, the early modern concept of "aria" epitomizes the intrinsic performativity of courtly culture. The productive tension between being and doing that lies at the heart of aria thus conceived resonates with the tension between doing noble deeds and being "of noble blood" that pervades early modern writing about courtiership and social rank. It resonates, too, with the tension that pervades prescriptive writing about genteel womanhood, in which such behaviors as abstaining from wine and meat (or from singing) were prescribed in order to preserve the supposedly essential coolness of a woman's body. The performativity of early modern culture resonates, in turn, with some important aspects of early twenty-first century life, notably the intellectual theories and day-to-day self-concepts by which many of us believe that we are what we do.

The tension between being and doing fills the Italian word "musica," which can be both a noun denoting the craft composed of music making's many skills and a form of the verb denoting the act of bringing disparate elements together into a harmonious, meaningful whole. It is a tension that pervades this book, not least because it is the central tension Francesca explored in her published collection of solo songs and duets. Her explorations are nowhere more bold than in her ingenious take-offs on the romanesca, which show users of her book how to use the form as a medium in which to stretch or reorient the conventions that framed them. Inspired by Francesca's most adventurous romanescas, and by her skilled fusion of being and doing, I mean this book to stretch and reorient the conventions that frame its genre. I hope to have brought into being, for a time, a different way of doing music history.

Acknowledgments

The Italian philosopher Luisa Muraro argues that the primal feminist act is the expression of gratitude. I begin with Francesca herself, for having changed my thinking, and my life, far beyond my wildest dreams.

I thank the staffs of the Archivi di Stato in Florence (especially Doctor Paola Peruzzi), Lucca (especially Sergio Nelli), Modena, Mantua, and Rome; of the Archivi vescovili in Florence and Lucca (especially Sister Giuseppina), and the archive of the Opera di Santa Maria del Fiore in Florence (especially Doctor Lorenzo Fabbri); of the Archivio Segreto Vaticano and the Archivio Storico Capitolino in Rome; of the Biblioteca Laurenziana, Biblioteca Riccardiana, Biblioteca Marucelliana, Biblioteca Governativa di Lucca, Biblioteca Casanatense, Biblioteca Conservatorio Santa Cecilia, Biblioteca Universitaria di Roma, Biblioteca Nazionale Vittorio Emanuele di Roma, and the Bibliothèque Nationale in Paris; and of the Galleria degli Uffizi.

I thank Cardinal Archbishop Ennio Antonelli of Florence and Reverend Mother Osanna Gobbetto, superior of the Monastero Domenicano Santa Croce in Florence, for generously granting permission to use the cloister's archive. I am grateful to Sisters Rosanna and Antonina for opening the door there and bringing strong coffee in the afternoons.

I owe more than I can ever say to the always gracious and generous staff of the Casa Buonarroti in Florence, especially to the director, Doctor Pina Ragioniera, and to Elena, Maurizio, and Susanna.

Research for this book has been supported by grants from American Council of Learned Societies, the National Endowment for the Humanities, the University of Virginia, New York University and by a month-long residency at the Terza Università di Roma. The project began with the support of an NEH Fellowship for Independent Scholars in 1990–1991 and ended when I was a Frederick Burkhart Residential Fellow at Villa I Tatti in 2001–2002. I am grateful to all these institutions, but more grateful to the people who enabled my work. Jane Bowers, Tim Carter, Susan McClary, Ellen Rosand, Howard Smither, Gary Tomlinson, and the late Philip Brett supported my applications for grants. Thanks, too, to Walter Kaiser, director of I Tatti when I was there, for his sharp and provocative wit; to the matchlessly intelligent and helpful librarians there, especially Michael Rocke and Kathryn Bosi, for their extraordinary warmth and generosity, Ilaria della Monica and the late Stefano Corsi for swift and accurate bibliographic help, and Manuela Michelloni for forcing me to speak Italian as we trudged up the hill from the early bus; to the staff, especially Nelda Ferace (for calling me "Bestia"), Alexa Mason (for countless rides and her social grace), Patrizia Carella, Donatella Pieraccini (for approving my interest in Francesco de' Gregori's music), Liliana Ciullini, Rosanna Gaspari, and Gennaro Giustino; and to my cohort for fabulous conversations, advice, *feste*, and wine, especially Geraldine Albers, Kurt Barstow, Cammy Brothers, Andrew and Jaclyn Blume, Marilina Cirillo and Giorgio Falzerano, Andrew Dell'Antonio and Susan Jackson, Bruce Edelstein, Iain Fenlon, Arthur Field, Katherine Gill, Catherine Goguël, Paul Hill, Chris Hughes, Lawrence Jenkins, Christiane Klapisch, Robert Leporatti, Christian Moevs, Caroline Murphy, Jonathan Nelson, Deanna Shemek, and Ty Miller.

For their generous help in matters large and small I thank Claudio Annibaldi, James Barrett, Renae Bernstein, Lorenzo Bianconi, Christine Brandes, Jeanice Brooks, Anna Maria Busse-Berger, Annamaria Cecconi, Janie Cole, Gino Corti, Emily Van Evera, Dinko Fabris, Jean Grundy Fanelli, Annegret Fauser, Alfonso Fedi, Gabriele Giacomelli, Lisa Goldenberg-Stoppato, Bonnie Gordon, Warren Kirkendale, Thomas Kuehn, Giuseppina LaFace, Stefano Lorenzetti, Anne MacNeil, Brian Mann, Arnaldo Morelli, John Nádas, Paul O'Dette, Anne Jacobsen Schutte, Mary Springfels, Nina Treadwell, and Richard Wistreich. I thank Amy Brosius, Paula Matthusen, and Eve Straussman-Pflanzer for expert research assistance and Paola Bonifazio for help with translations.

I owe a special debt to Tim Carter, Kelley Harness, and John Walter Hill; without their generous sharing of research tips and research finds this book could not exist. And I thank the four scholars who read drafts of this manuscript for the University of Chicago Press, especially Professor Carter and the anonymous Reader 2 for the bracing and extremely helpful detail of their comments. They made this a much better book.

For countless gestures of support, and for the inspiration of often penetrating questions, I thank my former colleagues at the University of Virginia, especially Elizabeth Hudson, Michelle Kisliuk, Fred Maus, Marita McClymonds, Susan McKinnon, Farzaneh Milani, Stephan Prock, and Alicyn Warren; my current colleagues at New York University, especially Michael Beckerman, Stanley Boorman, Kyra Gaunt, Elizabeth Hoffman, Jairo Moreno, and Ana Maria Ochòa Gautier; all my students; and some truly dedicated friends, Sarah Fagg, Patrice Giansante, Jill Gordon, Julia Griffin, Marion Guck, the late Corinne Guntzel, Lydia Hamessley, Vicki Hawes, Ellie Hisama, Martha Mockus, Glenn Munkvold, Trina Myers, Susan Patrick, Kevin Phelps, Annie Janeiro Randall, Tom Renckens, Sandra Saari, and Wynne Stuart. I am indebted to Elizabeth Wood for everything—the inspiration of her own beautiful writing, the piercing insight of her questions, and the generosity and sweetness with which she offers criticism. Similarly, the intelligence, playfulness, and friendship Marilina Cirillo has so generously shared with me since our year at I Tatti continues to sustain me.

The people of St. Stephen's Lutheran Church in Syracuse, New York, kindly granted me leave from my position as their music director to begin this work, and the friendship offered by the people of Santa Felicita in Florence sustained me during long months of archival work and writing. I especially thank my fellow choir members Maria "Lala" Galgani and her daughter Ludovica, Maria Pea, Eleonora and Giuliana; Leonisia, Signora Guicciardini, and the *ragazzi della media* whom I tried to turn into a children's choir; and most of all Don Mino Tagliacozzi, whose preaching and kindness reopened my heart to life's joy. Vi ringrazio tutti.

The late Finn McCool, Cuchulainn O'Houlihoulihoulihan, Bridget Kelly Black, and Francesca Katchini attended to this work as only creatures of their kind can; I thank them and their worthy successors, Ginger Rogers and Fred Astaire.

But there is no one to whom I owe more gratitude than to my partner, Margaret McFadden. Peerless as a teacher, a thinker, and a human being, she has so far exceeded what one might imagine by such words as "patience," "love" or "support" that I can only bow my head in acknowledgement. When she generously welcomed Francesca into our shared life, neither of us dreamed how long she would choose to stay. I owe this book to Margaret's steadfast generosity of spirit, but much more important, I owe her all the sweetness in my life.

Abbreviations

F-Pn	Paris, Bibliothèque Nationale
GB-Lb	London, British Library
I-Bc	Bologna, Civico Museo Bibliografico Musicale
I-Faa	Florence, Archivio Arcivescovile
I-Fas	Florence, Archivio di Stato
	MdP: Mediceo del Principato
I-FcasaB	Florence, Casa Buonarroti
	A.B.: Archivio Buonarroti
I-Fd	Florence, Archivio dell'Opera del Duomo
I-FEas	Ferrara, Archivio di Stato
I-Fgu	Florence, Galleria degli Uffizi
I-Fm	Florence, Biblioteca Marucelliana
I-Fn	Florence, Biblioteca Nazionale Centrale
I-Fr	Florence, Biblioteca Riccardiana e Moreniana
I-Las	Lucca, Archivio di Stato
I-Lbg	Lucca, Biblioteca Governativa
I-MNas	Mantua, Archivio di Stato
I-MOas	Modena, Archivio di Stato
I-MOe	Modena, Biblioteca Estense
I-Rasc	Rome, Archivio Storico Capitolino
	F.O.: Fondo Orsini
I-Rasv	Rome, Archivio Segreto Vaticano
I-Rcas	Rome, Biblioteca Casantense
I-Rsc	Rome, Biblioteca musicale Santa Cecilia, conservatorio
I-Rvat	Rome, Biblioteca Apostolica Vaticana
I-Vnm	Venice, Biblioteca Nazionale Marciana
US-Nypl	New York Public Library

Note to the Reader

Editorial Principles

All the musical examples are based on seventeenth-century printed sources. Note values and original slurring have been retained, as have original bar lines, except where indicated. I have used instrumental beaming for ornamented vocal passages so as to make the relation of ornaments and syllables to the beat absolutely clear. Continuo figures use modern symbols. Accidentals in the source pertain to the measure in which they appear. Editorial accidentals and continuo figures are in square brackets. Examples from *La liberazione di Ruggiero* use the text as printed in the score.

In my discussions of music, I have used the Helmholz system of pitch naming (middle C = c′). Single uppercase letters refer to major sonorities (G) and single lowercase letters refer to minor sonorities (g).

Throughout the book, Italian spelling and punctuation have been normalized silently, following the guidelines of Giuseppina LaFace Bianconi ("Filologia dei testi poetici nella musica vocale italiana," *Acta musicologica* 66 [1994]: 1–21).

Dates in the text have been modernized to reflect the modern practice of beginning the year on January 1, except in appendix B, containing letters of Francesca Caccini, where I have noted both the date as written in Florentine style (beginning a year on 25 March) and, as relevant, the modern date (for example, 22 March 1613/14 denotes 1613 in Florence and 1614 in Rome).

Names

In seventeenth-century Italy, a woman's birth name was her lifelong legal name, no matter how often she married; yet many women signed letters or were known in public documents by both birth and married names. Thus, wherever possible I refer to a married woman first by her full name as it would have been written in the seventeenth century—given name, maiden name, and, as relevant, the name of the family into which she married (for example, Arcangiola Palladini ne' Broumans, that is, "Arcangiola Palladini among the Broumans," or Vittoria Concarini ne' Archilei). Thereafter I refer to each woman by her birth name. The exception is Vittoria Archilei, who is almost universally known only by her married name.

I refer to members of the Caccini family by their first names to avoid confusion.

I refer to Medici grand dukes so as to make their place in the order of succession clear (for example, Cosimo I or Ferdinando I), and I refer to women members of the Medici family as they signed their names—Catherine de' Medici for the sixteenth-century French queen and Marie de' Medici for the seventeenth-century one; Christine de Lorraine, Maria Magdalena, and Vittoria della Rovere for the Tuscan grand duchesses; Caterina de' Medici for the seventeenth-century duchess of Mantua.

Honorifics

I have not expanded the following abbreviations of honorific titles found in sources.

Cav.re	Cavaliere	Oss.mo	Osservandissimo
Col.mo	Colendissimo	R.do	Reverendo
D.	Don	S.A.	Sua Altezza
Ecc.mo	Eccellentissimo	S.A.S	Sua Altezza Serenissima
G.D./G.D.ssa	Granduca/Granduchessa	Ser.ma	Serenissima
Ill.re/Ill.mo	Illustre/Illustrissimo	S.r/S.ra	Signore/Signora
L.A./L.L.A.A.	Loro Altezze	V.A.	Vostra Altezza
M.o	Maestro	V.A.S.	Vostra Altezza Serenissima
N.S.	Nostro Signore	V.E.	Vostra Eccellenza
		V.S.	Vostra Signoria

Excerpts from Francesca Caccini's Compositions on the Accompanying CD

1. "Ardo infelice, e palesar non tento," stanza 1, from *Il primo libro delle musiche* (1618), p. 9. Emily Van Evera, soprano; Eric Milnes, harpsichord.

2. "Maria, dolce Maria," from *Il primo libro*, pp. 17–18. Emily Van Evera, soprano; Eric Milnes, harpsichord.

3. "Ecco, ch'io verso il sangue," from *Il primo libro*, pp. 24–28. Emily Van Evera, soprano; Eric Milnes, harpsichord; Andrew Parrott, organ; Maria Cleary, double harp; Fredrik Bock, theorbo; Erin Headley, lirone.

4. "Lasciatemi qui solo," from *Il primo libro*, pp. 38–43. Emily Van Evera, soprano; Eric Milnes, harpsichord; Maria Cleary, double harp.

5. "O che nuovo stupor," stanza 1, from *Il primo libro*, pp. 43–44. Emily Van Evera, soprano; Eric Milnes, harpsichord; Maria Cleary, double harp; Adrian Butterfield, baroque violin; Erin Headley, viol.

6. "Rendi alle mie speranze il verde, e fiori," from *Il primo libro*, pp. 62–64. Emily Van Evera, soprano; Eric Milnes, harpsichord.

7. "Haec dies," from *Il primo libro*, pp. 72–73. Emily Van Evera, soprano; Eric Milnes, harpsichord; Andrew Parrott, organ.

8. "*Chi desia di saper che cosa è amore,*" from *Il primo libro*, p. 90. Emily Van Evera, soprano; Fredrik Bock, baroque guitar.

9. "*Se muove a giurar fede,*" from *Il primo libro*, p. 94. Emily Van Evera, soprano; Eric Milnes, harpsichord; Mélisande Corriveau, viol.

10. "*Dispiegate,*" from *Il primo libro*, p. 97. Emily Van Evera, soprano; Fredrik Bock, baroque guitar; Erin Headley, viol.

11. "*Ferma, ferma crudele,*" Alcina to Ruggiero, from *La liberazione di Ruggiero* (1625), pp. 53–54. Emily Van Evera, soprano; Eric Milnes, harpsichord.

12. "*Deh, se non hai pietà del mio languire,*" Alcina to Ruggiero, from *La liberazione di Ruggiero*, pp. 55–56. Emily Van Evera, soprano; Eric Milnes, harpsichord.

Adrian Hunter, recording production and engineering.

Figliuola del celebratissimo Giulio Romano

1

Francesca Caccini was born Friday, 18 September 1587, six and seven-eighths hours after sunset, in the Florentine parish of San Michele Visdomini, under the sign of Virgo.[1] The oldest legitimate child of Giulio Caccini and the firstborn of her mother, the singer Lucia di Filippo Gagnolandi, she was baptized later that day in Florence's Baptistry. Her godmother, Francesca del Signor Rustico Piccardini, the wife of a horse trainer in the Medici's service, held her at the font, along with Girolamo Guicciardini, whom her official godfather, Pandolfo de' Bardi, had sent as his substitute.[2] Afterward, the Piccardini and Bardi families probably sponsored a banquet to honor her parents and her birth, although by tradition the festivities would have been muted because the couple's first child was a girl.[3]

In early modern Italy the birth of a girl was taken as a sign that one parent or the other was not strong enough to have produced a fully formed male child. Moreover, unlike a male child (who would inherit, build, and pass on his father's property), a female child would drain her father's patrimony when, in keeping with the dowry system, he had to pay another family or a religious institution to accept responsibility for her in adulthood.[4] Francesca's father took his responsibility to dower his baby daughter seriously. On 8 April 1588, when she was almost seven months old, Giulio signed contracts in his mentor Giovanni de' Bardi's city home according to whose terms land and farm buildings in Fiesole were sold to one Bartolemeo da Brucianese. Of the 1,120 scudi that Giulio realized from the sale, 600 were to be deposited in Giulio's account at the

Monte di Pietà, Florence's principal dowry bank. Twenty years later, those 600 scudi would be transferred to the account of Francesca's first husband, in partial payment of her dowry.[5]

For most of her contemporaries and for posterity, Francesca was first known in the way women in patriarchal societies usually are: as the daughter of her father, "the most celebrated Giulio Romano."[6] What did that mean for Francesca?

To be the daughter of Giulio Caccini meant to have been born into an ambitious family of ambiguous social rank.[7] Born in Rome on 8 October 1551, Giulio Caccini was the second son of a woodworker from Montopoli, near Pisa, so ambitious to improve his children's circumstances that he had moved his household to Rome. All three of Michelangelo Caccini's sons were successful artistic workers. The eldest, Orazio, became *maestro di cappella* at Santa Maria Maggiore in Rome; the youngest, Giovanni Battista, became one of Florence's most fashionable sculptor-architects; Giulio was among the most highly praised singers and singing teachers in Italian history. When Francesca was born, Giulio was thirty-six, already the father of an eight-year-old natural son, Pompeo, and the second most highly paid musician on the staff of the Medici household, earning sixteen scudi per month.[8]

Musicians of the Medici household were construed by their masters less as employees than as members of a relational web called the *famiglia*. When he had entered the Medici's service in the mid-1560s, Giulio Caccini had surrendered his rights over his artistic and intellectual work, over his and his children's marriages, and over his and his family's whereabouts. In exchange, the Medici guaranteed that he and his family would enjoy the ruling family's favors, which were likely to include dowry assistance for daughters, job placements for sons, and pensions for those too old or ill to continue useful work. In addition, musical service in the Medici famiglia promised a modest but steady income, a housing allowance, and access to gifts for extraordinary service; these were as likely to come from the Medici's princely guests as from family members. Giulio's position in the Medici household thus all but guaranteed that his daughter Francesca would experience some kind of intervention by the grand duke in her education and marriage, and it guaranteed all his children access to powerful people and to dreams of their own empowerment.

Giulio Caccini was a sometimes difficult man who chafed at the gap between his actual social rank and that of people in the elite world he served. His contemporaries knew him to participate in such common but slightly disreputable activities as gambling, speculating in currency and stocks, and openly longing to be treated as an equal by the aristocrats among whom he so often moved.[9] Giulio wrote boastful letters to his patrons, shamelessly took credit for the virtuosa performances for which his two wives and his eldest daughters were praised, and often complained to the court that he needed money.[10] Indeed, although he had at least two sources of income other than his salary—a business trafficking in "cipolle" (probably bulb plants, an attractive commodity for investment) and the most active singing studio in Florence—his claim of financial woes may have been justified, for by 1606 he was the father of at least ten children by three women.[11] Giulio could be a good father, tirelessly promoting the interests of his children, but he could also be a paternal tyrant and a deadbeat. In 1602, his son Pompeo allowed himself to be charged with raping Ginevra Mazziere, to whom he had been teaching a part in the opera *L'Euridice*, so that the courts would require him to marry the girl and thus overrule Giulio's implacable opposition to the union.[12]

A decade later, in 1611, Giulio reneged for so long on the dowry he had contracted to pay his daughter Settimia's husband, Alessandro Ghivizzani, that the Ghivizzani family abducted her and held her for ransom in Lucca. Giulio, the twenty-two-year-old Francesca, and Settimia herself wrote to Medici cousin Virginio Orsini, Duke of Bracciano, imploring that he ask the grand duchess to order the court's payment of the balance due.[13] Giulio's letters about the matter imply that the court's failure to honor its obligation to one of its servants was to blame for the imbroglio. Yet other letters insinuate that Giulio was at fault for supposing that his family's professional excellence entitled them to special treatment. In fact, Giulio's proud breaching of the boundaries of social rank often caused him to depend on the intercession of his social betters for rescue. At age sixty, the infirm and financially strapped Giulio was placed under house arrest for refusing to cede the right of way to the higher-born Ottavio Archilei (son of fellow court musicians Vittoria and Antonio). Nearly everyone in Florence's musical and courtly establishments wrote letters on his behalf before the city authorities would set him free.[14]

The years of Francesca's childhood were not tranquil. In 1588 her mother Lucia—and all the rest of Florence's musical women—had been fired as part of the policy of the new grand duke, Ferdinando I, of purging Francesco I's luxuries from the court. Giulio immediately sought work that would include stipends for himself and his wife elsewhere, negotiating unsuccessfully for a position at Ferrara in 1589 and again in 1592. When Lucia died on 8 January 1593, Giulio was left with three children under the age of six, in addition to the fourteen-year-old Pompeo, and with no immediate hope of a second salary to offset expenses. Giulio was fired six months later because of a dispute over the affections of a courtesan known only as "la Gamberella," whose singing lessons with Giulio were subsidized by her lover Antonio Salviati, a patrician banker whose complaint Ferdinando I could not ignore.[15] Struggling to support himself and his family with the revenues from his singing studio, his financial trading, and his performing, in 1594 Giulio somehow found the resources to enter a long-term lease agreement with the Arte della Lana for property near Santissima Annunziata and to marry Margherita di Agostino della Scala, "Bargialli," an eighteen-year-old singer from so poor a family she brought only one hundred scudi as a dowry.[16] Giulio declined tantalizing offers of support from consortia of gentlemen in Florence and Genoa in 1595 but seems not to have returned to the stability of court service until October 1600.[17] Then, only days before the wedding of Marie de' Medici to Henri IV of France, he returned to the Medici payroll with his old monthly stipend of sixteen scudi.

The Caccini household teemed with activity. It was frequented by Giulio's many music pupils and by the poets, painters, musicians and melophiles of Florence's elite classes who flocked to visit the celebrated Giulio Romano and his increasingly celebrated family.[18] At least one such melophile, Sinolfo Ottieri, sometimes joined Francesca's and Settimia's music making, lavishing them with gifts of jewels and "treating them with such reverence and humility that he seemed to be dealing with princesses."[19] Amid the commotion, Giulio arranged to educate his eldest daughter—whom Bronzini characterized as "a girl of the sharpest intelligence"—as if she had been a child of the propertied class destined to life as a donna at court, like Tarqinia Molza, or as a learned monastic woman, like Isotta Nogarola.[20] Francesca studied Latin, rhetoric, poetics, geometry, astrology, philosophy, contemporary languages, "humanistic studies," and even a little Greek until the sudden death of her tutor interrupted that study.[21] She inclined so much to her books that Bronzini would claim, "If she had been allowed (as were Lastheneia and Axiothea, the disciples of Plato) to go in boys' clothing to public school she would have done as well as other renowned women and people of our time." Especially devoted to geometry, astrology, and "the occult sciences," Francesca also acquired a fine chancellory hand. Music, Bronzini reported, was something she had at first studied "only as a pastime, and to please her father."[22]

The effect of such a childhood on such a girl can only be imagined. It seems possible that the intellectually gifted Francesca could have internalized, along with her lessons, her father's ambition, his pride in the achievement of personal excellence, a taste for hubbub, and an anxious, internally confused sense of herself as both dependent on the power of others and worthy to be treated as if she were a princess. But because she was a daughter, not a son, of the celebrated Giulio Romano, this was not the sum of her formation. She had also been educated in the social graces expected of a gentlewoman, trained to behave in ways that would allow her a much smoother social life than that of her sometimes ill-mannered father.

The Institution of Womanhood

A rich body of advice literature concerning ways to train girls for genteel womanhood circulated in early modern Italy.[23] Whether they were erudite *letterati*, enterprising publishers, or hacks, authors affirmed that three interrelated virtues constituted the center of gravity for the institution of womanhood: *castità, onestà,* and *continenza.* Together they enclosed and policed a metaphysical space that defined a woman's relationship to the authority of fathers and, eventually, of husbands. A woman of onestà was absolutely faithful to her word, to her family, and eventually to her husband and his family; accommodating no efforts to breach her fidelity to authority, she was a person of unimpeachable integrity. A woman of castità was physically and morally untouched by desire. Mere physical intactness was not the whole of chastity, nor even its most important component. The crucial element was a woman's refusal of bodily or spiritual pollution, pollution that could as easily come from ideas, from dancing, or from overly spiced food as it could from the sexual intrusions of a man's body through the perimeters of hers.[24]

To withdraw modestly from overstimulation was both to preserve and to demonstrate one's castità, and, as almost all who wrote about the subject observed, the reputation for castità was as crucial as the fact of it. Continenza, the third of these virtues, subsumed the others, for it was the virtue of self-containment. Demonstrated and elaborated most conclusively by adult married women, continenza linked a woman's personal onestà and castità to her wifely role as conservatrix of her husband's patrimony. A woman of continenza exercised moderation in her *governo della casa* (oversight of household expenses), her personal adornment, and her choices of food, wines, entertainments, and household guests. From an economic and political point of view, continenza was the crowning virtue of the ideal wife, who lived to preserve her husband's property.[25] Her personal loyalty, her physical and spiritual chastity, her protection of her husband's home against inappropriate intrusions and of his patrimony from excessive expense—each was a sign of the other, the womanly virtues inextricably linked to each other by a notion of preserving and policing boundaries.[26]

How might a girl such as Francesca have learned these overlapping concepts of enclosure? Training in onestà began with a girl's first games and toys. She was only to play in the presence of her mother, her wet-nurse, or other girls, lest in the presence of a boy she learn inadvertently to love him and the love prove difficult to uproot.[27] Her toys were to model the tools she would later use in household management, so she would learn by play to lead a virtuous, chaste, industrious, and useful life. She was to be told stories that would develop her devotion to God, and she was to learn obedience and the self-discipline required for excellence from her father, learning to think of him as ruling the household as a prince ruled his state, with absolute authority. Fathers were never to forget the need to demonstrate their authority, however great their affection for their child. It was fathers—the only men Dolce mentioned as present in a young girl's life—who were charged with disciplining their daughters, exhorted to ensure that their daughters "weep often, and learn sadness so they might laugh and live happily when they are old."[28]

At the time of weaning (about age four) a girl would be taught to read and to sew.[29] Most writers specified that women's literacy should be different from men's; it should be a matter of reading, not writing, of receiving knowledge, not producing it. Properly both an ornament and a means to deepen a self-aware spirituality, a woman's literacy was not intrinsic to her identity, and it was not, as it was for men, the crucial means by which persuasion could intervene in relationships of power.[30] By contrast, sewing and related skills defined womanhood across the boundaries of social class. Poor women needed to know spinning and weaving to help support their families, while wealthy girls—even princesses—were to spin and weave to avoid wasting their time amid the idle talk of young female attendants and women courtiers, lest their frail minds wander off in uncontrollably frivolous directions: "What sort of talk is theirs? . . . Feminine thoughts are for the most part speedy, unstable, light, erring, and they don't know where to stop. . . . They [upper-class women and princesses] should not imitate the females of Persia who pass their days sitting among their eunuchs in banquets and songs and continuous pleasures and lusts."[31] Usefully tending to her textiles to prevent her mind from wandering, a virtuous woman would learn to focus her mind as a practice of constancy, a female virtue that was prerequisite to the total loyalty implied by onestà.

Because reading, too, could focus the mind, parents were advised exactly what their daughters ought to read in order to minimize their flightiness, develop their piety, and learn the moral philosophy needed for the prudent management of a household.[32] Patristic writings by Ambrose, Augustine, and Jerome, Latin histories by Cicero, Livy, and Quintus Curcius, and the ethical writings of Plato and Seneca were all recommended for girls, unlike the Horace, Ovid, and Virgil that Bronzini claimed Francesca had studied. Modern or lascivious vernacular books such as the works of Boccaccio were forbidden, although virtuous girls could read Petrarch, Dante, Bembo, the *Arcadia* of Sannazaro, the *morali* and dialogues of Sperone Speroni, and Castiglione's *Il libro del cortigiano,* as well as books about the Virgin Mary.[33]

Beyond the literacy and numeracy required to manage a household, learning was believed to develop girls' moral character. Constant study would preserve their onestà because it would so completely occupy their minds that they would be oblivious to dances, parties, and banquets.[34] Learned women were understood to be better equipped than ignorant ones to defend their castità, which they should be prepared to defend to the death.[35] But women need not (and should not) disperse their learning as boys and men did, in public demonstrations of prudence, eloquence, skill at governing, inventiveness, memory, art, industry, justice, liberality, and generosity. Instead, a woman's learning was to be contained within her self. As she learned to focus her mind she would become better able to resist the temptations of worldly festival, to manage her home well, and to tend to the health of her soul. Her attention thus turned inward, a learned woman could easily maintain what one writer called "the queen of women's virtues," her castità.[36]

A well-reared girl was expected to display her synthesis of genteel womanhood as "timidity and bashfulness: which happen to be virtually the base and foundation of the whole edifice of virtue," and by shunning personal adornment, drinking wine in moderation, avoiding meat, and fasting only when it was necessary to "enervate the body's strength and chill its heat."[37] Fasting and abstinence from meat would have been tacitly understood to serve two purposes directly related to womanhood. First, chilling the body literally preserved its femaleness, which pre-modern doctors believed to be signified by an inversion of the genitals caused by insufficient bodily heat. Second, because sexual desire was understood to result from heat, chilling the body was a way of controlling the capacity for sexual agency.[38] Most authors, however, recommended a restrained, chilling diet to ensure that "the mind be the master of the body, which serves."[39] Indeed, control of the body by the mind remained the theme of other prescriptions for ladylike behavior. Clothing was to be moderate and modest. No face coloring, mascara, perfume, or chemicals for dying or curling the hair should be used. A young woman should rise early and be constantly occupied "because idleness is the enemy of virtue, because leisure makes vile and earthly love grow."[40] If she appeared in public, an unmarried woman should be accompanied by her mother or another adult woman, her face was to be covered with a veil, and she should take care to walk neither so quickly as to signal flightiness nor so slowly as to suggest arrogance or pride. Nor should she ever laugh, lest she be deemed frivolous. "As for talking," the oft-reprinted Ludovico Dolce remarked, "I do not praise her using many words. . . . I do not want her to be mute, however, but [I want] that she seldom speak."[41] Elaborating his point for several pages, he concluded: "to gather many words into one, [the] most beautiful praise of a woman is her silence. Knowing how to dance, play music and sing is neither praise- nor blameworthy in a girl."[42]

"To please her father"

Like most musical women of her time, regardless of social rank, Francesca studied music to please her father by satisfying his ambitions.[43] Probably she began to learn music at about the time she learned to read. If contemporary sources about the way nonprofessionals learned virtuoso singing are to be believed, she would have begun singing the ritual song of Catholicism, plainchant. Morally suitable for children because it could teach them the spiritual practice of prayer, singing plainchant could also teach children fundamental musicality because of the repertoire's narrow range, emphasis on firm tonal centers, and simple but sophisticated rules for communicating the grammar and syntax of psalm-based texts through melodic gestures that either suspended the desire for closure or satisfied it. Sometime after she had learned to sing Francesca would have begun to study instrumental music making. She eventually mastered keyboards, viols, harp, lute, theorbo, and Spanish guitar, probably studying with professionals her father hired to teach her at home for an hour or more at a time. By the age of nine or ten, she would have learned the rudiments of contemporary modal theory, including the notion that particular sets of pitches could communicate affect as well as a text's grammar by exploiting different parts of a voice's range and by "tuning" the voice to specific mathematical relationships in the cosmos. To improve her ability to monitor the sounds and sights her body produced, Francesca would likely have practiced singing in a room with an echo, in front of a mirror.[44]

Musical training for genteel girls was understood to reinforce their enculturation to the institution of womanhood. Like her concentration on textiles and texts, music making gave a girl a decorous way to avert her gaze from those of her betters or of potentially desirous men. As Annibale Guasco wrote his daughter Lavinia: "if you should find yourself in the presence of your mistress when she is accompanied by the Lord Duke, or his courtiers . . . keep your head and eyes bent over your canvas and needle, or your clavichord and songbook, . . . without letting your gaze dart all around, for that would be interpreted not just as lack of self-restraint but as wantonness."[45] A girl's musical skill was to be hoarded like her dowry or her chastity. Genteel women were to practice their music alone in their rooms, as insurance against the unlikely chance that they might someday be asked to make music for others. A perfect outlet for the virtuous industry that protected them from the temptations of idleness, a girl's musical practice and resulting skill demonstrated her family's ability to invest in their daughter, if not necessarily to invest for her through the transfer of property into a dowry account.[46] Perhaps most important, a girl's musical training was a means by which she learned to submit to her father's discipline and to internalize the memory of that discipline as a memory of his investment in her,

a memory she would contemplate whenever she practiced. As Guasco wrote to
Lavinia:

> [Practice] imagining your father is with you in your chamber and at an ap-
> propriate moment exhorting and commanding you to it and that you are doing
> it more willingly out of reverence for him than you would do it for yourself. This
> fear must motivate you not only when you are away from me and subject to a rule
> other than mine but even when I am in my grave and nothing remains of me
> but a memory. . . . By thinking in this manner, you will be able to judge rightly
> whether I would have just cause to consider myself held in contempt if, upon
> entering your chamber, I saw you treating with little regard every small gift I had
> lovingly offered you. . . . [W]hat greater gift, acquired with what greater labor on
> my part, could I bestow on you, than the skills which I am now commending to
> you[?] . . . [Remember that] you are bound, under pain of mortal sin, to honor
> your father.[47]

Such memories could only reinforce the womanly virtues of onestà and
continenza.

Unlike Lavinia Guasco, Francesca Caccini learned much of her music directly
from a man who was considered the greatest singing teacher of his time, and
who was considered to have been the "father of a new kind of music, a singing
without song."[48] Her lessons in a home aswarm with other pupils and musicians
must have been especially intense; they surely included complete immersion in
the principles of her father's new kind of music, principles he presented to the
world in his 1602 book *Le nuove musiche*, along with twenty-four examples.[49] A
singer would usually perform this music alone, improvising an accompaniment
on lute, theorbo, harp, or keyboard and singing in a way that hovered between
speech and song. All musical choices, including constantly flexible dynamics
and the improvisation of ornaments, would be guided by a single fundamental principle—the imitation in music of the conceits that informed the song's
words. As Giulio's humanist mentors would have put it, paraphrasing Aristotle,
music should obey its text as a child does its father, a pupil its teacher, or a servant its master.

Read for both what they say and what they assume can be left unsaid, *Le
nuove musiche*'s verbal and musical texts allow one to speculate on what Giulio
taught his daughter Francesca. One thing she surely learned was her father's
claim for his new music's aesthetic origins in the principles of ancient Greek
music, a claim most persuasively made in his book's preface. The preface begins
by rambling gratuitously from subject to subject: Giulio's youthful study (subsidized by Grand Duke Francesco de' Medici) with the Neapolitan singer Scipione della Palla; his concern that his songs circulated too widely, in versions

so corrupt he described them as "tattered and torn"; his frustration with the confused textures produced by the counterpoint of part-songs. Coming suddenly into focus halfway through, Giulio's preface attributes his discovery of a new kind of music to his study amid the "nobility . . . musicians . . . poets and philosophers" who formed the humanist circle of the soldier-scholar Giovanni de' Bardi in the 1570s and 1580s. From Bardi's group Giulio learned "to follow that style so praised by Plato . . . who maintained music to be nothing other than rhythmic speech with pitch added"; he decided "to introduce a kind of music by which anyone could almost speak in music."[50] Giulio's new music, then, was best understood as a renewed music guided by the ancient aesthetic principles propounded by local humanist scholars.

The preface's sudden focus at the mention of Bardi's name instantiates in writing the expressive advantage Bardi and Giulio claimed for solo song over part-song; as solo song synthesized music's conflicting elements rather than confusing them as part-song did, so Bardi's humanist ideas synthesized Giulio's rambling thoughts. Further, the reference aligning Bardi's influence with a passage from Plato's *Republic* triggers memories of the classical materials cited by Bardi's circle. Few of these were focused on aesthetics, rhetoric, or music theory. Rather, they were mainly political treatises in which music was discussed only insofar as its practices affect the training of rulers or the health of the state. Moreover, the reference to Bardi points to a circle of men who were deeply enmeshed in shaping the artistic policy of Grand Duke Francesco I de' Medici's court and to Bardi's other important collaboration with Giulio Caccini, the creation of Tuscany's first ensemble of musical women, who provided virtuosa vocal chamber music under Giulio's direction until its disbanding in 1588. Bardi's name, that is, points to an unwritten history entangling Giulio's new soloistic music with Medicean power, a history Francesca could have learned directly from her father and his friends.

By the time Francesca was born, members of the Medici family had wielded hegemonic power over Tuscany for more than a century, a power won by wealth, brute force, extravagant patronage of the classical scholarship now called humanism, and the claim that a single person's view of reality provided better political leadership than the inevitable confusion of competing views that characterized republican democracy. But in 1587 the Medici's right to rule Tuscany as absolute princes was still relatively new. Cosimo I had been installed as duke in 1537 following the murder of his cousin Alessandro by exiled advocates of republican democracy and the ensuing defeat of those exiles by imperial troops. Cosimo swiftly consolidated his rule by war, the replacement of elected officials with newly ennobled appointed ones, and a cultural program designed to promote Tuscany's intellectual and artistic production as the best in the world.[51] Just as swiftly, he confirmed Tuscany's feudal allegiance to the Hapsburg empire by marrying the Neapolitan princess Eleanora da Toledo, who bore him two potential heirs, Francesco and Ferdinando. The elder son, Francesco I, succeeded Cosimo in 1574 and continued his father's policies. But Francesco's love affair with the merchant-class Venetian Bianca Cappello, his taste for introspective, private luxuries, and, worst of all, his inability to produce a legitimate heir marred both his reputation and his political usefulness. In 1587 Francesco and Bianca Cappello were murdered in their separate beds, within hours of each other. With the dynasty's very survival at stake, Ferdinando resigned his cardinalate and returned to serve as grand duke. Ferdinando I married his French cousin Christine de Lorraine in 1589 and set her to rearing their children in the country villa of Castello. Thus ensuring the biological survival of his father's Florentine-Neapolitan dynasty, Ferdinando demonstrated the vitality of Medici rule by showing himself a frugal steward of private and state resources, by using the diplomatic alliances he had forged at Rome to establish Tuscany as a world power, and by continuing his father's policy of promoting Florence's cultural supremacy to encourage local elites' pride in their city's excellence.

Although he had at first fired most of Francesco's musicians, including the ensemble of women favored by Bianca Cappello, in repudiation of his brother's wanton ways, by the turn of the seventeenth century Ferdinando had gathered back around him the musicians and scholars whose efforts to revive the supposed power and political utility of ancient music Francesco had quietly sponsored.[52] Included in that number were Giovanni de' Bardi and Giulio Caccini, men whose self-proclaimed creation of a new, overwhelmingly powerful kind of solo singing from the fusion of Neapolitan technique with Florentine humanist ideas might be likened to Giorgio Vasari's propagandistic paean to Florentine visual culture, *The Lives of the Artists.* When Francesca learned to make her father's classically justified "new music," she had to have known that her music could have been received, in part, as embodying Medicean dynastic power in sound. To please her father, she would have mastered the details of his singing without song.

Singing Lessons

Giulio's new kind of music depended as much on the distinctive expressive use of two singing techniques as it did on the relationships between words and music. These techniques, breath control and *gorgheggiando* (literally, warbling) both foregrounded aspects of singers' bodily self-mastery that had implications for their performances of gender and sex. Thus, they are likely to have been critical to Francesca's habits of being and eventually to her embodied self-concept.

Giulio's ideas about breath control are well known to musicians. To ensure good intonation he advocated marking the beginnings of sung words by landing directly on the desired pitch and decreasing—or, less often, increasing and decreasing—the sound's intensity until the next word began.[53] Applied to entire phrases, the constantly changing intensity of sound from word to word imitated the dynamic shape of speech, resulting in extremely clear declamation of a song's words. Each new word would seem to elicit from the singer's body an increased volume of breath that literally animated the words into song; the sound would die away as flesh does without the soul, until revived by a new word. If heard as arising from a singer's response to the text, such dynamic shading could sound like emotional fluidity, and it could imply that the singer's very body was controlled by the conceits, images, and feelings inscribed in the text.

The apparent responsiveness of a singer's constantly changing breath was best produced, Giulio argued, by bodies that produced their voices naturally, rather than by the steady, high-speed forcing of air through the vocal folds that characterizes men's falsetto singing. At the cusp of the seventeenth century this mattered, because high voices were thought to be best suited to texts of high emotions or rhetorical power.[54] In effect, Giulio implied that the bodies that were naturally suited to envoicing expressive nuance and rhetorical power were those of castrati and adult women.[55] As people who were socially inferior, even abject, in their nonvocal lives, they might also have seemed naturally suited to obeying, with their bodies, the conceits of a song's text. Giulio's preference for natural voices, then, foreshadowed the curious combination of social abjection and performing power that would characterize European modernity's performance culture. It also resonated with the contradictory feelings of abject dependence and performance-based entitlement that were part of his and his eldest daughter's personalities.

It is possible, too, that in the early seventeenth century people would have perceived the actions that produced Caccinian dynamic control as a way of articulating intrasubjective order. To produce the required ebb and flow of sonic intensity, a singer's diaphragm would have had to be in almost constant motion, changing the relative volume of chest and abdomen in the torso to control the movement of air into and out of the body. In the terminology of the sixteenth-century physician Francesco Sansovino, this constant changing of the proportion between chest and abdomen changed the proportion of a body's "nobile" and "ignobile"—its rational and bestial, or masterly and servile—parts.[56] Thus Francesca may have understood in her disciplined singer's gut that in her father's singing without song she controlled precisely the proportions of reason and sensuality, mastery and obedience within herself. She might, thereby, have been able to imagine her virtuosa breath control as analogous to the womanly self-control demanded by the virtue of continenza and as a component of what a twenty-first-century person would call agency.

Gorgheggiando—starting and stopping vocal sound by the split-second, infinitesimal opening and closing of the vocal folds as the air stream passed through—also required virtuosa self-control on the part of a singer. In part because gorgheggiando cannot physically be produced unless the intensity of the air stream remains low, it draws attention to the most intimate space of the throat with a sweet, gentle sound. Giulio did not claim to have invented this technique, but in the preface to *Le nuove musiche* he boasted that he had taught his two wives and his two eldest daughters to control the speed of their gorgheggiando at will.[57] Once they had mastered its speed, they could use throat articulation to ensure the absolute clarity of each note in the short ornaments called *trilli, gruppi,* and *cascate* as well as in the longer, often phrase-length *passaggi* to which Giulio's humanist advisors had uniformly objected as merely sensual pleasures. Yet throat articulation could emphasize the proper rule of words over music in the singing without song. Used on the penultimate note of a phrase, a trillo drew especially sensual attention to the desire for musical closure, emphasizing the penultimate syllable of a poetic line or thought. Used to articulate the melodic curve of a longer passaggio, throat articulation could enable each note of the phrase to be as discrete and independent from its neighbors as were the words of spoken language. Passages of untexted vocality that critics might dismiss as merely titillating to the ears could approach the condition of mentally controlled language because they were articulated by a singer's conscious control over her throat's utterance.

Articulating the boundary of the body as the resistance of the vocal folds to the exit of the *anima* as breath, and the boundary between vocality and silence, gorgheggiando dazzled in part because it added to a singer's display of self-mastery a second level of subtle, last-minute control over her breath's release. But while gorgheggiando was easily interpreted as an especially delicate gesture of bodily *continenza*, Francesca would have known that her body's prodigious control of her breath and throat was just as easily taken as a sign of something like sexual agency, for it controlled her body's heat.

Because it was known to be produced by rapid vibrations of the vocal folds, any naturally high voice was associated with the generative power of fire.[58] Thus Francesca's voice poured from her body as heat, filling her throat with heat. Given that ancient medical writers still widely read in early modern Europe likened a woman's throat to her uterus and her uvula to her clitoris, the heat-filled throat of a female singer might logically have been understood as a space linked disturbingly to the possibility of sexual self-pleasuring.[59] If the heat of her singing throat was a natural result of her femaleness, the rapid, controlled articulation of the vocal folds with which she sang ornaments and trills surely added to that heat. Indeed, Sansovino argued that the voices most suited to highly flexible, ornamented singing came from bodies that were naturally cold and wet—the bodies of women and castrati—because they were most able to tolerate a build-up of heat.[60]

One way of controlling a body's heat was to control the breath, for in the most common view of early modern medicine the purpose of breathing was to control the body's heat. Inhalation cooled the body, and exhalation released the hot, noxious fumes produced by the heart, the body's furnace.[61] Body heat, in turn, was understood to affect both biological sex and sexual desire. Hot and therefore dry bodies were manly ones, efficient burners of the body's fuel. Cold and therefore wet bodies were effeminate. Whether their coldness was produced by the fasting recommended for girls or by the surgical removal of heat-producing testicles, they burned fuel inefficiently, excreting uncombusted resources such as the peculiarly female fluids milk and menstrual blood. Hot, dry bodies were necessary for imaginative thought, were susceptible to sexual arousal and, under the right circumstances, released seed for reproduction in the moment of orgasm. Thus when women's bodies were heated by the intentional sexual stimulation of their partners—or, as ancient medicine taught, by singing or dancing professionally—their bodies began to resemble the efficiently combusting, imaginatively thinking, and sexually ready bodies of men.[62] In turn, when a singer such as Francesca displayed her mastery over both her breath's release and the heat of her throat, she inevitably displayed control over her humoral sex and over her readiness for sexual arousal. In the aesthetic regime of Giulio's new kind of music, this dangerously empowering mastery was meant to be controlled by the onestà with which her musical choices respected the authority of her song's poetic conceits.

The preface to *Le nuove musiche* concludes with various short ornaments in notation, followed by several extended examples of how an improvising singer might combine short and long ornaments to produce multiple close readings of a text. These examples offer vividly evocative evidence of the flexibility he might have taught his daughter. The very multiplicity of Giulio's examples teaches that the most faithful respect for a text's authority allowed singers considerable freedom in their interpretive choices, even were they to choose (as Giulio does in examples 1.1 to 1.3) to further constrain their choices by improvising within the conventions of a common aria like the agitated romanesca.[63] A singer might choose, as in example 1.1, to improvise a melody whose upward gestures on the word "non" contradict the romanesca's conventionally descending tune, enacting as melodic struggle a resistance to languor that fails when the word itself is sung.

Or she might choose, as in example 1.2, to emphasize the almost nonverbal exclamation "deh," struggling vainly to fill it with the energy of dotted-rhythm ornaments, while delivering the word "languire" on a single middling pitch that is bereft of animating musical energy.

Ex. 1.1, Giulio Caccini, *Le nuove musiche* (1602), preface, "Deh, non languire" (Oh, don't languish)

Ex. 1.2, Giulio Caccini, *Le nuove musiche* (1602), "Deh, non languire," second version

Ex. 1.3, Giulio Caccini, *Le nuove musiche* (1602), "Deh, non languire," fourth version

Or her voice might collapse onto the pitch marking languor almost at once, long before the feeling is named, as in example 1.3, resisting only with the slightest of ornaments until her voice, resting on the apparently unadorned "languire," shrinks in intensity only to grow again in executing the *esclamatione affetuosa* that the book's preface had explicitly named as a sonic emblem of languor.

Giulio's most provocative lesson in interpretive agency is his proposed reading of the single word "parto" from his little romanesca's second line, "Ahimè, ch'io moro! Parto." (Alas, I die! I leave.) "Parto" is the most lavishly ornamented word among all Giulio's examples, a veritable tour de force of gorgheggiando gruppi, trilli, ribatute di gola, and passaggi crammed into a phrase that sustains the first vowel for so long that the word "parto" risks being wholly unintelligible to listeners (see example 1. 4).

Giulio seems to break entirely with the aesthetic principle by which all his previous ornaments had been justified: the principle that in the new kind of music all musical choices should serve the conceit of a poetic text, as the ser-

Ex. 1.4, Giulio Caccini, *Le nuove musiche* (1602), "Parto" (I leave)

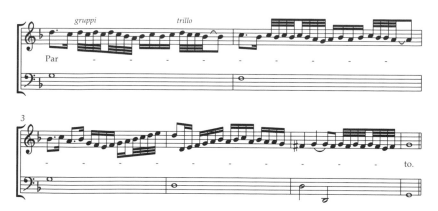

vants of a household do its master, or children their father. It is as if "parto" has metaphorically left the house, refused the authority of a musical phrase's proper master and, especially in its old-fashioned scalewise, mode-articulating passaggio from a low e′ to d″, behaved according to wholly musical rules beyond the control of verbal reason. And yet, in a way the phrase "parto" obeys both the imperatives of the new kind of music and the conceit of the text by enacting its own meaning—"I leave." In this case, to obey is to disobey, extravagantly, and to disobey is to obey. A lesson in Baroque paradox and in resistance (however temporary) to the tyrannies embedded in a power regime constructed of mind-body, master-servant, teacher-pupil dyads, it was a lesson that Francesca would develop into the wit that informed her adult art.

"Le donne di Giulio Romano"

Francesca's identity as the daughter of Giulio Romano had surely been impressed on her contemporaries by the circumstances of her earliest public music making. She is first known to have performed as one of the women of her father's household in two musical entertainments produced for the marriage of Marie de' Medici (the niece of Grand Duke Ferdinando I) to Henri IV, king of France, in October 1600. Ensemble singers in the production of Jacopo Peri and Ottavio Rinuccini's *L'Euridice* that the banker Jacopo Corsi had donated to the marriage festivities as his gift, Giulio's women also took all the female parts in his setting of Gabriello Chiabrera's spectacular *Il rapimento di Cefalo*, the theatrical fable commissioned and staged by the Medici themselves.[64] Despite Ferdinando I's command that the official description should not "name so many musicians," that account particularly praised the music Giulio had composed and the performance he had drawn from "four women of his family with angelic voices excellently disciplined by him in singing, and in singing and acting from the stage."[65] For the next decade, Giulio and his well-disciplined women were to be the only musicians named in official descriptions of Medici court music making.

In that decade, "le donne di Giulio Romano" served Ferdinando I and his heirs as substitutes for the ensemble of women Ferdinando had dismantled a decade earlier. That ensemble had been formed by Giulio Caccini at the command of Francesco I, partly in emulation of Ferrara's famed *musica segreta*.[66] Coming from other cities to serve as *dame* or *donne* to the women of the Este family and provided with generous dowries, stipends, and noble husbands, the four women in Ferrara's ensemble had served their duchesses by participating with them in plays and *balletti* produced solely for the pleasure of the immediate family. But they also served at the duke's command, singing for guests with whom he wanted to share the open secret of Ferrarese court life: the spectacle of women's perfect vocal and gestural fidelity to the minutely detailed notation of manuscript scores that he ostentatiously displayed. Both their extravagantly ornamented singing and the sensual pleasure it produced in listeners were to be understood as controlled by the duke's authority as it had been delegated to the ensemble's composer-directors, Ippolito Fiorini and Luzzasco Luzzaschi. Thus performances of Ferrara's musica segreta displayed the duke's patriarchal control of women's bodies and, in their seductively beautiful fidelity to the scores' symbolic inscription of his power, the women's corresponding onestà. Both were easily construed as representing the Este duke's absolute power over the people of his tiny principality.

As reconstructed after 1600 in the form of "le donne di Giulio Romano," Florence's ensemble of women brilliantly adapted the Ferrarese model to Ferdinando I's self-fashioning. Following Florentine tradition in many arts, the singers were not imported from other courts but were home-grown, not nobly born but upwardly mobile artisan-class girls, not performing in slavish obedience to written notes but seeming to improvise freely their responses to others' words as they had been taught to do under the authority of a Tuscan subject who, like the grand duke, had begun his career in Rome. The ensemble always performed for occasions when Ferdinando I's biological family was on symbolic display: the marriage of his niece in 1600, the simultaneously personal and political visit of Cardinals del Monte and Montalto in 1602, and, with notable regularity, when the Medici family gathered to attend the offices of Holy Week in the passageway that linked their palaces in Florence and Pisa to the adjoining parish churches.[67] For these latter performances, the Caccini women sang under Giulio's direction from the very space occupied by the Medici family—the passageway that linked their private to their public lives, a space from which their princely bodies could not be seen by the people who gathered to share their parish worship. Thus, in the only performance moments when the donne di Giulio Romano might be heard by ordinary Tuscans, the voices of women from Giulio's famiglia could easily have seemed like extensions of the princely famiglia beside whom they stood. In these performances, then, the voices of the donne di Giulio Romano were the outward and audible signs of the ruling family's presence, modeling in sound and social reality the Medicean concept of patronage through the trope of famiglia and the Aristotelian image of the family as the model for a well-ordered state.

When Bronzini wrote that Francesca was at first serious about her music to please her father, he evoked his contemporaries' memories of her artistic roots in these youthful performances of obedience to personal, patronage, and political tropes of family. At every level of her being—personality, education, performance history, even perhaps in terms of her performance-induced flexibility of gender and sex—Francesca was a product both of her father's investment in her and of Medicean power. The erudition, excellence, and political utility that Bronzini would attribute to her adult work in the service of Ferdinando I's widow and daughter-in-law could thus seem always to have been contained within the virtues she shared with those women: the fidelity to paternal and husbandly authority that was onestà and the concern to preserve and reproduce a family's patrimony for another generation that was continenza.

"To win the girl";
or, Francesca as Object of Desire

2

At the age of twenty, Francesca would be appointed as a musica on the staff of the Granducato of Tuscany. The position, which allowed her father access to her talents until his own retirement, was to be the one in which Francesca would enjoy the most fully professional, productive career any European woman musician had yet known. The story of her hiring is made up of three unusually well-documented tales: that of her family's 1605 sojourn at the French court of Henri IV and his Florentine wife Marie de' Medici, when Francesca's performances transformed her into an object of royal desire; that of her father's 1606 negotiation to place her in the service of the Montalto-Peretti family, Rome's most important patrons of new music; and that of her first known composition for the stage, written with Michelangelo Buonarroti the younger for the Medici court's 1607 Carnival celebration.

Common to all three tales is the relationship of artistic servants to their masters in early seventeenth-century Italy—a relationship that resembled that of daughters to their fathers in a patriarchal sex-gender system. As fathers exchanged daughters to create and sustain relationships between their families, so princely households exchanged performances and artistic workers. A father who was, like Giulio Caccini, an artistic servant seeking his daughter's lifelong security needed to recognize opportunities to make his child the object of patrons' desire and, as necessary, to encourage patrons' competition for his child's services as if she were the prize in a game. Giulio, Francesca, and, eventually, their friend Buonarroti played that game to pique Grand Duchess Christine de Lorraine's desire to win the girl, a victory that led directly to

Francesca's hiring and her marriage to an impoverished if handsome colleague, both at the command of the grand duchess.

The Caccini in Paris

On 24 August 1604, King Henri IV of France and his wife, Marie de' Medici, each wrote letters to Florence asking the grand duke and grand duchess, respectively, to "borrow for several months" the services of "Giulio Caccini's ensemble, and his daughters."[1] After a five-week delay caused in part by Giulio's ill health, on 30 September he left for France with his wife, two daughters, a son, a boy singing pupil, two carriages, six mules, and 450 scudi, more than twice his annual salary, to cover the expenses of a sojourn that would last nine months.[2] On the way, the troupe stopped at Modena to sing for the Este family, at least once singing with Princess Giulia d'Este, whom a Florentine diplomat described as a woman of "rarest intellect."[3] The family was delayed in Milan for five days because Francesca was ill with tertian fever (a form of malaria), and they spent another five days in Turin, where their performances for the duke and duchess of Savoy earned the Caccini girls gifts of jewels.[4] Everywhere, Giulio reported in his letters, they were treated as guests; thus, he had not needed to spend any of the travel allowance on food or lodging.[5] Arriving in Paris by 6 December, 1604, the family was given rooms in the home of the Florentine resident ambassador, Girolamo Gondi, along with kitchen privileges, firewood, and an allotment of wine.[6] There, according to Giulio, the ambassadors from Spain and Venice and an Austrian archduke came to hear them sing.[7] The family received a gift of one hundred scudi from the queen's favorite, Concino Concini, and a another one hundred scudi from Concini's wife, Leonora Doni Gagliari, who served as dama d'onore to France's Medici queen. Leonora's gift was to allow Giulio to "dress my women in French fashion," a fashion they reportedly endured more happily than the French fashion of kissing, which they emphatically rejected.[8] During the next few months, the Caccini consort would perform perhaps half a dozen times for the French sovereigns, sometimes alone and sometimes with the king's chamber singers.[9]

For the rest of his life Giulio would cite his family's Paris sojourn as if it had been the high point of his professional career. A moment when he was the object of royal desire as a performer, teacher, and ensemble director, it served in his letters as evidence that he deserved the respect and the favors he continually sought from his masters in Tuscany. Yet the voluminous epistolary record of the family's trip to Paris tells a slightly different story.

By all accounts the Caccini's reception at the French court was at first decidedly cool. Indeed, the Florentine diplomat Bacio Giovannino reported that Henri and Marie had quarreled over who would pay the family's expenses, each accusing the other of having initiated the request for their services.[10] Concini reported to Florence that Giulio behaved at court in a way that was "ill-bred and ill-advised," attracting irritation at his arrogance rather than admiration for his excellence.[11] But one evening in February 1605 the family's fortunes changed, when Francesca's performance of French songs before the king made everyone marvel—and made the king declare her the best singer in all of France.[12] The following day, both Giulio and Giovannino wrote home with the news that Francesca had been offered a position serving the French court.[13] Writing as an artistic servant to his patron the grand duke, Giulio asked permission to negotiate the terms of both musical service and marriage for Francesca, in whose person he shared patriarchal rights with his master. Writing to the secretaries of Tuscany's ministry of state, the meticulously gossipy Giovannino reported that the French queen was so keen to have Francesca that she was willing "to give the other (Settimia) enough that she could marry."

Seizing the opportunity, Giulio at once began to act as much as Francesca's father as he did as the director of a visiting ensemble. He worked tirelessly to leverage her desirability into courtly offers that would benefit the entire family. In two months of intense negotiation, the duc d'Umène would offer Pompeo Caccini a place as a painter at Fontainebleau and the duchesse de Guise would offer a place and a dowry for Settimia.[14] Eventually, Giulio's letters would make it seem that someone in France wanted everyone in his entourage, whether individually or as an ensemble, since even his wife Margherita had "trills that never failed to astound Their Majesties."[15] During the negotiations just one person, known only as "Monsù le Grandi," is reported to have consulted Francesca about her preferences, accosting her, according to Giulio, the very evening of her dazzling performance to ask if she would be willing to stay in France.[16] No one saw fit to record her reply. By late April, all thought of the Caccini's service to the French court had ended. Giovannini reported that Giulio had been hesitant to leave Francesca in France, married to a Frenchman.[17] No matter how persistently Concini had negotiated on his behalf—in compliance, Giovannini wrote, with Grand Duchess Christine's will—and no matter how determined Queen Marie had been to take her, Giulio's hesitancy had finally caused the queen's desire for Francesca's service to chill.[18]

Giovannini's letter contradicts the usual supposition of music historians that the grand duke had denied Giulio permission to leave Francesca in France. No letter from the grand duke survives to clarify the point. But there is ample evidence that neither Giulio's nor Ferdinando's interests would have been served had she remained there and that Giulio had shrewdly exploited the French court's escalating desire for his family's services in an effort to better their circumstances at home. As early as 1 March 1605, Giulio had written the grand duke's nephew, Virginio Orsini, expressing reluctance to part with Francesca—

a reluctance he expressed in terms both of the labor he had invested in her and of her usefulness to his own ability to serve his Tuscan prince: "I would be forever sorry to deprive myself in Italy of those labors that could make me shine for as long as I live, besides the convenience I have had of being able to serve my patrons, which is what I value above everything else."[19] He went on to contextualize Francesca's transformative performance of French songs as only one element of the ensemble's excellence, which Giulio's labor had produced in service to Tuscany: "[A]lthough in the beginning we had some difficulty, finally at the end, having heard us again with their ensemble and made every comparison, and hearing with what facility little Francesca sang in French, with such good expression of the words, making their Majesties and all these princes marvel, . . . they said that there was no one in France who sang better than she, and that this was the best music in France, which I heard from the King's own mouth."[20]

Giulio's letter to Orsini reminds one that the Caccini family's entire Paris sojourn had been undertaken at the command of their Tuscan patrons. Their journey and their work in France served to strengthen the Tuscan-French alliance that Marie de' Medici's uncle, Grand Duke Ferdinando, and her husband Henri IV had sealed in the customary way, by the exchange of a woman in marriage. In the gift economy that characterized early modern social networks, that alliance would have been strengthened by the request, the response, and the fact of sharing particularly gifted artistic servants. As the very singers whom Ferdinando had allowed to be named in the official description of the Franco-Florentine wedding of 1600, Giulio Romano, his donne, and those dependent on him constituted an especially evocative gift. In the terms of the performance studies scholar Richard Schechner, their performances promised to "restore the behavior" of an already fraying alliance by re-creating the sonic splendor and sovereign vocal magic of the 1600 celebrations.[21] The Caccini's work in Paris, then, was as much political service to the grand duke as it was musical service to the French king and queen. The warming of the French court signaled the success of that service.

When Francesca's expressive performance of French song moved the king to praise and the queen to desire, the possibilities for the Caccini to serve their granducato by serving the French dramatically changed. As a learned Tuscan girl whose performances displayed both knowledge of the French language and, in her mastery of French singing style, a literal ability to incorporate French ways, Francesca may have struck both king and queen as all that Marie de' Medici was not.[22] The prospect of Francesca's long-term service in France may, therefore, have both reminded the queen of her own happier youth and represented the fantasy of a Tuscan woman's assimilation into France that was embedded in her marriage to Henri. At the same time, because Francesca was to have been married to a suitable Frenchman, she would have literally replicated at a different level of society the political work of the queen's marriage: the strengthening of Franco-Florentine ties through the exogamous exchange of women. For the French, and especially for the Medicean French queen, this must have been a tempting prospect.

But had Francesca remained in France, perhaps with her father's entire family ensemble, they would have performed at the command of the French king. Their subjection to Henri's will might have seemed, to some, to symbolize Tuscany's subjection to the greater power of the French monarchy. Because Ferdinando's political and personal investment in the French alliance had cooled by 1605, even the appearance of his servants' subjection to Henri may have seemed unthinkable. Giulio and his consort would best serve their prince by returning home intact, with the added value that Francesca's performance had brought them: the value of having been the object of genuinely royal desire that Tuscan patriarchy had denied.

The person whose performance had unexpectedly elicited that royal desire, the seventeen-year-old "little Francesca," came to seem irreplaceable to both her father and his patrons. Thus concentric circles of patriarchal power converged to seal her fate, regardless of what her own will might have been. Still, Francesca must have known that it had been her virtuosity that shifted the family's fortune, as she must have known that her performance had begun to shift the dynamics of her relationship with her father. In Paris, he had become as much the father of "little Francesca" as she was "the daughter of Giulio Romano."

Negotiations with the Peretti-Montalto Clan

The Caccini family left Paris in early May 1605 armed with letters of recommendation to ensure safe travel and fifteen hundred scudi from the king's and the queen's treasuries.[23] As before, they had hardly any travel expenses, for as they retraced their journey through Lyons, Turin, Milan, and Modena they lodged wherever possible at princely households, making music in exchange for hospitality.[24] By late June all but Francesca had returned to Florence. Left in Modena until mid-November 1605, Francesca taught Giulia d'Este, whose family was negotiating her marriage to a French prince, "to sing certain songs in French."[25] She must have done her work well, for Giulia's mother, Duchess Virginia Medici d'Este, expressed reluctance to let such a virtuosa go.[26]

The Medici court diary and the surviving letters of the court are silent about the Caccini for the next two years, but a flurry of documents from the first quarter of 1607 reveals Giulio to have been busy during that period. Acting simultaneously as his daughters' father, as the granducato's servant, and as a musician whose own work at court depended on his ongoing access to his daughters' performance skills, he had negotiated to place Francesca and Settimia in two households of an extended Roman family linked by marriage and political alliance to the Medici—the melophile family of the princes Peretti, headed by the vice-chancellor of the Papal States, Alessandro Peretti Damasceni, known as Cardinal Montalto.

On 7 January 1607 Giulio wrote Prince Virginio Orsini, Ferdinando I de' Medici's nephew and Cardinal Montalto's brother-in-law, to ask for lodging in Rome for as long as it took him, his wife, and Settimia to present Francesca to the service of Orsini's sister-in-law "Princess Peretti," born Margherita della Somaglia. Evidently his Medici patrons fully approved: "[H]aving told me that since service to Cardinal Montalto and service to them is the same thing, they know they can send for Cecchina and for Signora Ippolita anytime, as confidently as His Lordship has when he wanted Signora Vittoria."[27] For Giulio to have described Francesca as entering the service of the Princess Peretti, not that of her husband Prince Michele Peretti, almost certainly meant that her contract would have been modeled on those of the women who had formed Ferrara's musica segreta a generation earlier.[28] Like them, she was to be on the payroll of the princess and to serve at her command as a way of preserving her chastity and, just as important, her reputation for chastity. Prince Peretti would neither command her nor pay for her body's pleasurable, desire-inducing, implicitly sexualized performances, except insofar as he could command her through his wife.

However indirectly, Francesca must have been expected to serve the prince, the only lay heir to the fortune accumulated when his great-uncle Felice Peretti (1520–1590) had become Pope Sixtus V in 1585. Everyone in Michele Peretti's household in turn indirectly served his even wealthier older brother, Cardinal Montalto. Boasting an annual income of more than one hundred thousand scudi, Montalto was one of the most energetic and enthusiastic patrons of the new virtuosic solo music in early modern Italy.[29] It was with Montalto that Giulio had negotiated Francesca's placement. To serve in Montalto's musical establishment would have meant working with Rome's most acclaimed musicians, Giovanni Bernardino Nannino, Orazio Michi, Cesare Marotta, and one of the best singers then working, Marotta's virtuosa wife Ippolita Recupito. All of them like Francesca brilliant improvisers, they were well paid for work intended to dazzle Montalto's guests by projecting through their highly individualized music making their patron's heroic capacities for "individuality, stupefaction, force, power, persuasion, influence, and domination."[30]

Service with so distinguished a musical entourage could have been a thrilling professional environment for Francesca—assuming that she had by then resolved to channel her intellectual energy toward the life of a musical virtuosa. Yet there is some evidence that such service had its unpleasant side, requiring the capacity to accept without complaint the patrons' stark objectification of their servants for the sake of displaying princely power. Cesare Marotta wrote of one evening when he and Ippolita were commanded on a half-day's notice to perform for about two and a half hours at the Bentivoglio country palace for the Duke and Duchess of Massa, the Bentivoglio family and their entourage, and Cardinal Mellini. Evidently their performances pleased everyone, and Ippolita received a diamond wand for her trouble. But from her husband's letter we know that the cost to Ippolita of that evening was especially high: "Ippolita did as well as possible, sang a few things, although with very great difficulty, because she is in her sixth month of what has been a very difficult pregnancy. . . . I can assure you that she could hardly breathe, and as a consequence could not sing at her usual level."[31]

Neither Marotta nor Recupita could decline an order from the cardinal, not even an order that asked a pregnant woman to take a carriage ride across the city and sing in a style largely dependent on breath control for its success before an audience primarily composed of unmarried, nominally celibate men. Although Marotta's letter alluded to his wife's physical discomfort, he left unstated her social discomfort: as a woman who merited the title "dama," she had not been raised to present her pregnant body to the gaze of men outside her immediate family. To do so breached her continenza.[32] Almost certainly the Bentivoglio family, Montalto himself, and their guests gave no thought to Ippolita's embarrassment; they would have assumed her performance to have been within the bounds of their famiglia. Moreover, like her husband or any other paid musician, Ippolita was only a means for her patrons' entertainment, an object whose virtuosity could be displayed and collectively enjoyed as a sign of the cardinal's power. As a woman, however, Ippolita was doubly objectified, forced to display her sexual difference in its most dramatic and uncomfortable form. As much by their discomfort as by their musical virtuosity, Recupita and Marotta performed Montalto's power in the social and sexual hierarchies of Rome—the power of an unmarried Prince of the Church, untainted by contact with women, to command a married man to command and accompany the performance of his pregnant and ill wife in a space outside the couple's or the cardinal's household.

Francesca could have expected much the same treatment—double objectification based on social rank and sex and the use of her performances to demonstrate the power of Rome's aristocracy of celibate men over women and married men. But Francesca may not have been meant to confront such power alone. As noted above, according to Giulio's plan, approved by his patrons, his musical daughters were both to be in Rome.

Giulio had opened his January 1607 letter asking lodging from Orsini with elaborate if belated condolences on the September 1606 death of Orsini's wife, Flavia Peretti.[33] His condolences ended with an elliptical but suggestive remark about Settimia's particularly strong response to Flavia's death: "Of Settimia's [grief] I will not speak, because Your Excellence knows that she could not have lost more, even if she had lost me, her father."[34] It is possible to read this remark as suggesting only an important emotional bond between Settimia and the musically and poetically gifted princess who had until fourteen months earlier lived at the Florentine court. But it seems equally possible to read it in relation to a curious remark Giulio had made about Settimia in a letter he wrote Orsini from Paris two years earlier. Reporting that he had been asked to leave Settimia in service to the duchesse de Guise, Giulio reported, as well, that he had given a cagey reply intended to protect Orsini's interests: "Madame de Guise then asked me for Settimia, and made these gentlemen talk to me, attesting every one of them to the good treatment she would have, to which I replied that if the other one [Francesca] remained I wanted this one for myself, without naming Your Excellency, because you are a friend of the duc de Guise, her brother."[35] Taken together, the two remarks suggest that Orsini and his wife had a very special interest in Settimia's future. Indeed, it seems possible that as early as late winter 1605 Giulio—with the presumed approval of his patrons—had discussed placing Settimia in the service of Flavia Peretti.[36]

Had there been such an arrangement, then a parallel arrangement for Francesca in the household of Prince Michele Peretti (through service to his wife) would have ensured that each Peretti household in Rome had a virtuosa on staff. Each woman's performances would have signaled her household's power, as Ippolita Recupita's did the cardinal's. In addition, however, having a Caccini daughter in each household would have given the extended Peretti family a *concerto delle donne* of almost unimaginable collective virtuosity. Projecting the family's power as transcending household boundaries, such an ensemble would simultaneously have articulated the hierarchy of households within the clan. As the senior singer, Recupita would sing the cardinal's household as the source of the others' power and wealth; Francesca, the next most senior, would sing the lay brother's secular power; Settimia, the youngest, most beautiful, and least educated of the three, would have sung for the household with the least prestige, that of the Peretti sister living in Rome. Stylistically sounding the harmonious entwining of Recupita's Neapolitan virtuosity with the Florentines' more austere, language-driven singing without song, such an ensemble could have embodied the Peretti's most important extra-Roman alliances, those with Tuscany and Naples. And because (as Giulio had noted in his letter to Orsini) the same ensemble would have been available to the Medici at any time, its every performance would have renewed the alliance between two princely families. First formed in the politicking by which Cardinal Ferdinando de' Medici had ensured Felice Peretti's election as Pope in 1585, that alliance had been sealed at the level of princely marriage by Flavia Peretti's marriage to Virginio Orsini, Ferdinando's nephew. From his Medici patrons' point of view, then, Giulio's agreement to place his daughters with the Peretti would have enabled the exchange of musicians between the families both to articulate anew a political and kinship alliance and continually to restore the alliance as behavior in every performance.

When Flavia Peretti ne' Orsini died unexpectedly after bearing her twelfth child in September 1606, the vision of intertwined Medici and Peretti musical splendor died with her. So did Giulio Caccini's plan to place his daughters in situations ensuring them dowries and husbands while ensuring himself and his patrons access to their skills. All had good reason to rethink their agreement to place Francesca amid the Peretti, if she were to go to Rome alone. As it would turn out, although Francesca would enjoy lively ties to the Peretti and Orsini households for years to come, she would never directly serve either Margherita della Somaglia or Cardinal Montalto. New circumstances that emerged between 7 January and 5 March 1607, including her own apparent debut as a theatrical composer, led to Francesca's placement at home.

Two months after Giulio had all but announced his arrival in Rome to place Francesca in service, he wrote letters to two differently situated readers explaining the reasons why he would not do so. Exactly parallel in their rhetorical structure yet exactly opposite in their factual claims, the two letters—to Virginio Orsini and Grand Duchess Christine—show how skilled play with (and from within) contradictory statements could grant musicians of the Caccini's social rank some self-determination in a patronage system built on princes' prestige games.[37]

Each letter began with gratitude for the favors Giulio and his family had received from their patron: to Orsini, Giulio was grateful for the offer of lodging in Rome with which his earlier letter had been answered; to Christine, he was grateful for unnamed favors during a recent "grave illness." Each letter then narrowed the scope of Giulio's gratitude in a way that transformed the expression of thanks into an implicit sharing of information: to Orsini, the narrowing focused on how much the Caccini daughters had looked forward to their trip so they could honor him for all the other favors he had done them; to Christine, the narrowing focused first on Giulio's gratitude for her gift to Francesca of a dress to thank the girl for "having worked such a little thing in [her] service" and then on his claim that Francesca had done the work "only from the pure will she has always had to serve Your Highness." Each letter then moved to its rhetorical center, a statement of Giulio's action in relation to the Montalto affair that seemed logically related to that which preceded it. To Orsini, Montalto's brother-in-law, he wrote that he would postpone his trip because he had heard that Montalto's interest in Francesca had chilled.[38] To the grand duchess he wrote that he had pretended to Cardinal Montalto to have heard that his interest in Francesca had chilled.[39]

Although the two major statements directly contradict each other, the action they signified had the same result: Giulio had broken his agreement with Montalto for Francesca's services. As Michelangelo Buonarroti would write Christine the next day, it was clear that "interest in the relationship had chilled, on one part or the other."[40] It mattered not one whit to Francesca's future which side had initiated the chill, so long as Orsini and Christine each responded to Giulio's letters in the way he suggested benevolent patrons should: for Giulio's letters to the pair end almost as they had begun, equal and opposite requests balancing equal and opposite gratitude to complete the perfect contradiction. Giulio asked Orsini outright for help in mending his relationship with the Montalto. But Giulio only implied what he needed from the grand duchess, reminding her that without Francesca his consort would break apart; that when her son, the fast-maturing Prince Cosimo, would come to power he would be well served by "a subject as virtuosa and valuable" as Francesca; and that he, Giulio, had given up a promised dowry when he broke his agreement with Montalto. Elliptical though his letter to Christine may be, it is perfectly clear how Giulio wanted his patron to respond. When added to the "small thing" Francesca had done for the grand duchess, Giulio's gift—the deception of a prince and the sacrifice of a dowry—merited more than a dress in response. Or, rather, they merited not just any dress but the official dress of Medici court service.

La stiava

What did Francesca do that could have merited her appointment to the musical staff of a granducato that had only recently been content to let her go to Rome? The answer seems to lie in a set of documents entwined with those that tell the story of the abortive Montalto plan. Those documents detail the plans and production of the court's principal entertainment for Carnival 1607, a *barriera* invented, designed, and scripted by Michelangelo Buonarroti the younger known as *La stiava*, for which the nineteen-year-old Francesca composed what the court's official diary described as "una musica stupenda," a music that does not survive.[41]

Although the preparations for *La stiava* are among the most well documented in Medicean theatrical history, it is impossible to know from the surviving evidence exactly when Buonarroti had turned to Francesca as his barriera's composer.[42] Among his papers Buonarroti saved a letter from one of Christine's secretaries, Curtio Picchena, dated 29 January 1607, in which Picchena gently rejected Buonarroti's idea for a barriera on the subject of the Horatii and Curiatii.[43] Christine approved a barriera in principle, but she wanted one that would end with dancing by cast members and guests and that could reuse costumes from previous entertainments. By 5 February Picchena had written again to ask for the *invenzione*.[44] In a letter to the grand duchess dated the same day, Buonarroti defended himself against the implied charge of slowness. He had been trying to serve as quickly as possible by carrying the verses as they were finished, bit by bit, to the house of Giulio Romano, "whose daughter I have asked with the advice and consent of her father to do the music, and it is very beautiful . . . as soon as the music is finished I will send it to Your Serene Highness."[45]

Francesca, who a month earlier had been described by her father as eager to leave for Rome, had suddenly been asked to compose music for the final entertainment of the Medici court's Carnival at Pisa, the apogee of a season that would include a *commedia in musica* written and composed by the skilled amateur poet and musician Cardinal Ferdinando Gonzaga. By Sunday, 18 February, Francesca had evidently composed all of the show's music: a sinfonia "for many instruments" to which the cast would enter, more than eighty lines of monologue and dialogue in recitative style, and a strophic five-voice chorus to which the company and, eventually, select members of the audience would dance in the Italian and the French styles. According to a letter from her father to Buonarroti, by that Sunday Francesca had "had the parts sung many times" under her supervision, and she had written them "in a way that they can be revised there," during final rehearsals in Pisa that she would apparently not attend.[46] Receiving a last-minute addition to the text that very day, she had composed music for it at once and was sending it to Pisa that evening with her brother Pompeo.[47] By then, less than four weeks after the earliest time Buonarroti could have asked for it, Francesca's work was done. She had only to wait in Florence to learn how her music for a court entertainment that seemed particularly important to the grand duchess would be received.

Christine's unusual interest in *La stiava* is apparent both from her direct interventions in the invenzione and in the way she directed that both the show and her relationship to it be represented in an official description that she asked Buonarroti to write.[48] Clearly Christine wanted *La stiava* to be received as having been created through her power. Just as clearly she wanted the show's sonorous effects to be represented as symbolically more important than its visual and spectacular effects. The latter concern in turn made the music seem, in Buonarroti's description, like a symbolic discourse in which female power and voice were possible. Thus Christine emphasized the importance to her of Francesca's work providing *La stiava* with "una musica stupenda."

In response to Christine's rejection of his first idea for the show, on 5 February Buonarroti sent Christine a drastically revised invenzione centered on Tuscan knights' changing responses to the existence of a Persian slave woman (played by a man) in their midst.[49] Seeing her to be beautiful, the men would at first decide to fight among themselves for the right to take her as their prize. But the apparent slave was to interrupt their preparations for combat, her sorrowfully sung narrative revealing that she was the king of Persia's daughter, captured by pirates en route to her planned marriage with the king of India. Hearing her to be no slave at all, but twice a queen, the knights would change the reason for their combat: they would fight for the honor of escorting her to her proper consort. Though presented amid many of the usual Florentine trappings of spectacle—music, brilliantly colored costumes, mock battles, and solo and ensemble song—one overarching theme of the plot was the transformation of a woman from an object of desire, competition, and exchange to a sovereign subject, a transformation wrought by the intervention of her own self-defining voice.

Picchena reported that the grand duchess was "infinitely pleased" with the new idea, although she questioned some details of the planned staging and commanded one change of plot: the knights were to be moved to combat not by the slave's beauty but by her "nobility, or novelty, or other evident merits."[50] This change had two critical effects on the resulting scenario, one on its gender politics and one on the relative importance of the music. First, the conventional connection between a woman's beauty and men's competitive desire to possess her would be severed, and with it the logic by which women traditionally have been blamed for their own objectification. The plot's principal theme was thus strengthened. Second, the first version's quite sharp distinction between sight and sound as ways the men might know this woman would be blurred; in Christine's revision their intended objectification of the slave as the prize for combat might or might not have seemed to depend on their having seen the desirable qualities that Buonarroti's text would ascribe to her. Because her visible beauty was not supposed to matter, they would know her majesty by the sound of her voice in dialogue with the voices of her guards. Sound would become the privileged means by which these men (and by extension the audience) might know the truth about the woman among them. Thus, whether intentionally or not, Christine's change elided the slave's self-transformation from mute object to speaking subject, from slave to queen, with the implications that hearing was the most reliable way to know, and music the most reliable representation of stable, orderly reality. That change, in turn, increased the likely importance of the music to the show's success as an indirect representation of the grand duchess's own authority.

A close reading of Buonarroti's description suggests very strongly that she meant *La stiava* to signal a turning point in her own relationship to the power of the Granducato of Tuscany. Never meant to be printed but instead to be circulated in manuscript to the court of Christine's father, the Duke of Lorraine, the very existence of a description reveals that *La stiava* served Christine as a representation of power that she needed her poet both to memorialize and to interpret for posterity. Yet because the manuscript would circulate only among a limited, easily controlled audience, Christine would inflect her projection of power so that it would blur the distinction between the public and the private. Her official interpretation of the show's origins and meanings would be known to only a few.

Thus, only a few would know that she allowed Buonarroti to attribute the *invenzione* to her, a false claim of authorship on her behalf that was surely intended as a metaphorical claim to something like sovereign authority.[51] Yet like her choice to circulate the description privately, Christine's claim of authorship was oddly muted, with the responsibility for the claim doubly deflected. The description attributed the will behind *La stiava*'s invention and production to her son, Prince Cosimo. He had wanted an entertainment that would display the "valor" of his courtiers at Carnival, and his mother had invented and produced it. Therefore her falsely claimed authorship appeared to arise from her maternal desire to serve and please her son by realizing his will for masculine self-display.[52] Thus, Christine's claim to power was very carefully situated so as to seem recognizably feminine and maternal, an almost (but not quite) passive will to power consistent with womanly *onestà*.

Curiously absent from the description (and, in fact, from the whole enterprise) was Grand Duke Ferdinando I, to whom both authority and de facto authorship of courtly entertainments ought logically to have been attributed.[53] But in the winter of 1607 Ferdinando had already been gravely ill for months, often unable to attend to the correspondence of state for weeks at a time.[54] In his stead, his French wife heard the reports of ministers read to her daily, choosing which matters could wait for his attention and which she would decide herself in consultation with his ministers. Everyone in the Medici secretariat must have known what the text of *La stiava* sought subtly and entertainingly to proclaim: that the foreign-born Grand Duchess of Tuscany was the de facto sovereign, intervening to control, redefine, even redirect local politics. But neither the general mass of Ferdinando's subjects nor foreign powers were meant to understand—that is, to see—the extent to which Christine exercised de facto sovereignty. Understandably, Christine meant to inform her family in Lorraine of her circumstances but to do so subtly, through the manuscript description, her claim of de facto regency presented through a gesture of modest *continenza*.

Managed so as to be both chastely out of public sight and only indirectly acknowledged in writing, Christine's assumption of power was nonetheless known in the Tuscan court's oral culture. Thus it seems particularly logical that the foreign woman's unexpected power in *La stiava* should have been made to seem a matter of voice. According to Buonarroti's description, when the slave's voice intervened with words and music meant to convey powerfully her experience, her guards and the knights onstage responded with "the action of *meraviglia*," of marveling. The stage action of marveling is quite precisely described as the knights' bodily miming of the affections expressed by the slave's exchange with her guards: "While the stiava and the soldiers sang, the knights by their various acts and postures moved according to the words and conceits of whoever was singing in turn, performing now pride, now pity, now kindness as was wanted by this or that affect, as was fitting to represent constant marveling at the discovery that this stiava had been a queen."[55] Clearly, the knights were represented as experiencing the slave girl's intrinsic sovereignty in the pressure that her voice's sounds—words and music—exerted over their feelings and the postures of their bodies. They knew her sovereignty in the experience of being so dominated by her voice, and that visceral knowledge led them to change both their perception of the woman before them and the reason they meant to engage in combat in front of her.

It is significant that the spectacle of stylized combat as a performance of masculinity was not affected by Christine's commands concerning the show, nor was it affected by the slave's onstage intervention; only the (pre)text, so to speak, for masculine combat had changed. Just as significant, even in describing the combat Buonarroti privileged sound as the medium through which the audience recognized the difference between two social worlds, experiencing that moment as a special source of delight.[56] The noise of arms and of drums being beaten signified the eruption of male homosocial competition, the discourse that the slave's sovereign singing had caused to be rejustified as performing chivalrous rivalry rather than greedy competition for a prize. In sharp contrast, the sound of singing and musical instruments signified a heterosocial world in which the voice of a woman singing could define her own social position as a subject, not an object (if always a subject defined in relation to powerful men). Further, because of the defining power that the heterosocial sounds of music exercised over the homosocial sounds of combat noise in this show, music was represented as a discourse in which a woman's intervening voice could exert a similar defining power over the world around her. In Buonarroti's description of *La stiava*, then, the orderly sounds of music formed the discourse that represented Christine's authority over the disorderly, though still sensually pleasurable, sounds of male combat. Wisely staged at Carnival so that it could be received as only a playful representation of a world turned upside down, *La stiava* nonetheless represented with total accuracy the situation of the Medici household: a foreign woman had taken up enough de facto power to redirect the combative energies of the men at her court. The "musica stupenda," then, was no small thing, but the very music that represented Christine's invisible but very real power as the rule of sonic order over disorder. For Francesca to have created the music through which the grand duchess could claim her power—to have created it on short notice, to the pleasure of the whole court, without breaching the decorum of proper womanhood in either representation or reality—surely made her a valuable prize indeed to the grand duchess.

La stiava, Vocality, and the Rules of the Game

La stiava represented Christine's power as resting on the primacy of hetero-social values that acknowledged the legitimacy of a woman's voice, no matter how abject that woman may have appeared, no matter how veiled her intrinsic self-sovereignty needed to be. Christine seems to have been grateful that Francesca's music served that representation well. But the barriera's representations also addressed directly Francesca's situation as a female musical servant. The figure of the slave brought vividly to onstage life the internal contradiction between servitude and symbolic performance of sovereignty that was intrinsic to both the ideology and the bodily practices of the Caccinian new way of singing. In addition, the figure of the slave was, like Francesca, at first perceived only as an object of desire, competition, and exogamous exchange through which others could articulate their own relative prestige, with no thought to her independent experience or desire. As Buonarroti had conceived her, the slave was as effective a figure for the girl who composed her voice as she was for that composer's sovereign.

The slave's onstage intervention changed the rules by which she was herself to be an object of competition and exchange. When the slave's voice and singing impressed her own affects on the affects and bodily postures of the knights who were prepared to fight over her as a prize, she moved them—literally—to respect both her family's desires for her destiny and her own. Changing these men's hearts by singing so powerfully as to make them feel as she did, the slave's voice transformed her in their perception from an object to a subject with a life trajectory of her own. Her singing thus proposed to change, at least on the Medici court's Carnival stage, the rules of the traditional patriarchal game by which women and servants were exchanged as signs of their princes' power. But the effectiveness of the slave's vocality in changing the rules of a game in which she was to have been the prize depended on Christine's directives to Buonarroti to privilege sound over sight as a means of knowledge in the fictive world of their little show. Thus the power of a subordinated woman to reveal herself by her voice, and thereby change her onstage fate, depended on the greater power of the offstage woman who had already changed the rules. Buonarroti (and Francesca) acknowledged the dynamic between these different kinds of power in the slave's final solo number, when she expressed her grateful dependence on the grace of the grand duchess, bowing before her as she sang from the stage:

> O gentle servitude
> O sweet prison, and not unworthy yoke . . .
> . . . I see Christiana, in whose noble breast
> the royal virtue of pietà is locked,
> Whence I hope one day
> For a happy return
> of the tear-stained Queen to her Indian home.[57]

By the new rules of the game the slave's realization of her own desire depended on another woman's capacity for *pietà*—for pity, piety, and altruistically generous acts—rather than on the desires and competitive exchange of prizes among men.

In the letter to the grand duchess that he drafted on 6 March 1607 to accompany his first draft of the description, Buonarroti reported on his quiet efforts to learn what Giulio Caccini intended to do with his daughter.[58] When Giulio had declined to tell him, saying he would prefer to write the grand duchess directly, Buonarroti had turned to sources in Rome, whence he learned that "the business is quite cold on both sides now, such that I think it a sure result that not much will be needed to win the girl freely without new concerns that might appear or other bothersome resistance."[59] Buonarroti's letter thus links Christine's apparent interest in Francesca, Giulio's breaking of his contract with Montalto (and his 5 March 1607 letter to Christine about it, cited above), and the official story of *La stiava*. The link implies a collusion among these three parties over Francesca's future.

Very possibly only Buonarroti, acting as a broker between Christine and Giulio, knew how the others planned to move in a game that was still a competition to "win the girl," a game in which Christine was determined to take the prize. Moreover, the letter encourages reading the show and its description as crafted by Buonarroti to be part of the stylized struggle over Francesca. Possibly always understood as in part constituting Buonarroti's broker-like moves in that game, the texts of *La stiava* suggest that Francesca had at first been treated as a prize and then treated almost as a queen though she was a token of kinship between heads of household that understood themselves to own her. At some point, and perhaps in connection with her assumption of a de facto regency, Christine entered that game. Removing Francesca from the game, Christine both protected herself from having to play the game of exchange by the rules of androcentric, patriarchal Rome and behaved as a patron whose actions were congruous with the virtues of womanhood. For when Christine "won the girl" she conserved for Tuscany one of its most valuable artistic servants, a girl who literally embodied the Medicean patrimony that was its new way of singing. Winning the girl was, for Christine, a way of exhibiting her own continenza.

Reader, She Married Him

In his biography of Francesca, Bronzini claimed that Christine had arranged both for the training in "counterpoint and passaggi" that enabled her composing career and for her marriages. Although his claim about counterpoint cannot be corroborated, his claim about her first marriage can be. In an eighteenth-century annotation to a copy of her marriage contract in the Riccardi family archive, G. P. Lami asserted that it had been "on the orders of the grand duchess" that Francesca Caccini married Giovanni Battista Signorini in November 1607. According both to a lawsuit Francesca was to file in 1639 and Lami's biography of the banker Riccardo Riccardi, the banker was to have paid Signorini a dowry of one thousand scudi for Francesca, plus six hundred scudi toward dowering any daughter that might be born.[60] In fact, Francesca married Signorini on 4 November 1607 in her father's home in the parish of Santa Maria Maggiore.[61] Riccardi and the husband of her godmother, Rustico Piccardini, were the official witnesses. Despite his representations to the grand duchess that he might not be able to dower Francesca properly, on 22 November 1607 Giulio, not Riccardi, paid her dowry, transferring to Signorini's account at the Monte di Pietà six hundred scudi as partial payment on a dowry of one thousand scudi.[62] A dowry contract notarized by the Monte's chief financial officer, Noferi Maccanti, identified the payment as the partial proceeds of Giulio's April 1588 sale of a Fiesole farm and stated that it completed his obligation to Signorini. In the presence of two notaries, Giulio and his eighteen-year-old son Giovanni Battista, and with the consent of the Fiesole farm's heir, Signorini acknowledged his previous receipt of four hundred scudi. He also gave his wife, "although absent," a wedding gift of fifty lire (there were seven lire in a scudo), promising to comply with the laws regarding restitution of dowries.[63]

What sort of man did Francesca marry on the orders of her grand duchess? Born 15 January 1576, Giovanni Battista Signorini was the second son of a respectable artisan-class family.[64] Originally apprenticed as a wind player to the group known as the Franciosini, by the late 1590s Signorini appeared in court records as a tenor and string player as well. By then, too, he was considered a steady enough person to have been entrusted with the coaching, accompaniment, and domestic arrangements of the Medici court's concerto di castrati. It may have been his work as coach to the castrati that led to Signorini's casting in the small role of First Soldier in La stiava; conceivably he also coached and monitored the performances of the two principal singers, the young castrato

Giovannino, who had been supposed to sing the slave's part, and the even younger Fabio, who had taken the role of Second Soldier.

Evidently Signorini was poor and had hoped for years that the grand duchess would help him find a wife with money. On 27 September 1603, as part of a series of letters evaluating the usefulness and administration of the court's music-making establishment, court steward Enea Vaini had written Christine about two singers with special needs. The bass known as Pienza needed to have some travel expenses reimbursed, and Signorini needed to marry: "Gio' Battista del Franciosino, one of the vocal ensemble and the wind consort, wishes you to assign to whomever might seem right to you the proposition that, with your protection, he marry the only daughter of the former dyer Benedetto di Borgo. . . . Being well born, Gio. Battista knows how inappropriate it is to marry beneath one's station; and having arranged for his two sisters, selling the little he had of land and other goods, he is said to be virtuous, [he] has no debts, and [he] treats people well. But because this girl will be an heir, I believe he will have competitors of quality, with property, ahead of him."[65] About ten days later Vaini wrote Christine that Borgo found Signorini to be virtuous but poor, entirely dependent on his court stipend of 120 scudi annually. Unless the grand duchess intended to use force against him, the dyer intended to accept as his son-in-law a man whose yearly income from property was two hundred scudi: "It did not seem right to me to use Your Highness' authority in such a hopeless case, and Gio Battista is calm about it, and consoled by having learned from this business that Your Highness has such good will [as] to favor him in a similar effort."[66]

Little else is known about Signorini. In a letter of 1616 the poet Jacopo Cicognini recommended casting him in the title role of a projected work called *L'Adone* for Cardinal Ludovisi "because he is very handsome."[67] The annotations to an anonymous astrological chart now in Florence's Biblioteca Nazionale described him as an "esempio dell'huomo ozioso," that is, as a man who cultivated intellectual pursuits in leisure and avoided the bustling "negozio" of business. In dictating his own testament, which was to be the only trace of his voice in documented history, Signorini spoke warmly of his wife, acknowledging with unusual grace her disproportionate contribution to the household's wealth—revealing himself to be a poor man who treated others well, even at the end.

From a post-Romantic perspective, Francesca's marriage could seem like the end to her story: her music-making body, her sexuality, her voice, her labor, her learning, and her compositional ability had passed from one man's possession to another man's. By the logic of the late-modern "marriage plot," Francesca's voice ought then to have been silenced. Yet we know that instead Francesca's marriage to Signorini marked the beginning of her adult career, an opening of her compositional and epistolary throat that let her voices enter the documented world. Almost all her known compositions and two-thirds of her surviving letters come from the period of her first marriage, 1607–1626. On 15 November 1607, the newly married Francesca joined the ranks of musicians "provisioned" by the Grand Duke of Tuscany at an initial stipend of 120 scudi annually that matched her husband's.[68] A servant of the granducato, she would spend most of her working life serving among the women of a court whose center of gravity was Grand Duchess Christine.

However starkly the dowry contract represents Francesca's marriage as an exchange of property between men, that representation is but part of the truth, because both Giulio Caccini and G. B. Signorini were bound by the will of the Medici famiglia. That is, at another level of truth that was no metaphor but was material reality, Francesca's marriage marked only a change in her location within that larger famiglia. Freed from a father who, however well-intentioned, claimed his daughter's virtuosity as his property, Francesca had been given over to the care of a kind, handsome, unambitious man who would have reason to be grateful to the grand duchess for giving him a wife both learned and talented, whose virtuosity could bring him wealth. But the fact that their marriage merely changed her place within the famiglia meant that the social relation the marriage articulated and strengthened was not only a horizontal bond between the men who exchanged coins and contracts at the office of the Monte di Pietà in Piazza San Stefano. In addition, the marriage strengthened Giulio's, Giovanni's, and Francesca's vertical bonds to the woman who had ordered it. The men were the objects of her generosity, but Francesca had been and would remain the object of her desire and power—because she had shown herself able to give voice to them. The residue of that desire and power lent an intimate charge to their relationship during many shared years in the gynocentric spaces of the Medici court.

Power, Desire, and Women among Themselves

TOLOMEO: Is it any wonder . . . that Cecchina turned out to be excellent in music (since ordinarily good fruit comes from good seed), having been given this Art from the womb of her mother Lucia Gangoletti [*sic*], the first wife of her father and her parent, no less excellent and miraculous in singing than Giulio Romano? But continue.

LEONORA: At the pleasure of the Most Serene Grand Duke Ferdinando I of happy memory, and of Madama the Most Serene Grand Duchess Christine, Princess of Lorraine, her special patron and benefactrix . . . this young girl began to apply her mind to counterpoint and to passaggi, in a short time mastering both, [and] created compositions such that they were highly esteemed, requested and prized by the leading men of the profession, and by great princes.[1]

For all that posterity remembers Francesca Caccini primarily as the daughter of Giulio Romano, that is not how Bronzini introduced her in his biographical sketch. Rather, he introduced her as he did all the women worthies in *Della dignità e nobiltà delle donne*, through her relationship with a woman: "sister of the above-mentioned Settimia." Alluding to Giulio only in passing, Bronzini moved on to list Francesca's musical skills, her obedience to her father, her music making's miraculous power over others, and her noteworthy education. In the passage quoted above, his interlocutor Tolomeo interrupts Leonora just as she mentions Francesca's work as a composer, prompting an exchange that implies that Francesca's composing career had been produced by two women.[2] Tolomeo unequivocally attributes Francesca's musical excellence to the seed of her long-dead mother Lucia, seeming to affirm the second-century physician Galen's view that women as well as men contributed the seed to which a mother's nurturing body gave the material form that would become a child. But because Tolomeo mentions Giulio while failing to acknowledge his contribution of seed, there is something off about Tolomeo's remark. It almost erases Giulio's parental role in producing the composer Francesca, leaving a textual void that is filled when Leonora continues her story. She unequivocally attributes the development of Francesca's composing talents to the grand duke and duchess, but notes in particular Francesca's "special patron and benefactrix," Christine de Lorraine. In this moment, Bronzini's text allows a reader to slip from Galen's view of reproduction to Aristotle's—to, that is, the view that only one parent provided the seed while the other provided the nourishment needed for the seed's development. If a reader makes that slip, Bronzini could seem to imply that as a composer Francesca had two mothers, Lucia and Christine, whose gendered contribution of seed and nourishment defy easy characterization.

Surely the strangest moment in Bronzini's narrative about Francesca, this passage betrays what may have been the preferred view of Francesca in the women's world that circled around the Medici princesses in early seventeenth-century Tuscany. The women of that world, and perhaps especially the woman who was its center, Christine de Lorraine, may have wanted to believe that their world had produced Francesca's career, her prestige, and what they fantasized to be her music's performative and political power. In an effort to explain how they might have held such a view, this chapter explores the dynamics of power and desire at Tuscany's "women's court"—the court Francesca Caccini served for thirty years.

Christine de Lorraine, Her Court, and Her Desire to Command

Christine de Lorraine had been dispatched to live in one or another of Ferdinando I's country palaces almost as soon as he married her.[3] There, far from the dangerous tumult of urban political life, she was to await her husband's conjugal visits and to bear and raise his children. Like many Italian princesses, she was also to preside over an extended household of his female relatives as they waited for marriage or as they bore and raised their own husbands' children. Thus, as a new bride Christine took command of a household that included her husband's nieces Marie de' Medici (future queen of France), Leonora de' Medici (future Duchess of Mantua) and Flavia Peretti (sister of Pope Sixtus V and the new bride of Ferdinando I's nephew Virginio Orsini). She commanded, as well, a small army of butlers, maids, cooks, wet-nurses, stewards, gatekeepers, gardeners, laundresses, and men charged with maintaining the stalls, horses, and carriages. Further, she had ultimate authority over the staffs of well-born women who served each of the four princesses, in two ranks. *Dame* (singular, *dama*) were women from aristocratic families who served as the princesses' companions, and *donne* (singular, *donna*) were more often girls from the middling classes who performed bodily services (helping their princesses dress, do their hair and makeup, and eat and drink) and entertained them by singing, dancing, or playing any of several common courtly games. Finally, Christine commanded two categories of servants whose service to the household was intermittent, not requiring long-term residence among the princesses. *Ingegnii* or virtuosi were poets, musicians, and tutors of the household children, their work depending mainly on intelligence and imagination rather than on bodily strength. *Segretarii* were borrowed from the enormous bureaucracy of the Tuscan state. Often of sufficient social status to be good marriage prospects for the dame and donne, many secretaries were destined for lives in diplomatic service. Those who served the women's court well enjoyed the lifelong affection, loyalty, and favor of their princesses.

Insofar as it can be known from epistolary and financial records, Christine, her nieces, and their courts lived more or less as readers of Baldassare Castiglione's *Il libro del cortigiano* would expect. They made music, danced, rehearsed and produced small plays for their own amusement, played card or ball games, and hunted, often with the professional advice of virtuosi and ingegni; they heard letters read to them by secretaries and dictated letters in response; they interceded with their male relations on behalf of less powerful people who asked their help; they raised their own and each other's children; and they monitored one another's onestà, castità, and continenza.

Like any courtly community, the women's court at Tuscany came eventually to be marked by patterns of behavior that suited the woman who reigned over it. Who was this woman?

Her Florentine subjects knew Christine de Lorraine to be the granddaughter of King Henri II of France and the Florentine woman he had reluctantly taken as his queen, Catherine de' Medici.[4] Born in 1565 as one of the nine children her mother Claude de France bore her father, Duke Charles de Lorraine, Christine had been raised by her grandmother after her mother's death in childbirth when she was ten. Catherine treated Christine like a daughter. She ensured that the girl understood the importance of learning, and she encouraged her participation in the balli, hunts, and riding exhibitions Catherine herself enjoyed. Most important, Catherine taught Christine prudence, piety, and good judgment, the tools by which the first Medici to be a French queen had turned royal widowhood into a de facto regency that allowed her to rule France for nearly thirty years. Christine would use the same tools when she, in turn, ruled as her adoptive nation's de facto regent.

When Ferdinando de' Medici had resigned his cardinalate in 1587 to succeed his brother Francesco as Tuscany's grand duke, he had immediately sought a wife with whom to create the third generation of Medici rulers necessary to ensuring that the family be a dynasty.[5] Emissaries of Henri III proposed Christine, promising a dowry of six hundred thousand scudi and the resolution of various property disputes between France and Tuscany. Seeing marriage to Christine as a way to offset via kinship alliance the granducato's feudal subservience to the Hapsburgs, Ferdinando accepted. By the time their marriage was celebrated in April 1589, Christine's grandmother Catherine had died, leaving her even more wealth to bring Tuscany: an additional two hundred thousand scudi, Catherine's palace in Paris, and her presumptive rights as heir to the Duchy of Urbino, land which, if joined to Tuscany, promised to give the Tuscan fleet access to Adriatic as well as Mediterranean ports. Although Christine was still in mourning for her grandmother, her marriage had been celebrated with unparalleled splendor in Florence, culminating in the *intermedi* to Giovanni Bargagli's comedy *La pellegrina* so well known to historians of music and spectacle.[6]

Tall, slim until middle age, described by some as beautiful, Christine had at first struck Florentines as vivacious, innocent but not naive, brilliant but not affected, impressive for her graceful courage when her progress through France en route to marriage had been threatened by civil unrest in Marseilles.[7] Within a year of her wedding she had borne Ferdinando an heir; by 1604 she had brought eight of her nine subsequent pregnancies to term.[8] Bronzini spent pages praising Christine's humility, her always-generous response to subjects who appealed to her for favors, her observant and deeply felt piety, and her special concern for the needs of widows, unhappily married women, and impoverished girls. But even Bronzini made no claim that she was learned or especially intelligent. Christine was, however, a woman whose majestic face and gestures showed her to be "born to reign and command."[9]

Christine eventually shared dominion over the Medici world of women with her daughter-in-law Maria Magdalena d'Austria, whose 1608 marriage to Christine's and Ferdinando's heir, Cosimo II, was meant to balance the French alliance embodied in Christine.[10] Short and tending toward stoutness, cheerful, robust, and athletic, Magdalena was the physical opposite of her mother-in-law. Yet she, too, produced more than enough heirs for the dynasty, bearing five sons and three daughters in her thirteen years of marriage. Praised by Bronzini for her piety, high spirits, and superb horsemanship more than for intelligence or learning, Magdalena nonetheless took great pride in ensuring that all her children, girls as well as boys, were extremely well educated and well read, taught by the greatest virtuosi, virtuose, ingegni, and ingegne of the age. Like Christine, Magdalena was observantly pious. And like Christine, she had lost her mother figure unexpectedly during her journey to Tuscany, a kind of shared loss that might in part account for the unusually affectionate relationship that secretaries and diplomats attributed to them.

Whatever their respective merits or relationship, the misadventures of the regency they were destined to share from 1621 to 1628 caused both women to be dismissed by post-Enlightenment historians as incompetent spendthrifts and superstitious zealots susceptible to every "vanity" of court life.[11] Their supposed zealotry led them to endow countless new monasteries and convents in Tuscany that drained both tax and labor resources from the state; their supposed susceptibility to courtly vanity led them to spend lavishly on court spectacles and to encourage their courtiers to do the same. But both tendencies can be understood as strategies by which Christine and Magdalena sought to preserve their own reputations for continenza while they concentrated on the essential work of regency: preserving the state intact for the next generation of men.

Preceding Magdalena in Tuscany by nearly twenty years, and destined to outlive her, Christine was by far the dominant woman of the pair; it was she who had created the patterns through which the female power that these histories denigrate would circulate. Neither Christine nor those patterns are well understood by histories that are mainly concerned with the long-term interests of the Tuscan state. Like the state, and like Ferdinando's decision to send his wife to the country, such histories have the effect of keeping Christine, the women around her, and the relationships among them out of sight. Enforcing a sort of historiographical modesty, they contradict the evidence of contemporary documents. These reveal Christine to have been at once high-spirited and pious, hungry for power and deft in its use, systematically kind to other women in some circumstances and ruthless to them in others. Although the woman revealed in these documents may seldom have been revealed to the Tuscan population at large, she is likely to have been the woman that the elite women and virtuose of her court knew, the woman whose conflicting desires in relation to power moved the system of relationships that circulated around her.

In startlingly direct letters to her sometime secretary Curtio Picchena, Christine revealed herself to be sharply aware that she needed to live within social conventions that contradicted her own will. Moreover, she named the contradictions in ways that show those forces to have been the constricting traces of institutional womanhood. On 2 November 1604 Christine wrote Picchena from Villa Ambrogiana to ask that he thank her husband for his gift of fruit—a case of fertility-inducing pomegranates to which, she reported, her children had laid siege. Amid her cheery domestic news, Christine noted her own internal struggle between obedience to her husband—the womanly virtue of onestà—

and her desire to join him at Livorno: "I envy [the Grand Duke] being in Livorno in this good weather, and if I were the padrona of my own will I would have enjoyed it myself: but obedience prevails in me more than any other thing, which makes me go and stay where I am told; even when [it is] far from my lord, so that I am like a plant without the sun."[12]

In another letter to Picchena written a few days later Christine developed this theme, explaining that both by personality and by upbringing she could not stay still. But, she reported, she had discovered a legitimate (and gender-appropriate) way to satisfy her restlessness without either directly disobeying her husband or needing to ask his permission. She and her retinue traveled to local holy sites, in what amounted to pilgrimages undertaken mainly for the exercise and the diversion. Christine seemed well aware that this habit tested the limits of her husband's intentions about how far afield from Villa Ambrogiana she could go:

> As for our news, I will tell you how yesterday, since the *tramontana* [northwest wind] died down, the duchess [Flavia Peretti Orsini] and I together with all our children went to the Madonna di Baltinaccio. And the prince, Don Francesco, Sig.r Paolo and Sig.r Alessandro went and returned on horseback, beautifully at full tilt. I want to go to mass tomorrow morning to the Madonna di Monsummano, and dine there, and return from there in the evening, because it is less far from here than Poggio, where His Highness gave me permission to go. There I will pray for the grand duke as I ought. My nature, and the way in which I was raised make it so that I cannot stay put. I did not wait for permission from His Highness because I won't stay long enough to sleep over, and I believe that he won't take it amiss as he has never denied me going to devotions. I want His Highness to know not only what I do, but also my thoughts, and if the weather were not so beautiful I wouldn't organize myself to go, having no obligation to make this trip beyond my pleasure, and pastime.[13]

Skillfully playing uxorial and religious piety against each other, Christine had used one trope meant to contain women to cancel the other so she could evade both constraint and opprobrium.[14] In her zeal to realize her desire, to be sovereign of her own will, Christine turned piety into a pastime and into a successful means of resisting patriarchal authority in full view of her retinue. This was but one instance of a drive that would lead one of the horseback-riding boys in that party, Paolo Giordano Orsini, later to describe Christine as a woman who "so desires to command that she puts this desire ahead of the reputation of . . . her son."[15]

Satisfying her desire to resist containment by the pieties of elite womanhood while remaining intelligible to her husband, his court, and their subjects in terms of those pieties, Christine was invited by life's accidents to satisfy her desire to command, as well. As the ladies who literally stood ready to serve her during audiences certainly knew, Christine's desire to command had been both nourished and satisfied long before her husband's death. As early as January 1600, Bartolomeo Cenami, the ambassador from Lucca to the Tuscan court, had reported Christine's routine presence at state meetings and the shrewd calculation of her interventions: "Madama was present at this meeting, as His Highness is introducing her [to such matters] so that she will be well-informed in any situation that God might present her, and she inserts herself willingly from the natural desire everyone has to govern. . . . She has occasionally shown herself not to agree so fully with the opinion of the archbishop [of Pisa], but experience has shown how much the grand duke needs and values his opinions, so with much prudence she complies and lets him enjoy reputation and greatness."[16]

By the winter of 1606–1607, the "situation that God might present" was at hand. As the grand duke's health and attention failed, state business was increasingly concluded by Christine. She issued "orders of the grand duke" that approved or amended judgments of the Ruota Civil (Florence's civil court), and she supervised the state's finances as administered by the Depositeria Generale.[17] All decisions recorded in First Secretary Belisario Vinta's minutes for 1607 begin with the words "Madama dice" (Madama says), a heading that affirmed within the secretariat what would never be completely clear to Tuscany's subjects: by early 1607 Christine de Lorraine was the de facto sovereign of Tuscany, a role she would continue to play intermittently through her son Cosimo II's reign.

Christine's centrality to the government of Tuscany in the first decade of the century was well known to diplomats posted in Florence and to their governments. Resident diplomats experienced exclusion from her audiences as a wound to their reputation as well as to their authority to negotiate for their princes.[18] Yet the image that emerges from Modenese diplomatic reports and the letters of Tuscan secretaries to each other is one of a sovereignty shared by Christine, her often-ill son Cosimo II when his health permitted, and her daughter-in-law Maria Magdalena.[19] The diplomats portrayed Christine as exercising power within this shared sovereignty in three ways. First, she acted as an intercessor with her son in matters of bureaucratic appointments, adding the weight of her approval to an ambassador's or a prince's recommendation.[20] Second, in matters concerning members of the Medici's biological or bureaucratic famiglia; concerning women, dowries, and marriages; or concerning the management of convents, Christine enjoyed not intercessory but absolute power that could, in her hands, be harsh. For example, when in January 1612 her nephew Don Cosimo Medici killed Giorgio Bentivoglio in the via Larga because of a woman, he was brought to the grand duchess to explain himself. The

Modenese ambassador reported that "Madama, fiercely indignant, not only did not accept his excuses but reproved him vigorously."[21] She did more than reprove Cosimo. When he tried to flee the authorities, she ordered the gates of the city closed and ordered the Florentine police to conduct a house-to-house search. Discovered hiding in a Benedictine chapel, Cosimo was arrested and banished to Malta.

The fierce indignation that Christine showed her nephew paled beside the outrage she displayed in 1620, when an incident erupted that directly involved her authority over the famiglia, over elite women's well-being, and over Florence's convents. On the morning of 2 July Sinolfo Ottieri, son-in-law of the late First Secretary Belisario Vinta and husband of Christine's dama Tommasa Vinta, was arrested in the convent of Santa Verdiana.[22] Ottieri had been found in the cell of one of the sisters, Suora Maria Vittoria Frescobaldi, an illegitimate daughter of Ferdinando's nephew Virginio Orsini, who paid for the singing lessons with Francesca Caccini that had made Frescobaldi the best singer in Florence. Ottieri claimed he had only been singing and making music with Frescobaldi, lured by her brilliant romanescas, but Frescobaldi claimed that he had entered her room by force and raped her. As church and state tussled over the authority to punish all concerned, the archbishop of Candia, who was investigating the case, visited Christine, who had "sworn on her faith that 'as soon as Sinolfo is in our hands he will see the severest punishment, loss of life and more'; and if it were a brother or son of the Grand Duke, Her Highness said several times that she would like to give the world an example of her righteous justice."[23]

The heat of Christine's wrath concerning the scandal did not stem wholly from its offense to her apparent control over the areas delegated to her authority in Cosimo II's granducato. Instead, it was likely to have been fueled by the tension she felt at having to exercise power in the third way noted by the diplomats. The scandal erupted during one of the many periods in her son's short reign when he was too ill to engage in the daily business of governing, periods during which Christine acted as head of state.

Throughout 1619 and 1620 the Modenese resident diplomat Paolo Boiardi reported regularly on Cosimo's health, noting as exceptional the occasions when he was well enough to stand through an audience or watch a comedy produced by his children and their *famigliari*.[24] By July 1620, he reported, all diplomatic business was being taken to Christine "because the most Serene Grand Duke is no longer in a condition to negotiate."[25]

So it would be until Cosimo's death on 28 February 1621. At the reading of his will two days later, a regency was declared, under the nominal command of Cosimo's widow Maria Magdalena. It was she who, with Christine's assistance, would have the authority to use the seal of state, to sign policies, and to receive the accounts of the fortress where the gold was kept.[26] In his brief history of the Tuscan governments for his colleagues in Lucca's diplomatic service, envoy Alessandro Lamberti in 1626 matter-of-factly reported both the extent of Christine's real power during the second decade of the century and the shrewdness with which she satisfied her desire to command while seeming to step aside so Magdalena could satisfy the same desire:

> Madama, with marvelous moderation of spirit, has relinquished the nearly
> absolute power she exercised during the life of her son, and without any of the
> usual argument between mother-in-law and daughter-in-law not only cheerfully
> renounced in favor of the archduchess but (both) in reality and in appearance
> joined everyone else in praising the new leader. Nonetheless she retains control
> over all the business, and without opposing the will or caprice of the archduch-
> ess in things of minor importance, in big and important matters [Christine]
> directs or transforms or moderates the archduchess' ideas. Using the most
> trusted ministers, she has preserved the unity and peace of the ducal household
> and kept the governance of the state united and consistent.[27]

Christine remained a respected force in Tuscany's governance throughout the regency and afterward, during the reign of her grandson Ferdinando II. She continued to give advice occasionally on matters of state and always to hear the ministers' reports, until her death in December 1636.[28]

The Women's Court and the Traffic in Women

The acknowledged seat of power for both Tuscan grand duchesses was the dynamic system of relationships that linked elite women (aristocrats and virtuose) to each other through the constant circulation of desire and power in their relationships with Medici princesses. A gynocentric universe almost parallel to the all-male secretariat through which Christine and Magdalena worked to rule the state, the Tuscan women's court was populated by women who witnessed the authority and real-world power of the grand duchesses on whom they waited. In men's eyes they were bound together by the weaknesses, virtues, and dangers assumed to characterize their gender. In their own eyes they were bound by shared experiences of sex-segregated spaces, pilgrimages, pastimes, and games. More important, they continually shared in the grand duchesses' detailed management of their participation in the two institutions that articulated and governed their sexual difference from men: the institution of marriage, which governed heterosocial and heterosexual relations; and the institution of monastic life in *monasterii di monache* (now called convents), which claimed authority over ostensibly religious homosocial communities of women. Thus policing their own and each others' sexualities (and therefore policing the range of bodily differences on which the gender system was based), the elite women who circulated through the Tuscan women's court participated in a culture that extended the grand duchess's authority to traffic in the artistic servants of her *famiglia* to a nearly absolute authority to traffic in elite women.

The relationships that constituted the women's court left traces amid the voluminous preserved correspondence of the grand duchesses.[29] Hundreds of these letters consisted of formulaic greetings at Christmas, Easter, or other religious holidays, equally formulaic expressions of congratulations or condolence, and exchanges about who would be godmother to whose new child. These letters that seem to have no content nonetheless had a purpose. Articulating social relations between the parties to the exchange, the letters were the least material instances of the constantly circulating gifts by which the social world around the grand duchesses was sustained. These courtesy letters exchanged among women often included advice about health, especially reproductive health, and accompanied gifts of herbs, ointments, and special foods or religious relics offered as aids to improve fertility, ease a difficult pregnancy, or help the recipient produce a male child.[30] Neither more gendered nor more frivolous than the exchange of wines, horses, and military advice by which the Medici men sustained their social networks, it was these women's traffic in folk remedies and relics that drew Enlightenment historians' accusations of superstition and zealotry. Superstitious and scientifically implausible though they may have been, when letters and gifts such as these came from the grand duchess, they sustained her authority in an area of overwhelming concern to elite women: their ability to provide their husbands with heirs. The stability of their marriages, and therefore their place in the social order, depended on this ability. Whether or not Christine or Magdalena was involved, however, these exchanges all sustained women's relationships with each other and to the kinship network through which those relationships served the interests of their men.

But the defining activity of the women's court was not their traffic in relics so much as it was their traffic in women themselves, many of whose marriages they had arranged and continued to superintend. Christine's authority to negotiate marriages for elite women in her extended household and beyond seems all but indistinguishable from her absolute authority to command in all details the marriages of Medici household and civil servants. Acting through her staff, Christine investigated the genealogical and financial histories of proposed marriage partners, reserving to herself the right to reject a marriage if the partners were not financially and socially suited to each other.[31] This oversight sustained and expanded the concept of the household as a famiglia, a concept that had been central to her late husband Ferdinando I's fashioning of the Tuscan state in terms of Aristotle's favorite metaphor for political order. In her management of the marriages of the famiglia's women and men, Christine seems to have been expected to act as a benevolent parent, or, as the archbishop of Siena had once exhorted her to be, a "mother-guardian" of other women's onestà.[32]

Christine had no less authority over the marriages of the princely class than over those of her servants. One compact set of documents about the 1610 marriage of Fulvia Salviati to Bartolomeo dal Monte, preserved among Christine's letters, provides a convenient example of how closely Christine monitored the prenuptial negotiations of princesses whose marriages she could command.[33] The orphaned Fulvia's interests were represented by her mother's brother, the prince of Mirandola, and her father's sister, Marchese Maddalena Salviati, both concerned with separating Fulvia's promised dowry of thirty thousand scudi from another twenty thousand scudi that she had inherited from her mother. The Salviati side wanted written assurance that Fulvia would have full access to the private income from her mother's wealth, with no interference from the Dal Monte. Bartolomeo, too, was represented by family: both his biological father Francesco, a general in the Tuscan army, and his adoptive father Giovanni Battista Dal Monte, a general serving the Republic of Venice. The elder Dal Monte, who intended to name Bartolomeo heir to an estate yielding twelve hundred scudi annually, implied that Fulvia ought to spend her mother's money for her own maintenance and support if she did not intend to "turn it to the benefit of the house that she enters." Christine's negotiators—Donato dell'Antella, his nephew Niccolò, and the envoy to Venice, Girolamo Guicciardini—were adamant that the Dal Monte promise in writing that Fulvia would "be received into their house in Florence and there, with said Marchese Bartolomeo, be treated, provided and maintained as is appropriate to their station and quality." Eventually both families agreed to Christine's terms and signed a marriage contract that began, "Be it known that under the happy auspices and benign protection of the Serenissima Grand Duchess of Tuscany, Mother, the following family relationship has been negotiated and established." The contract specified that the time, the expenses, and the exchange of clothing and jewels at the ring and the wedding ceremonies would be commanded by the grand duchess.[34]

Once Christine had been involved in another woman's marriage, she remained attentive to that woman's marital conditions for life, commenting on the advisability of a second marriage or rescuing women from physical or financial abuse. Older women considering second marriages were explicitly granted the right to make their own choices. Thus, when in 1622 Tommasa Vinta found herself "still young, without a husband, and with no one to govern her affairs," Christine dispatched Andrea Cioli to persuade Vinta to consider remarriage.[35] Vinta rejected Cioli's argument, declaring she would send a notarized statement to the Regents asserting that she did not want to hear another word about remarriage; that she had sought the counsel of God in the matter, having no faith in the advice of men; and that she had not yet had a reply.[36] As one secretary involved in the negotiation wrote to the other: "Madama has heard of your exchanges with Signora Tommasa Vinta up to now, and on the one hand she approved [Vinta's] opinion, given the poor luck she had with her first husband; [but] on the other hand, it doesn't seem to her that, given her youth and the need she has to take care of herself and her property, she can go on like this; [Christine] approves that you give her time to return to consulting with God, and to thinking about her condition."[37]

In another instance, Madama graciously granted a "command" to her former dama Costanza Medici to marry Giovanni Battista Malvessi in 1628, despite Costanza's refusal many years earlier to await such a command before marrying a man who had subsequently beaten and abused her.[38] Christine's marriage order affirmed her dama's right to have made her own mistakes, while affirming her own right to issue the command that constituted full approval. Similarly, when Maria Magdalena advised Lucrezia Seta against a second marriage that she had proposed to a poorer man, Giovanni Cini, Magdalena assured Seta that she had other options and that she was free to ignore the archduchess's advice: "Reflect according to your own sense of prudence, as there will be no shortage of subjects more proportionate to your wealth and quality in this city (with) whom you could remarry. . . . We have no other purpose in this business than your own benefit and reputation . . . and now that we have done what seemed to be our duty, we leave it to you to think, and to resolve it for yourself, as you are old enough to know your own mind."[39]

The culture nourished by the grand duchesses' management of Tuscany's "traffic in women," then, included respect for women's ability to make intelligent decisions about their heterosexual arrangements. In this world, mature women could enjoy kinds of power that contemporary prescriptive culture sought to deny them, the power to realize their own sexual and economic desires.

Not all the women in this network were able to manage their own affairs, nor were they all treated well by the husbands assigned to them. Such women could hope for systematic advocacy on their behalf from other women who were bound, as they were, by an obligation to honor the exchange of courtesy letters, reproductive aids, and sexual partners through collective responsibility for marriage's sometimes unfortunate results. When Leonora Orsini, married to a duke of the Sforza family, needed to be rescued from her husband's repeated beatings, a network of princesses across central and northern Italy responded with epistolary shock, indignation, and arrangements for help. That help enabled Leonora and her children to take refuge in various convents, finally writing Christine for sanctuary in Medici villas on 24 May 1616: "Forced by the continuous scoldings and beatings and worse that I received from Sig.re the Duke of Sforza, I fled with the intention never to return into his hands, where I would not be able to save my soul or my honor or my life."[40]

The grand duchesses' ongoing responsibility to protect other women in bad marriages extended beyond the princesses' class. In early November 1628, Magdalena wrote the Auditore of Siena about the ill treatment suffered by one of her former donne: "We cannot nor should we tolerate that gentildonne who have served us and been married from our household should find themselves unhappy and distressed because of their husbands. It displeases us infinitely therefore to hear that this happens in that city, and to the person of Ippolita Agostini, because of her husband Bolgherini's evil ways, whence he has wanted to beat her and throw her out of the house, without the slightest regard for her merit."[41] Magdalena wanted the auditore to remedy the situation, first by talking to Bolgherini. Specifically, he was to tell him that if the beatings did not stop "we will make him aware of his error, and in such a way that he will have the memory of it forever, and be an example to others."[42]

The Medici princesses were also perceived to offer redress when a marriage turned financially abusive, either through nonpayment of a dowry or the failure of a dead husband's family to restore a woman's dowry as required by law.[43] Although dowry abuse was under the jurisdiction of the Ruota civile (civil court), if a marriage had been brokered and dowered in part by the Medici women, problems were referred to them in the usually realized hope that the grand duchess would impose financial order. Thus it was at Christine's personal command that in 1610 the Depositeria Generale paid six hundred scudi toward Settimia Caccini's overdue dowry, rescuing the eighteen-year-old virtuosa bride from a father-in-law who had abducted her to Lucca and apparently meant to hold her there by force until her dowry was paid.[44] Christine was believed to be able to force her courtiers and staff to deal honorably with their dowry obligations, assuming their finances allowed. For example, several long and piteous letters in 1627 implore Christine to force a retired bailiff of the court, Francesco Saracinelli, to restore the dowry paid to his family when Victoria Tornabuoni married his brother.[45]

In fact, women of all social ranks could appeal to the grand duchess's generosity when they were desperate enough, and when the cause of the desperation ultimately arose from their condition as women in conflict with the institutions that governed their sexual difference. A 1613 letter written on behalf of a Sienese baker's daughter made pregnant by the physician for whom she worked successfully sought and received a dowry of six hundred scudi, equivalent to the kind of dowry a Medici cook might have received.[46] In 1603 the thirty-five-year-old spinster Vittoria Ardinghelli, wanting to enter a convent, petitioned Christine to force her brothers to pay the dowry they had promised to the convent.[47] Similarly, a woman cook at the Abbazia di San Salvatore whose daughter had been molested by a group of intoxicated gentlemen begged the grand duchess "by the viscera of Our Lord" to give her girl justice.[48] It seems, then, that even non-elite women understood themselves to be protected by the grand duchesses' quasi-maternal obligation to advocate for other women, whatever their condition.[49]

Christine did not always use her authority to protect the agency of other women in relation to marriages she could command. It is clear from the letters she exchanged with her pious great-niece Camilla Orsini that she all but forced the girl into marriage for the sake of her brothers' political and financial alliances in Rome. Orsini had tried to avoid her arranged marriage to the Roman prince Marc'Antonio Borghese (nephew of Pope Paul V) by claiming a monastic calling, going so far as to wear for two years the habit of the Monastero della Concezione, where she boarded as a pupil.[50] Curtio Picchena reported to Christine's daughter Caterina, then duchess of Mantua, that in May 1619 Camilla's brother Paolo Giordano removed his sister personally from the convent, taking her to the family home at Bagnaia to force her to marry; meanwhile, Caterina's brother Cardinal Carlo de' Medici had been dispatched to distract their sister Claudia, "who has the most ardent love for Orsina."[51] On learning in July that marriage negotiations were all but complete, Christine wrote Camilla, consoling her that she would find the will of God by serving the interests of her family: "From what Paolo Giordano writes to my son the Grand Duke, and to me, I understand that the contract to marry Your Excellency to the Prince of Sulmona has been renewed, news which has brought me as much contentment as I could have wanted. And this [is] because it confirms for me that it is the will of God that Your Excellency follow the first vocation. . . . as I recognize in Your Excellency that you will dispose of yourself according to the will and interests of your brothers, I am persuaded that Your Excellency will find it easy therein to do Our Lord's will."[52]

Camilla succumbed to Christine's overt manipulation of their shared piety, accepting her framing of her surrender in her first letter to Christine as a married woman: "Your Highness will have heard of the finalizing of my marriage to the Prince of Sulmona, and even if I have always inclined with my spirit toward religion, it seemed to me nonetheless that I needed to strip myself, finally, of my feelings, not only because thus I have honored the will of God and the service of my family and my brothers, but because I can also take from it the satisfaction of your Highness' pleasure, [you] to whose prudent and loving advice it is my duty to obey with all readiness because of the good feeling and extraordinary kindness Your Highness has shown me at all times."[53]

❧

The epistolary evidence shows the Medici grand duchesses to have had absolute authority to negotiate, approve, and command the terms of literally hundreds of marriages, authority that preempted the rights of fathers and guardians across very large swaths both of the Tuscan population and of central Italy's princely class. Responsible for ensuring the horizontal articulation of kinship among people who were already bound by loyalty or blood into vertical relations of service to the granducato, Christine exercised absolute sovereignty over the sex-gender system of e Tuscany's elite as if she were not so much a mother and guardian as the head of a tribe.

This authority may have had implications for the experiences that women had of themselves. As Gayle Rubin explained a generation ago, the exogamous exchange of female persons to form kinship relations is typically managed by men.[54] This traffic in women, she argued, reinforces the homosocial relations among the male persons who engage in it. The female persons thus exchanged learn to know themselves as only secondarily significant to the social fabric that constitutes what human beings call "the world"; this knowledge produces the self-perception of being an object, not a subject. For Rubin, as for her contemporary Luce Irigaray, this is also the self-perception we in the modern world have come to mean by the word "woman."[55]

In her 1978 essay "Commodities among Themselves," Irigaray theorized that if female persons actively exchanged each other in exogamous heterosexual networks, the male homosocial foundation of traditional patriarchal culture would be exposed, and the female persons involved in exchange would know themselves to be subjects as well as objects of desire. One logical conclusion to draw from Irigaray's theory is that when such female persons participated in heterosexual acts, they would perceive those acts as substitutes for the necessarily more important relations with other female persons through which they had identified themselves as both subjects and objects, the relations through which they had found their places in the social world. Such female persons would understand themselves in ways that are very different from the range of ways most female persons in the developed world understand themselves today. As Irigaray put it, they would not be women as we know them, even though we might persist in referring to them with that word.

The sex-gender system over which Christine and Magdalena presided was not that Irigaray imagined. Although elite females were not exchanged as commodities intended to strengthen the intrinsically homosocial kinship bonds among men, they also did not generally exchange each other as commodities among themselves. Instead, without removing the compulsion for females to participate in heterosexuality for the sake of their family's patrimony, this system sutured elite women into primary kinship relations with the grand duchess-mother who managed their exchange, and, through her person, into allegiance to the Tuscan state. Moreover, to the extent that their allegiance was inscribed in their psyches the way it was inscribed in documents—in the rhetoric of family loyalty—it was inscribed by means of a very fundamental trope of genteel womanhood: the unshakeable integrity of commitment to family that was onestà.

Thus elite females became ideal subjects in an absolutist state of which Christine was the affective center. This, I propose, was the world in which Bronzini's story of Francesca as an artist produced by the interaction of two women could make sense. It was, too, the world that Francesca's 1625 *balletto La liberazione di Ruggiero* assumed its audience understood.[56]

%

If Christine's sovereignty over the Tuscan traffic in elite women served the interests of the Tuscan state, it also allowed every female person in it to imagine herself as the object of another female person's desire and power. Therefore, every such person could imagine herself, through the mirror of sexual (in)difference, as also a female subject with the right to act powerfully in the service of her own desires. Indeed, Christine's papers are full of letters from other women who seem deliberately to have emulated the patterns of her power in an effort to realize their own benevolent desires. Perhaps none is so rich as one that Camilla Orsini wrote barely a month after her marriage, soliciting Christine's help in ensuring the placement in a convent of an impoverished servant's daughter: "The ancient, faithful service to my house of Bernardino, Knight Hospitaller of St. John of Jerusalem, is well known to you, which persuades me that you cannot refuse the business (appropriate to my gratitude) that I bring to your Highness on his behalf. He has a daughter serving there among the girls of S.r Vittorio, who wants to serve God in some religious order, but not being able to pay her expenses he would like by a special grace of Your Highness for you to have her accepted as a servant in the Monastero della Concezione. I, too, petition you for the same grace."[57]

Camilla's densely allusive letter shows her to have been still keenly aware that she remained subordinate to the grand duchess. Yet she seems eager to begin a reciprocal relationship through which, as married women of the princess class, the pair could exchange gifts meant to articulate and preserve a multitude of social relations. Camilla proposed to put in circulation favors between women (between Camilla and her servant's daughter, between Christine and Camilla, and therefore between Christine and the servant's daughter); favors between the princess class and the faithfully serving class; and a real woman who was to be moved horizontally from one place in the social world to another in keeping with her own and Camilla's desires. Camilla piquantly joined their desires by her explicit request that the girl be placed in the Monastero della Concezione, the very spot from which she had been abducted into marriage only months earlier. It is almost as if Camilla meant to imply that Christine both owed her the favor of acknowledging a girl's genuine vocation and owed the monastero a nun.

The latter implication suggests that both Camilla and Christine understood marriage placements and convent placements to be complementary parts of the sex-gender system, held in careful balance by the grand duchesses' absolute authority over all the institutions meant to control female sexual difference.[58] Convents represented, in spatial and social terms, women's right to refuse compulsory heterosexuality. Under the Medici grand duchesses, choosing a monastic life did not mean sacrificing access to friends, fashion, money, or the pleasures of commercial exchange, and it certainly did not mean sacrificing access to music, dancing, and theater. Indeed, all of these were prominent features of the "abuses" for which Florence's elite convents were ineffectually condemned by church authorities for the whole thirty years of Christine's de facto regency. Instead, to choose monastic life could mean to choose a life of female homosocial luxury and pleasure, freed by monastic walls and decorum from the disapproving scrutiny of men.

The grand duchesses' correspondence is even richer in letters about Florence's convents than in letters concerning the management of marriages. Much of that correspondence sprang from their insatiable desire for *licenze*—official documents from the church suspending the rules by which the cardinals and bishops who had convened as the Council of Trent had, in the sixteenth century, tried to restore their idea of pious, homosocial order to the communal lives of monastic women.[59] Acting on behalf of petitioning women and men alike, the grand duchesses instructed their diplomats in Rome to procure licenze allowing the full range of abuses that the council had meant to abolish. They successfully sponsored petitions for girls as young as ten to embark on monastic novitiates, a liberty that encouraged the coerced monacations of girls too young to resist but significantly improved a convent's cash flow when the girls' dowries were paid. They advocated the pleas of sisters, aunts, and cousins from the same family and those of girls who had been boarders together to enter a single community. Such group professions, which kept families together and kinship ties strong, were opposed by the church because they led to bloc voting in chapter meetings and, therefore, to resentment from sisters who felt that their individual "voice and vote" in their communities could be overwhelmed. Further, the grand duchesses ensured that elite secular women who sought refuge from abusive families could live inside convents with their servants. Often leaving substantial legacies to the communities in which they had been sheltered before their deaths, in life these women had no obligation to participate in the prayer life or work life of the community, and therefore they disrupted discipline.

Above all, however, the grand duchesses competed fiercely with the princesses of other courts over the number of licenze they could have in a year authorizing them to enter cloistered communities, attend or participate in services, take their meals in the refectory or the gardens, and to bring their dame, donne, children, and servants in tow. And they successfully gathered the sheaves of licenze necessary to build and staff palazzi adjoining the monasterii into which Medici princesses withdrew, at San Giovannino, Le Murate, and La Crocetta. The latter kinds of licenze ensured that certain convent walls in Florence were especially porous, breached at all hours of the day and night by masons, carpenters, tradespeople, and music teachers as well as by supposedly zealous princesses and their retinues.[60] Taken together with Christine's great generosity in dowering entrants such as the one Camilla Orsini had proposed, her court's traffic in licenze ensured that many women within convents would be even more grateful for her interventions in their lives than their married sisters would be. For Christine unwaveringly seconded the desires of women who sought relaxation of Trent's strict rules and the desires of women who, like her, cherished the freedom convents provided for homosocial pastimes.

One result was the unsavory reputation that Florence's convents had in Rome. According to a scathing report by the governors and confessors of convents in the Diocese of Florence to the Sacra Congregazione dei Vescovi e Regolari (Holy Congregation of Bishops and Regular Clergy), a "relaxation of religious observance" characterized all the convents of the diocese.[61] Norms for training girls to be nuns via systematic novitiates were widely ignored, as were the required vows of poverty intended to dissolve differences of wealth and social rank in a community. Instead of pooling their resources in a common fund as the Council of Trent had advised, in Florence "everyone waits to receive gifts; and the consecrations of nuns have gone so far that each nun spends about 200 scudi to be consecrated, almost all of which money goes for gifts and food." The governors and confessors sternly urged that the rule about pooling of funds be enforced in order to wrest control over their incomes from individual nuns: "nor should you take for an excuse that the nuns spend their private incomes for the benefit of the convent, because under this pretext they all do exactly what they want with their income, never contributing to the community but living like property owners." Economic inequality among the sisters led, they argued, to competition, vanity, and a tendency for administrative offices to be distributed more on the basis of apparent wealth than on the basis of spiritual merit or competence. Further, Florentine nuns neither worked nor prayed but spent their days in unvirtuous practices, including transforming the *parlatorii* (parlors) into "shops for every sort of vanity that secular women wear, and these nuns even manufacture some of them, so that the parlatorii are filled with fashions and boxes of haberdashery, and thus many unvirtuous friendships are formed."[62]

For women who used convents as refuges from the constraints of heterosexual domesticity, none of the practices that struck the governors and confessors as disorderly would have seemed problematic. Indeed, they make the world behind Florence's convent walls seem like a female utopia. In the proclaimed sanctity of cloistered space, women were free from men's efforts to control their bodies via the complementary tropes of heterosexual love and chastity. They were free to sing, dance, and play games without such pastimes' being constantly perceived as strategies of courtship or seduction. In the exchange of finery, jewels, and loans to finance such exchanges, they were also free of men's efforts to control their economic behavior via the ideology of continenza. But for nuns who had chosen monastic life out of deep spiritual conviction, the Medici princesses' literally licentious interferences were both offensive and dystopian, threatening to destroy monasticism's promise of serenely spiritual, sheltered lives. Inevitably, communities that accommodated the licentious princesses and their retinues were riven by the conflicting desires of very differently oriented women. No such community was shaken as badly as the Monastero Santa Maria Annunziata, known as Le Murate, a place Christine held especially dear as the community that had sheltered her grandmother Catherine from Florence's republican rebels from 1527 to 1529.

In March 1615 an unnamed advocate of some sisters there had written Rome to report "the gravest discord."[63] Two years earlier, "as a result of favor from the laity" and a dishonest confessor, Angelica Caterina Cybo, a member of the Medici family, had been named abbess, though three-fourths of the sisters had voted against her. Reasoning that if they could not trust the confessor to report their votes they should not trust him with their spiritual lives, the sisters had petitioned for a new confessor. When passed by the archbishop to the abbess, their petition had of course been denied. Year after year the sisters of Le Murate petitioned for a substitute confessor, their petition always denied in favor of a man whose reappointment Christine preferred.[64] The rebel sisters linked their pleas for a substitute confessor to complaints about licenze for secular people to come and go in service of the four Medici princesses among them, and complaints about the behavior of the princesses themselves: "Genuflecting, we wish Your Holiness would deign to give us the grace [to declare] that in our convent there will be no more lay residents, because they cause great confusion even if there are 180 of us and 8 of them, because they are always multiplying, and they do nothing but hold court here and there; they sing, they dance, they play games."[65] The lay women did more than this, however; they brought gold and jewelry into the convent to show off, inducing several nuns to go hundreds of scudi in debt to buy equivalent jewels and fashions.[66]

Years' worth of irritation finally broke into open rebellion on Palm Sunday, 1620, when the leaders of the dissident faction stood at Mass and voiced their refusal to take communion from the clergy assigned to them. After several undocumented months of dispute, on 8 October 1620, 47 of Le Murate's 180 nuns petitioned the Sacra Congregazione for permission to break irrevocably with the mother house, where their lives had changed from "bondage worse than that of [the Jews] in Egypt" to being like the lives of "slaves in chains."[67] The ongoing quarrel about the community's confessor is but a minor point in the rebels' blistering indictment of Le Murate's governance and patronage. Listed among the authors of their bondage are the archbishop of Florence, their confessor Vincenzo Querci, their former abbess Angelica Caterina Cybo and her successor Ippolita Acciauoli (who, they said, "adores [Cybo] more than God, and would do anything for her"), all of them implicated because they are "related to each other and the Medici, and do whatever they want."[68] They complained that the Medici princesses wanted the confessor for themselves and that "with their ladies [they] want to come into the convent for sacraments and . . . to give the habit to nuns themselves, and do the profession of vows, and do everything at their pleasure even when no priest will come."[69]

The Medici women's apparent usurpations of priestly authority were not, however, the shock that prompted these nuns' petition to secede. Rather, it was a pending Medici building project that finally broke the community of Le Murate in two: "The Signore want the liberty to build entire palaces . . . and to bolt the doors to us so that the sisters cannot go where they go and cannot see what they are doing. One need only remember what happened not long ago at Santa Verdiana because of leaving a young woman at her liberty."[70] The sisters did more than allude vaguely to the discovery of Suora Maria Vittoria Frescobaldi and Sinolfo Ottieri together in her cell to seal their case against the Medici. They accused the four Medici inhabitants of Le Murate of behaving entirely as though they still lived in the secular world. "We do not accept that one is a nun, even if she wears the habit, [if she] lives at liberty as if in the secular world, apart from us in sleeping quarters, servants and eating, although eating in the refectory when it pleases her, and all four are like this . . . [and] have refused to go through the novitiate like everyone else."[71] By his own admission exasperated beyond endurance by the troublemakers, the archbishop of Florence wrote the Sacra Congregazione approving the secession of the forty-seven dissident sisters and conceding some points about the behavior of the resident Medici princesses and about the new wing to be built for their accommodation. But his judgment was not to be binding.

Bundled together with all the other documents labeled "Murate" in the archives of the Sacra Congregazione for 1620 is an unsigned, undated memo from the Medici secretariat that asserts the resolution to which the Church would agree. Enumerating Christine's will point by point in each of the arguments about Le Murate, the memo framed its recommendation with the coldest reminder of the basis on which she claimed dominion over the sisters' space: "The Monastero of Le Murate in Florence, living under the protection of their Highnesses of Tuscany, by whom they are subsidized at the rate of 1,200 scudi a year, and other accounts and donations without which these nuns could not maintain themselves; and Madama having built an addition of 18 rooms at the expense of more than 4,000 scudi contiguous to this Monastery and united with it in a cloistering order by the Archbishop, who also chose as governor Vincenzo Querci."[72] In effect, the Medici owned Le Murate because it would collapse without their financial support. Consequently they claimed the right to appoint its governor and confessor, to deny the plea of dissident nuns to move elsewhere, to demand perpetual silence concerning the matter of the passageway linking old and new wings, and to authorize the archbishop to suspend (temporarily) the voice and vote of dissident nuns as punishment for the trouble they had caused, threatening them with imprisonment if their disobedience continued.

This document brings to an emotionally brutal conclusion a story in which too many contradictory urges in Christine's world converged. Her apparently genuine piety was offset in this case by her own conception of convents as sites where her court could enjoy pleasures and pastimes free from the gaze or restrictions of men. Her loyalty to Le Murate was offset by her presumption of absolute power, now that she had command of her own will. Her lifelong advocacy for other women collided with her equally lifelong blindness to the independent desires that those she could command might have. Instead of being balanced each against the other to make a structure by means of which a peaceful resolution might be found, the contradictions became entangled with Christine's unchecked desire to command. In full sight of the courtly women bound to her through the kinship web spun of courtesy letters and relics, marriages and licenze, Christine badly mismanaged the trouble at Le Murate. Dismissing the women there with the casually ruthless contempt born of wealth and class, she shattered forever her own relationship with a place she had long loved, she shattered the community there, and she shattered any illusion an elite woman might have had that participation in Christine's courtly world gave her safety from the realities of absolute power. In the end it was Christine's brute force, not any of the male bureaucracies through which her desire to command was mediated, that destroyed this particular homosocial paradise.

Bronzini's weird but vivid story implying that Francesca's career had been produced by two women comes into sharp focus when one understands the equally weird world of the Medici court's women. His fictional world mirrored the real world Francesca served, as it reflected the likely way women perceived themselves in relation to the peculiar sex-gender system over which the grand duchesses ruled. Bronzini located Francesca in that world as an object of exchange between women (Lucia and Christine), and therefore, in Irigaray's analysis, as a person too aware of her own capacity to be both subject and object of female desire to be a woman as conventionally conceived. Indeed, he located her as a person liable to imagine that she could use the power available to her to realize her own desires. For Bronzini, and indeed for history, Francesca was to be a person like the grand duchess, whose gender was unstable though her sex and apparent sexuality were not; and she was to be a person whose management of her own desire to command would be equally troubled. For Bronzini also projected Francesca as always subordinate to the woman whose parallel initiatives to train and to marry her had moved Francesca from one place in the social world to another, always in a relation of paradoxically empowered subordination.[73] Francesca was to serve, and she was to serve a woman who could be heedless of exactly the independent desires for power her management of Tuscan womanhood encouraged.

Bronzini had a story to explain the way the Medici princesses envisioned their subordinates' contributions to their own absolute, gynocentric power: his story of how the Muses came to be collectively associated with music making. The Muses, he wrote, were sisters who were enslaved and sold into the service of Megado, daughter of the ill-tempered, tyrannical King Macaro of Lesbos. By teaching the daughter and her long-suffering mother to sing and to accompany their songs on the kithara, the muses temporarily dissolved the social difference between sovereign and slave. In turn, the music-making of mother and daughter placated Macaro's ire, restoring harmony and balance to the Island of Lesbos. Thereafter, Bronzini claimed, the Argive word that had meant "female servant," *musi,* came to refer both to the female figures themselves (to whom he attributed deep knowledge of the cosmos' web of resemblances) and to the medium through which that knowledge emerged as power in the world: music. The politically transformative power of these curiously Lesbian muses was a power Bronzini attributed to Francesca—the power an erudite female servant and teacher might occasionally share with women whose access to governing power was guaranteed by the privileges of blood. It was a relationship of power that would serve Francesca and Christine well.

Musica to the Granducato

4

On 15 November 1607 Francesca entered the service of the Granducato of Tuscany as a musica, with an initial stipend of 10 scudi per month that would soon double.[1] Until May 1627 she would provide virtuosa solo singing, both improvised and *sopra'l libro* (by the book); sing with others in church, chamber, and theatrical settings; compose new music and coach its performance in all three settings; play lute, theorbo, harpsichord, guitar, harp, "and every sort of stringed instrument" as performance circumstances required; evaluate the performance abilities of others; teach singing, instrumental performance, and composition to girls and young women whose study with her was subsidized by a court eager to transform Florence's new way of making music into a tradition; and teach music to some of the ruling family's children.[2] Like her female colleagues, Francesca worked from day to day among the court's women, in circumstances that protected her reputation for continenza. Yet, alone among the court's women musicians, Francesca was as likely to be trusted with composing all or part of a court spectacle as was Marco da Gagliano or Jacopo Peri. Francesca's versatility made her a highly useful servant. Her work among the women who quietly ruled Tuscany during the long regencies made her a powerful one, able both to capitalize on her familiarity with her patrons and to give eloquent, entertaining voice to their concerns. In a world that conceived music as a discourse of power, Francesca's experience at the women's court and her particular musical strengths allowed her to bring into being, as sound, experiences of virtuous female mastery that served her women patrons' artistic and political aims. That circumstance, as much as any accident of her birth, accounts for her remarkable career.

A Musica among Women

Writing sometime after Francesca left the granducato's service in 1627, Bronzini left a long description of her performances as a familiar of the women's court might remember them. Based, he claimed, on his own memories, it is worth quoting at length for the way it evokes Francesca's presence as a charming woman whose musical erudition and skill, not her beauty or charm, transformed her listeners' minds and hearts:

> Even though she had not been favored by the gifts of nature, she was nonetheless friendly and admirable, never tiresome or resentful but merry and charming, and presented herself first of all with sweet and graceful manners toward everyone. And whether playing, singing or pleasantly talking, she worked such stunning effects in the minds of her listeners that she changed them from what they had been.
>
> Many times, finding myself where she was, together with many noble persons, we heard the marvelous woman accompany her own Phrygian song with such grace, whether on harpsichord, lute or theorbo, and work such stunning effects in the minds of her listeners that she made them pliant, agreeable, or many other things by turn, so that it was a wonder, to tell the truth something almost unbelievable. This same woman, whenever it suited her (no less than, indeed maybe far more than Amphion) so ignited wonder and daring in the breasts of the people that they would have done anything, no matter how difficult. At other times she changed her listeners with a *maniera*[3] . . . such that . . . wanting to sweeten the ferocity and cruelty of hearts, with the gentlest song she brought forth in them sweet, pleasing and human ways, such that they set their annoyances aside for the sweetness of delights, the merriment of song, and the preciousness of sound, and in this way drew them in toward herself. . . . Other times . . . making herself heard . . . in that music called Dorian (which has the intrinsic virtue of elevating the low and earthbound in human minds to the level of sublime contemplation), with such sweetness she made other people's minds climb to the contemplation of celestial things, such that she transformed (I daresay one could say) human beings into gods. What will I say of her Lydian music? Which when heard took the mantle of joy away from hearts and faces, so that, wrapped only in the sadness of melancholy and the denseness of dark clouds, there was nothing to do but weep? . . .
>
> Our miraculous Cecchina knew not only these three maniere of songs, but many others that created various effects in human minds. Some of them bent

the irascible of heart to agreeable meekness and some the lust in the will of others to praiseworthy temperance. With the soft sound of her playing and the sweetness of her song she invited every breast (even if opposed to chaste intentions) to pure continenza and onestà, for which her own modesty and integrity shone equal to those most renowned for these virtues. Some other maniere that she knew could bring the sick and weak of body to longed-for health and recovery of their strength.[4]

Bronzini's characterization of Francesca's performances contrasts sharply with his admiring accounts of her best-known female contemporaries. He does not praise her, as he did her sister Settimia, for "miraculous passaggi," throat articulation that "surpassed any quivering nightingale," and "so well-formed and harmonious a body, and so chaste a soul, as to awaken chaste, virtuous and celestial love in whoever sees or hears her."[5] Nor does he praise her as he did the virtuosa Adriana Basile, whose performances of distilled sadness or joy left listeners "stunned, almost out of themselves."[6] Instead, Bronzini remembers Francesca as a person whose mastery over every aspect of musical craft enabled her to use musical performance as an instrument of benevolent power, power like that he had elsewhere attributed to Amphion, whose "prudence and gentle eloquence" brought disparate listeners into community.[7]

Court records show Francesca to have performed only rarely in staged entertainments that the court sponsored for large audiences invited from among Florence's elite. She was no stage diva, but rather a singer who almost always performed music she was acknowledged to have composed, most often in private.[8] Performed before or after meals for the grand duke, his family, their dame and donne, and the visiting dignitaries they invited to share their domestic pleasures, Francesca's Dorian or Phrygian song may have been intended and received as complementing political arguments made earlier in the day. During the receptions that Maria Magdalena held in her bedroom for the gentildonne of Florence to celebrate a successful childbirth, her music may have been intended and received as reinforcing the womanly virtues of all who were there. When, sometimes alone and sometimes with others, she made music at the bedsides of the dying Cosimo II and, later, of his widow Magdalena, Francesca may have seemed actually to heal her patrons, as well as to distract them. That is, if Bronzini is to be believed, Francesca's work in private circumstances could always have seemed political as well as artistic, and always transformative.

Yet Francesca also served her patrons in circumstances that are difficult to describe as political—performing with her pupils, the dame and donne of the women's court, and the princely children in ad hoc entertainments she composed and prepared either for their sovereigns' or their own amusement.[9] Despite Bronzini's memory that her music could bend any listener to her will, in these circumstances Francesca's patrons treated her not at all as a person of power but as the servant she was. She could be ordered to appear at any palace, including the winter compound at Pisa, on short notice.[10] Once there, she might wait for hours, even days, to make whatever music they wanted to hear. Sometimes Francesca performed not for her patrons' pleasure but for their evaluation, for she was called on to preview excerpts from entertainments that were still being written and to justify any inexpert, under-rehearsed, or still unfinished parts to patrons who were concerned that work under her direction might reflect poorly on their own excellence. As she wrote to Buonarroti on 18 December 1614:

> although we have rehearsed our music in the presence of the Serenissima [Magdalena] and Madama [Christine], the grand duke has not heard us yet, even though we wait from day to day to be thus commanded; indeed, one evening we were gathered waiting to do so until three hours after dark, but because of the impediment of an ambassador we had to put it off for another evening and that was lucky, since Madama asked me why Signora Giralda could not yet sing her solo, and I told her that it was because you had not yet had the time to do the verses because your nephew was in danger of dying.[11]

Francesca's reply to Christine shows the quick thinking that enabled her to survive her subservience at court. Quick to explain away Giralda's apparent lapse, she avoided making it seem like her own and protected Buonarroti from criticism by playing on Christine's sympathy. She deflected Christine's criticism, too, by performing her own prologue and ending for the show to such good effect that she reported that Christine and Magdalena had laughed "from the heart, and their laughter filled the room."[12]

These letters suggest that Francesca may have served as composer and music director of all entertainments originating in the women's court, including many that went unrecorded in Tinghi's diary. The 1614 letters show Buonarroti sending texts directly to her as soon as he finished them, so that she could compose and teach them to Magdalena's dame.[13] Even as she prepared the group for one performance, Francesca alerted Buonarroti to the likelihood that he would soon be asked to devise another: "You should start thinking about some little comedy for eleven actors, for that's how many we are, and it should be with a pleasing, new and varied invention, to make one laugh, and with varied characters, because even though we don't have a sure decision, I have enough in hand to want to give you a warning, so you won't be caught off guard."[14]

Nine days later she wrote with more details, asking Buonarroti to keep them secret. In the course of rehearsing the current show, the dame had decided to ask Magdalena for permission to do a comedy "among themselves," permission they had been granted the year before.[15] Waiting for her reply, the eight women and three girls had discussed among themselves what kind of comedy it should be. Francesca, who as a girl had played both Beco, the handsome boy who wins the title character in G. A. Berni's satire *La Catrina,* and a lovesick nymph, may have brought her long experience to bear on the results.[16] Communicating their decisions directly to Buonarroti, Francesca enabled them all to evade Christine's or Magdalena's meddling, as well as the upsetting effects of their tendency to issue last-minute, peremptory commands. Yet her instructions to Buonarroti have a peremptory tone of their own: "The comedy ought to be in 5 acts, or 3, as you judge best, and the intermedi should have scherzi [light, strophic poems] like those you have made before that we can sing among ourselves; the quality of the comedy should be *civile,* with aged lovers, sad servant boys, comic serving girls . . . so long as it is varied, high-spirited and without long speeches . . . there are no teenage girls or babies, but only three girls between eleven and twelve years old. The rest of us are adults. Enough said, except that I can tell you that the whole comedy could be built around Signora Giralda as a sad teenage boy and Signora Medici as a serving girl. That's how we left it."[17]

If the company ever received both the permission and the text necessary to their comedy, it went unrecorded in the court's official diary. Yet it seems likely that this group constituted what Francesca would call, years later, her troupe ("compagnia"), a troupe responsible for performing the dozens of informal comedies and scenarios for the court that can be found among Buonarroti's papers.[18] Perhaps more important, Francesca's letter shows her to have engaged the power dynamic at court quite differently than Bronzini's description of her might suggest.

Francesca's service to the women's court put her at the intersection of powerful forces that linked all concerned in relations of mutual dependence. As subject to the grand duchesses' commands as any other musical servant, she nonetheless enjoyed a certain familiarity with them, both by virtue of her frequent presence among them and by virtue of her familiarity with their dame and donne. Because these young women were of much higher social rank than she, they, too, might have thought they could command Francesca. Yet in matters of performance she commanded them, and they depended on her to command them well, for she composed and taught them parts in which they could "do themselves honor" in the eyes of their patrons.[19] They depended on her, as well, to protect them from criticism and to ask poets such as Buonarroti for suitable material. Buonarroti, too, depended on Francesca, and not only because she could give him advance notice and bossy advice about an imminent command. Francesca was sometimes unexpectedly asked by her patrons to comment on a colleague's work, a situation that could serve the colleague well or ill.[20]

More often, Francesca could serve a poet by seizing the opportunity that an unspecified command for music could afford her to present her settings of his newest poetry as their joint service to their patrons. Her letters asking that Buonarroti send specific poems, by name, and the large number of poems in his ephemera that are inscribed to Francesca in the margins suggest that she depended on him for a constant supply of new verse that she could "match . . . in the part that is mine, that is, in composing and singing it . . . to their Highnesses."[21] Mutual dependence forced dame, poets, and musica to collaborate in mutual service to each others' interests so that they could serve their patrons well.

In 1614 Francesca's usefulness to her patrons changed, and with it, her fortunes. On 10 December her stipend leapt suddenly to twenty scudi per month, making her the best-paid musician and one of the highest-paid workers of any kind at court.[22] That April the court had for the first time denied Virginio Orsini's request that she be detailed to his household in Rome, as if she were too precious to be shared.[23] Tinghi began to name her as an individual in the official diary of court performances, rather than as "the daughter of Giulio Romano," whom she seemed to replace. By 1616 she had eclipsed Vittoria Archilei, too, becoming the most prestigious among a new generation of women musicians that included Angelica Sciamerone ne' Belli, Arcangela Palladini ne' Broumans, and eventually still younger women who had been Francesca's or Jacopo Peri's pupils: Maria Botti, Emilia Grazii, and Caterina and Angelica Parigi. Indeed, by 1616 Francesca was treated as the equal of her father's old rival Peri, for they were the two virtuosi sent to Rome that May as part of Carlo de' Medici's retinue when he claimed his cardinalate.[24] What could account for Francesca's remarkable rise?

It was the luck of the versatile, quick-witted, musically erudite Francesca to find herself at the musical center of the women's court when, in late March 1614, Christine's buoyantly healthy second son Francesco suddenly fell ill, dying in late May.[25] Grief turned to fear in early September when the always fragile Cosimo II fell briefly ill with fever and vomiting that returned in early December, keeping him bedridden the entire month.[26] In December 1614, Christine was face to face with the prospect that, instead of fading as her son grew into his role as grand duke, her de facto regency might soon become a de jure one. The women's court amid which Francesca's gender had destined her to serve was to be the center of political gravity for the granducato. From that center, her every performance mattered to the state.

Francesca as Composer of Court Spectacles

Immersed as she was in service to the women's court, where women commanded and men turned commands into action, Francesca had also long been immersed in a system for the production of court spectacles in which authority was mostly shared among men who knew her as her father's daughter. Tacking between two worlds, she composed music for spectacles that gave voice, in the politicized, semi-public performances of the granducato's court, to the sensibility of the women's court.

As the granducato's orders for Buonarroti's 1619 comedy *La fiera* show, once a poet's plan for a spectacle had been approved, several staff members shared responsibility for administering the realization of his plan.[27] The superintendent of buildings was to manage the design of the performance space and provide for stage machines, acting on the advice of the court architect. Acting on the poet's advice, the guardaroba was to provide costumes; the superintendent of music was to distribute the composition work and choose the singers; and the maggiordomo was to ensure that those who wrote or copied the music and the spoken parts were paid promptly, so that parts could be distributed in ample time for rehearsal. This was the system that Francesca's letter on behalf of the court's dame, telling Buonarroti what kind of comedy they wanted, had dodged.

The orders for *La fiera* are consistent with other evidence that suggests it was normal at the Tuscan court for theatrical composing to be divided among several musicians. Those who were to compose were likely to assume that the parts they wrote would be assigned to their pupils and protegées, to whom they could teach the parts.[28] Thus the system for production of large-scale court spectacles resembled the one that Francesca's letter described at the women's court, except that the pool of musicians on whom a poet might draw was larger, encouraging competition and even envy among them. A letter from Christine to Buonarroti about his 1614 comedy *Il passatempo* implies that there was such a pool, perhaps determined for each entertainment according to its likely needs. Given the choice for *Il passatempo* of Jacopo Peri, Francesca, Lorenzo Allegri or the Frenchman Antonio Gai, to all of whom he might have assigned scenes or parts, Buonarroti replied to Christine: "I assigned it all to Signora Francesca."[29]

More often, entertainments were composed by teams. Because Tinghi ignored the system of joint musical authorship, it is difficult to know how often Francesca was part of such a team, but other sources make it clear that she collaborated with women and men. She shared the composition of the 1611 *Mascherata di ninfe di Senna* with her sister Settimia, Vittoria Archilei, and Jacopo Peri. According to both Tinghi's diary and Buonarroti's working manuscripts, Francesca and Marco da Gagliano shared responsibility for composing *La fiera*. The poet Jacopo Cicognini reported that she composed the parts of Sant'Agata, Eternità, and the priestesses of Venus for his *Il martirio di Sant'Agata* (1622), and Giovanni Battista da Gagliano composed the rest. Kelley Harness has shown that Francesca composed the parts of Cordula and Urania for Andrea Salvadori's *La regina Sant'Orsola* (1624), attributed by Tinghi to Marco da

Gagliano. Harness's discovery opens the possibility Francesca may have contributed more often to the court's theatrical life than can now be proved.

In terms of sheer numbers, Francesca's career as a composer of court spectacles compares well with those of her best-known contemporaries, Peri and Marco da Gagliano. Each composed at least one full-length entertainment intended in part to celebrate a dynastic marriage; each composed several full-length entertainments for Carnival; each collaborated with the others in composing such entertainments or in composing sacred operas; each composed a myriad of ephemeral balli and intermedi. Yet Francesca's career had a distinct profile, one that invites the inference that her assignments were gendered, or grounded in the sensibility of the women's court. Unlike Peri or Gagliano, Francesca never composed for an entertainment with a classical or tragic subject. Unlike them, she seldom composed for the dance-based entertainments that Cosimo II and Magdalena so loved to offer to Florence's elite. Unlike them, after writing the music for *La stiava* she never again composed for an entertainment based on mock combat. Instead, unlike Peri and Gagliano, Francesca composed music for entertainments that celebrated the marriages of Magdalena's dame. The day of dancing and feasts celebrating the marriage of Elizabeth Destain to Attilio Incontri in May 1611 was followed by the first performance of Buonarroti's comedy *La Tancia,* with music by Francesca, in Don Antonio de' Medici's home. A similarly festive celebration of Sofia Binestan's marriage to one Cavaliere Castiglione in February 1615 was followed by the performance of Francesca's *Ballo delle zingare*. In the 1620s she composed several little shows for the princely children to perform for their mother or grandmother. And in 1625 she composed all the sung music for the pastiche of comedy, *balletto di dame* and *balletto di cavallo* known as *La liberazione di Ruggiero.*

Before the composition of *La liberazione,* Francesca's contributions to Buonarroti's *La Tancia, Il passatempo,* and *La fiera* were probably the most historically important theatrical works of her career, for they are widely considered three of the most important comedies of the early Baroque. Each included song scenes (some verisimilar and some not) and intermedi between the acts in which ensembles commented obliquely on the main action through song and dance. Thus each bore a stronger structural resemblance to a mid-twentieth-century North American musical with dialogue, songs, and production numbers than to the entirely-sung dramas such as *La Dafne, L'Euridice,* and *Il rapimento del Cefalo* with which court-based composers had experimented at the turn of the seventeenth century, the experiments that have come to be considered the principal forerunners of opera. Indeed, Buonarroti's comedies determinedly mock the classicizing pieties of high culture. Mocking even more sharply the conventions of heterosexual love, each asserts women's right to sexual agency, to mobility in their community, and to voice. Thus each brought to the official performance culture of the granducato—to the attention of the Tuscan elite and of the state's guests—the sensibility of the women's court. The urgency of such work to her patrons' interests helped to drive Francesca's career.

The plot of *La Tancia* turns on the struggle between a rich, self-important urbanite and an emotionally honest peasant for the hand of the girl whom the comedy's title names. Buonarroti's comedy is justly famous for mixing once up-to-date jokes about telescopes with scenes of nearly incomprehensible, occasionally obscene patter in Tuscan dialect. But at the heart of the comedy lay a characterization of Tancia herself both as a natural virtuosa of the most beautifully ornamented Tuscan song and as a woman who thought she had the right to decide how her beauty and sexuality would be disposed in marriage.[30] Pietro, the city man, admires her singing in terms that seem borrowed haphazardly from Giulio's preface to *Le nuove musiche* or Vincenzo Galilei's unlikely comparisons of Tuscan folk song to the *melodia* of ancient Greece. Yet Pietro's exuberant demonstration of the virtuoso improvised singing that he believes to be his Florentine birthright is so extravagantly awful that it drives everyone else screaming from the stage.[31] His intellectualizing, musical clumsiness, and belief in the power of money to make him excellent in all things converge both to satirize the pretensions of the "new music" and to demonstrate the arrogance that the virtuosa Tancia rejects at the show's end. Instantly popular with its audience and with those to whom manuscript copies of the script circulated, *La Tancia* remained in the local repertoire for years, its music eagerly sought for productions at the Monastero di San Miniato in 1618 and in Rovezzano in 1619. Pietro's ridiculous song and Tancia's evident virtuosity notwithstanding, Francesca's music for the show was locally remembered as easy, although the Rovezzano producer, Zanobi Braccii, worried that it might not be easy enough for the youths with whom he worked.[32]

A deliberate pastiche of styles that the narrators Pastime, Restoration after Labors, and Laughter propose as possible entertainments for ladies of the court, Buonarroti's *Il passatempo* systematically mocked the amorous conceits of all dramatic genres—civil (political) comedy, tragedy, *commedie rusticale* such as *La Tancia*, "Spanish" action dramas, and pastoral scenes of idealized love between shepherds and nymphs. As rich with musical numbers as *La Tancia*, the song scenes and intermedi of *Il passatempo* were not means of creating character and dramatic tension to drive a plot so much as they were means of performing absurdity. The only fully musical scene known to survive is a brief *egloga* (eclogue).[33] This love scene between the shepherd Tirsi and his nymph Filli shows unflinchingly the conclusion all such scenes must logically reach: a woman's surrender to her lover leads to her silence and her disappearance from the heterosocial world they share into a world of constructed femininity inaccessible to him. Poetically, the joke lies in the irrevocable fracturing of the classical alexandrines by which Tirsi declares his love. When Filli unexpectedly responds, she disrupts his high-style eloquence by replying in the short rhyming lines of the canzonetta.[34] Forced by courtesy to reply in kind, Tirsi struggles awkwardly to fit his notions of love into Filli's style. Only when she disappears can he return to the grandiloquent style in which he is comfortable, a style he now turns to lament. But with Filli no longer there to hear him Tirsi cannot sustain the alexandrines; he falters into alternating long and short lines that, reversing Orpheus, command woods, hills, beaches, trees, rivers, and fountains to join his silence instead of his song. Francesca's setting constructs the joke differently in music. To demonstrate that she hears Tirsi's pleas, Filli's music shifts from the natural tonal world they had shared to a world marked by flats on the page and by such traditional markers of femininity in sound as cross-relations and unresolved dissonances. When her tonal language finally is stabilized, Filli cadences firmly in the "flat" tonal world of femininity and softness, a world as unreachable by Tirsi as the nearly cloistered world of women and children to which married women and the women of the court were necessarily consigned.

However perfectly the scene realizes the prophecy of the song with which *Il passatempo* had opened, "To whoever wants to know what Love is / . . . I will say it is nothing but sorrow," the egloga's joke on the absurdities of pastoral love is only one among many. The delight of the show lay in the utter illogic and disunity of its construction and in its creators' virtuosity at mastering all genres.[35] At the same time, the show's pastiche construction ensured a finale in which Cosimo II and Magdalena's shared passion for costumed dancing could be indulged without any twisting of narrative logic. It became instead the stabilizing point of the evening. The plot of the concluding *Ballo della cortesia*, the discovery of Florence by a woman rising from the sea to find safe haven under the benevolence of a woman named Christiana, evoked a familiar local myth. Implicitly, the number proposes that the audience might similarly find safety from the most heterogeneous of fictive worlds if they joined their sovereigns' well-ordered dance. The two authors' masterful mixing of genres, then, served their patrons as much as it delighted them, for like the mastery over all the modes that Bronzini attributed to Francesca, Buonarroti and Francesca's mastery over genre transparently symbolized a political mastery over heterogeneity that the Medici could claim as their own.

Buonarroti's 1619 comedy *La fiera* was both his most ambitious play and his most problematic. Like *Il passatempo* constructed as a pastiche, *La fiera* mocked every scene-type of contemporary drama from comic to violent to lamenting and cast a gimlet eye on every imaginable problem of Florentine court and civic life.[36] Although the first performance reportedly lasted only three and a half hours, Buonarroti endlessly reconceived the text of *La fiera*, leaving a mass of manuscript material he intended to be a gargantuan concatenation of scenes organized into five spectacles in five acts each, to be performed on five succes-sive days. As a result it is impossible to decipher from his manuscripts exactly what form *La fiera* took in 1619, but it is clear from marginal annotations that Francesca, Marco da Gagliano, and possibly Arcangela Palladini shared the work of producing the musical numbers, none of which survives.[37] These in-cluded comic intermedi for syphilitics, prisoners, and ensembles of such char-acters as Commerce, Deceit, Fraud, and Self-interest, scenes full of singing, dancing women circulating unescorted through the streets, and lament scenes for women alone whose untoward circumstances, in turn, ranged from con-ventional abandonment to public childbirth (both easily construed as resulting from unsupervised dancing in the streets). Although usually very much to her taste, the irreverence of *La fiera* unexpectedly provoked Christine's ire. She took offense, among other things, at the scene of public childbirth, which she felt showed a disrespect for women that should not be allowed to seem funny.[38]

A Figure for Female Excellence

Christine had been concerned that the court's entertainments represent re-spect for women at least since the 1607 preparations for *La stiava*. Indeed, the theme of respect for women's authority runs through much of her correspon-dence, both that intervening in the court's artistic program and that concerned with more substantive matters of state. Her concern was not personal. If the official culture of Tuscany were not premised on a respect for women's author-ity, she and her daughter-in-law could not do what the accidents of history re-quired of them. They could not manage the always restive elites who staffed the state's bureaucracies, and they could not, thereby, preserve the state for its male Medici heirs. Thus representations of women's perspective and performances by women that could command a respect for female virtù became, in the 1610s and 1620s, crucial to the health of the state.

Some of the performances that Francesca gave under the auspices of the granducato's court seem likely to have been both intended and received as eliciting a respect for women that reflected on the women she served. That, at least, would explain the frequency with which Francesca's performances were mentioned after 1618 in Tinghi's diary of "all the public things that His Serene Highness shall do, and all that happens daily at court."[39] Always both private and political, her performances in the most intimate circumstances of the rul-ing family's life, among princely children she can be assumed to have taught, may have seemed likely to have real effects on the family's physical and men-tal health. But it was on the rare occasions when Francesca's music was heard outside such circumstances that it could both elicit respect for women and fig-ure in sound the palpable but invisible power of the women who ruled. Two performance events from Francesca's maturity are well-enough documented to allow their partial reconstruction: her performance in Santa Felicita on Holy Thursday in 1618 and a set of performances that she gave in Rome in the winter of 1623–1624. Together they illustrate the range of ways Francesca could have served, in performance and in memory, as a figure for female Medicean excellence that commanded respect.

On 9 April 1618 Francesca provided part of the music for the office for Holy Week that the Medici family heard, singing from the *corridoio* that linked Palazzo Pitti to the Uffizi with a passage through the back gallery of the palace's parish church, Santa Felicita. From that year to 1625, Francesca's name is the first one mentioned in Tinghi's increasingly detailed accounts of the Holy Week music.[40] Since 1602 Francesca had been the single most regular participant in such performances, which were in turn the single most regular performance event by which the Medici represented themselves to their people. Always, the Medici family heard the offices from the passageway that linked the palace where they would spend Easter to its parish church.[41] One to three ensembles of the court's "musici"—its male musicians—placed in the church joined one or two ensembles of its musical "donne," placed in the passageway, next to their sovereigns, to perform evening offices with music so "stupendous" that it attracted crowds of listeners.[42] Like the princely family beside whom they stood, the women musicians could see and hear everything in the space. Like their princes, the women musicians remained invisible to the listening crowds.

Holy Week in 1618 was unusually memorable. Cosimo was well known to be recovering still from a longer and more serious illness than had beset him in 1614, and the weather that winter had been catastrophically bad.[43] An endless round of hailstorms and rain that showed no sign of stopping had left the fields flooded, threatening "universal penury and famine." According to Bronzini, Magdalena took the initiative to organize Forty Hours devotions in San Lorenzo, hiring a Capuchin preacher and ordering the court architects to create a model of heaven, purgatory, and hell in the church. Every parish and confraternity in the city and suburbs would receive a plenary indulgence if they processed to San Lorenzo to pray and hear the preaching.

On Holy Thursday it was the turn of Santa Felicita, the palace's parish. In a gesture of surprising humility and solidarity, Magdalena and the princely family took their turn in the streets among their people. According to Curtio Picchena, Cosimo's younger brother Don Lorenzo led, holding a cross aloft; he was followed by princes Ferdinando (age seven) and Giovan Carlo (age six) and the signori and gentlemen of the court. Magdalena followed, bearing a slightly smaller cross, as she led her sister-in-law Princess Claudia, her daughters Margherita and Anna, their cousin Camilla Orsini, all the dame and donne, and the rest of the parish across the city on foot. Once at San Lorenzo, Magdalena "ardently prayed for the well being of the people, the cessation of the rains, and the return of good weather."[44] Then she led her parish silently home, later returning with them to Santa Felicita to hear the offices.

The music performed that year came from four directions—from two groups of men in the church and two groups of women in the corridoio, including Arcangela Palladini, Angelica Sciamerone, and Francesca. As the Sienese poet Gismondo Santi would describe it in a fifteen-stanza poem, Francesca's performance swept all others from memory. Her music, "like a stairway to the empyrean choir," began with a prelude on "touched strings" (probably a lute or theorbo), in which notes "turned around their mates, uniting in discords and concords" so as to make "avid ears" long for resolution. Bringing her prelude to rest, he wrote:

> [Now] she bends her flexible voice like a bow
> Now lets it shake, now widens it, now brings it into focus
> Now she lengthens its pace, now turns it on itself, now splits its line,
> Now spins a finely focused thread of sound, now raises her voice, now blurs it
> Now makes it grave and low
> Now draws it in, now turns it harsh, now sweetens it
> Marking her musical voyages in tempo
> With trills, with gruppi, and with passaggi.
>   Sometimes she hastens its flight with false notes
> And deliberately tunes dissonances
> But while she seems to offend, [she is] opening
> A more delightful path to harmonic sweetness;
> As a beloved woman kindles still more love
> in her lover with disdainful harshness,
> A physician mixes artfully the bitter
> with the sweet, [or] a painter [mixes] darkness with light.[45]

Citing in these and subsequent stanzas all the tricks of dynamic variety, register, timbre, ornament, and harmony that comprised the Caccinian "new way" of singing, Santi portrays Francesca to have been as much a master of singing's details as she was, for Bronzini, a master of its effects. Such virtuosity would have compelled respect and wonder in any year. Inseparable in her patrons' and her listeners' minds from the Medici past, and enacted from the threshold between a principality's private, invisible power and its palpable public effects, Francesca's performance must have commanded quite precisely her listeners' respect for the elision of princely power and female virtù. But the performance Santi described was likely to have surpassed merely general effects; her listeners would have received her song through knowledge of its moment. The miracu-

lous multiplicity of the vocal and musical effects her performance drew together
may have resonated for her listeners with Magdalena's initiative, that very week,
to direct the energies of every parish and confraternity toward common prayer.
Indeed, Santi remembered Francesca's performance as producing a similar
unity of response among her listeners:

> You would have seen every listener fixed
> While the singing lasted, not batting an eye
> Eager that the hours of that day would turn eternal
> [That] the son of Latona [Apollo] stop his chariot
> and then [you would have seen them]
> Applaud these songful melodies with peaceful murmurs;
> Remaining every one of them separated from himself
> With his Body on Earth, and his Soul in Paradise.[46]

Silencing by the softness of her voce di camera and her lute, and compelling
attention to her mastery of every kind of musical detail, Francesca bound her
listeners together in stunned wonder at a kind of leadership they might easily
have attributed to Magdalena. An idea of leadership that used gentle means
rather than force, it brought others out of themselves—out of the narrowness
of individual, embodied self-interest—to work toward the common good. In
Santi's description, its performance as music can seem to have produced both
spiritual and political ecstasy.

   If Francesca's performances for Holy Week can be understood to have represented Magdalena's emergent leadership to the Tuscans able to elbow their
way into Santa Felicita, her performances in Cardinal Carlo de' Medici's Roman
household, in the winter of 1623–1624, can be understood to have represented
female Florentine excellence in the service of the regency's foreign policy. Unlike the visit paid in 1616, when she had served along with Jacopo Peri, in 1623–
1624 Francesca was the unquestioned leader of the musicians detailed to the
cardinal; she was the only Florentine musician mentioned in any account of the
season. Francesca and her performances, potential and real, were her patrons'
gift to the Florentine Maffeo Barberini, whose election as Pope Urban VIII all
Rome celebrated that winter.[47] Like any gift, Francesca's presence was intended
to affect the relationship between the parties to the exchange. By sending a musician whose performances they had increasingly limited to their own court's
private space, Magdalena and Christine acknowledged Barberini as no longer
their subject but a fellow head of state whom they invited to intimacy. Moreover, by sending Francesca they represented the apogee of Tuscan musicality,
and by extension Tuscan power, as taking female form.

   From October 1623 to late February 1624, Francesca performed at banquets

that Cardinal Carlo hosted for the best-known melophiles and the most powerful cardinals of Rome, at *veglie* (social gatherings) for Rome's elite women
hosted in the rooms of the Tuscan ambassador's wife, or for private visitors to
the lodgings the court had secured for her.[48] Performing either just before or just
after a meal, often for several hours at a time, she sometimes sang *all'improviso*
and sometimes not, sometimes alone and sometimes with Adriana Basile, the
widely admired virtuosa whose presence in Rome was the Duke of Mantua's
gift. Not until the last Sunday in January 1624 was she called to perform for the
new pope in his private apartments. There, before a tiny audience that included
the pope's brother Carlo Barberini, his sister-in-law Costanza Magalotti, Lucrezia Vaini, and Francesca's husband, she sang two of the pope's own Latin
odes to him, as well as two odes by Horace, a madrigal to the Virgin by Buonarroti that particularly pleased the pope, and poetry by Andrea Salvadori that she
delivered so well that the mathematician Mario Guiducci would write, "[S]he
could not have done more to enhance his reputation." As Orso d'Elci wrote to
Magdalena, "[S]he honored herself and her service to this whole court."[49]

Nothing more is known about how the pope received the Medici women's
gift. But accounts of her performance for the poet Giambattista Marino and
members of his Accademia degli Umoristi in November 1623 provide indirect
evidence of the way Francesca's music-making was valued in Rome. For months
the Florentine Antimo Galli had argued with Marino about the relative merits
of Adriana Basile, whose performances Marino found ravishing, and Francesca,
whom Marino had never heard: "But the man, unable to believe there could be
another like her [Adriana], hardly gave me a hearing. Finally he let us take him
[to hear Francesca] . . . she sent immediately for his poem *L'Adone*, and finding
in it certain stanzas she sang them, improvising without even having read them,
and he couldn't have been more stunned. Going the next evening to hear Adriana sing the same verses, he began to appreciate the difference and returned
last night to Cecchina, praising her above all the exponents of this profession,
having been forced to confess that she is more knowledgeable and more a master of the art."[50] More aesthetic than political, Marino's judgment nevertheless
identified the exact value of Francesca's presence as a gift: she was the most
learned and masterful exponent of her art, a woman who dazzled not by beauty
or her ability to elicit profound emotional response but by an intelligence in
turning poetry into music that she had dramatized as effortless.

Marino's judgment of Francesca would be magnified by a competition between her and Adriana scheduled at Cardinal Carlo's palace the following Sunday evening and by Francesca's performance for the Accademia degli Umoristi
on November 26 that was memorialized by poems the members recited in her
honor the following day.[51] Four of these, written by Basile's brother Giovanni
Battista, survive in a collection of poetry he published under the pseudonym

Gianfrancesco Maria Materdona.[52] Basile's craft as a poet was not equal to capturing either Francesca's performances or his sister's. But while his poetry is pedestrian, the themes through which he framed Francesca's effects shed light on the ways her performances and persona were received.

Unlike Bronzini and Santi, Basile seems to have been unmoved by the variety of Francesca's musical effects. Instead, in a sestina about her performance of a passage from Marino's *L'Adone*, he focused on her ability so to confound categories as to unmoor him from his ability to construe reality.[53] Tossed in his own mind between such opposites as "woman/goddess," "goddess/angel," and "heaven/earth," he describes himself as having been "intoxicated by song, intoxicated by sound," and "raptured" by the harmony made by Francesca's "graceful hand, learned mouth." He attributes to Francesca, too, an ability so to reorganize a listener's perception of life's binaries as to reverse them, saying that if the beast who had bitten Adonis had heard how sweet she made his death, he would not have bitten him. Yet in the poem's last stanza Basile captures Francesca in his own binary logic, contrasting the beast's "pitiless mouth" with her "learned, noble mouth," which restored Adonis to life.[54]

Like Bronzini and Marino, Basile made a point of attributing Francesca's power as a performer to her learning. Hers was an erudite mouth, not a sensual one; her music enraptured listeners' souls, not their bodies. It was therefore by chaste and reasonable means that her song forced listeners to reconsider the a priori assumptions and conventional tropes by which they were accustomed to interpret the world. Although Basile is unlikely to have had in mind the Tuscan regents' agenda in sending her to Rome as their gift, his account of Francesca shows how her performances must have served it.

By focusing on Francesca's singing about Adonis' death, Basile powerfully insinuated a comparison with Orpheus, who sang of this very death before his own in Ovid's *Metamorphoses*.[55] Two sonnets Basile addressed to her made the Orphic allusion explicit, while construing her Orphic power to be both feminine and Florentine. Playing on memories of a real storm that swept the Tiber into the low-lying areas around the Campo de Fiori in December 1623, Basile's first sonnet attributed the flood on Francesca's doorstep to singing so remarkable that even the Tiber rushed to kiss her feet.[56] His tercets named her as the embodiment in Tuscany of a virtù that responded to the Thracian's and as a woman who did anew what a man had first done. Extending the comparison by means of the humoral theory of sexual difference, Basile pointed out that whereas Orpheus' masculine—and therefore dry—lira stopped the flow of rivers, Francesca's feminine—and therefore moist—*plettra* drew water to her.[57] Indeed, Basile seems to have imagined water as Francesca's natural medium, for his sonnet on her return to Florence likens Francesca's song to rain moistening Tuscany's shores, while her siren-like self miraculously walked ashore

from the waters of the Arno.[58] Basile thus linked Francesca to one of Florence's
favorite symbols of its intellectual and artistic fertility: a woman caught between two worlds, whether she be the Virgin of the Assumption or a Venus
continually reborn.[59] Thus, he elided Francesca's humoral femininity with her
fiorentinità in a way that captured the liminality on which Orphic power depends. As he projected it, however, Francesca's liminality differed profoundly
from that of Orpheus. For Orpheus liminality was essential, a result of being
the son of Apollo and a mortal woman. For Francesca, as for Venus, the Virgin,
and the women whose regency she had been sent to represent, liminality was
not essential but performative, the result of moving between incommensurate,
contradictory worlds.

Moving between such worlds was not only a trope by which to project Francesca's access to something like Orpheus' musical power. Moving between the curiously gendered, gynocentric world of the women's court and the androcentric
world of the granducato's musical establishment was a governing condition of
Francesca's life. Moreover, the conditions of her service required that she move
gracefully, in both worlds, between subordination to authority and the exercise
of authority, between serving her patrons as a privately performing diva whose
excellence brought honor to them and serving them by waiting around in their
palaces' hallways, ever ready to make music for their pleasure. She spent her
time at court literally in between vectors of power that she might need, at any
moment, to redirect for the sake of tending the relations of mutual dependence
on which her ability to serve relied. Francesca thus seems to have been known
at court for an attentive listening to the conversations around her that gave her
social, not merely musical, power. Mario Guiducci wrote Buonarroti that Francesca would tell him, in person, things about her visit to the papal court that he
preferred not to write. Orso d'Elci advised Magdalena that Francesca herself
would tell her patron how the gift of her presence had been received.[60] The social power that came from having needed to listen well to everyone around her
may have guided Francesca when, as Bronzini wrote, she made listeners "pliant
or agreeable . . . by turns."

Yet Bronzini, who had heard Francesca perform in Rome, would never have
compared Francesca to Orpheus. To do so would have linked her dangerously
to a mythical musician who was both misogynist and corrupt, according to one
of *Della dignità*'s interlocutors, "for having introduced that infamous abuse of
which it is better not to speak."[61] Instead, he likened her to Amphion, whose
playing of the lyre caused stones to move of their own power, forming the walls
of Thebes. Of all the musicians mentioned in classical myth, Amphion was the
one who most directly figured musical power as political power. For Bronzini,

then, and for his patrons, the usefulness of Francesca's musical prowess was fundamentally neither magical nor aesthetic but political. Her service to the Medici women directly aided the granducato.

Bronzini was very specific about what he understood the story of Amphion to mean: "[I]t means nothing but that he with his prudence and gentle eloquence could lead the men of that religion who lived dispersed through the fields and woods to live civilly in the same city." His understanding of Amphion as mastering human heterogeneity may have been crucial to Bronzini's account of Francesca's performances. No matter what the particulars of the situation were, Francesca's music making transformed her listeners, turning negative energy toward the good—the agreeable, the bold, the chaste, the healthy, the sublime, or toward a "laugh from the heart." But Francesca's mastery of the particulars was part of Bronzini's point about her. She had mastered the heterogeneity of maniere, of vocal techniques, of instruments, even of the heterogeneous elements of harmony and affect in a particular moment of song, mixing them together, Antimo Galli's letter suggests, with that pretense to utter nonchalance treasured in courtly Italy as *sprezzatura*.[62] These were effects that could not help but accustom her listeners to the experience of being subject to a certain kind of woman whom they might imagine to resemble Christine or Magdalena—an erudite and subtle woman who with nonchalant mastery always took account of particulars, always enabled concord and discord, bitter and sweet, to live civilly together.

Who Was This Woman?

5

Bronzini's, Tinghi's, Marino's, and Basile's representations of Francesca's presence all come from listeners' ideas of how a musician's work (or life) should be valued. As sources, they encourage a narrative like that of chapter 4, focused on Francesca's ability to inhabit the multifaceted role that her birth, the conditions of her service, and the desires of her patrons assigned her. Such a narrative gives barely a glimpse of the woman behind the role, the woman of the quick reply, the woman who conspired with others to ensure that the comedy they wanted would be half-complete before permission was granted, the woman who represented herself, in her letters, as having come to her nonchalant erudition by a life of constant study. In the terms of the philosopher Adriana Cavarero, that narrative shows what Francesca was—a musica who served a woman-dominated granducato—but not who. This chapter provides glimpses of who she was in relationships with others when she was not confined to the physical and discursive spaces of her service to the court.[1]

Francesca at Home

Francesca did not live among the people she served. Instead, like most artistic and artisanal workers, she had a home in the city. It was at home that she did most of the work for which she was especially valued (and compensated): teaching, coaching, and composing. A refuge from the court and yet a hive of activity mostly destined to serve that court, Francesca's home both was and was not a site of autonomy, privacy, and the possibility of independent subjectivity. Never a place of solitude and unhurried reflection—never, that is, a "room of her own"—the home Francesca shared with her first husband, Giovanni Battista Signorini, was also not a place that trapped her in the conventions of gender.

In the first years of their marriage Francesca and Signorini may have lived in one of Giulio Caccini's properties, either the house at the Croce del Trebbio (just southeast of Piazza Santa Maria Novella) or the one on via Sebastiano (now via Gino Capponi, 42).[2] Only in April 1610 did Signorini finalize the customary investment of Francesca's dowry in easily liquidated real estate, combining her 1,000 scudi with 455 more that she gave him to buy property on the via Valfonda.[3] Thus the couple lived less than five minutes' walk from Giulio's home at Croce del Trebbio, close to his sculptor brother Giovanni's home on the via della Scala and to the homes of several of Giovanni's children on the same street. Like these homes, the Caccini-Signorini property occupied a neighborhood of artisans clustered around a few homes of great wealth. The couple's nearest neighbors in the 1620s were the notary Giulio Casini and the sculptor Orazio Mochi to the east and the investment banker Riccardo Riccardi to the west. But for the wall that separated them from Riccardi's land, the Caccini-Signorini could have watched the sun set behind a classical vision of bucolic luxury: woods, statuary carefully chosen from archeological sites in Rome, a "wooded labyrinth covered in woven vines," and a palace that housed one of Florence's richest classical libraries.[4] Another wall separated them from gardens of Santa Maria Novella to the south. Thus the Caccini-Signorini could have shared with Riccardi and their monastic neighbors the fantasy that they lived far from the bustle, energy, and violence of the city.

Francesca's profession required constant negotiation with the city and its bustle. Probably she walked or rode in borrowed carriages when she moved about town to the various monasterii where she visited, taught, or performed for the Medici princesses, to the rooms of the Palazzo Vecchio and the Uffizi that were used for performances, to the Palazzo Pitti and Villa Imperiale across the Arno where she performed chamber music for the grand duke's family, and to the suburban villas to which the women's court so often repaired. Even her days at home would have been disrupted by the delivery of mail several times a day, often by couriers who might wait for her response to the court's commands for musical work, reports on work in progress, news about rehearsal times, costumes and so on, or reports on the progress of her court-supported music pupils.[5] Thus whatever visual fantasy of the contemplative life her home's view to the south or west might have encouraged, her home was no retreat from the world but a principal place of work.

When Giovanni Battista Signorini died in late December 1626, his will waived the usual requirement that there be an inventory of his property.[6] Without an inventory, however, it still is possible to imagine something about the Caccini-Signorini home on the basis of property records. According to tax records, by 1619 the Signorini property consisted of a large house and a smaller adjoining one "made from it," with stalls and a kitchen garden.[7] When Francesca sold the property in August 1630, the larger house and its garden were rented to the career diplomat Domenico Pandolfini for fifty scudi annually; two years later the city census reported Pandolfini's household as having eleven "mouths."[8] The smaller house and stalls were rented for twenty-seven scudi annually to Guido Gagnolandi, whose household in 1632 included four "mouths."[9] Thus the property on the via Valfonda must have been quite spacious for a married couple who would have no children (of their own) for the first fifteen years of their marriage.

How might that space have been laid out, and how might it have been used? Inventories of two analogous households allow one to imagine some answers. The 1639 inventory of their near neighbor Orazio Mochi suggests how artisans' houses on the via Valfonda were laid out, and the 1627 inventory of their colleague at court Domenico Belli, a singer, composer, and teacher, suggests how musicians used space within their homes.

Valued at 600 scudi, Orazio Mochi's single house and garden must have been larger than the smaller of the Signorini houses, valued at 540 scudi, but substantially smaller than the larger one, valued at 910 scudi.[10] Yet Mochi's house was not small: his ground floor included two camere, a courtyard that opened onto the vegetable garden, and a cantina; his first floor had a sala (a large room or hall), camera, *antecamera* and kitchen; and his second floor (the top floor) had another sala, camera, and antecamera, the latter opening onto a *terrazzo* (balcony) with a view. The Mochi inventory does not describe the uses or contents of the rooms, but the inventory of Belli's house does, and it suggests the quality of life possible for a musical household that earned a little less than half the combined income of the Caccini-Signorini.[11] When Belli died in 1627, he shared two homes with his wife, the court singer Angelica Sciamerone, and their two children: a house he rented near the Ponte Vecchio and a smaller rented house near the Badia in Fiesole.[12]

His city home consisted of fourteen rooms on the ground and first floors. The living space on the first floor included a hall with a long table, chairs, and stools; a camera with beds, bedding, linens, clothing, and footstools, an adjoining salottino with two chests containing more clothes, and an antecamera with an *armadio* (armoire) for more linens as well as the family's valuables: three gold rings (one with four diamonds that was Angelica's wedding ring, one with two diamonds, and one with a pearl), gold chains that had been baptism gifts for their children, and share certificates for the Monte di Pietà. Each room was decorated with several paintings. By contrast with the upper rooms, the ground-floor spaces were filled with the tools and materials of the household's work: a cantina, terrace, and adjoining room contained demijohns for wine, sacks of grain, and firewood; another room open to the courtyard contained a sarcophagus "with its lid," and the room nearest the street contained miscellaneous household goods. The pantry and kitchen were across the courtyard on the side farthest from the street. It was in the pantry, next to fifty-four plates and a larder full of food, that the Sciamerone-Belli pair stored about half of their music books, including six folio-sized books of manuscript compositions. On the other side of the kitchen from the pantry two rooms provided additional storage: one held paintings, pots, and pans, and the other held the family's hats and coats along with many more music books, both printed and manuscript. Finally, above the space open to the courtyard (where the inventory taker had found the sarcophagus and lid) was a room with four *viole da sonare* in canvas cases, a lute in its case, three *chitarrone*, and still more music books. Belli's harpsichord, a *sordellina* (Neapolitan-style bagpipe), and many more paintings were reportedly stored in his rented house in Fiesole.

It seems likely that the Caccini-Signorini, too, would, have lived above the ground floor of their larger house on the via Valfonda. They probably would have devoted at least as much space as the Sciamerone-Belli household to storing musical instruments and both manuscript and printed books of music. In the 1620s the Caccini-Signorini instrument collection included a harpsichord painted by Lodovico Cigoli that Francesca had inherited from her father and five instruments that Signorini had on consignment from the Medici household: a *lira doppia* (double lyre) with its bow in a wooden and leather case, a bass transverse flute, two double sordelline, and a simple sordellina.[13] The Caccini-Signorini music library may have stored multiple copies of Francesca's *Primo libro delle musiche* and *La liberazione di Ruggiero*, along with the manuscript and printed music they would have found useful in their daily work lives. If Bronzini's claims about her wide intellectual interests are to be believed, Francesca must have owned a fair number of nonmusical books, as well as the large amount of poetry that any improvising singer needed. Whether she would have stored her books in the pantry, like Domenico Belli, is anyone's guess.

Signorini's will implied that most of the wealth of his household had come from his wife's labor. Yet there is no reason to believe that the couple's roles in relation to household management were unusual. Most likely Francesca managed the domestic work of their home. Like any other woman of her time, she would have ordered the food, cloth, and other supplies, administered the work of servants, and kept records of the household's cash transactions.[14] As the housewifely manager of the petty cash, Francesca would have managed exactly the kind of wealth that her labor produced: gifts, jewels, and salary payments, which were made in cash. Signorini would have managed financial matters that required engagement with public institutions: income they might have had from rental property, shares they might have owned in one of the savings institutions known as monti or in a business, the collection of debts owed to them, and the household's relationship with banks, notaries, and the city's government magistracies. But because the Caccini-Signorini household owned no property other than the houses they occupied, Signorini had little to manage. He needed to meet his tax obligations as a Florentine citizen, he needed to collect and invest the thousand-scudi dowry that Riccardo Riccardi had promised at the time he and Francesca married, and when their daughter Margherita was born in February 1622, he needed to collect from Riccardi's heirs and deposit in the Monte di Pietà the six-hundred-scudi dowry that Riccardi had promised to any daughter they might produce. He did none of these things, thus earning the comment of the court astrologer that he was "an example of a man of otium"—that is, of a man who cultivated the leisure to study and reflect that Florentine humanists revered as an ideal life.[15]

"Otium was inimical to her"

A masculine privilege in most homes, otium was widely viewed as offering nothing but temptation to women: it was to counteract this temptation that women of all classes were exhorted to pass their time industriously working with yarn, thread, and cloth, with virtuous study, or with music. Responding to this norm, Bronzini took care to describe Francesca as constantly busy, "composing new styles of songs that various groups asked of her, all of which she copied in her own hand beautifully; in addition to this, every week she wrote more than twenty letters to various ladies and gentlemen (so as not to fail, in her natural kindness and courtesy, to respond to everyone); with all of this (I say) in only two months of summer, and in the worst of the heat, she composed, wrote (in her own hand) and recopied in her own hand, in good form, such big works (seen by me) that I do not know any man (however diligent he was) who could have done in two years, or [who] could ever do, what she did in just those two months."[16] Bronzini presents the tantalizing image of an industrious Francesca composing music for clients other than the granducato and thus points to a nearly unknown aspect of her musical career. Surviving letters show that she composed madrigals for the daughters of Virginio Orsini when they were pupils at Florence's Monastero della Concezione; intermedi for Caterina Picchena (daughter of the court secretary Curtio) to perform with her girlfriends between the acts of Giovanni Cecchi's comedy La serpe; and "four nice little songs . . . with written parts for a keyboard instrument" for Neri Alberi of Arezzo to give to a nun in his city.[17]

Although he specifically wrote about Francesca's copies of her own compositions, not those of others, Bronzini's comments about her copying and her fine hand have prompted speculation about another virtuous activity with which Francesca may have avoided idleness. John Walter Hill has persuasively proposed that Francesca may have been the copyist of one of the manuscripts that transmits Florentine song repertoire from her father's generation, the so-called Barbera manuscript.[18] Hill cites a well-known letter from 1614 in which Giulio Caccini said Francesca had "filled three books with over three hundred works with all those passages of invention others imagine, and with the best ornaments, that could come from anyone who professed solo singing."[19] He proposes that Francesca may have copied several other such manuscripts, too. If that were so, Giulio's comments imply that one might read the ornaments and passaggi of those manuscripts as evidence of either Francesca's performing practice or her pedagogical practice. Given the closeness in date between Giulio's apparent reference to her copying and the publication of his own *Nuove musiche e nuova maniera di scriverle*, one might further speculate that Francesca shared responsibility with her father for standardizing the new way of writing this music that he claimed to have invented in his collection's preface.

Whatever her role in copying may have been, Francesca, too, made a point of claiming she was constantly busy with study, with teaching, and with composition, and at least once was so overcommitted that she went to bed in exhaustion. Writing to Virginio Orsini on 22 March 1614, she framed her eagerness to serve him the following summer in the claim that she meant to offer "certain new studies that I have undertaken in the last year . . . that I think would at least not displease you by their novelty."[20] A few years later, writing to Buonarroti from Genoa, Francesca expressed an even stronger commitment to a life of study: "[L]ife would leave me before the desire to study and the passion I have always brought to virtù, because this is worth more than any treasure or fame."[21] Indeed, writing to Andrea Cioli from Lucca when she was no longer a Medici dependent, Francesca looked back on her service to the granducato as a time of "constant study for forty years," the fruits of which she hoped to pass on to her daughter.[22] All three letters firmly tie Francesca's studies to her professional development, and all three show her life of study to have unfolded in intense, busy relation to other people rather than in the solitude implied by humanist ideas of otium.

One of the most important ways in which Francesca's study affected others was in her work as a teacher. Indeed, her contemporary Antonio Brunelli described her as "a maestra of good and graceful singing, and as such . . . recognized and admired by the world."[23] As early as May 1612 Francesca was assigned by the court to teach two of three artisan-class girls whose parents evidently hoped they would become salaried musiche, Emilia d'Orazio di Giuseppe Grazi and either Caterina di Domenico Avanzelli or Lucretia di Battista detto il Mancino. Each of these students was given three scudi per month for room and board, while Francesca's monthly stipend was raised from her entry level of ten scudi to twelve for teaching both. Thus it was in part because of her teaching that Francesca would become the court's most highly paid musician by 1614.[24] A memo reporting to the court on Emilia Grazi's progress in 1623 indicates just what Francesca was expected to teach, noting "the girl is very studious and could be capable of great success, and where her voice is not all it could be she compensates in many other ways such as by her playing and composing."[25] Besides her court-subsidized pupils and the notorious Suora Maria Vittoria Frescobaldi, Francesca may have taught the daughters of Curtio Picchena and the physician Lorenzo Parigi, and from time to time her *scuola* (training) prepared the dame, donne, and Medici children for their ad hoc performances at the women's court. It may be that she taught them all to sing, play, and compose—a range of skills that could provide the musical equivalent of agency.

Teaching was important to Francesca as a site of her honor as well as an investment of her knowledge in another person that she could not bear to see it wasted or spoiled. When her cloistered pupil Frescobaldi was permitted to sing after an enforced three-year silence, Francesca wrote Virginio Orsini volunteering to help her "regain what she has lost . . . to obey your Excellency, and also for my honor, so that my efforts will no longer be buried alive."[26] Years later, facing the prospect that her own daughter would be educated at the court's expense in La Crocetta, Francesca pleaded for permission to continue as her teacher lest "in the hands of strangers . . . she lose all that she has learned, and I remain with all my time wasted, and with no fruit . . . from the virtù I taught her."[27]

A letter that Francesca wrote to Andrea Cioli, a court secretary, in March 1619 shows how her performance, teaching, and composing service to the court converged to produce an industrious life with no room for idleness, short of the enforced idleness of a sickbed.[28] The letter points, as well, to the relationships that shaped Francesca's role as maestra of a studio of young female musicians that amounted to a production unit of the granducato's service:

My most respected padrone and lord,

   Because of my many labors in recent days I am in bed with a little medicine to rest, and therefore I could not reply to you this morning. Now I tell you that it is not possible that I could [even] think of composing and teaching to these girls music for the seventy lines [of poetry] you have sent, in only the three days between today and Saturday because these girls and I, we are tired from having had to learn the Offices for Holy Week in only two weeks, and the half hour of music to sing in the archduchess's chapel for the Feast of the Holy Sacrament, which took me two months to teach them, because these are little girls that do not yet sing from parts and they learn by force of study and practice. I am greatly mortified that I cannot show myself as ready to serve my most serene padroni in this matter as I have been in all others, and willingly, and, if S.r Ottavio Rinuccini had given at least 10 days' advance notice we would have been able to strain ourselves, and our not doing it is not because we cannot endure the effort but for the shortness of time, and the impossibility of our few forces. For this reason I return the words to you and beg you to explain vividly to Her/His Highness because I am so sure of the pietà and benevolence of my serene padroni that I do not doubt at all that I will be excused and pitied, because in their service I will never look at any sort of labor as effort, and I have no other desire but to serve well and promptly and with that end I bow to you, begging you anew to excuse and help me with Her/His Highness and I thank you so much for the good office you have done me with this service that I press on you: I will remain very obliged to you for it, and because you are my protector I am of good hope and again I urge it on you, praying Our Lord to grant your every desired happiness. From home 25 March 1619,

I bow to your wife, and remind her that I am her very devoted servant,

[Your] ever very obliged servant,

Francesca Caccini ne' Signorini Malaspina[29]

As the maestra of "these girls that I teach," Francesca was clearly expected to do more than teach them singing, playing, and composing: she was both to compose for them and to teach them their parts, however much practice it took. Fruits of her pedagogical labor, these girls were also to be both co-producers and raw material for her compositional work—as much the material with which she composed as were modes, harmonies, ornaments, and passaggi. Thus her honor—her reputation for musical excellence—depended on her girls' labor as much as their honor depended on hers. Yet precisely because she was their maestra, she had absolute authority over them that was delegated by the court, an authority like that of their own parents, that of a padrona over servants or of a prince over his subjects. With her authority came the obligation that Francesca protect her pupils' well-being as a parent, padrona, or prince would. When the heedlessness of the court's characteristically last-minute command caught them all on the point of exhaustion, Francesca's rhetoric of excuse and pity intervened between her patrons and her "little girls" to protect the whole studio from overwork and from the embarrassment of an under-rehearsed performance.

Francesca's authority as maestra of these girls echoed in its way the grand duchesses' similar authority to command or protect those in their power.[30] Because the power flow in her household resembled the power flow in theirs, Francesca matched the strange microclimate of gender politics that was the Medici court between 1610 and 1630; as a result she may have known a presumption of the right to power and authority that could be described in twenty-first-century terms as "female privilege." That presumed female privilege, linked as it logically was to her pride in her position as a maestra, her gender-based access to private moments with the grand duke's family and her apparent favor among its members, seems to have attracted some colleagues' ire. Her responses to two incidents that took place in the mid-1620s support the contemporary claim that the "merry and charming" Francesca whom Bronzini knew could be fierce when threatened.

"As fierce and restless . . . as she was capable"

In the autumn of 1624, Francesca was at the center of artistic in-fighting that erupted over the court's plans to remount Andrea Salvadori's sacred opera *La regina Sant'Orsola* for production during Carnival in 1625. Kelley Harness has recently read the letters from the court's superintendent of performance, Ferdinando Saracinelli, that recount the dispute as evidence of Archduchess Maria Magdalena's direct involvement with the details of her regency's spectacles.[31] I focus instead on the way the incident illuminates Francesca's responses to her work environment and others' responses to her.

Originally conceived for performance during celebrations of Princess Claudia's marriage to Federigo della Rovere in February 1621 that had been cancelled because of Cosimo II's death, *Sant'Orsola* had been staged in October 1624 for the visiting Archduke of Styria. The music for *Sant'Orsola* had been composed by at least four musicians—Mutio Effrem, Jacopo Peri, Marco da Gagliano, and Francesca—each of them writing the music to be performed by members of the studio over which they presided. For the February 1625 revival, the poet Andrea Salvadori wanted the title role, which in October had been sung by Loreto Vittori to music of Marco da Gagliano, to be sung by Francesca's pupil Maria Botti. In Salvadori's plan, the archduchess's castrato Domenico Sarti would replace Botti in the part of Urania, which Francesca had written for her, but Francesca objected, "saying that since she composed this part, it would seem owed to her that her brother Scipione sing it."[32] A pupil of Peri's was to be recast as well, and Saracinelli had asked Salvadori and Francesca to decide what to do about the chorus of saintly virgins, given that at least one of them, Emilia Grazi, was pregnant. In the first of several interventions, the archduchess denied Francesca the right to reassign the music she had composed for Urania, instead ordering that the part be given to Sarti, adding that "if la Cecchina wants some part for her brother . . . give him that of Emilia."[33]

Although hardly unexpected given the power structure of artistic servitude, Magdalena's usurpation of Francesca's presumptive property rights over the part she had composed must have piqued, leaving her pride vulnerable to a second attack on her authority as a maestra, this time from almost all sides. A month later simmering tensions exploded in a storm of charges, counter-charges, and tantrums that increasingly focused on Francesca. Saracinelli re-ported that Francesca had been accused of abusing and perhaps beating her pupil Maria Botti, and that in any case she was failing to teach the girl her new part adequately.

These two accusations reverberated through the remainder of Saracinelli's letters, all but obscuring the several resolutions of the casting dispute that suc-cessive auditions judged by Magdalena or Cardinal Carlo de' Medici proposed. Francesca responded by turning on the antagonist nearest to hand—Salvadori, whose addition of new verses to the part of Urania required that Francesca compose it anew—"so harshly that someone had to intervene to inject a little calm," and exclaiming "Misericordia!" and other unquoted epithets every time Botti's failure to learn became apparent.[34] Dispelling the charges as best he could, Saracinelli patiently reported to the court that "in all the time that Maria has been at Signora Francesca's house I have never seen her not honor her like a daughter."[35] He added that the girl was failing in part because Giovanni Bat-tista da Gagliano had been teaching her the part as his brother Marco had com-posed it, and Francesca was teaching her the part that Mutio Effrem had com-posed for Arcangela Palladini in 1621 and in part because Marco da Gagliano had "stolen" liberally from Effrem's setting in the first place. Though Francesca accused her of singing the part badly on purpose, and Saracinelli described her as a girl of unsurpassed impertinence, Maria Botti may have had good reason to be confused.[36]

In the end, Magdalena's firmness, Saracinelli's diplomacy, and Francesca's steadfast refusal to express any further opinions about the casting enabled the practical details to be resolved. Francesca's rights in her combined pedagogi-cal and compositional work were restored when she was assigned to compose and teach a new part for Botti to sing as Urania. Sarti was assigned to sing Gagliano's version of the part of Sant'Orsola, a part he already knew. But in his last letters about the matter Saracinelli revealed his concern that the violence of the imbroglio had centered on Francesca. "I begin to wonder," he wrote a colleague, "if it will be possible for la Cecchina to survive, because I know these emotions, and those tongues, and . . . what they have said on other occasions."[37] On at least one such occasion, he had reported that Marco da Gagliano and Jacopo Peri had falsely insinuated to Magdalena that Francesca's pupil Emilia Grazi was "useless."[38] It seems possible, then, if no by no means certain, that the pair were among those whom Saracinelli accused of continuing to "behave in order to impede this woman so that she cannot serve Her Most Serene High-ness well."[39]

The whole story shows that Francesca could be a focus of tension among the artistic workers at court, as her father had been before her. When she was a target of her colleagues' calumny, of challenges to her authority, or of her pupils' disloyalty, she could be hot-tempered in response. The second story, told by the writer Andrea Cavalcante, shows Francesca to be equally capable of waiting to taste her vengeance cold.

Cavalcante's story survives as a long aside that interrupts his narrative of Andrea Salvadori's life much as Francesca's vendetta against him interrupted the womanizing poet's career.[40] As Cavalcante told it:

In his youth Andrea was quite a handsome man, if of olive complexion, and like those who find themselves among musicians and singers, and who delight more than a bit in little notes inserted into other documents, upon becoming infatuated with one of these women, when one of them was needed in the production of one of these shows he was partial toward whoever attracted his affection, accommodating the parts and the music to favor the one who was in his heart. Francesca Caccini, a woman as fierce and restless as she was capable in singing and acting, could not abide this behavior, and began to expose and talk about him, first in passing and behind his back, and then openly and to his face, revealing his intentions and designs and the origin of his favoritism. Because of this he was immediately disdained. Seeing himself in conflict with all these women who, because of these slanders, knew all about every occasion and circumstance, he could get no good from any of these things whence he once had solicitude, so that not only the princes and princesses but the whole palace took continuous and wonderful pleasure at his expense. In response he took his pen and composed many, many graceful but very biting *ottave* against women singers, describing with artifice and wit, as he knew very well how to do, the least likeable habits and qualities of Cecchina. She, raising a bigger ruckus, plunged the court into disorder, and it took a lot of effort to quiet her, and the authority of the Most Serene Padrona intervening to make peace between them. But their minds were so ruined and poisoned that they did not reconcile. When it became necessary to create a spectacle for the marriage of the above named [duke] of Parma, Salvadori had put in order the story of Iole and Ercole, in which prepared work he took pleasure, and delight, having had time and leisure to satisfy himself. It had already been set to music, the [stage] machines sketched and the parts assigned when Francesca took her best revenge, like a man who waits for the worst place and time. Finding herself one day with the Most Serene bride, she sang the part that was to have been hers, and praised the verses and the workmanship of it, adding: "Serenissima, every thing will go well, and I like it. I have only one remaining doubt."

—"What is that?" prompted the princess.

—"I would say it," responded the other, "but what do I know? I don't want to go on. It's enough [to say that] Your Highness knows how the court is."

Burning to know, the bride commanded her to speak up without further thought or concern.

—"Well," the good Cecchina replied, "Serenissima, although I am a woman, reflecting on the plot I wondered if some wag might not say that Your Highness wanted to teach your Serene Husband to spin [like Hercules, who disguised himself as a woman at the court of his lover Oomphale]."[41]

This idea pierced the princess's heart to the quick, and taking the occasion of joking with the archduchess her mother, when she saw her most disposed to please her, she begged her to grant a favor. The mother immediately replied,

"One, two, or as many as you want, my daughter."

—"But Your Highness mustn't change your mind afterward," the bride replied, "because it would upset me not to get this favor."

—"No, of course not," replied the archduchess.

—"The favor is that Your Highness command either that there be no comedy or at least that the subject be changed."

Asked what reason had prompted her to this, she said, "Up until now I have never thought to teach my husband to spin, but [only] to love, revere, and obey him; I don't want it to seem that Hercules could be taught to spin in this house."

[The archduchess] savored the liveliness of the idea, the grace, the witty peculiarity and the self-possession with which her daughter brought it up, and calling Salvadori, commanded him that within eight days he should have another comedy in order, because the one on Hercules would be valuable on another occasion. He knew by what hand he had been struck, but he had to be quiet, and he obeyed without reply. It is true that to have such little vengeance as was allowed him in I know not what show he put the part of Discordia on Caccini's back. Exulting at this, she always said that the response was not equal to the blow.

Like the biting ottave against women singers he attributed to Salvadori, Cavalcante's story can be taken to represent Francesca's least likeable qualities: an opportunistic alertness to others' weaknesses, a capacity for manipulation, and a taste for vengeance. More broadly, his story captures perfectly the power that Francesca's familiarity with the women's court could give her and the damage a courtly antagonist might incur from that power. Cavalcante seems to appreciate Francesca's willingness to use her access for her own ends, as he appreciates her wit, her impeccable timing, and her resilience in response to Salvadori's counterblows—as if he admired her ability to win some rounds in the courtly world's often vindictive games.

Read with knowledge of the dynamics that prevailed at Tuscany's women's court, Cavalcante's story can seem, as well, to make other points about who Francesca was in her world. Her vendetta against the womanizing Salvadori can be taken as an instance of advocating for other women, intervening to defend their continenza and their onestà. Moreover, her self-styled gynocentric interpretation of Salvadori's *Iole et Ercole* scenario yields an astute reading of its sexual politics. An interpretation of Hercules that drew on that commonplace of courtly women's reading, Ovid's *Heroides*, would necessarily evoke his reduction to spinning among the women who served Oomphale, one of the tales that supported the Classical view of men surrounded by women as effeminate.[42] It is conceivable that Princess Margherita's fiancé, Odoardo Farnese, could have received Salvadori's plot that way and taken umbrage. Given that they had tried for years to break the contract promising Cosimo II's first available daughter as his bride, he had ample reason to suspect the Medici of disrespect. But the image of a feminized Hercules enslaved among women could have had wider resonances. It could all too easily have elicited ordinary Tuscans' ongoing anxiety about their own entrapment in a gynocracy. Francesca's intervention defended the Medici princesses whom she served from both kinds of trouble. At the same time, for Francesca to interpret the image of the irrepressibly womanizing Hercules as effeminate was to direct another barb at Salvadori. Implying that his womanizing, too, was a symptom of effeminacy, it was the equivalent of hoisting him by his own petard. Only a woman of sharp intelligence, with access to the powerful, could have done so much work with so few words.

Indeed, from the perspective of the women's court Francesca's revenge against Salvadori might have seemed very much like a defense of other women, of the musiche on whom he preyed and of the princesses they served, for whom his scenario might have caused real political trouble. In Magdalena's laughing collusion with her musical servant's revenge, one might even detect just a hint of the fantasy about the Muses' complicity with the princesses of Lesbos that Bronzini had spun.[43]

Voice Lessons:
Introducing the *Primo libro delle musiche*

In August 1618, Francesca published the longest and one of the most varied collections of solo song to be produced in her generation. Cited by her contemporaries as evidence of her importance as a composer in the new Florentine style, Francesca's *Primo libro delle musiche* was taken in the twentieth century as evidence for her practice as a performer.[1] Yet because it includes examples of every genre a solo singer needed to master, arranged in the order in which music pupils typically encountered them, Francesca's book has also been taken as evidence of her pedagogical prowess.[2] Surely all these things, it is just as surely a rich trove of new repertoire for performers of early music to explore.

Francesca's *Primo libro* is also evidence of her engagement with the problem of claiming the cultural authority that condenses into the word "voice." Because such a claim was as imperative and problematic for the elite women she served as it was for her, Francesca's claim to voice could not help but strengthen the analogous claims of the powerful women around her. Whatever her intentions might have been in choosing to publish her work, her choice could have served any of these women as symbolic as well as literal voice lessons.

This chapter and the following two explore ways in which Francesca's book and the musiche in it might have engaged the problem of women's cultural authority in terms of voice. After introducing the most basic facts about the *Primo libro*'s repertoire, organization, and physical survival in our time, this chapter probes the known circumstances surrounding Francesca's presentation of her music in print and the meanings that her contemporaries attached to the book. I argue that her choice was shaped by circumstances at court that encouraged ambitious musicians to publish their work, by her intention to mark publicly her own coming of age as the master of her family's craft, and by her expressed, contradictory fears about the way her claim to a distinctive compositional identity would be received. In chapter 7, I argue that a straightforward progress through Francesca's *Primo libro* can reveal her to have addressed in these songs the issues that Sandra Gilbert and Susan Gubar theorized a generation ago as "anxiety of authorship."[3] The interaction of her songs' texts with the lessons in vocal technique, music theory, or form taught by those songs transformed that vague anxiety into specifically embodied anxieties of voice that successful performance of these songs would symbolically overcome. In chapter 8, I show that the division of the book's fictional world by the table of contents into spiritual and temporal halves becomes an unavoidable fact after the songs at the book's midpoint allowed her pupil to perform a certain level of vocal and musical mastery. Through the diametrically opposed repertoires of liturgical Latin songs and sexually candid canzonette Francesca taught contrasting approaches to the construction of distinctly modern songs.

The *Primo libro delle musiche* as Repertoire and as a Book

At first glance, Francesca's *Primo libro* seems like a compendium of early modern vocal genres: sonnets, a recitative soliloquy, solo and duet madrigals, arias of various kinds, motets, hymns, and canzonette. Their pedagogical order strongly suggests that Francesca intended her book to demonstrate the range of skills she was prepared to teach and that she expected some of her book's users to be aspiring singers and their teachers.[4] The *tavola* (table) printed as the book's last page identifies each song by genre, making the book especially easy to use. In addition, the contents are grouped into nineteen *spirituali* (twelve Italian and seven Latin texts) and seventeen *temporali*. By creating an order that does not match the order of songs in the book, this grouping would have facilitated teaching for each of the venues in which Francesca is known to have taught nonprofessional singers: Florence's convents, and the women's court.

Depending on genre and text, some of these songs are ravishing examples of "expressiveness." That is, some songs express desire ("Ardo infelice, e palesar non tento," "Io mi distruggo," "Rendi alle mie speranze"), loss ("Lasciatemi qui solo"), or anguish ("Ferma, Signore, arresta," "Ecco, ch'io verso il sangue") through Francesca's idiosyncratic choices from the harmonic, contrapuntal, and motivic gestures that twentieth- and twenty-first century scholars have labeled "expressive" in early modern music. Some songs are mysteriously compelling despite the absence of so-called expressive devices, communicating ecstasy ("Maria, dolce Maria") or tranquility ("Jesu corona virginum") rather than agony, through melodies so well organized and harmonies so modern as to render the deceptively simple songs unforgettable. Some are funny ("La pastorella mia," "Non so se quel sorriso," "Ch'Amor sia nuda"). But the songs that show Francesca's wit are funniest when their texts are understood in relation to the musical and vocal challenges they pose to potential singers. Most of the jokes seem to be meant for the performer; they might not ever be amusing (or audible) to a listener. All of the songs reveal Francesca to have taken extraordinary care over the notation of her music, focusing special attention on the rhythmic placement of syllables and words, especially within passaggi, on phrasing as indicated by slurs, and on the precise notation of the rhythmically and melodically fluid, melismatic passaggi—so demanding of throat and breath control—that become prominent toward the center of the book.

Although her contemporary Pietro della Valle described her as an accomplished poet, there is no evidence that Francesca wrote any of the texts in her *Primo libro*.[5] At least seventeen of the twenty-nine Italian texts can be attributed to someone else. Twelve songs, making up exactly one-third of the book, set texts by her lifelong friend and colleague Michelangelo Buonarroti; three of these are excerpts from their theatrical collaborations for the Medici court: "La pastorella mia" from *La Tancia* (1611) and "Io veggio" and "Chi desia saper" from *Il passatempo* (1614). At least two other texts—the sacred sonnet "Che fai, misero core?" and the recitative soliloquy "Ardo infelice"—were by Andrea Salvadori. Two of the four duets (the madrigal "Io mi distruggo" and the refrain canzonetta "S'io men vò, morirò") set poems found in Florentine manuscripts once owned by the amateur poet and musician Francesco Gualterotti, a nephew of Giovanni de' Bardi. One canzonetta, "Dispiegate guancie amate," sets verses by the Genoese poet (and longtime friend of Gabriello Chiabrera) Ansaldo Cebà. All but one of the Latin songs set common liturgical texts (see table 6.1).

Several things are striking about Francesca's poetic choices. First, although Bronzini was to claim she had "produced exceptional compositions, Latin and vernacular, spiritual and secular, on moral poetry by the most famous poets," if she ever composed music for the poetry of Petrarch, Bembo, Ariosto, Tasso, Guarini, Chiabrera, or Marino, she chose not to publish it.[6] Second, she seems not to have published songs that set texts by any of the women poets whose works circulated in the early seventeenth century. Instead, she presented her music to the world mainly through the poetry of people whose work was currently fashionable, whom she knew personally, with whom she collaborated often. In choosing not to borrow canonic poets' glory, Francesca chose not to invite singers and critics to evaluate either her relation to the historical canon of Italy's great poets or her relation to their great musical settings. Instead, in their radical contemporaneity, Francesca's poetic choices constitute evidence of the Florentine court's taste for poetry with performatively contorted syntax and

Table 6.1. Contents of Francesca Caccini, *Il primo libro delle musiche* (1618)

First line	Genre according to print	Poet or text source
Chi è costei, che qual sorgente aurora	Sonnet	Anonymous; paraphrases first antiphon of Matins, Feast of the Assumption
Che fai, misero core, ecco ch'in croce	Sonnet	Andrea Salvadori, "Fiori di Calvario," *Poesie* (1668), p. 24
Ardo infelice, e palesar non tento	Ottave	Andrea Salvadori, I-Fn, MS Palatino 251, fols. 356–358
Maria, dolce Maria	Madrigal	Michelangelo Buonarroti, I-FcasaB, A.B. 82, fol. 378; A.B. 84, fol. 200
Nel camino aspro, et erto	Madrigal	Michelangelo Buonarroti, I-FcasaB, A.B. 82, fol. 380v; A.B. 84, fol. 200v
Pietà, mercede, aita	Madrigal	Michelangelo Buonarroti, I-FcasaB, A.B. 84, fol. 199v
Ferma, Signore, arresta	Madrigal	Michelangelo Buonarroti, I-FcasaB, A.B. 82, fol. 376; A.B. 84, fol. 199v
Ecco, ch'io verso il sangue	Aria	?Michelangelo Buonarroti, I-FcasaB, A.B. 95, fol. 504; paraphrases the Improperia of the Good Friday liturgy
Deh, chi già mai potrà, Vergine bella	Ottave romanesca	Anonymous
Nube gentil che di lucente velo	Ottave sopra la romanesca	Anonymous
Io mi distruggo, et ardo	Madrigal for 2 voices	Anonymous, I-Fr, Mor. 309, fol. 38a
Lasciatemi qui solo	Aria	Anonymous
O che nuovo stupor mirate intorno	Aria allegra	Michelangelo Buonarroti, I-FcasaB, A.B. 82, fol. 357; A.B. 84, fol. 185v; paraphrases I-Fn, MS Palatino 251, no. 96, "O che nuovo miracolo"
Su le piume de' venti	Aria allegra	Anonymous
Giunto è'l dì, che dovea'l cielo	Aria allegra	Michelangelo Buonarroti, I-FcasaB, A.B. 82, fol. 375; A.B. 84, fol. 179r–v
Io veggio i campi verdeggiar fecondi	Ottave sopra la romanesca	Michelangelo Buonarroti, *Il Passatempo*, 1614, I-FcasaB, A.B. 62, fasc. 1, fols. 31v–32r

La pastorella mia	Ottave sopra la romanesca	Michelangelo Buonarroti, *La Tancia*, 1611, I-FcasaB, A.B. 61, fasc. 3, fol. 265r, act 2, scene 5
Rendi alle mie speranze il verde, e i fiori	Ottave sopra la romanesca	Michelangelo Buonarroti, I-FcasaB, A.B. 84, fol. 195v
Dove io credea le mie speranze verde	Sopra la romanesca	Anonymous; partly paraphrases Ottavio Rinuccini, "Lasciatemi morire," from *L'Arianna* (1608), lines 860–862
Laudate Dominum	Motet	Psalm 150
Haec dies	Motet	Psalm 118; 24, antiphon from First Lauds for Easter morning
Regina Caeli laetare	Motet	Marian antiphon for Compline, Sundays between Easter and Pentecost
Adorate Dominum	Motet	Respond for Compline, Vigil of Epiphany, plus Psalm 97:4
Beate Sebastiane	Motet	Third antiphon of third nocturne, Matins, for Christmas
Te lucis ante terminorum	Hymn	Hymn for Compline, attributed to St. Ambrose
Jesu corona virginum	Hymn	Hymn for Vespers, Common of Virgins, in Eastertide, attributed to St. Ambrose
S'io men vò	Canzonetta for 2 voices	Anonymous
Non so se quel sorriso	Canzonetta	Michelangelo Buonarroti, I-FcasaB, A.B. 84, fol. 214
Chi desia di saper che cosa è Amore	Canzonetta	Michelangelo Buonarroti, *Il passatempo*, 1614, I-FcasaB, A.B. 62, fasc. 1, fol. 3
Che t'ho fatt'io?	Canzonetta	I-Fn, MS Palatino 251, fol. 329
O vive rose	Canzonetta for 2 voices	Anonymous
Se muove a giurar fede	Canzonetta	Anonymous
Ch'Amor sia nudo, e pur con l'ali al tergo	Canzonetta	Anonymous
Fresch'aurette	Canzonetta for 2 voices	Anonymous
Dispiegate	Canzonetta	Ansaldo Cebà
O chiome belle	Canzonetta	Anonymous

proto-Baroque theatricality. Moreover, Francesca's choices allowed her to avoid public compositional engagement with the Petrarchan tradition's extremely hierarchical representations of gender. Finally, her choices depict her as a person who collaborated actively with men in the ongoing production of the Medici court's artistic life. She was not the isolated creator of musico-poetic texts, as some have imagined, but a woman in the thick of things who chose to project herself that way in the self-presenting medium of print.

Just as there is no poem set in Francesca's *Primo libro* that can credibly be attributed to her, there is no song in the collection that can be traced to any of her known performances. Thus there is no reason to suppose that these songs directly document the performing virtuosity for which she was renowned. Indeed, Francesca might have deliberately eschewed publishing songs that would have been associated with her performances. Published texts as detailed in their prescriptions for performance as these could easily encourage users to imagine themselves imitating and even inhabiting the most intimate gestures of a first performer's body. Conceivably, such a fantasy could have compromised Caccini's carefully cultivated reputation for modesty.

Thinking about the *Primo libro* as a material object raises some questions that any scholar or performer using the book might keep in mind. Three copies survive: one in the Bibliothèque Nationale de France, one in the Biblioteca Estense in Modena, and one in the Biblioteca Nazionale Centrale in Florence.[7] Each measuring about 22 cm by 33 cm in its current binding, each printed in upright score format, each is slightly different from the other two in textual details. The Paris copy has some handwritten corrections that the other two copies accommodate either by paste-overs or by changes in the printed text, suggesting that it might be the earliest of several "states" created by in-press corrections. All three copies include a significant number of handwritten corrections of minute musical or textual flaws, ranging from continuo figures and accidentals to the most finicky details of where syllables or slurs begin and end. Almost all of these corrections are clearly in Francesca's hand.

The Florence copy, the latest and best preserved of the three, is nicely bound in faded nineteenth-century paper that once bore stylized pink flowers and green leaves on a ground of cream. Vellum binding tape on the spine bears the author's name, the book's title, and the shelf number. Two binders' pages of excellent paper enclose Francesca's book, which is printed on paper that seems worn, floppy with use. The title page is full of print; several sizes of print draw the eye equally to the multiplicity of the *musiche* and to the honorific title of the book's official patron, Cardinal de' Medici.[8] Hardly less striking is the size of the composer's name. Yet the dedication page that follows graphically reconstructs the power relations between composer and dedicatee. The cardinal, with all his titles, is named at the top, in large roman letters, but the composer's name seems unusually tiny and distant, far even from the body of the short dedicatory letter. In the tininess of her name one can almost hear Francesca adopting the self-effacing voice of a "timid and bashful" woman determined to perform her insignificance in the world, her distance from its power. Comparison of this page with the dedication of Andrea Falconieri's *Il quinto libro delle musiche*, the next music book to come from Zanobi Pignoni's press and (conveniently) the next book on the Florence library's shelf, show Falconieri and his gentleman patron to be not nearly so separate as Caccini and her cardinal. Although Falconieri's name is also printed in tiny type, because it is placed closer to the body of his dedication letter his name does not look so disproportionately small (see figures 6.1 and 6.2).

The comparison with Falconieri's book yields another important distinction. At thirty-six pages, Falconieri's book is so light and slim that it bends in the hand like a thin magazine. It feels ephemeral. Francesca's book, at ninety-nine pages, fills the hand with weight and substance. If it were a magazine, it would be as heavy as *Vogue*.[9]

Turning the old, crackly pages of Francesca's book to get a sense of the contents, a reader in Florence's Biblioteca Nazionale cannot help but notice the plethora of handwritten annotations or the gradual increase in the number and length of graces and passaggi on the pages: these reach a kind of climax roughly midway through the book, when there seem to be many more notes on a page than there are words. After that point, the visual impact of the pages approaches something like balance: the stanzas or songs all seem to be about the same length. By the end, however, because the book ends with a set of strictly strophic canzonette, the proportion of words to music on the page is reverse of what it was at the midpoint: there are many more words than notes. Turning the pages thus leads to a provocative surprise. The tavola lists the contents of the book, grouped by genre in a way that would be convenient to singers, singing teachers, and their pupils. But the division of the repertoire into spirituali and temporali intrigues, because it tracks a path through the book that does not match the actual order of contents. If one tries to follow the tavola's order in the Biblioteca Nazionale, the task soon forces one to make the pages' crackling sound again and again as one flips back and forth noisily. The noise of following the tavola contradicts the orderliness of its binary division, reminding me of Buonarroti's admiring comment that the contrast in *La stiava* between heterosocial music and homosocial noise was among the most delicious moments of the show. Whenever I have worked with one of the copies of Francesca's book, either flipping noisily to follow the tavola or turning the pages one by one, I have wondered what this extremely meticulous woman might have meant by the tavola's literal invocation of music's opposite in her world, its literal creation of noise.[10]

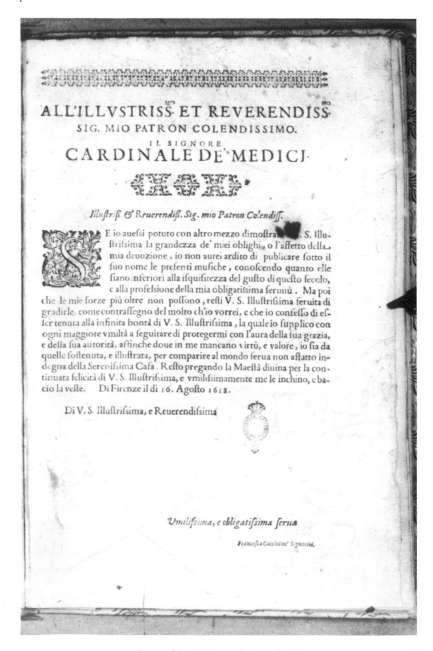

Figure 6.1. Francesca Caccini, *Il primo libro delle musiche* (1618), dedication page. Reproduced by permission of the Ministero per i Beni e le Attività Culturali/Biblioteca Nazionale di Firenze.

Two very differently situated chroniclers of Florentine culture cited Francesca's *Primo libro* as material evidence that she was more than one of the great virtuose of her generation: as one could see from her book, each asserted, Francesca alone of these women was a prolific, publicly acknowledged composer. This is the most important meaning Francesca's book had in her world. The

Figure 6.2. Andrea Falconieri, *Il quinto libro delle musiche* (1618), dedication page. Reproduced by permission of the Ministero per i Beni e le Attività Culturali/Biblioteca Nazionale di Firenze.

musician and composer Severo Bonini said little more about Francesca than that.[11] Intent on writing one of the earliest historical narratives to claim the new *stile recitativo* as a Florentine invention, Bonini preferred instead to focus on her sister Settimia's and her daughter Margherita's conventionally gendered excellence as performers and the equally gendered excellence of her father and

of Jacopo Peri, Francesco Rasi, and Marco da Gagliano as composers. Cristoforo Bronzini, by contrast, was intent on producing an encyclopedic account of
women's achievements that would portray Florentine women at the apogee in
every category and project thereby the worldview of the Medici women among
whom Francesca so often worked.

Bronzini alluded twice to Francesca's engagement with print culture, both
times amid passages that emphasized her identity as a composer. In the first instance, he invited readers to confirm her inventiveness and excellence in composition by examining the book. Coming at the end of a winding sentence that
specifies the breadth of her professional skills, his invitation seems intended
to support the claim that she surpassed all the other women musicians about
whom his interlocutors had spoken because she was so excellent a composer:

> And truly, in relation to the aforementioned women (by you so highly and
> liberally praised above) our Cecchina not only showed and shows herself
> equally excellent in music (and in playing excellently the harp, harpsichord, lute,
> theorbo, guitar, and every sort of stringed instrument, and in singing with great
> grace to their accompaniment the most artful Latin odes that she composed
> herself, but also the odes of Horace, the heroic verses of Virgil, with such good
> pronunciation, and marvelous Italian arias, and French, Spanish, and German
> songs that she set to beautiful arias, and compositions in Genoese dialect no
> longer heard by anyone, with the most difficult, sweet and artful passaggi) but
> in inventiveness of her rare compositions, there is no one to surpass her and
> few who come near or equal her; her excellence in composition often stunned
> the most praiseworthy swans of Florence, as one can see from the much praised
> works brought to light in 1618.[12]

Rhetorically folding her multiple virtuosities into her identity as a composer,
as if he were literally bundling together individual gifts, Bronzini revealed how
he and his intended readers might have understood the persona of a composer,
regardless of gender. A composer, in Bronzini's rhetoric, is a synoptic musician,
one who focuses her constituent musical skills in the act of musical invention.
At the same time, his insistent cataloguing of Francesca's multiple skills in this
passage invited readers (and potential exegetes) to imagine that her instrumental prowess and all-around musical virtuosity might have informed the book as
much as they informed the performative wonders generally attributed to her
singing.

The second time Bronzini mentioned Francesca's publication, he did so at
the end of a passage presenting her as meticulous, industrious, and prolific.
Citing a range of genres in which she composed that might have come straight
from her book's tavola, he sought to refute any reader's suspicion that she com-

posed trivialities or, as he put it, *bagatelle:* "And perhaps she applied herself to bagatelles? No sir, she produced exceptional compositions, Latin and vernacular, spiritual and secular, on moral poetry by the most famous poets who ever wrote: odes of Horace; madrigals, sonnets, canzone, psalms, motets, hymns and other spiritual works in every genre."[13]

By carefully balancing reports of Francesca's prolixity with an insistence on her industry and passion for order, Bronzini implicitly defended her against the possibility that her compositional fluency could be construed as unchecked, intrinsically feminine excess. Indirectly, his comment might seem, too, to align her composerly work with the literary fashion for encyclopedic texts in which he so extravagantly participated. All of his points are borne out by the way Francesca's *Primo libro* as a material object sits in a user's hand. The book seems heavy in every sense, projecting in mental and physical weight a solidity and a professional mastery that are the opposite of bagatelles. Yet if Bronzini is to be believed the *Primo libro* represents only a fraction of Francesca's work as a composer, and not the only fraction she had hoped to see in print. For Bronzini also reported that "because of the huge amount of material she had composed, she would have published new things, if she had not been forbidden to do so by the doctors [Medici] and their Serene Highnesses (for the sake of preserving her person, as she had been gravely ill)."[14] Thus Bronzini's account confirms that the meticulous, industrious, prolific Francesca was eager to publish her work. Doubtless she understood as well as he and Bonini did how publication could construct her public image as inventive, productive, and synoptic and could, thereby, advance her career.

Indeed, Bronzini allows performers and scholars to draw some tentative conclusions from the peculiarities that characterize the repertoire, the poetry, and the physical presentation of Francesca's book. First, although his report that she was unusually concerned with order in her autograph manuscripts could be read as referring only to her fine calligraphy, when combined with the evidence of her persnickety notation it suggests that the contradiction between the order of songs in the book and the order printed in its tavola might need to be taken seriously. Francesca may have meant the mental noise of a puzzle to be solved. Second, if, as Bronzini suggests, the *Primo libro* represents only a slice of Francesca's compositional output at the time, one she had intended would be quickly followed by another, then her choices of repertoire and of poets must have been calculated, perhaps as a musical, aesthetic, even intellectual self-introduction. She can be imagined, then, as having meant to show that she was a serious composer, sensitive to pedagogical needs and active in all genres, who worked in the thick of the most up-to-date poetic culture—a composer of her moment, rather than a composer to be defined by her relation to Italian culture's "procession of educated men."[15] As aware as Bonini and Bronzini of how rarely women were imagined to be fully professional composers, however admired they were as improvisers, she may well have published repertoire she had not performed both to preserve her reputation for modesty and to ensure that her claim to the status of composer—and thereby to the musical equivalent of authorial voice—was absolutely clear.[16]

The Impetus to Publish

In Francesca's youth, the Medici establishment had systematically suppressed composers' names in the documents of official court memory and allowed a local musical press to languish, beset by costly litigation and chronic lack of capital. Grand Duke Ferdinando I had articulated his preference that musicians be anonymous in his critique of Buonarroti's draft descrizione of the festivities for Marie de' Medici's 1600 wedding to King Henri IV of France, commenting drily that "it is not necessary to name so many musicians." Often read as a prince's annoyed response to the squabbling in print among his music superintendent Emilio de' Cavalieri and two staff musicians, Jacopo Peri and Giulio Caccini, Ferdinando's comment can also be taken as an effort to absorb their claims of authorship in one of his own.[17] In the prefaces to printed scores of their music Cavalieri, Peri, and Giulio Caccini had each claimed, in 1600, to have invented the new kind of solo song, stile recitativo, that was to be so closely linked in its aesthetic justifications to Medicean patronage. Moreover, in his preface each man had claimed to be the first to use the stile recitativo effectively in a new kind of theatrical spectacle. Ferdinando's comment to Buonarroti caused the poet to leave almost all musicians nameless in the court's official representation of the event. The erasure of composers' names from the public record seems to have become court policy, for although various performers would be named over the course of the next decade, from 1600 to 1612 Giulio Caccini was to be the only composer identified either in Tinghi's diary or in official descriptions of such events.[18] Thus seeming to have no individual human authors, the musical marvels of Ferdinando's court could seem to have emerged almost as if by the magic of the granducato's will. Ferdinando had appropriated all authorship to himself; his servants would have access to apparent authorship only "as an agent of the prince."[19]

A few years later the court's policy of suppressing its familiars' right to authorial voice changed. Beginning in 1612, Tinghi's diary became ever more punctilious in recording the names of those who had composed music for important court events, as did the trickle of official printed descrizioni.[20] In 1614, three high-born musical amateurs who were close to the court invested in the printing business that Zanobi Pignoni had acquired from his former employers, the heirs of Cristoforo Marescotti.[21] The one Florentine printing firm with a history of publishing music, Pignoni's business published six music books in its first year of operation; by 1620 he would have published twelve, all containing music composed by Tuscan subjects or associated with the Medici court. Furthermore, the court seems to have released its tight grip on permissions to print, for between 1614 and 1620 twenty books of music by Tuscan composers would appear in Venice, and six in Rome. Access to musical authorship became the norm for Tuscan musicians who came of age between 1615 and 1620.

Francesca's decision to publish in 1618 and her desire to publish again soon thereafter came in the middle of this sudden flowering. Although the court's policies seem to have been gender-neutral, Francesca's gender may have affected her claim to authorial voice in two ways. First, it seems possible that her decision might have been more strongly encouraged than most, because the publication of her work could have served the emerging cultural program to prepare the people of Tuscany for a de jure regency in the ever-more-likely event of Cosimo II's death. Second, she may have deliberately chosen to publish with the parochial Pignoni rather than with a Venetian printer to avoid seeming to have trafficked commercially in so culturally charged a commodity as the written signs of her voice.[22]

By mid-April 1618, the archdeacon of Florence had read and approved for publication the first six "days" of Bronzini's *Della dignità e nobiltà delle donne*.[23] Thus both his project and Francesca's must have been conceived and largely completed in the autumn of 1617, when Cosimo II was widely believed to be dying. From September until shortly before Christmas that year he had lain ill with the tubercular fever that would kill him four years later. Although no firm evidence explains Bronzini's motivation for beginning his project, the timing is suggestive. His text argued forcefully for the moral, intellectual, and political equality of women and men, justifying the possibility of women's rule over men in Classical and Christian philosophy, historical and extravagant praise for the virtues of the woman whom everyone in Florence believed would soon be regent: Archduchess Maria Magdalena of Austria. Given that Bronzini would eventually use Francesca's *Primo libro* as evidence that the apogee of female musical accomplishment had been achieved by a Florentine, one trained to excellence at the command of Magdalena's mother-in-law Christine, it seems possible that Francesca's book could have been perceived by the court as part of a larger project. Francesca's access to authorship, then, might have seemed to her patrons to be as an agent of a (female) prince.

In choosing to have her musiche published locally rather than by one of the Venetian firms that had given some of her father's other protegés wide distribution of their work, Francesca can seem to have resorted to a firm that has been dismissed as a vanity press. To be sure, there is no evidence that any of the music that Pignoni printed earned profits either for composers or for the firm;

but wide commercial distribution and profit-making may have been beside the point for the composers. Publishing with Pignoni gave composers modern-seeming objects that they could use instead of old-fashioned presentation manuscripts as gifts by which to sustain relationships with patrons. The twenty-first-century locations of Francesca's book suggest she may have used her book this way. According to the provenance materials of the respective libraries, the Florence copy came from the Medici patrimony, the Modena copy from the personal library of the melophile Modenese cardinal Alessandro d'Este, and the Paris copy from the collection of Prince Marc'Antonio Borghese. Because these were households with which Francesca had well-established relationships, she would have been likely to send them copies of her book as a courtesy that acknowledged and renewed the relationship of patronage.[24] Such private circulation of books attesting to her mastery as a teacher and composer could enhance Francesca's prestige, as well as her patrons', while ensuring that she was able to control completely access to her musicality, and therefore to any fantasy of intimacy with her physical and authorial voices. Francesca's publication with Pignoni, therefore, might not have been a strategy of vanity so much as a way to ensure just enough public circulation of her authorial voice to make her the equal of her male colleagues while preserving her reputation for the womanly virtù of continenza.

Anxieties of Authorship

By the time Francesca's *Primo libro* was in circulation, in the late summer and fall of 1618, she was the professionally mature musica, fully immersed in her profession's social network, that one might imagine from her book's self-presentation and Bronzini's account. Her oral advocacy had apparently facilitated the appointment of Vincenzo Calestani as substitute organist at the Duomo in Pisa, and her combined oral and written intercession with court secretary Andrea Cioli had evidently helped the guitarist Andrea Falconieri gain permission to publish his music in Florence with Pignoni. Unabashed to ask both an appointment and a carriage of the grand duchess's dama d'onore, Angelica Badii, she had been equally unafraid—if embarrassed—to acknowledge her own drive in a letter to Angelica's husband, Cioli: "In truth I am embarrassed by my presumption with you, but I know how very courteously and discretely you will indulge me, knowing how much, once I have begun it, I would want to bring this business to a victorious end."[25] Yet she had known considerable anxiety before bringing the business of her own book to such an end.

No known documents survive to explain directly Francesca's motives for gathering her musiche for publication. Nor do any known documents illuminate the mechanics by which she secured the financing, editing, permissions, privileges, and distribution of her book. Yet a 1,400-word letter she wrote to Buonarroti from Pisa in February 1617/18 provides something far more rare: a glimpse of a musical author's situation on the cusp of publication, after the material had been chosen, copied and edited, the permissions won and the contracts signed, when only the book's frontmatter, its dedication and an introductory *discorso*, remained to be written. Francesca's letter moves from an ebullient, even smart-alecky account of her interactions with her patrons to concerns about the conventions of ghostwritten introductory texts that precipitated a crisis of interlocking anxieties about appearances, arrogance, and authorship that she could not resolve alone.

Characteristically, Francesca began with the news and a vivid portrait of her work amid the ruling family:

> The canzonetta that you sent about the Holy Face of Our Lord gives me great satisfaction, and for the little that I know, I judge it very beautiful. Now it remains for me to match it with my part, that is, in composing and singing it. I will find the occasion to sing it for their Highnesses, and I hope it won't be hard, although I can't give a firm promise, not knowing when I will be there and given the surprises that can happen. Suffice to say that I won't fail in my part and I'll tell you all about it. I arrived here and His Highness called for me immediately, as he has done almost every day, with great pleasure to all the patrons, and Monsignor Strozzi was there twice. The second day His Highness made me sing excerpts from *Il passatempo*, on which occasion the grand duke and Madama in particular talked about you with great affection and praise, and the grand duke asked me if you had shown me anything of your *Fiera*, that is, of the most recent show their Highnesses ordered from you, and I replied that I had seen a few things pertaining to the music, but that from what I had understood from you it would be very different from *Il passatempo*, and that I believed for sure that it would prove the best show that had ever been done in the palace. Twice I've had conversations with them, and I think that before I return I will be able to bring you good news, because if the [Medici] ball bounces to my hand I won't let it get away.[26]

News of her book quickly released a whirlpool of anxiety—not about the book but about an imbroglio over the authorship of its frontmatter:

> The business of my print went so well that you will marvel when you know about it, but I would rather tell you in person for various reasons. And to come to the point, I tell you that because of my unexpected departure from Florence I was not able to be favored by you with the discorso that I wanted, but only by the [dedication?] letter, and that with some trouble. Now having found it convenient

to have it [the discorso] done for me here, based on conceits I wrote out myself; and because I could not do otherwise, I showed it as if it were my work, and I had to do that to not reveal that you had done it for me; . . . In any case the person who wrote the introduction wanted to do the letter, too, and asked that I take it so the letter and the discorso would be in the same style. Now I did not make a fuss, first because I know that it will make little difference to you and secondly to not reveal that [the letter] isn't mine, so as not to seem too partial to my own work. I accepted it, but not in a way that I cannot back out. I cannot write you other particulars for now but in person I will tell you who, and how, and everything. However, before I do anything else, so that I don't deceive myself (as one is used to doing in one's own things) I want to know from you, since I have bothered you, if it is to your taste, because if it is not, I do not want it, because before I would displease you or behave rudely to you I would drop the print and all the rest of it. But write and tell me your opinion as soon as you can, with no deference at all, so that passion won't deceive me. Because I know you love me and hold my reputation dear, and want me to enjoy the benevolence of everyone, indeed want that benevolence to grow. I send you the letter and the discorso first so that you could do me the favor of correcting the language and second, edit out everything that you know will not be good and might even minimally prejudice me, and add what you know to be missing. I beg you with every feeling not to fail me in this favor, but sincerely, without ceremony, [do] as you would do for something of your own that mattered a lot to you. I will be forever in your debt for this, among all the other kindnesses for which I owe you, and please do me the favor of keeping the whole thing secret, and send it back to me up here, so I can then send it there to the gentleman who has responsibility for it. As for my father, I don't believe that he will have reason to be upset with me because I left so unexpectedly, as you know, and as soon as I had the order I sent him all the pieces from up here so he could look them over and see if they seem ready to print. Suffice to say that whether you speak with my father or with anyone else about it, you should seem surprised and distant from the whole thing, and as for keeping or rejecting these writings that I send you don't pull any punches because this is a person I can handle in my own way, and I have already by taking [his work] and sending it to others. And so no one can guess anything, I asked it to be given to me personally so I could have it for a few days to consider it with a mind checking for its suitability; and thus whatever you send me I will say are my revisions, and I will recopy them in my own hand, so you can say whatever you want freely. I beg you for promptness because I am in a great rush. And you shouldn't respond by mail but via the court, as people come every day from Florence. Send the letter the way that seems best to you, remember us, and forgive my long-windedness, and give me news of yourself and the city. Together with

my husband I kiss your hands and pray Our Lord for every real blessing. Pisa,
23 February 1618.
Her Most Serene Highness is well, cured, but not up yet.

> Always most ready to serve you,
> Francesca Caccini Signorini[27]

Though perhaps embarrassing, Francesca's situation would hardly seem
worth all the worry, were her sense of voice not already embattled. A postscript
so long that she had to finish it by writing around the edges of the paper finally
identified the dead center of her fears: that one false move in the conventionally
borrowed voice of "her" discorso would seem arrogant, and would cast doubt
on her musically authorial voice:

> [I]f it were possible, in the place where the discorso praises the virtuosi of
> Florence, I would like to name my father in a way that he would be honored, and
> to speak of him as maestro of others, but . . . I would not like it to seem that I
> did not claim him as my origin out of arrogance, but I want to recognize him
> as a master, but without eliciting prejudice against me, and without the simple-
> minded being able to believe that these works have been perfected and finished
> and revised by him. I have been told that as a daughter it is not good manners
> for me to praise my father; but I want to turn it entirely over to you; I would not
> want, on the other hand, to be taken for arrogant and I would want to give my
> father some satisfaction. I appeal to you, and all my hope I have placed in you, so
> because the anxiety of time did not allow me to be favored by you in everything
> at least don't fail to favor me in this that I beg.[28]

In the end, there would be no discorso. The book would be introduced only by
the most formulaic of dedication letters, one that bears no trace of Francesca's
several epistolary voices.

Although she never described it that way, Francesca's particular dilemma was
gendered, peculiar to her identity as the daughter of Giulio Romano. A son
of Giulio's who was masterful enough to publish his own works also would
have worried about how to praise his father without seeming indirectly to praise
himself. Yet if a Caccini son at age thirty had published music in the tradition
his father could legitimately claim to have helped invent, his action would have
seemed to signal only that the son had come of age—the musical equivalent of
any artisan's son taking over management of the family business. Such a son
might have been troubled by some elements of the Oedipal competition with
his father that Harold Bloom called "anxiety of influence," but it is unthinkable that his authorship of his own works, good or bad, would have been ques-

tioned.[29] But Francesca, stepping forward to claim her parent's place as master of the family craft, experienced both anxiety of influence and some of the feelings that Gilbert and Gubar described as a characteristically female authorial complaint, "anxiety of authorship."[30]

Francesca's anxiety of authorship was not constructed quite as it was for the mainly Anglophone nineteenth-century women about whom Gilbert and Gubar wrote. Although consistently self-deprecatory in her written critiques of others, Francesca did not disparage her own creative work in ways that differ appreciably from the conventions common to men. Nor did she admit in any extant writings to "a fear that she [could] not create" or a fear that "the act of writing [would] isolate or destroy her."[31] Perhaps emboldened by the power of the women who quietly ruled Tuscany, Francesca seems to have been certain of her rightful place among Florence's virtuosi and certain about the merit of her work.[32] Her anxiety focused not on her own capacities but on what others ("the simple-minded") would make of her work: it was their gendered reception that she feared.

Francesca's mere participation in the convention of ghostwritten dedications was the proximate cause of her anxiety.[33] In having allowed herself to cede responsibility for her book's verbal authorial voice, she had both opened the door for the simple-minded to assume that she might similarly have feigned her musically authorial voice and opened a door onto her own memories of having that voice appropriated by her father. Giulio had long used the prerogatives of patriarchy to occupy the space of his daughter's musical identity. In 1605 he had used the favor her virtuosity had earned with the French king to bargain on Pompeo and Settimia Caccini's behalf.[34] Two years later, he deflected Buonarroti's gratitude for Francesca's labor on *La stiava*, calling the thanks "superfluous, because we all serve you willingly."[35] For years afterward, the court diarist who singled out Giulio as the one local composer who would be consistently named had described Francesca's service only through her filial relationship to her father. Thus for Francesca Caccini, the long decade and a half during which the granducato had appropriated all musicians' authorial voices had been an era of twofold appropriation: that of her sovereign and that of her father. Needing as she therefore did to exert twice the effort of her male colleagues against the habit of having her authorial voice usurped, it is little wonder that Francesca feared both to mention her father and to fail to mention him, and little wonder that she feared the undermining misattributions that might come from "the simple-minded."

Given Francesca's reluctance to show her book's contents to her father until all the work, negotiations, and ghostwriting had been done, and her exhortation that Buonarroti feign ignorance of the project if Giulio brought it up, it seems possible that she meant her book to distance her work from his and to claim an artistic identity independent of that of the daughter of Giulio Romano. Yet by 23 February 1618 she had sent her father a draft of the book for his comments, and at least three other letters, all with no reply. Earlier in her long postscript, Caccini asked Buonarroti to send news of her father, betraying still another level of anxiety. The coils of anxiety about arrogance that circle around the figure of her father in the postscript may have arisen not only from a general (and gendered) anxiety of authorship and from fear for the aging Giulio's health, but also from her nervous anticipation that his silence might signal both his irritation at her independence and his negative artistic judgment.

Because no letters between father and daughter are known to survive, it is impossible to know whether Giulio's long-claimed ownership of Francesca's musical voices ever caused expressed tension between them, nor is it possible to know, directly, what he thought of her work. A few days after Francesca wrote to Buonarroti, Giulio wrote to Andrea Cioli, asking the secretary to send Francesca an enclosed letter, probably a response to her work, through the court's private postal system.[36] Written in an untroubled, genial tone, the letter claims that two previous replies had been lost in the ordinary mail. Whatever Giulio might have said in those letters, some sense that he acknowledged Francesca as his artistic heir can be read in the final codicil of his will. Dated in early December 1618, about ten days before his death, the codicil rearranged Giulio's legacies to the women of his family, leaving Francesca "a keyboard instrument hand-painted by Cigoli," a symbolic tool of a singer-teacher-composer's trade.[37]

Being, Doing, and Allegories of Voice

7

Asinger or scholar who is attentive to texts and who leafs through Franceca's *Primo libro* cannot help but notice the book's overt self-reflexivity. It is full of adjacent songs that seem to be in dialogue. "Che fai?" (What are you doing?), asks the second song; "Ardo," (I burn), responds the third. "Rispondi" (Respond), commands the refrain of the eighth; "Deh chi già mai potrà cantar tua lode," (Alas, who could ever sing your praises), replies the next. Closer reading reveals self-reflexive moments within songs, too, when text and music together direct attention to the same problem in terms so opposite that they seem to mock each other. The opening of "Non so" (I don't know)—sung above music's ultimate assertion of certainty, a V–I cadence—is one such moment, so concisely self-contradicting as to impose the speaker's epistemological dilemma on a listener forced to choose which discourse, words or music, to believe. Often, the self-reflexive moments point so obviously to the musical challenge the song poses as to make a would-be performer want to laugh. In those moments of laughter the lesson of the song fuses to the song itself so that the song becomes a device for remembering the lesson. Tactics of a skilled and witty teacher, such moments seem like so many knowing winks in Francesca's text, traces by which one can spot her pedagogical intentions today.

Perhaps no such gesture is as obvious as Francesca's choice to open her book with a pair of songs that pose opposite kinds of questions in opposite poetic voices that are, themselves, constructed of contradictions. "Chi è costei?" (Who is she?) and "Che fai?" demand ontological and performative replies, respectively.[1] Yet each song links being to doing and implies that who one is and what

113

one does are linked in a reflexive cycle—as, indeed, they were in the etiquettes of survival at a princely court.[2] The ontological quandary of "Chi è costei?" springs from the speaker's vision of a woman (the Virgin of the Assumption) moving miraculously through the previously masculine spaces of paradise. Her motion, musically constructed by rising transpositions of a bass line and chord progression played by the performer's hands but never given voice, contradicts the fixity intrinsic to the concept of being. Consistent as it is with the early modern idea that the feminine was by definition mutable, that motion nonetheless constitutes both the means and the essence of a miracle. This woman's mutability produces not abjection but glory. By contrast, the performative emphasis of "Che fai?" springs from the lips of the crucified Christ, a man literally nailed to the spot. His breathlessly self-interrupting voice, sung above tonally stable harmonies, demands that his listeners change the actions of their souls by identifying with his condition and his transcendence of crucifixion's principal torment, the inability to control one's breath. Consistent with the early modern notion that the masculine was by definition fixed, this man's nearly strangled vocalization of fixity is, like his mother's speechless movement through the heavens, both the means and the essence of a miracle. Yet however much his fixity is also acknowledged to produce not abjection, but glory, Christ's masculine stability is presented as a torment to be overcome, while his mother's feminine mobility is pure glory.

This pair of songs functions as a double exordium to Francesca's book, presenting paradoxes of gender and problems of musical technique as interrelated dilemmas to be simultaneously resolved. Learning to navigate musical space like the speechless Virgin and to master vocality and breath like the speaking Christ, promises "being" miraculous in the fusion of musical sound and speech that is song and "being" miraculously free of containment within either gender's norms. In this chapter I read the first half of Francesca's *Primo libro* as responding to her exordium's twin questions with a set of lessons in how to sing that also constitute a set of lessons in how to be.[3] Constructing a self-reflexive course of study that winks simultaneously at problems of vocality and problems of womanhood, Francesca's book can have taught her female pupils to liberate their voices, physical and improvisatory, as a way of liberating their selves from an exaggerated obedience to the conventions of womanhood that could paralyze or silence them. I show how Francesca's songs systematically address a music pupil's anxieties about breath control, about expanding her range, about coordinating hands and voice in a self-accompanied performance, about the conventions of pitch and form in terms of which she might improvise or compose music that spoke her musical will. Grounded in the skills of hand, diaphragm, throat, and mouth, each song adds to a pupil's understanding of the means of musical representation available to chamber singers in early modern culture. As they lead a pupil toward the entwined mastery of her own body and of representation required for an improvising singer to produce a "voice," Francesca's lessons can have taught the ongoing evasion of containment that was the preferred way of being for women at Christine de Lorraine's restless, peripatetic court.

To interpret the cultural work of Francesca's *Primo libro* thus is not to discount the beauty, expressive power, or inventive wit of these songs, nor to detract from appreciation of their importance as documents of Florence's new music as its second-generation practitioners developed it. These songs and duets surely document the results of what Francesca would describe as her own "years of study" as they document the techniques by which she taught her best pupils to improvise and compose. In particular, the sly inventiveness of her romanescas evokes the freedom this simple antecedent-consequent formula granted to performers. As flexible as a twentieth-century blues, the romanesca as Francesca presents it seems to have encouraged singers to create, from recognizable and conventional materials, sounding narrative structures unlike any that had existed before. The taste for building narratives both traditional in their elements and unpredictable in their forms can be understood to have been one of Francesca's fundamental interests as an artist working on the threshold of the new sensibility that came to be called Baroque.

Anxiety of Authorship as Anxiety of Voice: The Problem of Breath

"I burn unhappily, and try not to reveal it."[4] Thus begins the third song of the *Primo libro*, as if responding to the questions of being and doing with which the book opens.[5] Embodying the self-contradiction of its first line, the song thwarts expectations. It responds to Christ's question with a decidedly secular complaint about unrevealable, and therefore unrequited, secular love. Moreover, its six stanzas of ottava rima are not to be sung in the strophic, metrically marked style of an aria, as one might expect, but as a through-composed recitative soliloquy. By setting Andrea Salvadori's ottave instead as a recitative soliloquy, Francesca marked the song as articulating the principal moral dilemma of the book.[6] By staging that dilemma through the recitative soliloquy's most common poetic voice, that of lament, she acknowledged the gendered convention that assigned the work of voicing painful internal contradiction to women. But by choosing to set this particular text, in which a person of indeterminate gender laments not the loss of a lover but her own fearful incapacity to communicate desire, Francesca challenged the gendering of the lament.[7] She used "Ardo infelice" to stage the problem of women's speech, translating what theorists centuries later would call anxiety of authorship into anxieties of voice that are left largely unresolved, as her speaker fails to find a rhetoric through which to speak—in a way that is intelligible to others—of her own desire.

Aflame with passion, the speaker of Salvadori's stanzas so fears revealing her desire that she silences her own public speech. She relies instead on the inexact eloquence that writers of prescriptive literature since Aristotle had preferred in women: the eloquence of silence. Interpreting silence to allow the speechless language of her body to communicate, Salvadori's protagonist tries in vain to reveal her desire through the visible signs of her pallid face and tears and the audible signs of breathlessness, sighs, and what she calls "interrupted speech." By the poem's end she finds a way to be always near her beloved, but because her passion remains invisible, the beloved's uncomprehending gaze causes her "death." We know this to be the death of agency, not the "little death" of sexual consummation, because she has styled herself a "Clizia novella," evoking the sea nymph of Ovid's tale whose expressed desire for Apollo caused her sister to be buried alive and the nymph herself to be transformed into a sunflower condemned to follow with her gaze Apollo's star across the sky.[8]

Francesca translated the protagonist's bashfully ineffectual efforts at self-revelation into an interlocking set of vocal and musical challenges that might easily bedevil a neophyte—all of them based in the breathlessness that Clizia hopes will narrate her desire. To represent this breathlessness literally, Francesca peppered her vocal line with rests that interrupt the otherwise fluent declamation of a poetic line or interrupt passaggi in a way that invites the singer to choose whether the rests should be dramatized as sighs or simply used as opportunities to sneak a breath. Moving more deeply into a singer's understanding of breath as it related to the release of the anima's energy and, through that release, to register, Caccini mapped the effects of breathlessness on the singer's ability to move through musical space. All but paralyzed at the outset in a middle register that hovers around the soliloquy's tonic g, the singer's voice rises every time she considers self-revelation, only to sink back to the tonic or below when her breath, like her courage, fails her (see example 7.1). Digging deeper still into the self-silencing implications of breathlessness for a singer, Caccini extended the breath-based problem of register to two abstract problems of musical design that throughout the song's six stanzas generate a purely sonic experience of constant struggle between conflicting tonal systems. By setting the song in g-mollis, Caccini had evoked the traditional connotations of the old-fashioned transposed Hypdorian mode—piety, submissiveness, tears—that arose from the physical cause of the mode's low range, a lack of animating energy caused by a lack of breath.[9] But when the singer first suggests that her body be read as the text of her desire, at measure 4, an errant b-natural slips into her line: foreign

Ex. 7.1. Francesca Caccini, *Il primo libro delle musiche* (1618), 9, "Ardo infelice," mm. 1–7

I burn unhappily, and try not to reveal
My fire to the one who consumes me;
My torment can be easily read in my face
And the breathlessness of my heart narrates my desire.

to the signature and foreign to the mode, it is a tiny gesture of energy, as if her body almost involuntarily reached toward the higher register that her song will consistently link to self-revelation and desire.[10] (Listen to track 1.)

However tiny a gesture, the b-natural and the audible brightness to which it points become a recurring problem for the performer as her voice struggles toward a higher range while her hands struggle to play the brightened harmonies of a durus world on her instrument. The b-natural's pull of her voice upward seems to express both the speaker's desire and her effort to make her body speak what her words will not say, while the same note's pull of her harmonies toward brightness leads, eventually, to the sun-like presence of the beloved. Just as consistently, womanish tears, ineffectual self-representation, and the beloved's failure to understand her unspoken feelings collapse the song, both voice and harmonies, back into a g-mollis world, as at the end of the second stanza (see example 7.2).[11]

Struggling again and again against her own fear and against the way others receive her obedience to the conventions that constrain her speech and desire, in the end this singer's music accommodates the most timid implication of that

Ex. 7.2. Francesca Caccini, *Il primo libro delle musiche* (1618), 10, "Ardo infelice," mm. 24–35

The messengers of my suffering go forth.

Bitterest burning tears

I scatter to reveal my desires

But nothing works, and my weeping [is] not seen

Or is believed to have another cause.

involuntary b-natural's gasp of desire. Instructed by the composer's handwritten corrections in all surviving copies of the book to sing cheerfully once she is allowed to be close to her beloved, she shifts to a still g-centered world that assimilates the b-natural.[12] In the fifth stanza she sings scalewise passaggi that follow her lover's "sojourn" into the higher register that marks eloquence; by the sixth stanza's conclusion her voice has once more collapsed to its middle register. Again she fills the range d' to d" with a passaggio that seems to articulate her only partly satisfied desire by evoking the old Hypomixolydian mode, the mode of wifely petition in which, one might imagine, the b-natural of her desire is now safely contained. Like the mythical Clizia, then, Francesca's singer remained rooted to the spot, her faltering breath unable to lift her voice to a permanently higher register or her harmonies from the centering on g, where her song began. Francesca's structuring of her soliloquy as a narrative of hopeless desire built from breathlessness thus succeeds because breath fails. Still breathless, and thus unable to control either the release of her anima as voice or her body's heat, the singer performs her own complicity with the social forces that would silence any woman's desire.[13] But she is made to perform that complicity as a correctable lack of self-control. In the final line, Francesca forces the singer to insert a rest that all but forces her to contradict the more obvious meaning of the words—"you will know that your glances are to blame for my death"—and to say "the blame is mine." Thus did the singing teacher Francesca drive her point home: this singer's anxieties of voice could have been overcome by the somatic self-discipline of breath control (see example 7.3).

Having thus staged anxiety of authorship as anxiety of voice, Francesca staged the resolution of these anxieties over the course of the next sixteen songs. She chose and ordered these songs' texts so that they articulate both the authorization of voice by powerful others and the gradual transformation of her singing subject's responses from fear to uncertainty to growing confidence to, finally, the complete disappearance of her own bashful, self-reflexive identification behind the formal structures of the romanesca and behind the personae of theatrical songs. Just as important, Francesca organized the sixteen songs so that each constituted a lesson in some aspect of the improvising chamber singer's art: breath control; the construction of goal-directed phrases via progression through the circle of fifths; the coordination of hands and voice, melody and harmony, in controlling a song's momentum; ways of organizing musical responses to a text to illuminate individual words and a poem's overall conceit; practice with different kinds of arias, with composing new arias based on audible traces of traditional ones, and with ensemble singing; and finally, a revisiting of the lament. By the time a pupil reaches the set of four romanescas at the center of the book, she could have acquired both the cultural authority and the self-mastery to control her own songs' representations.

Ex. 7.3. Francesca Caccini, *Il primo libro delle musiche* (1618), 15, "Ardo infelice," mm. 107–111

Loving eyes, wicked eyes, you will know too late

That the blame [cause?] for my death is your glances.

Authorizing Voice: The Name of the Mother and the Call of the Son

Francesca staged this acquisition through a set of spiritual songs—four madrigals and an aria—that begins by deriving the grace that is song from the silent Virgin and ends by demanding that new voices respond to the voice of her crucified son.[14] Developing the figures and themes through which her book's double exordium had linked being to doing, as if these five new songs formed a rhetorical ornament to the opening pair, Francesca thus opens a space between gendered opposites within which a singer can conquer fear of voice. Responding directly to the question "Chi è costei?," the song "Maria, dolce Maria" dramatizes the emergence of an ecstatic vocality in coordination with ecstatically moving harmonies and of a musicality that allows the performer to control her own ecstasy in the name of Christendom's archetypal authorizing woman. Responding directly to the question "Che fai?," the song "Ecco, ch'io verso il sangue" (Look, I pour forth blood) allows the singer to use her new vocality to practice and project the angry reproach intrinsic to lament through the unimpeachably justified voice of Christ, and, embodying his voice, to command other voices to respond. The three songs that come between give a pupil practice in organizing both her harmonies and her voice's melodic surface to support the rhetorical conceits of her text.

From the very beginning, Francesca's "Maria, dolce Maria" invites the singer to enliven certain words with little graces that fill those words with an extra release of voiced anima from her body (see example 7.4). Linking these words in a chain of associations that fill the intervallic space of the word that inspires them—Maria—the singer's voice also fills the words that name Maria's attributes ("soave" [gentle], "sacrato" [consecrated]) and actions ("imparadis'il core" [enraptures my heart], "m'infiammi di celeste amore" [enflames me with heavenly love]) with graces that sing her speechless body's responses to speech. It is almost as if a female Word were being made flesh, as if this song enacted the incarnation of song itself, not from a woman's words but from a Word that is the name of a Woman. Indeed, when that first Word returns in the middle of measure 9, the name "Maria" is enlivened by the sonic and somatic energy it seems to release, energy that finally pours forth untrammeled from the singer's throat in the stunning passaggio on the song's only first-person statement, "io canto (I sing)."[15] (See example 7.4.) (Listen to track 2.)

By lengthening the time the word "canto" occupies, Francesca ensured that the singer's breath will control every aspect of the song. Introduced by a cadence to the song's final of F, her rapture into song all but stops the harmonic motion that had been gradually quickening in response to the Word. Exaggerating the effect of the contorted syntax by which the poet's words simultaneously desire and defer the enrapturing word "Maria," the extravagant passaggio performs the act of singing as a complex act of self-control, an act by which the singer's body controls both what her words will say and how much ecstasy her soul will be allowed. Creating a moment that fuses self-censorship to prolonged spiritualized ecstasy, by sustaining the moment of speechless song the passaggio allows a singer to release her voice from the prison of word-dominated song as wrought by her own spiritual discipline and control of her breath.

The singer's enactment of spiritual ecstasy is as much a matter of the harmonic momentum that her hands produce on an accompanying instrument as it is a matter of literal voice. Her hands begin in relative stillness, playing only two chords, ones we would call tonic and dominant, below the first phrase. As her voice fills with graces, her hands touch a wider range of harmonies, harmonies that are as if enraptured by the goal-directed pattern of root movement by fifth in response to the words "Che'l cor m'infiammi de celeste amore." From that moment to the end of the song, nearly all harmonic motion consists of links in the chain of fifths that it inspires (F–B♭–E♭–a–d–g–G–C–F). Indeed, the dizzying fall of the harmony's root movement through the circle of fifths that begins in measure 5 is only prevented from cycling endlessly by the singer's insistence on certain words, notably "io canto," and by the inspiring word

Ex. 7.4. Francesca Caccini, *Il primo libro delle musiche* (1618), 17, "Maria, dolce Maria," mm. 1–11

Maria, sweet Maria,
Name so gentle
That pronouncing it enraptures the heart,
Name sacred and holy
That inflames my heart with celestial love,
Maria, never as long as I sing
[Can my tongue
A happier word
Pull from my breast than to say "Maria."]

Ex. 7.5. Francesca Caccini, *Il primo libro delle musiche* (1618), 18, "Maria, dolce Maria,"
mm. 23–28

That makes every heart serene, every soul happy.

itself, "Maria." By the time s/he has reached this cadence, though, the singer
has swirled through the circle of fifths two and a half times, enacting in the
musical miniature of harmonic motion the spiritual ecstasy so dear to Baroque
religious representation. It is an ecstasy in which the powerful tension between
a voice that prolongs musical time and a pair of hands that work to propel time
forward threatens to fracture the performer's effort to sustain a unitary self.

In apparent response to poetic lines that recover equilibrium by describing the sacred name as consoling and tranquil, the singer's voice and hands
together begin to rise through the circle of fifths, as if both need to reclaim the
song's tonal space by this equal and opposite motion. But it is not quite equal,
for there is no building of sonic energy in the voice through the accumulation
of short graces, as at the song's opening. Instead, the sonic energy seems to be
shared equally by voice and hands as they move in a roughly homorhythmic
motion that performs as intrasubjective unity the serenity the Virgin's name can
also bring. The singer's ultimately untroubled vocality is thus made to seem
born of and in the Name of the Mother: the singer's authorization to sing, and
her first demonstration of vocal and spiritual self-control, are represented and
performed as rooted in the authority of another woman (see example 7.5).

The next three songs reinforce the lessons of "Maria, dolce Maria" and build
on them. All introduce a new component of empowered vocality: the construc-

tion of a melodic line by the varied repetition of motives calculated to show the relation of ideas to one another or the effect that reinterpretation of a word might have. Thus, in "Pietà, mercede, aita," a pupil learns that when the opening word is taken to cry out for pity, she should give voice to it with a diminished fourth or fifth, but when it is taken to mean the piety of solidarity with others, these intervals' difficulty is washed away on a glorious rush of passaggiando voice that signifies the formerly breathless singer's recovery of self-control in community with others. In "Ferma, Signore, arresta," a madrigal whose text seeks to defer God's judgment until the speaker has time to convert, the singer both enacts her fear of criticism and tempts it by her song's too-literal reading of the text. She stops her song cold with an authentic cadence to stop the "terrible sentence" of final judgment, as if she were utterly ignorant of the poem's overall narrative of conversion. When her conversion from a frivolous attention to detail to intelligent engagement with the poem's narrative comes, the singer gains control of her song, marshalling the forces of effective self-expression that she learned from the three previous madrigals. Boldly rising melodic ideas explore both ends of her mode's characteristic range. Short phrases with sharp rhythmic profiles repeated at different pitch levels give her melody a motivic coherence that makes it memorable. Strong progressions through the circle of fifths by her hands support her voice's increasingly focused delivery of poetic lines. And passaggi link her desire for consecration to God's accepting response by opening each phrase into the same intervallic space. Rhetorically effective for the first time, the pupil's sung speech in "Ferma, Signore" calls forth the voice of Christ himself again in the set's final song, the aria "Ecco, ch'io verso il sangue."

No pupil could fail to compare "Ecco" with the book's exordial song in the voice of Christ, "Che fai?" Supported by harmonies that writhe ineffectually against a web of nearly unrelieved dissonance, the voice of the latter song's Christ had performed both his suffering and its promise of salvation directly, as matters of breath. Dramatizing the suffocating effect of crucifixion in the song's constantly broken, gasping phrases, Francesca had created a final phrase that asked the singer to perform both the release of Christ's anima in death and his invitation to salvation as a final torrential passaggio that displayed her capacity to sustain a breath (see example 7.6).

But if the singer of Caccini's "Che fai?" had been asked to give voice to a Christ of doing, not being, the singer of "Ecco, ch'io verso il sangue" is asked to give voice to a Christ whose crucifixion she performs as the ontological condition of hybridity.[16] Caught between through-composed and strophic form, Christ's recitative-like song always loops back to a refrain whose insistent ending on the mode's dominant prompts an eternally unsatisfied desire for rest. Neither choppiness of phrasing nor inexorably sinking register links this voice's liminality to problems of breath. Instead, Francesca calculated shifts between

Ex. 7.6. Francesca Caccini, *Il primo libro delle musiche* (1618), 8, "Che fai, misero core, ecco ch'in croce," mm. 43–45

For your salvation there are so many doors

mollis and durus to cast the transposed motives that connect textual ideas in intensely different sonic lights. Creating thus a motivically tight, dramatically colored vocal line that depends on her singer's ability to support her sound in the high register of eloquence, Francesca gives voice to a Christ who sings as contradictions between flat and sharp pitch worlds the contradictions between human and divine being that he embodies and sustains.

Like the protagonist of "Ardo infelice," the Christ that Francesca has constructed for "Ecco" experiences human life in the mollis world, where b-flat is normal, but pours out his intrasubjective reality in the durus world, where b-natural is the norm.[17] At the first mention of outpoured blood the performer's hands shift her harmonies from the mollis world implied by her voice to the brightness of an unnaturally major tonic triad, through a knot of surrounding dissonances—as if to capture the sight of fresh blood's brightness before it dries brown in the air. Unlike the protagonist of "Ardo," however, the Christ of "Ecco" can encompass both worlds, an ability shown most effectively when he sings the word that identifies him as master, "Signore," above a shocking upward slide from c″ to c-sharp″ that is to be harmonized either by successive diminished triads or by a mollis a-dim-6 sonority followed by a durus A-6/4 (see example 7.7a, especially measures 5–6).

Able in subsequent verses to link the durus directly to his audience's heedlessness, Christ can recover his fundamentally mollis voice even when the expression of his body's innerness—again in the twin fluids of anima and blood—is forced by a soldier's blade piercing his chest. He can absorb even that blow of symbolic mishearing and assimilate the crucial pitch of cantus durus into his mollis experience (see example 7.7b).

Ex. 7.7a. Francesca Caccini, *Il primo libro delle musiche* (1618), 24, "Ecco, ch'io verso il sangue," mm. 1–13

Behold, I pour forth blood.

Behold, I approach death.

Calm your scorn, O Israel,

Already you see your pale Lord on the Cross.

People so beloved,

People so ungrateful,

Respond, my people.

In what did I ever offend you?

What have I done to you?

Ex. 7.7b. Francesca Caccini, *Il primo libro delle musiche* (1618), 27, "Ecco, ch'io verso il sangue," mm. 44–48

And safe on the banks
[I] brought you out of the stormy battlefield.
You, [who] so that I would faint
Open my chest with iron.

Why can Christ do what Clizia could not? What has the singer learned that enables this triumph of sustaining contradiction?

In terms of these five spiritual songs, she has learned grace. Grace has consistently been figured as an outpouring of music that required bodily self-discipline, intrasubjective balance, practice navigating the mollis and the durus tonal worlds, logical motivic design—all in response to words, but slavishly obedient neither to those words nor to the word-dominated aesthetic so often proclaimed as fundamental to the Caccini family's new music. For the singer of "Ecco," those elements of grace converge in the refrain that grounds the end of each through-composed stanza in Christ's haunting demand for response (see example 7.7a, measures 12–13). Sung in the register of eloquence, not breathless bashfulness, artfully developed from a single motive into a phrase that incorporates the upward slide of the first stanza, directed again and again to a half-cadence that provokes but never satisfies desire, this refrain is one of the most memorable phrases in Francesca's book. More crucial to the efficacy of Christ's call than his words, the refrain displays a singer's mastery of her lessons: her control of breath and of the use of b-flat and b-natural that in "Ardo infelice" had signaled an involuntary breach of continenza, and her ability to give powerful voice to desire by the musical work of her voice and hands alone. By the things she does to ventriloquize this authoritative voice of Christ, she practices being a person who could give hauntingly memorable voice to desire, could reproach those who by failing to hear the cause of another's suffering worsen it, or could demand that other voices respond. (Listen to track 3.)

Voice, Desire, and Anxiety of Genre

"Alas, who could ever sing praises equal to your grandeur, beautiful Virgin?" replies the first line of the next song, "Deh, chi già mai potrà."[18] Retreating to a bashfulness not heard since "Ardo infelice," the singer is asked by this text to retreat, as well, to a dependence on the speechless eloquence of the body all too worthy of Clizia: her tears, she says, will tell her story, and her silence will be her trumpet.[19] Feminizing the vocality being taught, the affective retreat marks the beginning of a new set of lessons that will lead a pupil with a firm technical foundation toward mastery of the conventions by which improvising singers created distinctive musical voices in the daily practice of their craft. Two profoundly different examples of the most fashionable framework for improvisation of the era, the aria di romanesca, introduce a pupil to the astounding flexibility with which a conventional framework can be made to challenge its own apparent constraints. A soprano-bass duet unambiguously representing sexual desire gives invaluable practice in the coordination of improvised ornaments, responding to the long-standing Florentine critique of the ornamented part song as an aesthetic impossibility. And in the culminating lesson Francesca's pupil is taught to respond in a way that is at once feminine, Florentine, and singerly to the genre that most fully instantiated the constraints of convention on women's voice. A direct challenge to Monteverdi's 1608 lament for Arianna, Francesca's masterful "Lasciatemi qui solo" treats the Monteverdi lament as if it were an aria for improvisation—one convention among many that a singer could turn to her own use. Building from Monteverdi's aria a song so focused in its communication of a grave desire for death that it overwhelms, Francesca made "Lasciatemi qui solo" a near-perfect example of the power of the Florentine aesthetic. By casting it in the poetic voice of a man, Francesca simultaneously obeyed the cultural convention that linked unity of being and doing to masculinity and challenged the convention that assigned the cultural work of lamenting to women's voices. With this song the anxiety of genre that was implicit in the lamenting voice of Clizia is finally dispelled.

It seems that in this section of her book Francesca's interest was to teach how a pupil might conceive such a reconstruction of convention. Thus she first introduced the most common aria for improvised singing of narrative poetry, the romanesca. As with any aria, the singer constructed the romanesca's characteristic way of being by reference to certain melodic and harmonic gestures. S/he would usually divide the text into couplets that function as two-line stanzas of a strophic song. These stanzas consisted of musically antecedent and consequent

Ex. 7.8. Scheme of a romanesca

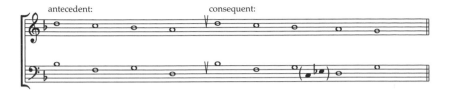

phrases: the antecedent descended from the fifth degree of a scale to its second degree, and the consequent returned to the fifth, then descended all the way to the "final" to give closure to a thought. For accompaniment the singer would touch harmonies that, too, produced antecedent and consequent phrases: in the simplest twenty-first-century terms, the antecedent phrase would move B♭–F–g–D, and the consequent moved B♭–F–g–D–g. Conventionally written as a mollis Dorian song transposed to g, its implied 3/2 rhythm constantly evoking its origin as a dance song, the romanesca was a genre of oral tradition (see example 7.8).[20] Thus its formula, however simple, was independent of the intellectualized tradition that sustained the contradictory pitch systems of mode and system with which Clizia had struggled. Endlessly elastic, transposable to any key, susceptible to almost infinite ornamentation and expansion, it was a perfect aria through which a singer might explore the malleability of convention and learn to use her ingenuity to bend convention to her own desire.

With "Deh chi già mai potrà" Francesca introduced the singer to the romanesca's patterns as they most often appeared in print (see example 7.9).[21] The angular bass line that would be produced by the simplest version of the supporting chords is filled in so that it moves stepwise. Although obscured by the barring, the 3/2 dance rhythm unmistakably accents the harmonic pattern's points of arrival, ensuring that the work of the performer's hands is easy and secure so she can concentrate on the work her voice must do. That work performs the romanesca's characteristic affect of excitability as restlessly ornamented melody that frequently defies both the aria's overall direction of vocal descent and her own hands' articulation of points of arrival.[22] Raising the coordination challenge of "Maria, dolce Maria" to a new level and prescribing the articulation of short syllables so that they are almost swallowed on their sixteenth notes (as they would be in speech), "Deh chi già mai potrà" demands much more concentration and skill from a performer than anything that has come before. Thus even as her melody arches in agitated, often mimetic response to poetic words or conceits rather than in response to the harmonic signals of her own hands, the internal equilibrium required of the singer contradicts her words' heralded retreat into silence and tears.

Ex. 7.9. Francesca Caccini, *Il primo libro delle musiche* (1618), 29, "Deh, chi già mai potrà, Vergine bella,"mm. 1–12, showing nodes of a romanesca tune and bass line and rebarred to show its characteristic rhythm

> Oh, who could ever be able, beautiful Virgin,
>
> To sing your praise [in a way] equal to your grandeur?

If "Deh chi già mai potrà" teaches a singer how to be in a romanesca's patterns, "Nube gentil" (Gentle cloud) gives the first lesson in how to do unexpected things with the pattern, to manipulate listeners' desire.[23] The anonymous text draws attention to the lesson, addressing a cloud as a veil that conceals "the King of Glory," gives the sun its rays, and seems to have the power to withhold and then restore the sun to the sky; the sun is knowledge of God, and the cloud that which obscures it. In Francesca's song the romanesca pattern represents the elusive sun. Bits of the expected vocal descent, bits of the usual chord pattern, and bits of the characteristic 3/2 rhythm are audible but out of order, bringing an ever-greater desire for an unequivocal statement of the pattern. That desire is never fully satisfied. It is shamelessly elicited by the performer's control over the form of her listeners' experience rather than by her increasingly disciplined control over her physical voice. For a singer who began her journey with "Ardo infelice," the shift of her attention to matters of form and representation is an important step toward acquiring an improviser's equivalent of authorial voice.

Desire is certainly the subject of the duet that follows, "Io mi distruggo" (I destroy myself), a duet so textually and musically explicit in its performances of longing, union, and fantastically ornamented singing as to leave little doubt that it is as much a lesson in sexuality as in vocality.[24] For, like sex, singing improvised ornaments with a partner requires that each singer pay careful attention to the other's body, breath, gestures, and timing so that moments of individual expression and moments that need precise somatic unanimity will be performed well. Although these physical requirements were modestly ignored by contemporary aestheticians of song, almost everyone who wrote about ornamented singing in Francesca's time understood it as a vocality of the body that pleased by its sensuality alone. Rejection of such singing as disorderly, especially when done in ensemble, had been fundamental to the claims that Giulio's mentors encouraged him to make for his new kind of music. Thus Francesca's demonstration here of how beautiful and orderly it could be suggests that she meant both to refer to those claims and to respond to them. Singers of "Io mi distruggo" could find solutions to the problems of both vocality and sexuality in her careful construction of complementarity, as the starkly differentiated voices of soprano and bass echoed and supported each other's turns at ornamental self-display, coming together only at rare, easily coordinated moments of cadence or homorhythmic, syllabically uttered words of mutual desire. A female pupil who could not sustain any sonic expression of desire when she began "Ardo infelice" could find in this duet a paradise of expressed and reciprocated desire constructed by the actions of voice.

Both the baby steps toward turning the romanesca into a means of provoking desire and the experience of performing a duet of reciprocal desire lead Francesca's pupil to a staged confrontation with Claudio Monteverdi's lament for Arianna, the lament that, according to Severo Bonini, was so widely known that "there was no house that, having a keyboard or theorbo, did not also have her lament."[25] Dodging both the Oedipal anxiety of influence that would kill a precursor author by besting him and the feminine anxiety of authorship that longed to borrow authority from a female precursor, in performing Francesca's "Lasciatemi qui solo" a singer takes possession of the genre.[26]

Francesca opened and closed the stanzas of her strophic lament with phrases that unmistakably evoke the opening and closing phrases of the first section of Monteverdi's lament.[27] Thus, like Monteverdi she encircled her lamenter in verbal and musical variants of a phrase so determinedly asking for death that the contrasting phrase in between, turning rhetorically outward to address others, cannot break free (see example 7.10).

But whereas Monteverdi (and the poet Ottaviano Rinuccini) left that formal inscription of isolation behind to explore in successive sections of recitative soliloquy Arianna's conflicted feelings of desire, envy, rage, and regret, Francesca chose to develop the first of these. Her song's successive stanzas frame her speaker's resigned farewells to the world in phrases reminiscent of Monteverdi's music that welcome rather than struggle against death. In effect, Francesca treats Monteverdi's opening and closing phrases as though they were among the gestures of an aria in the improviser's oral tradition—a set of choices about range, affect, phrase structure, and mode by which a singer could perform a way of being and by which she could build any structure she might choose.[28]

Francesca built a strophic song that fused Monteverdi's opening gestures to her own mastery of tonal desire. Above a glacially slow bass line and harmonic rhythm, the singer first asks for solitary death on the single mid-range a′. Falling very slowly through successive phrases, the singer's voice reaches what will come to seem, in later stanzas, like its inevitable goal—the quoted refrain "lasciatemi morire," which cadences in d-Dorian. Quoting in measure 3 the piteous rise from a′ to b-flat′ that so poignantly marked the opening phrase of Monteverdi's Arianna, like her Francesca's lamenter seems to internalize the motive, moving it into the bass line in measure 6. Like Monteverdi's Arianna, too, she takes advantage of the equally mollis and durus qualities of the Dorian mode, playing the a′-to-b′ gesture in its durus form in the bass below dire, if fleeting, dissonances in measure 14, on the way to the refrain that so desires death. Each succeeding stanza elaborates the irresistible force pulling the singer's melody toward its final: fleetingly passaggiato farewells to the world's living creatures only add to the strain of a listener's desire for the tonic and for the familiar, lovingly elaborated paraphrase of Monteverdi's "lasciatemi morire" that itself becomes an object of desire. Overwhelming by its austere, dignified, ineluctable desire for death, the lament is a showpiece revealing what fidelity to the Florentine aesthetic of focused affect could allow one to do. (Listen to track 4.)

Today, singers and audiences who encounter "Lasciatemi qui solo" invariably hear it, at first, as a woman's song, despite the details in the text that unambiguously identify the poetic speaker as male. Although this confusion is surely exacerbated by an exaggerated sense of the genre's gendering, Francesca's choice to make Monteverdi's music for Arianna the theme of her own aria ensured that the musical voice of her lamenter would be received as partly that of Arianna. Thus her aria is likely to have bedazzled its first singers' and listeners' perceptions of gender as well, even as it would have provided them with a perfect example of the unspoken gender dynamics of early seventeenth-century Italy's musical aesthetics. In "Lasciatemi qui solo," the words, which rule (as, according to Giovanni de' Bardi and Monteverdi, the mind does the body), clearly speak in the voice of a fictive man, and the music, which serves those words (as the body does the mind), just as clearly "speaks" in the voice of a fictive woman. The voice of the aria as a whole, however, is neither male nor female. Hovering between these poles, the aria's voice can sound to us like the artistic voice of a third sex; in the seventeenth century it may have sounded like a voice that sustained the contradiction between binary gender norms and the belief that all human beings shared a single sex.[29]

Still, if we take seriously the notion that this aria was meant to be understood as giving the musical voice of a woman to the poetic voice of a man, we must acknowledge that the musical voice was in part built from the fictional voice of Arianna that Monteverdi had created. The assimilation of her voice, in particular her piteous a'-to-b-flat' motive, into other musical gestures is the essential act of each stanza. As the mark of Arianna's voice moves into the bass line in its mollis and durus forms, the voice that assimilates it falls again and again from dominant to tonic with a force as irresistible as gravity. That assimilating voice makes the desire for death's self-silencing overwhelm both the speaker and listeners, invading and constructing our experience more powerfully than do Monteverdi's gestures. If the musical voice is indeed that of a woman, then it is a woman's voice that overwhelms us. Thus by quoting Monteverdi's lament and by treating it as an aria in terms of which she could create her own reality, Francesca marked the music of her "Lasciatemi qui solo" as the terrain on which she would contest the terms of Monteverdi's ubiquitous, culturally powerful construction of woman's voice. Torn asunder by registral and harmonic strife, a voice of rhetorical, affective, and sonic disorder, this voice was the one Francesca had parodied in her book's opening soliloquy, "Ardo infelice"—the very voice she projected as born of a womanly fear to speak, that rendered her Clizia breathless. Francesca surely meant to engulf this construction in the overwhelming tonal logic of her own song.

"Lasciatemi morire." Inevitably, we must ask what death, or whose, "Lasciatemi qui solo" makes us desire. The most transparent answer would acknowledge that the one who dies is a fictional man who sings his desire to die to the world's pleasures through the fictional voice of a woman, a voice he has appropriated to express his needs. Yet the "voice of a woman" that he appropriates, Arianna's voice, is overwhelmed by the voice of another woman: the once-living Francesca, not a fiction. Her music created—for the song's protagonist, for the female pupils who would sing it, and for us—an overwhelming desire for the silence of this man, of his self-serving constructions of a woman's voice, and of

Ex. 7.10. Francesca Caccini, *Il primo libro delle musiche* (1618), 38, "Lasciatemi qui solo," mm. 1–9, with phrases of Claudio Monteverdi,

"Lasciatemi morire," from *L'Arianna* (as published in 1623) for comparison

Leave me alone here.

Return, O birds, to your nest.

While my soul is sorrow,

I breathe [expire] on this beach.

I want no others with me

But a cold rock

And my fatal suffering.

Let me die.

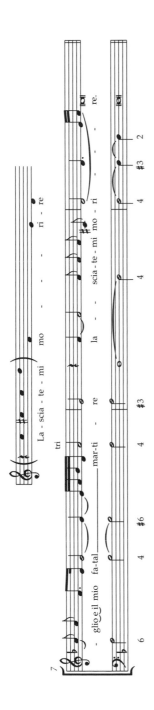

the anxieties of voice that they caused. We desire the death of that beautiful but imprisoning genre of beset womanhood, the lament.

Taking Possession

Francesca's "Lasciatemi qui solo" provides us, as it provided her pupils, with the spectacle of a woman musician taking full possession of the musical genre that most fully instantiated the paradoxes limiting her access to voice in her culture. In the Mediterranean world, the cultural work of vocalizing laments has long been delegated to women of all social ranks.[30] It was the musical equivalent of spinning, weaving, and sewing—a performance par excellence of womanhood itself. As a result, the lament was both an authorized genre of female vocality and a genre in which women enjoyed authority without raising questions about their virtue. Yet the lament limited women's vocal authority to performing the work of their communities' pain. However valuable that work, and however convenient laments might have been as channels through which women could release their individual frustrations, anger, or unrealized desires, the aural experience of women's voices raised in lament perpetuated in real life the association of public female vocality with pain, disruption, and social disorder. Those associations, in turn, led to an understandable cultural desire both to praise a lamenting woman's rhetorical skill and to silence her disorderly voice. Moreover, the association of women's voices with laments framed those voices, denying them authority in other contexts and making other manifestations of female vocality seem transgressive or unnatural. By taking possession of the lament, Francesca engaged both sides of the paradox: the authority for female vocality implicit in the genre and the tendency of that authority to limit female vocality to the cultural work of pain. By treating Monteverdi's lament as simply one aria among many, she demonstrated that she had a being independent of what the genre permitted her to do and that she could shape the tropes of the lament rather than be shaped by them. Thus by example she showed her female pupils a dynamic between being and doing in relation to cultural convention that could allow them to recognize each convention of womanhood as no more than one aria among many—no more, that is, than a set of performance materials that invited them to improvise momentary self-performances suitable to their needs.

But if the conventions for performing womanhood might be thought of as only arias, invitations to create new ways of being by the myriad ways in which one might improvise on the old ones, what did Francesca bring into being for her pupils with "Lasciatemi qui solo"? She brought into being a lament that is neither disorderly nor hysterical but rather sings both sadness and desire with dignity. Further, she brought into being something the traditional multisectional, emotionally uncontrolled lament denied every woman: the possibility of being a unified desiring subject who, by taking possession of the arias that were the basis of an improviser's art, could take possession of her own musical will. Thus Francesca's "Lasciatemi qui solo" performed for her pupils the work of the lament as a genre: the articulation of the threshold between one state of being and another.[31] In the succeeding lessons, a set of three "arie allegre" (cheerful ways of being) followed by a set of four romanescas, Francesca provided examples of different ways to construct arias by reorganizing arias already circulating in oral culture or not; with ritornellos, with double ritornellos, or with no ritornellos; with refrain structures or without. These lessons reinforce the lesson of "Lasciatemi qui solo," namely, that an improvising singer can bring herself into many different ways of being by the way she chooses to arrange—to compose—the elements of an aria. In the end, they move beyond treating arias as allegories of social convention to be obeyed or, by artful, twisting recomposition, made one's own, and turn the force of allegory back onto the singer. The self comes to seem like an aria, a set of well-practiced conventions for how to be that could be arranged at will to create, satisfy, or express desire. To take possession of arias, then, could lead to self-possession, that is, to taking possession of the ways in which one's performances, chosen in dialogue with culture, bring one's several selves into being again and again.

"O che nuovo stupor!" Arie Allegre and Female Desire

A set of three spiritual arie allegre (cheerful strophic songs) follows. Setting texts suitable for Christmas ("O che nuovo stupor" [O what new astonishment]), the Ascension ("Su le piume del vento" [On the wings of the wind]), and the Assumption ("Giunto è il dì" [The day has arrived]), each associates the cheerful affect that the set's rubric prescribes with praise of miraculous motion across the threshold between earthly and celestial space. Expressing cheerfulness presents a pupil with new challenges: the lightning speed with which her mouth and tongue must move to execute Francesca's fastidious transcriptions of speech's shifting rhythms, colors, and pitch contours, the breath control needed to sustain a sense of line across long phrases that encompass both the crystalline delivery of words and the eruptions of ornaments within those words, and a restless harmonic rhythm that requires her to navigate her instrument with unhesitating precision. Her hands supporting nearly every word with a different sound, the singer must thus move through musical space like a dancer, each word a step of her whole person that articulates part of the design that is her song. Neither silenced nor paralyzed by internal contradictions, no longer in thrall to the convention authorizing her vocality only for the work of pain, she is ready to learn how to create musical ways of being—arias—of her own.

"O che nuovo stupor," the first of the three arie allegre, exemplifies their lessons. A Christmastide canzonetta by Buonarotti, its text articulates both wonder at Christ's birth and the speaker's desire to go visit the child and his mother.[32] For some in Francesca's immediate circle, the text may also have evoked Buonarroti's metrically identical secular canzonetta, "O che nuovo splendore," in which a girl's renewed ability to sing leads her to express desire and to run through fields of flowers toward the arms and kisses of her lover.[33] But for any seventeenth-century Florentine, either text was immediately recognizable as a parody of "O che nuovo miracolo," the final number of the intermedi for G. B. Bargagli's *La pellegrina*, which had celebrated Christine de Lorraine's marriage to Ferdinando I in 1589. "O che nuovo miracolo" had brought into temporary being onstage a golden age of song and dance to a newly composed tune that would later be known as the "aria del Gran Duca." Thus Francesca reflexively winks at the birth of a golden age for her pupil as the logical consequence of having overcome the cultural forces condensed into the lament and therefore having found a voice for her desire.

Francesca's aria for "O che nuovo stupor" enacts the wink by quoting the aria del Gran Duca in a way that emphasized its similarity to the ever-flexible romanesca (see example 7.11). Moving on to new material for the next three poetic lines, she closed each stanza with a differently ornamented, long-breathed romanesca consequent. It invited listeners to hear the ritornello's motivic basis in alternately partial and complete stepwise descents to a tonic *and* each subsequent stanza's opening reference to the aria del Gran Duca as allusions to the romanesca.[34]

Francesca does more than wink at her creation of a new aria from two bits of oral tradition. By impeccably aligning the romanesca-like phrases with the poetic lines through which her singer gives voice to first-person desire—"andiam" and so on in the refrain, "Io vò" and "Voglio" in the stanzas—she ensures that the musical novelty between the quoted phrases aligns with the objects of desire.

Having thus created an aria in which desire is a constant dynamic between subject and object, tradition and novelty, Francesca showed in each new stanza how supply her aria could respond to successive stanzas' elaborations of poetic themes. She focused on the interaction of ornament and declamatory rhythm by which her singer could enact the desires of which she spoke without disturbing the aria's strophic frame. Thus ornaments fill the accented syllables of such verbs as "andiam" or "cantar" with tonally directed, mimetic passaggi that, because they do what they say, constitute miniatures of musically performative speech. Ornaments to nouns and pronouns can both draw attention to the deictic level of speech and enact the singer's desire, as when a passaggio

Ex. 7.11. Francesca Caccini, *Il primo libro delle musiche* (1618), 43, "O che nuovo stupor," mm. 1–19, with allusions to the *romanesca* bass line of "O che nuovo miracolo" (*l'aria del granduca*) indicated

Oh, what new wonder, look around

At midnight [it seems like] day.

See the sky open, hear the sound

Of angelic choirs.

Come, let's go, let's look for Jesus, shepherds.

(continued)

Ex.7.11 (*Continued*)

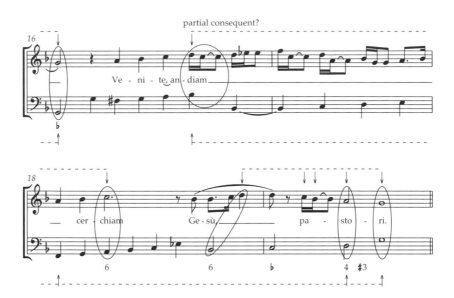

showers the pronoun that stands for the baby Jesus' feet with the hot breath of the speaker's sighs.[35]

More often, however, ornaments given to nouns shift the accent of a poetic line or prolong a word for emphasis. Francesca also lavished attention on the rhythmic function of phrases within stanzas and of stanzas within the strophic form. An unusually high density of ornamental or metrically shifting gestures distinguishes the fourth line of each stanza, as if in response to the third line's naming of a miraculous, intimate exchange between human and divine. Such accentual irregularities entirely pervade the third of the aria's four stanzas. The aria's structure of feeling remains intact, but its previous metrical patterns shatter as the singer's words break through clichés to imagine the object of her desire: her kisses warming a baby's bare, trembling feet. This is the crux of Francesca's "nuovo stupor"—a way of being and doing by which a woman's voice can express irreproachable, irrepressible, high-spirited desire. (Listen to track 5.)

An attentive pupil whose study had begun in earnest with "Ardo infelice" could not help but see in the set of arie allegre another "nuovo stupor." The set disentangles once and for all the vexed relationship expressed in "Ardo" between mollis and durus modes that share the tonic g, projecting them through separate arias—separate ways of being. The g-mollis shared by "O che nuovo stupor" and the Assumption aria "Giunto è'l dì" seems to be linked by these texts to female desire for closeness to the Virgin, her infant Son, and an imaginary drenched with fertility; the g-durus, via the Ascension text "Su le piume del vento," seems to be linked to the challenge of following in Christ's footsteps on a stony ascending path. This disentangling seems, in turn, prerequisite to confronting the lessons of the four romanescas that constitute the final set. In these lessons, Francesca first explores the implications of transposing romanescas, in relation to the construction of dramatic personae, and then shows how the full range of romanesca techniques, including transposition, could be used to move through new symbolic spaces that defied the rigidity of cultural rules. Separately and together, these lessons were crucial to knowing how not to fall back into either musical or allegorical anxiety of voice.

Changing Places

Once a basic skill for improvising musicians, transposing the romanesca required understanding how it could combine with the conventional ways of organizing musical sounds to communicate meaning, mode, and system. Francesca's "Io veggio i campi verdeggiar fecondi" (I see fertile fields turning green) and "La pastorella mia tra i fiori è il giglio" (My shepherdess is a lily among flowers) are the only published examples of transposed romanescas known to exist. Both demonstrate clearly that she understood the romanesca to be a tune (that is, a general melodic contour with its harmony), a rhythm, and a way of interpreting the world by means of the abstract principle of an antecedent-consequent dynamic. Transposed away from its conventional notation as a g-mollis song evoking some form of the transposed Dorian, the romanesca allowed the creation of distinctive ways of being that could be understood as allegories of virtual selves accommodating to changes of context. That, at least, is the allegory—the wink at her lesson—that Francesca's two examples encourage, for each was a song from a recent courtly entertainment, sung by a persona whose defining characteristic was being out of place.

"Io veggio," which originally opened the final number of *Il passatempo* on Carnival night in 1614, was sung by "a Syrian woman" who, as the first of a boatload of shipwrecked women to come ashore, reports on the local conditions.[36] At first recognizable only by the rhythm of the bass line, her romanesca signaled her foreignness most audibly by its transposition down a fourth, conferring authoritative gravity on her voice by its register and by the evocation of an authentic Dorian mode. As if following her gaze's sweep back and forth and back again across the landscape, her voice hovers around a′, extending the antecedent across three lines of poetry. Her melody and harmony explored the places where the romanesca tune and the conventional cadences of a mode on d aligned (the A in measure 6, the F in measure 8), coming to a conclusion about neither until each quatrain's fourth line fell happily through a romanesca consequent to the conclusion in d that she had made her listeners desire (see example 7.12).

"La pastorella mia" had originated in the 1611 rustic comedy *La Tancia*.[37]

Ex. 7.12. Francesca Caccini, *Il primo libro delle musiche* (1618), 56, " Io veggio campi verdeggiar fecondi," mm. 1–11

I see fertile fields turning green

And flowering banks, hills all around

And trees heavy with apples and leaves

And a beach adorned with an infinity of villas.

There it was the defining song of Pietro, a Florentine gentleman in love with the countryside and the songs of a peasant girl he encounters near Fiesole. Marked in previous scenes as a possible singer by his ubiquitous chitarrone, his critique of the peasant girl's surprisingly artful singing, and his vain pretensions to the elite but archaic tradition of improvised singing of *strambotti*, in act 2, scene 5, Pietro burst spontaneously into this song to exult in his imagined triumph of love. He had taken the peasant girl whose singing so pleased him by bribing her father to force their marriage. "Improvising" to his trusty chitarrone, he sang a parody of Jacopo Sannazaro's "La pastorella mia, dispietata e rigida" to praise rather than condemn his peasant girl: unlike Sannazaro's rigid and dismissive girl, Pietro's shepherdess was a lily, a fragrant rose, a ruby, and a goddess of love. Choosing to sing the romanesca in a g-durus mode that can be taken for Hypomixolydian, Pietro stumbled into a confrontation with the most daunting transposition of the romanesca, the awkward shift of an aria whose natural tune is mollis into a durus tonal world.[38]

At first his romanesca was, like the Syrian woman's, identifiable only by its characteristic rhythm. Laughably combined with a melody that began by quoting the eighth psalm tone instead of the romanesca tune, the song's first phrase marked Pietro as a musical *pasticcione*—a bungler whose errors come from the ill-considered mixing of motley elements. Yet the psalm tone shared with the romanesca both an antecedent-consequent structure and an eventual descent from the fifth to the first scale degree. Over the course of four couplets of gradually expanding range and increasingly inspired ornaments, Pietro found a way to develop a more or less Hypomixolydian melody from his psalm tone and to create a song in which the mode's conventional cadences mesh with the romanesca's rhythm, phrase structure, and final d to g melodic descent. As good a lesson in the technical problems of transposing romanescas as it was an irretrievably awkward comic song, on stage "La pastorella mia" was received by Pietro's listeners with shrieks and hands clasped to ears, a sign in song that Pietro, like his romanesca, remained out of place and that his shepherd girl, La Tancia, would not in the end be his.[39]

Doing as Being

With the last two romanescas of her book, Francesca backed away from the theatrical directness of "Io veggio" and "La pastorella mia" and returned to the idea of song that had motivated the failed efforts of Clizia: the idea that singing could be an action by which a person might so move the very humors of her listeners as to change them. Demonstrating how a performer might do things with song to change others' ways of being (as well as her own), Francesca taught her pupils vocality as an instrument of power.

Her first example, "Rendi alle mie speranze il verde e i fiori" (Restore to my hopes green leaves and flowers), gives voice to a lover's plea that Amor reverse his/her misfortune with a romanesca that is all restless, excitable doing.[40] The lover's voice strains to reverse the romanesca's descent from the middle of the first line, while the lover's hands "fall" through harmonies that move backward through the circle of fifths to exaggerate the aria's mollis side (Bb–Eb, then C–F–Bb) and support the voice's postponement, until the middle of the poem's second line, of an unadorned romanesca descent that his words link to the "rigid and severe" austerity that has crushed the lover's hopes of spring (see example 7.13, measures 1–7). As the lover repeats the line the ornaments contradict the words and the severity of the pattern that they name, staging an almost compulsive resistance to the two disciplines that might dictate the terms of a song: the claims of text and the conventions of a preexisting aria.

Although in the next couplet the lover asks Amor to dispel sighs and tears, the very terms of silenced self-expression on which Clizia had fecklessly relied, a long passaggio begins the work even before the lover gets to the multiply stated, multiply ornamented imperative "disgombra omai" (dispel now). Singing the imperative three times, each time with longer and more elaborate passaggi, the lover enacts the desired affective change by prodigious breath control, by control of musical time with a long passaggio to emphasize the word "omai" (now), and by staging, through the presence of e-flats in the voice's scalewise runs, a melodic trace of the tonally backwards motion toward the double mollis system in the song's opening line (see example 7.13, measures 11–17). Continuing to perform with the voice the actions asked of others, the lover twice breaks the word "frangi" (break), first filling it with a passaggio so long that the word loses intelligibility and then breaking the passaggio itself, insinuating, in the voice's suddenly articulated descent from a g to the phrase's cadential c, the possibility that the intransigent pattern of the romanesca has been broken by transposition (see example 7.13, measures 19–20). In the end, however, finally singing not resistance to others' patterns but the desire to see pity in the beloved's eyes, the lover creates the sound of that pity in a passaggio as spectacular for its precise tonal enactment of the change sought as for its display of breath control. (Listen to track 6.)

In "Rendi alle mie speranze" the singer's voice enacts resistance to the potential constraints of both too-literal service to the word and too literal a performance of the romanesca. S/he resists each in its own terms, enacting the poem's desire by breaking its words asunder with ornaments and breaking out of the romanesca's rigidity by constant ornamenting that both hints at internal transposition and brings the aria's pitch pattern in and out of phase with its characteristic rhythm. A pupil could learn from this song an ingenious extension of a lesson that Francesca could have learned from the examples of

Ex. 7.13. Francesca Caccini, *Il primo libro delle musiche* (1618), 62–64, "Rendi alle mie speranze il verdi," entire

> Restore to my hopes the green leaves and flowers
> That scorn, rigid and severe, took away,
> And [all] sighs, tears, and sorrows
> Dispel now from my sad thought.
> You who break hard hearts in their chests,
> Move the proud heart of my lady.
> Love, [you] who conquers all and can do all,
> Let me see mercy in her eyes.

Ex.7.13. (*Continued*)

(*continued*)

Ex.7.13. (*Continued*)

(*continued*)

Ex.7.13. (*Continued*)

ornamentation in her father's *Le nuove musiche:* the subversive principle of obedient disobedience. Here the effect of doubly obedient disobedience opens a
space built of doubly sustained contradiction, a space filled not so much with
words or musical form as with a singer seizing the power to change others by
displaying mastery of her own body and will.

In her book's final romanesca, "Dove io credea le mie speranze vere" (Where
I believed my hopes to be true), Francesca invited her pupil to revisit the figure of Arianna as Monteverdi and Rinuccini had so powerfully created her and
to perform that figure in dynamic tension with the Arianna that Ovid and his
sixteenth-century commentator Giovanni Anguillara had caused early modern
culture to forget. This Arianna is not the helpless and abandoned woman
weeping at the water's edge but the thinking woman who had daily crossed the
threshold of Daedalus's labyrinth to navigate the subterranean perils of forbidden desire with the simplest attribute of virtuous womanhood, a thread. Constructing this Arianna's labyrinthine reflections on her fate as a refrain aria that,
like "Lasciatemi qui solo," parodies the Monteverdi-Rinuccini text, Francesca
used the infinitely malleable, transposable romanesca as the means by which a
musical Arianna could navigate the apparent contradictions of womanhood, to
give pensive, unlamenting, and unchastised voice to her experience.

Francesca evoked Monteverdi's Arianna powerfully by means of a text developed from the last three lines of the lament as it circulated in the early seventeenth century. In these lines, Arianna invited others to see her suffering
as an emblem warning others not to "love and trust too much"—that is, not
to choose their sexual partners but to accept the choice of husband that their
families made for them.[41]

Mirate di che duol m'han fatto erede	See the sorrow of which I have been made heir
L'amor mio, la mia fede e l'altrui inganno	By my love, my trust, and another's lie.
Così va chi troppo ama e troppo crede.	So it goes [for one] who loves and trusts too much.[42]

Quoting those lines in a different order as a third stanza, the anonymous poet of "Dove io credea" had spun another song around it, each stanza drawing a slightly different conclusion about the causes of Arianna's fate, and each connected to the Rinuccini by its final line, sung twice as a refrain to all stanzas:

> Dove io credea le mie speranze vere,
> Io vi trovai smarrita più la fede:
> > Così va chi troppo ama e troppo crede
> > Così va chi troppo ama e troppo crede.
> Il cor sincero che con fede amava,
> Senza speme tradito al fin si vede:
> > Così va . . .
> Il mio amor, la mia fede, e l'altrui inganno
> D'un infinito duol m'han fatto erede:
> > Così va . . .
> Lasso, ch'io pur m'accorgo et ard'il veggio
> Che fede non puo dar chi non ha fede:
> > Così va . . . [43]

To tie her pupil's song loosely to Monteverdi's setting of the whole lament, Francesca set each second statement of the refrain "Così va" to a melody that seems to graft the rising half of his lament's most memorable outcry to the descent and bass line of the consequent of a romanesca. Far more than the tantalizing allusion to Monteverdi's phrase, however, Francesca's repeated quotation of the romanesca's consequent for the conclusion both emphasizes its moralizing, objectifying effect and casts the romanesca itself as an emblem of conventionality. In subsequent stanzas the singer of "Dove io" subjects the refrain to ever more extravagant ornamentation, performing the word "troppo" with an excess that is simultaneously funny and defiant. Her ornamental excess, produced by her control of her breath and her body's heat, both resists the rigid judgment of the moral and performs symbolically the very excess against which it was meant to have warned: a woman's excessively realized desire to be padrona of her own will (see example 7.14).

The nonrefrain sections of this strophic aria seem at first to be based only loosely on the romanesca's characteristic gestures. Performers and listeners alike seek in vain the bass line or the dancing rhythm by which Francesca's earlier experiments with romanescas could be deciphered. Even the use of antecedent and consequent that governs the flow of ideas in each stanza's couplet seems garbled by a cadence pattern that creates and satisfies a tonal desire for F that can seem extraneous to the obvious g-mollis romanesca refrain. Yet the

Ex. 7.14. Francesca Caccini, *Il primo libro delle musiche* (1618), 65–68, "Dov'io credea le mie speranze vere," each of the four refrains, mm. 7–8, 15–16, 23–24, and 32–34

So it goes for one who too much loves and too much trusts.

stanza's opening gesture, rising to arrive at an accented d″ on the first line's poetic caesura and then beginning a stepwise descent toward g′, so strongly evokes the romanesca as to make all that intervenes before the final refrain's explicit romanesca seem to be framed by the aria (see example 7.15). Across the song's four stanzas, the romanesca frame implies a strong causal link between

Arianna's credulity, her sincerity, her love, her sighing outburst "Lasso," and the moral condemnation articulated by the final, ever-more excessive refrain: in g-mollis, she can seem to be the helpless, sexualized Arianna of lament.

As if set off in parentheses, three intervening phrases mark with perfect authentic cadences to F, its dominant C, and F the singer's unequivocal definition of F as an alternative tonal space within the g-mollis romanesca frame (see example 7.15). Within that space Arianna considers the causes of her predicament somewhat differently than the g framework implies. It is from the tonal space centered on F that she "dares to see," in the fourth stanza, that her predicament results as much from Teseo's untrustworthiness as from her womanish vulnerability to his lies. Within that space, too, it is easy to see, to perform, and to hear the unadorned descent from c″ to f′ of the first refrain as a transposition of the romanesca aria in its most severe form. And it is almost equally easy to see, to perform, and to hear the descent from d″ in the stanza's first phrase as

Ex. 7.15. Francesca Caccini, *Il primo libro delle musiche* (1618), 65, "Dov'io credea," mm. 1–8
Where I believed my hopes [to be] true
There I found my trust most damaged.

having slipped past its apparent goal of g′ into an F-centered world. A singer and her listeners can experience themselves as deceived by that first phrase's slide, learning its consequences just a little late, and can imagine vividly how Arianna, with her onestà, could have been betrayed by someone for whom onestà was not a value. Tricked along with her into an F-centered world, we can identify with her starkly chaste envoicing of the refrain (see example 7.15).

Repeated with equal austerity in each of the four stanzas, this chaste yet unafraid conclusion, articulated through the romanesca transposed to F, complements and complicates the self-disciplined sensual excesses of the refrain on g. Francesca may have meant her song's internal play with the romanesca on F to tap a distinctly nonexcitable valence of the aria. Jeanice Brooks has shown that in the courtly world of Catherine de' Medici, where Christine de Lorraine was raised, the romanesca could evoke an aura of widowish, chaste constancy.[44] By singing Rinuccini's moralizing conclusion twice, as a romanesca at two different pitch levels, Francesca's pupil thus could perform two kinds of womanhood at once: in F she sings the experience, the reasoning, and the conclusions of an Arianna who faces the chastening consequences of her own excessive onestà, and in g she sings an Arianna whose increasingly extravagant ornaments reclaim her right to control her own body and who resists thereby the force of the Rinuccini refrain to silence and contain female sexuality. In the constant excesses of her g-centered refrain and the excessive constancy with which she repeats Rinuccini's words, Francesca's Arianna shows her greatest fidelity to be to the work of giving voice to the relationship between her own complicated experience of womanhood and the conventional emblem of womanhood that was Rinuccini's moral.

This is because the moment of Arianna's deception, her romanesca antecedent's slide past g′ to f′, becomes in strophic repetition an opportunity to reflect on and eventually understand her situation. By her retreat from the aria's g-centered surface to the unexpected tonal space of F, Francesca's Arianna creates in sound a representation of interiority where her thoughts can seem to unfold in private autonomy. Furthermore, because listeners expecting her to sing a straightforward, tonally stable romanesca will find her articulation of a completely separate space difficult to follow and comprehend, Arianna's retreat to F can seem to protect the borders of her interiority and thus protect the privacy of her thought. In this hearing, Arianna's retreat from immediate intelligibility in terms of convention performs her psychic and affective continenza. Yet Francesca's Arianna is neither unintelligible nor silenced by her performative retreat into virtuous continenza. She always returns to the g-centered surface of her song. There she can seem to express the conclusions drawn during her retreats into F-centered, virtuously private thought by her increasingly defiant insistence on transforming Rinuccini's moralizing words into an emblem of vocal excess intelligible to her contemporaries as sexual and singerly self-control. Singing her thoughts' journey from depth to surface, surface to depth, in a constant cycle of doing and being, this Arianna brings a complicated, expressive, dynamic self into being while she brings into being as song, with the exaggerated passaggio on "troppo," a final, oppositional hint that belief in Rinuccini's moral might constitute the most dangerous excess of all.

Thus with the Arianna of "Dove io credea" Francesca invited her female pupil to encompass the contradiction between virtue and vocality—that is, between the need to preserve her continenza and the desire to reveal her self in speech or song—on which the paralyzed Clizia of "Ardo infelice" had foundered. Rather than obeying either imperative, rather than trying to ignore the contradiction, Francesca's aria for Arianna articulated both parts of the contradiction clearly and showed her pupil how to trace a path between them in terms of a single musical thread. Inner experience and its outward expression are made of the same bits of cultural convention. This song teaches that the key to self-expression lies in organizing those bits in ways that represent one's inner world to an outer one. But precisely because both her song's surface and its depths were so overtly constructed of the same bits, the performative gestures that constituted the romanesca thread, the voice of Francesca's Arianna could not be taken for anything other than a product of artifice. It was an aria like any other, made of conventional gestures that a skilled singer or composer could combine conventionally or not as might suit her will—the musical equivalent of a self-made mask. Thus in the end Caccini's resolution for her own and her female pupils' anxiety of voice lay in an affirmation of artifice. By ensuring that a woman's performance of the gestures of desire could never be mistaken for desire itself, the systematic affirmation of artifice as the means of womanhood's vocality preserved the boundary of every woman's innerness. Artifice was the *technē* of a music-making woman's continenza, while the ingenious recombinative play with which she fused ways of doing into ways of being was its poiesis, bringing forth an almost infinite range of voices that could serve as her own.

After Arianna

8

The aria "Dove io credea" closed the first half of Francesca's *Primo libro delle musiche* in the poetic voice of Arianna. Like Arianna, a pupil who had reached this point in the book had found her voice. Moreover, she knew how to craft her own ways of being in the world from the simplest materials of her culture, how to navigate between different levels of reality, and how to encompass contradictions rather than trying to resolve them. But her training was not finished. This chapter traces the lessons of Francesca's book after her rehabilitation of Arianna for her pupils.

Francesca presents two repertoires that are pertinent to the work of an improvising singer at court. A set of Latin songs of praise prepares her to participate either in the devotional singing that dame, donne and professionals offered in the princely family's private chapels or in the often elaborate singing from behind the grate for which several of Tuscany's elite monasterii di monache were known. A set of sexually knowing canzonette prepares her to improvise the songful delivery of fashionable love poetry or to learn quickly the canzonetta-based dance songs from which most of the court's theatrical entertainments were made.

At first glance, these repertoires seem very different. Yet their texts share the increasingly self-assured affect that pervaded the book after "Lasciatemi qui solo" and an impersonal, even formulaic poetic tone. Francesca set such texts to music that is clever, beautiful, ecstatic, even sexy. Although they are the most stylistically modern pieces in her book, these songs are never quite what musicians today would describe as "expressive." She eschews entirely the dissonance, the harmonic, tonal, and rhythmic disorder, and the sense of hopeless struggle that to us connote the expression of inner truth and in her time connoted women's traditional work of pain. Thus the Latin songs and the canzonette follow logically from her book's rejection of the work of pain, best instantiated in her Arianna's embrace of artifice instead of unmediated expressivity. Moreover, the apparent binary opposition between these most spiritual and most sexual repertoires instantiates a paradox embodied by Arianna. The clever but too-trusting (or too eager?) lover of a fickle man, her singing caused her to be loved by a god; she accepted from Bacchus's hands a crown visible to humans as the constellation Virgo.[1] In the second half of her book, then, Francesca invited her pupils to embrace the rehabilitated Arianna's condition and to learn to perform her sensibility as music. Premised musically on high spirits, self-possession, and the use of artifice to preserve continenza, this sensibility resonated with the aesthetic of early Baroque courtly life and with the practices of the women at Christine de Lorraine's court, for whom piety and pastime were interchangeable.

Although not quite interchangeable, the Latin songs and canzonette are linked by two preoccupations. Respectively the least and the most obviously word-dominated repertoires in her book, both sets engage the problem of rehabilitating music (and therefore musicians) from the subservience to text that her father and his mentors had advocated.[2] And almost all create structures of being, however large or small, that seem deliberately to sustain rather than resolve contradictions. The Latin set explores the relations between a word's meaning and sound, between a recitative vocality and a metrically marked one reminiscent of instrumental music and dance, and between the vocalized "speech" of a singer's voice and the contribution that her hands' instrumental music made to meaning. The canzonette add exploration of duet textures, refrain forms, explicit contradiction between semantic meaning and musical gesture, contrasts between major and minor modes, and the relation of poetic meters to musical rhythms.

Because none of these binary pairs are gendered, the songs in this half of the book can seem opaque to feminist interpretation. Not overtly concerned with womanhood, the Latin examples in particular invite consideration, instead, as lessons in how to evade the culture of word-dominated song, to create songs that celebrate the music itself. Yet the very elision of a musical escape from language's domination and a textual escape from all reference to womanhood suggests that the two escapes might have been related. The Latin set's systematic projection of music's equality with language can seem to assert the equality of the feminized term in early modern metaphors prescribing that in song the music should obey the words as a servant does her master, the body does the mind, and so forth. But such an interpretation needs to be balanced by a recognition that the Latin songs' textual escape from gender trouble might have been part of the point for Francesca and for her pupils. As their frequent retreats to the homosociality of convents enabled courtly women to escape the pressures of a womanhood premised on compulsory heterosexuality, so these motets and hymns may have allowed Francesca's pupils to escape the insistent sexualizing of passaggiato singing and, by extension, of all music that could seem independent of language. In Latin, the language of spiritual and scholarly retreat, they could practice extravagantly melismatic singing and call it ecstasy, and they could learn how applying the most basic principle of rhetoric—development by a figure of repetition—might transform musical sound into a discourse parallel and equal to language. Such lessons prepared them to confront the return of domination by the word in canzonette whose texts explicitly linked the relation between word and music to the contradictions of sexual love.

"Laudate . . . Alleluia" and the Silent Speech of the Hand

Francesca opened the set of Latin-language songs with a psalm-motet.[3] It is curious that she did not choose Psalm 149, "Cantate Dominum canticum novum," the psalm that most directly commands praise of the Lord in new songs.[4] Instead, she chose Psalm 150, which commands that the Lord be praised with instrumental music of every sort: "Praise the Lord . . . with the sound of trumpets / . . . with psaltery and kithara / . . . with drum and dance." It commands, that is, that praise be offered in a music governed by its own principles, rather than by the principles that govern human language. Francesca's choice implies that the lessons of the set will reexamine the subservience of music to language that was so cherished in the official aesthetic of her time and that those lessons will show how music might communicate and develop ideas on its own terms. In the four motets that follow, Francesca's emphasis on extravagantly passaggiato singing and on matters of musical rhetoric make music and language into parallel discourses, responsive to each other and to a larger motivating idea.[5] These parallel discourses converge in the two hymns that end the set, culminating in a deceptively simple setting of "Jesu corona virginum" that is so musically patterned that its music and words are inseparably fixed in a listener's or performer's heart.

Three things catch the eye of a singer reading through Francesca's setting of "Laudate Dominum." First, the richly ornamented, constantly varied phrases promise ample occasion to practice passaggiato singing (see example 8.1a). Second, the exuberant melodic inventiveness of each phrase is balanced by motivic economy, as ten of fourteen phrases begin with one of two head motives that

Ex. 8.1. Francesca Caccini, *Il primo libro delle musiche* (1618), 69–71, "Laudate Dominum"

(a) Measures 1–11

Praise the Lord in his sanctuary,

Praise him in the firmament of his power,

Praise him for his mighty acts,

Praise him according to the multitude of his greatness.

(b) head motives

(c) Measures 35–43

Alleluia.

set the insistently repeated imperative "Laudate" (see example 8.1b). Third, instead of the expected doxology, a six-fold, triple-meter "Alleluia" based on new melodic material concludes the psalm (see example 8.1c). It is easy to see the motet as responding to the psalm's verbal command to praise the Lord with proliferating music that culminates in the ecstatic vocalization of "Alleluia"—a

Ex. 8.1. (*Continued*)

singer's ultimate obedient response to the command to praise him with *sound*, with music itself.

But as soon as a singer's hands reach for an instrument to perform "reading" by other means, three additional features of the motet become palpable. First, her hands articulate the motet's g-mollis tonality, much more crisply than does her voice. After a static oscillation between tonic and dominant in the first measure, her bass line sounds the entire ambitus of g-Dorian at measures 3–4. The cadence points of B♭, F, d, and g that she articulates for the first two verses of the psalm (measures 1–11), perfectly establish the mode at the outset, and the cadences on d, B♭, and g reconfirm it after a middle section that explores different corners of musical space.[6] Second, the performer knows more fully through her hands than through her voice that Francesca's tonal choices imposed a musical A-B-A′ form on the conceptually strophic form of the psalm's six antecedent-consequent sentences. Thus the performer realizes a reading of the psalm as *exordium* (verses 1–2, measures 1–11), *narratio* (verses 3–6, measures 12–40), and *peroratio* ("Alleluia," measures 41–48). That reading, in turn, emphasizes the performer's sense that the semantically vacant alleluia section is her most profound response to the psalm's command and her sense that the motet's midsection is necessary to the emergence of her voice's wordless praise. Third, only when the performer reads the motet with hands and voice together can she realize that in the *narratio* the bass line echoes the motive to which her voice most often sings "Laudate." The sound of the imperative to praise the Lord in music has always already been the music it commands (see example 8.2).

Serving as an exordium to the Latin set, "Laudate Dominum" instantiates its lessons. Practice in melismatic singing that does little to interpret or enact the meaning of individual words is justified as obedience to a celestial command. At the same time, the harmonic work of the pupil's hands articulates a musical design that complements the psalm's form and therefore enriches the expressive effect of the whole. The motivic interaction of voice and hands, seeming to develop the idea "Laudate Dominum" by figures of repetition, shows how easily meaning can cross the border between words and music.[7]

These lessons are reinforced in the second motet, a setting of the first antiphon sung at Lauds on Easter morning, "Haec dies."[8] To sing Francesca's "Haec dies" is to move from stammering repetition of the antiphon's first words ("this is the day") through the gradual emergence the declarative response ("this is the day / this is the day the Lord has made / this is the day the Lord had made, we will rejoice and be glad in it"). Each phrase feels like new, increasingly luxuriant growth emerging from the motive of an ascending third to which the opening words are first sung, creating a phrase rhythm of gradually rising intensity. Midway through the motet, the accumulating musical energy with which the singer fills the words bursts free of ordinary language in a set

Ex. 8.2. Francesca Caccini, *Il primo libro delle musiche* (1618), 69–71, "Laudate Dominum"

   (a) Measures 14–15

     Praise him [with lyre].

   (b) Measures 17–18

     Praise him with timbrel and choral dance.

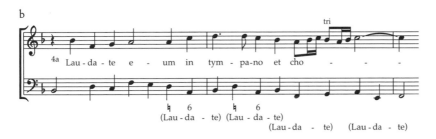

of melismatic, syncopated, triple-meter alleluias notated so as to challenge any singer's need for breath (see example 8.3).[9] Though they may seem to be free of ordinary language, these breathless alleluias also grow from the initial rising third. As that third generates the new melody of the alleluias and echoes (as the memory of its words) throughout the bass line, the third's rising impulse overtakes the alleluia's harmony, as well. Complementing this string of alleluias, the performer's hands articulate cadences that rise through the circle of fifths (B♭–F–C–g). (Listen to track 7.)

    In this first set of alleluias, then, the rising implicit in the sung words "Haec dies" has utterly filled the performer and the audible world that is the motet. But, of course, these words respond to Christ's resurrection. To perform these alleluias is to dramatize a gradually dawning, ecstatic awareness of the resurrection that exceeds any merely verbal response. Indeed, after the alleluias the musical phrases for "exultemus" (we will rejoice) and "letemur in ea" (we will be glad in it) become interchangeable; like the alleluias, they seem ecstatic, not semantic, elements of a musical design that shows the relationship of ideas without depending on language. Made present in the realized musical implications of the opening rising third, the unspoken miracle of the resurrection can seem to have made the independence of music and words dissolve.

    The motet that follows, a setting of the Marian antiphon for Eastertide, "Regina caeli laetare," asks the pupil to confront the relationship between words and music in terms of a text that interrupts the greeting-praise-petition

Ex. 8.3. Francesca Caccini, *Il primo libro delle musiche* (1618), 72, "Haec dies," mm. 1–12
　　This is the day the Lord has made.
　　Let us rejoice and be glad.

formula of ordinary prayer with recurrent alleluias.[10] Responding straightforwardly to the text's formal prompt, Francesca created a through-composed motet that requires the performer to switch rapidly between passaggiato recitative for the semantically rich words of ordinary prayer and the strongly metrical, dance-like style, already synonymous with the word it sets, for the alleluias (see example 8.4).[11] The rapid switching challenges the performer to make an aurally coherent whole—in effect, to mediate between vocalities that in the previous motets stood for linguistic and supralinguistic responses to divinity. If

Ex. 8.4. Francesca Caccini, *Il primo libro delle musiche* (1618), 74, "Regina Caeli laetare,"
mm. 1–6.

Queen of Heaven, rejoice, alleluia.

she succeeds, she can imagine that she has performed this praise song as an imitation of the Virgin's most miraculous attribute: her ability to mediate, in her body, between human and divine.

The harmonies Francesca conceived for her performer's hands ease the transition from one vocality to another. Each recitative statement ends above an inconclusive first-inversion chord that functions as a dominant to the first chord of the alleluia phrase that follows it. Thus the linguistic and the supralinguistic are in equilibrium, bound together in something like a cause-and-effect dynamic in which the supralinguistic provides closure and stability. Francesca exploits the dynamic between vocalities further by harmonizing the recitative phrases that address the Virgin so that they explore different areas of the motet's mode, implying cadences that are always confirmed by the responding alleluia. The result adumbrates something like a ritornello form in which the language-driven recitative phrases function as episodes whose tonal explorations are stabilized by ritornellos on "alleluia" (see table 8.1).[12]

Although the set of Latin songs seems, as a whole, to evade issues of gender, "Regina caeli laetare" invites comparison with Marian songs that appeared earlier in the book (especially "Chi è costei?" and "Maria dolce Maria"). In all three, Francesca used the figure of the Virgin as the pretext for a study in chaste musical motion and equilibrium.[13] In "Regina caeli laetare," the Virgin figured as queen of heaven is the pretext, too, for a concept of gynocentric vocality that mediates between feminine mutability in its recitative phrases and, in the ritornello function of its ever-changing alleluias, a stability that Francesca's culture associated with the masculine. Moreover, the queen of heaven prompts a praise song in which words and music complement each other in the production of meaning, for the motet's words allow the attribution of specific meanings to

Table 8.1. Harmonic motion of "Regina Caeli laetare"

Latin text	Tonal motion	English translation
Regina Caeli laetare	F → C6	Queen of heaven, rejoice,
Alleluia, alleluia, alleluia	g → Bb	
Quia quem meruisi portare	Bb → D6	For he whom you were worthy to bear
Alleluia, alleluia, alleluia	g → g	
Resurrexit, resurrexit sicut dixit.	g → G	Has risen, has risen as he said.
Alleluia, alleluia, alleluia.	C → F	
Ora pro nobis Deum.	F → A	Pray for us to God.
Alleluia, alleluia, alleluia.	a → F	

the regions of the F-mollis tonal world to which the recitative phrases point. The singer praises the Virgin in B♭; she addresses her as worthy to bear her Son in g, a sound world that mention of his resurrection miraculously lifts to G; and she prays that the Virgin intercede with God the Father in a music that reaches, with a Phrygian cadence on A, the brightest, most sharp-feeling limit of her mollis world. Without the music's clearly articulated tonal motion these would have seemed more like attributes of the Virgin than like distinct places within the queen of heaven's relational world. The mediating queen of heaven, and the song that her presence prompts, thus hold words and music, stability and change, semantic and ecstatic expression in equilibrium. Like her secular counterpart Arianna, she enables contradictions to be sustained.

Read by themselves, the texts of the final two motets can seem semantically empty. "Adorate Dominum" combines a liturgical respond's succinct command that angels move beyond praise to adopt the affect of adoration with a psalm verse often sung as part of an antiphon for Matins on Christmas. The text of "Beate Sebastiane" alludes to none of Saint Sebastian's attributes—not even, explicitly, the presumably apposite miracle by which he restored the mute Zoë to her voice.[14] Instead of commanding specific musical responses to their words, these motet texts depend on ideas introduced and developed in Francesca's music for their meaning.

"Adorate Dominum" is a showpiece of passaggiato singing. Like "Regina caeli laetare," it requires a singer to switch rapidly from ornamented recitative to alleluia refrains.[15] More strikingly, the motet is a lesson exploring the many different ways in which a wholly nonverbal idea can be developed. As every phrase of "Laudate Dominum" had derived from one or the other of the motives with which the singer uttered its command, every phrase of "Adorate Dominum" derives in some way from the bass line beneath the command sung in its opening measures. Treated as a head motive, the bass line is easy to track as it is shortened, lengthened, ornamented, reharmonized, and transposed beneath the rich variety of the vocal line (see example 8.5).

For a listener, the result is a sense that a coherent but nonlinear sound world is constantly regenerating, created from phrases that are elusively reminiscent of each other and of their common source. For a performer, the motet is an exhilarating challenge that requires total concentration on the proliferating variations and combinations of variations that she must produce with hands and voice. In forcing that intensity of concentration, Francesca's music for "Adorate Dominum" could induce in the performer one of the states of consciousness that characterize a mystic's ecstasy. It would thereby induce the affect that the words command.

"Beate Sebastiane" requires even more concentration on the part of a performer, for its highly ornamented vocal line is accompanied by a bass line and a harmonic rhythm that are in rapid perpetual motion. The curiously unprayerful text seems to point with a winking slyness otherwise absent from the Latin set to this motet's principal lesson: how best to solve voice-leading problems posed by the cross-relation caused when major triads whose roots are a third apart sound one after the other. First played beneath the sustained final syllable of her text's address to the saint in measure 2, the cross-relation in the bass is made to seem as if it had knocked the singer's (or the saint's) verbal rhythm askew. As the text reminds Sebastian that "you have known justice" (cognovit iustitiam) in measure 3, the performer's vocal line recovers cheery equilibrium while her knowing, correct hands avoid a cross-relation that might seem to be implied by the continuo figures. Evoking, after all, Jacobus de Voragine's description of the mute Zoë's plea to Sebastian "by the signs of her hands," the performer's hands execute five more solutions to the cross-relation, associated with the words "you have seen great wonders" (et vidit mirabilia magna) and "you have persuaded" (et exoravit) (see example 8.6).

Here, the text can seem to serve the musical interests of teacher and performer alike: these phrases function as mnemonic devices for ways in which the musical phoneme of the cross-relation was conventionally used to serve language. Moreover, as in "Haec dies," Francesca's music speaks a part of the scene that is not articulated in language. Most important, perhaps, Francesca both frees and gives explicit meaning to the speech of a pupil's hands. Thus she addresses, once and for all, a lingering problem posed by the recitative soliloquy "Ardo infelice," whose speaker sought in tears, sighs, and breathlessness a way for her body to speak the desire she dared not voice. "Beate Sebastiane" teaches how a potentially tongue-tied Clizia might, like Zoë, communicate well by the signs of her hands.

Ex. 8.5. Francesca Caccini, *Il primo libro delle musiche* (1618), 76–77, "Adorate Dominum," with variants of the head motive marked

    (a) Measures 1–7

        Adore the Lord.

    (b) Measures 9–19

        The Lord has made known his salvation.

Ex. 8.6. Francesca Caccini, *Il primo libro delle musiche* (1618), 78, "Beate Sebastiane," mm. 1–12

Blessed Sebastian, you have known justice

And have seen great wonders

And have persuaded.

Indeed, "Beate Sebastiane" emphasizes how important the performer's hands have been all along. Throughout Francesca's book, the performer's hands have supported the liberation of her physical voice, and they have been the instruments of her emerging compositional voice, articulating formal and tonal relations, developing motives in ways that added meanings beyond those that servile obedience to language could provide. Although the five motets have offered the performer ample opportunities for passaggiato singing, none of the motets has taught new vocal techniques. Instead, the motets have been primarily lessons in composition, ways of developing ideas in sound rather than speech. They have therefore all directed a pupil's attention to her hands. Francesca's interest in teaching her performer's hands to speak resonates with Bronzini's surprising emphasis on the instrumental performance, and specifically the "learned hands" and "silent speech of the hands" of the women musicians whose achievements he catalogues. By rehabilitating the hand as an organ of respectable female musicality, Bronzini and Francesca alike evade the reduction of female musicality to the easily sexualized throat. In so doing, both evoked the Aristotelian and Galenic understanding of the hand as the body part most strongly associated with reason—the part that in "its difficulty and beauty . . . reveals God's intentions as no other part can."[16] The hand, then, could function as an instrument of reason in a way that a singer's throat, when ecstatic passaggi denied it speech, could not.

Only in the motets' ecstatic alleluias could a pupil's physical voice be as free from the rule of language as her hands, most often when her hands "spoke" harmonic or motivic reminiscences of the words to which her alleluias respond. In the set's concluding hymns, "Te lucis ante terminum" and "Jesu corona virginum," the contributions of voice and hands, semantic language and ecstasy, recitative and regularly phrased, dance-like song converge.

Both hymns are homophonic, largely homorhythmic settings of freely composed melodies whose triple meter, regular phrases and eruptions of passaggiato singing could not but remind a pupil of the alleluia style in the previous motets. Thus the hymns function as do those motets' concluding alleluias, as examples of ecstatic song that respond to the psalmist's command and that are now, miraculously, filled with language. Because Francesca chose not to allude to the plainchant melodies associated with these hymns, each shows clearly how the figures of repetition used in the motets could be used to create melodies of far greater motivic economy than can any of the freely composed arias she had presented earlier in her book. Moreover, both hymn melodies scrupulously respond to their texts' shared meter, iambic dimeter. The longest accent comes on the fourth syllable of eight, usually as the result of a vocal ornament that may or may not have any relation to the meaning of the word.[17] In these hymns, Francesca's music responds to the metrical, not the semantic, qualities of the poets' language.

Similar though they be, the two hymns exemplify opposite approaches to the homophonic, homorhythmic texture that could seem to figure an equality of voice and hands or of linguistic and harmonic or tonal discourses in song. Thus, the hymns function as a double peroration, ensuring that the Latin set avoids seeming to resolve any binary opposites. In "Te lucis" the voice and the bass line move almost entirely in parallel motion, except for the lines of the hymn that ask for God's protection and for safety from bodily pollution. It is as if contrary motion between the hands and the voice were dangerous to unanimity of expression. "Jesu corona virginum" confronts that danger, for contrary motion governs the relationship between hands and voice in almost every phrase. But their contrariness is more than a matter of texture: while the performer sings the words to a melody that is little more than a rhythmically animated articulation of the ambitus and cadence points of the Dorian mode, her hands navigate a d-centered tonal world via transpositions of the romanesca's bass or root movement by fifths to produce highly goal-directed phrases. The resulting play of contraries produces a hymn whose melody is modal while its harmonies seem tonal, a crowning glory of sustained contradiction that, like the Jesus to whom it is addressed, partakes of two natures at once.

Reading for Rhythm, Reading for Love: Francesca's Canzonette

The first line of the opening canzonetta, "S'io men vò, morirò" (If I leave, I shall die) contradicts any reader's sense that either hymn could have ended her journey. Indeed, both hymns foreground the convergence of words and music through the shared element in which their capacities most resemble each other: rhythm. The relation of verbal and musical rhythms is the pedagogical focus of the ten canzonette with which the book concludes. Arranged so as to present a systematic introduction to the problems of reading in improvised song the metrical rhythms of fashionable love poetry, these canzonette also critique the assumption of an imbalance of power between lovers that is fundamental to traditional poetic conceptions of love. Instead, they develop the ideal of mutuality implicit in the Latin set's final hymns, enacting that ideal primarily through rhythmic rather than textural relationships. In their irony, sexual candor, embrace of contradiction, and eventual retreat to emotionally opaque but brilliant displays of artifice, Francesca's canzonette provide performers with texts through which they might emulate the self-revealing, self-concealing Arianna.

Like the hymns that precede them, these homophonic, often homorhythmic songs make scant use of passaggiato singing, except to emphasize the texts' poetic meter, and even scanter use of dissonance. Hence, far more than the motets and hymns, the canzonette seem today to be light or light-hearted rather than serious and expressive music. To the extent that one might nonetheless imagine them to express something, they do so neither by the assumption of amorous pain nor primarily by pitch relations, but by the performative and pedagogical play of rhythm, both verbal and musical. Thus this is a repertoire that challenges twentieth- and twenty-first-century scholars' elision of neo-Petrarchan amorous suffering with expressiveness and our acquiescence to the early modern assertion that, in an ideal song, music obeys language as servants obey their masters, pupils their teachers, children their fathers, and—in the world of the Medici court—a people their prince. If she had thought about her lessons in terms of the political imagery associated with Giulio Caccini's "new kind of music," a seventeenth-century singer finishing her course of study with Francesca Caccini's canzonette could well have learned to model in her music making an alternative ideal. In that model, music and words could coexist, complement and even helpfully contradict each other, in relationships characterized not by subservience and domination but by mutual respect. Like the relationships that contemporaries reported between Christine and Grand Duke Ferdinando and between Maria Magdalena and Grand Duke Cosimo, and like the relationship that Giovanni Battista Signorini's will implies he had with his wife Francesca, this would have been a model very like the ideal relationship between women and men that Bronzini's *Della dignità e nobiltà delle donne* presented again and again.[18]

The text to the set's first solo song, "Non so se quel sorriso," explicitly complains of reading trouble: a man's epistemological confusion as he tries to "read" the meanings of a beloved's smile and gaze.[19] His problem illuminates that of the self-silencing speaker in "Ardo infelice" from a new angle: a voiceless woman is as much a problem for others as for herself. Francesca translates the amorous obtuseness of the speaker in "Non so" into a comic inability to read his own text in music. As if unable to choose the right musical gesture for his words, he contradicts his opening admission of uncertainty by singing the words "Non so" while his hands sound harmony's most decisive gesture of certainty, a perfect authentic cadence (see example 8.7). It soon becomes clear that he has trouble reading a poetic line, too, for he fails to reach another cadence until the eleventh syllable he sings. He has mistaken a perfectly ordinary seven-syllable line for an eleven-syllable one, producing an unnecessary enjambment that emphasizes his paranoia, and compounded his mistake by prolonging what would ordinarily be an unaccented syllable with an ornament (see example 8.7, measure 6).

Laughably confused even after he rights himself metrically at the end of the poem's second line, in Francesca's setting he goes on to perform a different accent pattern for each of the stanza's seven-syllable lines.[20]

Ex. 8.7. Francesca Caccini, *Il primo libro delle musiche* (1618), 89, "Non so se quel sorriso,"
mm. 1–7

I don't know if that smile
Mocks me or confides in me.

1 2 3 4 5 6 7	Non so se quel sorriso	I don't know if that smile
1 2 3 4 5 6 7	Mi schernisc'o m'affida	Mocks me or confides in me
1 2 3 4 5 6 7	Se quel mirami fisso	If that glance fixed on me
1 2 3 4 5 6 7	M'allett'o mi diffida	Allures me or distrusts me
1 2 3 4 5 6 7	Già schernit'e deriso	already mocked and derided
1 2 3 4 5 6 7	Da bella donn'infida	By a beautiful unfaithful woman
1 2 3 4 5 6 7	Non vorrei piu che'l core	I don't want anymore for my heart
1 2 3 4 5 6 7	Fosse strazio d'amore	To be a torment of love

The song delivers Buonarroti's poem brilliantly—as if it were impassioned speech—by a combination of metrical accents, agogic accents (those caused by ornamentation and those not caused by it) and harmonic accents articulated by a surprising number of authentic cadences, often oddly placed. Yet the singer's inability to distinguish at first between a seven- and an eleven-syllable line points to an uncertainty that could bedevil anyone sight-reading or listening to neo-Petrarchan love poetry, which was ordinarily written in a free (and unpredictably accented) alternation of such lines. The speaker's never-resolved inability to construe seven-syllable lines metrically is an obvious metaphor for his inability to construe his lady's smiles and glances—his inability, that is, to construe the silent, silenced gestures to which such poetry limited women's speech. Thus this song implies that Francesca's lessons in the poetic and musical metrics of the new post-Petrarchan canzonette could be construed as simultaneously lessons in new conceits for love.

In linking a singer's sensitivity as a reader of poetic meter to a poetic persona's sensitivity as a reader of lovers, Francesca grounded her canzonette in the poetic reforms of her older contemporary, the poet Gabriello Chiabrera. Francesca is sure to have known his ideas well when she was a girl. He was close enough to her father to have agreed to be godfather to her brother Michelangelo in 1598, and Giulio's 1602 collection *Le nuove musiche* had named the poet as the creator of a new kind of canzonetta that assimilated the metrical ideas of ancient poetry into the relatively unaffected conceits of popular part-songs.[21] However directly she may have absorbed Chiabrera's intertwined ideas about poetry's metrics and representations of love, his ideas may have been fresh in Francesca's mind as she gathered material for her *Primo libro*, since she and her husband had spent several weeks during May 1617 in Genoa, lodging near the poet in a palace belonging to Gianfrancesco Brignole.[22]

Writing long after his experiments had set a new fashion for courtly *poesia per musica*, Chiabrera explained his intentions in the dialogue *Il Geri*,[23] which critiques the poetic techniques and the amorous conceits of traditional Italian lyrics equally and interchangeably. Chiabrera's spokesman in the dialogue, the Florentine *letterato* Giovanni Francesco Geri, advocated poetry that expressed the simple, honest emotions of lovers free of elaborate conceits because "ninety of a hundred [lovers] will ignore what Socrates divinely taught Phaedrus, and everything that Plato had said with such grandeur in the dialogue of his *Symposium.* . . . [I]f you say to me, didn't Dante and Petrarch want to adorn their rhymes, I say, they did it superbly, and they knew how to do it, but the lover not supplied with such learning will pour out his pains and his pleasures more simply; so why must one work at high and proud-sounding verse?"[24]

Geri explicitly linked the quest for a more natural poetic voice for love to his advocacy of Latin and Greek poetry's relatively simple metrics. Declaring the canonic eleven-syllable line of Tuscan poetry indistinguishable from ordinary prose unless it was sung by someone who could impose poetry's pauses and accents by "reading aloud," he advocated using classical poetic feet to measure Tuscan poetry's limpid lines. Further, he urged the acceptance of stanzas like those of Horace and Pindar that deliberately combined long and short lines, likening both kinds of poetic modernity to the discoveries of Columbus and Galileo.[25] The two solo canzonette that follow "Non so" explore its speaker's quest for knowledge in terms of precisely such stanzas and in matters of love.

"Chi desia di saper che cosa è Amore" responds to the amorous uncertainties of "Non so" through the persona of Pastime, who sang this indictment of both love and the desire for certainty to open the 1614 Carnival entertainment *Il passatempo*.[26] Carefully packed bundles of contradictions, the stanzas of the strophic song require the singer to perform contradiction itself as the only sure thing about love and the only sure way to read Michelangelo Buonarroti's intrinsically contradictory text. For Buonarroti had crafted Pastime's signature song as a set of palindromic, metrically mixed stanzas. In each a couplet of poetically high-style eleven-syllable lines invoked a lover's quest for certainty; these framed three poetically low-style eight-syllable lines that declared love to be sorrow, madness, torment—the whole range of amorous sufferings of which Petrarchan love lyrics complain. Francesca's setting deepened the contradiction of poetic styles, and therefore the mockery of love poetry's clichés, by mismatching poetic and musical styles. Her Pastime reads the high-style eleven-syllable lines aloud to a musically low-style triple-meter tune in F and switches to a musically high-style declamatory recitative in d to read the poetically low-style eight-syllable lines that indict love (see example 8.8). Thus vocality and tonality switch to match the lines' affective content while contradicting the connotation of their meter. Francesca's recitative can seem to lend exaggerated seriousness to the enumeration of love's torments, as if Buonarroti's low-style meter envoiced a down-to-earth truth that penetrates the mask of sophistication presented by Pastime's framing eleven-syllable lines. Or her recitative can seem to mock the self-important, self-absorbed seriousness of the complaining Petrarchan lover. Either way, or both, Pastime's constant alternation between internally contradictory phrases of song denies the clarity that the persona of "Non so" had sought. For Pastime, love is not one way or the other but always both ways at once. "Chi desia di saper" teaches the singer of "Non so" to read both texts and love ironically, in insouciant (and comical) performances of paradox. (Listen to track 8.)

"Che t'ho fatt'io?" (What have I done to you?), too, explores the relationship of short and long lines and of low and high styles in poetry, music, and love.[27] The anonymous text begins and ends its first stanza with the question that its first five syllables pose to an interlocutor who seems to want the speaker dead. Protesting in eleven-syllable lines that s/he could not reciprocate love if s/he were dead, s/he also protests that the interlocutor should know the questioner's dependence and desire.

Francesca's setting poses the question in more ways than one. First, she accented the five-syllable line itself in three different ways by deft manipulation of its relation to barline accents and authentic cadences. Each delivers the refrain's challenge in a different way—Che t'ho fatt'io? (What have I done to you?), Che t'ho fatt'io? (What have I done to you?) and Che t'ho fatt'io? (What have I done to you?). See example 8.9.

Second, and more important, Francesca ensured that the question would pervade the stanza, while turning the canzonetta into a kind of metrical etude that so emphasizes the five-syllable unit of the opening question as to make it "do" something to the poem's eleven-syllable lines. At the end of the first such line, and in the middle of the second, she repeats the musical idea to which the opening question was sung, forcing listeners to hear each eleven-syllable line in terms of that opening five-syllable question (see example 8.9 and table 8.2).

Ex. 8.8. Francesca Caccini, *Il primo libro delle musiche* (1618), 90, "Chi desia di saper che cosa è Amore," first stanza

[To] whoever wants to know what Love is

I will say, it is nothing if not heat,

It is nothing if not pain,

It is nothing if not fear,

It is nothing if not madness.

I will say, it is nothing if not heat

[To] whoever wants to know what Love is.

The rhythmic effect is to make a five-syllable unit the most regularly recurring aural pattern. It functions as a poetic foot does, measuring and therefore rereading each of the three eleven-syllable lines in its own image. In addition, as in "Chi desia di saper," Francesca switches from the low-style metrically regular canzonetta vocality to high-style recitative when the text turns to the language

Ex. 8.9. Francesca Caccini, *Il primo libro delle musiche* (1618), 91, "Che t'ho fatt'io?," first stanza

What have I done to you
That you so want
My death so that I won't be able to love you?
Don't you know that I live only by your splendor?
Alas, hard heart, alas, bend your desire.
What have I done to you?

Table 8.2a. "Che t'ho fatt'io" as written in I-Fn, MS Palatino 251, fol. 329

Italian text	Syllables	English translation
Che t'ho fatt'io	5	What have I done to you
Che tanto brami	5	That you so want
La morete mia perch'io non t'ami	11	My death, so that I will not be able to love you?
Non sai ch'io vivo sol del tuo splendore?	11	Don't you know that I live only by your splendor?
Ahi, duro core, ohimè, piega'l desio.	11	Alas, hard heart, alas, desire yields.
Che t'ho fatt'io?	5	What have I done to you?

Table 8.2b. "Che t'ho fatt'io" as Francesca's setting reads it.

Italian text	Syllables	Vocality
Che t'ho fatt'io	5	
Che tanto brami	5	
La morte mia	5	
perch'io non t'ami?	5	Canzonetta vocality
Non sai	2	
ch'io vivo sol	5 (tronco)	
del tuo splendore?	5	
Ahi, duro core,	5	
ohimè	2	
piega'l desio	5	Recitative vocality
Che t'ho fatt'io?	5	
Che t'ho fatt'io?	5	

Note: Boldface indicates repetition of the opening motive; italic indicates repetition of "Non sai" motive at "ohimè."

of amorous suffering and desire, showing how the five-syllable unit can read a line independent of metrical accents (see example 8.9 and table 8.2 again).

The opening question of "Che t'ho fatt'io" serves wonderfully as a mnemonic device for the five-syllable line, and therefore for a lesson that foreshadows the reading by poetic feet that Chiabrera advocated. Moreover, reading everything, even the eleven-syllable lines, almost entirely in terms of five-syllable units emphasizes this stanza's first-person statements. Its "I" can easily be identified with the low-style meter (asking the high-style line what it has done), with the musical devices that have imposed that low-style meter's perspective on the high-style lines, with the musician who sings the poem, or with a lover of either sex. Whichever way one might interpret it, the questioning "I" is the inferior partner of a binary, forced to suffer even though it acknowledges the other's splendor. Yet the agency seized by the questioning, reading "I" does no damage to the eleven-syllable lines. Indeed, both in canzonetta-style and recitative phrases, reading by five-syllable units lends drama and emotional clarity to the singer's delivery of text. A pupil might or might not draw a larger inference from the drama and clarity provided by her initiative as a reader and her ability to perform a sustained contradiction. "Che t'ho fatt'io" could seem a harmless preparatory exercise in Chiabreran reading, or it could seem harmlessly to substitute mutuality for the asymmetrical power relationship that traditional poetry assumed to be the foundation of the endlessly painful relationship it called love.[28]

Indeed, mutuality lies at the heart of the two duets for soprano and bass with which Francesca framed these three songs in her book. By setting amorous texts as duets for voice types that so easily suggest a gendered pair of lovers, Francesca rewrote the implied dynamics of sexual love.[29] If sung as a solo song, the text of "S'io men vò, morirò" (If I leave, I will die) might seem to give voice to one person's self-absorbed desire to sustain an amorous encounter until s/he achieves a proper "little death."[30] But sung as a duet, the text becomes simultaneously an exercise in the mutually negotiated solution of a rhythmic problem about line endings and a startlingly explicit representation of two lovers' quest for mutually satisfying sex. Similarly, if sung by one voice, "O vive rose" might seem conventionally objectifying as it urges another person's lips to surrender to the speaker's desire.[31] As a duet, however, it gives voice to two lovers' desire for each other's surrender and, implicitly, each lover's response to the plea that s/he cede to the desire others can see in her/his eyes. Thus Francesca shifts away from a dynamic of active and passive, speaking and silent partners and toward a relationship between two subjects. Their voices enact mutual desire through their simultaneous performances of a common text brought into being by their bodily acts.

"S'io men vò" vividly represents sexual love by requiring its performers to act out musically the contradictory desires of lovers to sustain their encounter and to come to mutually satisfying ends.[32] Francesca capitalized on the poem's refrain-and-verse structure to dramatize the contradiction. The refrain moves tonally from an F-centered opening toward d at the mention of death and departure, while the verses move steadfastly back to F. The constant oscillation between tonal centers, matched by a constant shifting between imitative and homophonic singing, binds the singers in an internally contradictory force of their own bodies' making. As in sexual acts, their bodies produce joyful contact and painful separation in an alternation they seem to sustain as love. Within that alternation, they struggle to create musically satisfactory endings to poetic lines that end alternately on accented and unaccented syllables. (In Italian, such lines are called *tronco* and *piano*, respectively.)[33] In each section, soprano and bass approach these line endings differently, always managing to end together. The result is easily perceived as a representation in texture and rhythm of mutually satisfying sexual endings created by lovers who respect each other's differences.

The metrical problem and several possible solutions are established in the opening refrain, but the sexiness of Francesca's proposed solution for the pair is more easily seen in the verse.

Refrain:

S'io men vò, morirò (6 syllables,   If I leave I will die.
   understood as 7, tronco)

Ahi, crudel dipartita (7 syllables, piano)   Oh, cruel departure.

Verse:

S'ora il cor non ha virtù (tronco)   If now the heart has no strength

Contra il duol di sua ferita (piano)   Against the pain of its wounding

Come lei non miri più (tronco)   How could it see her still,

Chi salvar potrà mia vita (piano)   She who could save me for living?

The soprano begins lines one, two and four, each time imitated by the bass three half-notes later. Entering second, and therefore always with less time to sing before a cadence, the bass relies less than does the soprano on agogic accents provided by ornaments than on the unadorned rhythmic declamation of syllables in relation to the music's perceived meter. Yet by means of a distinctive reading of the text, each singer contributes to metrical play that allows them to accommodate tronco and piano endings. The interplay of the singers' individual readings and individual bodily acts thus produces something greater than either voice alone, a coming to temporary closure that shifts the way their singing measures time itself. "S'io men vò" thus represents good sex as resulting from play with individual differences, in a relationship of mutual respect (see example 8.10).

The lovers who sing "O vive rose" (O living roses) also seem interested in sustaining a relationship of mutual desire. As each asks the other's lips to cede to the passion already gleaming from laughing, burning eyes, these voices brush past each other like the lips their words address, avoiding both homophonic union and harmonic cadence until fully half the text has been breathlessly sung (see example 8.11).

The singers mark the shift between praise and petition in the poem's modes of address by shifting their relationship to each other and to their voices' shared articulation of the poem's rhythms. Whereas their quest for each others' elusive

Ex. 8.10. Francesca Caccini, *Il primo libro delle musiche* (1618), 86, "S'io men vò, morirò," mm. 16–34, with metrical shifts marked

If now the heart has no strength
Against the pain of its wounding,
How could it see her still,
She who could save me for living?

Ex. 8.11. Francesca Caccini, *Il primo libro delle musiche* (1618), 92, "O vive rose," mm. 1–8

O living roses,
Loving lips,
If in a lovely face
In a lovely smile,
You move proudly . . .

lips had led them to ignore, too, their words' metrical structure, their lips now meet: in perfect homorhythmic declamation of their mutual plea's cleanly accented five-syllable lines, each mouth cedes to the other, then opens with the other into a shared ornament, in parallel tenths, on the word "omai" (now) (see example 8.12).

Afterward they move slightly apart, each voice ornamenting a shared accented vowel in its own way before joining the other for the articulation of consonants in perfect unity. But here, in the temporal luxury of two seven-syllable lines, the ultimate ecstasy is not the homophony of their kiss but a return to the texture of praise, as a way of reaching clearly articulated, shared harmonic goals. On the last line of the stanza loosely imitative phrases, led first by the bass at the octave, then by the soprano at the fifth, allow each singer to linger in a different way on particular words on the way to joining the other's lips in another shared move toward the cadence.

Each duet could serve as a mnemonic to teach the technical skills that improvising ensemble singers would need if they were to read the metrical challenges of poems in compatible ways, but the erotically charged achievement of equilibrium in difference breaks free of musical pedagogy on at least two levels. First, these duets provide opportunities for singers to rehearse a decidedly non-Petrarchan kind of love. In the world created by these duets, each partner to love's shared text has agency, voice, and the right to express desire; each can both lead and follow; each shares with the other responsibility for reading and performing the text of their relationship well. In this world, love's pain is gone. Second, these duets' sexual explicitness show that Francesca's persistent affirmation of sustained contradiction as a principle of musical architecture in the second half of her book had direct implications for the normative relations of gender and sex that framed her, her pupils', and her patrons' everyday lives.

Brilliant miniatures from which both emotional and sexual intensity gradually evaporate, the last five songs of Francesca's book are lessons in the artifice of singing Chiabreran poetry to create emotionally detached structures of paradox that gainsay any examination of what the speaker may feel. Thus they seem deliberately to withdraw from the confusions of traditional love and traditional lyrics into a delighted play with internal contradictions, as if a woman's agency in love required that she be an adept of paradox.

The first of these songs, "Se muove a giurar fede," returns to the tone of aphoristic pronouncements about love foreshadowed by "Chi desia saper."[34] Francesca matched the oddly old-fashioned image of a lover swearing fealty to

Ex. 8.12. Francesca Caccini, *Il primo libro delle musiche* (1618), 92, "O vive rose," mm. 9–11
Cede now,
Fragrant lips.

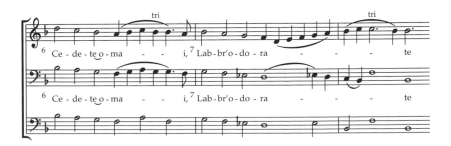

the court of Love with a lovely, rhythmically fluid melody from which all hint of musical contradiction seems to have been banished. Yet she took advantage of the poem's technical self-contradictions to construct a lesson in measuring the classic seven- and eleven-syllable lines of the Italian love lyric in proper poetic feet. The poem's metrical scheme, 7–7–11 / 7–7–11, breaks it into matched, symmetrical halves, but both the syntax and the rhyme scheme that supports it divide the stanza into an "if" clause of four lines followed by a "then" clause consisting of a couplet.

Se muove a giurar fede	a7	If [a lover] moves to swear fealty
Al Tribunal d'amore	b7	To the court of Love,
E non stemprarsi, e non versar dolore	c11	And loss of self and outpoured pain
Un amator si crede	a7	He believes he can avoid,
Ei non sa con quel legge	c7	[Then] he does not know with what law
Amore i servi suoi govern'e regge	c11	Love governs and rules his servants.[35]

Enacting the lover's mistake as an internal technical contradiction, the poem challenges a singer who would read it to perform the mistake while drawing attention to it *as* a mistake, and to perform, in the final line, Love's rule of law.

Francesca's smooth melody tempts the singer to read her amorously misguided lines as if ignorant of their metrical implications. The result is a melody whose accents convey a fluidity and grace familiar from sixteenth-century love lyrics.

Se muove a giurar fede	a7	1 2 3 4 5 6 7
Al Tribunal d'Amore	b7	1 2 3 4 5 6 7
E non stemprarsi e non versar dolore	b11	1 2 3 4 5 6 7 8 9 10 11
Un amator si crede	a7	1 2 3 4 5 6 7

Though the second and fourth lines have almost the same pattern of accents, and the first and third are each "off" in a different way, there is a unifying measure that would reconcile these differences as the five-syllable unit of "Che t'ho fatt'io" had done. The lover doesn't know that, however, until Francesca's music imposes iambs on the song's twice-sung, law-enforcing final line—an imposition that makes Love's (and the iamb's) law seem almost to dance.

Ei non sa con quel legge	c7	1 2 3 4 5 6 7
Amore i servi suoi govern'e regge	c11	1 2 3 4 5 6 7 8 9 10 11

Love's law and a Chiabreran reading of long lines in terms of poetic feet are metaphors for each other, so indissolubly fused that no pupil who learned the technique from this song could ever forget the lesson. Poetry and love each have a discipline that one is eventually compelled to obey. Yet as a glance at the example's final phrase shows, s/he would also have learned that even such laws allowed the possibility of agency, for Francesca presents two quite different realizations of the metrically disciplined, law-giving line. No system of discipline, it seems, need suppress entirely a singing reader's capacity for inventiveness (see example 8.13). (Listen to track 9.)

"Ch'Amor sia nudo, e pur con l'ali al tergo," like "Se muove," focuses on the abstract qualities of love. The poem systematically contrasts clichéd images of Amor from conventional love poetry: those that focus on the disembodied and the celestial are mocked as vanity, while those that bring Love into individual embodied experience are proclaimed to be truth.[36]

Ex. 8.13. Francesca Caccini, *Il primo libro delle musiche* (1618), 94, "Se muove a giurar fede," mm. 25–41

Love governs and rules his servants.

Ch'amor sia nudo e pur con l'ali al tergo	a11	[The idea] that love is naked and with winged back,
Stia sotto il cielo e non procuri albergo	a11	Lodges beneath the sky and seeks no other shelter,
E vanità.	b5	Is vanity.
Ma che per gli occhi egli discen'al petto	c11	But [the idea] that [it is] through the eyes that he enters breasts,
& ivi posi & ivi abbia ricetto	c11	And there rests and there is received,
E verità.	b5	That is truth.

Francesca, however, invites a singer to mock both ideas of love by exploiting the technical opposition between the irregularly accented, dithering eleven-syllable lines of high-style love lyrics and the pithy, summarily judgmental tronco five-syllable lines of modern mixed-style poetry. She emphasized the clarity and rhythmic decisiveness of the two short tronco lines by setting both to the same sharply defined melodic motive and by underlining both with strong authentic cadences. As the singer declares the short lines' parallel but opposite judgments with equal clarity, the distinction between long and short lines, tradition and modernity, becomes more important musically than the distinction between vanity and truth. Indeed, because the pronouncement "E vanità" (example 8.14 a) articulates a cadence on the song's dominant, and the pronouncement "E verità" cadences on both the dominant and the tonic, the relationship that binds "vanità" and "verità" is doubly strong. Melodically and rhythmically identical, in the repetition of "verità" (example 8.14b) they are also linked by the dominant-tonic relation that is the musical equivalent of cause and effect.

Thus projecting "vanità" as both exactly equivalent to "verità" and leading inexorably to it, Francesca's song directly contradicts the meaning of its text's words by faithfully reading the intrinsic music that is that text's rhythm. The result is a song in which the thematic and technical (semantic and sonic) oppositions of the poem cancel each other out, creating in musical miniature something like a liar's paradox: in terms of love, vanità is verità, and vice versa, while everything said in the eleven-syllable line seems like so much neo-Petrarchan cant. To be enjoyed for their own sake, the mutually cancelling oppositions construct the song as a game from which there is no epistemologically correct exit. Wittily triumphant over all the neo-Petrarchan conceits ensuing stanzas proclaim, the contradictions between "vanità" and "verità," between unruly eleven-syllable lines and perfectly ordered tronco five-syllable ones, and between poem and song cancel each other out, and construct a kind of hexagonal paradox in which differences sustain each other in a plan of a distinctively Baroque wit.

Ex. 8.14. Francesca Caccini, *Il primo libro delle musiche* (1618), 95, "Ch'Amor sia nudo e pur con l'ali al tergo"

    (a) Measures 7–8

        That is vanity.

    (b) Measures 15–17

        That is truth.

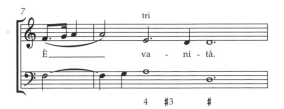

The breathless dance song "Fresch'aurette" engages registral and metrical differences by rendering them utterly unproblematic, while requiring the singers to perform heroic feats of breath control and unanimous declamation.[37] An almost perfectly homophonic duet for soprano and bass, the song requires these two voices to coordinate the rapid syllabic delivery of two four-syllable lines that run into an eight-syllable line before the singers are granted the briefest of chances to breathe, at the comically self-reflexive words "or qui spirate" (now here you [both] breathe) (see example 8.15).

Thus the partners whose mouths had known perfect coordination in only one phrase of "O vive rose" here sustain perfect coordination of their tongues' articulation of consonants, their mouths' shaping of rapidly changing vowels, their bodies' release and only brief intake of the "fresch'aurette" of air that would cool their bodies' ardor. Paradoxically, both the challenge and the pleasure of singing this utterly word-dominated patter song are bodily. Perfect union in the shared delivery of text requires a perfect union of bodies whose differences from each other are marked only by register and who can, paradoxically if briefly, read love's shared text as if they were one embodied voice born of superb, virtuosic breath control.

Almost wholly composed of happily sustained contradictions and encompassed opposites, Francesca's setting of Ansaldo Cebà's "Dispiegate guancie amate" practically floats on air.[38] Cebà's poem invites construction through binary opposites, for his six-line stanzas twice juxtapose two four-syllable lines,

Ex. 8.15. Francesca Caccini, *Il primo libro delle musiche* (1618), 96, "Fresch'aurette," mm. 1–3
Fresh breezelets,
Charming airs,
Sweet breaths now, here, [you] breathe.

each accented differently, with an eight-syllable line whose accent pattern is the sum of those different four-syllable parts.

Dispiegate	a4	1234	Unfurl,
Guancie amate	a4	1234	Beloved cheeks,
Quella porpor'acerbetta	b8	12345678	That little purple bud
Che perdenti	c4	1234	So that losing
Che dolenti	c4	1234	So that grieving
Sian le rose	b8	12345678	Will be the roses
in su l'erbetta			in the meadow.

Thus in each stanza of poetry opposite ways of articulating four syllables are twice articulated, first as different, then as complementary parts of a larger whole, as if the poem obeyed its own first verb—the command to unfold or unfurl.

Careful to respect Cebà's metrical and syntactical strategy, Francesca created a song that unfurls as rhythm, as melody, as harmony, and eventually as tonality, while it sustains equilibrium in a dizzying number of contradictory forces. The singer's first accent unfurls as a scalewise passaggio, while the enjambment of the two four-syllable lines carries the action of unfurling forward through the naming of the verb's object. Although a half rest allows the singing reader to pause, no harmonic cadence punctuates the space between the elided four-syllable lines and the following eight-syllable line that completes the sentence. Instead harmony and melody gradually unfurl as well, the voice rising from the tonic g′ to pause on the dominant, then rising again to an f″ from which it falls back easily to cadence on the mediant b-flat′. The bass line, meanwhile, falls stepwise from tonic through dominant to mediant, opening the sonic space that the song occupies, only to rise again to articulate an authentic cadence. By her equally careful joining and separating of metrically different units of text to enact the text's imperative, Francesca ensured that her music would effortlessly complement Cebà's words. The claims of form and content, music and verbal parts of the whole are held in a shimmering, delicate balance of reading in song (see example 8.16). (Listen to track 10.)

Francesca transformed at least three other potentially conflicting forces in the song from contradictory to complementary partners. First, to articulate the conventional short-short-long-short (1234) pattern of a four-syllable unit, whether free-standing or as part of an eight-syllable line, she aligned metrical accents with ornaments that gave agogic emphasis. As a result, ornamented and unornamented phrases alternate: ornamentation, the bugaboo of many

Ex. 8.16. Francesca Caccini, *Il primo libro delle musiche* (1618), 97, "Dispiegate," first stanza

Unfurl,
Beloved cheeks,
That little purple bud
So that losing
So that grieving
Will be the roses in the meadow.

critics of virtuoso or virtuosa singing, is in equilibrium with syllabic declamatory style, the bugaboo of those who criticized the Florentine new music's monotony.[39] Second, Francesca's always meticulous placement of syllables and slurs articulates a perfectly regular combination of 3/2 and 3/1 metrical units for each eight-syllable unit (3/2 + 3/1 + 3/2). By combining two musical ways of measuring time, this unit complements in musical terms Cebà's play with two poetic ways of measuring time, while it coordinates the delivery of his text with a standard rhythmic pattern for dancing. Third, Francesca chose two fundamentally different ways of defining a tonic to articulate the two halves of each stanza. In the first half, voice and hands unfurl melody and bass through a g-mollis scale, articulating the old-fashioned mode precisely by pausing on the dominant and then cadencing on the system-defining mediant. But in the second half of the song, the bass line differentiates itself from the still-stepwise voice's motion, moving instead in the more angular style of fully modern, tonal bass line to articulate the return to g by rising (on the accented beats of the 3/2 + 3/1 + 3/2 pattern) through the circle of fifths (F–C–g–D–g). Seamlessly, with the semblance of effortless ease that courtly culture knew as *sprezzatura,* the singer's exquisitely trained "guancie amate" (beloved [breath-controlling] cheeks) unfurl a song that is the sum of all the lessons that have gone before.

A song of vocal, tonal, and rhythmic mastery that exceeds all expectations of mere obedience to words, a song that makes contradiction and paradox seem natural, "Dispiegate" is, too, a song that has left the sensibility of struggle, so familiar from early seventeenth-century music, far behind. Its smooth, thoroughly modern virtuosity can tempt both performer and listener to join the singing persona of "Dispiegate" in ignoring the text's unequivocal expression of desire. The purple bud that the singer wants to be revealed could be a harmless flower opening in the grass, of course, but it could just as easily be someone's (anyone's) sexual organ. Almost as shocking as her song's multiple enactments of the unfurling she desires is the singer's performance of denial, produced by a brilliantly steadfast development in music of the song's technical unfurling. Herein lies this set's ultimate contradiction—and the entire book's ultimate performance of voice in relation to womanhood. For by focusing her attention on music—on the music of Cebà's language and on music's capacity to develop an idea—the singer of Francesca's "Dispiegate" instantiates the fundamental paradox of womanhood as constructed by patriarchal interests. A woman of castità, onestà, and continenza needed simultaneously to deny her sexuality (her desire and her knowledge of desire) and to unfurl it for the satisfaction of socially legitimated desire. But if "Dispiegate" allows the performance of patriarchal womanhood, it also so multiply performs its unfurlings as to be a musical performance of desire realized. And it gives a woman such as Clizia a way to give voice to her desire: drape it in the artifices of self-control, which can confer denial and deniability at will, and you can be heard without being hurt.

※

In her *Primo libro delle musiche,* Francesca advertised herself as able to teach others the full range of musical skills—of body, breath, and mind—by which they might create their own meanings in the discursive world. A pupil who studied the book diligently, from cover to cover, stood to learn the myriad tricks of a musica's trade and much more. She could have learned that control of her own body (hands, breath, and voice) would free her physical voice; that a refusal to be limited to the work of pain could free her compositional voice, so that she could take possession of the means by which to represent herself; that agency in self-representation—that is, a deliberate use of artifice—could preserve her continenza; that it was the nature of song itself to stage and sustain contradictions; and that words and music, voice and hands, being and doing were all equally important to intelligible communication, able to interact cooperatively, like post-Petrarchan lovers, in relationships based not on obedience to hierarchy but on mutual responsiveness. She might well have inferred that the musica's multifaceted craft was always, therefore, an art worthy of Arianna.

The surprising sexual candor of Francesca's canzonette suggests that her court-subsidized teaching of young girls might have been assumed to include lessons in how to negotiate sexual love's dangers, doubts, and delights through savvy acceptance of its paradoxes.[40] Such lessons might have reflected an awareness that understanding sexuality would be crucial for girls and young women who would, like their teacher, exercise a craft of bodily self-display that, however disciplined, was all too easily an occasion for sexual danger. Such an assumption would be consistent with Francesca's attention, in the first half of her book, to aligning lessons in breath control, range, phrasing, harmony, and composition with texts that drew attention to the problem of finding cultural authority for women's voices. For Francesca's gynocentric clientele, to teach lessons in musicality and sexuality simultaneously was no paradox created of wit alone. It was the defining paradox of every musical woman's life.

La liberazione di Ruggiero amid the Politics of Regency

9

Late on the morning of 3 February 1625, 160 gentildonne of Florence, their husbands, and an unknown number of foreign guests rode in carriages past the Palazzo Pitti, through the Porta San Pier Gattolino (now Porta Romana) on the city's southeastern side, and half a mile up a broad tree-lined avenue to the villa atop the nearest hill to the south.[1] Recently renovated, renamed, and dedicated to "the leisure and delight of Tuscany's future grand duchesses," Villa Imperiale was to be opened to Florence's elite for the first time that day.[2] As they arrived, the guests of Archduchess Maria Magdalena left their carriages in a grassy courtyard guarded by two squadrons of armed cavalry and entered the palace by a side door, under the watchful eye of Commander Inolfo de' Bardi. All were greeted by Cardinal Carlo de' Medici, and the gentildonne were escorted to designated bench seats by Marchese Guicciardini.[3] Protected by her maestro di camera and two guards, the archduchess waited with the wives of Modena's and Lucca's ambassadors in a newly frescoed antechamber. When her specially invited male guests—the papal nuncio, the prince of Malta, and ambassadors from Modena, Lucca, and Venice—arrived, she joined them and the others for the Medici court's most private welcoming of their Hapsburg nephew, Crown Prince Władisław Sigismund of Poland, who was there to attend Carnival. A *commedia in musica* was to be followed by a *balletto di dame* that would in turn be followed by a *balletto a cavallo* in the courtyard. Afterward, the gentildonne would be served at lunch by the cavalieri who had performed in the horse ballet, while the male guests watched through the arches of interior windows.[4]

Breaking with the Medici court's practice, Magdalena had assigned sole authority for the commedia's music to the preeminent musician of the women's court, thirty-seven-year-old Francesca Caccini.[5] A veteran composer of court spectacles, Francesca worked largely without supervision. Although Magdalena attended five rehearsals of the balletto di dame and seventeen rehearsals of the balletto di cavallo, she attended only the last two of the commedia's rehearsals.[6] Because the work that Francesca, librettist Ferdinando Saracinelli, and architect Giulio Parigi had done for that day was especially important to Magdalena's presentation of herself to her people, the regent supported the printing of a score that Francesca prepared for the commedia, of Saracinelli's libretto, and of five engravings that Alfonso Parigi made of the stage pictures and effects his father had designed.[7] Known from these publications as *La liberazione di Ruggiero dall'isola d'Alcina*, the commedia entered the canons of music history as a single work; it came to be known, inaccurately, as the first opera composed by a woman, and therefore for centuries Francesca Caccini's principal claim to fame.

La liberazione is clearly not an opera. It is, as its sources' title pages attest, a "balletto composto in musica"—an entirely sung, plotted entertainment meant to end in dancing that, in keeping with Florentine preference under the late Cosimo II, featured named dame and gentiluomini of the court whose performances deliberately dissolved the barrier between representation and reality. Opera or not, *La liberazione* is precious because it is one of the few full-length works of early modern music theater by a single composer to survive. It is no less precious for the accuracy with which it represented the sights, sounds, and dynamics of Tuscany's women's court, for the startling modernity with which it represented political power in terms of sex, and for the wit with which it simultaneously exposed and allayed anxieties about the gynocentric universe amid which the show's composer and its patron flourished. Moreover, as I will show, in February 1625 the genre designation "balletto" gave the show political heft.

The choices of the artistic team who created *La liberazione* and the meanings available to the show's first audience were shaped by the political climate of Magdalena's regency and by the congeries of images, spectacles, and representations through which she projected her authority and persona. This chapter situates *La liberazione* in relation to Magdalena's regency, analyzing the ways its genre, location, stage pictures and libretto addressed her subjects' anxieties about female rule and supported her political agenda. The next shows how Francesca's music for *La liberazione* complicates and enriches the meanings one might attribute to it, showing her to have served her patron well while displaying her own mastery of the means by which music could be a medium for the performance and representation of power.

Magdalena's Regency and Gender Trouble

By the time Carnival arrived in 1625, the long de facto regency of Christine de Lorraine had been transformed into a de jure one headed by her daughter-in-law, Maria Magdalena d'Austria. Four years earlier, on 28 February 1621, thirty-year-old Grand Duke Cosimo II had died after seven years' illness, naming his widow principal regent until their eleven-year-old son Ferdinando II achieved his majority.[8] Although he had long intended that his brother, Cardinal Carlo de' Medici, would share the regency with Magdalena, in a final codicil Cosimo excluded his spendthrift brother from both political and fiscal authority and ordered their mother Christine to serve as co-regent.[9]

Magdalena had long been dismissed by visitors to the court as merely affable.[10] Yet Christine and Cosimo had prepared Magdalena systematically for regency, as Christine's letters to the life-long diplomat Orso d'Elci explained.[11] Having focused first on governo della casa, the personal and financial management of the enormous staff known as the famiglia, by 1610 Magdalena was attending all briefings by the Consulta (the grand duke's cabinet) and was invited to comment on matters related to Spain and to German-speaking Europe. By late August 1611, Christine had ordered d'Elci, then ambassador to Spain, to make sure the Spanish king knew that his sister-in-law Magdalena also heard all petitions to the Consulta di Giustizia e Grazia (Tuscany's court of last resort) and would soon be assigned to other matters concerning external affairs, "because she can no longer call herself a foreigner" and because she had shown herself to be intelligent and capable.[12] According to a letter that Belisario Vinta, the first secretary, had written d'Elci earlier that year, Christine strove to ensure that her respect for her daughter-in-law was matched by "reciprocal benevolence" between them.[13] Evidently Vinta believed Christine's efforts to be successful, for he described the princely family—husband, wife, mother, and children—as extraordinarily united by affection and shared opinions.[14] A source of domestic tranquility in both personal and political registers during Cosimo II's lifetime, the unanimity, mutual affection, and respect that bound his mother and his widow ensured that their shared regency would strike some Tuscan subjects as a threateningly close-knit gynocracy.

But her closeness with Christine was not the only gender trouble that Magdalena's regency posed. Unlike her reserved, elegant mother-in-law, who was descended from the Medici, Magdalena had long struck her Tuscan subjects as an odd sort of woman. As a girl she had been reported to be unusually robust, cheerful, physically active, and so humorally hot as not to have menstruated until she was seventeen—the last a considerable worry to the Tuscan diplomats who had negotiated her marriage to Cosimo.[15] Fulfilling the papal nuncio's prediction that she would bear children easily in spite of her unnatural heat, Magdalena had given the sickly Cosimo eight children in the first ten years of their marriage, five of them boys.[16] An enthusiastic dancer, horsewoman, and huntress capable of personally killing wild boar with either bow or gun, Magdalena had never lost a certain pride in her Austrian Hapsburg identity. That pride extended to an earthy discomfort with the refined courtesies that characterized Florentine social exchanges, a disdain for the tendency of even chaste and noble Mediterranean women to paint themselves with makeup, and a craving for German butter and schmalz that she asked visitors to Austria to send her by the barrel.[17] Whether Magdalena could still call herself a foreigner or not, her pride in her imperial connections lent a foreign air to her decidedly unfamiliar performances of womanhood.

Magdalena's oddness was so pronounced as to have been a principal theme of the biography that her apologist, Bronzini, drafted for the first volume of *Della dignità e nobiltà delle donne.*[18] Praising her imperial lineage and her piety equally, Bronzini declared his patron to be prudent, merciful, devout, generous to charitable institutions, and so perfectly unanimous with her husband in the governance of household and state that the two were like mirrors of each other. Moreover, Bronzini praised Magdalena lavishly for her attention to her children's education and her "true and zealous" interest that her dame and damigelle be as well versed as she in womanly arts, in grammar, rhetoric, and arithmetic, and in dancing, riding, and fencing according to their gifts.[19] Bronzini elaborated this portrait of his archduchess in a way that implied that her eventual political power could rest on the same virile, bellicose capacities as a man's: "Since childhood she concentrated on great and virile deeds, and trained her tender arm so much to things of horsemanship, arms, archery, and hunting gun, and [so] accustomed her white hand to bend the bow, [and] aim arrows and balls of lead in hunting, that it seemed that there were few people who could equal her. She looked at birds, and few or none escaped her hands. She stared at stags and boar, and infallibly striking them in the middle of the forehead with her bow, she killed them; despite the right breast on her chest and a husband at her side, no one could deny that she seemed a new Amazon in Tuscany."[20] Even if one allows that Bronzini intended to flatter his patron, his text suggests that many Tuscans would have imagined the reins of their regency to have been in the hands of a disturbingly mannish woman.

Contextualizing a Virile Gynocracy

Bronzini's *Della dignità*, published between 1622 and 1632 and surviving in twenty-two manuscript volumes, is best understood as the intellectual foundation of a cultural program to justify the regency that Cosimo's fragile health had long heralded as inevitable. Cast in the conventional form of a dialogue among leisured women and men, its twenty-four "days" of conversation continually asserted the equality of women and men as both an absolute value and as a necessary condition for the well-ordered state.[21] This argument would echo in the last vocal scene of *La liberazione*.

Bronzini's interlocutors elaborated his argument with a seemingly endless proliferation of examples that served two interlocking purposes. First, the countless examples of women rulers and regents from myth, fiction, and history situated Magdalena's regency in a rich tradition of women who defended their families' and their nations' patrimonies by whatever means necessary. No matter how different the circumstances and methods of rule of each, in Bronzini's narrative all were examples of integrity, self-sacrifice, and heroic fidelity to the interests of their people. All exemplified, that is, a transformation into public virtue of womanly *continenza* and *onestà*. Second, the proliferating examples widened the context both for Magdalena's political power and for her foreignness by presenting encyclopedic knowledge of female excellence in all fields. Although almost all the historical or living women about whom Bronzini wrote were elite, the sheer abundance of examples ensured that many different types of excellent women—some of them oddly gendered—would populate the world he constructed in his readers' imaginations. Cross-dressed women warriors, fictional and historical, thus could resonate with the cross-dressed Lastheneia, who wore boys' clothes to hear Plato lecture, with women who rode into battle beside their husbands, and with women who withdrew virginally into convents or the studios of their fathers' homes to pursue intellectual interests in chaste and pious privacy. In the resonance of their differences and their common participation in the distinctive womanly virtues of modesty, industry, graciousness, and devotion to the Virgin, the hundreds of women whom Bronzini's interlocutors discussed collectively constituted a vision of women's multiplicity, capacity for self-discipline, and underutilized potential. This crowd of women who exceeded the conventional limits of womanhood functioned as a backdrop against which Magdalena's similar excesses could seem not deviant but part of a rich, baroquely varied norm.

Bronzini's project found echoes in the archduchess's redecoration of Villa Imperiale. The villa had been associated with proud womanly excellence since shortly after the first Medici grand duke, Cosimo I, confiscated the palace from the Salviati family in 1564. The following year it was his gift to his daughter Isabella, who used it as her Florentine residence after her marriage to Paolo Giordano Orsini I. A woman whose "wit, beauty and talent made her conspicuous," who spoke French, Spanish, and Latin fluently, and who was said to have been skilled both as a poet and as an improvising musician, in 1576 Isabella had been murdered by her husband for her open adultery.[22] For decades Isabella's villa lay understandably abandoned by the Medici and the Orsini families, despite its proximity to Palazzo Pitti and its grand views.[23] When Magdalena acquired title to the property in 1619, she had ordered the road connecting it to the city gate to be widened and solicited designs for its rehabilitation.[24] In 1622, Giulio Parigi won the bid for a project that was to last two years, cost thirty-five thousand scudi, and provide much-needed work for hundreds of artists and artisans during a time of economic crisis.[25]

Among the most politically salient aspects of the project were the frescoes commissioned from Matteo Rosselli's workshop for Magdalena's audience room, antechamber, and bedroom.[26] Like Bronzini's text, Rosselli's frescoes surrounded the archduchess with representations of powerful, unimpeachably virtuous women from history and myth. Magdalena held audiences at Villa Imperiale beneath the figures of heroic queens whose stories Bronzini's *Della dignità* had told: Clothilda, Mathilda, Pulcherria, Galla Placidia, Costanza, Augusta, Isabella of Spain, and Saint Ursula, whose martyrdom saving Cologne from spiritual and political barbarians was painted as if it were a historically verifiable fact. She slept and dressed beneath images of Christendom's heroic women: Saints Cecilia, Agatha, and Ursula, plus Judith, Mary Magdalen, and the Virgin Mary.

Villa Imperiale served Magdalena, her children, and her household as a private retreat from the official state palaces of Pitti and Palazzo Vecchio and as the place from which she launched her hunting expeditions. But the political valences of Villa Imperiale exceeded its aura of sovereign privacy, female seclusion, and indulgence in virile pastimes. By rehabilitating the palace of Isabella de' Medici in the way that she did, Magdalena had linked the memory of the most intellectually ambitious and sexually dangerous of the Medici women to the unquestionable virtue of the exceptional, excessive women painted on the villa's ceilings. She thus claimed for herself (and future generations of princesses) an unlikely melding of female Medicean ambition, sexual agency, and political virtù. *La liberazione*, then, would be performed in a space that Magdalena had infused with an almost defiant affirmation of womanly power, the space in which she meant her personification of Medici power to be understood.

"Born a virago": Magdalena as Patron and the Question of Genre

Kelley Harness has written about the broad pattern of artistic and theatrical patronage during Magdalena's regency. Bronzini's sketch of the archduchess adds depth to our knowledge of Magdalena as a patron by describing her habit of personally superintending the preparation of court spectacles meant to display Medicean power during her husband's reign.[27] Attributing the success and political effectiveness of certain entertainments to Magdalena's interventions in their preparation, Bronzini implied that she had mastered the art of political representation on which any princely government depends: "Born a virago . . . just by watching the discipline of the court's signori . . . she learned as well as her husband . . . how to manage horses and arms. Nor was there ever a festa or a torneo of horseback knights . . . at which she did not want to be present, to watch everything rehearsed, holding the script with great attention, not as a curious spectator but as a schooled and diligent observer, to remind and to comment (as she often did) on this or that which was lacking, and to give her opinions with great judgment."[28]

Bronzini elaborated his claim by describing in detail her direction of two spectacles, the equestrian spectacle *La guerra di bellezza*, staged in Piazza Santa Croce in 1616, and *La liberazione di Tirreno*, performed for the marriage of Cosimo II's sister Caterina to Duke Ferdinando Gonzaga of Mantua in 1617.[29] Writing of *La guerra*, Bronzini dutifully noted its music, decoration, costumes, and stage machines, but he reserved the ultimate praise of a Baroque performance—"fù meraviglia e stupor" ([it produced] wonder and awe)—for the agility and skill with which the riders of forty-two prized horses executed the maneuvers of stylized war, for the "fierce and terrible battle of the people on foot," and for the concluding balletto that the horses danced to a corrente:[30] Its "variety, beauty and fame," he wrote, were "recounted in other Italian and European cities by those who were present to see it, as a sign of the level of perfection Cosimo II's equestrian ballets had achieved. When the show was over, wherever the noble cavalry passed pedestrians, infinite crowds of the *popolo*, and all Florence rejoiced that through the actions of its lord the ancient spectacles of Rome and Athens had been renewed."[31]

Remarkably, the elements of *La guerra* that produced "meraviglia e stupor," international fame, and admiring crowds of Tuscan subjects in the streets were the very elements that Bronzini claimed were coached not by the Tuscan people's lord, but by his wife. Bronzini thus cast Magdalena as an ideal political wife whose expert work, literally behind the scenes, ensured that the people's admiring awe would be directed toward her husband. Read with the knowledge that by 1616 Magdalena also participated behind the scenes in the daily work of government, Bronzini's description implies she might similarly have used her virago's knowledge of manly things to advance Cosimo's position in matters of state.

Bronzini's description of Magdalena's equally fruitful attention to *La liberazione di Tirreno* seems aimed at making a slightly different point. More elaborate than *La guerra di bellezza*, *Tirreno* was for Bronzini "miraculous" for its stage machines, costumes, musical performances by Florence's best singers (including "ten virtuosissime women and girls"), and for the beautiful inventiveness of its staged battles and balletto di cavallo. But *Tirreno* elicited "meraviglia e stupor," he wrote, by virtue of the intricate balletti in which Magdalena and Cosimo II led carefully selected members of their court: "The Gordian knot was never woven as well as were these artful and most noble balletti led and performed by the most Serene Highnesses, [and] by a good number of dame and cavalieri at court . . . with the greatest agility and lightness that one can imagine; one saw the dance weave and unweave in such a way, and with such facility and felicity that it brought at once delight and pleasure, meraviglia and stupor, to whoever watched. It is no marvel that it succeeded so well, because (as I said before) the archduchess of whom we are speaking wanted always to be present when all the parts were rehearsed, before they were made public, and to have her prudent judgment taken into account."[32]

Again Bronzini attributed to Magdalena's intervention the element that had produced wonder and awe. In seventeenth-century Florence his claim had a powerful political valence, for half a century's worth of court spectacle had been based on a principle articulated in the second book of Plato's *Laws*. Rhythm and dance, Plato wrote, were gifts of the gods "whereby they cause us to move . . . linking us one with another"; they were the media for performing as embodied social action a social harmony governed by one of the universe's eternal principles, rhythm.[33] For Cosimo and Magdalena to have led *Tirreno's* balletti (as they had done so many others) was for them to have led their courtiers' performance of social harmony. Bronzini's emphasis on the balletti's intricate weavings and unweavings specifically invoked the common trope of sixteenth-century court dances as labyrinthine, enacting a dynamic relationship between apparent order and apparent chaos that was understood always to be governed by the higher-level order of a cosmic, divinely given rhythm.[34] For the virile Magdalena's "prudent judgments" to have ensured the felicity of *Tirreno's* balletti was, therefore, for her to have shown herself capable of governing the intricately shifting relationships that constituted the Tuscan state.

In light of Bronzini's representations of her patronage, Magdalena's choice to commission a "balletto composto in musica" for performance in the palace that was the seat of her gynocracy seems both intensely personalizing and intensely political.[35] Eliding her image as a virago capable of managing horses and arms in war, her ability to manage social order in times of peace, and her reputed attention to detail, the dances into which Francesca's commedia in musica would dissolve were sure to be seen as performances over which the archduchess had exercised personal artistic control. Thus *La liberazione*, though not an opera, had the political importance usually associated with one: it was likely to have seemed like a model in music and spectacle of Magdalena's gynocratic reign.

The 1624–1625 Season

Magdalena had commissioned *La liberazione di Ruggiero* as part of a four-month season of state entertainments intended to celebrate the visits of her brother, Archduke Karl of Styria, during October 1624 and at Carnival in 1625, and the visit for the latter of their nephew, Crown Prince Władisław, then renowned for his decisive rout of a Turkish army at the battle of Khotyn in 1621.[36] These visits were more political than personal; both were key to Magdalena's effort to align Tuscany and the Papal States with the Hapsburg Empire in a "Catholic league" dedicated to opposing both Lutheran heresy and French territorial ambitions on the Italian peninsula.[37] Magdalena's enthusiastic advocacy of the league was to be her boldest act as the Tuscan head of state, an effort to return its fortunes to the imperial protection to which Cosimo I had pledged himself vassal in 1537. Reversing the generation-long Tuscan "tilt" toward alliance with France initiated by her father-in-law Ferdinando I and sustained by his widow Christine, Magdalena meant to confirm the new alliance's seriousness in the same currency Ferdinando had used: the exchange of women. She meant to marry her second daughter, twelve-year-old Margherita de' Medici, to the handsome and cultivated Władisław.[38]

To celebrate both her own emergence as a world leader and the restoration of Tuscany's centrality in world affairs, Magdalena ordered a two-part entertainment program for the 1624–1625 season. A preliminary autumn season would honor Archduke Karl as he, his sister, and her ministers worked out details of a draft treaty that he would carry to the Spanish king. When Karl returned in the winter with a revised text, ready for Magdalena's and Władisław's signatures, the first full-fledged Carnival season of Magdalena's regency would celebrate both the new alliance and the betrothal meant to seal it.[39] Serving both as a kind of thematic bridge in the state's self-presentation and a demonstration of Magdalena's economy with Medicean resources, the show that had first welcomed Karl, *La regina Sant'Orsola*, was to be restaged in late January 1625. It would be followed by two entirely new entertainments: the complicated pastiche that was *La liberazione di Ruggiero*, and the musical barriera *La precedenza delle dame*. All three addressed the gender trouble that hovered around the virago archduchess's reign.

The official offering of fourteen-year-old Ferdinando II, paid for from the granducato's funds and staged in the theater of the Uffizi, Andrea Salvadori's sacred opera *La regina Sant'Orsola* had been written for the 1622 marriage of Princess Claudia de' Medici to Federico della Rovere, prince of Urbino.[40] Salvadori's drama elaborated one of the most common tropes of the widowed regents' will to power: the Catholic image of the virgin-martyr. His portrayal of Saint Ursula's defense of Cologne against the Huns showed how the womanly virtues of onestà and continenza could be projected beyond personal concerns, inspiring a resistance to invasion that could preserve intact a Catholic state. The 1624–1625 productions of *Sant'Orsola* were richly baroque.[41] Designed by Giulio Parigi, choreographed by Agnolo Ricci, composed by a team that included Marco and Giovanni Battista da Gagliano, Jacopo Peri, and Francesca Caccini, *Sant'Orsola* assimilated nearly every convention of court spectacle into its narrative. Aquatic, infernal, and celestial scenes evoked intermedi, an earthquake effect by which Jesus smote the heathens showed off a stage machine recycled from *La liberazione di Tirreno*, lament scenes for women and men filled the air with the sounds of powerful feeling, and an elaborately staged combat scene projected by its careful choreography Tuscany's ability to deploy troops effectively. The show concluded with a balletto through which the huge cast both embodied and celebrated the collaborative harmony of heaven and earth as symbolized in Christian terms. The virginal, virile Christian Ursula ascended to Paradise on a celestial cloud, surrounded by saints and angels, her body drawn heavenward by the warlike yet loving will of Jesus, at whose command onstage social order was restored.

La precedenza delle dame was a barriera—a stylized swordfight that takes place across a barrier—staged on 10 February 1625 as the offering of young Ferdinando's brother, thirteen-year-old Giovan Carlo de' Medici, in their uncle Cardinal Carlo's city palace, the Casino.[42] To music by Jacopo Peri and Marco da Gagliano, "young gentlemen of Florence" in two squadrons represented Mars and his swordsmen in battle with Athena and the armed girls who were her companions. According to Andrea Salvadori's published text, the battle had high stakes. If Mars were to win, women's bodies would forever be constrained in long skirts, and women would be forced to acknowledge themselves as forever the servants of men. But if Athena were to win, men would be obliged to treat women as equal consorts, not as domestics subject to endless tyranny. Their choreographed, long-practiced battle ended when Jove descended on a cloud amid a chorus of gods to pronounce Athena and her beautiful warriors victorious over arrogant Mars. Henceforth, Jove declared, "Every good soul, and every fierce heart must cede to the power of feminine beauty."[43] In the bold words and battlefield victory of Athena the audience could have perceived a spectacularized affirmation of the archduchess's image as a woman warrior surrounded by similar women. At the same time, because the barriera was sung and fought by her sons and their cohort among the noble youth of Florence, *La precedenza* demonstrated vividly that whether Tuscany's young men were dressed girlishly or not, during Magdalena's reign they were being well schooled in the arts of war.

In the figures of Ursula and Athena, both entertainments interpreted female virility, homosociality, and resistance to male ardor as saintly heroism and benevolent self-sacrifice on behalf of others. Moreover, by presenting female masculinity in masculine spaces, both shows naturalized the nonnormative qualities of the archduchess. But neither directly addressed men's fears of what would happen if they were to be trapped in a female homosocial world. *La liberazione* would address and allay those fears and would most directly affirm Magdalena's political program.

La liberazione di Ruggiero

When Magdalena's guests crossed the threshold of Villa Imperiale on 3 February 1625, they knew they were entering a gynocentric and gynocratic world. There, they would brush against the sexually dangerous ghost of Isabella de' Medici, and they would be wholly subject to female command. Their experience of Medicean gynocracy was to be set against one of recent literature's great gynophobic stories: the rescue of a young knight (Ruggiero) from a feminizing sorceress (Alcina) by a benevolent, magically bi-gendered one (Melissa), told in cantos six through ten of Ludovico Ariosto's *Orlando furioso*.[44]

The curtain that had been hung at one end of a balcony opened on an aquatic scene. Neptune, the traditional figure of Medicean naval might, entered to welcome his guests. With his Polish "tributary," a singer representing the River Vistula, he sang a double prologue in honor of Prince Władisław (see figure 9.1).[45]

Figure 9.1. Alfonso Parigi, first scene, wherein Neptune appears, *La liberazione di Ruggiero* (1625). Reproduced by permission of the Ministero per i Beni e le Attività Culturali/Galleria degli Uffizi, Firenze.

Figure 9.2. Alfonso Parigi, second scene, Alcina's island, *La liberazione di Ruggiero* (1625). Reproduced by permission of the Ministero per i Beni e le Attività Culturali/Galleria degli Uffizi, Firenze.

At the end of the prologue, trees rose from the sea to transform the aquatic scene into a pastoral one, Alcina's elegant garden of delights (see figure 9.2).

Melissa entered on a dolphin's back to explain, in what amounted to a second prologue, the action that would follow. Acting on behalf of the warrior-princess Bradamante, Melissa would rescue Ruggiero from Alcina's pleasure-filled spell, restoring him both to his military duty and to his sexual duty to found the Este dynasty as Bradamante's husband.[46] As Melissa exited, Ruggiero, Alcina, and her retinue of singing and dancing *damigelle* (maidens) appeared. After a dangerously miscommunicated exchange of lovers' vows, Ruggiero and Alcina temporarily parted. Alcina returned to her palace to tend to matters of state, leaving Ruggiero amid rhythmically swaying trees to be entertained by her damigelle, a shepherd, and a siren.[47] Their singing of increasingly seductive, poetically entangling paeans to love's delights lulled Ruggiero to sleep. Melissa returned, disguised as the aged African warrior Atlante. Her/his stern exhortation that Ruggiero return to battle awakened the lad both physically and spiritually.[48] Freed from his sensualist's stupor, the remorseful and newly resolute Ruggiero prepared to leave the stage with Atlante. But the pair were stopped by apparently disembodied song that seemed to emanate from nowhere and everywhere:

the pleas of the plants in Alcina's garden, discarded lovers of the sorceress who begged that they, too, might one day be liberated from the sorceress's spell.[49] Hearing Alcina return, the plants hurriedly advised Ruggiero and Melissa/Atlante to leave the stage.

Alcina returned with her damigelle to find Ruggiero gone. One of her damigelle, who, "hidden among the branches . . . saw and heard all," recounted a version of Ruggiero's liberation that was slightly different from the one represented onstage: she emphasized Melissa's gender transformation and her message from Bradamante but ignored Atlante's exhortation to war.[50] In response, Alcina vowed to win Ruggiero back with a stereotypically feminine display of "sweet notes" and "wet cheeks."[51] Rather than lament, Alcina confronted Ruggiero, demanding that he remain long enough at least to acknowledge her pain, his sins against the chivalric code, and his memories of their lovemaking's pleasures.[52] When he still spurned her, Alcina and her damigelle responded first with sorrow, then with ever-increasing rage. Alcina called on monsters of land and sea to avenge her loss as the scene that had been her garden was engulfed by flames.[53] Transformed from a beautiful woman into a monster, Alcina rode offstage amid her kind on a dragon's back (see figure 9.3).

Figure 9.3. Alfonso Parigi, third scene, Alcina's island ablaze, *La liberazione di Ruggiero* (1625). Reproduced by permission of the Ministero per i Beni e le Attività Culturali/Galleria degli Uffizi, Firenze.

Figure 9.4. Alfonso Parigi, fourth scene, wherein knights and ladies emerge from the caves; afterward, knights on horseback emerge. From *La liberazione di Ruggiero* (1625). Reproduced by permission of the Ministero per i Beni e le Attività Culturali/Galleria degli Uffizi, Firenze.

From the suddenly rocky, dry remains of Alcina's garden, dame who were once plants emerged at Melissa's command and "wove graceful dances" (see figure 9.4).[54]

Their first dance ended, one of the dame begged Melissa to liberate their still-imprisoned male partners as well.[55] Dispelling all occasion for lament in response to the dama's plea, Melissa freed the men. After dame and cavalieri danced together, the mountains and rocks onstage vanished, revealing a piazza where twenty-four cavalieri indicated their intention to perform a horseback ballet.[56] Audience and performers alike then left the loggia and repaired to an even vaster space. Settling at specifically assigned vantage points above or near the villa's lawn, they watched the horse ballet and Melissa's triumphant return, in a cart drawn by centaurs, to review the horses and riders (see figure 9.5).[57]

Giulio Parigi's plan for the stage pictures and scenic rhythm powerfully shaped the spectators' experience. After the early change from the aquatic prologue to the pastoral scene of Alcina's island, the visual world of *La liberazione* remained static until nearly the end of the show, mirroring Ruggiero's onstage entrapment in a world of pleasure. When it finally came, the consumption of Alcina's island by fire liberated spectators, players, and the workers who operated the stage machines into a world of suddenly rapid change that eventually required everyone to move. Lending a startlingly asymmetrical (indeed, baroque) shape to the audience's experience, *La liberazione*'s scenic rhythm focused attention not on Ruggiero's liberation but on the fire as a moment so transformative that it literally changed everything (and everyone) in the room. It was the fire that purged the wateriness that had for so long marked the stage as a humorally feminine, isolated space, replacing it with the ruggedly dry, humorally masculinized space in which all would be freed from complacent constraint. Because fire scenes depended on the expertise of explosives experts from the military, the experience could have seemed to restore masculinity by means of an implicitly masculine artifice of war, that is, it seemed to work the masculine magic of liberation that the show's plot attributed to Melissa's impersonation of Atlante.

But the fire seems not to have been wrought directly by Melissa's magic. All the sources that describe the first performance of *La liberazione* link the moment of immasculating fire directly to Alcina's magic—to the moment when she rejected as futile the feminine strategies of song and tears and instead marshaled magic and monsters to her defense.[58] The fire that precipitated all other scene changes was unmistakably Alcina's response to the damage Melissa had caused in her relational world. Thus both the fire and the liberating change it

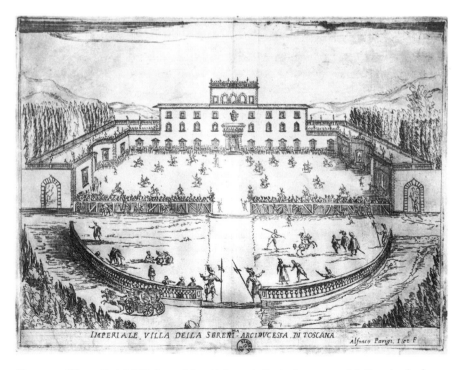

Figure 9.5. Alfonso Parigi, Villa Imperiale with horse ballet in the courtyard, believed to be from *La liberazione di Ruggiero* (1625). Reproduced by permission of the Ministero per i Beni e le Attività Culturali/Galleria degli Uffizi, Firenze.

unleashed could easily have been understood as produced by the response of one commanding woman to another, a response with humorally healing, socially desirable, "liberating" effects that leapt past the boundary of the stage to have consequences in the spectators' world. Parigi's scene design, then, elaborated the story of Ruggiero's liberation in a way that affirmed two commanding women's capacity to collaborate with each other in the creation of accelerating, beneficial, liberating change. At the same time, because the final scene required all the spectators to move, *La liberazione*'s scenic plan transformed the archduchess's guests into performers. As did the horses and dancers, the audience moved in response to effects produced at powerful women's command. Parigi's design compelled both on- and off-stage worlds to experience something like gynocracy as producing their liberation.

Spectators more attuned to details of plot and poetry than to scenic rhythm would have perceived Saracinelli's 685-line libretto as producing a symmetrical design for their experience, one that hinged, literally, on the two different, partly true representations of Ruggiero's liberation: Melissa's appearance as Atlante and the messenger's narrative account.[59] Saracinelli shrewdly juxtaposed poetic styles and well-chosen stock scenes to articulate his design. Before the liberation, two distinct poetic styles articulated a class-based social hierarchy. Ruggiero, Alcina, and Melissa sang *versi sciolti* (blank verse) that evoked high style and high-minded conceits; by contrast, the damigelle, shepherd, and siren who entertained Ruggiero and the ex-lovers she had trapped in the bodies of her garden's plants sang in short-lined, canzonetta-like stanzas. After the liberation, the hierarchy of styles was loosened. At that point Saracinelli added two stock scenes for women, familiar from the emerging conventions of *favole in musica*, that greatly expanded the range of female perspectives to which *La liberazione* gave voice: a messenger's description of transformation so catastrophic to her listener as to be painful to the ears, and a protagonist's struggle to recover her loss through lament.[60]

Both the messenger scene and Alcina's long complaint seem to affirm the conflation of women's public voices with the cultural work of pain, but they also invited the audience to reconsider their relationship to contemporary ideas of womanhood—perhaps to sympathize with the evil Alcina. Still, even if listeners responded sympathetically to Alcina's long speech, their assumptions about female embodiment may have made them hear her excessive vocality as producing excess bodily heat. Whether perceived as causing a monstrously accumulating readiness for sexual contact or an equally monstrous masculinization, Alcina's extravagant speech could thus have seemed to cause both her reversion to monstrous physical form and her recourse to the masculine magic of a stage fire. Because it provided an account of Ruggiero's liberation that was more complete than the one presented onstage, the messenger scene raised the possibility that reality seemed different to women than to men. Given that neither version of the liberation encompassed the whole story as told by Ariosto, attentive listeners could have concluded both that the knowledge exchanged among women was necessary to any whole and that their own presumed omniscience was but partial (and gendered) knowledge. Saracinelli thus made relationships among women, including those among relatively minor damigelle, seem necessary to constitute the (epistemo)logical world of the show.

A Tale of Two Women

The interaction of Saracinelli's symmetrical plot with Parigi's asymmetrical scenic rhythm, on one hand, and Saracinelli's focus on the liberation scenes with Parigi's alternative focus on Alcina's liberating fire, on the other, produces a tension that encourages an audience to understand the show's liberations beyond the level of plot—as produced, like the show itself, by the interaction of verbal and nonverbal "magics" over which each sorceress had control. Together, Saracinelli and Parigi ensured that their audience would receive the story of Ruggiero's liberation as primarily a tale of two magically powerful women and the conflicted yet complementary relationship between them. Ruggiero was little more than a token through whose exchange these women articulated the distribution of power. Indeed, *La liberazione* can be perceived as a fictional world constituted by the exchange of a man between two women, an exchange that restored him to productive sexuality and articulated the women's relationship as one of dominance and submission. Odd though it may be, the sex-gender system of *La liberazione* thus includes all the elements of heteronormativity. Moreover, it reflects remarkably well the system by which elite women managed each others' marriages in Tuscany, reinforcing a patrilineal circulation of economic power while ensuring that women could perceive themselves to be subjects as well as objects. Perhaps best described as female patriarchy, this was a system that justified Magdalena's plan to use her daughter's sexuality as a token in a diplomatic exchange.

Another way to think about the prominence of the two sorceresses in *La liberazione* is to imagine them as two versions of a single troubling figure, the commanding virago. Melissa is clearly a figure for Magdalena, effortlessly controlling her relationship to binaries that might have controlled others and, alone among the work's characters, existing both outside the plot (as the narrator of the show's second prologue) and inside it. Because she seemed both to transcend and to control the boundary between reality and representation that the setting at Villa Imperiale blurred, Melissa alone seemed capable of breaking representation's spell and liberating the audience to enter new social and spatial relationships. Even within the plot that her own prologue can seem to

have spun, Melissa's magic lay in her capacity to choose between binary opposites at will—to choose whether she would act as a woman or a man, a European or an African.[61] When she appeared to Ruggiero in the guise of the African
Atlante, Melissa projected gender and ethnic masquerades that seemed little
more than rhetorical strategies chosen to meet her listener's expectations. Yet
like all masquerades, Melissa's so vividly performed an identity other than her
own that it affirmed all the more strongly her European, womanly identity once
the disguise of African masculinity was dropped. By representing masculinity
as a masquerade that a powerful woman might employ for the purpose of restoring sexual, gender, and social order, and by using ethnic masquerade to dis-
place ambiguities of gender and sex to a place geographically far from Austria,
the source of Magdalena's identity, the figure of Melissa deftly managed local
anxieties about Magdalena's mannish, foreign ways. Melissa, who seemed to
exercise princely control over the contradictions of gender and ethnicity within
her own persona, implied that the virago archduchess whose power she so obviously represented could do the same.

Alcina seems like Melissa's polar opposite, an incarnation of the traditional
Mediterranean sorceress whose charms transformed lovers and rivals into animals, plants, or monsters, last represented on the Tuscan stage in 1617 as Circe
in *La liberazione di Tirreno*. Although nothing like a virago, the Circe-Alcina type
was no less terrifying to men, for she elicited men's fear of female sexuality as
the cause of their own effeminating desires and their even deeper fear of female
sexual difference as itself monstrous. Far less comprehensible to men in her
intentions and methods than the strategically virile virgin-martyrs, Athenas,
and Melissas of androcentric imagination, Alcina threatened social order both
by affirming female sexual subjectivity and by detaching all sexuality from its
social utility in reproduction. Yet for all that she evoked a dangerously exaggerated femininity, she eventually rejected the feminine rhetorics of song and
tears in favor of magic, monsters, and fire. Indeed, it was at the very moment
when Ariosto's story would have led audiences to believe that Alcina's power
had failed, revealing her true nature to all, that *La liberazione*'s Alcina wielded
the magic that beneficially masculinized the performing space and revealed her
own monstrosity. Whatever the staged transformation of Alcina's body might
have been, the monstrous Alcina could easily have seemed in that moment to
act with the power of a virago. But unlike Melissa's, Alcina's suddenly revealed
mannishness would have seemed no contingent, strategically chosen disguise.
Instead, this Alcina would have seemed both committed to unproductive sexuality and a virago at her core. As pure a threat to heteropatriarchy as could be
imagined in female form, it was this monstrosity of essential gender and sexual
disorder that *La liberazione*'s narrative sent flying from the Tuscan stage astride
another monster's back.

"Donne con Donne"

The essentially monstrous Alcina was brought to two obvious expressions of sexual excess—proliferating speech and explosive heat—in response to the magic of another oddly gendered female. To a twenty-first-century sensibility the relationship between the two seems a little queer.[62] Might this relationship—one that *La liberazione* ensured its audience would experience as beneficial—have seemed queer in 1625? If so, how might the hint of queer doings have interacted with the political work that *La liberazione* seems likely to have done?

Certainly, female homoeroticism was part of the early modern imaginary. Abundant evidence attests to anxious fantasies about the erotic lives of courtly women left to themselves.[63] The Abbé de Brantôme's picaresque tales of life at the French court of Catherine de' Medici, for example, portray some women there as exchanging erotic intimacies.[64] Describing a wide range of relationships with the vague description *donne con donne*, Brantôme emphasized that although convention linked such behavior to *putains* (prostitutes), females of the highest rank exchanged various combinations of physical and affective intimacy. Some *dames galantes* were so immersed in mutual pleasure or so emotionally attached to each other as to have cuckolded their husbands, he thought. Others treated their relationships as mere pastimes. According to Brantôme, so long as these relationships did not involve the use of dildos they were neither scandalous nor unnatural. Indeed, Brantôme restored such relationships to usefulness in a heteronormative gender system, suggesting that dames galantes, especially unmarried girls and widows, could use erotic and affective intimacy with each other to satisfy desire without risking pregnancy or dishonor. Such intimacies, he added, could prepare girls well for the heterosexual intimacies of marriage.

Brantôme's notions about female homoeroticism were surely known at the Tuscan court, if only because his titillating anecdotes came from the very court where Christine de Lorraine had been raised; he had been careful to exempt both Christine and her beloved grandmother from participation in that court's prevailing culture of donne con donne eroticism. Yet it seems possible that gossips hostile to Christine's long regency, now shared with Magdalena, would have used their reading of Brantôme to develop whispered sexual slanders against the pair's firmly gynocentric social world. Thus when Magdalena and her artistic staff chose to stage *La liberazione* at Villa Imperiale, the palace at the heart of that world, they may have meant to confront rumors of courtly women exchanging erotic pleasures (as well as knowledge, men, and magic) among themselves. Indeed, the choice of plot could hardly have been better designed to address exactly this aspect of the regency's gender trouble, for *La liberazione* was recognizably set somewhere in northwestern Africa.[65] A setting that invited guests to identify Ruggiero's "liberation" as the redirecting of his sexual and political allegiances toward the north, the show's location also invited them to compare Alcina with the notorious sorceresses of Fez as described in Leo Africanus's widely circulating travelogue: "People call these women *Sahacat,* which in Latin signifies *Fricatrices,* because they have a damnable custom to commit unlawful Venerie among themselves. . . . If fair women come unto them at any time, these abominable witches will burn in lust towards them no less than lusty gentlemen do toward young maids. . . . There are even some which being allured with the delight of this abominable vice, will desire the companie of these witches."[66]

Committed to unproductive sexuality, responsive in the easily sexualized registers of excessive speech and somatic fire to the power of another woman, recognized as having captured dame as well as cavalieri in the arboreal thrall of her island, Alcina could surely have evoked this passage (or any of the similar ones recycled through mid- and late-sixteenth-century literature) for the 1625 audience of *La liberazione.*[67] She might, that is, have been received as an African sexual renegade whose monstrosity encompassed possibilities that a twenty-first-century audience could call "lesbian." As such, Alcina represented in the most monstrous possible form the perils of entrapment in anachronistic, unproductive allegiances that could sap any hero's will to act effectively in response to a suddenly changing world. Her antagonist Melissa's magical ability to be a virago or not, to be an African or not, taught the onstage Ruggiero (and the audience that watched) a liberating flexibility in relation to the categories of identity and identification on which such allegiances might be based. Ultimately, Melissa embodied as virtuous, liberating, and restorative the policy of Tuscany's female princes—their break with the state's anachronistic dependence on political and sexual alliances to other Italian princes and their shift toward alliances with the Hapsburg network of world powers.

Yet the possible "lesbian" resonance between Alcina and the sorceresses of Fez queers her incendiary relationship with Melissa, allowing the staged complementarity of their magics to seem like a representation of donne con donne eroticism. *La liberazione*'s unequivocal representation of the two sorceresses in a dominant-submissive relationship could have been interpreted to portray them as a conventionally gendered couple, however oddly sexed. That portrayal could in turn have rendered their collaborative restoration of the show's onstage gender order a logical outcome of their shared commitment to gender complementarity.[68] Certainly, Melissa's dominance ensured that her commitment to productive heterosexuality would prevail. Thus *La liberazione* may have allowed its audience to revisit a common suspicion about the pleasures that circulated among women left to themselves, leaving mental space for individuals to allay any fears or savor any pleasures that suspicion might provoke. The show all but acknowledges the existence of donne con donne eroticism at the regents' court, while in the liberation of the courtly women whom Alcina had entrapped, and in their explicit pleas for male partners, it affirmed something like Brantôme's view. Even if female homosociality included homoeroticism, it need not threaten full participation in the reproductive heterosexuality and hierarchical gender that together constituted a heteronormative social order.

Indeed, in the fictive world of *La liberazione* it was the stylized donne con donne eroticism of Melissa's and Alcina's complementary magics that produced the conditions in which that social order would flourish, preparing young women for erotic pleasures with men. Moreover, the dynamic between these two extraordinary females clearly produced the politically important liberations of both Ruggiero and the spectators who identified with him. Together, Melissa and Alcina liberated Ruggiero from unproductive sexual and ethnic identifications, redirecting his energy toward sexually and politically productive identification with a militant Christendom centered in Europe. And together they liberated the audience from the thrilling but stifling, intentionally tangled thralls of represented and real confinement in a gynocentric space.

As political theater intended to support Magdalena's policy initiatives, *La liberazione* clearly had the potential to liberate her subjects from their worst fears about a gynocratic regime. But according to Florentine assumptions about the uses of spectacle and music to support the state, it could not have had a serious effect on its audience—could not have literally moved their bodies from their seats and their minds from their fears—without its music.

Performance, Musical Design, and Politics in *La liberazione di Ruggiero*

10

*L*a liberazione is the only entertainment from Francesca's pen to survive nearly whole. That the score was published under Magdalena's aegis implies that Francesca's music was important to the show's success and to the memories of its performance that Magdalena wanted to be circulated and preserved. Indeed, *La liberazione*—funny, inventive, and moving by turns—proved entertaining enough to be produced again three years later, under the patronage of the Polish prince whose Tuscan sojourn it had first marked. Liberated from its ontological status as an event into transportable and transhistorical existence as a work, *La liberazione*'s representation of the paradoxes that can link power regimes we consider public to the ones that govern gender and sexuality continues to ensure its intermittent salience as a semi-canonic work.

The interpretive perspectives on *La liberazione* that I offer here are informed by two idiosyncratic preoccupations.[1] First, I have developed my interpretations by thinking through my experience of the performances of *La liberazione* that I saw at Düdingen, Switzerland, in May 1999, under the direction of Gabriel Garrido and Ruth Orthmann.[2] Because I came to these performances after a decade of archival work, the sensibility of my presentist response had been formed to a historicist cultural literacy of the sort Gary Tomlinson once proposed as a technique for unraveling the meanings of early music texts.[3] The interior dialogue between my presentist self and my historicist self encouraged me to think about *La liberazione*'s power in performance through two events—one the week-long set of technical rehearsals and performances I witnessed in 1999, the other a late-morning entertainment at court in 1625. Acknowledging that

my responses are based on a particular performance has forced me to acknowledge, too, that during the performance I experienced vivid, out-of-time recombinations of events that were liberated from the show's narrative, but not unre-
lated to it. Those recombinations so illuminated my experience that I have tried
to replicate it here. Through close readings of *La liberazione*'s central scenes, in
relation to each other but out of narrative order, I show how Francesca's music
encouraged her audiences to understand Ruggiero (and the humans trapped as
plants in Alcina's garden) as liberated not from Alcina's evil spell but from the
results of gynophobia.

Second, I have tried to think about Francesca's contribution to *La liberazione*
through the aesthetic to which Bronzini referred in *Della dignità e nobiltà delle
donne* when he repeatedly claimed that the world was made of geometry and
music.[4] If Francesca or her patrons believed such a thing, however incoherently,
her compositional work could never have seemed to them only a matter of providing music that delivered Saracinelli's words well—least of all when, as in the
winter of 1625, matters of state were at stake. Instead, they must have understood her charge to have been the creation of a parallel universe made of music,
in which musical relationships could bring into being real experiences of the
dynamic that is power. I show that Francesca's sound design for *La liberazione*
met that challenge, modeling in sound a notion of liberation as the reorganization of power relations in the performance space, leading men and women alike
to find places in a harmonious moral universe guided by a female hand.

La liberazione as Entertaining Performance

Three scenes in *La liberazione* make an especially strong impression in live
performance—the fabulously campy lament scene for a chorus of enchanted
plants, the highly ornamented yet unforgettable strophic aria that a siren sings,
and Alcina's long complaint against Ruggiero's abandonment. Two of the three
were explicitly constructed in *La liberazione* as self-conscious performances,
meant to elicit a response from Ruggiero: the siren was to entertain him, and
Alcina sought to win him back by the ostentatious display of feminine song and
tears. Yet these two scenes are just as easily construed as performances of a single male fantasy: the alluring siren who promises amorous delight and the insa-
tiably demanding monster into which she could turn constituted the before and
after of a young man's heterosexual infatuation. Each entertaining in its own
way, these scenes' sounds, formal techniques, and representations bounce off
each other in memory, and bounce as well against the experience of the third, a
scene that seems at first neither a performance nor a projection of young men's
experience of female sexuality. That third scene, featuring the enchanted plants
of Alcina's garden, stages the experiences of once-human creatures whom

Alcina has reduced to a lower form of life. Creatures assumed to have neither subjectivities nor voices, whose reception of cultural performances had never been imagined by those who trafficked in the conventions of representation, the plants, too, perform for Ruggiero, begging him to secure their return to full humanity.

When I first saw *La liberazione* performed, it was the scene of the enchanted plants that sprang me out of the assumption that I knew *La liberazione* because I knew its score so well.[5] In a flash, as the plants bewailed their fate, an out-of-time parallel track opened in my mind where for the rest of the evening I experienced the fruitful collision of performance moments with each other as avidly as I watched the show's narrative unfold before my eyes. Richard Schechner has theorized a way to account for my experience. He has likened the liminal and ludic space that performance can open in the mind to the subjunctive mood in language.[6] In the years since 1999, I have come to think that Francesca may have hoped to create just such a subjunctive experience. For at the moment my mind opened to perceive *La liberazione* in two dimensions at once, I experienced the power of performed music to intervene in the normative relations of which "the world" is made. The song of the plants adjusted power relations among the figures onstage, and that shift all but burst across the proscenium to change both my relation to the staged events and my relation to perception itself. Sprung unwittingly into a new state of consciousness, I was myself temporarily liberated. I think it was no accident that this moment of meraviglia e stupor was the moment after Ruggiero's onstage liberation, the moment when liberation began to move, however slowly, through all the silenced, motionless, listening creatures in the room.

In the subjunctive space that the Düdingen performance opened in my mind, I felt that the scene of the spatially, socially, and discursively constrained enchanted plants performed with wit and pathos exactly the condition imposed on women by societies that cater to the gynophobia elicited by Alcina's and the siren's songs. Thus I came to understand the three most memorable, most entertaining, most easily excerpted scenes of *La liberazione* as constituting an internal intertextual web centered on performances of womanhood, each of which is a foil for the other two. Set, so to speak, perpendicular to the entwined narratives by which action, stagecraft, poetry, and plot construct the show's world as one made and ruled by women, the web formed by these three scenes crystallizes Ruggiero's experience of that world, fuses it to the audience's experience, and represents powerfully the spell that needs to be broken. Taken together, these scenes imply that it is not the spell of musical or sexual allure that traps Ruggiero on Alcina's island, but the spell of his own gynophobic fantasies. They further imply that Melissa's liberation of Ruggiero liberates women and men alike—the chorus of enchanted plants—from the compulsion to perform themselves and their relationships through the conventions about womanhood and gender in which gynophobic fantasies result.

A Paradox of Plants

It is at the exact midpoint of the show, in the moment after Ruggiero's liberation, that the enchanted plants begin to sing. Persuaded by Atlante (he thinks) to abandon Alcina and return to the field of war, the chastened Ruggiero has moved to exit when a disembodied tenor voice calls to him by name. Singing rhythmically repetitious phrases that descend inexorably (and dependently) in parallel tenths with the bass, the voice pleads that Ruggiero listen to the bitter fate of the plants.[7] Suddenly the garden fills with song, a five-part chorus accompanied by viols, *organo di legno*, and keyboards that echoes the first plant's music and affect. Ruggiero and Atlante listen on, agape at a moment of theatrical and musical wonder.

Surprising in its beauty and emotional power, the scene of the enchanted plants is a little masterpiece of paradox.[8] Comprised of miniatures yet one of the longest scene complexes in *La liberazione*, the scene in 1625 would have unleashed a cascade of associations in listeners' minds: plants were among the entities most often claimed to have been moved by the musical magic of Orpheus; some plants—notably the laurel tree and the sunflower—had once been women (Daphne who became a tree to escape Apollo's rape, Clizia who became a flower as punishment for loving Apollo too much); given Giulio Caccini's equal fame as a teacher of women singers and a cultivator of citruses and roses, they might be a joke on the probable casting of the show from among his daughter's pupils; given the Medici family's creation of the gardens at Castello—the traditional women's villa—as an allegory of the Tuscan state, and given the meaning of "Fiorenza"—flowering place—they might be the Florentines (*fiorentini*) themselves. Moreover, in its astonishingly pure distillation of pathos the scene would have given its listeners a nearly perfect realization, in miniature, of the Bardian aesthetic that demanded music so focus its expressive gestures as to overwhelm audiences. But all this density of reference, all this focus of musically expressive power, emerged from the unseen orifices of . . . well, of plants. The campy improbability of the moment—poking fun at the very aesthetic it realized—must have been every bit as overwhelming as the plants' pathos and proliferating meanings, so overwhelming the audience's responses that they would not know whether to laugh or cry. And that, perhaps, would have been the first of the scene's powerful effects, for the lament of the plants could paralyze the expanding responses of its listeners as surely as root and bark paralyzed the bodies of its singers.

Francesca constructed the scene of the enchanted plants as two miniature strophic songs entwined around each other, and entwined in turn around the straightforward recitative responses of the plants' onstage listeners, Melissa and Ruggiero. The first strophic song consists of three six-line stanzas, each set to a mere fourteen bars of music. Sung by tenor, soprano and tenor plants respectively, each stanza's plaintively descending melody began bound to its bass by parallel motion, and bound to a single rhythmic idea. Twice, Francesca's melody asks the singer to leap fruitlessly toward the upper limit of the mode on d, reaching it on a third try only to sink back down by step through the mode's whole range (see example 10.1).

Ex. 10.1. Francesca Caccini, *La liberazione di Ruggiero* (1625), 37–38, First Plant to Ruggiero
Ruggiero, for the bitter injuries
Of these plaintive plants,
Oh! Feel pity in your heart.
We shall remain very sad
And deprived of every hope
If your virtù leaves.

Entangled with the plaints of individual plants are two stanzas of a five-part ensemble refrain, and its instrumental ritornello. Francesca packed a surprising number of relationships among parts into the nine bars (thirty seconds) of music. Each linked motivically to the solo plants' rhythmic surface, and each restricted to a narrow range, the five voices (soprano 1, soprano 2, alto, tenor, and bass) form, in this tiny bit of music, five different homophonic subgroups (AB; AT; S1AT; S1T; and S2 A) around two points of imitation (one involving all five parts, the other S1 and T only). Obscuring the words in direct violation of local aesthetic standards, Francesca's counterpoint required her singers literally to perform a cramped struggle to change their relations with each other within a space both temporally and registrally confined. By scoring the echoing ritornello for the "infernal" sonorities of the theater—viols, trombones, organo di legno and keyboards in low clefs—she colored the feeling of claustrophobic confinement with the sounds of hell. Form, rhythm, texture, tonality, register and timbre—every parameter of sound and performing gesture thus modeled the experience of imprisonment, and produced a distilled, comic example of one favorite seventeenth-century paradox, the beautifully hopeless struggle against constraint.[9] But even as one smiles for Francesca's wit, the emotional effect of so miniaturizing failed struggle can be overwhelmingly sad (see example 10.2).

Onstage in *La liberazione*, both Ruggiero and Melissa respond to the plants' pathos. Ruggiero's suggestion that their suffering might be praised as virtù elicits a soprano and then a tenor stanza of further pleading, followed by a reprise of the choral lament. Melissa responds then, above harmonies so goal-directed as to promise in music as well as words their eventual release. In the moment, however, they are not so much released as reorganized, transformed from performers of collective but leaderless complaint into a chorus whose newly homophonic texture added unanimity of utterance to their unanimity of affect. But transformation was not yet liberation. Still trapped in d-mollis, and now trapped as well in the strictly homophonic texture Medicean aesthetics prescribed for ensembles, the still-immobilized plants ended their scene with a dance song in 3/2 ("Itene liete") whose words wished Ruggiero and Melissa well in their quest of the plants' eventual liberation. As the rhythmic voices of these bodies rooted to the spot celebrated a fantasy liberation into dance, Francesca's music again ensured the plants' fate would seem both comical and sad. Exchanging the virtù of hopeless struggle for the modified rapture of living vicariously through others' exploits, they change both affect and words without changing either their condition or their apparent subordination to others' power.[10] Thus the plants prophesy one paradox of *La liberazione di Ruggiero*. In this show neither they nor Ruggiero would ever be free of Melissa's show-biz magic (see table 10.1).

Ex. 10.2. Francesca Caccini, *La liberazione di Ruggiero* (1625), 38, chorus of enchanted plants, with ritornello

Oh, how much merit, oh, how much
Praise you will have, if you calm our weeping.

Ritornello (4 viols, 4 trombones, organo di legno, and keyboards)

Table 10.1. *La liberazione*, scene of the enchanted plants

Character	Incipit	Tonal area	Meter	Length	Form
Tenor plant	Vs. 1: *Ruggier' de danni asprissimi*	d-mollis	c	14 mm.	⎫
Chorus à 5	Refrain: *O quanto merto*	d-mollis		9 mm.	⎬ A
Ritornello à 4		d-mollis		4 mm.	⎭
Ruggiero	Recit: *O miserabil vita*	d-durus		7 mm.	B
Soprano plant	Vs. 2: *Qual scempio miserabile*	d-mollis		14 mm.	⎫
Tenor plant	Vs. 3: *Fanne quinci rimuovere*	d-mollis		14 mm.	⎬ A´
Chorus à 5	Refrain: *quanto merto*	d-mollis		9 mm.	⎬
Ritornello à 4		d-mollis		4 mm.	⎭
Melissa	Recit: *Consolatevi o Piante*	d-mollis		12 mm.	C
Chorus à 5	Vs. 1: *Itene lieti mentre noi qui*	d-mollis	c3	9 mm.	⎫
Ritornello SSB		d-mollis		4 mm.	⎬ D
Chorus à 5	Vs. 2: *Su'l vil terreno*	d-mollis		9 mm.	⎭

At Düdingen in 1999, the women and men who sang the plants were barely visible behind a green scrim. That production choice made me realize where, in 1625, a Florentine audience would most often have heard voices that came from everywhere and nowhere at once. It would have been at the concerts performed from behind the grates in those Florentine churches that were attached to communities of cloistered women. Heard through memories of unseen music from behind grates, the scene of enchanted plants provoked for me a sudden awareness of the whole system for the containment of women for which the grate of a cloister stood—a system predicated on men's fear of entanglement by sirens, or by sorceresses like Alcina. Thus I heard the plants' compressed condition to stand for courtly women's entrapment in the miniaturized expectations their culture had of them. Their embodied, daily lives hidden away in the country villas to which court women were consigned with their retinues for months at a time, or in the cloisters that they visited for amusement and prayer, such women were expected to find virtù in suffering while men found it in action, and to find happiness in supporting the public action of their champions rather than in taking public action themselves. Only women born to what Tasso had called the virtù donnesche—the immasculate virtù required of women born to rule—escaped the confines of such expectations.[11] Like me, I thought, the people who heard this scene in February 1625 may have heard in the plants' complaint against infernal confinement the voice of women's seldom-acknowledged pain, as well as a critique of the gender system that confined them. Like me, they may thus have heard the show's two more obvious performances of womanhood—the siren's song and Alcina's complaint—as staging men's fantasies and fears of women's sexuality, fantasies and fears from which Melissa's magic promised to liberate both women and men.

A Siren Song

The very idea that the Circe-like Alcina commanded a siren to entertain Ruggiero must have struck everyone in 1625 as ridiculous, redundantly piling one atop the other two figures for women's power to reduce heroes to besotted beasts. Francesca captured both the scene's over-the-top comedy and its paranoid doubling of gynophobic fantasy in the form of her siren's song, ensuring that the scene could be heard to poke musical and theatrical fun both at the poetic conceit that likened women musicians to sirens and at men's imagined vulnerability to feminine wiles.

The song culminated a scene of progressively entangling forms. From the moment Ruggiero and Alcina had entered the stage, strophic songs had surrounded their recitative in webs of musical rather than verbal pleasure. Francesca scored the strophic canzonette Alcina's damigelle spun around the pair's apparent exchange of vows so that the girls' voices constantly change their relationship to each other within the texture.[12] Charming, distracting, deceptively simple, the girls' stanzas entertain in part because no ear can distinguish which girl carries the tune. When Alcina left the stage to tend to "the cares of the realm," a shepherd had sung love's praises in a strophic song for which Caccini composed slyly elusive ABA' stanzas and a tonally static ritornello for three flutes that evoked the erotic allure of the pastoral.[13] But for Ruggiero's final entrapment by the siren, Francesca created a whirlpool of musical pleasure, as shown in the chart below.[14] A strophic song built of palindromic stanzas at first left Ruggiero capable of reasonable, recitative response. But by repeating an interior phrase as the instrumental ritornello between stanzas two and three, Francesca spun a song that stuns the casual ear, making the song's form both alluring and momentarily unintelligible.

The delightful but not dazzling passaggi, slippery harmonies where line-ending cadences ought to be, and formal indecipherability of the siren's little song tighten the last knot by which Ruggiero's capacity for reason was bound in threads of song. Only one phrase could linger in a listener's memory, its crisp goal-directed harmonies bearing their words' command even in its instrumental ritornello reprise: "follow Love, follow Love." The command lulled Ruggiero to the intellectually lazy, sensually satisfied sleep of a man drugged by the performance of his own fantasy that a woman's love was pleasurable entanglement (see example. 10.3).[15]

The siren's song seems stylistically remote from the compression into tight spaces of the enchanted plants' scene. Yet *La liberazione*'s plot sources would have led the first audience to suppose that exactly such performances had entrapped Alcina's former lovers in similarly entwining strophic forms of their own, until they were reduced to the irrational, spiritually paralyzed condition of plants. That debasement was, in turn, understood by at least one sixteenth-century critic of *Orlando furioso* to have represented through metaphors of sexuality the illegitimate power of tyrants over their people.[16] Thus along the axis of narrative the scenes of the siren and of the plants could have musically engaged their first listeners' fears about their own vulnerabilities both to female sexuality and its political counterpart, tyranny from the absolute gynocracy that ruled Tuscany. Calculated to seduce listeners as surely as, respectively, they seduced and moved Ruggiero, both scenes were calculated, too, to make the audience laugh at the absurdity of their fears.

Perceived in the subjunctive mood of performance, these two scenes can prompt understanding of a causality neither represented nor implied by the plot alone. For if one imagined the plants as representing women forced to live within the often literally immobilizing constraints men's obsession with controlling female sexuality imposed, then the plants' lamentable condition would

Ex. 10.3. Francesca Caccini, *La liberazione di Ruggiero* (1625), 31–33, Siren to Ruggiero, with ritornello

Whoever in the flower of youth

Wants to enjoy sweetness of soul,

Follow Love,

Who dissolves

Every nuisance, every pain.

Follow Love, follow Love

[You who] in the flower of youth

Want to enjoy sweetness of soul.

seem to result not from sirens' singing so much as from the gynophobic fantasy
the siren represents. It was the figure of the siren—the projection of men's fear
that they would, themselves, lack sexual self-control—that caused the compression of real women's lives and voices into miniaturized forms. In *La liberazione*,
the siren and the plants marked as slithery seductiveness and wooden chastity
the opposite ends of the continuum on which both contemporary gender relations and conventional representations of womanhood were mapped. Their
scenes are opposites, too, as performances of power. Lovely and ingenious as it
is, the Siren's song produces only a detached admiration in a listener offstage.
Incapable of changing the dynamics in the room, it is too flimsy a representation of women's supposedly irresistible power to justify the cultural imperative
of women's containment in the bodies of trees. Not so Alcina's complaint.

Alcina's Complaint

Like the siren's song and the scene of the enchanted plants, Alcina's complaint
against Ruggiero's abandonment was both brilliant and over the top. As exag-
geratedly long as the plants' lament had been brief, Alcina's insistently vocal
response to Ruggiero's "liberation" eventually climaxed in the spectacle of a
woman having sung herself and her world afire. The scene's incendiary climax
must have struck at least some in the first audience as a hilarious sendup of
conventional warnings against the humoral and sexual dangers of overheating
that could result from excessive female speech.[17] But long before the confla-
gration Alcina's song had exceeded the conventions of the lament/complaint
scene, performing the worst nightmare of gynophobic fantasy—the spectacle
of a woman whose sexuality and desire burst her own subjectivity's boundaries
to spread unchecked, engulfing the sonic world.

Unlike the damigelle, shepherd and siren who were subject to her, Alcina had
never sung canzonetta stanzas, nor in rounded forms. Her onstage social rank
guaranteed that when she heard of Ruggiero's liberation, Alcina would confront
him with a through-composed recitative soliloquy.[18] Thus her listeners would
incline to hear her prolonged, musically and emotionally rich speech as articulating one of the moral themes of the show. Moreover, because both she and
her retinue framed the speech as an opportunity to "see what divine beauty can
do with sweet weeping," Alcina's speech would have been heard at least in part
through the conventions of lament.[19] A genre then understood to articulate, in
ritual and in drama, the threshold of fundamental change, the soliloquy lament
all but demanded that there be change in response to its moral dilemma.[20] Thus
more than any other scene in *La liberazione*, Alcina's complaint staged the power
of music to rearrange the relations of which the world was made.

Francesca constructed the scene's core address to Ruggiero from three motivically dissimilar sections. For the first, "Ferma, ferma crudele," she created a melodic surface of dense motivic consistency.[21] Alcina's every statement is built of only two rhythmic gestures, a trochee (long-short) or a dactyl (long-short-short), freely combined. Her economy of rhythm lends Alcina's words the force of direct speech, while it sustains a similar economy of melodic gestures, mostly limited to triad outlines emphasizing a sustained harmony in the bass, or multiple ways of filling a single intervallic space. The most prominent of the latter can be heard in developments of the phrase that sets the opening line. Vaguely reminiscent of the beginning of Alcina's speeches to Ruggiero in the earlier garden scene, this opening phrase serves as a kind of musical thesis for "Ferma, ferma crudele," establishing the diminished fourth c'' to $g\#'$ as a space her melody will fill over and over again (see example. 10.4a). Recurring transposed over the next two phrases, the diminished 4th overtly creates a musical equivalent for the assonance that links such words as "spietato" (m. 4) and "ingrato" (m. 5–6). These links take on a peculiar enharmonic twist in the microtonally close sound of the major third a-sharp$'$ to f-sharp$'$ on the word "pianto" (m. 7–8) to the earlier b$'$-flat to f-sharp$'$ of "spietato." The density of these gestures at the speech's beginning are enough to make a listener cringe in expectation during all subsequent descents from d'' or c'', and to hear the many phrase endings that unexpectedly sharp a final pitch as related to the qualities in Ruggiero—he is "spietato" (pitiless) and "ingrate" (ungrateful)—that cause Alcina's tears. Thus, toward the end of the second stanza the extraordinary c#-g#-a# motion at "pene e doglie" (punishment and pain) (see example. 10.4b) can seem like a transformation of the opening motive, a strained conflation of the opening c'' to the extraordinary sharpness, in a musically literal sense, with which Ruggiero's sudden disdain wounded Alcina. It is a moment so musically wondrous as almost to make a listener forget that Alcina's words here speak of pain. That seems likely to have been part of Francesca's point, if not Alcina's, for Francesca thus ensured that the performance of a woman's pain would entertain, as an example of meraviglia. (Listen to track 11.)

In constructing the surface of "Ferma, ferma crudele" so economically, Francesca also ensured that she would seem at the beginning of her scene to perform one cardinal virtù of womanhood, continenza (the conservation of resources). But Alcina's surface continenza is belied by the tantalizing quality of her harmonies. Nearly every phrase of "Ferma, ferma crudele" ends by pausing either above an artificially major triad or above an 11 #10 suspension, or both (see example 10.4 again). Because both gestures typically signified the penultimate chord of a phrase, they arouse listeners' desires. Alcina's control of surface rhetoric and provocative harmonies combine to create a precise image in sound of the threat she posed to the social order. Capable of exciting others' tonal desires, and satisfying them or not at will, she seems in perfect control

Ex. 10.4. Francesca Caccini, *La liberazione di Ruggiero* (1625), 53–54, Alcina to Ruggiero
  (a) Stop, stop, cruel one,
        Where are you going, pitiless one,
        Where do you leave me, ingrate, [to be the] prey of weeping?
  (b) You will see your failing and my fidelity
        And [you will see] that between pain and grieving,
        Here [in my face] it gathers as much sorrow as the world has.

of the way she performs what Ruggiero and her other audiences expect from a lamenting woman—a sonic disorder that stands for the disorder of female sexual agency beyond the control of men.[22] Francesca's Alcina complains like a woman remarkably self-possessed.

But Ruggiero interrupts. Francesca ensures his interruption would seem to transform Alcina into the phantom of his fantasies, for at his prompting her Alcina literally changes tune. Dropping almost all pretense at motivic economy, in the second section of her soliloquy Alcina twists constantly between the mollis system his short recitative had proposed to her and the durus in which she tries to rekindle his desire.[23] Against her song's resulting fabric of cross-relations, Alcina's fleetingly sustained sevenths and ninths and her pauses on artificially major triads create still more desire for a tonal closure that never comes. At once alluring and disturbing, Alcina's harmonies sound a music of hurt feeling and proliferating desire that compels attention. As her music fills the ears and sensibilities of her listeners, the Alcina who is reduced to little else than en-voiced desire perfectly matches the gynophobic fantasy of a sexually insatiable woman. Yet at the moment her desire finds response in a damigella's voice, the Alcina Francesca has constructed becomes something more. A woman whose voiced distress moves another woman to supportive response, a woman whose desires are satisfied in the register of music by another woman's voice, Alcina evokes every terror embedded in the word gynophobia—fear of women's desire, of women's collective power, and of donne con donne intimacy that might, like the intimacies of women with the sorceresses of Fez, usurp the heterosexual prerogatives of men. (Listen to track 12.)

"O, cruelty of a tiger! o heart of stone!"[24] One of Alcina's damigelle thus interrupts her complaint, not to offer the familiar cliché of a confidante consol-ing her padrona but to berate Ruggiero on Alcina's behalf. Holding her voice to a narrow range and a restrained, speech-like recitative that signals a certain kind of self-control, the damigella addresses Ruggiero in Alcina's language of unanswered harmonic desire. Saturated with Alcinian harmonies that function like unresolved dominants, peppered with dissonances so unexpectedly harsh as to make a listener gasp, in less than a minute (sixteen bars of printed music) the damigella's interjection expands the tonal world onstage to fill four adja-cent hexachords (from the quadruple-mollis based on A-flat to the mollis based on F). Virtually unheard-of minor sonorities rooted on b-flat and e-flat ground the sung pitches d″-flat and g′-flat. Thereby the sounds of shared female com-plaint and unsatisfied female desire spread throughout the entire world of pitches recognized by early seventeenth-century music theory (see table 10.2, and example. 10.5).

The very image in jangling, discordant sound of women's supposed affinity for disorder, the moment most easily able to tap the Tuscan audience's fear of gynocracy, this frightening and delicious gynocentric moment can nonetheless be heard as the most orderly section of Alcina's complaint. The tonally exces-sive opening and closing phrases of the damigella's interjection return as ele-ments of a texted ritornello, first in another damigella's interjected echo and then in Alcina's own, increasingly angry voice. Thus the damigella's opening accusation—the voice of one woman hearing and objecting to the mistreatment of another—seems to articulate a new thesis for the scene as a whole. That new thesis liberates Alcina from harmonically wayward, ineffectual pleading to har-monically focused, tonally stable expressions of ire. Rather than entangling Al-cina in rounded form as the siren's song had entangled Ruggiero, the refrains "O ferità di Tigre" and "che neghi pace" seem to empower her. They frame her

Table 10.2. Tonal expansion from "Ferma, ferma" to "O ferità di Tigre," Alcina's complaint

Db	Ab	Eb/eb	Bb/b	F/f	C/c	g/G	d/D	a/A	e/E	b/B	f#/F#
					| →	Ferma, ferma crudele				→ |	
			| →	Deh, se non hai pietà				→ |			
	| →	O ferità di Tigre							→ |		

Note: Upper and lower case refer to major and minor sonorities, respectively. Both upper- and lowercase, separated by a slash, indicate that both major and minor sonorities are used above this root.

Ex. 10.5. Francesca Caccini, *La liberazione di Ruggiero* (1625), 56, First Damigella to Ruggiero

O cruelty of a tiger, O heart of stone

To an imploring woman, to a woman lover,

The most faithful and constant

Who ever scattered sighs or pleas,

Still you deny pity, and deny peace?

turn to rage in a formal coherence that is based in the responsiveness of women to other women's pain (see example. 10.5)

By contrast with the feeble threat posed by the siren's song, this is a performance of female sexuality powerful and frightening enough almost to merit the containment of women symbolized by the lamenting plants. And indeed, Ruggiero interrupts again to reject this performance as loathsome, but his judgment no longer affects Alcina's song. Emboldened by the gynocentric reception of other women, she refuses to be silenced, singing for minutes more until her extravagant vocality causes her world to burst into liberating, orgasmic, masculinizing—and hilarious—flame. Long after the fire and the liberation of the plants into dance, it is the intense and active sympathy, the intervocality among individual women in "O ferità" that lingers in the ear. It overwhelms, and in the dark dissonance of its irresistibly spreading harmonies it all but demands to be heard (in the subjunctive) as an explosion across musical space of the once-compressed agony that had been sung in the miniaturized lamenting chorus of the plants. Because nothing after this scene matches the musical and affective power of Alcina's dialogue with her damigelle, nothing contains its force on its own overwhelming terms. Instead, memories linger of women's voices sharing insatiable harmonies that refused either narrative or subjunctive (en)closure—the remembered sounds of a shared lament that liberated lamenting and thus, at least partly, liberated the plants from lament.

In 1625, the pull of this scene on the affective responses of its audience seem likely to have been as strong as it was for me in 1999. The women in the audience were likely to have received "O ferità" through their experience of a world in which elite women identified with each others' concerns, managed each others' sexual arrangements, and advocated for redress of each others' grievances as an all but obligatory performance of their gender and status. From their point of view the damigella's homovocal elaboration of Alcina's pain through the paradox of tonal expansion and enclosing form may have seemed both sexually innocent and very real, a rare confirmation from the stage of a world in which women's responsiveness to each other both constituted daily life and successfully managed proliferating desire and distress. However inclined they were by residual gynophobia to fear the homovocality as sexual, elite men may, too, have recognized a representation onstage of their social reality—a world in which their participation in the economy of productive sexuality was policed by the collective action of mutually empowering women.

Yet in the very moment of perceiving these elements of their real world so accurately represented onstage, because they were subject to music of overwhelming affective force, women and men alike might have experienced themselves as more vulnerable to the spell-binding power of performance than ever before.[25] The scene had shifted the axis along which that power moved. No longer contained in the onstage fiction of "Alcina's island," the spell-binding power of performance involved their feelings and identifications directly. Like the liberations enacted onstage, that shift marked a shift from gynophobic to gynocentric perceptions, both represented and real, that was the crucial political work of the show.

Liberation and Gender

The interaction of these three scenes in my head convinced me that the spell from which Ruggiero needed liberation could be taken for a figment of his gynophobic imagination. The fiorentini in the audience like the onstage plants, needed liberation too. But because the effects of gynophobia are different on women and men, they needed separate liberations. Or so I came to think as

I reflected that these three scenes surround the tidy pair of scenes that present Ruggiero's liberation, from different perspectives.[26] Straddling the scene of the enchanted plants, Melissa's speech liberating Ruggiero and the damigella's factually richer account of the same event forced a doubled liberation of the audience's identification with Ruggiero's masculinist standpoint. Presented as a performance of masculinity among men, Melissa's scene shows masculine authority to be nothing more than a set of magic tricks that anyone could perform, regardless of sex, and that depend on masculinist assumptions for their effect. Presented as a performance of women's behavior among themselves, free from the expectations of men, the damigella's account shows the whole truth of the liberating moment to be knowable only by those who "hidden among the branches/ . . . heard it all."[27] Considerably less compelling in performance than the scenes around them, these two scenes interrupt the spell the show casts on the audience: the interruption allowed the audience time to think, and to feel the axis of performance's power shift toward them.

"Atlante comes to you"

When Melissa arrives onstage to liberate Ruggiero, she finds him deep in the sleep to which the siren's song had lulled him. Starkly different from the siren's soul-entangling performance of feminine allure that immediately precedes it, Melissa's voice as Atlante awakens Ruggiero's manly soul from its effeminated torpor.[28] Melissa/Atlante's starkly syllabic, declamatory style would force any listener's attention to his admonishing and exhorting words. Centered firmly in the Dorian mode, his/her speech models vocal self-restraint in its registral confinement to the mode's lower fifth, while her/his harmonies' systematic cadencing on every pitch of the mode showed s/he could fully inhabit the mode of heroes, sovereigns and gods. Authoritative both in sound and style, Melissa/Atlante's speech moves listeners to the action s/he commands through a harmonic language consisting almost entirely of cadences or cadence-derived progressions around the circle of fifths.[29] Moreover, Melissa/Atlante articulates the beginning of each new thought above static harmonies before pressing forward, vocally and harmonically, toward questions and conclusions that seem to follow from the harmonically static premise. His/her phrases thus seem both logical and magical at once, for the words declaimed above a single chord demand all a listener's attention, while the whole feels like a moment of suspended time that suddenly rushes forward into action (see example. 10.6).

To a twenty-first-century ear, Melissa/Atlante's speech can sound incantatory, or magical in a stagey, "open-sesame" way meant for the ears of a child.[30] In 1625, however, Melissa's speech as Atlante may also have reminded listeners of a remarkable moment of musical magic in Monteverdi's 1607 entertainment

Ex. 10.6. Francesca Caccini, *La liberazione di Ruggiero* (1625), 35–36, Melissa, disguised as Atlante, to Ruggiero

(a) Atlante comes to you
   To know what folly
   Forces you to disgrace yourself in these parts.

(b) Fool that you are, remove
   From your warrior arms
   And your virile neck these necklaces and charms.
   Leave the evil sorceress
   And move to confront the enemy troops,
   If your fine soul still desires glory.

L'Orfeo. In the first-act speech "Rosa del Ciel," Monteverdi had projected Orfeo's power over nature through a displayed control over harmonic rhythm—stasis followed by motion—that stopped and then restarted the motion of the sun in the sky. Because Orfeo's display of musical power had been directly linked to expression of his masculine, heterosexual desire, *La liberazione*'s 1625 audience could well have heard Melissa's performance of Atlante's authority as inextricable from the performance of masculinity.[31] But Francesca projected the voice of Melissa/Atlante's magically compelling authority through the alto register. A register in which she is known to have sung, it was easily filled by the natural voice of a person of either sex. Thus Francesca's music ensured that Melissa's masculine authority would seem a matter of neither bodily sex nor bodily disguise, but a matter of style—the style of the recitative her father's friends had theorized a generation earlier as suitable for the well-ordered (Medicean) state. It was her appropriation of the austere Medicean musical style that gave Melissa power over Ruggiero. Francesca thus directly translated Maria Magdalena's legally authorized use of Medicean political style into the sounds from which she constructed Melissa's voice. Like Melissa, Magdalena need not be perceived as usurping masculine prerogatives when she adapted the "voice" of Medicean power.

Politically useful though this scene's projection of Magdalena's political style may have been, by comparison with the tunefully attractive music that preceded it this scene is hard to hear now as anything other than a masterpiece of deliberate musical tedium. It may have been thus received in 1625 as well. That Ruggiero should have been awakened and stirred to manly deeds by so tedious a song might well have provoked laughs among those in the audience who remembered the scathing comments with which the first experiments in Medicean recitative had been dismissed. His response exposed Ruggiero as a musical dolt, and therefore no longer the onstage listener on whose responses the audience would want to model their own reception of *La liberazione*'s performances. Thus the spell that Ruggiero's preconceptions and fantasies cast over the show would have been broken for the fiorentini who identified with him. At the same time, those who heard Francesca's construction of Melissa/Atlante's voice as a laughable elision of masculinity, pseudo-Orphic magic, and self-important tedium would be liberated from the spell by which gender norms arbitrarily assigned authority and "magic" to voices assumed to come from the bodies of men. Masculine authority would have been exposed as little more than a magic show, and a boring one at that. Men who might nonetheless find it stirring would be made to seem as foolish as they were to have been lulled to unreasoning sleep by the formally entangling magic of a siren's song. In each case, they were accomplices (perhaps even agents) of their own bedazzlement, victims of their own fantasies.

It is at the end of this scene, liberating the stage from belief in Ruggiero's fantasies, that the plants begin to sing the plaintive music that, at Düdingen, shifted all the power in the room. Revealing themselves to have consciousness, affect and will that had been both incommunicable and imperceptible as long as Ruggiero and those who listened with him were caught in gynophobia's spell, the plants' very existence as singing, listening beings further undermines Ruggiero's centrality. The plants replace Ruggiero as the ideal audience, and their liberation replaces Ruggiero's as the show's goal. By unveiling to the fiorentini in the audience a vision of women's conversation among themselves, the next scene moves toward that goal. Their voices and thoughts free of the sexualizing fantasies of men, the scene some fiorentini might have dismissed as a joke on female eavesdropping and gossip reveals women among themselves to produce a fuller account of the truth than had been available to the stage's "men." The truth of what women could know from their position "hidden among the branches," where they could hear everything, finally breaks the spell of gender hierarchy.

"I heard it all"

After the liberation and the scene of the enchanted plants, Alcina and her court return to the cheerful sound of the damigelle's strophic singing. Seeing her gifts to Ruggiero abandoned on the ground, Alcina stops, aghast, and asks "who among you, branches, leaves or fountains" could tell where he had gone.[32] A female messenger steps forward to describe Melissa/Atlante's liberation of Ruggiero as she witnessed it, eavesdropping (like many a courtier) while "hidden among the branches."[33] Redundant in terms of the show's narrative, her speech recounts both the liberation the audience has just witnessed and its aftermath, Melissa's wondrous self-transformation from man to woman so as to restore Ruggiero's memory of his commitment to Bradamante. Thus the narrative content of her speech reveals the staged scene to have been narrowly androcentric. Ignoring elements of the tale interesting to women, the show had seduced the audience into sharing only Ruggiero's perception. Restoring in a woman's voice well-known parts of Ariosto's tale, the messenger's speech restored as well the audience's memory that women often experienced reality differently than did men, and engaged each other differently than men might imagine. Furthermore, because Melissa's marvel of gender transcendence was the crucial difference in the messenger's account, the scene implied that the differentiating category of gender could, itself, be understood as the boundary marked by the branches among which the messenger hid. Occupied by the plants' leafily immobilized bodies, that borderland of gender could seem to be the magic spell constraining everyone's experiences of knowledge and power, and the space in which liberation would come.

While much of the scene's work liberating an audience's reception is done by the messenger's words, at least three elements of Francesca's musical construction added meanings not otherwise present—all of them meanings that liberated the sounds of women's voices from the narrow, sexualizing, gynophobic projections of men. First, the damigelle's cheerily strophic singing at their entrance seems calculated to convey innocence—both their innocence of impending catastrophe, and their innocence of the expectation that their singing would be heard by men. The similarity of their singing here to their formally intertwining songs in the first garden scene implies that a reception liberated from Ruggiero's sexualizing preconceptions would never have heard their music as part of Alcina's seductive plan. Not intended to amuse or entice men, the damigelle's singing suddenly seems only an ingenuous way girls and women might pass the time. Second, unlike the female messengers in such favole in musica as Peri's *L'Euridice* and Monteverdi's *L'Orfeo*, the female messenger in *La liberazione* tells her story to a stage full of women. Intervening in a sound world dominated by soprano and alto voices, her voice is not registrally intrusive, nor is her part dissonant with her own or others' harmonies. Thus Francesca liberated the stock scene of the female messenger from the conventions by which it had staged gynophobia through the registral and tonal wrongness of a woman's voice in androcentric spaces.[34] In the sound world of *La liberazione* a woman's voice need not be burdened with audible signs marking the very action of her speech as socially, sexually or sonically transgressive.

Third, the messenger in *La liberazione* delivers her account in a voice very like that of the liberating Melissa. Limited to a narrow range filled either with triad outlines or repeated notes, the messenger's mostly consonant recitative focuses listeners' attention on her words. The sudden slowing of her harmonies at "Odi strano successo" (Hear this strange event) and "Ma senti, o meraviglia" (But listen, what a marvel) draws aural attention to herself, her voice, and her words and emphasizes her capacity to mimic Melissa's incantatory style. Citing that style, she can be heard to claim the right to participate in its power. But she anticipates the magic of Alcina as well, for her harmonies produce unexpectedly bright phrase endings by shifting suddenly between two major sonorities whose roots are a third apart. Thus the messenger's narrative produces miracles of tonal motion to which Melissa, singing as Atlante, did not aspire; it is recognizably a voice of reason that seems to control its accompanying harmonic marvels. Tonal magic, an emphatically female standpoint, and the Medicean style of reason and self-control combine to give the messenger a fully authoritative voice. Francesca thus presented to the *fiorentini* a female vocality freed of men's sexualizing hearing, one in which women might be both innocent and intelligent, might speak the truths they know, and might wield the power to reorganize social relationships—the geometry of which political and musical worlds were made. This liberation of women's vocality leads naturally to the damigelle's participation in the excesses of Alcina's complaint that ultimately transformed onstage and offstage relationships of power.

Modeling Liberation in Sound

My critical focus on the central moments in *La liberazione* responds both to the power of these scenes in their Düdingen performance and to Francesca's construction of the show as a concatenation of easily excerpted scenes. Reflective of a courtly practice that most often assigned the creation and preparation of certain scenes in a single show to several different studios, that construction is particularly noticeable in *La liberazione* because so much of its pre-liberation world consists of shows within shows staged for Ruggiero's benefit. While two scenes after the liberation—the scene of the enchanted plants and Alcina's complaint—are also clearly aimed at him, neither seems intended to seem like entertainment. Rather, as befits Ruggiero's liberated condition, these scenes are made to seem real, functioning as narrative not entertainment no matter how powerfully they cast their musical and theatrical spells.

The shift from entertainment to narrative is but one of the ways that *La liberazione*, as a whole, instantiates the liberation of Ruggiero and the fiorentini as a shift from the paralyzing spell of one regime to the presumably liberating dynamic of another. Indeed, Francesca's sound design for the show, as it can be inferred from the published score, interacted fruitfully with Saracinelli's and Parigi's plans for it, presenting the process of liberation through changing the relations of sounds to each other and of individual characters' relations to music-making. First, Francesca's tonal plan matches Parigi's scenic rhythm.[35] Before the liberation, we hear a world remarkable for its tonal stability. The music of everything and every one centers on one of two closely related "keys," G/g and C. At and after the liberation, the tonal world widens, first gradually and then explosively in Alcina's long scene of complaint, finally settling around F for the exchange between Alcina and her monsters that sets their world aflame. Expansion of the tonal universe by female agency thus seems to cause the noisy stage magic of the fire and the ensuing rapid changes of scene that liberate the dame and cavalieri who had been plants, and, ultimately, the audience. Moreover, change in the world made of sounds seems to cause changes in the real one. Those real changes, in turn, lead to a recovered tonal equilibrium in the final scenes, a world made of sounds that can accommodate the changing perspectives represented by changing tonal centers. Not surprisingly, given *La liberazione's* teleological logic, the score's conclusion does not conflate tonal equilibrium with closure: the final eight-part chorus, after the horse ballet, is in F, the key from which Alcina's comically monstrous excess released the stage's fire, but not the key in which the show began.

Second, Francesca used shifts in singing style to portray the liberation as a re-organization of the power dynamics among the show's personae. Before the liberation, the contrast between strophic or rounded canzonetta-like song forms, and through-composed, speechlike recitative articulates the class-based social hierarchy implied by Saracinelli's text. The principal characters sing in recitative, while the watery spirits of the prologue and Alcina's nameless underlings—the damigelle, the shepherd, and the siren—sing the tuneful, aurally appealing but verbally insignificant canzonettas. After the liberation, these styles are redistributed, eventually articulating a hierarchy based on normativity not class. For a brief time all but the still-trapped plants sing in recitative. But as Alcina's complaint grows increasingly irate, she, her damigelle, and the monsters whom they call to her aid revert to rounded forms before they flee the stage. Hearing this trajectory, it is easy to reflect that the rounded, strophic forms of the pre-liberation world had functioned like its tonal stasis, entrapping performers and audience alike in a comfortable, if dangerously complacent, sound world.

Third, Francesca used harmonic language to delineate clearly both the gender trouble of that comfortable pre-liberation sound world and its post-liberation resolution. Before the liberation, only Ruggiero sings with the dissonances and surprising harmonies that in 1625 could sound, simultaneously, like "expressiveness" and like audible symptoms of the sonic disorder then considered feminine. Thus he sings like a man whose immersion in the world of women has made him effeminate. After the liberation, only female characters—the messenger who tells Alcina about Ruggiero's liberation, Alcina's companions, and Alcina herself—sing in this feminine style. Their "expressive" singing marks the liberation as restoring gender order. But because Alcina and her damigelle's femininely extreme harmonies expanded this fictive world's tonal and sonic universe, the gender order that is restored attributes to the musically feminine the liberation from narrow, dangerously complacent perception that is the obvious goal of the show.

All three—tonal, formal and stylistic planning—combine to reinforce the feeling of liberation from merely entertaining scenes to ones that seem, in their narrative power, to represent the onstage world as awakening to rapid musical and scenic transformation. It is as if the whole of *La liberazione* had been conceived to take the shape of Melissa's liberating soliloquy. Like her incantatory speech, it has hovered over static harmonies to present a premise, and then moved toward closure with such commanding force as to bring the 1625 audience to its feet, and to the windows of Villa Imperiale whence they could see, over the backs of the dancing horses, their city's place in the world anew.

Nothing could have better served the archduchess's political agenda.

But on what moment does Francesca' design, in sound, of transformative change seem to turn? Ruggiero's liberation? The scene of the enchanted plants? Alcina's multiply explosive complaint? I hear Francesca's sound design for *La liberazione* to be characteristically equivocal. That is, like some of the canzonette in her *Primo libro*, or like her Arianna's romanesca "Dove io credea," Francesca's *La liberazione* invites multiple interpretations, and invites reflection on the relationship between them.

Table 10.3 shows one way of receiving *La liberazione*'s overall design, centered on a scene near the mid-point of Saracinelli's libretto—Melissa's liberating exchange with Ruggiero.[36] In this hearing, Melissa's three long soliloquies in C stand out. Her opening soliloquy announcing her intentions, and her closing one, exhorting heroes to shun the caves of worldly pomp and return to the light, anchor the show's form in the voice of Medicean (and Platonic) reason, and reveal her to be narrator, agent and explicator of the show's many liberations.[37] In this hearing, too, Ruggiero's liberation is made to seem central, like the necessary condition for the plants' awakening, and for the reparative scenes on the post-liberation (right-hand) side of the chart that systematically reinterpret the pre-liberation scenes on the left-hand side. The plants' shift from multiply entangling contrapuntal lament to a homophonic dance song can seem to undo the spell of the multiply entangling siren's song. The expansion of knowledge represented by the messenger's through-composed narrative of liberation can seem to undo the spell of the shepherd's strophic fantasy of pastoral love. Alcina's complaint, aided by her damigelle, could seem to reinterpret the relationship she and Ruggiero had sung in the garden, so that what had once seemed like love seems like mutual antipathy. The still-rounded, homophonic chorus of monsters who come to Alcina's aid can seem to reinterpret (homophobically?) the overly intertwined vocalities of the damigelle who had introduced the garden scene. The concluding balletti can seem to liberate the desire to dance that the two opening *sinfonie* might have prompted at the show's beginning. And the through-composed dialogue between Melissa and a *"dama disincantata"* ("liberated lady") that interrupts the dancing can seem to liberate from intertwined strophic forms the dialogue prologue between Neptune and the Polish river Vistula with which hierarchical power had been enacted. In spite of all its surface teleology, leading to the liberation of the audience from their seats, *La liberazione* can thus be heard to unfold as a palindrome. Presenting a model of liberation as the progressive breaking of musical spells, it therefore presents a model in sound of liberation as the systematic reorganization of perception, gender, power, and

Table 10.3. Sound design of *La liberazione* with Melissa's liberation of Ruggiero at its center

Liberation C (thru)

Scene of Enchanted Plants d (doubly strophic + thru)
Liberation described G–g (thru)
Alcina, damigelle, etc. a–c–f–d (thru + rounded)
Monsters F (thru, canzonetta style)
Melissa's soliloquy C (thru)
Balletto di dame (no music)
Dialogue epilogue g–D (thru)
Balletto + chorus G
Balletto di cavallo
Chorus F

Siren g (strophic, palindrome)
Shepherd G (strophic, aba')
Ruggiero and Alcina's love scene G (thru)
Damigelle G (strophic)
Melissa's soliloquy C (thru)
Sinfonia C
Dialogue prologue G–g–g (strophic)
Sinfonia G

| Water/ Island | Fire/ Dry Land | Courtyard |

mobility on a theatrical stage. In 1625 the model was made to seem so powerful that it compelled just such a reorganization among those who heard it.

But however beautiful his lovesick, effeminate speeches are in Alcina's garden, and however resolute his brief interruptions to her complaint, the fact remains that Ruggiero is not much of a presence in *La liberazione*. Indeed, after his liberation he falls increasingly silent, seeming to vanish altogether before the fire. Moreover, nothing about the scene of his liberation makes it a moment of either musical or theatrical *meraviglia*. Nothing, that is, matches the improbable *meraviglia e stupor* generated by sound in the scene of the enchanted plants.

Table 10.4 shows a way of receiving *La liberazione* in which the plants, not Ruggiero, occupy the center of the palindrome, as the principal objects of Melissa's—and the show's—liberatory magic. In this hearing, the multiply entangled, contrapuntally lamenting plants' release into a homophonic dance song obviously reflects in miniature Francesca's overall design for the show. Cramped, confining entanglements (that, not coincidentally, impede the intelligibility that defined rational speech) are replaced by clarity, intelligibility, reason, and hope. Melissa remains the agent of transformation, for the hopeful chorus responds to her short speech in d, "Consolatevi," which stands at almost the exact midpoint of the libretto.[38] In this hearing, too, Ruggiero's liberation remains a necessary condition for all others, but he is not the center of the action. Rather, his liberation prompts that action—the liberation of women, if one has heard the hard-to-locate voices of the plants through memories of a cloister's grate, and the liberation of all fiorentini. It is with the plants at the center of Francesca's palindrome that one can hear the messenger's account of Ruggiero's liberation as breaking the spell of the narrowly androcentric version the audience has seen. With the plants at the center, too, one can hear Alcina's long complaint as responding neither only to her love scene with Ruggiero nor only to the figure of the siren, but to the entire garden scene—liberating the grievances of wronged womanhood, representing women as each others' advocates in times of distress, and, in her eventual fiery self-exile before Melissa's superior magic, revealing women to be capable of channeling each others' energies to constructive ends. The resulting representation of liberation, still modeled in sound as the reorganization of power relationships, equates the accuracy and breadth of perception in the liberated world with the inclusion of gynocentric perspectives, as well as with obedience to the authority of a benevolent woman endowed with "magical" power (see table 10.4).

In performance, however, it is easy to hear Alcina's complaint as the most musically intense scene, its tonal expansion the moment of greatest musical *meraviglia*. To hear it thus is to experience the scenes that follow as confusing, jumbled, even disturbing in their rapid change and the consequent denial of

Table 10.4. Sound design of *La Liberazione* with scene of enchanted plants at its center

	Water/ Island	Fire/ Dry Land	Courtyard
Scene of enchanted plants d̲			
(doubly strophic contrapuntal lament + strophic, homophonic dance song)			
	Liberation C̲ (thru)	Liberation described G̲–g (thru)	
	Siren g (strophic, palindrome)	Alcina, damigelle, etc. a̲–c̲–f̲–d̲ (thru + rounded)	
	Shepherd G̲ (strophic, aba')		
	Ruggiero and Alcina's love scene G̲ (thru)		
	Damigelle G̲ (strophic)	Monsters F̲ (thru, canzonetta style)	
	Melissa's soliloquy C̲ (thru)	Melissa's soliloquy C̲ (thru)	
	Sinfonia C̲	Balletto di dame (no music)	
	Dialogue prologue G̲–g–g (strophic)	Dialogue epilogue g–G̲ (thru)	
	Sinfonia G̲	Balletto + chorus G̲	
			Balletto di cavallo
			Chorus F̲
	Water/ Island	**Fire/ Dry Land**	**Courtyard**

prolonged aural pleasure that would balance the harmonic and tonal extrava-
gance of Alcina's scene. The dances' tranquillity comes as such a relief that one
can fail to notice that in the "liberated" world no one but Melissa is allowed
individual voice. A single moment disrupts the forward rush toward that world.
Disrupting the fantasy of closure created by the first dance, the balletto di dame,
a lone woman emerges, lamenting.[39]

Dispelling Lament

A phrase in the middle of her plaintive, palindromic song tugs at the ear, so
brief that it can pass without conscious recognition. Sung to the words "noi
nel pianto mestissimo" (we, in saddest weeping), it is the first phrase from
the scene of the enchanted plants, identifying the singer as a former plant,
and thus instantaneously both validating a hearing of the enchanted plants
through memories of a cloister's grate and inviting fleeting confrontation with
the show's homoerotic subtext (see example. 10.7a and compare with example. 10.1). More directly, her voice singing that phrase at the literal center of
her own palindromic song supports a hearing of the plants' scene as the center
of Francesca's large-scale palindromic design. But the miniature exchange the
"dama disincantata" has with Melissa does more than support a plant-centered
hearing of Francesca's sound design. It responds to the lingering memories of
Alcina's complaint, and thereby delivers a moral to La liberazione that, unlike
Melissa's soliloquy to heroes, encompasses everyone in the performance space
in a harmonious social order based on the liberation of women.

On either side of her tell-tale phrase, the dama disincantata's song recom-
bines elements of all the performances of womanhood she might have heard
from her life "among the branches." Before that phrase, her song slithers
Alcina-like from mollis to durus, in performed time little more than a flash
whose pause on a bright E-major sonority piques desire for the a on which her
citation of the plants' song begins (measures 7–9). Afterward, her harmonies
reorganize the Alcinian move toward a into a Melissa-like progression through
the circle of fifths to A, drawing both aural logic and audible agency from her
citation of Melissa's vocality (measures 10–14). But she wraps the whole in a
palindromic refrain in g (measures 1–6, 16-end), her leaps into and away from
dissonances fusing the sonic markers of lament to memories of the siren's entanglement. It is as if the tropes of lament (and Alcina's haunting lament lingering in the ear) were the last threads tying her to the musical prison of enchanted plants.

Melissa responds to break the spell. Singing her only unprepared dissonance,
a shocking minor ninth of empathy with the "aspri tormenti" (harsh torments)
she means to dispel, Melissa twice commands "Non più non più lamenti" (la-

Ex. 10.7. Francesca Caccini, *La liberazione di Ruggiero*, 67–68, lady freed from enchantment

(a) Pour forth, eyes, pour forth
Bitterest tears
Until heaven gives up
The desired prisoner-lovers.
If others beseech mercy
In sweetest song,
We, in saddest weeping
which distills through the eyes Love and Fidelity,
Perhaps will find, someday, compassion;
Eyes, therefore, pour forth,
Pour forth bitter tears
Until heaven gives up
The desired prisoner-lovers.

(b) Our breasts cannot
Know joys and delights
Until love returns
The heart to our hearts.

ment no more, no more). Her magic works. The dama responds by naming her desire—the liberation of the men—to a crisply goal-directed romanesca phrase (see example 10.7b). Satisfied that the dama is finally free, Melissa returns to her incantatory style. Her command that the men emerge and dance ends above a suddenly major chord on D, sounding for the first time her own desire, which is answered immediately by the chorus of *cavalieri liberati* in G.

Melissa's banishment of the dama's palindromic lament is not only a proto-feminist act that finally liberates the dama to speak plainly her desire, and to enjoy its satisfaction in dance. So explicitly to banish lament from an onstage fiction made of music was to follow a Platonic imperative for the relation of music to the state. Both in the *Republic* and in the *Laws* Plato had argued that the musicians of a well-ordered polis should reject plaintive modes and laments as effeminating threats to the health of the state. To fiorentini schooled in both the classicizing political theory of the Medici and the proto-feminist propaganda through which Magdalena's regency was continually justified, the message could not have been more clear. The health of the polis Melissa's magic had liberated—the health of the liberated Tuscan state—depended on empathetic relationships among women, insofar as such relationships ensured that all women and men would be free from enclosure in the assumptions about gender embedded in the debilitating tropes of lament. Or, as Bronzini had put it in *Della dignità delle donne:* "Equality . . . in ancient republics was always the keystone and the base on which rested public and private happiness . . . [equality] fostered peace . . . love and concord, [and] conserved . . . the relations of all members of the body politic."[40] Liberated, the relations of the Tuscan body politic would be performed as dance.

The Score as Portrait of Its Artist

In late November, 1624, the man who supervised music and spectacle at the Medici court, and would be her librettist for *La liberazione*, wrote that certain of Francesca's male colleagues behaved "in order to impede this woman, so that she cannot serve Her Most Serene Highness well."[41] Both experience of *La liberazione* and study of its published score show how well Francesca could serve when freed from such impediments. For, more than either Saracinelli's libretto or Parigi's scenic plan, it is Francesca's music that highlights the show's intended aim—the interlocking liberations of Ruggiero, of women, and of the *fiorentini* from narrow, entrapping perceptions of the relationships that could constitute their world.

The score shows, too, that Francesca was as shrewd, savvy and meticulous in conceiving the whole of an entirely musical commedia as she was in creating the entertaining, sometimes compelling moments that were its parts. Given that, in her time as in ours, a focus on details was understood as feminine while mastery of complex wholes was assumed to be masculine, she thus seems to have been, as a composer, every bit as liberated from the arbitrary constraints of gender as her sound design allowed the musical denizens of *La liberazione* to be.[42]

Frustratingly, the score does not include any of the music for dancing. Either Francesca did not compose that music, or someone decided that it should not be published. Given the importance of the concluding dances in *La liberazione*, the omission seems strange.

One way to explain the omission, admittedly speculative, is to think through the prestige hierarchies of musical labor, as they interacted with gender norms. People of noble rank composed and even published music for voices, but typically it was dancing masters and instrumentalists—musical artisans with low status in their profession—who composed the audible music that accompanied dancing's inaudible order. Public attribution of even some dances to a woman's pen would have weakened the strategy by which respectable women musicians' honor was usually upheld—the pretense that, regardless of their actual social rank, their musicality found expression only in activities suitable for dame and donne.

The effect of this omission, however, exceeds mere protection of Francesca's reputation. By representing unequivocally Francesca's music as having caused *La liberazione*'s spectacular stage fire, and the unrepresented chain of balletic liberations that ensued, the score could seem to have represented her music's effect as so overwhelming as to be unrepresentable. Seeming to inspire in her audience not only stupefied meraviglia but the energy to change themselves, their relations with each other, and their perspective on the world, Francesca is made to seem able to conceive music that had actually intervened in the human geometry of Tuscan politics. Thus through the interplay of its preserved musical notes and its omissions, the score represented Francesca's musical power as analogous to her patron's political power. "Whenever it suited her," he wrote, "(no less than, indeed maybe far more than Amphion) [she] so ignited wonder and daring in the breasts of the people that they would have done anything, no matter how difficult."[43]

Cataclysms of Widowhood

11

After composing *La liberazione*, Caccini continued for a time to serve the Medici court. She led the choir that sang from the corridoio during Holy Week; she entertained the archduchess while she lay ill in bed and was otherwise visited only by her immediate family, her physicians, and (presumably) her body servants; and she performed in Magdalena's apartments at Pitti and at Villa Imperiale for the granducato's most important guests—Magdalena's brother Archduke Leopold of Austria in May 1625, Cardinal Legate Francesco Barberini in September 1626, and Cardinal Legate Francesco Cennini in April 1627. Tinghi's diary made no mention of Francesca's participation, if any, in the court's principal public spectacles after the performance of *La liberazione*, the intermedi performed for the remarriage of the widowed Princess Claudia de' Medici to Archduke Leopold on 25 March 1626, and the sacred opera *La Giuditta*, produced as the most public welcome to Cardinal Legate Barberini six months later.[1] Yet there is reason to believe Caccini might have been working on a commission from abroad. Two letters that Prince Władisław wrote Magdalena in July 1626 confirm that he had commissioned two stage works from Caccini for performance at his court, one on the subject of Saint Sigismund and the other on a subject of her choice, "non spirituale."[2] By July 1626 Władisław evidently had negotiated by letter the details of these commissions directly with Francesca and with one of the court's staff supervisors, Jacopo Salviati. All that Władisław asked of his aunt was that she give the command that would authorize Francesca to begin work. Thus, late in 1626 Francesca had the opportunity, born of the success of *La liberazione,* greatly to expand her reputation by composing work for a foreign head of state. She was at the peak of her career.

But on 29 December Francesca's husband of nineteen years died at home after passing a black kidney stone that was the size of an egg.[3] Signorini's death set off a chain reaction of changes in Francesca's civil, economic, and professional status that would radically transform who she was in her world. It would end her public career but not her work as a teacher and composer, and it allowed her eventually to realize her father's dream of parlaying professional excellence into a permanent rise in social rank. Although they may seem to yield little of interest to traditional musicology, the stories of Francesca's widowings afford vivid glimpses of her life and of her personality. They afford, as well, glimpses of the way a person formed by experience as a virtuosa musica could engage the social institutions of gender and class that shaped what prescriptive literature considered the last stage of a woman's life: widowhood.

Signorini dictated his testament to the notary Paolo Lapi on Tuesday, 23 December 1626. Referring to his wife with rare warmth and respect, he explicitly placed his trust in her good will and rectitude as he confessed before witnesses that he had long been the marriage's economically weaker partner. Beyond the obligatory restitution of his wife's dowry, Signorini had nothing to leave his widow and child but a few bits of furniture and petty debts. He declared with shocking specificity that "the entire cost and value of these [houses] and the improvements, decorations and other additions to them were all executed from the effects and the money of the aforementioned Signora Francesca his wife, and therefore as he said above he intends and wills that the aforementioned houses belong to her as her own property."[4] Lest there be any mistake about the identity of the household's supporter, Signorini declared openly that

> two sorts of wealth and income had come into his household through the person of the aforementioned Signora Francesca his wife, and one was the annual stipend that the Most Serene Padroni had given her and the other the many bonuses and gifts that both the aforementioned Most Serene Padroni and other princes and important people had given him on many and varied occasions. And all these provisions were spent and used, along with his, in the service of the household, so that by their own will he had been able to advance himself and his family with the dignity and grandeur that he had done, and wanting both to thank her and to ease his conscience and satisfy every claim, for the sake of truth and good and affection he declared and declares that except for the clothes on his back, a few lire, and things like the bed he bought at the time of their marriage, and a few other linens, household goods, and furniture well known to the aforementioned Signora Francesca, all the other linens, household goods, fur-

nishings, and effects and everything remaining that can be found in the aforementioned house belong entirely to the aforementioned Signora Francesca.[5]

Assigning to Francesca title to property that had been hers all along, Signorini
asked that his widow, "who had treated him with a generous, affectionate and
noble heart in the affairs of this world," pay the expenses of his funeral and of
subsequent prayers for his soul from her own resources, rather than from his
meager estate.[6] Further, he asked that she hold a note for a dowry obligation
of his concerning an unnamed girl and, in the event his estate could not cover
the debt, that "for the sake of the reciprocal love, affection and good will that
they had shared for many years" she pay the fifty scudi from her own funds.[7]
Signorini also named her guardian of their child, Margherita, and charged
Francesca to "keep such accounts for her as will be useful, and to teach her the
sciences and arts that she herself knows, and any others that might be useful
and . . . to help with her own wealth as might be needed to establish her well."[8]
In short, Signorini left his widow his affection, her own property and financial
obligations that his estate could offer her no means to meet. He left to posterity
certain knowledge that their gender roles in the economic institution of marriage had been reversed, for such prosperity as they knew seems to have been
the fruit of her labor.[9] In the loss of a man so warmly at ease in an unconven-
tional marriage, Francesca had much to mourn and much to worry about as she
faced the obligations and institutional constraints of widowhood.

Francesca's first obligation as a widow was to organize her husband's funeral. In keeping with Florentine custom, Signorini was buried the day after he
died, in the tomb kept by his burial society, the Compagnia del Santo Rosario
della Gloriosissima Vergine Maria, in Santa Maria Novella.[10] Probably acting
via instructions to her household servants or possibly to male relatives, Francesca must have arranged for professionals known as *beccamorti* to bathe, shave,
and dress Signorini's body for burial and carry it to a bier they would have prepared in her home's main room.[11] She also would have sent someone to notify
the clergy at Santa Maria Novella, who would send a delegation of priests and
friars to intone the seven penitential psalms from one side of the bier. Francesca would have cut her hair to signify her renunciation of sexuality, donned
mourning clothes appropriate to her social rank, and led the ritual lamenting
by Signorini's female relatives and women friends.[12] No elegantly improvised
lament on the death of an imaginary Adonis, the mourning song Francesca and
the other women were likely to have improvised for her handsome husband was
meant to sound disorganized. Rising from the benches on one side of the room
to which all women mourners were confined, its ritual sonic disorder was to
emphasize in sound as well as space the sexual segregation that was a crucial
element of Florentine funerary rites.[13]

Francesca, or someone acting on her behalf, would also have organized a funeral cortege to accompany Signorini's body through the streets en route to burial. Led by clergy, the first mourners in the procession would have carried the banners of civil organizations to which Signorini had belonged: the Ordre de Saint Michel, the Compagnia del Santo Rosario, the neighborhood of Florence in which his citizenship had been inscribed (Ruote of Santa Croce), and the Magistrato dei nove, a civil court with jurisdiction over foreigners living in the city, on which he had recently served.[14] Signorini's body would follow, held aloft by close friends, relatives, or members of his craft and possibly decorated with a symbol of his craft. A carefully ordered procession of kin (his brothers, brothers-in-law, cousins, and nephews), friends, neighbors, fellow craftsmen, and acquaintances would have brought up the rear. The women's laments would continue until the body left the house, but no women would participate in the public rite. Instead, widows, women relatives, and women friends stayed at home to prepare food and drink for the male mourners when they returned from the chanted requiem mass and the burial ceremony.[15] Sexual segregation was thus enforced again, as Francesca (along with her virtuosa relatives, pupils, colleagues, and friends) served the men.

Even as Signorini's mourners lingered in her home, Francesca would have been forced to consider immediately the contradictory options that confronted every widow under Florentine law. A widow could continue living as part of her husband's family, with their children; she could live independently, near her husband's family, who would be charged with their children's care; or she could remarry, a choice that by law required her to renounce custody of children from her first marriage.[16] If she were still young enough to bear children, pressure from her family to remarry could be great; a widow could be forced to declare her willingness to remarry as early as the evening of her husband's funeral.[17]

As a thirty-nine-year-old woman in a household built with her own rather than her husband's wealth, responsible for his debts and for educating and dowering their daughter, Francesca would have had no interest in remaining among the Signorini. Under the law, her mutually exclusive options were to return to the authority of the Caccini clan for a remarriage that they would arrange, and therefore to renounce forever custody of her child, or to try to live independently so she could care for the undowered girl. But as a woman of the Medici famiglia, Francesca's future was most likely to be determined by the Medici princesses, who were accustomed to managing marriage's traffic in women.

Two letters that Francesca wrote Buonarroti in the weeks after Signorini's death reveal her struggle through grief and hurt pride to ensure that she had some say in the way her concerns were represented by the men around her to the female patriarchs of the Medici court. On 1 January 1627, two days after Signorini's burial, Francesca wrote:

I have delayed going to the palace until now, having waited for you to come see me as have some other loving friends of my late husband, because I want to confer with you about some of my concerns before I deal with them. But because my cousin Orazio told me this evening that rather than come here you would have gone to see him, while I remained outside of everything, amazed; having (as I do) to go to the palace the day after tomorrow, that is, Saturday, I resolved against my will to ask you to favor me with a visit this evening, so you can do me the favor of saying whether, together with my poor husband, you want to be among those who have abandoned me. Enough. If you do me the favor we shall talk about everything, and because I have less judgment than you, indeed, have none at all, I will not say you should not see my cousin, but you should know that it is with you, and not with my cousin, that I wish to speak.[18]

Presumably Francesca had postponed going to the palace because she knew her presence there would precipitate discussions about her future, discussions for which she hoped conversation with Buonarroti would help her prepare. Her cousin Orazio, the oldest male in her generation and therefore the head of her birth family, seems already to have discussed her future with Buonarroti, apparently without consulting her. Formidable and important to the musical life of the court as she may have been, as a widow Francesca was as "outside of things, amazed" as any ordinary woman would be.[19] Unaccustomed to being treated like an object with neither will nor voice of her own, Francesca expressed both pique and a preference to have Buonarroti, who knew her as an artist, represent her interests.

Although she never mentioned the conflict between remarriage and custody of her daughter, in her second letter to Buonarroti Francesca implied that she saw the defense of her daughter's interests as all but inextricable from defense of her own: she wanted custody. At the same time, her letter reveals almost inadvertently the effects of widowhood's shocks on her self-concept. Anxious about her sudden dependence on men's understanding of the law, she offered reciprocity for Buonarroti's help in the only currency she had—what she could do as an artist who was responsive to others:

Since you wrote me I know nothing [further], but I ask you to do me the favor to let me know something; I know that I have two months after the death of my poor husband to assume the guardianship, but because I have a certain dispute with the Marzichi, against me and against my daughter as her father's heir, if I have not assumed guardianship I cannot act for my daughter, but I would like to assume guardianship and, for this reason, I would like to know what one has to do to obtain it; and I sympathize infinitely with your troublesome preoccupations but since I have already begun to bother you I will continue to do so, with the same confidence; do me the favor of telling me what I have to do, and have compassion on someone like me who has no one in the world to look out for her interests, [she] whom I offer to you in exchange for your courtesy, whenever I can, and whatever I am worth; and if I am worth nothing it is the fault of my luck not of my will: [I] who have been, am, and will be always as responsive as can be to your every command.[20]

"The sirens will be joined together"

Whatever Buonarroti, Orazio Caccini, or Francesca may have said to the grand duchesses, Signorini's death had opened the question of Francesca's future at an unlucky time. In early 1627 Christine and Magdalena were preoccupied with the still unsettled marriage prospects of Princess Margherita, whose promised union with Odoardo Farnese, Duke of Parma, they continued to avoid.[21] Moreover, as the majority (in 1628) of Ferdinando II approached, both women recognized the need to shift public perceptions of the granducato's power away from images of benevolent gynocracy and toward unmistakably masculine ones. Themselves rumored to be planning withdrawals from obvious participation in public life, they may have seen that their use of Francesca as a public figure for female excellence might conveniently be withdrawn.[22] Her sudden widowing gave them and her the occasion to organize Francesca's withdrawal— a withdrawal from the pleasures and burdens of serving Florence's gynocentric court into what would turn out to be the silencing privacy of life as a Lucchese gentildonna.

By 4 October 1627, Francesca had married a fifty-six-year-old minor nobleman in Lucca.[23] A July letter to Christine's secretary Dimurgo Lambardi described her new husband-to-be, Tommaso Raffaelli, as a man who "makes his living from property, [and is] more a musician than a cavaliere. He has an inherited villa which, if you ask at Monte San Quirico, is about a mile from the city in a place where there are many beautiful villas owned by gentlemen, and where there are very large gatherings for conversation. From what one hears the wedding will certainly be in a few weeks, at which time I will give you a detailed account."[24] The wedding was postponed several times, for Lambardi's informant, the Tuscan agent Orazio Tuccarelli, reported on 13 August: "One believes that the sirens will be joined together for sure this coming September, and because the gentleman is well-regarded in this profession . . . Lucca will be transformed into a new Parnassus. . . . I will be informed of every particular so as to send you the news."[25] By mid-September, Tuccarelli would write: "[T]he friend who keeps me advised of Signora Francesca's affairs told me that she has sent many things to the home of her bridegroom, and that the wedding will be before the end of this month, which I believe without a doubt because of having seen the bridegroom today, who seemed like a Ganymede to me, although grey-haired, very well-dressed and graceful."[26]

These reports, sent to the secretary who was most closely involved in her management of elite women's marriages, suggest that the grand duchess meant to monitor Francesca's remarriage as closely as she did those of former dame and donne. Yet they also suggest that she may have approved the marriage without knowing much about Tommaso Raffaelli personally: it seems possible, then, that Francesca, Orazio, or Buonarroti had chosen the noble amateur musician as a suitable husband, despite the fact that he could seem "like a Ganymede," that is, like a pretty man whose presence evoked the younger, passive partner of male sodomy despite his age and gray hair.

Little else is known about Raffaelli. Born in 1571 to Antonio Raffaelli and Laura Bartolomei, Tommaso descended from a Mantuan immigrant, Antonio del Tornaio, who had acquired the family's farms, olive groves, and vineyard in the area of Fondagno in the mid-fifteenth century.[27] By the late 1620s the Raffaelli family ranked among the nobility of Lucca—the 104 families who were qualified by birth to serve in government and who declared themselves and their heirs to be the Lucchese republic's ruling class.[28] The Raffaelli fortune was meager by comparison with those of Lucca's great banking and silk-trade families: in 1599, the combined net worth of Tommaso and his brother Alessandro was assessed at about 10,000 scudi; that of the scion of Lucca's wealthiest banking family, Girolamo di Lodovico Buonvisi, was assessed at 907,000 scudi.[29]

Tommaso Raffaelli is said to have frequented the musical *accademie* hosted by Cesare Lucchesini and his wife, the poet Laura Guidiccione, in the 1590s and early 1600s, acquiring there a lifelong passion for the newest music.[30] After Lucchesini's group foundered in 1606 Raffaelli organized his own, convening his interlocutors at the villa near Monte San Quilici that he and his brother had inherited in 1597 rather than in his city palace on the via Fillungo.[31] At the villa that Tommaso shared with his nephew Girolamo after Alessandro's death, he housed a collection of musical instruments so extensive that the musical savant Adriano Banchieri called it a "museo armonico" when he visited it in the 1620s.[32] Tommaso seems to have been a bachelor until 1627. Rising political pressure to ensure the reproduction of noble bloodlines may have contributed to his interest, that year, in finding a wife who could guarantee him a legitimate son and heir.[33]

Just as nothing is known about who might have proposed the Caccini-Raffaelli match, almost nothing is known about the life that Tommaso and Francesca led. The letter in which Banchieri thanked Raffaelli for a tour of his instrument collection mentions that he had heard in Bologna "of your acquisition, in Lucca, in the household of the illustrious Vincenzo Buonvisi, of Signora Francesca Caccini," but no other evidence survives to indicate that Francesca served the Buonvisi as she had served the Medici.[34] Indeed, marriage to the noble Raffaelli seems to have allowed the long-overworked Francesca to retire from her performing life, perhaps into the life of private study for which Bronzini implied she had longed. Francesca is known to have refused requests that she sing in the entertainments planned at Parma to celebrate the long-delayed marriage of her former pupil Princess Margherita to Duke Odoardo Farnese. According to Antonio Goretti, Francesca had let it be known that "she absolutely wishes not to sing anymore, having taken a gentleman for her husband."[35] Yet there is evidence that she used her connections to Florence's musical establishment, her theatrical savvy, and her skill as a composer to enable her husband's literary academy, the Accademia degli Oscuri, to produce what would be remembered as a dazzling (and extravagant) set of intermedi for Carnival in 1628. As the Oscuri's secretary, Francesco Minutoli, wrote: "[T]he richness of the costumes reached such a level that those who had seen such things at great courts on similar occasions confessed not to have seen their equal; the perfection of the intermedi's words was so well accompanied by the excellence of the musicians, particularly of Domenichino, of Tatini, and of Brunelli's tenor from Pisa, that it made people wonder aloud which should be judged the best . . . many Genovese and Florentine gentlemen . . . confessed they would never have believed it possible to bring such excellences together."[36]

So thrilled were the Oscuri by their intermedi's success, and so concerned that textually imperfect copies had begun to circulate in Italy, that they authorized publication of both the poet Lelio Altogradi's words and "in one part of the book . . . the music . . . exactly the way it was performed."[37] But although the Oscuri's secretary lavishly praised Tommaso Raffaelli for the prudence, generosity, and skill with which his well-informed musical judgments had ensured that the performance met the highest standard possible, no document ever noted who had composed, prepared, or directed the music. It is tempting to suppose that the composer was Francesca and that the Oscuri's uncharacteristically costly and cosmopolitan Carnival had been produced from the union of the two "sirens."

"Padrona, donna, e madonna"

Lucca's new Parnassus turned out to be short-lived. The total collapse of the Buonvisi banking empire in 1629 deflated the entire city's taste for extravagant display, and by February 1630 Tommaso Raffaelli was ill enough to dictate his will.[38] He died on 16 April, leaving Francesca a widow for the second time in four years. Her second husband, however, had more to leave her than his debts and his bed. Thanking her in his will for "the many and great loving courtesies and the most welcome companionship that she has given him, and that he hopes she will give until his death, for the great value, prudence, and good qualities of this woman that said *testatore* truly admires in her," he named her "padrona, donna, e madonna" of all that he owned.[39] She was to be executrix of his estate until the majority of their infant son Tommasino and usufructrix for life, so long as she educated the boy well and raised him in a household commensurate with his noble status. Liberating her from all obligations to account for her management of the property, Raffaelli specified repeatedly that his heirs' privileges and benefits were contingent on their obedience to his widow if they were children or their respect for her if they were adults. He went so far as to authorize Francesca to evict them from Raffaelli property if they challenged her authority.[40] Further, by specifically asking his neighbors Girolamo Bernardini and Vincenzo Buonvisi to take his widow and child under the kind of protection they had afforded him, Tommaso bequeathed to them his place in the social fabric of Lucca's elite.[41] By the terms of Tommaso's testament, then, Francesca was set for life. So was her daughter Margherita, who had evidently not been left behind in Florence. Raffaelli left the girl two hundred scudi to be paid toward a dowry, should she need it, in recognition that "following her mother's example [she] . . . made and continues to make many kind gestures toward said testatore, as if her were her true father."[42]

Whatever grief Francesca might have felt at the fracturing of what seems to have been an affectionate little family, in 1630 she wasted no time in taking up her obligation to assure the economic security of her children. In early June she executed contracts with the Raffaelli estate's farmers on her son's behalf, and by late July she sold the two houses in the via Valfonda in Florence that represented the assets of her dowry.[43] Specifying terms of payment very like the ones that had enabled Giulio's 1588 sale of a Fiesole farm to accumulate into her dowry, she may have meant the sale to add to Raffaelli's small dowry for Margherita.[44] With no need ever again to exchange either her musical services or her voice for a living, with her financial obligations to both her children under firm control, and with no strong ties either to Lucca or to the Raffaelli family, at age forty-three Francesca stood on the verge of being "padrona, donna e madonna"—except that she had evidently made a bargain with her Medici princesses concerning custody of her daughter, a bargain that she now wanted to renounce.

On 19 March 1631, Francesca wrote to the first secretary of Tuscany, Andrea Cioli, a fifteen-hundred-word letter in a tiny, precise version of her usually sprawling script. Remarkable for an epistolary voice that mixes rhetorical traces of Giulio Caccini's daughter with the rhetoric of Margherita Signorini's devoted mother, with the pride of a passionate teacher, and with a servant's virtuosa manipulation of her princess's expected responses, the letter speaks the subjectivity of the immensely complicated woman Francesca Caccini had become, as she sought finally to take possession of her own life:[45]

My most illustrious lord,

It is many months that I have owed you a greeting by letter, but because of the troubles endured in that city, I dared not bother you, knowing that you had other things on your mind.[46] Now that I understand that they begin to pass, by the grace of God, I write to rejoice with you about it, and at the same time to remind you of my infinite obligation [to you], and to tell you that immediately after my return from there I informed myself, through an experienced confidant, [about] the difficulties that it had been suggested I might have in my wish to leave here with my son. And he was assured that there is neither law nor statute that could limit my liberty, adducing very clear reasons to me that for brevity I will leave aside. And I wanted to tell you everything as verification of this truth, as I remembered having discussed the contrary with Madama Serenissima and with you. I must also tell you, because I will never lose memory of the way that you have protected me with their most serene highnesses, and of the favor that you gave me, and [because] in those parts I have no other patron nor protector than you, I leave aside every fear of seeming too importunate to you, [and] I write with every confidence and trust, to beg that you with your usual benevolence will assist me in my very great distress.

I must in a little while send my daughter into the service of Madama Serenissima, and her serene highness persists in her intention of wanting her completely separated from [me], and under the discipline of other people, [but] because I find myself today in a very different condition than I was when her serene highness asked me for this daughter and I gave her, I had better speak my feeling and my thoughts without waiting any longer on vain hopes [about] what might follow, as I have done until now. I sought openly to know how this business might go to be able to accommodate my [new] situation, something about which I have been up in the air since I discovered this thought of Madama Serenissima that neither I nor others would have ever been able to imagine, there being natural reasons to have believed just the opposite. Sir, to bother you less, I would like to be able to tell you my need in only two lines, but not being able to, I will say only the most necessary things, with the greatest brevity that I can.

I say therefore that today I find myself alone, without my company, abandoned, in a foreign country, and I have nothing in the world but these children: nor have I hope for any other help, or other recourse in the needs and infirmities that I might have except from them, if it shall please God to spare them to me, and they similarly have no one else but me. And these are not my imaginings but the pure truth, so we need to hold each other dear, and united one to the other, so long as God doesn't separate us by death. And if it would have pleased the divine majesty (whose will one cannot question) to send death to this daughter I would have remained grief-stricken for the rest of my life, seeming to myself left as a miserable ghost with no vestige of virtù, and so I believe it would have seemed to her, if she were to have lost me, and her brother. Now consider, illustrious sir, and everyone, in what way I would be able to allow myself to abandon this daughter in her and my greatest need, and completely transfer her from me, if God [who] could take her from me, by his grace and goodness allows me to keep her. As for virtù, I say that a father and mother can have no greater desire than to make themselves anew in their children, leaving them heirs of their professions and virtù [skills]. Now if the blessed God gave me only one daughter, with such aptitudes and inclinations toward my profession that (speaking with every due modesty) I am sure not to have labored in vain, in continuous study for forty years, because I have somewhere suitable to leave all my efforts and study after my death, for what reason and how could I have the heart to abandon her, in the best part of her training, and put her in the hands of strangers, with the sure risk that in a short time she would lose all that she had learned, and I would remain with all my time wasted, and with no profit from her in my need, nor from the virtù that I taught her. I don't know whether this should be called prudence or cruelty, I leave it for you to consider, not being able [myself] to conclude otherwise than that I don't know anyone who could teach, superintend, and guide my daughter better than I, and woe to those who have no mother and no father.

Now, having no other intention or greater desire than to obey Madama's every nod, and to give her highness every satisfaction possible from myself and my daughter; and recognizing how [grateful I should be for] my daughter's good fortune, and for the great honor that her serene highness has done her in having wanted to choose and accept her as her servant, given the above-mentioned things I find myself the most afflicted creature that could ever be found, and I don't know or desire any other comfort or remedy than death, if it would have pleased God to send it to me to end for once so many tribulations, of which there have been so many, so many that if God had not given me strength I could not have endured them, because I don't know what to do with myself, or what resolution to make. It does not seem to me that this my maternal and reasonable feeling deserves Madama Serenissima's displeasure and disfavor, nor [does it deserve] the damaging of this poor daughter, who even though she is young, has enough sense to recognize [both] her good fortune and how much the loss of her mother would matter.

Sir, I have no other refuge, nor other hope, but in your protection and benevolence, and I implore you, with every strong feeling and gesture of respect, that you undertake to express to Madama Serenissima my thoughts and my feeling in such a way as will seem best to you, and that you do me the grace to extract from her highness (once she has heard [you]) what is needed to continue this negotiation and the final resolution and intention of Madama Serenissima that could accommodate my affairs, because from the time that her highness took this daughter until now I have been constantly up in the air. And full of embarrassment at having seen everyone at court, and many from outside it, keep their distance from me, and not respond to my letters any more, including even the very nun who dealt with me in this matter. And when her highness wanted news of this daughter and her studies, she wrote to Tuccarelli and he came to my house, and without saying so much as a word to me from Madama Serenissima spoke with my daughter as if I were not her mother, or were not even in the world. Then when I came there (except for you, illustrious sir, by your grace) everyone avoided me, let alone sought to see me, and if it hadn't been for your favor I would not even have seen the most serene patrons. When I returned Tuccarelli came again by order of her highness to see that my daughter was cured, with his usual manner; and not finding me at home, he led my people to understand that perhaps it would be his job to take my daughter to Florence, without me, this past October, this notwithstanding that I am absolute guardian of my son and free padrona while I live of all that there is, and if he dies before eighteen, of every other thing [I am] free padrona except for the real estate that is mine for usufruct, and that I am padrona of my own liberty, and I can (as you said, sir), padrona that I am, return if I want to my homeland, not having committed crimes for which I deserve exile. Just the same, given the above mentioned behaviors I would not, could not, should not without the entire pleasure and protection of all the serene highnesses, nor do I think you would advise me otherwise, nor would it be in the best interests of my son. I implore you anew, therefore, with all the feeling that I can, that you undertake to help me out of so much affliction, since if you don't get me out of it I truly don't know what to do. [In exchange] for such relief I will live forever as your obliged slave, and I will be always ready to acknowledge you with all the effects that my weak powers grant me. I remind you of the service my father and our whole household have given you, and the affection that we have all always had for you, for the memory of which [I hope] you might decide to trouble yourself for me in this my necessity, and with humblest bows to you and to your wife I pray our Lord and God to give you every true and desired happiness.

From Lucca 19 March 1631.

Ever [your] most obliged servant
Francesca Raffaelli

Francesca's Return *in Patria*

Written in Francesca's most eloquent epistolary voice, this letter points both to likely facts about her remarriage and second widowhood and to the kinship structures and institutions of womanhood that formed the emotional situation from which she wrote. The letter reveals that Francesca's privilege as a favored member of the Medici famiglia had temporarily released her from the harshest dilemma that Tuscan remarriage customs imposed on a widow. She seems not to have had to choose, in the short run, between remarriage and care for the daughter born of her first marriage. Instead, Christine had granted her physical custody of the girl until she reached a certain age, while the court assumed the economic burdens of legal guardianship by promising her an appointment in service, an education in a monastero di monache, and, probably, a dowry.[47] Christine had thus acted in place of the impoverished Signorini clan, substituting the protection of the Medici famiglia for that of the girl's patrilineal family; at the same time, insofar as Christine's offer resolved the most significant obstacle to Francesca's second marriage, she had also acted as if the Medici were the mother's patrilineal family. Christine had served as a de facto father to two generations of women, embodying the force of patriarchy in female form. Thus for the second time in her life, Francesca had profited from the female control of institutional heterosexuality that she had helped represent in the character of Melissa in *La liberazione*. Rather like the dama disincantata who appeared at the end of that show, Francesca meant to petition the woman whose benevolence had already liberated her from one social norm for a second liberation: Francesca wanted Cioli to persuade Christine to restore her to full maternity of her daughter and to restore her to the country that was her home.

The letter is as remarkable for its inscription of Francesca's conflicted feelings as it is for its evocation of the facts. Personal and professional isolation, intense family feeling apparently heightened by what may have been Margherita's early brush with the 1630 plague epidemic, and a passion to pass the fruits of a lifetime's study on to her child swirl around one another. The resulting eddy of feeling directly opposed Francesca's feelings of obligation to the grand duchess. Rather than mutually reinforcing each other, as intended by the kinship practices that knit a prince's dependents into a vast, pseudo-familial web, Francesca's loyalties to her biological family and her patronage famiglia conflicted so badly as nearly to tear her life apart. Francesca's indignation at Tuccarelli's behavior when he had come to check on her daughter's recovery crystallized the conflict. On one hand, she seems to speak from a surprisingly modern experience of a biological family's affective bonds: although she was, in the eyes of Tuscan law, "as if dead" to her daughter once she had ceded the economic responsibilities of guardianship to the court, she seemed to imagine human beings' bodily and affective relations with each other to be as important as the abstractions that constructed their relations in law.[48] On the other hand, her encounter with Tuccarelli reminded Francesca all too well that the seeming benevolence of Christine's maternalistic world—a world in which the interests of biological and patronage families were intended to overlap—extended only to the limit of the grand duchess's self-interest. No matter how intimate with her sovereigns she had been, no matter how highly they had valued her virtù and her person, Francesca was not ever to be treated by her princesses quite as if she had, herself, human feelings of the sort it was her craft to represent and perform. Yet if she was to preserve her little family, give value to her life by passing on her craft to her talented child, and free herself from the isolation of life in highly androcentric, artistically provincial Lucca, she needed Cioli to stage an eloquent appeal that would make the interests of her family and those of her patronage famiglia seem once again to align.

The middle section of the letter amounts to Francesca's coaching of Cioli's appeal. Wrapped in the stereotypically feminine tropes of the lament ("alone . . . abandoned, in a foreign country"), as ornamented by widowhood's special griefs, the very details through which Francesca seems to communicate feelings aim precisely at Christine's sympathies. Caccini and Cioli both knew that foreign-born widows had appealed to Christine's experience of widowhood far from her native France, as countless more had appealed on behalf of daughters. By evoking her own watchful anxiety at Margherita's sickbed, Francesca's letter cagily reminded Cioli to evoke Christine's lifetime of anxious watch over her own children's health. And by reminding him of her wish to preserve her artistic patrimony in her daughter, she implicitly encouraged him to link her concern to Christine's dedicated stewardship of the Medici principality. That stewardship had extended to assuming guardianship over her granddaughter Vittoria della Rovere when, a year before Francesca's second marriage had been arranged, Christine had remarried Vittoria's mother, Princess Claudia, to an Austrian archduke.[49] Given that Margherita Signorini and her eloquent mother would eventually be listed on the payroll of the young Vittoria, not her dowager grandmother, it seems likely that the relationship between Vittoria and Margherita was the exact place where the preservation of the Medici and Caccini patrimonies converged—the place where the interests of biological and patronage families could align.

Margherita and Princess Vittoria had been born but days apart in 1622, and each had been taken under the grand duchess's protection when she negotiated their mothers' second marriages. The two girls' mothers may well have expected them to know each other as musical companions. Christine may have imagined that Margherita would have served Vittoria as Francesca had served her grandmother, as the virtuosa artisan who would produce Vittoria's literal, public voice when she became Tuscany's next grand duchess. But for Margherita to serve Vittoria well, Francesca's letter implied, she would need to have been fully formed in the craft her mother had developed in a lifetime's obedience to Christine's commands.

On 24 May 1631, Cioli replied, reporting his success at clarifying what he must have understood to be Francesca's most pressing concern. It would be up to Francesca to decide when she (not some stranger) would deliver Margherita into service "because she will be received by their Highnesses willingly, and with that esteem for her virtù that you deserve for having taught them to her, and it will be also up to you when to come see her after you have left her, however many times you like, because you will always be welcome."[50] Her dignity, her maternity, and her ability to teach her daughter restored, two days later Francesca thanked Cioli for news that had brought her a "consolation equal to the bitterness [that] I had in my heart."[51]

Margherita Signorini's return to Florence under her mother Francesca Caccini's care was to be postponed by the recurring waves of plague and quarantine that swept Lucca and Florence over the next three years. Penitential processions seeking safety from the plague had begun at Lucca as early as 15 July 1630, barely five weeks after Francesca had taken charge of the Raffaelli estate and a month before she finalized the liquidation of her property in Florence.[52] Processions continued throughout the summer, but by 17 November 1630 Lucca's elders felt compelled to take stronger action. They quarantined three suburban communities, including Monte San Quilici, where the Raffaelli villa was located, and ordered all citizens to return to their city homes. In a desperate attempt to control the contagion by limiting personal freedom, the city forbade Lucca's women and children under the age of sixteen to leave their homes, allowing only one person from each household to go out for provisions, and then only on Tuesdays and Fridays. Grain prices were set artificially low to prevent famine, and Eastertide communion was ordered to be distributed in the doorways of homes. By August 1631, eight thousand people had died of plague in Lucca, and the city's public life had all but disappeared into the myriad privacies of homes under individual quarantine. Residents' most frequent contact with the outside world was their communal recitations of the rosary from the windows of palazzi under quarantine, recitations ordered by the Pope and led by the only people still allowed to move freely about the streets: parish priests. Only on 14 February 1633, nearly two years after Caccini had received Cioli's clarification of her authority over her daughter's delivery, did the quarantine of Lucca's population lift. But the news in early April of a second wave of plague in Florence, with a reported death toll of fifty or sixty people per day, led Lucca to close its gates again.[53] Not until 1 January 1634 were those imprisoned by Lucca's draconian quarantine officially free to travel. Unless they somehow evaded the quarantine, by then Francesca and her children had been locked inside their palazzo on the via Fillungo, fearing for their lives and engaging in daily prayers at their windows, for nearly three years.

Sometime during those three years Francesca and her Florentine patrons had conceived a new arrangement that would enable Francesca's return to her native city in a situation of such unquestioned onestà as to not risk her usufruct of Raffaelli's estate. On 22 June 1633 Christine's anxiously waiting secretaries received news from Rome that Pope Urban VIII had granted two licenze requested by the Tuscan ambassador Francesco Niccolini. Princesses Anna and Maria Maddalena de' Medici, living at La Crocetta, were granted permission to play musical instruments, and "the widow Francesca Caccini" was permitted "to enter the monastero of La Crocetta, with her girl."[54] The grand duchess herself was rumored to have petitioned the Pope in 1633 for permission to withdraw from the world to La Crocetta, a community she had already amply populated with widows and other secular women to serve her daughter Maria Maddalena and her two granddaughters, Anna and the future grand duchess, Vittoria della Rovere.[55] Neither Christine nor Francesca ever took advantage of their permission to withdraw completely into La Crocetta's nominally cloistered world. Christine continued to live either at Castello or La Quiete, while Francesca and her children were eventually to rent apartments in a home that Francesco Forte owned on Borgo Pinti, just behind La Crocetta.[56] Nonetheless, each seems to have found solace, community, and continued social power in a world of women they had helped create between 1610 and 1630. For Francesca, a return to her native Florence—as a gentildonna who could live independently with her children yet ground her social and artistic life amid princesses, dame and donne—promised to restore the gynocentric community of her youth, in which she had thrived before succumbing temporarily to the successive blows of widowhood.

Afterlives

12

I f the traditional narrative of women's lives ends at "reader, she married him," the narratives of music history typically treat a musician's withdrawal into private, nonprofessional music making as the equivalent of artistic death. In that sense, Francesca's life after her marriage to Tommaso Raffaelli was already a life after death. Her life as his widow, and therefore as a would-be gentildonna, in what was left of the Florence of her youth would be another such afterlife, for although she remained musically active in the 1630s Francesca would never again make music in a way that was important to the public record. This chapter tells the story of these afterlives—after she returned to the profoundly changed women's court in her homeland, after the death of her lifelong benefactrix Christine de Lorraine, and after her own disappearance from the documentary record, as traces of her life and the world she had known lived on in the lives of her daughter and granddaughter.

The Women's Court at La Crocetta

When Francesca, eleven-year-old Margherita Signorini, and five-year-old Tommaso Raffaelli returned to Florence in 1634, they lived apart from yet immersed in a populous, lively, but radically depoliticized women's court that continued to circulate around Christine de Lorraine.[1] Still as restlessly peripatetic as she had ensured it would be in her youth, Christine's court moved almost daily from her preferred suburban villa, Castello, to the institution that had become its urban center, the Monastero di Santa Croce (of the Dominican order), known as La Crocetta. As far as Tuscan subjects knew, the aging grand duchess and her court passed their days at La Crocetta in prayer and in caring for the Medici princesses who had been sent to live there.

Christine had taken an interest in La Crocetta as early as 1611, but her intense engagement with the community began in 1619, when her disabled daughter Maria Maddalena declared her intention to enter the Dominican community.[2] On the church's authority, Medici architects built a palazzo with an enclosed garden and a private passageway to the nearby church of Santissima Annunziata for the princess and her resident staff of four unmarried adult women and two seventeen-year-old donne. Two of La Crocetta's fifteen resident servants were to clean and cook for the princess's household, along with three or four more servants whom Christine sent daily to help with housekeeping chores.[3] La Crocetta soon became the urban home of all the unmarried princesses: it was the home of Christine's youngest daughter Claudia from 1623 until her remarriage in 1626, Claudia's daughter Vittoria della Rovere from 1623 until her marriage in 1637, and Archduchess Maria Magdalena's youngest daughter Anna from 1628 until 1637.[4] Like Princess Maria Maddalena, each had her own resident servants, each was served by additional staff who arrived daily on orders from the court, and each was permitted to enter and leave at will to enjoy holidays and good weather at Christine's favorite villas, Castello and La Quiete. Only after Christine's death and Vittoria della Rovere's marriage did La Crocetta cease to be the center of the women's court, the passageways that connected the palaces to monastic spaces dismantled and sealed by Florence's archbishop.[5]

Contemporary accounts indicate that in the 1630s La Crocetta embodied all the "abuses" of female monastic life for which the diocese of Florence had long been famous. Unlike the residents of Le Murate, however, those of La Crocetta seem to have embraced enthusiastically the glitter of what residents there still call "the epoch of the princesses." In his instructions to the community shortly after that epoch ended, confessor Anton Maria Riconesi sternly reminded the nuns that the princesses, their donne, servants, and guests had come and gone in the cloister at every hour of day and night, conversing and exchanging clothes, jewelry, and secular books with the nuns, and hosting lavish luncheons and dinners on major feasts.[6] The constant "uproar of carriages . . . and the cries and noise made by couriers, guards and others of the court who waited on her highness" interrupted even the quiet of La Crocetta's confessional.[7] Perhaps worst of all in Riconesi's eyes, the monastero "had become a court of princesses and ladies, and you became so many courtiers."[8]

La Crocetta's constant traffic in fashion, conversation, books and favors among women of all social ranks made it the principal site for the women's court whose private circulation of power had once complemented Christine's de facto regency. Yet the retreat of that court behind apparently cloistered walls coincided with a withering of its connection to the mechanisms of the Tuscan state. In the 1630s the most significant remaining link lay in the symbolic value that La Crocetta acquired when Christine used renewed petitions for the founder's beatification as a means by which the Medici regime could be seen to combat the epidemic of plague.[9]

The Monastero di Santa Croce had been founded by a determined visionary peasant girl turned anti-Savonarolan anchorite, Suor Domenica del Paradiso, who had miraculously raised funds to house a community of like-minded women in 1511. Local historians claimed her best-known visions to be interpretations of Medicean hegemony as angelically ordained, and she was believed to have freed the city from both plague and political crisis in 1527 by miraculously displacing the city's suffering onto her own feverish, bleeding, and plague-ridden body. Thus Christine's renewed pressure for beatification revived the memory of Suor Domenica as a highly partisan emblem of a womanly Medicean sanctity that could shield against both plague and the threat of civil disorder that it posed.

Christine's efforts were directly echoed by the decision of La Crocetta's prioress to circulate the founder's relics among selected victims of the plague, ones who were subsequently known to have been miraculously cured. Both efforts, in turn, complemented the practical, scientifically up-to-date quarantine standards of public hygiene imposed by the new grand duke, Ferdinando II, who had assumed power in 1628. La Crocetta's public image as a strictly observant, cloistered, and health-giving community came to symbolize both the image of Medicean rule as providing good government attuned to divine will and the safety that government promised to citizens who submitted to enclosure in the city's quarantine. Through its connection to La Crocetta, the informal women's court that convened there might seem to have retained some of the political importance it had had in the long years of regency. But in fact the distribution of Medicean power had become sharply gendered: the women were relegated to managing symbolic power, while the men managed practical affairs in the public world. Cut off from the exercise of public power, its very containment seen as a symbol of sanctified civil order, the community of secular and monastic women centered at La Crocetta can be seen with hindsight as itself something like a relic of the world to which Francesca might have thought she had returned. Like a relic, it retained in metonymic, miniaturized form energies that had once circulated as the power both to command and to make things happen in the real world.

Music at La Crocetta and Castello

Music had long been important to La Crocetta's communal life. Working with its meticulously detailed account books, Kelley Harness has shown that the monastic community there knew a rich musical life from the 1590s through the 1640s.[10] Instrumentalists from the court's ensembles joined organists, singers, and maestri from the Ospedale di Santa Maria Nuova, Santissima Annunziata, and the Duomo to provide timbrally rich, polychoral music for the community's principal feasts. Princess Maria Maddalena's arrival in the 1620s sparked both an increase in the community's theatrical life and the de facto appointment of Giovanni Battista da Gagliano as its maestro of musical performances.[11] Material that Harness has gathered corroborates Riconesi's complaint that spiritual comedies were frequently performed for residents and courtly guests with costumes, props, and musicians borrowed from the court. Francesca Caccini had been among those musicians in the 1620s. She is known to have visited Princess Maria Maddalena there, perhaps to teach her the instrumental performance that the 1633 licenza noted, and she evidently provided some music for Jacopo Cicognini's *Il martirio de Santa Caterina*, probably performed at La Crocetta on 27 November 1625.[12]

Music also played a part in the unofficial courtly life of La Crocetta that its account books do not record. It was to this life that Francesca and her daughter Margarita Signorini seem to have contributed in the 1630s as paid members of the overlapping staffs of Christine de Lorraine and her granddaughter Vittoria della Rovere.[13] In those years the core mission of the court at La Crocetta was to educate the Medici's two youngest princesses, especially Vittoria, who, betrothed to her cousin Ferdinando II as an infant, was destined to be Tuscany's next grand duchess. In a 1633 letter to her daughter Princess Maria Maddalena, Christine outlined the way she expected eleven-year-old Vittoria to spend her days, "so as to accustom herself to Christian and virtuous practices appropriate to a princess of her quality."[14] Christine specified that those practices should include about two and a half hours daily spent "playing an instrument." At least two women from outside the community taught music at La Crocetta. Princesses Anna and Vittoria evidently listened with pleasure to the Roman harpist Costanza della Porta when she visited Florence in 1635 "as an opportunity to pass the time, and to learn."[15] They may have learned not from personal study but from observing the lessons that della Porta gave Margherita Signorini that year at Christine's request. Francesca, whose licenza to come and go as she pleased with her daughter had been written on the same page as Princess Anna's licenza to play instruments, and who received a stipend as a musica from Vittoria's household, was the other woman who taught music at La Crocetta. Although the evidence that she taught the princesses is only circumstantial, her letters from the 1630s clearly indicate that she taught canzonette spirituale to nuns—in direct violation of the terms of her licenza, which forbade her to talk or engage in business with any nuns.[16]

Like Lavinia Guasco in the 1580s or any girl in early modern Italy, Vittoria must have been expected to learn music in close association with the womanly virtues of onestà and continenza. But unlike most girls, and most princesses, she seems likely to have learned those virtues, and the respect for a teacher that modeled respect for domestic and political authority, from a woman—in the case of Francesca, a woman quite accustomed to authority. Indeed, Christine's letter about Vittoria's education named the girl's respect for her teachers' authority over her education "no less than . . . [that for] a mother" as among the practices appropriate to a princess of her quality.[17] In a sense, then, Francesca's probable work as Vittoria's teacher might be viewed as political work, as part of a program to teach her the respect for women's authority that would enable the future grand duchess to wield authority as easily as her grandmother had done.

Francesca and her daughter seem to have contributed, too, to the impromptu musical life of the women's court when it adjourned for holidays to Christine's home at Castello. As her mother had decades earlier, Margherita Signorini seems to have performed for Christine to help her pass the time, especially when she lay ill. Mother and daughter seem to have participated as well in the domestic performances of little comedies by which the princesses and their dame and donne amused themselves, their grandmother, and her guests, and in entertainments their grandmother ordered for the princesses.[18]

Nine letters that Christine's secretary Ugo Cacciotti exchanged with Michelangelo Buonarroti in February 1634/35 reveal the process by which such entertainments were developed, in a swift progress from invention by professionals to performance by amateurs.[19] On Wednesday, 4 February, Cacciotti asked Buonarroti to provide up to eight stanzas of verse "at once erudite and witty" for a birthday surprise that Christine planned for Vittoria the following Sunday.[20] A cook had been commissioned to create from sugar a miniature palace, supported by four columns with chests at their bases that were to be filled with the "gloves, handbags, and other galanterie" that were to be Christine's gifts to Vittoria.[21] Christine wanted three or four costumed personae to deliver the gifts after singing verses that, Cacciotti emphasized, needed to be funny. "The direction of the singing," he noted, "will be good, because Signora Francesca Caccini and her daughter are here, even though neither of them yet knows this thought of Madama."[22] A flurry of letters between the two men followed as Cacciotti sought Buonarroti's advice about costumes and props that might help the under-rehearsed singers remember their parts. The personae, he decided, could be costumed as peasant girls hiding their parts in bunches of flowers that they carried. Francesca, he noted drily, "nowadays would be better as their mother-in-law."[23] Cembali were to be added to the performance area so that the singers would not have to "depend entirely on their memory for the singing" that Francesca had conceived for two performers singing alternate stanzas of Buonarroti's poetry.[24] Buonarotti's final draft arrived at Castello on Sunday morning. According to a letter Cacciotti wrote the following Thursday, the surprise went "prettily," even though Francesca had left Castello an hour before it began.[25]

At first glance, the story that these letters tell includes all the features of Francesca's earlier life as a musica amid the women of the Medici court: the last-minute spontaneity of the patrons and their artists' corresponding need for haste and improvisatory skills, the use of props and supporting instruments to compensate for lack of rehearsal, her own role composing and teaching music for verses that Buonarroti had written but hours earlier, and the limited but very real authority she had over other women by virtue of her skills. But the fact that this little show is known only through letters between men implies that Francesca's relationship to the circulation of power in the courtly world had changed, reverting to something like the relationship she had known as an unmarried girl. For though Francesca seems still to have been the person on whose musical inventiveness and skill the show's success would depend, she seems not to have been involved in communicating Christine's intentions from the world of women with the power to command to the world of men with the power to get things done. No longer in constant motion between those two worlds, Francesca was stuck as firmly in a woman's world as was Christine—or as were the leafy denizens of Alcina's garden before the liberation. Within that world, her music making served not to extend the power of princely women into the wider world but to create the medium through which women's affection and respect for one another could circulate as the bodily actions that produce musical sound and voice.

Between Musica and Dama

Mainly making music that served what Riconesi had called the court's "vanities," Francesca in the 1630s could seem to have all but retired from the profession in which she had once showed so much ambition and skill and to which she had still seemed so devoted in her 1631 letter to Cioli. But although it ensured that she would not again live and work in a way that twenty-first-century musicians and feminists could describe with the admiring phrase "fully professional," the enclosure of Francesca's musical virtù in a world of women seems likely to have served her interests. It preserved the reputation for onestà and continenza that were critical to her status as the widowed guardian of a noble son. Francesca's new social location was perfectly represented by the place her name occupied in the financial records of the women's court. Inscribed exactly between the court's gentildonne and its servants as "Francesca Caccini Raffaelli, musica," she was still identified to the paymasters by what she could do rather than simply by who she was. Ambivalent as it was, this was a social position Francesca worked hard to sustain, for her own sake and for the sake of the children with whose social rank her own was completely intertwined.

Nothing better defined a courtier's social location and access to social power than her or his successful trafficking in favors. Although surviving documents provide only an incomplete record, it seems that as a married woman Francesca participated in that part of the courtier's game. When the beneficiaries of her favors were men—Vincenzo Calestani, Andrea Falconieri, Lorenzo Papi, or her cousin Fra Damiziano—Francesca traded on the social familiarity that her virtù had won for her to secure the intervention of powerful men. [26] Only when her own circumstances or those of her female relatives were at stake did she trade indirectly on her family's years of faithful service to the Medici.[27]

As a widow in the 1630s, however, Francesca seems to have focused exclusively on seeking favors for herself, her daughter, or other women. She sought Buonarroti's poetry for her daughter and "some nuns" to sing.[28] Twice she asked his help in arranging a meeting with Jacopo Soldani, then tutor to Prince Leopoldo.[29] On two other occasions she wrote Buonarroti on behalf of needy widows: in September 1635 she asked that he help one Lisabetta outfit her daughter for profession as a nun (a cause to which the princesses had already given), and in December 1636 she asked that he aid Maddalena Quoreli, a widow "in greater need" than Francesca chose to put in writing.[30] When Francesca recommended these two to Buonarroti's generosity, she participated in a small way in the practice of women advocating for other women that had long been the lifeblood of Christine's court: she behaved as a gentildonna rather than a servant. Her style in advocating for these women was as important to that behavior as its substance. Presenting each widow's worth in terms of her intrinsic goodness rather than in terms of her family, Medici service, usefulness to others, or skill, Francesca represented herself as a person who valued others for who she knew them to be rather than for what they could do.

In these letters Francesca's self-presentation could imply an unexpected sweetness or disinterested generosity in her character, once she was liberated from the compulsion to promote one's own interests that courtly culture imposed on its underlings. But her acts of generosity on behalf of women too needy to offer favors in return also enabled Francesca to portray herself as above the mere traffic in favors, as if she were the gentildonna her maternal obligations to her son required her to be. Francesca had tried to consolidate that status in January 1635/36 by petitioning Christine to appoint her to the court as a dama, with court-supported servants of her own, a petition subsequent records show to have been denied.[31] A month later, when her stepmother Margherita died, leaving an undowered, incapacitated adult daughter behind, Francesca was to learn that her social location between musica and gentildonna at the women's court was a place of almost no social power.[32] Described as "storpiata" (crippled or maimed) in Giulio's will, Dianora Caccini had been deemed unfit for either marriage or monastic life. Nonetheless, Giulio's final codicil left her only sixteen scudi annually and entrusted her care to his widow, his son-in-law Giovanni Battista Signorini, and his cousin Benedetto Mainardi.[33] When Giulio's eldest legitimate son, Giovanni Battista, had threatened to evict Margherita and Dianora from their home in 1624, Francesca—not her husband—had hand-carried a memo describing their plight from the Arte della Lana to the court in Pisa, argued their case in person before Curtio Picchena, and ensured thereby their right to a home.[34] The day after Margherita's burial on 8 February 1636, it would be Francesca, not any of her siblings then living in Florence, who sought to protect Dianora, if she could, from the prospect of homelessness or impoverished dependence on the brother who had once tried to evict her.

Francesca wrote the maggiordomo of the household at La Crocetta, Ortensia Guadagni ne' Salviati, asking her first to obtain Christine's permission to discuss the matter with Francesca's agent, Selvaggia de' Medici, then to request a licenza allowing Dianora to live either in a convent or a home for unmarried girls, and, finally, to ask Christine to "favor" Dianora by supplementing her meager income.[35] Eschewing genteel claims about Dianora's intrinsic goodness, Francesca used the rhetoric of mutual obligation that governed relations of service within a patronage famiglia, reminding Salviati that "Madama does such works of charity all the time, and for people who do not have the merit of having served the serenissima house as my father did for sixty years, and my stepmother for twenty, and I for my entire life."[36]

But this rhetoric failed her, perhaps because she was no longer quite the lifelong servant she made herself out to be. Thanks to her usufruct of the Raffaelli estate, Francesca was financially able to take her of her sister herself. Yet as she explained to Ugo Cacciotti two days later:

> It was never my thought to bring the daughter of my stepmother, my sister, into my home, because I cannot aggravate my son with either the expense or the inconvenience, but rather, if she could have had the consolation and sufficient dowry, and if it could have been done, to put her in some charitable place. But if it cannot be done, I have judged it to be all right, and necessary, that her brother take her into his home under his care, and he cannot escape it since I have already executed Madama's thought and will in the matter: and I beg you to do me

the favor of kissing her highness's robe, and humbly thanking her in my name for the honor that she did in having thought about the interests of my sister.[37]

In the intervening days Christine had granted some kind of favor to Dianora Caccini, probably a financial contribution to her support, but she seems not to have been willing or able to procure a licenza for her. Although Tuscany's diplomats had inundated the Vatican for twenty years with requests for licenze from women whose petitions Christine had supported, all the beneficiaries were either elite by birth or especially suited to a kind of work that needed to be done for cloistered members of the princess class. Dianora Caccini was neither. Moreover, the sister who petitioned on her behalf was neither quite a servant to whose family certain kinds of generosity were owed nor enough of a gentildonna ever to have been able to reciprocate by expediting a similar favor for the grand duchess. Indeed, from the perspective of locally circulating biographical fact, Francesca owed both her old identity as a servant and her new one as a gentildonna directly to Christine. Francesca was as dependent on her patron's disinterested generosity as the penniless Lisabetta had been on hers. But even the generosity of a sovereign had its limits, especially when its price would have to be paid from the dwindling political capital the Medici had in Urban VIII's Rome, and paid in the currency of licenze on which the monastic households of Princesses Vittoria and Anna continued to depend. Thus even though, as one secretary had recently written another, the grand duchess continued to "feel affection for S.ra Caccini, and [she] esteems and honors her virtù," the licenza that Francesca had sought marked the limit of Christine's generosity toward a person whose very life her generosity had made.[38]

Square 43: Your Patron Dies

When she responded to Francesca's plea with only partial grace, Christine, nearly seventy-seven, was well aware that she was slipping fast into physical decline. In July 1636 she would write Camilla Orsini ne' Borghese in Rome: "Beginning as I am to suffer the mishaps that age brings, I beg Your Excellency to remember me in your prayers. . . . To tell Your Excellency the truth, because of the grand duchess's [Vittoria's] youth and Princess Anna's needs, I would like to prolong my life in the service of this House."[39] But by late November, the once restlessly energetic leader of monastic visits and pilgrimages was confined to bed with symptoms her secretaries described as constant pain, weakness, near blindness, and gathering deafness. Leaving La Crocetta on 28 November, her granddaughters joined the vigil at Christine's bedside in Castello, where her enforced idleness and perhaps her pain were soothed by the singing and playing of fourteen-year-old Margherita Signorini, "the daughter of la Cecchina musica."[40] On 20 December, the woman on whom the Medici, their vast service and kinship famiglia, and indeed all of Tuscany had depended for thirty years of stability, generosity, and grace died quietly in her bed.[41] Christine's death ended what had been the most enduring relationship of Francesca's life.

The Spaniard Alonso de Barros had recognized the devastating effects of a patron's death when he labeled the most problematic square of his board game The Courtier's Philosophy, number 43, with the rubric "Your patron dies." As in life, players landing on square 43 were required to start the game over.[42] Even in a world where the death of a patron could be turned into ludic fun, Christine's death might have struck some in her court as a genuine catastrophe that exceeded individual courtiers' self-interest. As the center of Tuscan political gravity for thirty years, Christine had been responsible for policies and spectacles that had seemed to realize the golden age of stability, wealth, and power predicted by the intermedi created for her marriage in 1589. Marking what would turn out to be the end of the granducato's pretensions to be a political or artistic great power, her death also marked the end of a time in which Tuscany's dependence on a foreign-born woman to be the nerve center of local and international power had temporarily suspended the deep masculinist bias of local tradition. Thus passed an era in which women of many social ranks enjoyed, as a reflection of Christine's power, implicit authority over their own and other women's lives.

Whatever she may have felt at the loss of her patron, professional savvy and maternal concern seem to have fused in Francesca's first response to her impending encounter with "square 43." On 10 December 1636 she petitioned the dying Christine to authorize immediate payment of an already granted clothing allowance that signified Margherita's inscription in her service, winning a very generous commitment of twenty-four scudi (two months' salary) just for Christmas.[43] On 19 December she wrote Ugo Cacciotti to urge that he have Christine sign the authorizing memo, "so my daughter could have the dress that she needs for this Christmas, and now there is not much time."[44] Had Margherita's allowance been authorized in writing by Christine, she would have been as fully inscribed as possible as an individual musica in the written record of Christine's patronage obligations—obligations that Francesca knew the Medici famiglia would honor after her death. But Christine died the next day, without signing Cacciotti's memo. Remaining only an anonymous daughter under her mother's name on Christine's staff list, Margherita was more vulnerable than Francesca had hoped she would be to the staff review that began on the first of January.[45]

Sparked by Ferdinando II's order to evaluate and reassign his grandmother's staff as appropriate, that staff review unfolded amid a perfect scenario for staff to begin their relationships of service anew: preparations for the week of festivities that would celebrate the mid-July consummation of Ferdinando's marriage to his cousin Vittora della Rovere.[46] By late January 1637, a sovereign command for Margherita's performance in one of the scheduled comedies found Francesca trapped between the contradictory interests of her daughter and her son. On 27 January, Vittoria della Rovere wrote her cousin and future brother-in-law Prince Giovan Carlo, who was in charge of the wedding festivities: "I have revealed openly to Margherita, the daughter of Cecchina musica, that it was the firm will of the grand duke, my lord and bridegroom, that she should sing and act in a comedy; and, furthermore, because my own [will] is not nor shall it ever be anything but the same as his highness's, I commanded the same Margherita to obey promptly. But the mother is the one who opposes it, on the premise that by being seen on a stage the daughter could lose her future and have that much more trouble either marrying or becoming a nun."[47]

Vittoria was not the only one trying by command or persuasion to secure Margherita's services. One Cavaliere Usimbardi also wrote Giovan Carlo of his attempt to intervene with Francesca: "I have obeyed Your Highness in making every intercession possible with Signora Francesca, to dispose her toward allowing her daughter to act onstage, in accordance with the will of the most serene grand duke. But she told me that she had given her reasons to Father Centuriono and that she already believed her daughter to have been excused. And that no other or greater reason forced her to show the opposite of her usual obedience than her concern not to compromise either the reputation of her daughter, or that of her son, by having allowed [the girl] to act publicly on stage. It falls to me to tell your highness, to whom I humbly bow, that this matter is a lost cause."[48]

To disobey so steadfastly her sovereigns' wishes for their own wedding, at the very moment when her own and her daughter's future at court were under review, was so risky that Francesca's expressed reasons must have been offered in good faith. She may selfishly have feared that his half-sister's performance, albeit on the grand duke's stage, would blemish the noble status of her son and thus be grounds for some ambitious Raffaelli to contest both her custody and the usufruct on which her own independence and class pretensions were based. But Francesca may also have hoped that her refusal would have redefined Margherita's position in a new Medici famiglia that was still forming. If she succeeded in portraying her girl as a musical virtuosa whose relationship to young Tommaso Raffaelli gave her the right to say no to her sovereigns, Francesca might have done more than preserve Margherita's suitability for a good marriage or convent placement. She might have shown her daughter how, if she remained in a service relationship to the court, she could mix expressed respect for her patrons, an expressed concern for the conventions of genteel womanhood, and a strong sense of personal pride when she responded to commands. Francesca might, that is, have taught Margherita how to exercise her right to agency—her right to disobey—without directly challenging the hierarchy from within which she had no choice but to seem "always most ready to serve." At the same time, by redefining Margherita in relation to the Raffaelli's noble status, Francesca may have hoped to change the court's view of her daughter, to spare her daughter the life of compulsory music-making that she had known.

Afterlives, 1

"Today I find myself alone, without company, abandoned, . . . and I have nothing in the world but these children."[49] When Francesca wrote this piteous if accurate description of her life as a widow in Lucca, she may not have imagined that she prophesied the condition to which she would return in Florence once she had arrived at square 43. Although she and her daughter continued to be provided for by the Medici and to live in Borgo Pinti until at least 1641, after the middle of 1637 neither was a court familiar important enough that her actions or concerns were reported. However rich or impoverished, cheerful or strained, affectionate or aloof her private life with her children may have been, it seems from the few documentary traces to survive that in her last known years Francesca concentrated her energy and intelligence on the private womanly work of providing for her children. The erratically preserved records of Lucca's Offizio delle Vedove e Pupille indicate that she continued to manage Tommaso Raffaelli's estate for their son, sometimes acting through her brother-in-law Padre Costantino Raffaelli to collect and pay small debts related to the land's agricultural use.[50] And in April 1639 she embarked on an ill-advised effort to collect on a dowry promise signed in 1607 by one of the richest members of the new "noble" class that the Medici had created, the investment banker, humanist scholar, and amateur poet Riccardo Riccardi.[51] Almost certainly, the effort was aimed at amassing a substantial dowry for her daughter.

According to depositions taken sometime before 12 April 1639, Francesca had "acted on her own behalf and for her daughter," presenting an *apoca* (a kind of promissory note) for payment by Riccardi's heirs, his nephews Cosimo and Gabriello. Dated and signed by Riccardi on 7 October 1607, the apoca promised to pay Francesca's first husband Giovanni Battista Signorini 1,000 scudi toward her dowry and 600 more to dower any daughter that would be born of their imminent marriage.[52] Besides asking for payment of the principal, Francesca had asked to be paid interest of 5 percent per annum on her own never-paid dowry, beginning from the date of her marriage. Once the interest was calculated, Francesca's claim amounted to nearly 2,500 scudi, a claim large enough that even the Riccardi brothers, whose annual household expenses totaled 19,680 scudi, could neither ignore it nor pay Francesca off to avoid the nuisance of litigation.[53] Instead, Cosimo Riccardi (acting for himself and his brother, who was ambassador to Spain) took Francesca to court.

Everything the Riccardi heirs said in court about the apoca and everything said by the family archivist Giovanni Lami in the eighteenth century affirms that the document itself was valid.[54] But when Cosimo Riccardi appealed to the Ruota Civile with jurisdiction over Signorini's *gonfalone* (neighborhood of origin) in Santa Croce on 12 April 1639, he rejected her claim on several grounds. He asserted that Francesca had no legal standing to collect payment, that in any case too much time had passed since the contract was signed, that she had not given proper notice of her intent to collect, and that the promise had been conditional on Signorini's taking a position with the Uffizio della Dogana, which he had not done because he had received better compensation from some other position the grand duchess arranged for him. "Given the request and given the norms of the law," the judge granted Riccardi's request for an injunction prohibiting further discussion of the case and ordered that Francesca not dare to cash the apoca against Cosimo Riccardi's accounts, that she be charged with court costs, and that she appear in court to explain herself.[55] By the next day Francesca had replied through her attorney Ferdinando Mainardi to the summons and injunction delivered to her in Borgo Pinti. Because she had declared herself injured by the injunction, the judge reserved the right to hear her side of the case.[56] Three months later, on Wednesday, 13 July 1639, Mainardi appeared in court on her behalf, repeating her claim but accepting that most of what had been said on Cosimo's side had been true. Nonetheless, he added, some parts of it were not true, and Cosimo had not acted according to the norms outlined by the statutes of the Comune di Firenze. Therefore he asked that the injunction against Francesca be lifted, along with the requirement that she pay court costs.[57]

There all record of the case ends. What remains is the question why Francesca would have tried to cash in a thirty-two-year-old piece of financial paper that she must have located among her first husband's effects. Since there is no evidence that the Raffaelli estate had suffered losses disproportionate to others suffered in the general agricultural recession in Lucca, the best guess is that Francesca sought to gather a substantial dowry for the seventeen-year-old Margherita. If the twenty-five hundred scudi that Francesca had hoped to gain had been added to the sixteen hundred scudi that she had realized from the sale of the property on the via Valfonda, Francesca could have given her girl a dowry roughly four times the size of her own—a dowry fit for a real member of the gentildonna class that Francesca would have won independent of whatever good will she and Margherita may still have enjoyed from the unhappily married Ferdinando II and Vittoria della Rovere.

After August 1639, publicly preserved traces of Francesca Caccini's life dwindle rapidly to a vanishing point, without any unambiguous indication of when or where she died. On 8 May 1641 Ferdinando II's secretary Perseo Falconieri drafted a letter patent for his patron's signature and seal that articulated Francesca's position in the Medici famiglia with exquisite precision: "Francesca Caccini Raffaelli having long served us as a musica, to our extraordinary satisfaction and with particular fame for her singular value in that profession, we have desired with this [document] to make public the benefits [assigned because] of her merit with this house, declaring expressly as we do, that she lives under our protection, so that her virtù should remain more fruitfully marked by the possession of the greatest prerogatives and honors that our most welcome, worthy and esteemed servants currently enjoy."[58] Although preserved among passports and letters of introduction asking other princes to protect court functionaries as they traveled abroad, this letter seems not to have been a travel document so much as it was an official certificate of Francesca's status. No longer serving the Medici as a musica, and apparently no longer anywhere inscribed in a courtly pay record, she had long ago earned the right to all the privileges that Medici protection could afford, without any obligation ever to trade service for protection again. Yet six weeks later, on 18 June 1641, she wrote Paolo Giordano Orsini, heir of her old patron Virginio Orsini, asking for temporary lodging in his Roman palace at Monte Giordano, ending her letter with the old, conventional rhetoric that acknowledged princely favors with a self-effacing promise of perpetual service: "I find myself at the moment in urgent need of moving to that city, for business that matters a great deal to me, with which I could be engaged for a month and half at the most. . . . I beg you to pardon my boldness and confidence toward you, prompted by your infinite goodness, benevolence, and courtesy, to which all who serve you are obliged. I shall always serve your excellency and her excellency your duchess with all my forces and weak talents, in all that Your Excellence shall command."[59] Four days later, Orsini replied that he had no room because "in addition to my famiglia I have the duke of Sforza and all his people here."[60]

With that letter, Francesca Caccini Raffaelli's life disappears from the documentary record in the three communities where she is known to have lived, Rome, Lucca, and Florence. Almost certainly neither resisting (en)closure to the last, as I sometimes fantasize, nor cast out from the Medici famiglia to die in obscurity as punishment for feminine artistic ambition, as others have imagined, Francesca may simply have retreated to the life of study she claimed to have loved. Her privacy would have been guaranteed by the well-earned protection of the Medici and by the privileges of her son Tommaso's property and social rank. By February 1645 she was no longer his guardian.[61] She may have died by then or remarried and therefore forfeited her rights in the Raffaelli estate; she may have somehow evaded the mid-century policies against such things and withdrawn into any of several more or less cloistered communities; she may have followed some princess she had known at court such as Princess Anna, when she married and went to Innsbruck, or the duchess of Guise when she left La Crocetta and returned to France. Or she may have been the "Francisca (daughter of) J: Romani" who received the last sacraments at San Concordio, near Pontetetto, just south of Lucca, on 21 August 1646, and who was buried the next day from the parish that governed San Concordio, San Piero Maggiore, to which Tommaso Raffaelli by then belonged.[62]

Afterlives, 2

"As for virtù, I say that a father and mother can have no greater desire than to make themselves anew in their children, leaving them heirs of their professions and virtù. Now if the blessed God gave me only one daughter, with such aptitudes and inclinations toward my profession that (speaking with every due modesty), [then] I am sure not to have labored in vain, in continuous study for forty years."[63]

The survival of her knowledge and virtù in the bodies of those she had taught seems to have been a way Francesca understood her own life of study and virtù would have meaning, a way through which the afterlives of her posterity would be known. No artistic heir seems ever to have been as important to her as her daughter, in whom Francesca's musical virtù and ease with authority lived on. By June 1641, when her mother needed to be in Rome for business, nineteen-year-old Margherita Signorini had been living at the Franciscan Monastero di San Girolamo sulla costa for eight months.[64] A deposit toward her dowry was made at the Monte di Pietà in July 1641, presumably by a procuratore acting on her behalf. The clerk who noted the deposit described Margherita as the daughter of "Francesco Signiorini Malaspina," inscribing into the public records of Florence's most venerable financial institution a mistaken perception about Francesca's gender that seems, with hindsight, both easy to understand and a remarkably accurate accident of fate.[65] Francesca may or may not have been in Florence then, as she may or may not have been present a year later when Margherita professed on the feast day of her community's patron, San Girolamo, 30 September 1642.[66] Taking a name eerily opposite to the qualities sometimes ascribed to her mother, Margherita Signorini lived as Suor Placida Maria until her death in 1690.[67] For a time in the middle of the century Suor Placida Maria was one of the most renowned singers in Florence, a living tribute to her mother's training. As Severo Bonini wrote: "[Margherita,] . . . nourished at [Francesca's] loving breast and in the tastes of her [mother's] sweet milk, grown older became so polished and brilliant in the profession of singing that everyone raced to hear her, admiring her smooth voice, almost like resonant silver pipes, full of trills and articulated ornaments accompanied with miraculous and feeling-filled dynamic shadings. Now, having consecrated her so pure heart to God, and left every earthly pomp, she enjoys an angelic life with other virgins in the pure cloister of San Girolamo sulla costa, where in some feasts of the year great numbers of virtuosi and noble people compete to hear her sing the divine praises, alone or in concert with other virtuose virgins who are her companions."[68]

Besides singing from behind the grate, Suor Placida Maria may have composed, coached, and performed in the musical numbers of Suor Maria Clemente Ruoti's many convent plays, perhaps including *Il natal di Cristo* (1657), which featured musical intermedi that, based on the manuscript's descriptions, seem to have been unusually sophisticated.[69] Almost certainly, she was one of the targets of the Inquisition's 1660 order banning the performance of *canto figurato* (polyphony) in Florence's monasterii di monache, for the order singles out the community at San Girolamo as having claimed that it did not have to submit to any prohibitions issued by church authorities.[70] Yet despite her virtuosity and possible contribution to disorder in their adjoining church, Suor Placida Maria seems never to have acted with an arrogance that would cause her sisters distress.[71] Taken ill in 1654 and temporarily relieved of her obligation to participate in the community's work, by 1662 she was well enough to serve again, for in that year she was chosen to manage the *foresteria* and to serve as maestra to two novices. During the next twenty years she served in both capacities several times, occasionally sold her own embroidery and figurines she had had sent from Lucca to her lifelong acquaintance Vittoria della Rovere, and served as sacristan and maestra di sala late in life.[72] The Fathers of Ognissanti were paid for officiating at her burial in San Girolamo on 1 May 1690.

In the middle of the seventeenth century, three men—an astrologer who seems not to have known her well and the musical chroniclers Pietro della Valle and Severo Bonini, who did—remembered Francesca Caccini for her miraculous singing and playing, her literary and musical mastery, her composing, and her teaching of a new music for which Florence itself claimed the rights of authorship. None of these men commented on Francesca's human qualities, although another who may have known her when he was a child, Andrea Cavalcante, thought her "a woman as fierce and restless as she was capable." But at least one man living in the middle of the seventeenth century might seem to have commented indirectly on Francesca's legacy of human rather than merely musical virtù. Her son Tommaso remembered her fondly enough in 1656 to name his first child, born near what would have been Francesca's sixty-ninth birthday, after his mother.[73]

Although born in Lucca, Maria Francesca Raffaelli certainly knew who her grandmother had been in Florence, for from the age of seven to the age of sixteen she was a boarding student in her aunt Margherita Signorini's convent, San Girolamo sulla costa.[74] For at least the last three years of her time there, the young Francesca Raffaelli's room and board at San Girolamo were paid for by Vittoria della Rovere, whom her aunt and her grandmother had known so well at La Crocetta in the 1630s.[75] San Girolamo's surviving records fail to show who taught what to the community's pupils, but it seems possible that the young Francesca could have learned from her aunt Suor Placida Maria the "arts and sciences" that Giovanni Battista Signorini had charged his widow with teaching their daughter, the craft built of forty years' study that Francesca Caccini Raffaelli had so wanted to pass on. Sometime after 1671 Maria Francesca Raffaelli entered Vittoria della Rovere's service as a dama, achieving thereby the social rank toward which her grandmother Francesca and great-grandfather Giulio had aspired. She married a minor Florentine nobleman, Giovanni Battista Bucetti, with whom she had a long, childless marriage. A favorite of the grand duchess, praised by another woman as "the most witty and gracious dama I have ever known," Maria Francesca Raffaelli died at home on the via dei Bardi on 9 January 1733.[76] She left expensive, fancifully designed jewelry to particular women in gratitude for their "most courteous and noble friendship," to her niece, and to her sister-in-law Maria Mazzoni ne' Raffaelli. Her estate went to her brother Domenico, who had inherited their father Tommaso's lands and investments in 1694.[77] The second Francesca Raffaelli is buried in the church of San Agostino delle Calze, a monastery church on the Costa San Giorgio endowed by the woman who had most enabled her grandmother to be a virtuosa, a gentildonna, and a composer with whose worth posterity continues to reckon, Grand Duchess Christine de Lorraine.

Francesca Caccini's Known
Performances and Compositions

Table A1. Francesca Caccini's known costumed, theatrical performances, 1607–1627

Date	Location	Description	Source
19 Oct. 1608	Pitti	Intermedi for Buonarroti's *Il giudizio di Paride*, esp. the 3rd by Bardi on the theme of Calypso and her entrapping nymphs and the final one. Sang "contralto," played chitarrone and guitar; not a soloist but an ensemble singer.	Tinghi I, 227–229; I-FcasaB, A.B. 60, 61v for Francesca's part; Carter, "Music . . . Wedding," 89–107
14 Feb. 1611	Pitti	*Mascherata di ninfe di Senna*, balletto by Rinuccini, music mostly by Peri, featuring fishermen and nymphs. Francesca appeared as a nymph soloist and in a trio of nymphs for which she composed the music.	Tinghi I, 321v–322; Solerti, *Musica*, 61–62. Text is in Solerti, *Albori* II, 283–294. See also table A4.
06 May 1613	Pitti	*Ninfe di Senna*, repeated for marriage of Renee de Lorraine, princess of Umene, and Mario Sforza, duke of Onano.	Tinghi I, 491; Solerti, *Musica*, 73–75
24 Feb. 1615	Pitti, Salone delle Commedie	*Il ballo delle zingare*, Francesca sang principal gypsy, composed all the music to Ferdinando Saracinelli's text; Margherita Caccini, Sig.ra Artemisia, and Sig.ra Laura were also in the cast; performed for the marriage of dama Sofia Binestan "Todesca" to Cav. re Castiglione, provveditore di Livorno	Tinghi, 648v–651; Solerti, *Musica*, 89. See also table A4.
11 Feb. 1619	Pitti	*La fiera*, comedy for Carnival; marginal notes in I-FcasaB, A.B. 65 script indicate that Francesca may have sung some scenes	Tinghi II, 188v; Solerti, *Musica*, 143–144. See also table A4.
06 Jan. 1620	Pitti, Cosimo's rooms	*Lode della Befana*, with "fanciulle"	Tinghi II, 232v; Solerti, *Musica*, 151. See also table A4.
01 Mar. 1620	Pitti, Cosimo's rooms	*Fiume Danubio et altre* [Sunday of Carnival]: "SAS con l'Arciduchessa et i sig.ri fillioli et Madama . . . stettero a sentire e vedere una festa et ballo a cavallo dalle dame della Ser. ma l'Arciduchessa et i sig.ri fillioli et Madama . . . stettero a sentire e vedere una festa et ballo a cavallo dalle dame della Ser. ma Arciduchessa. . . . La Cecchina con le sue fanciulle vestite rappresentante fiume Danubio et due altri fiumi, Albia et . . . che riescono nel Danubio, cantando in musica rendevano obbedienza al Danubio; et fatto questo comparsero 6 dame dell'Arciduchessa in maschera, mostrando d'essere cavalieri a cavallo, fecero un	Tinghi II, 238r–v; Solerti, *Musica*, 153. See also table A4.

Date	Location	Description	Reference
03 Mar. 1620	Pitti, Cosimo's rooms	balletto mostrando combattere, et erano nominati e' cavalli marinai et ballorono leggiadrissimamente; et durò ½ ore. . . . Composto detto ballo da dette Dame dell' Arciduchessa." *Ballo delle Nazioni* "Erando tutte le dame di loro AA . . . vi erano la Cecchina con le sue filiole, et altri musici in diversi abiti, che cantorno in musica di belli versi."	Tinghi II, 238r–v; Solerti, *Musica*, 153–154. See also table A4
22 July 1620	Pitti, Christine's rooms	"Preparata una prospettiva boschereccia per recitarvi una pastoralina recitata dalla principesse filliole et dalle dame della Ser. Arciduchessa in abito di pastori et ninfe, dove recitarono una operina composta [di Salvadori] . . . et cantato le musiche della Cecchina et dalle sue fanciulle . . . et fecero un ballo o balletto fatto nuovamente, dove durò per mezza ora."	Tinghi II, 259r; Solerti, *Musica*, 155. See also table A4.
14 Sept. 1623	Pitti, Maddalena's rooms	"Festicina recitata dalla due principesse Margherita et Anna et da Leopoldo et Francesco, et due dame . . . et nella musica a sonare v'era la Francesca Caccini . . . il suo marito et le sue fanciulle et il suo fratello."	Tinghi II, 619v; Solerti, *Musica*, 169 See also table A4.
07 Oct. 1623	Pitti, Maddalena's rooms	"*Allegoria della nascita di Maria Maddalena* . . . comparsero le due principesse Margherita et Anna . . . et il principe Francesco et Leopoldo . . . rappresentante la principessa Margherita l'Austria imperiale, et principe Francesco rappresentante il fiume Danubio, che venivano a rallegrarsi con la Toscana del felice natale della regina de"Toscani; et poi il principe Leopoldo in forma di Amore divino veniva a rallegrarsi con queste . . . poi tutte insieme con altre figure che erono le dame, fecero un balletto con diverse mutanze alla todesca, alla francese, alla spagniola, et alla italiana. Cantato da Diana et da altre Muse molte belle stanze et il ballo insegnato da Santino . . . et le stanze cantate et sonate dalla Cecchina musica; composto l'opera dal prete Salvadore maestro di dette principesse."	Tinghi II, 633v; Solerti, *Musica*, 169. See also table A4.

Table A2. Francesca's chamber music performances, (uncostumed) 1607–1627

Date	Location	Description	Source
29 Oct. 1608	Pitti, "salotto mezzano delle stanze dei forestieri"	After dinner, for Cardinals del Monte, Sforza, Montalto, Farnese, and Este and Cosimo II, Christine, Magdalena, Archduke Karl, Don Francesco de' Medici, Prince Peretti, "vi fu le musiche delle donne di Giulio Romano et altri in trattenimenti."	Tinghi I, 233v; Solerti, *Musica*, 51
01 Dec. 1610	Pitti, in room assigned to Spanish ambassador	After dinner with Abbate Orsini "si fece musica in camera sua dalle filiole di Giulio Romano."	Tinghi I, 313r; Solerti, *Musica*, 59
28 Dec. 1610	?	Monteverdi wrote by letter that he had heard her sing in Florence and play chitarrone (theorbo), lute, and keyboard.	I-MNas Autogr. 6, f. 108b
31 May 1611?	home of Giulio Romano	After dinner, Cardinal Ferdinando Gonzaga and Cosimo II went "a casa Giulio Romano a sentire cantare."	Tinghi I, 335r
16 June 1611	her own home	During the day, Cardinal Ferdinando Gonzaga, Cosimo II, and Don Lorenzo de' Medici went "a sentire musica a casa la figliola di Giulio Romano."	Tinghi I, 336v
08 Aug. 1611	Pitti, rooms of Magdalena	Magdalena was visited by the wife of the ambassador of Lucca and "numero grande di gentildonne fiorentine" to celebrate the birth (of Prince Gian Carlo, b. 4 July 1611); "vi fece musica delle filiole di Giulio Romano."	Tinghi I, 340v; Solerti, *Musica*, 62
Spring 1613	Rome	With Signorini "serving" the household of Virginio Orsini	I-Rasc, F.O. 1, 124/2, no. 233, letter of F.C. to V. Orsini, 4 May 1613; F.O.1, 124/1, no. 204, letter of Piero Strozzi to V. Orsini at beginning of trip, 3 March 1613
13 June 1613	Pitti, Magdalena's rooms	Magdalena was visited by the wife of the ambassador of Lucca and fifty "gentildonne fiorentine" to celebrate the safe birth of a third male child; she was "in bed, half dressed"; "vi fece musica dalla Vittoria Archilei et dalla Cecchina di Giulio Romano [poi nella prima anticamerasi fece musica grande da M.o Marco Gagliano et da suoi musici]."	Tinghi I, 501r; Solerti, *Musica*, 75

Date	Place	Description	Sources
Spring 1616	Rome	In retinue of Cardinal Carlo de' Medici for his installation	I-Fas, Carte Strozziane I, 13, fol. 130v; I-FcasaB, A.B. 44, no. 444, letter of Francesca to Buonarroti, 20 May 1616, thanking him for a canzonetta he has sent to Rome
Spring 1617	Genoa, Lucca	Self-reported singing in Lucca and in Genoa at the household of G. F. Brignole in the presence of G. Chiabrera	I-FcasaB, A.B. 44, no. 446, letter of Francesca to Buonarroti describing performances in Lucca and Genoa, 26 May 1617; A.B. 44, no. 527, letter of Gabriello Chiabrera describing her reception in Genoa, 26 June 1617
Feb. 1618	Pisa	Called suddenly to serve the court at Pisa, 13 February	I-FcasaB, A.B. 63, fol. 129v, letter of Francesca to Buonarroti, 13 Feb. 1618; Tinghi II, 13r–v reports Cosimo II taken suddenly ill 11 Feb. 1618, entertained in various ways
09 Nov. 1619	Pitti	Cosimo II, feeling better, got up from bed, tended to "negoti," rested, "si fece musica della Cecchina et dalle sue fanciulle."	Tinghi II, 227bis r
Jan.–Feb. 1620	Pitti	Cosimo II, in bed, tended to "negoti" and "la sera senti cantare di musica al solito da soliti music" [Tinghi II, 234r, specifies that Cosimo had sent for the bass Giandomenico Puliaschi, a priest in Rome, lodged him in the palace with Fioravanti, and been entertained by him "tante volte et solo et in compagnia della Cecchina et delle sue fanciulle et con l'Arcangiola ricamatore (Palladini) et con altri musici . . . et cosi ogni sera S.A. lo fa cantare." Diary entries mentioning such music include 9 Jan. 1620, fol. 233r; 12 Jan. 1620, f. 233v; 17 Jan. 1620, f. 233v, when he sang with a daughter of Lorenzo Parigi; 22 Jan. 1620; 24 Jan. 1620, both on fol. 233v; 26 Jan. 1620,	I-Fas, MdP 6108, fol. 1026, letter of Curtio Picchena to Caterina de'Medici, 4 Feb. 1620 f. 1026, describes Puliaschi and Francesca singing humorous songs: "si fanno comporre delle frottole che racontano la vita di qualcuno che il Gran Duca ha, gusto di far entrare in valigia, come ultimamente

(continued)

Table A2 (*Continued*)

Date	Location	Description	Source
		fol. 234v, specifically mentioning music made by Puliaschi and "Cecchina et sue fanciulle"; fol. 235 describes "the usual music" Cosimo heard on 3, 4, 5, 6 Feb. 1620 "dalle sudette donne et il detto Giandomenico."	maestro Simone Cerusico [his doctor] et simile, et le canta la Cecchina son la sua solita grazia."
		Cosimo heard "the usual music" between negoti and supper on 17, 18, 19 and 20 Feb. 1620.	Tinghi II, 237r–v
27 Feb. 1620	Pitti, Cosimo's rooms	In the evening, Cosimo heard "musica della Cecchina."	Tinghi II, 238r
31 Mar. 1620	Pitti, Cosimo's rooms	At 20 "hours" of daylight, after taking broth, Cosimo was entertained by singing of "l'Adriana (Basile), la Cecchina et l'altre fanciulle."	Tinghi II, 247r; Solerti, *Musica*, 155
6 June 1620	Pitti, Cosimo's rooms	Cosimo, in bed, heard "l'Adriana, la Cecchina et altri musici," as did his guest Cardinal Lenzi, before supper.	Tinghi II, 252r; Solerti, *Musica*, 155
	Pitti, Cosimo's rooms	(On 9, 10, and 11 June 1620, Adriana Basile "et altri musici" played and sang for Cosimo. Basile left on 14 June.)	Tinghi II, 252v–253r
26 June 1620	Pitti, Cosimo's rooms	Cosimo, in bed with gout and eating poorly, amused himself "a sentire di musica la Cecchina con le sue fanciulle."	Tinghi II, 254v; Solerti, *Musica*, 155
1 July 1620	Pitti, Cosimo's rooms	Cosimo, after eating, amused himself "a sentire cantare la Cecchina et le sue fanciulle" before evening.	Tinghi II, 255r
2 Aug. 1620	Pitti, Cosimo's rooms	Cosimo, after medication and a meal, "fece cantare di musica della Cecchina et dalle sue fanciulle," perhaps while being visited by Christine, Magdalena, and his brothers before evening.	Tinghi II, 260v
17 Aug. 1620	Pitti, Cosimo's rooms	Cosimo, after eating well, amused himself with various virtuosi "et a sentire cantare di musica dalla Cecchina" before turning to his negoti.	Tinghi II, 262v; Solerti, *Musica*, 155
19 Aug. 1620	Pitti, Cosimo's rooms	Cosimo, after visits from doctors and family and being up a while, dined, returned to bed, and amused himself with virtuosi, tended to his negoti, and then amused himself "a sentire cantare la Cecchina con la sua fanciulla" before supper.	Tinghi II, 263r; Solerti, *Musica*, 155

		(On 20 Aug. 1620, Arcangiola Palladini and Mutio Effrem sang. Someone made music between negoti and evening on 27, 29, and 30 Aug. and 5, 6, and 11 Sept. 1620. Francesco Rasi sang for Cosimo on 10 and 11 Nov. 1620.)	Tinghi II, 263v–288r
12 Jan. 1621	Pitti, Cosimo's rooms	Cosimo, after visits from doctors and his family, amused himself with various things and in the evening before supper "a sentire la Cecchina con il marito."	Tinghi II, 296r; Solerti, *Musica*, 157
		(On 11 Jan. 1621 he heard Marco da Gagliano and the castrato di Doni; on 13 Jan. 1621 he heard Arcangiola Palladini and Muzio Effrem.)	Tinghi, 296r
15 Jan. 1621	Pitti, Cosimo's rooms	Cosimo, after giving several audiences in bed, in the evening heard "cantare di musica dalla Cecchina et della Settimia sua sorella venuta da Lucca, dalla Arcangiola (Palladini) et dal maestro di cappella (Marco da Gagliano)."	Tinghi II, 297r; Solerti, *Musica*, 158
17 Jan. 1621	Pitti, Cosimo's rooms	Cosimo, after medication, received all the family and amused himself with various things; in the evening he arranged that "si cantò di musica per fino a ore tre et cantò la Cecchina, la Settimia, l'Angelica, et tutti i musici a soliti" before supper. (These performances seem to have been repeated on 18 and 19 Jan 1620. Someone sang on the evening of 22 Jan. 1621. Cosimo became much sicker on 7 Feb., dying without apparently having heard any more chamber music on 28 Feb. 1621.)	Tinghi, II, 298r; Solerti, *Musica*, 158
11 June 1622	residence of Sig.ra Felice Pellicari	After lunch for the wife of the ambassador from Spain "vi andò la Cecchina a cantare con le sue fanciulle."	Tinghi II, 521r
July? 1622	Pitti, Christine's rooms	Princesses Margherita and Anna sang with Francesca to awaken Christine on St. Anne's day.	I-MNas, Archivio Gonzaga, busta 1132, fol. 213, letter of Alessandro Bartolini to Caterina de' Medici, 30 Aug. 1622
1 June 1623	Pitti, Magdalena's rooms	Regent Archduchess Maria Magdalena, in bed after taking a purgative, amused herself "a sentire cantare la Sig.ra Cecchina Musica."	Tinghi II, 586v

(continued)

Table A2 (*Continued*)

Date	Location	Description	Source
28 Oct. 1623	Rome, residence of Card. Carlo de' Medici	She arrived from Florence and immediately sang "allegramente"	I-Fas, MdP 3645, letter of Antimo Galli to Dimurgo Lambardi, 28 Oct. 1623
30 Oct. 1623	Rome, Trinità dei Monti	She sang for Cardinal Barberini, Taddeo Barberini, Monsignore Magalotti.	I-Fas, MdP 3645, letter of Galli to Lambardi, 30 Oct. 1623; I-Fas, MdP 3883, letter of the cardinal to unnamed recipient, 1 Nov. 1623, reports that the music was made by Francesca; I-Rvat, Urb. lat. 1093, f. 82or also reports on the music.
3 Nov. 1623	Rome, residence of Carlo de' Medici	With Adriana Basile, she sang before dinner for Cardinals Gaetano, Lodovisio, Capponi, Torres, and Ridolfi, Paolo Giordano Orsini, Ferdinando Orsini, and Abbate Peretti.	I-Fas, MdP 3645, letter of Galli to Lambardi, 3 Nov. 1623. I-Rvat, Urb. lat. 1093, fol. 821v, reports instrumental and vocal performances.
11 Nov. 1623	Rome, residence of Carlo de' Medici	The previous Thursday, she sang after dinner for the Mantuan ambassador and Bishop Monsuardo. By this date, she had also sung for the poet G. B. Marino, "improvising in a way that astonished him. . . . He celebrated her . . . greater knowledge and mastery of her art, rather better voice, more artfulness with *affetti*" than any other singer he had heard.	I-Fas, MdP 3645, letter of Galli to Lambardi, 11 Nov. 1623
23 Nov. 1623	Rome, residence of Carlo de' Medici	The previous Sunday Cardinal Barberino had come to hear her and Adriana sing "for many hours," leaving before dinner with the other guests, Cardinals Ludovisio, Borghese, Mellino, Valiero, Savello, Leni, Rivaroli, and Orsini.	I-Fas, MdP 3883, fol. 320v, letter of the cardinal to unnamed recipient, fol. 320v
25 Nov. 1623	Rome, residence of Carlo de' Medici	Francesca sang with an unnamed woman who played the harp excellently for a *veglia* organized by the wife of the Florentine ambassador for Duchess Sforza (Leonora Orsini) and the wives of Orazio Magalotti, Falconieri, and Neri Capponi.	I-Fas, MdP 3645, letter of Galli to Lambardi, 25 Nov. 1623
26 Nov. 1623	?	Marino and Accademici degli Umoristi "went to hear" Cecchina.	Ibid.

Date	Location	Description	Source
(27 Nov. 1623)	Rome, home of Paolo Mancini	Umoristi met to recite poems in Francesca's honor.	Ibid.)
4 Dec. 1623	Rome, residence of Carlo de' Medici	Adriana and Francesca sang during or after a banquet for Cardinals Este, Savoia, Barberino, Borghese, Savello, and Orsini. The letters of Giacinto Antonio Medici and Antimo Galli imply that the guest list included Abbate Perretti, the dukes of Zagarola and Cornie, and Prior Aldobrandini.	I-Fas, MdP 3883, fol. 334, letter of Agnolo Firenzuola to unnamed recipient. I-Rvat, Urb. lat. 1093, fol. 899r, 6 Dec. 1623, seems to refer to the same incident See also I-Fas, MdP 3645, letters of Giacinto Antonio Medici and Antimo Galli to unnamed recipients, 8 Dec. 1623.
17 Jan. 1624	Rome, residence of Carlo de' Medici	"Suoni e canti" were sung during or after a banquet for Cardinals Monte, Peretti, Bentivogli, Pio, and della Valletta, the duke of Nevers, and the French ambassador.	I-Rvat, Urb. Lat. 1054, fol. 35
3 Feb. 1624	Rome, rooms of Pope Urban VIII	On the previous Sunday Francesca sang for two hours for the Pope, including 3 of his odes in Latin, two by Horace, a madrigal to the Virgin by M. Buonarroti, and stanzas on Santa Cordulia by A. Salvadori. Other guests included Carlo Barberini, Costanza Magalotti (mother of Taddeo Barberini), Lucrezia Vaini, unnamed courtiers, and Francesca's husband G. B. Signorini.	I-FcasaB, A.B. 47, no. 1037, letter of Mario Guiducci to Buonarroti, 3 Feb. 1624
16 May 1624	Villa Guicciardini, at Piano d'Arcetri	Ferdinando II and Magdalena, received by Girolamo Guicciardini and his wife Simone, respectively, "si trattenero con sentire sonare et cantare la Sig.ra Cecchina musica et poi un altro concerto cantato dal Sig.r Angiolo Guicciardini e 2 altre musici."	Tinghi III, 39v
23 May 1624	Pitti	"Fu fatto musiche dalla Cecchina Caccini et venne le 2 principesse filliole . . . et cantarono" for the visiting Duke of Mantua.	Tinghi III, 42–43; Solerti, *Musica*, 172
29 May 1624	Magdalena's rooms	"fu cantato di musica dalla Cecchina"	Ibid.
30 May 1624	Magdalena's rooms	For a visit of M. Bethune, the French ambassador, "musica della Cecchina"	Ibid.
28 July 1624	Poggio Imperiale	For visit of Archduke Karl, "andono in camera della S.ra Aridu-chessa in conversazione alla domestica" (with Christine, Ferdinando II, Don Lorenzo, princes GiovanCarlo and Mattias) "comparse le due principesse Margherita et Anna, et principi Francesco et Leopoldo vestito in diversi abiti somiglianti le tre grazie,	Tinghi III, 73v; Solerti, *Musica*, 173

(continued)

Table A2 (*Continued*)

Date	Location	Description	Source
		et recitorno alcuni versi in lode della venuta del Arciduca in Italia et in Toscana et in Firenze, et dalla Cecchina et da altri cantato e sonato in lode di questa venuta composta da M. Salvadori loro maestro et dalla Cecchina e dal marito et dalla sua fanciulla furono cantati diversi madrigali et per spazio di mezz'ora ebbero gran piacere."	
3 Aug. 1624	Pitti, Magdalena's rooms	During the visit of Archduke Karl of Styria, "finito desinare andorno in camera della Ser.ma Arciduchessa che vi si cantò di musica dalla Cecchina et dalla sua fanciulla."	Tinghi III, 74r
5 May 1625	Poggio Imperiale	Magdalena, ill, was visited by Ferdinando II, other children, Christine, and Don Lorenzo, "Fu tratenuta dalla Cecchina musica."	Tinghi III, 125v
10 May 1625	Poggio Imperiale	Magdalena was visited by Christine, Princess Claudia, "fu trattenuta dalla Cecchina musica che cantò et sonò insieme con altri musici."	Tinghi III, 126v
26 May 1625	Poggio Imperiale	Magdalena was visited by Ferdinando II, Cardinal Carlo, Don Lorenzo, the princesses, Christine, "et il giorno si tratenne a sentire cantare di Musica dalla Sig.ra Francesca et altri musici per passare il tempo."	Tinghi III, 128v
13 Jan. 1626	Poggio Imperiale	Magdalena hosted Archduke Leopold in her rooms; "la Cecchina et altri cantorno di musica."	Tinghi III, 156v
17 Sept. 1626	Pitti	After dinner for Cardinal Legate Barberini and Cardinal Sacchetti, "si trattennero a sentire cantare la Cecchina."	Tinghi III, 180r
18 Apr. 1627	Poggio Imperiale	After dinner at Pitti, Cardinal Legate Cennini, Cardinal Carlo, Don Lorenzo, and others "andonno tutti in camera della Serenissima Arciduchessa et quivi fatta venire la S.ra Franc.a stettero a sentire cantare alcuni madrigali."	Tinghi III, 194v

Table A3. Francesca's performances for Holy Week, 1607–1627

Date	Location	Description	Source
7 Apr. 1610	S. Nicola (Pisa)	Three ensembles, "c'era la Vittoria e Antonio Archilei, et Giulio Romano con le due sue figliuole et la moglie et fecero una musica stupenda con gran gusto di S.A. et di tutto il popolo."	Tinghi I, 287v; Solerti, *Musica*, 58
30 Mar. 1611	S. Nicola	Four ensembles, "v'era una musica rara venuta di Firenze et si cantò a quattro cori et v'era le figliuole di Giulio romano."	Tinghi I, 326v
18 Apr. 1612	S. Felicita (Florence)	Three ensembles, "cioè due giù in chiesa cantata da musici di S.A. et uno là sù alto nella cappella di rimpetto a S.A.S. cantata da le figliuole di Giulio Romano; et dalla Vittoria Archilei, et da altre musici; et durò il matutino per fino alle ore una di notte: era la chiesa calcatissima di gente."	Tinghi I, 384; Solerti, *Musica*, 64
26 Mar. 1614	S. Nicola	"Si fece musica a 4 cori dai musicisti venuti di Firenze a posta, cioè due cori si fece in chiesa, et due sul corridore; uno dalla Vittoria et da Antonio Naldi, et l'altro dalla Francesca figliuola di Giulio Romano et da Giulio et dalla moglie, et dal marito di detta Francesca; dove fu musica stupendissima."	Tinghi I, 562r; Solerti, *Musica*, 85
30 Mar. 1616	S. Nicola	"Il giorno stetto all'uffizio in casa, cioè nella chiesa di S Nicola, et S.A. aveva fatto venire li suoi musici di Firenze et fece venire la Vittoria et la Cecchina et altre donne per cantare et fecero musica a 3 cori,"	Tinghi II, 32; Solerti, *Musica*, 106
22 Mar. 1617	S. Felicita	"Et a di 22 detto giorno del mercoledi santo S.A. udi la messa in casa et il giorno andò all'uffizio alla chiesa di S. Felicita per il corridore con la Ser.ma Arciduchessa ed il Cardinale et tutti gli figliuoli dove era fatto 3 cori di musici di S.A. et una le donne musiche a cantare et S.A. non usci di casa per rispetto alla purgha."	Tinghi II, 95v
9 Apr. 1618 [etc.]	S. Felicita	"Si fece musica a 4 cori, 2 in chiesa cantati dai musici di S.A., et 2 cori cantati sù ad alto nel corridore cantati dalla Francesca, dalla Aran-giola et dalla fanciulla figliuola di Filippo Sciameroni, la quale con melodia et devozione furno cantate." In Magdalena's private chapel, her dame and Christine's formed 2 ensembles and sang 3 Passion psalms and *Pange lingua* for 2 choruses, one "solito" and the other	Tinghi II, 133; Solerti, *Musica*, 129 See also I-Fas, MdP 6108, fol. 977r–v. letter of Curtio Picchena to Caterina de' Medici, 10 April 1618, describing Holy Thursday procession; I-Fn, Magl. VIII,

(continued)

Table A3 (*Continued*)

Date	Location	Description	Source
		comprised of Vittoria Archilei, dama Maria Medici, and a fanciulla de' Ricci. On Holy Saturday, the private singing of the dame ended with the *Stabat mater* for 2 choruses.	t1525/1, 70–76 for stanzas by Gismondo Santi describing Francesca's performance
27 Mar. 1619	S. Felicita	"S.A. fece venire l'ambasciatore di Francia con molti de sua gente . . . fù fatto musica a 3 cori dai musici di S.A. et dalle donne, la Cecchina, l'Arcangiola et altre." The next day, in Magdalena's private chapel, the Sacrament was exposed, along with a representation of Jacob's ladder and the Holy Face; there were 3 sermons; and "fu cantato laude in musica dalla Cecchina et le sue discepole et sonato dal suo marito et dal Bardella." On Holy Saturday, the dame sang Passion psalms and the *Stabat mater* as before.	Tinghi II, 194; Solerti, *Musica*, 144
15 Apr. 1620	Pitti, Magdalena's and Cosimo's rooms	[On Wednesday of Holy Week] "si cantò il matutino, con 3 cori di musica con istrumenti, et vi era la Cecchina, le sue fanciulle, l'Arcangiola, et la Vittoria et il castrato del Doni et messer Marco [da Gagliano] . . . et tutti i musici di S.A. et più eccellenti, e cantorno molti terzetti." On Good Friday, in Cosimo's rooms, "venne . . . la Cecchina et le sue fanciulle, et la principessa Margarita, figliuola di S.A., et cantò alcune laude insieme con due dame della Ser.ma Arciduchessa." On Holy Saturday, the same group sang Compline for Cosimo and Maddalena.	Tinghi II, 243; Solerti, *Musica*, 154
2 Apr. 1621	S. Felicita	"Era preparato di dire l'uffizio et le musiche a 3 cori, 2 in chiesa dei musici di S.A. . . . et l'altro sù ad alto nel corridore di donne, cioè la Francesca Caccini con le sue fanciulle, et l'Arcangiola con Muzio Effrem."	Tinghi II, 341; Solerti, *Musica*, 158
23 Mar. 1622	S. Nicola	"Loro A.S. avevono fatto venire di Firenze la Sig.ra Francesca Signorini et la Maria et la Emilia sua fanciulla et il fratello piccino, [Scipione Caccini] et Muzio Effrem con la Arcangiola et il pretino castrato suo discepolo..le donne in sul medesimo corridoio, et i musici in coro in chiesa . . . ." For the first time, Tinghi mentions the composers of this music: "E a di 24 . . . la musica del Sig.r Jacopo Peri,	Tinghi II, 485v; Solerti, *Musica*, 161. See also I-MNas, Archivio Gonzaga, busta 1132, fol. 13v, letter of Curzio Picchena, 25 Mar. 1622, who commented "non già Vittoria, la quale è ormai fatta assenta come vecchia. Ci è benvenuta la

		et quelle di ieri furno quelle Muzio Effrem, et quelle di oggi sono piaciute più."	Cecchina, benchè si è fresca del parto dalla sua bambina." Francesca gave birth to Margherita Signorini on 9 Feb. 1622; her baptism on 10 Feb. is noted at I-Fd, Battesimi Femine 1621, M.
12 Apr. 1623	S. Nicola	"Era venuto li musici di S.A., in particolare la Sig.ra Francesca Signorini, la Maria Botti, l'Angelica moglie di Domenico Belli, et fecero 4 cori, et le donne cantorno sul corridore et cantorno la composizione del Sig.r Jacopo Peri detto il Zazzerino."	Tinghi II, 575v; Solerti, *Musica*, 169
3 Apr. 1624	S. Nicola	"Et si fece la musica a 3 cori, cioè 2 cori in chiesa et un coro in sù corridore dove erano loro A.S. e cioè dalla Sgr.a Fran.ca Caccini, dalla [Maria] Botti sua fanciulla et dal suo fratello [Scipione] et del marito et erono tutti i musici di S.A. venuti di Firenze a questo effetto et furno musiche squisite et per eccellenza loro A. S. fecero venite i predicatori de cavalieri a sentire le musiche in sul corridore."	Tinghi III, 30v
26 Mar. 1625	S. Nicola	"Si fece 3 cori, 2 in chiesa et uno in sul corridore dove erano Loro Altezze, fatto dalla Francesca Caccini, musica di S.A.S. et dalle due fanciulle, et li altri cori fatti da musici di S.A.S. venuti tutti di Firenze a posta per questo effetto al numero di 48 … et finito l'uffizio loro Altezze andonno in sù l'altro corridore della Chiesa dove avevono fatto mettere il ritratto del Volto Santo et fatto un tabernacolo dove fù cantato dalla Sig.re Dama di loro A.ze salmi della meditatione della Passione del S.re Dio."	Tinghi III, 120v; Solerti, *Musica*, 184
?8 Apr. 1626	S. Felicita	"Andò all'uffizio a Santa Felicita cantato in musica a 3 cori secondo gl'anni passati."	Tinghi III, 164v
?31 Mar. 1627	S. Felicita	"S.A. … andò per il corridore a Santa Felicita a sentire l'uffizio che fù cantato in musica a 3 cori."	Tinghi III, 192v

Table A4. Francesca's theatrical compositions

Title	Date	Genre	Location/Occasion	Poet	Cast	Sources, Descriptions, Remarks
KNOWN WORKS:						
La stiava	24 Feb. 1607	barriera	Pisa/Carnival	M. Buonarroti	Fabio, Niccolò, G. B. Signorini	Tinghi I, fol. 173; Solerti, *Musica*, 39; I-FcasaB, A.B. 81, fols. 270–273r contain the invenzione and script; fol. 280r–v is the descrizione; fol. 277r–v is Buonarroti's draft letter of 6 Mar. 1606/07 re: Francesca's not entering Montalto's service. I-FcasaB, A.B. 44, no. 454, is a letter from F.C. to Buonarroti, 21 June 1626, asking for a copy of "la Stiava, e della quale io composi la musica 20 anni sono."
Ninfe di Senna	14 Feb. 1611	mascherata/ballo	Pitti/Carnival	O. Rinuccini	J. Peri, V. Archilei, S. Caccini, F. Caccini	Tinghi I, fols. 321v–322; Solerti, *Musica*, 62; Solerti, *Albori* II, 283–294 cites description by Jacopo Cicognini that includes the multiple author attributions. See also table A1.
	6 May 1613		Pitti/marriage of Renee de Lorraine to Mario Sforza, duke of Onano		J. Peri, V. Archilei, S. Caccini, F. Caccini	Solerti, *Albori* II, 283–294 cites description in a letter by Jacopo Cicognini, 14 Feb. 1613: "la prima fu cantata con la solita grazia e voce angelica dalla Vittoria Archilei, romana; la seconda con ogni suprema equisitezza dalla Signora Settimia, e la terza con

l'usata prontezza ed ammirazione universale dalla Signora Francesca, ambedue figliuole del celebratissimo Giulio romano; et la quarta ottava composta dalla medesima Signora Francesca con stile graziosissimo e vago, fu dalle predette unitamente cantata con si belle fughe e passaggi, che se Paride della virtù loro fosse stato eletto giudice per dare alla più eccellente donare il pomo d'oro, come irresoluto l'averebbe ripartito per onorare ciascheduna conforma al suo merito."

A balletto with the same title was performed for the marriage of Christine's parents, Claude de France and Charles de Lorraine. See Yates, *French Academies*, 60–61.

I-FcasaB, A.B. 61

Tinghi I, fol. 334r; Solerti, *Musica*, 62

Title	Date	Genre	Location / Occasion	Author	Performers	Source
La Tancia	25 May 1611	commedia rusticale	Casino di Don Ant.o de' Medici / 2nd day of celebrations for marriage of Elizabeth Destain, dama of	M. Buonarroti	Florentine boys	

(continued)

Table A4 (*Continued*)

Title	Date	Genre	Location/Occasion	Poet	Cast	Sources, Descriptions, Remarks
			Maria Magdalena, to Attilio Incontri			"La pastorella mia," act 2, scene 5 (A.B. 61. fasc.3, fol. 265v) in *Primo libro* (1618), 58–61
	May 1618?		San Miniato			I-FcasaB, A.B. 52, no. 1452, letter of 21 Jan 1618, Marc' Antonio Pieralli asking for advice to revive under Vicario Buontalenti at S. Miniato
	Summer 1619		Rovezzano			I-FcasaB, A.B. 43, no. 424, letter of 28 June 1619, Zanobi Braccij asking Buonarroti to help him get the "musiche" from Francesca Signorini, music she had offered him while visiting his garden, and promising not to use it if the songs prove too difficult for his students, so neither her music nor Buonarroti's show would be badly performed
Il passatempo	11 Feb. 1614	commedia	Pitti/Carnival	M. Buonarroti	?	I-FcasaB, A.B. 62 and 63
					?Francesca, ?wife of Mainardi; ?Angelica Sciamerone	I-FcasaB, A.B. 45, fol. 66ov, draft letter from Buonarroti to Christine attributes the music of *Il passatempo*, including its concluding ballo, "assolutamente alla S.ra Francesca"

Title	Date	Type	Place/Occasion	Librettist	Performers/Composers	Notes
					Cosimo II, Magdalena, as lead dancers in *Ballo della cortesia*	Tinghi I, 554r, attributes music of the concluding number of *Ballo della cortesia* to Peri; fols. 554v–557 describe it in detail. See Solerti, *Musica*, 81–85. Three letters of *cameriere* Domenico Montaguto to Buonarroti. I-FcasaB, A.B. 50, no. 1253, 6 Feb. 1614; no. 1254, 12 Feb. 1614; and no. 1255, 26 Feb. 1614, seem to refer to *Il passatempo*; the last indicates gifts that Cosimo II gave Francesca, the wife of Mainardi, and the daughter of "Pippo Sciamerone pittore" for their participation. "Chi desia saper che cosè Amor," opening song for "Il Passatempo in su la barca" (I-FcasaB, A.B. 62, fasc. 1, fol. 3) in *Primo libro*, 90. "Io veggio i campi verdeggiar," opening song of *Ballo della cortesia* (I-FcasaB, A.B. 62, fasc 1, fols. 31v–32r) in *Primo Libro*, 54–58. "Egloga pastorale. Tirsi et Filli. 'Pascomi sospir.'" (I-FcasaB, A.B. 62, fasc 1, fols. 20v–21v) in I-Ru, MS 279, fols. 61r–68r, attributed to F.C.
Ballo delle zingare	24 Feb. 1615	ballo	Pitti, Salone delle Commedie/marriage of Sofia Binestan,	F. Saracinelli	F. Caccini. M. Caccini, Artemisia, Laura	Tinghi I, fols. 648v–651r; Solerti, *Musica*, 89–92. See also table A1.

(*continued*)

Table A4 (*Continued*)

Title	Date	Genre	Location/Occasion	Poet	Cast	Sources, Descriptions, Remarks
			dama of Maria Magdalena, to Cav.re Castiglioni, proveditore of Livorno			
La fiera	11 Feb. 1619	comedy	Pitti/Carnival	M. Buonarroti	Francesca Caccini?	I-FcasaB, A.B. 64 is an autograph fair copy; A.B. 65 is a fair copy with some stage directions indicating cast or composers; Francesca is suggested as a performer legibly at A.B. 65, fol. 66v.
					Arcangiola Palladini?	I-FcasaB, A.B.44, no. 447, is a letter from Francesca to Buonarroti, 25 Jan. 1619 suggesting that "S.ra Arcangiola" might be better for composing a certain scene. Tinghi II, 188v; Solerti, *Musica*, 143–144, attributes the composition to Marco da Gagliano and Francesca.
Lode della Befana	6 Jan. 1620	stanzas in costume	Pitti, rooms of Cosimo/Epiphany	A. Salvadori?	F. Caccini, fanciulle	Tinghi II, 232v; Solerti, *Musica*, 151. See also table A1. I-Fas, MdP 6108, fol. 103v, letter of Curzio Picchena to Caterina de' Medici describing comic gifts (e.g., a carafe of water given to a drunken priest).

Intermedi to G. Cecchi's La Serpe	26 Feb. 1620	intermedio	home of Curtio Picchena, Pitti in rooms of princesses	?	Caterina Picchena, dame	Tinghi II, 238r; Solerti, *Musica*, 153 I-Fas, MdP 6108, fol. 1036, letter of Curtio Picchena to Caterina de' Medici, 4 Feb. 1620: "La mia figliuola fu una commedia qui in casa, dove recitano 12 fanciulle la maggior parte nobile, et 7 fanciullette, et perche il Gran Duca ha sentito ch'ella riuscira cosa garbata, vuole che si faccia una volta in Palazzo nelle stanza delle Principesse, et veramente la Cecchina v'ha fatto tre intermedii graziosissimi, et la mia figliuola recita una parte d'un Pagetto, che ha piu di 300 versi."
Fiume Danubio	1 Mar. 1620	festa and ballo a cavallo	Pitti	?	6 dame, F. Caccini, fanciulle	Tinghi II, 238r–v; Solerti, *Musica*, 153. See also table A1.
Ballo delle nazione	3 Mar. 1620	ballo	Pitti, Cosimo's rooms	Agnolo Ricci	dame, F. Caccini, fanciulle	Tinghi II, 238v; Solerti, *Musica*, 153. See also table A1. I-MOas, Ambasciatori. Firenze. Busta 47, letter of 7 Mar. 1620 from Paolo Emilio Boiardi describing both balli in a way that could be read to conflate them: "In questi ultimi giorni di Carnovale dalla bande della Ser.ma Arciduchessa si sono fatti lieti

(continued)

Table A4 (*Continued*)

Title	Date	Genre	Location/ Occasion	Poet	Cast	Sources, Descriptions, Remarks
						trattenimenti con l'intervento dei Sig.ri Principi, e Principesse all'improviso, et in particolare alcune dame hanno rappresentati i cavalli mariani, e combattuto con le mazze, spettacolo grato al Ser.mo G. Duca, che era in luogo che vedea tali ricreazioni, e vi si ballò anche all'usanza di Francia, Spagna, et Alemagna."
pastoralina	22 July 1620	pastoral	Christine's rooms	A. Salvadori	Princesses Margerita, Anna, Princes Francesco, Leopoldo, F. Caccini, fanciulle	Tinghi II, 259r; Solerti, *Musica*, 155. See also table A1.
Martirio di Sant'Agata	10 Feb. 1622	opera	Compagnia di S. Antonio	J. Cicognini	Compagnia di S. Antonio	Tinghi II, 472v; Solerti, *Musica*, 162. The libretto was printed by Giunti in Florence, 1624. In the preface, Cicognini attributed the parts of Agata, Eternità, and choruses of Venus' priestesses to Francesca, adding: "per lodarla basta solo l'haver nominato che ne fu il compositore, che come Donna eminente, e singolare ormai del Mondo per tale è conosciuta, e ammirata."

	Date	Genre	Location	Performers	Source/Notes
	22 June 1622		Casino of Carlo de' Medici/for the ambassador from Spain		G. B. Da Gagliano composed the rest of the score.
festicina	14 Sept. 1623	festicina	Pitti, loggia	Princesses Margherita, Anna; Princes Francesco, Leopoldo; dame Sig.ra Nerla and Sig.ra Peruzza; F. Caccini, her husband, her fanciulle, and her brother Scipione	Tinghi II, 619v; Solerti, *Musica*, 169. See also table A1.
Allegoria della nascita di Maria Maddalena	7 Oct. 1623	stanzas and balletto	Magdalena's rooms	Princesses Margherita, Anna; Princes Francesco, Leopoldo, dame, F. Caccini	Tinghi II, 633v; Solerti, *Musica*, 169. See also table A1.

(continued)

Table A4 (Continued)

Title	Date	Genre	Location/Occasion	Poet	Cast	Sources, Descriptions, Remarks
La regina S. Orsola	?? Oct. 1624	opera	Pitti/visit of Archduke Karl of Styria	A. Salvadori	Loreto Vittori, Campagnuolo, Maria Botti, Scipione Caccini, Castrato of Rinuccini	Tinghi III, 75v, 81v–84; Solerti, *Musica*, 173–174, 174–177
	28 Jan. 1625		Pitti/visit of Prince Wladislaw of Poland			I-Fas, MdP 111, fol. 182r–v, letter of Ferdinando Saracinelli to Magdalena, 23 Oct. 1624; ibid., fol. 108r, draft of reply, 26 Oct. 1624; ibid., draft of letter from Magdalena to Saracinelli, 30 Nov. 1624; I-Fas, MdP 1703 [unfoliated], letters of Saracinelli to unnamed, high-ranking man, 26, 27, 28 Nov. and 3 Dec. 1624, and letter of Saracinelli to "Prince Giulio," 2 Dec. 1624, trace a casting and composition imbroglio and imply that Francesca may have composed the parts of Cordula and Urania. See Harness, *Echoes*, chap. 3 and documents 3.1–3.10.

La liberazione di Ruggiero dall'isola d'Alcina	3 Feb. 1625	balletto	Villa (Poggio) Imperiale/ visit of Prince Władisław of Poland	F. Saracinelli	?	Tinghi III, 106r, 109v–111r; Solerti, *Musica*, 179–183 Score was published in Florence by Pietro Cecconcelli, 1625; copies are now at I-Rcas, I-Rsc, I-Vnm, F-Pn, GB-Lbm. Libretto was published in Florence by Cecconcelli, 1625; copies are now at I-Fn, I-Fm, US-Nypl. Score, libretto, and stage pictures are published in facsimile edition with introduction by Alessandro Magini (Florence: SPES, 1999).
mascherata	9 Feb. 1635	mascherata	Castello/ birthday of Vittoria della Rovere	M. Buonarroti	?	I-FcasaB, A.B. 44, nos. 460–465 are letters from Ugo Cacciotti to Buonarroti developing the idea; I-Fas, MdP 1454 [unfoliated] includes Buonarroti's replies on 6, 7 and 10 Feb. 1634/35. A.B. 84, fols. 556v–558r contain the text.
POSSIBLE WORKS:						
Stanze in Lode d'Austria	28 July 1624	?	Poggio Imperiale	Salvadori	Princesses Margherita, Anna; Princes Francesco, Leopoldo; Francesca, Signorini, fanciulla	Tinghi III, 73v

(continued)

Table A4 (*Continued*)

Title	Date	Genre	Location/ Occasion	Poet	Cast	Sources, Descriptions, Remarks
Il Martirio di S. Caterina	Carnival, 1627	opera	Compagnia di S. Antonio	Jacopo Cicognini	?	Libretto, I-Fr, Ricc. 3470, fols. 325v–429; I-Fas, CRSGF 134, no. 2, fol. 42v; see Harness, "Amazoni"
S. Sigismondo	?	opera	Poland	Salvadori ?		Commissioned by Prince Władisław of Poland in 1626 but not known to have been composed or produced. See I-Fas, MdP 4292, fol. 565, letter of Władisław to Magdalena, July 1626.
Intermedi?	Jan. 1628	intermedio	Lucca, Accademia degli Oscuri	Lelio Altogradi?	?	I-Lbg, MS 383 describes preparations for musically elaborate intermedi on the fable of Esione to a tragicomedy titled *Alissa*, directed (but not composed) by Tommaso Raffaelli

Letters of Francesca Caccini (1610–1641)

Note: Letters set off by vertical lines are not written by Francesca Caccini.

1a. I-Rasc, F.O., 1st ser. 119/2, no. 185, letter to Virginio Orsini dated
6 March 1609/10), with related documents

Ill.mo ed Ecc.mo Signor mio Oss.mo

L'obbligo che io devo a mio padre è infinito per infiniti rispetti, onde può credere
V.E. Ill.ma che tutt'i suoi travagli mi siano tante punture al cuore; io lo veggo som-
merso in molti e molti pensieri, sia per la dote della Settimia, sia per gli 70 [scudi]
che il Signor Depositario non gli ha pagati quest'anno come soleva; veggo che non
può vivere con questa provisione, e che i suoi negozi di mercato sono mancati assai, e che perciò sarà necessitato fare qualche stravagante resoluzione di sé. Mi sono
mossa da grandissima compassione e pietà a raccomandarlo a V.E. perché tutto il
mal suo sarebbe il nostro medesimo; e disgregato lui, possiamo dire sicuramente
che sia finito ogni nostro bene; però, per l'amor di Dio, V.E. ci faccia grazia, ché sua
Altezza abbia qualche riguardo alla sua lunga e fedel servitù e li faccia conoscere in
quanta stima mio Padre appresso a tutta Italia, ché ben l'abbiamo veduto nel viaggio
di Francia, e quanto onore faccia a loro Altezze in tutte / [v:] l'occasioni, e particolarmente con l'onorevolezza della casa sua in regalar virtuosamente tanti personaggi
che ci vengono, come V.E. sa, che tanto volte ha favorito con la sua presenza in compagnia d'altri Principi; ché certamente io ne sentirò tanto buon grado a V.E. Ill.ma
che oltre alla mia servitù, benché debolissima per esser donna, ma piena d'affetto di
buona volontà, non mancherò mai di pregar Iddio per il colmo d'ogni suo vero bene.
Con che ricordandomele, umilissima serva, le faccio debita riverenza. Di Firenze alli
6 di marzo 1609[10].

1b. I-Rasc, F.O., 1st ser., 119/2, no. 183, letter of Giulio Caccini to Virginio Orsini, 6 March 1609/10

Ill.mo ed ecc.mo s.r mio Oss.mo

Come V.E. Ill.ma sa, io maritai la Settimia mia figlia a questo soggetto della nostra professione per dar gusto a Madama Ser.ma, la quale desiderava che questo conserto non si disgregasse; ne ebbi riguardo che mi constasse acconto 500 [800?] scudi del mio, pensando che tanto più fosse grato a loro Altezze in conoscere tanto ottima volontà; i quali denari io poteva anco rispiarmare, se io avessi accettato l'offerte d'altri Principi, che la volevano a loro stipendi con obbligo di maritarla; onde, non solo non mi pare aver fatto cosa che le sia stata grata da me, ma che appresso loro Altezze stimino anco poco o nulla la mia servitù, non solo perché Madama Ser.ma non ha mai fatto sborsare alla mia figlia li 600 soldi della dote, che S.A. gli ha promessi, né per quanto V.E. ne l'abbia pregata né per parola data a me già corrono cinque mesi, nemmeno risposto a due memoriali dati e chiestimi da lei, ma mi viene di vantaggio levato quel sussidio che la felice memoria del Ser.mo G.D. Ferdinando mi aveva dato sulla Zecca, che erano ogni anno il primo di gennaio 70 scudi che mi pagava, ed ha pagati già tre anni continui il S.r Depositario per tanti cambi che poteva fare l'anno, e così vendite o compre di reali la Zecca e la Depositeria; perché essendo andato il Gennaio passato per li detti 70 scudi secondo il consueto, mi fu risposto dal Signor Depositario che se S.A. gliene passava parola, che me li avrebbe pagati; il che avendo detto più volte a loro Altezze mi hanno promesso di fare o di dire, e /[v:] finalmente non è successo altro. Ora perché io son tormentato dal mio genero e da suo padre, che vorrebbono la dote promessali, e li frutti decorsi per farne li fatti e bisogni loro, ed io non posso vivere con 16 scudi il mese, supplichiamo tutta la mia famiglia insieme V.E. Ill.ma che per l'amor di Dio voglia fare grazia che Madama Ser.ma sborsi questa dote, e a me sia mantenuto quello che S.A. di felice memoria mi ordinò delli 70 scudi l'anno sulla Zecca che tutto riconoscevano dalla bontà di V.E. Ill.ma alla quale viveremo eternamente obbligati: con la quale occasione V.E. potrà farmi anco grazia di ricordare a loro Altezze come io ho servito questa Ser.ma Casa già sono 45 anni, e mi son portato nella mia servitù sempre onoratamente, e che di presente servo con la mia moglie come se fosse stipendiata in tutte le occasioni, e ben volentieri, e continuamente, tanto interviene lei agli studi che si fanno per servire a loro Alt. nelle occasione, quanto fanno le mie figlie che sono stipendiate. Avrò forse trascorso troppo avanti ma V.E. ne incolpì la sua bontà, nella quale sa che abbiamo sempre sperato ogni bene. Tutte queste donne fanno debita riverenza a V.E. Ill.ma ed io con pregarle da Nostro S.re ogni vero bene me li ricordo sempre umilissimo e devotissimo servitore. / Di Firenze alli 6 di marzo 1609 / Di V. E. Ill.ma / Umilissimo servitore / Giulio Caccini di Roma.

1c. I-Rasc, F.O., 1st ser., 119/2, no. 184, letter of Settimia Caccini ne'
Ghivizzani to Virginio Orsini, 6 March 1609/10

Ill.mo ed Ecc.mo signor mio Oss.mo

Avendo scritto mio Padre a V.E. Ill.ma e raccomandatoli il negozio della mia dote
appresso Madama Ser.ma mi è parso con questa occasione debito mio di raccor-
darmele umilissima ed obbligatissima serva, e per questo e tutto benefizio mio, sappi
V.E. che io li viverò eternamente obligata, né si maravigli di tanta briga che ne li dia-
mo perché io non ho in questo mondo altri in chi io possa sperare aiuto e favore che
da V.E. Ill.ma, alla quale con ricordarmele, umilissima serva li faccio reverenza, e le
prego da Dio quanto desidera. Di Firenze alli 6 di marzo 1609 [10] / Di V.E. Ill.ma /
Umilissima Servitrice / Settimia Caccini di Roma / ne' Ghivizzani

2. I-Rasc, F.O., 1st ser., 121/1, no. 90, letter to Virginio Orsini, 5 March 1611/12

Ill.mo ed Ecc.mo S.r mio Oss.mo

Con quanto affetto di cuore io abbia insegnato a Suor Maria Vittoria per obbedire
al comandamento di V.E. Ill.ma oltre all'obbligo mio, lei per se stessa lo può considerare come anco può aver inteso per altre relazioni: ben mi duole che diciotto mesi,
che io ho continuato, restino ora in fruttiferi, avendomi detto la Badessa che non
vuole che Suor Maria Vittoria impari più musica, perché ne sa tanto che gli basta, il
che mi è parso mio debito farlo avvisato a V.E. acciò, se al suo ritorno non la troverà
a quel segno, ché io sperava (anzi diminuito quel acquisto che ha fatto in questo
tempo) V.E. sappia che in quanto alla volontà mia è stata sempre pronta, come sarà
in ogni occasione, ch'ella resterà servita di comandarmi; con che me le ricordo umilissima serva, pregandole da N.S. ogni vera felicità. Di Firenze alli 5 di marzo 1611 [12] /
Di V.E. Ill.ma / Umilissima e Obbligatissima Serva / Francesca Caccini Signorini

3. I-Rasc, F.O., 1st ser., 124/2, no. 233, letter to Virginio Orsini, 4 May 1613

Ill.mo ed Ecc.mo Signor mio Oss.mo

Poiché non potei alla mia partita ringraziare in voce V.E. Ill.ma dei regali, de'
quali (oltre a tant'altre grazie da me ricevute in Casa sua) ella per render più infinito
il numero degli obblighi miei, si compiacque onorarmi, mi è parso mio debito ringraziarla adesso; il che io fo con ogni umiltà, e con tutto l'affetto dell'animo, offeren-
dole prontissimente ogni occasione, nella quale ella conosce, ch'io la possa servire;
perch'io vivo sempre con questo particolar desiderio di riconoscere con la mia servitù
gl'infiniti benefizi che da V.E. ho ricevuto e continuamente ricevo. Subito ch'io fui in
Firenze, andai a far riverenza alle Signore sue figliuole, le quale si rallegronno assai
nell'aver nuove di V.E.; stanno benissimo e mi hanno comandato che per loro io le
faccia riverenza e sono restate molto soddisfatte di alcune informazioni che a l'una
diedi di Roma e all'altra di Francia. Feci, appresso, tutte le altre visite che ella mi
comandò e tutte queste signore e Suor Maria Vittoria ringraziano V.E. della memoria

ch'ella si degna tener di loro, e se le ricordono umilissime serve. Lunedì prossimo si farà il Ballo, nel quale io intervengo, sì che, essendo uscita di tutte le occupazioni, po / [v:] trò servire a V.E. Ill.ma di quei due madrigali che le promessi per quelle signore; e per più non la tediare insieme con mio marito le fo umilissima riverenza pregandole da N.S. ogni vero bene. Di Firenze alli 4 di maggio 1613 / Di V. E Ill.ma / Umilissima Serva / Francesca Caccini Signorini

4. I-Rasc, F.O., 1st ser., 126/5, no. 858, letter to Virginio Orsini, 11 May 1613

Ill.mo ed Ecc.mo Signor mio, e Padrone Oss.mo

Mando a V.E. Ill.ma i due madrigali che già le sono in obbligo; non so se saranno di suo intero gusto, sebbene in procurarlo non ho mancato di usarci ogni diligenzia, come farò sempre in tutte l'occasioni ch'ella mi porgerà di poterla servire; nelle quale mi troverà prontissima conforme agl'infiniti obblighi che le tengo. Prego V.E. che mi voglia far grazia di baciar le mani alla S.ra Camilla con tutte quell'altre Signore, e essendo sbrigata da tutto quello ch'io dovea operare per servizio dei Ser.mi Padroni in queste nozze, aspetto con sommo desiderio di poter venire a servire a V.E. Ill.ma; e con farle umilissima riverenza insieme con mio marito, prego N.S. per ogni sua vera felicità. Di Firenze alli 11 [or 15?] di maggio 1613. Di V.E. Ill.ma / Umilissima ed Obbligatissima Serva / Francesca Caccini Signorini

5. I-Rasc, F.O., 1st ser., 125/1, no. 164, letter to Virginio Orsini, 22 March 1613/14

Ill.mo ed Ecc.mo Signore e Padron mio sempre Oss.mo

Dalla Signora Maria Cavalcanti ho inteso come V.E. Ill.ma mi comanda ch'io le scriva qual volontà io abbia di ritornare a Roma; onde, per obbedire al suo comandamento e insieme soddisfare al continuo desiderio ch'io ho di poter servire a V.E., non posso intorno a ciò dirle se non che da lei maggior grazia ed onore non potrei ricevere (oltre a gli altri infiniti, che ho ricevuto) ch'ella m'intercedesse licenzia da miei Ser.mi Padroni di venire a passare la prossima estate a Roma, ché per meno tempo non mi pare di dovere mettermi in tal viaggio perché, invece di poter servire a V.E., altro non potrei fare che noiarla e incomodarla, sì come altra volta mi avvenne. Se avrò tanta buona fortuna che ciò possa seguire, io spero che maggiore occasione avrò di poterla servire di quella che ebbi l'anno passato per certi nuovi studi che ho fatto, i quali io non debbo ardire né ardisco di pensare che per lor proprio merito possano darle gusto; ma sebbene credo che almeno non le abbiano a dispiacere, per la novità che sempre suol dilettare; aspetterò adunque, con quel maggior desiderio ch'io possa, che segua l'effetto di quanto per sua bontà e amorevolezza ella mi promette per la lettera della S.ra Maria; e vivendo sempre desiderossima di riconoscere con la mia servitù quant'io sono obligata a V.E. Ill.ma, insieme con mio marito le fo umilissima riverenza con pregarle da N.S. le buone feste e il fine de' suoi desideri. Di Firenze alli 22. di marzo 1613.[14] / Di V.E. Ill.ma / Umiliss.ma e Obbligat.ma Serva / Francesca Caccini Signorini

6a. I-Rasc, F.O., 1sr ser., 127/4, no. 664, letter to Virginio Orsini, 18 or 28 April 1614 [very poor condition]

Ill.mo e Ecc.mo S.re e padrone mio sempre Oss.mo

Non manca de . . . . .ha la lettera di V.E per grazia del Ill.mo ed Ecc.mo Signor Paolo Giordano . . . . indegna . . . adesso a ringraziare V.E. dell'onore e grazia che . . . poggiar Loro Altezze Serenissime . . . ..persona insieme di potere avvisare a V.E. la risposta di LL.AA la quale ricevuta dopo 13 giorni e perché l'hanno negato, con la scusa del parto della Ser.ma, per servizio del quale io intervengo solo all'audiena una mezz'ora d'un giorno per cantare due canzonette, come già V.E. sa, ho creduto che non mol . . . .può supplire V.E. possa facilmente con qualch'altro offi . . . . . . mezzo di costà, intercedere grazia e licenzia dalla Ser.ma di tal servizio e perciò, con quel maggiore affetto e reverenza ch'io possa di tal grazia la prego e supplico; e s'ella vorrà . . . .rmi e onorarmi di tale, domando per grazia singularissima . . . . .dia avvisi e lo procuri grazia più presto, mi duol infinito . . . . . di poter servire a V.E. com'io vorrei io debba.. infastidirle . . . particolarmente . . . asprezza con estremo mio disgusto prego V.E. a compatta alla mia . . . la fortuna; perché spero in Dio che pure una volta si dovrà rivoltare e perché ho per . . . . . . che tale in preme dell'impedimento del parto della Ser.ma abbia a f.. i Padroni con l'i . . . . . . qualche persona diffida poi di doverla presto revedere e . . . ./[v:] . . . . Ecc.za Ill.ma perpetuamente obbligatissima insieme con mio marito li fo umilissima riverenza con prego sempre N.S. per ogni maggiore bene. Di Firenze alli [18 or 28] aprile 1614 / . . . . Il . . . / Umilissima e Obbligatissima Serva / Francesca Caccini Signorini

6b., I-Rasc,, F.O., 1st ser., 162/1, no. 167, letter of Paolo Giordano Orsini to Virginio Orsini, 15 April 1614, paragraph 3:

Non trova bene Madama Ser.ma che la Signora Francesca Caccini parta di qua dovendo la Ser.ma Arciduchessa / [v:] servirsene questa estate, e nel parto che sarà all'agosto ed in altre occasione; qui m'occorre dire a V.E. che nel parlare a queste Padrone ho scorto che non hanno gusto che la Francesca venga costà, che sia per avvio all'E.V. onde non ho fatto offizio in nome di V.E. se non con Madama, e trovata la durezza che V.E. vi sente non sono passato piu innanzi.

7. I-FcasaB, A.B. 44, no. 441, letter to Michelangelo Buonarroti,
18 December 1614

Molto Ill. S.r mio Oss.mo

La partita di V.S. così in fretta non meno mi dispiacque per il bisogno che ci era di lei, che per l'occasione, per la quale ella sì partì. Pure, per gli avvisi che V.S. mi dà, piglio speranza ~~della~~ che presto il suo nipote debba esser fuori del pericolo; ché così piaccia al N.S. Resto doppiamente obligata a V.S. dei versi che mi ha mandati per la S.ra Giralda, poiché mi vo immaginando con quanto fastidio ella gli debbe aver composti, avendo occasione di pensare ad altro che a poesia. Son venuti a proposito quanto sia possibile perché, sebbene abbiamo provato la nostra musica alla presenza della Serenissima e di Madama e delle Signore Principesse, non l'abbiamo ancora fatta udire al Gran Duca, sebbene aspettiamo di giorno in giorno d'esser comandate; anzi, ché una sera stemmo in punto ragunate sino a 3 ore di notte ma per l'impedimento d'uno ambasciatore si trasferì per un'altra sera; e questa è stata buona fortuna, poiché Madama dimandò perché ancora detta Signora Giralda non cantava sola; a che io risposi la cagione per la quale V.S. non aveva avuto tempo di farle i suoi versi e siccome il suo nipote si trovava in pericolo di morte, e prometto a V.S. che Madama ne mostrò tanto dispiacere, ché non poteva mostrarlo / [v:] maggiore. Il gusto poi che tutte ebbero dell'invenzione di V.S. e del mio prologo e licenza, e in somma di tutta la musica insieme, non lo posso scrivere, né esprimerlo, a V.S. basta che io l'assicuro; ché è un pezzo che io non ho visto ridere la Serenissima e Madama così di cuore e per tutta la stanza si sentì gran romor di risa e Madama, in particolare, disse tanto bene di V.S. che ella in verità non potrebbe desiderar davantaggio. Le serbo a bocca tutti i particolari. Solo gli dico che ella disse, alla Serenissima e a tutta l'audienza insieme con voce alta, che non ci era uno pari a V.S; e che V.S. sapeva comporre di tutti gli stili, e si sapeva accomodare a tutte l'occasioni e gravi e allegre, e facili e difficili, e in somma mostrava d'aver grandissimo gusto; in quanto a quelle dame si portorno benissimo e si feciono grande onore. Non voglio restar di avvisare a V.S. un'altro particolare che io mi era scordata, cioé che a Madama piacque sopra ogni cosa quel picco dei medici avari e lo ricordò 2 o tre volte. Adesso che canta la Signora Giralda, la festa sarà perfetta e appunto, prima che'l Grand Duca la senta, sarà in ordine. Mi rincresce quant'ella può credere che V.S. non ci abbia a essere; però non voglio mancare di avvisarla, che s'ella può, vada pensando a qualche com / [2 r:] medietta di 11 interlocutori, ché tante siamo appunto, e sia d'invenzione piacevole, nuova, e varia e da ridere e di variati personaggi; perché, sebbene non abbiamo resoluzione certa, ho tanto in mano che le voglio dar questo avviso, acciò ella non sia colta all'improvviso ma possa pensare intanto all'invenzione, per non avere poi occorrendo se non a distenderla; ma di grazia non parli di niente, mi perdoni se troppo l'ho infastidita; e piaccia a Dio ch'ella se ne possa tornare presto e con allegrezza e sanità del suo nipote; con qual fine le fo riverenza e mio marito se le ricorda servitore, mentre io le prego da Iddio ogni vero bene. Di Firenze a 18 di dicembre 1614 / Di V. S. Molto Ill.re / [PS:] Non mi sono servita di quei versi che V.S. mi mandò per la Signora Medicea, perché mi sono parsi più a proposito quelli altre di V.S. "Non passar tra quelle fronde" e gli ho messe sopra l'aria "Addio selvaggi monti" e tornano benissimo / Per servirla sempre prontissima / Francesca Caccini Signorini

8. I-Rasc, F.O., 1st ser., 126/1, no. 67, letter to Virginio Orsini, 26 December 1614

Ill.mo e Ecc.mo Signore e Padrone mio Sempre Oss.mo

Che V.E. Ill.ma abbia fatta abilitare Suor Maria Vittoria a poter cantare in chiesa, io sono sicurissima che non solo lei e io ne le restiamo obbligatissime ma tutta questa città insieme; e che ancora i nostri Ser.mi Padroni ne sentiranno molto gusto, perch'io so quanto abbiano sempre desiderato ch'ella possa cantare liberamente. Quanto all'avere detta Madre bisogno di qualche mia instruzione, io non debbo negarlo che sebbene ell'era ridotta a quel grado di perfezione che V.E. sa, può essere nondimeno che non si essendo potuta mai esercitare per 3 anni passati ella abbia perso qualche cosa, la quale io son prontissima (pur ch'io sia buona) di farle racquistare, per obbedire principalmente a V.E.; e anco per mio onore, dovendo non più viver sepolte tante mie fatiche; e sia certa V.E., che com'io non posso ricever grazia maggiore de' suoi comandamenti così non per donerò a fatica alcuna, per quant'io possa, per andare quanto più spesso al monastero; né di ciò mai sarò impedita volontariamente; e perché gl'infiniti obblighi ch'io le devo ricercano ch'io la serva in altra maggiore occasione che in questa di che ella mi comanda, supplico la benignità sua che voglia ricever sempre da me l'affetto della mia buona volontà, sino a che non piaccia a N.S. porgermi qualche degna occasione, dal quale io prego a V.E. Ill.ma ogni vera felicità, con farle umilissima reverenza insieme con mio marito. Di Fiorenza alli 26 di dicembre 1614 / Di V.E. Ill.ma / Umilissima e Obbligatissima Serva / Francesca Caccini Signorini

9. I-FcasaB, A.B. 44, no. 442, letter to Michelangelo Buonarroti, 27 December 1614

Molto Ill.re Signor mio Oss.mo

I meriti di V.S. sono tanti e di tal qualità ch'io non posso entrar in volerne trattare, perché l'ignoranza mia piuttosto gli oscurebbe che ella potesse spiegarne una minima parte; so bene che quantunque si debbano sempre stimare gli onori de principi grandi e in particolare dai loro vassalli. Con tutto ciò V.S. dalle nostre Serenissime Padrone non ha ricevuto favore o grazia alcuna nella quale non abbia avuto più lungo la verità che la buona e amorevole loro inclinazione verso di V.S. In quanto poi a me, so certo che V.S. sa benissimo che non le ho potuto fare onore alcuno, né anco quelle signore dame non hanno avuto bisogno della mia scuola per altro che per imparare quelle nuove composizioni, ché nel resto si sanno fare molto bene onore da loro, ma perché questi non sono i primi obblighi ch'io devo alla benignità di V.S., non mi confido però, ma tutto ricevo dalla sua amorevolezza. Ho sentito grandissimo gusto e contento che il suo nipote vada riacquistando la sanità; pure mi è doluto non meno, e della lunghezza del male, e della dubbia speranza che V.S. ci dà del suo presto ritorno. La Signora Giralda ha imparato benissimo i suoi versi e tuttavia stiamo in punto per quando saremo comandate dal Ser.mo Gran Duca, il quale ancora non ci ha udito; la cagione mi vo imaginando io che derivi dal non passar bene le cose, poiché ancora egli non è uscito di quel termine nel quale V.S. lo lasciò, cioè quando a letto e quando al lettuccio, né ancora è mai uscito di camera; pure com'ella si vada lo rimetto nel miglior giudizio di V.S.: e spero che se N.S. ponessi qualche fine alla febbre del suo nipote, V.S. sarebbe ancora a tempo. Non dubito punto che sebbene V.S. in luogo molto lontano dalle muse, e fra medici e ammalati, che essendo in lei la propria stanza e abitazione di tutto / [v:] Parnasso, nessun altra contrarietà abbia a poterle cacciarle dal lor proprio seggio o alterare la lor natura; però, occorrendo a V. S. di aver a pensare a quella Commedia, della quale io le scrissi, non ho altra difficoltà, senonché molte cose si conferiscono e discorrono in voci in simili occasioni che difficilmente si possono trattare e stabilire per lettera; pure converrà di mano in mano accomodarsi a quello che sarà possibile. Non ho resoluzione alcuna di detta Commedia, perché come sopra ho detto ci debbano essere altri fastidi che musiche e commedie; ma per soddisfare a quanto conosco essere il gusto di V.S o per dir meglio il bisogno suo, le dirò quanto si è trattato, ma pregandola però che resti fra di noi due con gran segretezza. Deve adunque saper V.S. che sull'occasione di questo poco trattenimento di queste Signore Dame è venuto a loro in pensiero di chiedere in grazia alla Serenissima di poter fare una Commedia in fra di loro perché l'anno passato ebbero licenza, sebbene per altri impedimenti non la fecero, onde seguendo che ella se ne contenti, la Commedia vorrebbe essere di 5 atti o 3, come giudicherà meglio V.S., e gli intermedi vorrebbono essere scherzi, come questi che V.S. ha fatti per potergli cantare fra di noi; la qualità della commedia dovrebbe essere civile con vecchi innamorati, servitori tristi, serve, buffoncelli. Insomma, a V.S. non sarebbe ~~volto~~ posto necessità nessuna ma potrebbe farla con quelli personaggi che ella volesse. Basta ch'ella fosse varia e allegra e non troppo lunghi ragionamenti; questo è quanto gli posso dire; che V.S. ci debba perdere / [2r:] tempo alcuno, a me non pare a proposito, sino a che io non sappia la certezza d'ogni cosa; quanto ho detto a V.S. di questo particolare l'ho fatto perché sono sicurissima che all'usanza nostra ordinaria la Serenissima manderebbe in una furia per V.S. e non ho voluto che V.S. sia colta all'improvviso, ma intanto per suo gusto vada pensando a quella invenzione che le paressi che fosse a proposito, per non aver a far altro che distenderla; V.S. riceva la mia buona volontà che il tutto ho fatto per levarle briga, sapendo quali sogliono essere le furie delle nostre feste Carnovale ~~che s~~ che cercherò d'intendere qualcosa e di tutto la ragguaglierò; anzi, caso che si concludesse quanto negozio, io gli avviserei quale avesse a essere la proposta parte di ciascheduna nelle quale non sono ragazze o bambine, ma solo 3 fanciullette di età tra gli 11 e i dodici anni. Il resto siamo tutte grandi, basta che solo gli posso dire come la Signora Giralda per un ragazzo tristo e la Signora Medici per una serva sono il caso per aggirare tutta la Commedia; e così fra noi siamo rimaste. Il resto le avviserò se occorrerà. V.S. mi perdono perché la sciopero troppo a leggere così gran bibbie; e per più non l'infastidire le fo riverenza e mio marito e mio padre se le ricordono servitori mentre io prego N.S. per ogni suo vero bene. Di Firenze alli 27 di dicembre 1614 / Di V.S. Molto Ill.re / per servirla sempre prontissima / Francesca Caccini Signorini

10. I-FcasaB, A.B. 44, no. 443, letter to Michelangelo Buonarroti, 16 January 1614/15

Molto Ill.re s.r mio oss.mo

È qui in casa mia il S.r Cavaliere Ferdinando Saracinelli però, avendomi detto che è stato a cercare di V.S. e non l'ha trovato in casa, fo intendere a V.S. come egli averebbe grandissimo gusto che ella senza suo scomodo si trasferisce questa sera fin qua, per essere insieme tutti, e il poeta e la musica, e per restare meco dell'ultima resoluzione di ciò che si abbia a mutare; V.S. farà grazia potendo a non mancare e quanto più presto può. Con qual fine le fo riverenza e le prego da N.S. ogni vero bene. Di casa alli 16 di gennaio 1614[15] / Di VS Molto Ill.re / per servirla sempre prontissima / Francesca Caccini Signorini

11. I-FcasaB, A.B. 44, no. 444, letter to Michelangelo Buonarroti, 20 May 1616, from Rome

Molto Ill.re Signor mio Oss.mo

Ringrazio V.S. della canzonetta allungata che mi ha mandato e mi duole che, per la mia ignoranza, essendomi lasciata intendere da V.S. diversamente da quello che era la mia intenzione, io non me ne potrò servire altrimente se non a che meglio non saprò farmi intendere a V.S. Sono in obbligo di ringraziarla perché in ogni modo V.S. non ha mancato di affaticarsi per favorirmi con tutta la prontezza; frattanto, sperando di esser presto a Firenze, le farò riverenza insieme con mio marito con pregar N.S. per ogni suo vero bene. Di Roma alli 28 di maggio 1616. Di V. S. Molto Illre. / Per servirla sempre / Francesca Caccini Signorini

12. I-FcasaB, A.B. 44, no. 445, letter to Michelangelo Buonarroti, 10 September 1616

Molto Ill.re S.r mio Oss.mo

Iersera mio marito mi domandò se V.S. mi avesse mandato o portato quelle parole; ora, rispondendoli io che non ne sapevo niente e non avevo avuto niente, mi ha commesso che io le mandi a ricordare a V.S. con pregarla che, se le fosse comodo, mi favorissi portarmele questa sera; e così l'ultima stanza di quella canzonetta "Miro vicino." V.S. ci perdoni la briga. Credo che saranno a tempo perché penso avere a ire a palazzo domani, se anderò a cantare a questo principe. E con baciarle la mano prego N.S. per ogni suo vero bene. Di casa alli 10 di settembre 1616 / Di V.S. Molto Ill.re / per servirla prontissima / Francesca Caccini Signorini

13. F-Pn

This consists of a report by Farrenc, pasted to the Paris copy of *La Liberazione di Ruggiero*, of a letter dated 22 April 1617 to one Cavaliere Roffa (in service to the Farnese at Rome), asking for a letter of introduction to the court at Parma, to be used on the return trip from Genoa and Milan.

14a. I-FcasaB, A.B. 44, no. 446, letter to Michelangelo Buonarroti, 26 May 1617, from Genoa:

Molto Ill.re S.re Oss.mo

Non mi sono scordata del debito ch'io avevo di scrivere a V.S. ma sì bene sono stata impedita da infinite occupazioni, le quali mai non lascierebbono me s'io talvolta non le fuggissi. Le do nuova come stiamo bene per grazia d'iddio; i favori, poi, e le cortesie che abbiamo avuti, di donde siamo passati e che ci sono fatte qui in questa città, sono più capaci e ⊕ di più credibili a vederli che a poterli esplicare, sí come parte ne dirò in viva voce a V.S. e gliene farò vedere molti effetti. Basta che in me prima mancherà la vita che il desiderio di studiare e l'affetto che ho sempre portato alla virtù, perché questa val più d'ogni tesoro e d'ogni grandezza. Diedi la lettera di V.S. a Signor Chiabrera, il quale ha risposto ed è qui da noi alloggiato nella medesima casa del Signor Giovanni Francesco Brignole, dove siamo alloggiati noi; ché veramente è casa che si può chiamare mare d'ogni bontà e d'ogni amorevolezza e cortesia; stiamo allegramente e come V.S. sa, quando il Signor Gabriello beve con tanto gusto, spesso gli fa dei brindisi e io gli rendo ragione per V.S. e / [v:] così spesso facciamo commemorazione di V.S.; e per ventura nelle nostre stanze abbiamo trovato tra molti ritratti delli uomini segnalati, il ritratto di Michelagnolo Buonarroti il quale ci ha dato e dà spessa materia di ragionare dei meriti di V.S.; e questo Signor ha sentito molto gusto che in Firenze sia un discendente di così grande uomo che porta i vestigi delle sue virtù e il suo proprio nome, come è V.S.; sì che, come ella sente, e ragionando e operando ci andiamo passando il tempo virtuosamente e allegramente; a Lucca, vive nella memoria di tutti la festa delle dame, la quale ha dato estremissimo gusto qua; ho cantato molte canzonette di V.S. ma questa non l'ho cimentata perché non si intende qua i propri vocaboli della nostra lingua come a Lucca. V.S. ci tenga in grazia sua e ci dia nuove di lei. Quest'altra settimana, ricevute le lettere di Firenze, subito ce ne andremo a Savona e di poi alla volta di Milano per Firenze. Intanto con baciarle le mani insieme con mio marito / [2, r:] prego N.S. per ogni suo bene. Di Genova alli 26 di maggio 1617 / D. V.S. Molto Ill.re / per servirla sempre prontissima / Francesca Caccini Signorini

14b. I-FCasaB, A.B. 44, no. 527, letter of Gabriello Chiabrera to Michelangelo Buonarroti, 26 May 1617

I primi giorni che la Signora Francesca giunse in Genova io mi trovai impedito sí che subito non potei esser in barca per visitarla e servirla; sono passati otto giorni, e mi sono venuto; ella mi ha consegnata la lettera di V.S. alla quale io rispondo; la parte, che reca l'eccellenza di questa donna è da me per quanto vaglio autenticato; e che lo possa fare con quiete all'animo me n'assicura il suo valore; qui ella è voluta per meravigliosa, e senza contraddizione; e in poco giorno la fama sua si è sparsa tutto che la città sia e numerosa e negoziosa dell'onore, ella ne riporterà poco meno di quello, ch'ella merita e di qui voglio sperare, che non sarà lasciata con le lodi sole, quantunque ancora si navighi alquanto lontano da porto; spero che questo suo

viaggio ci presterà materia/v: questo inverno a veggia di seco passare lunghi ragionamenti. Intanto io mi raccomando con tutto il core a V.S. pregandola ad amarmi e
comandarmi, e salutare il Signor Soldani e il Signor Galilei e Salvadori miei signori
che Dio sia sempre con loro. Di Genova li 26 di maggio 1617 / Di V.S. Molto Ill /
Servitore. Affettissimo / Gabriello Chiabrera

15a. I-FCasaB, A.B. 63, fol. 129v, letter to Michelangelo Buonarroti,
13 February 1618

Molto Ill.re S.r mio e P[ad]rone

Domattina per ordine del G.D. ci bisogna andare a Pisa; però, desiderando portare il mio libro finito, la prego che questa sera voglia favorirmi di quel servizio che
ella sa, perchè sebbene non so quello che io mi abbia a fare, voglio andare prov-
vista per non esser colta all'improviso. Gli bacio le mani e questa sera l'aspetto se il
tempo non mi ~~sov~~ impedisce. N.S. la conservi. / Di Casa alli 13 di febbraio 1618 /
Di V.S. Molto Ill.re / per servirla sempre del cuore / FCSg [written over her own closing: ho quasi messo in musica il sonetto spirituale però averò caro che V.S. senta e le
parole e la musica, e venga a buon ora, perché vorrei parlare se io potessi]

15b. I-FcasaB, A.B. 63, fol. 202

This document consists of notes for *Il Passatempo* written on undatable fragments
of a letter from Francesca to Buonarroti: fol. 202 r is very clearly just the address, "in
sua mano," and part of the fold, across which the beginnings of three lines of text can
be distinguished, "do", "al" and "be." The next fragment allows one to read these
text bits at the beginnings of lines: " rat" / "ce, se" / "non fugg" / "ta," / "chia" /
"be per" / "favo" / "se" / "cu" / "di se" / "non dic . . . " / "sarò in" / "in voce"

16. I-FcasaB, A.B. 44, no. 448, letter to Michelangelo Buonarroti,
23 February 1618, from Pisa

Molto Ill.re S.r mio Oss.mo

La canzonetta che V.S. mi ha mandata sopra il Volto Santissimo di N.S. è di mia
grandissima soddisfazione e, per quel poco ch'io so, la giudico bellissima. Resta ora
ch'io sappia corrispondere nella parte che tocca a me, cioè nel comporla e cantarla.
L'occasione di poterla cantare a loro Altezze io la procurerò e la spero, né l'ho per
difficile, sebbene non sapendo quanto io abbia da stare quassù e gli accidenti che
possono occorrere, io non gliene prometti sicura del tutto, basta che non mancherò
dalla mia parte e di tutto l'avviserò. Arrivai qui e subito Sua Altezza mandò per me,
sì come ha fatto quasi ogni giorno, dove si è stato con molto gusto di tutt'i padroni e
Monsignore Strozzi ci è stato 2 volte, al quale il secondo giorno Sua Altezza mi fece
cantare delle musiche del *Passatempo* nella quale occasione il Ser.mo Gran Duca e
Madama in particolare ragionò di V.S. con molto affetto e con molta lode e il Serenissimo Gran Duca mi domandò se V.S. mi aveva mostro cosa alcuna della sua *Fiera,*

cioè della ultima festa che V.S. ebbe l'ordine da loro Altezze. A che io risposi che aveva visto qualche eo-/ [1 v:] cosa appartenente alla musica ma, per quello che aveva inteso da V.S., era d'opinione che dovesse essere altra cosa del *Passatempo* e credeva sicuramente che fosse per riuscire la più bella festa che mai si fosse fatta in palazzo due volte n'ho già avuto ragionamento e credo, prima ch'io torni, avere a portare a V.S. qualche buona nuova, perché se la palla mi balza in mano non me la lascierò scappare; e'l negozio poi della mia stampa è andato tanto bene, ché V.S. si maraviglierà quando lo saprà. Ma gliene voglio serbare a bocca per diversi rispetti. E per venire alla conclusione, dico a V.S. che per la mia partita di Firenze così improvvisa non potei esser favorita da V.S. di quel discorso che io desiderava ma solo della lettera e a mala fatica. Ora, avendo io trovato quassù buona comodità di farmelo fare, con quei concetti però che ho dato io in carta, ho mostro la lettera per non poter far altro come cosa mia; e sono stata necessitata, per non dire chi me l'avesse fatta, per amor di quel particolare che le dissi, a pigliarne una che in tutti i modi me ha fatto voluto fare quel medesimo che mi ha fatto il discorso e pregato che io la pigli perché sia del medesimo stile del discorso; ora, io non ci ho fatto difficultà, prima perché so che a V.S. poco importerà e secondariamente per non voler dire che non sia mia, per non mi mostrare troppo parziale di me, l'ho accettata / [2 r:] Ma non in modo però che io non possa ritirarmi; non posso scrivere a V.S. altro particolare per adesso ma in voce poi gli dirò chi e come e ogni cosa; però prima che io faccia altro, acciò io non mi ingannasse (come si suol fare nelle sue proprie cose) io desidero sapere da V.S., da poi che io l'ho affaticata, se è suo gusto che io [. . .] mi serva di questa lettera e del discorso di un medesimo; ché se non è suo gusto non ne voglio far altro, ché prima che disgustar V.S. o usar malacreanza con lei, lascierei andare e la stampa e quanto ci è. Però senza rispetto alcuno mi scriva il suo parere o ordine di spedirmi; quanto prima però, acciò che la passione non mi ingannassi, perché io so che V.S. mi vuol bene e ha caro la mia reputazione. A che io mi mantenga la benevolenza dell'Universale, anzi me la vadia sempre augmentando, io le mando la lettere e il discorso, prima perché V.S. mi favorisca di correggermi la lingua, e secondariamente, levi tutto quello che ella conosce che non stia bene e possa minimamente, nonché assai, pregiudicarmi in cosa alcuna e aggiungere quello che ella conosce che ci mancassi. Io la supplico con ogni affetto a non mi mancare di questo favore ma, sinceramente e senza cerimonie, come se avessi a fare per cosa sua propria e che assai gli premesse; l'obbligo ch'io gliene averò sarà perpetuo e singulare fra tutti quelli che le devo. Mi farà bene, somma grazia, a tenerlo segretissimo e rimandarmelo in su, perché io poi lo manderò costà a quel gentiluomo che ne / [2 v:] ha la cura. Intorno a mio padre, non credo che avrà di che dolersi, poi che mi partì così improvvisamente come V.S. sa e di quassù, subito che ho avuto l'ordine, gli ho mandato tutte l'opere che gli dia una vista, se gli pare che possino stare per stamparsi. Basta per avviso di V.S., o con mio Padre o con altro che gliene parlassi, V.S. se ne mostri nuova e lontana del tutto; e intorno a porre o levare di queste scritture che le mando, V.S. non ci abbia riguardo alcuno perché è persona che ne posso fare a mio modo e ho a essere stata io, perché di già n'ho levate e poste delle altre; e perché non si possa immaginare niente, gliene ho chieste in mia mano per parecchi giorni, per poterle un poco considerare da me

a mente scarica; e così come V.S. me le manderà così dirò d'averle acconce io e le rico-
pierò prima di mia mano propria; sì che V.S. può farne liberamente quanto vuole. La
supplico bene della prontezza perché ho fretta grandissima e non bisogna che V.S.
mi risponda per l'ordinario ma per via della corte, perché ogni giorno vengono gente
di Firenze. V.S. la mandi la lettera per questa strada, come gli parrà meglio; si ricordi
di noi e mi perdoni la lunghezza; e mi dà qualche nuova di lei e della città. Io insieme
con mio marito le bacio le mani e prego N.S. per ogni suo vero ben. Di Pisa alli 23 di
febbraio 1618 / Di V.S. Molto Illre / S.A.S. sta bene e è guarita ma non si leva / per
servirla sempre prontissima / Francesca Caccini Signorini/ [3 r:]

Poscritta

Ricevei la canzonetta di V.S. e non è altrimenti andata male. Do nuova a V.S.,
come il primo o secondo giorno di quaresima canterò a loro Altezze la canzonetta di
V.S. sopra il Volto Santo e alla presenza di Monsignore Strozzi, e ne darò avviso e
ragguaglio a V.S. Desidero che mi dia qualche nuova di mio Padre perché di 4 lettere
che gli ho scrisse non mi ha mai risposto.

Stasera mi è comparsa una lettera di V.S. con un'altra copia della canzonetta sopra il Volto Santo e veramente che V.S. ha gran ragione di dolersi di me, quanto
all'apparenza, ma in verità non è così, perché ho indugiato a risponderli per mandarle queste scritture e sono tanto occupata che V.S. non se lo potrebbe mai dare
ad intendere ma a bocca meglio discorreremo. Raccomando a V.S. quella grazia che
le ho domandata nella lettera, cioè che con ogni sincerità mi dica il suo parere di
questa lettera e di questo discorso; e se si potessi io vorrei, dove nel discorso loda
i virtuosi di Firenze, nominar mio padre, di maniera tale che ne restasse onorato,
e parlarne come maestro degli altri, perché non vorrei che paresse che io non avessi
voluto dipendere da lui per superbia ma riconoscerlo per maestro, però senza mio
~~pregiud~~ pregiudizio ~~ne~~ e senza che i semplici potessero credere che le presente
opere mi fossero state perfezionate e finite e riviste da lui. Mi è stato detto che come
figliuola non è buona creanza che io lodi mio Padre; ma io me ne voglio rappor-
tare a V.S. totalmente ~~all'Univers~~; e non vorrei, dall'altra parte, farmi tenere per
superba e vorrei dare ancora a mio padre qualche soddisfazione. Mi raccomando a
V.S. e tutta la mia speranza ho posto in lei, ché poi che l'angustia del tempo non /
[sideways:] mi ha concesso di poter essere favorita da lei d'ogni cosa, almeno non
manchi di favorirmi in questo che prego. [rip in paper] bacio le mani e la prego a non
mi mancare. / [3 v:] Ringrazio la mia buona fortuna poiché, e Monsignore Strozzi e il
dubbio che V.S. ha avuto che non fosse persa la lettera sua prima, è stato cagione che
si sono viste le sue lettere a me gratissime e care sopra ogn'altra cosa.

17. I-Fas, MdP 1377, unnumbered letter to Angelica Badii ne' Cioli,
11 August 1618

Molto Ill.re S.ra e Prona Mia Oss.ma

Desiderei un giorno venire a stare due ore con V.S. e, se non li fosse incomodo,
quanto prima però la prego a favorirmi di mandare la carrozza per me e, se bene
volesse oggi, sarò in casa aspettando; se non potesse, quando potrà, verrò a ricevere

il favore, basta che sia con manco briga sua che sia possibile; le fo riverenza ed offerendomele con ogni prontezza ed affetto, prego N.S. che le conceda ogni vera felicità. Di casa alli 11 d'agosto 1618 / Di V.S. Molto Ill.re / Devotissima Serva / Francesca Caccini Signorini

18. I-Fas, MdP 1377, unnumbered letter to Andrea Cioli, 19 September 1618

Ill.mo Signor mio e Prone Oss.mo [*another hand: Zanobi Pignoni*]

Ho avviso sicuro come la parte avverrà di quel giovane che io raccomandai a V.S. Ill.ma sì [. . .] gagliardamente ed è tanto innanzi il negozio che fra pochi giorni senza dubbio sarà terminato. E perché io ho inteso come ancora V.S. Ill.ma non ha potuto farmi grazia di negoziare la supplica che le diede, perché io desidererei di fare dalla mia parte tutto quello che io posso, in favore del supplicante, e questo perché ci conosco il servizio del Principe, supplico V.S. Ill.ma che mi voglia per sua benignità fare questa grazia o di quanto prima trattare questo negozio con Sua Altezza. Se però conosce di poterlo e doverlo trattare, ovvero liberamente liberare questo giovane dalla speranza che ha in V.S. Ill.ma, perché possa o fermarsi di non infastidir più alcuno, ovvero servirsi di quel mezzo che a lui piacessi; io in verità mi vergogno con V.S. Ill.ma della mia presunzione ma so che, come cortesissima e discretissima, mi compatirà, imaginandosi quanto io, per averlo incominciato, desidererei tirare a fine vittoriosa questo negozio. Fo riverenza a V.S. Ill.ma e insieme alla Signora sua consorte e supplicandola perdonare alla mia sicurtà prego N.S. per ogni sua felicità. Di casa alli 19 di settembre 1618 / Di V. S. Ill.ma Servitrice Obbligatissima Francesca Caccini Signorini

19. I-FcasaB, A.B. 44, no. 449, letter to Michelangelo Buonarroti, 4 October 1618

Molto Ill.re Signor Oss.mo

Domattina saranno dati in lista a Signori Consoli dell'Arte della Lana dal maestro de' cherici di Santa Maria del Fiore 8 chierici per essere scritti a Messa. V.S. m'intendere meglio per descrizione, ora fra questo otto sarà il maestro di Scipione, il quale non è inferiore di merito a qualsivoglia di questi, siccome desidera mostrarsi nell'esamina. Ora, perché io ho inteso che il S.r Buonarroto fratello di V.S. è uno di questi Signori Consoli, io prego V.S. che mi voglia far grazia di fare offizio con lui, ché questo giovane sia nel numero di quei due che devono essere scritto tra questi otto. Il giovane ha nome Lorenzo di Marco Papi. V.S. non manchi di raccomandarlo e farlo raccomandare e al suo fratello e a S.ri suoi compagni. So che se il S.r suo fratello vorrà, si otterrà quanto si desidera per grazia e favore di V.S. Io la / [v:] prego quant'io posso e così a perdonarmi la briga che io le do e la sicurtà che io piglio; e con farla riverenza prego Iddio per ogni sua felicità. / Di casa alli 4 d'ottobre 1618 / Di V.S. Molto Ill.re / per servirla sempre prontissima / Francesca Caccini / Signorini

20. I-FcasaB, A.B. 44, no. 447, letter to Michelangelo Buonarroti,
25 January 1618/19

Molto Ill.re Signor mio Oss.mo

Ho pensato che quell'aria che V.S. ha gusto che canti infine introducendo o le
Dame o i Cavalieri del Ballo, la Signora Arcangiola sarà forse meglio che io la com-
ponga, se però piacerà a V.S.; e perciò l'avviso di questo, acciò che se non ha parlato
a quell'amico non ne parli e, quanto prima, faccia che io possa sbrigarmi per poter
pigliare un poco di riposo. Le bacio le mani e aspetto di rivederla. N.S. la prosperi.
Di casa alli 25 di gennaio 1618 [19] / Di V.S. Illre / Per servirla sempre / Francesca
Signorini Malaspina

21. I-Fas, MdP 1426, insert 1, letter to Andrea Cioli, 25 March 1619

Ill.mo Signore mio P.rone Oss.o

Per le molte fatiche durante alli giorni passati sono in letto con un poca di medicina per riposo e per ciò questa mattina non potei dare risposta a V.S. Ill.ma. Adesso
le dico come non è possibile che io possa pensare a fare cantare e imparare la musica di
questi settanta versi che mi ha mandato, a quelle fanciulle che io insegno, in sì poco
spazio di tre giorni, cioè per di qui a sabato prossimo, perché queste fanciulle e io
siamo affaticate per aver avuto a imparare in quindici giorni gli offizi della settimana
santa e una mezz'ora di musica per cantare alla Cappella della Ser.ma al Santissimo
Sacramento; le qual musiche ricercavano di tempo due mesi, perché queste sono fanciullette che non cantano ancora la parte e imparano per forza di studio e per pratica.
Ho grandissima mortificazione di non mi potere mostrare pronta al servizio de' miei
Ser.mi Padroni. In questo particolare, come in tutti gli altri, sono state di effetti e
son e di voluntà; e se il S.re Ottavio Rinuccini si fussi lasciato intendere al meno
dieci giorni avanti, ci saremmo potuto sforzare, ché quello che non si fa non è per
non durare fatica ma è per brevità / [42 v:] di tempo e per impossibilità delle nostre
poche forze. Perciò rimando a V.S. Ill.ma le parole e la supplico che voglia addurre
le mie vive ragione a S.A., perché io sono tanta sicura della pietà e benignità de miei
Ser.mi Padroni che non dubito punto di non avere a essere scusata [*sic*] e compatita,
perché per servizio loro non guarderò mai a fatica di sorte alcuna e non ho altro
desiderio che da ben servire e prontamente. E con tal fine a V.S. Ill.ma fo reverenza
supplicandole, di nuovo, a scusarmi e aiutarmi con S.A.; e la ringrazio sommamente
del buono uffizio che ha fatto per me di quel servizio che io li raccomandai: gliene
resto obbligatissima, e perché lei è mia protettore, ne stò con buonissima speranza e
di nuovo gliene raccomando con pregare N.S. che li conceda ogni desiderata felicità.
A casa li 25 di marzo 1619, Di V.S. Ill.ma Fo riverenza alla Signora sua consorte, e me
le ricordo serva devotissima / Servitrice sempre obbligatissima / Francesca Caccini
ne' Signorini Malaspina

22. I-FcasaB, A.B. 44, no. 450, letter to Michelangelo Buonarroti,
3 January 1620/21

Molto Ill.re Signor mio e P.rone Oss.mo

Io sto con quel sollevamento d'animo che V.S. può credere e desiderio di sapere
come stia V.S. della sua catarrale indisposizione; e molto più di non potere e visitarla
e servirla come vorrei. Però, facciami grazia ch'io lo sappia che per mio conforto
vò pensando che V.S. stia con buona salute ma abbia bisogno di riguardo e, particolarmente, di non uscire a queste brezze che veramente non possono essere più
acute e non basta per fuggirle le carrozze ben turate, sì come io lo provo; e perciò
attenda pure a star chiusa quanto può e, se si trova in grado di potere, favoriscami
di quella sua canzonetta che ha per intercalare "No ch'io non t'amo più, non t'amo
no," ché la desidero assai, e pensi ancora quando potrà di mantenermi la promessa
di quelle ottave rusticali e di quell'altre frottole, perché io vo pensando a nuovo modo
di pregarla, caso che ella volessi esser pregata dell'altro o se ella mi avessi promesso
per burlarmi; penserò ancora al modo di pregarla, perché ella mi risolva o di darmele
o di dirmi se mi burla per causa di qualche mio mancamento da me non conosciuto,
perché io stimo tutte le opere di V.S. quanto io sappi e possa e sopra ogn'altra cosa.
La saluto di tutto cuore, al mio solito, e restando sempre tutta di V.S., le prego dal
N.S. l'intera salute e ogni felicità. Di casa questo di 3 di gennaio 1620[21] / D VS
Molto Ill.re / Ser. D / Francesca [cut off at bottom]

23. I-FcasaB, A.B. 44, no. 451, letter to Michelangelo Buonarroti,
14 March 1621/22

Molto Ill.re Signor mio Oss.mo

Il mio marito desidera da V.S. quelle parole "Non, ch'io non t'amo più" e io la
prego di quell'altre sopra La Folia, le quali V.S. mi mostrò e poi, secondo me, se le
riprese; da poiché io non le trovo in luogo alcuno. E ci perdoni la briga. Ricordo a
V.S., con questa occasione, il servizio che sa; e se può o se vuole farmi la grazia desiderata sia di buonora e non verso la sera. Le fo riverenza e prego Iddio che le conceda
quello che desidera. Di casa questo dì 14 di marzo 1621[22] / Di V.S. Molto Ill.re /
S.D / [illegible]

24. I-FcasaB, A.B. 44, no. 453, letter to Michelangelo Buonarroti, 1 April 1622,
from Livorno

Molto Ill.re Signor mio, e Prone Oss.mo,

Conforme a quanto promessi a V.S., le do nuova di noi, come siamo in Livorno e
arrivammo iersera a 23 ore, dove staremo sino a che non siano partite le galere che
partiranno come sia addolcito il tempo, ché per al presente è molto crudo, con un
vento grande e contrario alla galere. Non ho da darle nuova alcuna, senonché doman-
tina il predicatore della chiesa de' Cavalieri di Pisa fa una predica qui in Duomo, per
ordine di Loro Altezze, a tutti i cavalieri e soldati che hanno a ire su le galere, che sarà

certo una grande e bella devozione, perché questo è un Padre di grandissimo valore e renderà tutta questa gente animosa e forte contr'ogni faticosa e difficile impresa. Intorno alla nostra tornata non ho certezza, senonché per tutto il presente mese noi saremo a Firenze, il quando è incerto, poiché si fanno 10 resoluzioni il giorno e poi non se ne conclude alle volte una sola, per quelle che si dice la Corte dopo qui non si tratterrà in Pisa più di 2 giorni e altrettanto a San Miniato al Tedesco e all'Ambrogiana; sì che staremo a vedere e noi faremo, di mano in mano, quanto da il padrone ci verrà ordinato e comandato. Intanto V.S. ci potrà favorire delle sue lettere che averemo tempo di riceverle e, volendo favorircene, potrà mandarle a Pisa e inviarle in casa del Signor Dottore Stefani, ché forse saremo ritornati là e, quando noi non ci fossimo, lui ce le invierà sicurissime. Stiamo tutti bene per grazia d'Iddio e così desideriamo che stia lei e, con questo fine, io le fo riverenza insieme con mio marito e Scipione; e salutandola di cuore, resto pre / [v:] gando il Signor per ogni sua maggiore felicità e la supplico a darci qualche nuova di Firenze, perché noi ne abbiamo pochissime; e di nuovo la saluto. Di Livorno, il di primo d'aprile 1622 / D.V.S. Molto Ill.re / per servirla sempre prontissima / Francesca Signorini Malaspina

25. I-Fas, MdP 1717, letter to Curtio Picchena[?], 25 March 1624

Ill.mo e Clarissimo Signor mio e Padrone sempre Oss.mo

Il Signor Provveditore dell'Arte della Lana ha procurato di rimediare che la mia matrigna non sia cavata di casa, conforme all'ordine che ha nel rescritto di Loro Alt. ma avendo trovato le parti molto ostinate e maligne, non ha voluto usar violenza senza l'ordine espresso delle Ser.me Alt. e perciò, avendo fatto l'informazione, me ha mandato, 2 giorni sono, il memoriale sigillato, e ha consigliato il mio marito che io lo porti. Io, dovendo venire fra sì pochi giorni costà, perché nel presentare il detto memoriale potrò aggiungere molte cose in voce che saranno di grande aiuto per conseguire la grazia che si desidera; e perciò, avendo noi accettato il consiglio del S.r Provveditore, porteremo il memoriale. E in quello istante che ricevetti la lettera di V.S. Ill.a, appunto voleva darle conto di tutto questo particolare. La ringrazio sommamente di tanta sua amorevolezza e tutti gliene viverem con obbligo perpetuo; e ci duole della sua indisposizione. Sabato sera prossimo saremo costà, se piacerà a Dio, dove meglio in voce l'informerò di tutto il negozio. Frattanto ricordandomele obbligatissima insieme con mio marito le fo riverenza e prego il Signore Dio per ogni sua maggior felicità. Di Firenze alli 25 di marzo 1624. Servitrice sempre obbligatissima / Di V.S. Ill.ma e Clarissima / Francesca Signorini Malaspina

26. I-FcasaB, A.B. 44, no. 454, letter to Michelangelo Buonarroti, 21 June 1626

Molto Ill.re Signor mio Oss.mo

Da persona alla quale siamo obbligati mi sono state chieste le parole di quella festa che V.S. fece a Pisa che si chiama *La stiava* e della quale io composi la musica 20 anni sono. Ora, io che non le ho, ho risposto alla detta persona che cercherò di fargliene avere. Ho fatto capitale della cortesia di V.S. e la supplico che voglia favorirmi di darmi queste parole; e perché io so che sono troppo più lunghe a scrivere d'un madrigale o d'una canzonetta, V.S. volendo favorirmi, potrà mandarmi la detta festa e io la farò copiare e subito la rimanderò a V.S. Mi perdoni la troppa sicurtà che non ho potuto far di meno. Il mio marito le fa riverenza, sì come fo io, pregando il S.re Iddio che le conceda quanto desidera. Di casa alli 21 di giugno 1626 Di V.S. Molto Ill.re / per servirla sempre prontissima / Francesca Signorini Malaspina

27. I-Fas, MdP 1449, letter to Dimurgo Lambardi, 15 September 1626

Molto Ill.re Signor mio oss.mo

Supplico V.S. a favorirmi di abboccarsi col S.r Balì Saracinelli perch'egli darà l'ordine a V.S. di poter spendere la parola di S.A.S. col Signor Cioli, per conto di quel servizio ch'io supplicai V.S. di farmi ed ella mi promesse. Essendo venuto il tempo di farlo, il Signor Balì è occupatissimo per questa festa che si fa all'Ill.mo Signor Cardinal Barberino e dice non aver tempo di poter cercare V.S.; e che se la vedrà gli darà l'ordine. Però mi faccia grazia di procurare di vederlo lei, ché gliene resterò con obbligo singulare; e procuri per grazia ch' il negozio abbia buono effetto. Intanto 'l rivedrò com'io si' fuori di queste occupazioni e le fo riverenza. N.S. le conceda quanto desidera. Di / casa alli 15 di settembre. 1626 / Di V.S. M.to Ill.re / per servirla sempre prontissima / Francesca Signorini Malaspina

28. I-FcasaB, A.B. 44, no. 455, letter to Michelangelo Buonarroti,
1 January 1626/27

Molto Ill.re Signor mio Oss.mo

Io ho indugiato d'andare a palazzo sino adesso, avendo aspettato V.S. che fosse venuto a vedermi, sì come hanno fatto alcuni altri amorevoli amici del mio marito (che sia in gloria), perché desideravo conferirle alcune mie cose avanti che io le trattasse; ma perché il Signor Orazio, mio cugino, a queste sera mi disse che dovendo V.S. venirci sarebbe andato per lui, restando io fuori di modo e d'ogni aspettazione, maravigliata, dovendo andare posdomani, cioè sabato, a palazzo, mi sono (benché contro ad ogni mia voglia) resoluta di pregarla a favorirmi questa sera di venire da me, perché mi faccia grazia di dirmi se, insieme col mio povero marito, ella vuol far compagnia agli altri che m'hanno, insieme con lui, abbandonata. Basta, se ella mi favorisca, discorreremo del tutto. E perché io ho meno giudizio di lei, anzi non punto, non le dirò che non vada per il mio cugino ma sì bene che a V.S. e non al mio cugino desidero parlare. Le fo riverenza e prego il Signore Iddio per ogni sua felicità. Di casa il primo di gennaio 1626[27] / Di VS Molto Ill.re / per servirla sempre prontissima / Francesca Signorini Malaspina

29. I-FcasaB, A.B. 44, no. 456, letter to Michelangelo Buonarroti,
13 January 1626/27

Molto Ill.re S.r mio Oss.mo

Poi che V.S. mi scrisse, non ho saputo niente; però la prego a farmi grazia che io
sappia qualche cosa. So che ho tempo due mesi a pigliar la tutela dopo la morte del
mio marito; ma perché io ho certa lite co' Marzichi, ché per la parte mia ci sono io
medesima e per il mio marito ci è la mia figliuola; perché se io non ho preso la tutela,
non posso agitare per la mia figliuola; però desidererei pigliar questa tutela e per
questo io desidererei ancora sapere che cosa si deve fare perché io la possa pigliare.
E compatisco infinitamente ai fastidi di V.S. e sue occupazioni; ma perché ho già
cominciato ad infastidirla, però seguito con la medesima sicurtà di darle briga. Mi
facci grazia che io sappia quello che ho da fare e abbia compassione di chi non ha per
sé persona al mondo sí come sono io; la quale le offerisco per contraccambio della
sua cortesia quando posso e quanto vaglio, e se non vaglio niente, colpa della fortuna
ma non della volontà: la quale fu, è, e sarà sempre prontissima ad ogni suo comandamento. Le fo riverenza e prego il signore Iddio per ogni suo maggiore bene e la saluto
di tutto cuore. Di casa alli 13 di gennaio 1626[27] / Di V.S. Molto Ill.re / Servitrice
sempre affettuosissima e obbligatissima di cuore / Francesca Signorini Malaspina

30a. I-Fas, MdP 1427, particolari F a Cioli, 77r–78r, letter to Andrea Cioli, 19
March 1631, from Lucca

Ill.mo signore mio P.rone Oss.mo

Sono molti mesi ch'io doveva far reverenza a V. S. Ill.ma con mia lettere, ma per
i travagli sopraggiunti in codesta città, non mi sono ardita infastidirla, sapendo non
le mancavano altre occupazioni. Adesso che, per grazia d'Iddio, intendo comincino
a passare, vengo a rallegrarmene con lei, e insieme a ricordarle la mia infinita ob-
bligazione, e darle conto come, subito dopo il mio ritorno di costà, informarmi di
persona pratica e confidente di quella difficoltà che mi erano state anteposte, circa
al voler io alienarmi di qua col mio figliuolo; ed essa fui assicurata come non ci era
legge né statuto che potesse impedirmi la mia libertà adducendomi ragioni vivissime
che per brevità tralascio, e tutto ho voluto dire a V.S. Ill.ma per giustificazione di
questa verità ricordandomi averne discorse con Madama Ser.ma e con lei contraria-
mente. Devo ancora dirle come non perderò mai la memoria della protezione che
tiene di me appresso le Ser.me Alt.e, e del favore che mi fece. E perché costà non ho
altro padrone né protettore di lei, deposto da parte ogni timore di parerle troppo
importuna, vengo con ogni confidenza e fiducia a supplicarla che voglia con la sua
solita benignità aiutarmi in un mio grandissimo travaglio, dovendo tra poco tempo
mandare la mia figliola al servizio di Madama Serenissima, e perseverando S.A.S.
tuttavia nel medesimo proposito di volerla in tutto alienata da me, e sotto la disci-
plina d'altre persone; perché ritrovandomi oggi in differentissimo stato da quello che
era quando S.A.S. mi domandò questa figliuola, e che io gliene diedi, conviene che
io dica il mio sentimento e le mie ragione senza star più aspettare su vane speranze

quello che deva seguire, come ho fatto sino adesso, e procuri sapere liberamente come abbia andare questo negozio per poter'oggi mai accomodare i fatti miei, sopra i quali sono stata sospesissima da poi in qua, ch'io scopersi questo pensiero di Mad.ma Ser.ma quale né io né altri si sarebbe mai potuto immaginare, essendo ragione naturale di aver creduto tutto l'opposto. Signor per meno tediarla, vorrei poter dirle il mio bisogno con due soli versi, ma non potendo, dirò solo le cose più necessarie con maggiore brevità ch'io possa.

Dico adunque come oggi mi ritrovo sola senza la mia compagnia, abbandonata, in patria forestiera, e non ho altro al mondo che questi figliuoli: né ho speranza ad altro aiuto e d'altro ricorso nei miei bisogni e nelle infermità ch'io posso avere che da loro, se piacerà a Dio di conservarmeli; e loro similmente non hanno altri che me, e queste non sono mie immaginazioni ma è la pura verità, sì che ci bisogna tenerci cari e uniti l'un'all'altro, mentre Iddio non ci separi con la morte; e quando piacesse alla Divina Maestà (al cui volere non si può replicare) mandare la morte a questa figliuola, io resterei afflittissima per tutto il tempo della mia vita, parendomi restare un'ombra miserabile senza vestigio di virtù; e così credo paresse a lei, s'ella perdesse me e il suo fratello. Ora consideri V.S. Ill.ma e ciascheduno, in qual modo io medesima abbia a poter permettere d'abbandonare questa figlia nel suo e mio maggiore bisogno, e in tutto alienarle da me se iddio che può tormela, per sua grazia e bontà, me la conserva. Quanto poi alla virtù, dico che maggiore desiderio non può avere un padre e una madre che rifar lor medesimi nei lor figliuoli, lasciandoli eredi delle lor professioni / [v:] e virtù. Ora, se Iddio benedetto m'ha data una sola figliuola e di tali attitudine e inclinazione alla mia professione che (parlando con ogni dovuta modestia) son sicura non essermi affaticata in vano nello studio continuo di quarant'anni che aver dove lasciare (e ben collocate) tutte le mie fatiche, e studi, dopo la morte mia, per qual ragione e come può bastarmi l'animo d'abbandonarla, né meglio dell'acquistare, e darla in mano di persone straniere, con rischio sicuro che in breve ella perde quanto ha acquistato; e io restare con tutto'l mio tempo perduto, e senz'alcun frutto di lei nei miei bisogni e delle virtù che le ho insegnato, non so se questa dovesse chiamarsi prudenza o crudeltà, lo lascierò nella consideratione di V. S. Ill., a non potendo concluder altro senonché non conosco persona che possa insegnare, sopratendere, e guidare la mia figlia meglio di me, e guai a chi non ha la madre e il padre. Adesso, non avendo altra intenzione e maggior desiderio che di obbedire ad ogni cenno di Madama Serenissima, e dare a S.A. di me e della mia figliuola ogni soddisfazione possibile, e riconoscendo, quanto io devo, la buona fortuna di questa figliuola e l'onor grande che le ha fatto S.A.S. in averla voluta eleggere e accettare per sua serva; stante le sopradette cose, mi ritrova la più afflitta creatura che già mai possa ritrovarsi, e non so né posso desiderare altro conforto o rimedio che la morte, se piacesse a Dio di mandarmela per finire una volta tante tribolazioni che sono state tanto; e tante sono che, se Iddio non mi desse vigore, non potrei più sofferirle, perché non so che armi né che partito prendermi, non mi parendo già per questo mio materno e ragionevole sentimento di meritare il disgusto e la disgrazia di Mad.ma Ser.ma, né il danno di questa povera figliuola la quale, sebbene è di poca età, ha però tanto giudizio che ben conosce la sua fortuna e quanto le importa la perdita di sua madre. Signore, io non ho altro refugio, né altra speranza, che nella sua protezione e benignità, e la supplico con ogni maggiore affetto e reverenza che voglia significare a Madama Ser.ma le mie ragioni e'l mio sentimento in quel modo che a lei parrà migliore, e farmi grazia di cavare liberamente da S.A.S. (udito, che l'abbia) quello che deve seguire di questo negozio, e l'ultima resolutione e intenzione di Madama Serenissima, per poter accomodare i miei affari perché, da quel tempo in qua che S.A.S. ebbe prese questa figliuola, sono stata sempre sospesissima. E piena di confusione per aver visto in un subito tutti di corte, e molti di fuore, alienarsi da me e non risponder più alle mie lettere, sino all'istessa monaca che trattò meco tutto questo negozio; e se tal volta S.A.S. ha voluto saper nuove di questa figlia e dei suoi studi, ha fatto scrivere addirittura al Tuccerelli e egli è venuto a casa mia, e senza dirmi pure una parola da parte di Mad.ma Ser.ma, ha parlato con la figliuola come se io non fosse sua madre o non fosse al mondo; quando io poi venni costà (fuor che V.S. Ill.a per sua grazia) tutti mi fuggirono, non che cercare di vedermi, e se non era il suo favore, non averei visto nemmeno i Ser.mi Padroni tornata ch'io fui; venne pure il Tuccerelli, per ordine di S.A.S., a vedere se la figliuola era guarita, col suo solito modo; e non mi trovando in casa, si lasciò intendere alle mie genti che forse sarebbe toccato a lui a condurre a Firenze la mia figliuola, senza me, l'ottobre prossimo passato. Onde, nonostante che io sia tutrice assoluta del mio figliuolo e padrona libera mentre viverò di quanto c'è, e morendo egli avanti 18 anni, d'ogni altre cose padrona liberissima fuori che di beni stabili dei quali sono in vita mia usufruttuaria, e che io sia padrona della mia libertà, e posse (come me disse V.S. Ill.ma) e padrone ch'io /

[78:] voglia venir alla mia patria, non avendo comesso errori per i quali io meriti l'esilio; tuttavia, stante le sudette dimostrazione, non lo farei, né poterei e doverei farlo, senza l'intero gusto e protezione di tutte l'Alt.e Ser.me, né credo V.S. Ill.ma mi consiglierebbe in contrario, né questo sarebbe il bisogno e benefizio del mio figliuolo; la supplico adunque di nuovo col maggiore affetto ch'io possa, che voglia aiutarmi uscire di tanta afflizione, ché se ella non me ne cava lei col suo potere, non so certo come farmi. Le viverò sempre schiava obbligatissima di tanto benefizio, e sarò sempre prontissima a riconoscerlo con tutti gli effetti che mi concederanno le mie debole forze; le ricordo la servitù di mio padre e di tutta la nostra casa verso di lei, e l'affetto che tutti le abbiamo sempre portato, per la cui memoria meno le rincresce l'affaticarsi per me in questa mia necessità, e con farle umilissima reverenza sì come alla Signora sua Consorte, prego il Signore Dio che le conceda ogni vera e desiderata felicità. Lucca alli 19 marzo 1631. / Di V.S. Ill.ma / Servitrice sempre obbligatissima / Francesca Raffaelli

30b. I-Fas, MdP 121, fol. 278, 24 May 1631

Alla S.ra Francesca Caccini Raffaelli 24 maggio 1631

Il Balì Cioli

Io indugiavo a rispondere alla lettera di V.S. per poterle dire che stava in suo arbitrio il tempo del condure qua la Signora sua figliola perche sarà da loro Alt.e ricevuta volentieri, e con quella stima delle sue virtù, che V.S. merita per avergliele insegnate, e che sarebbe anche in sua libertà il venire il a vederla, dopo che l'avesse lasciata, quante volte ella volesse, perché sarà sempre la benvenuta; ma finché duri il dispetto di cotesto contagio, del quale arrivano tuttavia qua molte cattive nuove, io non posso dare a V.S. quella consolazione, che sopra di ciò vorrei.

31. I-Fas, MdP 121, fol. 279, letter to Andrea Cioli, 26 May 1631

Ill.mo Signor mio, e Padrone Colendissimo

Conforme all'amaritudine ch'io avevo nell'animo, è stata la consolazione che ho ricevuto dalla risposta di V.S. Ill.ma, avendomi accertata di quello in che io stava molto sospesa, né le rendo quelle grazie maggiore che per me si possono, restandole singolarmente obbligata di tanto favore e grazia, fra tutti gli altri che da V.S. Ill.ma ho ricevuto; pregherò il Signore che voglia liberar questa città, acciò io possa venire a ricevere l'onore che mi ha fatto Madama Serenissima, e ringraziare personalmente V.S. Ill.ma, e servirla sempre con tutte le mie deboli forze; bacio le veste a Madama Serenissima e a tutte loro Altezze insieme con la mia figliuola, e a V.S. Ill.ma faccio umilissima riverenza, pregando il Signore che le conceda ogni desiderata felicità. Lucca questo di 26 maggio 1631 / Di V.S. Ill.ma / Servitrice sempre obbligatissima / Francesca Raffaelli

32. I-FcasaB, A.B. 52, no. 1543, letter to Michelangelo Buonarroti, 14 December 1634

Molto Ill.re S.re Oss.mio

Dall'Emilia intesi come V.S. aveva fatto molte canzonette spirituali sopra alcune arie che si cantavano sopra parole temporale; però, se fosse suo gusto, riceverei per favore e grazia, che me ne desse copia di tutte quante n'ha fatto, poichè averei occasione di servirmene per la mia ragazza; V.S. mi perdoni, se troppo l'incomodo. Averei ancora desiderio di trattare di un certo particolare col S.re Jacopo Soldani, ma per non aver io seco servitù né domestichezza tale che io m'ardissi a mandar a pregarlo che si pigliasse fastidio di venir a casa mia, se a V.S. venisse qualche occasione (venendo forse egli a casa dsua) di poterlo condur Lei da me, gliene resterei con obbligo particolare; se non potrà, pazienza. Con questa la reverisco, e pregandola a perdonarmi se troppo ardisco d'infastidirla, l'augurio da N.S. ogni desiderata felicità. Di casa alli 14 dicembre 1634. Di V. S. Molto Ill.re / per servirla sempre prontissima: / Francesca Raffaelli

33. I-FcasaB, A.B. 52, no. 1544, letter to Michelangelo Buonarroti, 14 September 1635

Moltto Ill.re signor mio Oss.mo

L'apportatrice di questa sarà Mona Lisabetta vedova e poverissima, la quale ha fatto una figliuola monaca nelle Convertite d e tutto di limosine. Io le ho fatto aver limosina dalle Ser.me S.re Principesse; e da molte altre signore adesso io so che V.S. è solito a far molto carità, e perchè il suo S.r Nipote è de' Buonuomini di San Martino, ho voluto provare se io potessi farli avere un poca di limosina, per ciò supplico V.S. a farmi grazia raccomandar detta donna a detto suo nipote che se può, e se ha niente da dispensare, le voglia fare un poca di limosina per poter comprare alcune cose necessarie a detta sua figliuola con alcune altre elemosine che le sono state fatte: questa è una buona donna, e la detta sua figliuola è una buona serva di Dio, come a suo tempo meglio le significherò in voce; mi perdoni la sicurtà, mentre la reverisco e le prego da Dio ogni felicità. Di casa alli 14 di settembre 1635 / Di V.S. Molto Ill.re / Servitrice / Francesca Raffaelli

34. I-Fas, MdP 1454, letter to Ortenzia Salviati, 9 February 1635/36

Ill.ma Signora Prona mia Col.ma

Per ovviare a scandali notabili, supplico V.S. Ill.ma a farmi grazia di ottener da Madama Ser.ma grazia di poter spender la sua parola in un negozio del quale le tratterà per me la S.ra Selvaggia Medici, da poiché non posso parlare io con V.S. Ill.ma, nemmeno a Madama Ser.ma; e così, oltre allo spenderla parola di S.A.S., procuri ottener licenza di poter trattare il negozio detto. Ci sarebbe ancora necessità di intercedere da S.A.S. tanta grazia che lei volessi per carità pigliarsi cura di far, mettere in qualche monastero se non di monache per amor della spesa, almeno di fanciulle la Dianora figliuola della mia matrigna che con 16 scudi di l'anno che lei ha da sé, e col favore di Madama, penso che si troverebbe. Signora V.S. Ill.ma è informata del tutto e sa benissimo come codesta fanciulla è restata si può dire senza alcuno che per lei sia salvo che per tanti giorni quanti bastino per cavarli di mano se averà niente. Sua madre si seppellì iermattina e mi duole non poter parlare sino a 23 del presente a Mad.ma Ser.ma però non potendo la supplico per quanto può abbracciar questa causa / [v:] che non si affaticherà senza merito poiché oltre alla carità ovvierà a molti scandali, che sono stati, e sono per nascere. Com'io possa parlare in voce potrò esplicarle quello che non si può per lettera. Basta che Madama ha fatto e fa continuamente simili opere pie e a persone che non hanno quel merito di servitù con la Ser.ma Casa che ha avuto mio padre d'anni 60 e la mia matrigna d'anni 22 e io di tutto'l tempo che ho. Le fo reverenza e la supplico a perdonarmi il fastidio che le do. Con pregarle da Dio ogni felicità. Di casa alli 9 di febbraio 1635 / Di. V.S. Ill.ma / Servitrice obbligatissima / Francesca Raffaelli

35. I-Fas, MdP 1454, letter to Ugo Caciotti, 11 February 1635/36

Molto Ill.re e molto R.do S.r mio oss.mo

Non fu mai mio pensiero di ritirarmi in casa la figliuola della mia matrigna mia sorella, perchè io non posso aggravare il mio figliuolo di tale spesa, ed incomodo di casa, ma sebbene, se ell'avesse avuto comodità e dote a sufficienza, e che si fosse potuto metterla in qualche luogo pio. Ma se non si potrà, ho giudicato che sia bene e che sia necessario, il suo fratello se la ritiri in casa sua sotto la sua custodia, e che lui non possa fuggirlo, sí che io già ho eseguito il pensiero e volontà di Madama Ser.ma:

e supplico V.S. a farmi grazia di baciar la veste per me a S.A.S. e ringraziarla umilmente in mio nome dell'onore che mi fa in aver avuto pensiero all'interessi di mia sorella; con che a V.S. bacio le mani con pregarle da N.S. ogni felicità. Firenze alli 11 di febbraio 1635 / Di V.S. Molto Ill.ri e molto R.do / Servitrice / Francesca Raffaelli

36. I-FcasaB, A.B. 52, no. 1545, letter to Michelangelo Buonarroti, 25 May 1636

Molto Ill.re Signor mio Oss.mo

Certe monache, m'hanno domandato con molta instanza, certe canzonette spirituali, composte (dicono) da V.S. sopra il metro medesimo di certe canzonette di Mantova, e rispondendogli io che non le ho (sí come è la verità) m'hanno replicato, che dico così, per non dargliene. Però mi sono resoluta di pregar V.S. che mi voglia far grazia di risposta a questa mia; acciò veghino dall'istessa sua risposta, che io in effetto non le ho; e che e quando V.S. volesse favorirmene d'alcuna, io l'ho domandate a lei adesso, e non l'avevo prima. La prego ancora a perdonarmi se troppo l'infastidisco, e per fine le fo reverenza. Di Casa il di 25 di maggio 1636 / Di V.S. molto Ill.re / per serverla sempre prontissima / Francesca Raffaelli

37. I-FcasaB, A.B. 52, no. 1546, letter to Michelangelo Buonarroti, 14 December 1636

Molto Ill.re Signor mio Oss.mo

Madonna Maddalena si raccomanda alla cortesia di V.S. e le ricorda quella carità che per me le fece domandare. Sta a casa dirimpetto alla rimessa della Signora Ortenzia Salviati dietro all'Annunziata la sua casa è al numero 27 e si ha a domandare di Madonna Maddalena Quorelli Vedova. Io la raccomando a V.S. e l'assicuro che la sua necessità è più grande assai di quella che io le significai. V.S. ci perdoni il fastidio, mentre le fo reverenza, e le prego da Dio ogni felicità. Di Casa alli 14 Dicembre 1636 / Di VS M.to Ill.re / per servirla prontissima / Francesca Raffaelli

38. I-Fas, MdP 1454, letter to Ugo Caciotti, 19 December 1636

Molto Ill.re Signor mio oss.mo

La Signora Ortenzia Salviati m'ha mandato a dire che aveva mandato il mandato dei 2 denari dell'abito della mia figliola al Signor Bufolini perché me li pagassi e avendo io mandato a pigliarli, m'ha fatto sapere che è restato con V.S. di far negoziare il memoriale con Madama Ser.ma e che subito negoziato V.S. gliene averebbe mandato; ma che sino adesso non l'ha per ancor ricevuto, però io ho preso espediente di mandare a supplicarla che mi voglia far grazia di sollecitare il detto memoriale sapendo che sta a lei acciò la mia figliuola possa avere in questo Natale il suo abito del quale ha di bisogno, ché ormai poco tempo ci resta; so qual sia la cortesia di V.S. e però, rimettandomi e confidandomi in quella, resto facendole reverenza e pregandole da Dio ogni felicità. Di Firenze alli 19 di dicembre 1636 / Di V.S. Molto Ill.re e molto R.do / Servitrice / Francesca Raffaelli

39. I-FcasaB, A.B. 52, no. 1547, letter to Michelangelo Buonarroti, 10 July 1637

Molto Ill.re signor mio Oss.mo

Prego V.S., per mia quiete, a farmi sapere se il mio instrumento è in camera del Signor P. Leopoldo, come mi disse Maso sarto e accordatore. Se però V.S. l'avesse inteso dal Signor Jacopo Soldani perché io ne sto con grand sospensione d'animo e caso che ci sia (come pur voglio credere) se il detto Signor Principe Leopoldo avesse inclinazione di comprarlo, mi farà grazia singulare V.S. a procurare d' col detto Signor Jacopo che le compri, ché si avrò per grazia grandissima che l'abbia più il S.r Principe che un'altro. In caso non lo voglia, V.S. mi farà favore grandissimo a procurare che il detto S.r Jacopo me lo faccia riportare a casa; acciò io lo posso dar via ad altri. V.S. mi perdoni che ben conosco usar con lei quella sicurtà che non devo, ma la mia costellazione di questi tempi mi sforza ad usar male creanze senza mia volontà e senza mia colpa. Le fo reverenza e le prego da Dio ogni bene. Di casa alli 10 di luglio 1637 / Di V.S. Molto Ill.re / Servitrice / Francesca Raffaelli

40a. I-Rasc, F.O., 1st ser., 186/3, no. 405, letter to Paolo Giordano Orsini, 18 June 1641

Ill.mo ed Ecc.mo S.r mio Padrone Col.mo

Mi ritrovo presentemente in urgente necessità di trasferirmi in codesta città per negozio che infinitamente mi preme; dal quale potrei esserci trattenuta circa un mese e mezzo al più, e dovendo io far capitale dell'alloggio di qualche amico, o padrone per detto tempo; per la servitù e devozione, che sino dalla nascita ho professato all'Ecc.mo Signor D. Virginio Padre di V.E. di felice memoria in tutto'l tempo, che detto S.re abitò in questa città, e che egli visse, di che V.E. molto bene può ricordarsi, e perché oltre di questo la prima volta ch'io venni in codesta città S.E. si compiacque onorarmi di darmi alloggio in casa sua a Monte Giordano, con quelle carezze, e onori, che mai mi scorderò, e che a ciascheduno sono noti; comandandomi di più che per mie occorrenze in codesta città, io non facessi mai capitale d'altra casa; per la medesima servitù adunque e devozione che io conservo, e professo a V.E. e le professerò sempre, non mi ardirei far capitale d'altro alloggio e protezione che della sua, sino a che da lei io non ne fossi licenziata; e per ciò per vera osservanza e affetto di servitù, io ho voluto significarle questa mia occorrenza di venire costà, per soddisfare al debito di vera serva, e alla mia infinita obligazione; acciò V.E. mi faccia grazia farmi sapere la sua volontà; perché (come vede) siamo in stagione che non / [v:] mi permette più trattenermi a venire, la prego, e supplico a voler perdonarmi questo ardire che ho usato con lei, perché mi ha dato questo animo, e questa confidenza, l'infinita sua bontà e benignità, e quella sua naturale cortesia alla quale ognuno che la serve si riconosce obbligato. Servirò sempre a V.E. e all'Ecc.ma Signora Duchessa sua, con tutte le mie forze e deboli talenti, in tutto che da loro Ecc.ze mi sarà comandato, e per fine devotamente e umilmente ad ambedue m'inchino. Firenze il dì 18 di giugno 1641 / Di V.E. Ill.ma / Umilissima e obligatissima Serva / Francesca Caccini Raffaelli//

40b. I-Rasc, F.O.. 1st ser., 310/2, no. 411, file copy of a letter to Francesca Caccini Raffaelli, 22 June 1641

Francesca Caccini Raffaelli

~~Ho della lettera di~~ Ho inteso dalla sua del 18 corrente il bisogno che ella ha di trasferirsi qua per un poco di tempo e come avrebbe gustato d'aver comodità ~~d'l~~ di potersene star ~~qui in quanto~~ in casa mia come ha fatto altre volte[.] In risposta devo dirle che mi trovo ~~di ogni~~ tutto il palazzo occupato perché, oltre alla famiglia mia ordinario, ho di più in casa il S.r Duca Sforza e la sua gente di maniera, che non mi resta un borso vacante; resto ben io con sentimento di non la poter dar questo comodo ~~servire~~ conforto e averei desiderato acciò ella continuasse il possesso che ha di valersi di questa casa ~~come potrà farvi altre occasione~~ desidero ben d'aver altre occasione ~~di poterli~~ d'impiegarmi in suo servizio e senz'altro [?preghi]

Cristoforo Bronzini,
Della dignità e nobiltà delle donne,
I-Fn, Magl. VIII, 1525/1, 54–77

Leonora: Vi ramenterei certo con particolar gusto la nostra virtuosissima Cecchina, ovvero Francesca, sorella della suddetta Settimia e figliuola anch'ella del celebratissimo Giulio Romano (musico e compositore famosissimo, e il primo inventore di quelle bellissime canzonette e arie di cantar maestrevole che oggi si cantono con tanto delicatezza e leggiadria appò ogni virtuoso e nobil spirito). E se il padre già diede in luce composizioni vaghissime, e questa rara e virtuosa donna sua figliuola non solamente ha dato in luce opere musicali molto pregiate, ma composto all'improvviso bellissime ode e artifiziosissimi versi latini, accompagnati poi da lei con suono e canto (come tante volte ha fatto e fa udire), e vedesse non solamente nella mia diletta e fortunata patria Fiorenza alla presenze delle Ser.me Altezze, dalle / [55] quali ed ella ed il ~~Signore Giovanni Battista Signorini Malaspina~~ suo consorte (virtuosissimo anche egli) vennero già nobilmente e liberalissimam.te ~~trattenuto e~~ trattati ma anco in altri principalissimi luoghi, alla presenza di grandissimi principi (e particolarmente in Roma, in Parigi, in Turino, in Milano, in Padova, in Verona, in Venezia, in Genova, in Parma, in Modena, in Bologna e in altri felicissimi stati che per brevità tralascio, dove molt'altre rare e virtuose persone si trovavano). E veramente che alle suddette donne (da voi così altamente celebrate di sopra) non solo si mostrò la nostra Cecchina (e tuttavia si mostra) di uguale eccellenza nella musica e nel sonare eccellentissimamente, sopra l'arpa, l'arpicordo, il liuto, la tiorba, e chitarra, con ogni sorte d'instrumento di corde, e cantarvi sopra con molta grazia, in lingua latina, ode artificiosissima composte da lei medesima, ma vi canta ancora le ode di Orazio, gl'eroici versi di Vergilio, con bellissimo pronuncio, ed arie italiane maravigliose, oltre le francese, e spagnuole e le tedesche, ridotte da lei in arie bellissime, e le composizione in lingua naturale genovese non più udite da altri sin qui, con passaggi difficilissimi, dolci ed artificiosissimi. E nelle invenzioni e sue rare composizioni, non è forse chi la superi e pochi appresso che l'agguaglino; la cui eccellenza / [56] nel comporre fa bene spesso stupire i più leggiadri cigni di Fiorenza, come dalle tante bramate opere sue, date in luce l'anno milleseicentodiciott' e intitolato *Il primo libro delle musiche a una, e due voci di Francesca* Cacci ~~Cacci~~ Caccini ~~ne'~~ *Signorini Malaspina* dedicate all'Ill.mo e R.mo allora Signore Cardinale de' Medici, si può vedere. Ma che oso io ragionare e dire di tante e tante rare qualità e parti di lei e della somma eccellenza nel canto e suono di questa veramente ~~miracolosa~~ maravigliosa e singolar Donna? La quale ancorché poco venisse favorita de doni di natura, fu ella nondimeno talmente amabile e mirabile che non punto tediosa, non punto rincrescevole ma lieta e graziosa, e prima di dolci e graziosissime maniere e modi a tutti si mostrava e tuttavia si mostra. E sempre sonando o cantando o piacevolmente favellando, oprava ed opra effetti di maniera stupendi negli animi degli ascoltanti, / [57] che gli trasmutava da quelli che erano. E per non esser tenuta né da voi né da altri né men da lei stessa (che sempre è stata amica della modestia e dell'onestà) troppo affezionata alle sue rare virtù, mi restringerò nel dirvi solamente che più volte essendom'io ritrovata con molte nobili persone, dove era lei, udimmo la meravigliosa donna accompagnare con tanta grazia, quando al suono d'un arpicordo, quando d'un liuto o di una tiorba, il suo canto Frigio, e operare effetti tanto stupendi negli animi degli ascoltanti che ora pieghevoli e piacevoli ed ora in tante altre guise gli disponeva, ché era un stupore e cosa nel vero quasi che incredibile. La stessa poi, ognivolta che a lei piaceva, cantando e sonando (non meno anzi vieppiù che il famoso musico Anfione) accendeva in modo tale i petti delle genti di stupore / [58] e di ardire che ad'ogni impresa (benché faticosa) si sarebbono poste. E altre volte di maniera alterava gli ascoltanti che (non meno del magno Alessandro, quando furioso e terribile, spaventando con gli atti, cercava l'armi per ucciderere [come uccise] il misero Clito un de piu suoi gran e amp'amici, il quale poiché l'ebbe morto, le pianse amaramente conoscendo che ingiustamenente ucciso l'aveva) gli faceva rimanere quasi insensati. Similmente a lei piacendo raddolciva la ferocità e la crudeltà de' cuori, con un canto talmente soave che faceva venire in loro voglie di maniera dolci, piacevoli ed umani, cosicché lasciate le noie da parte al dolce delle gioie, al giocondo del canto e al caro del suono, in cotal tono a sé li ritraeva. Altre volte, e particolarmente l'anno milleseicento e otto (e decimo ottavo della sua età) facendo ella sentire nelle regie e superbissimo nozze del Ser.mo Gran Duca Cosimo Secondo con la Ser.ma Arciduchessa d'Austria Maria Maddalena Gran Duchessa di Toscana, quella / [59] musica che Dorica si noma (la quale ha in se virtù d'innalzare il basso, e il terreno delle menti umane all'altezza delle contemplazioni ~~divine~~ sublimi) faceva con tal dolcezza salire le altrui menti alla contemplazione delle cose celesti che trasformava (oso qua se può dire) gl'uomini in dei.

Della musica Lidia che dirò io? La quale, udita, toglie in sì fatta guisa i manti di letizia al cuore e alla fronte che, solamente cinta del mesto delle malinconie e del denso delle nubi oscure, piena rimane solmente del pianto?

Queste tre maniere di musica (cioè Frigia, Dorica e Lidia), già molto dalla veneranda antichità poste (secondo l'occasioni) in uso, non pure da questa nostra rara donna si udivano apprese ma, in somma eccellenza e con sommo giudizio, a tempo usate. Né solamente queste tre maniere di canti ma molt'altre appresso eccellentissimamente la nostra mirabile Cecchina possedeva, le quali, essendo varie, anco vari effetti / [60] creavano nelle menti umane. Alcune delle quali piegavano l'iracondo del cuore alla piacevolezza della mansuetudine e alcune il lascivo delle volontà d'altrui al lodato della temperanza. Costei, col soave suono de' stromenti e col dolce del suo canto, invitava ogni petto (benché inimico di caste voglie) alla pura continenza ed onestà, per la cui virtù biancheggiava la di lei pudicizia ed onestà al pari delle più nominate in questa virtù. Alcune altre maniere ella ancora ne possedeva che lo infermo ed il debole del languente corpo, al bramato della sanità e al fermo della gagliardia, traevano; ma parmi di tacere per non venirvi a noia come forse potrebbe dubitare.

Tolomeo: Voi Signora Leonora (più che non fece già il Signor Onorio con quell'altra di nazione senese) di maniera procedete nelle lodi di questa vostra compatriota e virtuosa giovane che / [61] qualunque persona vi ode, ode voi al certo e vede lei vivamente al sicure.

Leo.: Sappiate Signore Tolomei ch'io non ne ho detto (si può dir) quasi nulla e che fin qui ha basciato di linearvi le principali, le più nobili e le più importanti parti di questa veramente virtuosa donna, della quale, sebbene mi potria bastare dirvi solamente che, essendo ella eccellentissima nella musica e nella geometria, sia anco eccellentissima in ogni cosa, poscia che (come ci scrisse P.sello) non è cosa al mondo fatta senza geometria e senza musica, tuttavia, per maggiore vostra e nostra sodisfatione insieme, vo' soggiugnervi di più: che, essendo la Cecchina fanciulla di acutissimo ingegno e datasi con spirito vivacissimo a compor versi, ne scrisse in vari soggetti elegantemente. Di dieci anni apprese benissimo le lettere latine e i principi delle lettere greche, nelle quali avrebbe fatto grandissimo progresso se la inopinata / [62] morte del suo caro maestro non se le interponeva, poscia che egli, per il bellissimo ingegno che vide in lei, li aveva già cominciata ad introdurre molto bene e nelle lettere greche e nella filosofia. Di dodici anni avendo udite Cicerone, Orazio, Ovidio e Vergilio, commentò da sua posta il Terzo e Quarto dell'Eneide; e se a lei fosse stato permesso (come già a Lastenia o Asiotea ed Asiate Falisca, eccellentissime nella filosofia, e discepole di Platone) di potere andare in abito virile alla pubbliche scuole e, come fanno oggi i nostri giovani, avrebbe senza forse fatto maggior riuscita che non fecero le già tanto famose ed altre nominate donne con altre persone de' nostri tempi che tanto s'inarborano. Cominciò anco in quella tenera età a imparare di scrivere dal Camerino (celebre scrittore del suo tempo) e fece tale e tanto onorata riuscita in questa professione che, avendo io veduti / [63] i suoi scritti e libri interi distesi di sua mano, gli giudicai più tosta opera del Maestro che scritture fatte da lei. Con tutto ciò alla presenza mia scrivendo ella con buona occasione alcune cose notate da lei, vidi con questi miei occhi la virtuosa giovane scrivere con tanta bella maniera e con sì bel carattere alcune lettere di cancelleresca corsiva formata che ne restai stupite.

Tol.: Attese ella ad altro?

Leo.: Attese oltre a ciò a tutte le sorti di belle e buone lettere: alla Umanità, alla Rettorica e alla Poesia; e però udì anco la Poetica d'Aristotele. (Commentò da se stessa i principali Poeti Latini e in breve sommario cavò da quello quanto giudicò poterle ritornare ad utile e fruttuoso acquista.) Attese anco alla sfera, nella quale e nell'Astrologia fece grandissimo profitto. Fu curiosissima di scienze occulte e se da persone spirituali non le venivano vietate, vi avrebbe fatta mirabile riuscita, tanto vi si trovava inclinata. / [64] Il minor studio ch'ella facesse in così tenera età ed anco sino alle tredici e quattordici anni (se bene di sette la fece il Signor Giulio suo padre cantare in Firenze alcune maestrevole, anzi maestevoli, arie e canzoni alla presenza della Serenissima Maria Medici e Cristianissima Regina di Francia, allora sposa) era tuttavia minore quello della Musica, del canto e del suono, ché se lo prendeva come per passatempo e più per compiacerne il Padre che per altro. Nientedimeno e nel canto e nel suono riuscì poi tanto eccellente che l'anno milleseicentotto e decimottavo della sua età (come si è detto) nelle nozze del Ser.mo Grand Duca con la Ser.ma Arciduchessa fece quella rara riuscita nel canto ed altre bellissime composizioni e invenzioni, che a tutto Italia e Francia fu nota.

Tol: Non fia maraviglia però che la Cecchina riuscisse così eccellente nella Musica (poiché ordinariamente di buon seme ne suol venire / [65] buon frutto) avendo ella dal ventre della madre recata quest'Arte, essendo che Lucia Gangoletti prima moglie di suo padre (la quale a suo tempo volle sentire il nostro Duca di Ferrara, che sia in gloria) fu non meno che Giulio Romano, suo genitore, eccellentissima e veramente mirabile nel canto? Ma seguite.

Leo.: Cominciò poi questa giovane, a compiacenza del Serenissimo Grand Duca Ferdinando Primo di felice ricordazione e di Madama Serenissima Gran Duchessa CRISTINA, Principessa di Lorena, sua signora e benefattrice singolarissima che nobilmente la maritò ~~nel sudetto signor Giovambattista Musico~~, et / [66] ~~virtuoso giovane (acciochè più egli da lei che lei da lui apparisse)~~ ad applicar l'animo al contrappunto e a passaggi; e in breve tempo, essendosi impadronita dell'uno e degli altri, fece composizioni tali che da primi uomini della professione e da Principi grandi furono poi sommamente stimate, richieste e pregiate.

Nell'Aritmetica e nelle sue / [67] numerose composizioni tenne sempre così bell'ordine e misura che le opere sue scritte a penna da lei non paion scritte per mano di donna ma stampate (anzi diligentemente intagliate per mano di eccellentissima persona in quest'arte); e con tutto che ella (come inimicissima dell'ozio ed amicissima delle virtuose fatiche; e come conosciuta per virtuosissima e per singolare in questa professione della Musica) si trovasse occupatissima nel comporre di continuo nuove foggie di canti che da diverse bande le venivano richieste e di proprio pugno le riscrivesse / [68] tutte e bene e in bonissima forma; ed oltre a ciò scrivesse anco ogni settimana più di una ventina di lettere a diversi Signore e Signori (per non mancare della sua natural gentilezza e creanza in rispondere ad ogniuno) con tutto ciò (dico) in due soli mesi di estate e nel maggior fervore del caldo compose, scrisse ~~di sua mano~~ e rescrisse di sua mano, in buona forma, tali e tante grande opere (vedute da me) che non so se uomo alcuno (per diligente che si fosse) in due anni continui avesse fatto o potuto mai fare quanto ella fece in que' due soli mesi. E forse ch'ella attese a compor' bagattelle? Signori no, percioché fece composizioni rarissime, latine e vulgari; spirituali e secolari; sopra poesie morali de' più famose poeti che abbino composto ode di Orazio; madrigali, sonetti, canzoni, salmi, motetti, inni ed altre opera spirituali / [69] d'ogni genere. E tuttavia in questa sua età di ventiotto anni, per la copia grandissima di che abbonda nel comporre, si sarebbe di nuovo posta a dar nuove cose in luce se, da' Medici e dalle Ser.me Altezze (per conservazione del suo individuo che da grave infirmità veniva oppresso) non le fosse stato ciò vietato. Taccio però molti altri particolari per non parere di essere troppo affezionata alle (già da tanti e tant'altri) celebrate virtù di lei; bastandomi sol dire in poche parole come già d [indecipherable passage crossed out] (con occasione dei stupendi e rarissimi concerti fatti la Settimana Santa in Firenze, nella chiesa di Santa Felicita, l'anno 1618, alla presenza di tutte le Ser.me Altezze e di nobiltà innumerabile) sentendo, oltre le altre virtuose donne che vi erano, cantare e sonare questa nostra virtuosissima Cecchina, e sola e in compagnia, e / [70] passeggiare e gorgheggiare a concorrenza con trilli bellissimi, anzi maravigliosissimi, eccellentemente scrisse e cantò di lei il valoroso Gismondo Santi, dicendo:

> Era'l dì, che per darne eterna vita
> Morte (sofferse Cristo acerba, e vile)
> Quando con Dame d'Arno in schiera unita
> In sacro Tempio entrò Donna gentile
> Tra le Muse, e le Musiche nodrita;
> Si ch'altra il sol non vide a lei simile.
> O nel tentar de le sonore corde.
> O nel temperar la voce al suon concorde.
>
>   Non quel cantor, che sovra a vivo legno
> L'onde fren cruciose, e'l vent'insano;
> Non quelche die cantando in cieco Regno
> A le fere, a le furie affetto umano;
> Non quel, che tratto i sassi al suo sì degno
> Plettro, il famoso alzò Muro Tebano,
> Può darsi al par di lei mirabil vanto
> D'esser emol de' gli Angeli nel canto
>
> [71]   Già con la voce il cantor Regio Ebreo
> E de' l'Arpe colpio nobil concerto
> Un infernal placava Angiolo Reo
> Al Rege ossesso il duol rendendo spento;
> Ella or fugar col doppio stil poteo
> Ogni nostro dell'alma aspro tormento;
> Ed'emola di lui col bel concerto
> Chiuder l'Inferno, il Ciel mostrarne aperto
>   O se quel gran Pittor, ch'al vivo espresse

D'ogni beltà l'esempio insieme accolto,
Poiché i più bei sembianti uniti messe.
Che vide in mille volti, in un sol volto,
così pennellegiar ancor potesse
D'ogni dolcezza un musical raccolto
Via più facil impresa a lui sarìa
Trovando in lei perfetta ogn'armonia.

    Di Partenope il Mar va risonando
Famoso per nutrir Cigni, e Sirene
Se stessi uccidon quei, dolce cantando
Queste apporton'altrui funeste pene;
[72] L'Arno sen' va più, che quel mar gloriando;
Che quest'armoniava in sen mantiene
Questa, ch'a' forza di Musiche note
Dar alla morte ancor la Vita puote.

    Dai cigni già nudrì l'Arno, canori
Che'l volo in fra la schiera ebber sublime,
Mentre un di Beatrice alzò gli onori,
L'altro di Laura i pregi in saggie rime;
Reca a l'Arno or costei glorie maggiori
Vantando in fra cantor le lodi prime,
Che non sol bei concetti in carmi espone;
Ma in Musica, e gli canta, e gli compone.

    S'ella godea di questa luce allora
Che Giove diede in luce il nume biondo
De le muse, a la squadra alta, e canora;
Perch'avea stile, a null'a altro secondo,
Pari emola d'Apollo eletta fora
Stata per guida in fra lo stuol giocondo;
Più, ch'un lascivo Dio degna ben'era
Diva imperara a virginale schiera.

[73]   E certo il sommo Musico immortale,
Che'l tutto in armonia mantiene, e crea
Della Musica eterna al Mondo frale
Volse lasciare armoniosa Idea
Infondendo in costei benché mal mortale
Armonie' alma di canora Dea
Perche'l concento suo dolce, e sonoro
Sia scala a quel de l'alto empireo coro

    Pria le corde or ritira, ed'or rallenta
Volgendo, e rivolgendo i lor mariti
Da quelle intorno avinti, a fare intenta
In discorde, concordia i suoni uniti,
Indi le fila armoniose tenta,

L'avide orecchie altrui con bassi inviti
Lusingando al concento al fine in tuono
Alto soavemente afforza il suono.

    Se melodia sì dolce al fonte in riva
Spars'avesse Minerva, e con tal'arte
La canna, ch'allor ruppe, intera, e viva
farebbe risona' per ogni parte;

[74] Tarda or le corde, unite insieme avviva
Presta or fiede, disgiunte a parte a parte,
Poscia la lingua scioglie, e varie sempre
Fabbre gentil di note, affina tempre.

    Or la volubil voce in arco tende,
Or la vibra, or la sparge, ora l'unisce,
Or l'allunga, or l'annoda, ora la fende,
Or l'assottiglia, e inalza, or la smarrisca,
Ora la tempra grave, e bassa rende,
Or l'innaspa, e l'inaspra, or l'addolcisce,
Segnando a tempo i musicali viaggi,
Or con trilli or con groppi, or con passaggi.

    Tal'or per false note il volo affretta,
E volontaria tempera durezze,
Ma mentre offender par, via più diletta
Scoprendo più l'armoniche dolcezze;
Tal a l'amor, amata Dama alletta
Gl'amanti più con sdegnosette asprezze;
Così col dolce il medico l'amaro
Mischia ad arte, e il Pittor l'oscur col chiaro.

[75]   Or lieta intesse, or melodia languente
Conforme a la parola allegra, o mesta,
Tal di pianti, e di canti empie sovente
Musico Rusigniol natia foresta,
L'unisona allor trattare si sente
Talor sovra a la quinta, il canto annesta
Or tra tutte s'avvolge, ed or di salto
Or per grado sen vola, or basso, or alto

    Or la voce in tre note intreccia al quanto
E triplicata forma, alt'armonia
Accompagnando co' sembianti intanto
In vago moto l'intrecciata via;
Poi quando vuol troncar l'ultimo canto
Nunzi, fia più canori, avanti in via,
Su la nota penultima s'aggira,
E dopo gran tirata al fin' respira.

    Veduto avresti intento ogn'uditore

Mentre'il canto durò, non batter ciglio
Bramoso, ch'a quel giorno eterni l'ore
Fermando il carro di Latona il figlio
[76]   E queste poi le melodie canore
Applauso far con placido bisbiglio;
Rimanendo ciascun da sé diviso
Col corpo in terra, e l'alma in Paradiso.

Priore: Bellissime ottave nel vero; degne di chi le fece e molto più di questa meritevol Donna, per cui furono fatte. Ora seguite, Sigora Leonora.

Leo: Seguirei volentieri, certo, e certo più che volentieri vi rementerei anco quale l'altra composizione bella "…..Bellissima Oda" fatta in lode di questa virtuosissima Donna da ingegno graziosissimo in Firenze e in Lucca, dove ora si trova nobilmente maritata; ma temo di non v'essere noiosa.
[Folio 76v includes another poem about Francesca, crossed out.]
"con speranza, che sia per aggradirle, se no altri; le signori votre almeno

Del Fonte di'Hippocrene.
Porgimi l'onda, ov'è più chiara, e fresca
Ond'io tra le sirene
Innalzi o febo, l'immortal FRANCESCA
Prestami l'aurea cetra; e questi accenti
Sian'meraviglie a le future genti.
Da Genitor' famoso [cioe Giulio romano]
De' bei studi d'Apollo ancor non stanco
Da' cigno armonioso
Tanto canoro più, quanto più bianco
Nacque Musa dell'Arno, onor di Flora
Cui riverente ancor l'Invidia onora.
Se con'nervose corde
Su varie cetre, o con le fila d'oro
All'Armonia concorda
Avvivò dotta man' legno canoro
Ben dimostrò che di valor sovrano
Però con gli Accenti contrastar la Mano
Dolcemente sospiri,
Mille note ricerchi in un momento
77:    Mentre non falsa gloria a lei s'ascriva
Invinicibil' e'l vero, e non s'oscura
Finta lode trapassa, o poco dura.

Notes

PREFACE

1. Adriano de la Fage, "La prima compositrice di opera in musica, e la sua opera," *Gazzetta musicale di Milano* 6, no. 45 (10 November 1847), 344–358. See also Romain Rolland, *Histoire de l'opéra en Europe avant Lully et Scarlatti* (Paris: E. Thorin, 1895), 114–115; August Ambrose, *Geschichte der Musik* (Leipzig: Leuchart, 1909), 4:295–296; Hugo Goldschmidt, *Studien zur Geschichte des italienischen Oper in 17. Jahrhundert* (Leipzig: Breitkopf & Härtel, 1901–1904), 1:174–179; and Federico Ghisi, "Ballet Entertainment in the Pitti Palace," *Musical Quarterly* 35 (1949): 421–436.

2. Cristoforo Bronzini, *Della dignità e nobiltà delle donne*, I-Fn, Magliabecchiana (hereafter Magl.) VIII. 1525/1, 56. See appendix C for a complete transcription of his sketch of Caccini. Like many courtly treatises, Bronzini's is in the form of a dialogue.

3. Bronzini, *Della dignità e nobiltà*, 50. No authenticated portraits of either Francesca or Settimia survive, although Cristofano Allori is known to have painted a miniature of Francesca in 1607, the year she married and entered the Medici's service. The portrait is mentioned in a poem that Gabriele Chiabrera addressed to the painter, "Mentre di più per te nascea," printed in Chiabrera, *Delle opere* (Venice: Geremia, 1730), 1:127–130, and in a family tree of the Caccini di Roma at I-Fr, MS 2098, fol. 127. The art historian Lisa Goldenberg-Stoppato speculates that this is the same miniature that Christine de Lorraine offered to send to Francesco Gonzaga of Mantua in 1621 and that it now hangs in Florence's Uffizi Gallery. Warren Kirkendale has persuasively argued that the cameo silhouette inscribed "Cecchina pulchritudinis immortalitati" and now owned by Wellesley College in Wellesley, Massachusetts, is a portrait not of Francesca but of a Florentine courtesan whose surname was Cecchina, not Caccini. See his *Emilio de' Cavalieri, Gentilhuomo Romano: His Life and Letters: His Role as Superintendent of All the Arts at the Medici Court, and His Musical Compositions.* Historia Musicae Cultores 86 (Florence: Olschki, 2001), 444.

4. For more on poems praising Francesca, see chapter 4.

5. Bronzini, *Della dignità e nobiltà*, 56.

6. Ibid., 56–57.

7. Adriana Cavarero, *Relating Narratives: Storytelling and Selfhood*, trans. Paul A. Kottman (London: Routledge, 2000; first published as *Tu che mi guardi, tu che mi racconti*, Milan: Feltrinelli, 1997).

8. On Buonarroti's contributions to seventeenth-century comedy, see Massimiliano Rossi, "Capricci frottole e tarsia di Michelangelo Buonarroti il giovane," *Studi secenteschi* 36 (1999): 151–180; Massimiliano Rossi, "I divertimenti accademici di Michelangelo Buonarroti il giovane (1568–1646)," in *Passare il tempo: La letterature del gioco e dell'intrattenimento del XII al XVI secolo* (Rome: Salerno Editrice, 1993), 777–789.

9. I-Fn, Magl. VIII. 1513–1538, includes the text of the four published volumes of Bronzini's *Della dignità e nobiltà delle donne* (Florence: Zanobi Pignoni, 1622–1634) along with eighteen volumes of fair-copy text (many with a second part consisting of draft material) that had been prepared for printing but never published and a three-volume index. I am extremely grateful to Kelley Harness for directing my attention to these volumes many years ago, in personal correspondence. For a more detailed account of Bronzini's ideas on music, see Suzanne Cusick, "Francesca among Women: A *Seicento* Gynecentric View," in *Musical Voices of Early Modern Women: Many-Headed Melodies*, ed. Thomasin LaMay, 425–445 (Burlington, VT: Ashgate, 2005).

10. Born near Ancona about 1580, Bronzini entered the Medici's service in 1615 after successful service as *caudatario* to several cardinals, the last of whom was Evangelista Pallotta. Once in the Medici's service, he began to frequent Florentine literary circles, becoming especially close to Baccio Bandinelli. He is known to have corresponded with the Venetian proto-feminist Lucrezia Marinelli, who visited him in Rome in 1624. Bronzini is believed to have died in Florence about 1640. On *Della dignità*, see especially chapter 9 and Constance Jordan, *Renaissance Feminism* (Ithaca: Cornell University Press, 1990).

11. Cristoforo Bronzini, *Della dignità e nobiltà delle donne: Settimana prima, Giornata prima* (Florence: Zanobi Pignoni, 1624) (hereafter Bronzini 1624), sig. H8v, as quoted in Jordan, *Renaissance Feminism*, 267.

12. Bronzini 1624, as quoted in Jordan, *Renaissance Feminism*, 266. See also her note 14, where she cites the original of this passage to sig. Bv.

13. I-Fn, Magl. VIII. 1525/1, 60. See appendix C.

14. Virginia Woolf, *A Room of One's Own* (London: Hogarth, 1929).

15. This concept of "aria" has very little to do with the notion, prevailing since the turn of the eighteenth century, that "aria" means a long, elaborate, song-like expression of emotion in an opera or oratorio. In the early seventeenth century, arias were by definition narrative responses to strophic poetry. Variations of the same aria—a tune with its harmonic support—were sung to a poem's successive stanzas to elaborate its conceits.

CHAPTER 1

1. I-Fd, Battesimi Femmine 1587, fol. 12v. Francesca's baptismal record contradicts the year of birth given in I-Fn, MS II.____.-105, fol. 85r, the horoscope used by Alessandro Ademollo and others as a source of biographical information about her. They also contradict a well-known passage in a dispatch of the Modenese ambassador Ercole Cortile of 8 April 1589 that described Giulio Caccini as childless, as part of a report on his suitabil-

ity for appointment to the staff of the Este dukes at Ferrara. See Anthony Newcomb, *The Madrigal at Ferrara* (Princeton: Princeton University Press, 1980), 58.

2. Pandolfo de' Bardi, d. 1599, was first cousin to the Giovanni de' Bardi who is well known to music historians. As *maestro di camera* to Francesco I de' Medici, he supervised all of the grand duke's public ceremonies and audiences. See Alessandro Magini, "I Conti de' Bardi di Vernio," in *Neoplatonismo, musica, letteratura nel Rinascimento: I de' Bardi di Vernio e L'Accademia della Crusca*, [Cahiers Accademia], ed. Piero Gargiulo, Alessandro Magini, and Stéphane Toussaint, 195–249 (Prato: Tipografia Cav. Alfredo Rindi, 2000), esp. 200–203. Rustico Piccardini is described as a "cavallerizzo," a horseman or riding master, on the grand duke's staff in 1598 in I-Fas, Manoscritti 131, fol. 80. By 1605 he was sufficiently valued to be served at the "tavolino" (little table) in the main dining room at Poggio a Caiano, along with "Signor Coloreto," "Signor Cosimo Medici," "Maestro Cesare Gualtieri," and the grand duke's maestro di casa, Ottaviano Buonaventura. See I-Fas, Carte Strozziane I, 30, fol. 112v.

3. On baptismal customs in Florence see Edward Muir, *Ritual in Early Modern Europe* (Cambridge: Cambridge University Press, 1997), 20–27. The ambivalence that greeted the birth of girls pervaded all levels of society, even the princely caste. See, e.g., I-Fas, MdP 66, fol. 42, draft letter of Ferdinando I de' Medici to Don Cesare d'Este, 13 April 1590, offering condolences on the birth of a daughter.

4. On the economic consequences of having female children, see Christiane Klapisch-Zuber, *Women, Family, and Ritual in Renaissance Italy*, trans. Lydia Cochrane (Chicago: University of Chicago Press, 1985), esp. chap. 5, 94–116, and chap. 6, 117–131.

5. The sale of Giulio's Fiesole property to Brucianese, witnessed by Medici court lutenist Cosimo Bottregari and a cloth worker named Fortunato Filippo, is recorded at I-Fas, Notarile Moderno, Protocolli 1993, Atti di Lorenzo Muti, 1588, fols. 54r–56r. As a favor to Giulio, Giovanni de' Bardi witnessed the signing of the receipt. Tax on the sale is recorded in I-Fn, Magliabecchiana (hereafter Magl.) XXVI. 139, 318, a copy of a notice presumed lost in Lib. Gab.D.236, fol. 134, no. 9: "M. Giulio di Michelagnolo Caccini Romano Musico di S.A.S. vende." The dowry contract for Francesca's marriage to Signorini is at I-Fas, Notarile Moderno, Protocolli 2171, Atti di Noferi Maccanti, 1607, item no. 36, fols. 26v–27v. I am grateful to Professor Gino Corti for his help in transcribing and translating these documents.

6. Cristoforo Bronzini, *Della dignità e nobiltà delle donne*, I-Fn, Magl. VIII. 1525/1, 54. See appendix C.

7. On the family origins of the Caccini, see Remo Giazotti, *Le due patrie di Giulio Romano* (Florence: Olschki, 1984). Michelangelo Caccini also had two daughters, Oretta and Dianora. The fullest biographical treatment of Giulio is in Warren Kirkendale, *The Court Musicians in Florence during the Principate of the Medici* (Florence: Olschki, 1993), 119–180.

8. I-Fas, Miscellanea Medicea 264, insert 20 H, "Ristretto del ruolo per l'anno 1586, Musici." See Kirkendale, *Court Musicians*, 119–120. By comparison, Francesca's godfather Pandolfo de' Bardi was paid 25.5.10 scudi per month. Giulio's salary suggests that he was held in very high regard.

9. See Howard Mayer Brown, "The Geography of Florentine Monody: Caccini at Home and Abroad," *Early Music* 9 (1981): 147–168. See Giazotti, *Le due patrie*, and Kirkendale, *Court Musicians*, 127–136, for this period in the life of the Caccini household.

10. Florentines resident at the French court of Henri IV and Marie de' Medici during the Caccini family's sojourn there in the winter of 1604–1605 complained about Giulio's bad manners. See chapter 2 for the particulars and for examples of Giulio's epistolary boastfulness.

11. Kirkendale, *Court Musicians*, 166, lists twenty-three musicians or amateurs who were Giulio's pupils. One letter about Giulio's financial dealings is at I-Rasc, F.O., 1st ser., 159/2, no. 303, 9 October 1615, cited by Kirkendale, *Court Musicians*, 158, n. 252. On p. 147 Kirkendale cites incompletely a 1603 letter from court major-domo Enea Vaini to his superiors that acknowledged that Giulio's wage might not match his usefulness and advocated that some supplement be found, either to accommodate the daughters or to help with brokerage commissions. The letter was first reported in Carlo Lozzi, "La musica e specialmente il melodramma alla corte medicea," *Rivista musicale italiana* 9 (1902): 297–338. Records in the Opera del Duomo in Florence show Giulio's known children to have been his "natural" son Pompeo (31 January 1579), born of an unknown woman; Francesca (18 September 1587), Giovanni Battista (25 June 1589), and Settimia (8 October 1591), born of Lucia Gagnolandi; and Michelangelo (3 August 1598), Dianora (27 September 1599), Giulio (20 April 1601), Lucia (7 June 1606), and Maria (known only by her death notice from December 1607), all born of Margherita della Scala. Giulio's will names another son, Scipione, whose baptismal record I have not found. In the 1620s, Francesca advocated for her *castrato* brother Scipione in the court's casting decisions. See chapter 5.

12. Timothy McGee recounts this tale in "Pompeo Caccini and 'Euridice': New Biographical Notes," *Renaissance and Reformation* 26 (1990): 81–99. I interpret the documents somewhat differently than does McGee, to whom I am grateful for several useful conversations about Caccini family dynamics. The first son of Pompeo and Ginevra, Jacopo Caccini, was baptized on 23 February 1603 in their parish of San Lorenzo. See I-Fd, Battesimi Maschi, 1602–1603, fol. 34.

13. Kirkendale, *Court Musicians*, 157–158, tells an abbreviated version of the story of Settimia's dowry.

14. To trace the story of this truly extraordinary imbroglio in chronological order, see I-Rasc, F.O., 1st ser., 159/3, no. 528, letter of Pier Federighi, 15 September 1615; 159/2, no. 323, letter of Vittoria Archilei, 2 October 1615; 159/2, no. 322, letter of Ottavio Archilei, 5 October 1615; 159/2, no. 303, letter of Giulio Caccini, 9 October 1615; 159/2, no. 520, letter of Camilla Orsini, 10 October; 159/4, no. 681, letter of Archduchess Maria Magdalena, 7 November 1615; 159/3, no. 476, letter of Pompeo Caccini, 9 November 1615; 159/2, no. 379, letter of Camilla Orsini, 14 November 1615; 159/2, no. 586, letter of Archduchess Maria Magdalena, 24 November 1615; 159/3, no. 435, letter of Ottavio Archilei, 24 November 1615; 159/3, no. 437, letter of Ottavio Archilei, 2 December 1615; and, finally, 159/1, no. 187, letter of Giulio Caccini thanking the person to whom all these letters were addressed, Paolo Giordano Orsini, for restoring his freedom as a favor to Archduchess Maria Magdalena, 7 December 1615.

15. Kirkendale, *Court Musicians*, 130–131, and nn. 138–140, based on I-Fas, MdP 844, fol. 74, and I-MOas Ambasciatori, Firenze, busta 35.

16. A trace of Giulio's agreement to the lease (*livello*) from the Arte della Lana is at I-Fn, Magl. XXVI. 133, p. 128: "M.o Giulio di Michelag.lo Caccini di Roma piglia a Livello dall'Arte della Lana. Franc.o Alba Cav.re di San Jacopo abita in Firenze Livello dall Arte

della Lana in Via de' Servi." A similar trace of Giulio's payment of tax on his second wife's dowry is at I-Fn, Magl. XXVI. 135, p. 134: "Giulio di Michelangnolo Caccini da Roma/Marg.ta di Agostino Bargialli." The paltry size of Margherita's dowry is recorded, possibly in error, in Giulio's first will, at I-Fas, Notarile Moderno 5503, Andrea Andreini, Testamento di 26 Dicembre 1612, fols. 1v–3v. On fol. 2r Giulio identified his second wife as Margherita "figliuola d'Agostino della Scala" and included restitution of her dowry among the debts that he acknowledged his estate owed her, alongside jewels and gifts worth six hundred scudi that she had received from the king of France that her husband had used for his own purposes and the three hundred scudi of her own money that she had spent to cover his medical expenses.

17. Kirkendale, *Court Musicians*, 119.

18. Adriana Basile, Giovanni de' Bardi, Michelangelo Buonarroti the younger, Gabriello Chiabrera, Ludovico Cardi (called il Cigoli), and the father-and-son painters Alessandro and Cristofano Allori, known as Bronzini, are among the best known of Giulio's frequent guests. See Kirkendale, *Court Musicians*, 159.

19. I-Fas, Otto di guardia e balìa, principato, 2793, fols. 29v–30v, deposition of Jacopo Cicognini in the trial of Sinolfo Ottieri, 27 March 1621.

20. On Molza's education and reputation, see Francesco Patrizi, *L'amorosa filosofia*, ed. John Charles Nelson (Florence: LeMonnier, 1963). On Nogarola, see Prudence Allen, *The Concept of Woman*, vol. 2, *The Early Humanist Reformation, 1250–1500* (Grand Rapids, MI: Eidmann, 2002), 944–969; Margaret L. King and Diana Robin, eds., *Isotta Nogarola: Complete Writings* (Chicago: University of Chicago Press, 2004).

21. Bronzini, *Della dignità*, 62. See appendix C. This list of subjects includes most of the disciplines that the theorist Giovanni Maria Artusi listed in his *L'Arte del contraponto ridotta in tavole* (Venice, 1586) as necessary to training a "musico perfetto," a person equally adept at musical theory and musical practice: if she lacked anything, it was training in history and dialectic. See Chadwick Jenkins, *"Ridotta alla perfettione:* Metaphysical History in the Musico-Theoretical Writings of Giovanni Maria Artusi," PhD diss., Columbia University, 2007.

22. Bronzini, *Della dignità*, 62. See appendix C.

23. Important to sustaining the sixteenth-century market for cheap printed books, most of this literature merely popularized tropes that had already circulated in Italian culture for a century. Three helpful English-language surveys of the literature about genteel womanhood are Ruth Kelso's *The Doctrine of the Renaissance Lady* (Urbana: University of Illinois Press, 1956), still the most comprehensive survey of the literature available in English; Ian MacLean's now-classic *The Renaissance Notion of Woman*, Cambridge Monographs in the History of Medicine (Cambridge: Cambridge University Press, 1980), which explicitly connects the expansion of a discourse about women and the fortunes of the printing industry; and Constance Jordan, *Renaissance Feminism* (Ithaca: Cornell University Press, 1990). Some important implications for music of the vast prescriptive literature concerning the creation of elite Renaissance women are skillfully drawn out by Stefano Lorenzetti in his monograph *Musica e identità nobiliare nell'Italia del Rinascimento: Educazione, mentalità, immaginario* (Florence: Olschki, 2003), esp. chap. 4, "L'altro polo."

24. Serafino Razzi, *Sermoni per le più solenne, così domeniche, come feste de' santi* (Florence: Bartolomeo Sermartelli, 1575), 211. See also Elissa Nova Chiavarra, "Ideologia e

comportamenti familiari nel predicatori Italiani tra Cinquecento e Settecento: Tematiche e Modelli," *Rivista storica italiana* 100, no. 3 (1988): 679–723, esp. 719–720 on the complexity of seventeenth-century ideas about virginity.

25. Leon Battista Alberti's highly influential *I Libri della famiglia* (1441) first defined the ideal Florentine wife. For a substantial summary of Alberti's argument, developed in and for the economic and political context of Florence, see Jordan, 47–53. Her note 53 on p. 47 provides further bibliography in English concerning Alberti's ideas. Renée Neu Watkins, *The Family in Renaissance Florence* (Columbia: University of South Carolina Press, 1969) is a translation with commentary of Alberti's *I Libri della famiglia.* Household governance is discussed in book 3.

26. The most widely known etiquette book of the sixteenth century, Baldassare Castiglione's *Il libro del cortigiano* (Florence: Giunta, 1528), is one of the many texts that elides the virtues of castità and continenza to create a distinctively female version of the latter. In book 3, devoted ostensibly to a description of the ideal courtly lady, the misogynist interlocutor Gasparo speaks of chastity and continence, entwined in women's behavior, serving men's interest in retaining certainty about their offspring and the passage of property from generation to generation.

27. This summary is based on the most often reprinted of the many treatises concerning womanhood, Ludovico Dolce's *L'istitutione delle donne* (Venice: G. Giolito de Ferrari, 1545). The last edition was published along with an edition of Angelo Firenzuola's *Le bellezze, le lodi, gli amori e i costumi delle donne* (Venice: Barezzo Barezzi, 1622).

28. See Chiavarra, "Ideologia," esp. 708–712, for a survey of the sermon literature that affirmed this view.

29. Sixteenth-century children were weaned sometime between the ages of three and seven, depending in large part on the ability of their parents to support a wetnurse.

30. Dolce, *L'istitutione,* 13r. See also Lorenzetti, *Musica e identità nobiliare,* 243, who develops his notion of the limited utility of female literacy from Leonardo Bruni's *De studiis et litteris liber,* written between 1422 and 1429 and dedicated to Battista Malatesta. Maria Ludovica Lenz, *Donne e Madonne: L'educazione femminile nel primo Rinascimento italiano* (Turin: Loescher Editore, 1982), 79, notes that Florentine women had no need for eloquence because the law forbade them to defend their own interests in civil court except through representation by a "protettore" or an attorney.

31. Dolce, *L'istitutione,* fol. 12r.

32. Ibid., fol. 18r.

33. Ibid., fol. 19r–v.

34. Ibid., fol. 17r.

35. Ibid., fol. 24r.

36. Dolce, ibid., calls learning an "istromento," or tool, on fol. 14, and calls chastity "la regina delle virtù donnesche" on fol. 28v.

37. Dolce, ibid., fol. 10v, uses the phrase "timidità e vergogna"; the second quotation, from fol. 24v, calls for female fasting that would "snervi le forze e raffredi il calore."

38. See Thomas Laqueur, *Making Sex: Body and Gender from the Greeks to Freud* (Cambridge: Harvard University Press, 1980).

39. Dolce, *L'istitutione,* fol. 24v: "l'animo sia padrone del corpo, che serva." For musically inclined readers this line may resonate with the famous metaphor used in the so-called Monteverdi-Artusi debate about the aesthetics of "modern music" at the turn of the seventeenth century. Giulio Cesare Monteverdi argued that in his brother Claudio's

music "l'oratione [the poetic conceit or rhetorical stance] sia la padrona e la musica la serva." Giulio Cesare Monteverdi, "Dichiaratione della lettera stampata nel quinto libro de' suoi madtrigali," in *Scherzi musicali a tre voci de Claudio Monteverdi* (Venice, 1607). Other readers may note a resonance with Aristotle's notion that as the mind rules the body, because it is the nature of the one to rule and of the other to obey, so it is "between the sexes: the male is by nature superior and the female inferior, the male ruler and the female subject." See Aristotle, *Politics,* I.ii.12, trans. H. Rackham (Cambridge: Harvard University Press, 1932), 21. Writing in 1545, Dolce could have intended to evoke the latter resonance; in any case, it would have been evoked in the minds of his classically educated readers.

40. Dolce, *L'istitutione,* fol. 25r.

41. Ibid., fol. 29r.

42. Ibid., fol. 31r. The juxtaposition of his praise of silence and his tolerance of music and dance may suggest that these arts could substitute for speech as means of self-expression.

43. The most accessible narrative of the way in which a girl's music lessons both served her father's ambitions for her future and implanted in her psyche the memories of patriarchal violence is Annibale Guasco, *Ragionamenti ad Lavinia sua figliola della maniera di governarsi in corte* (Turin: Eredi del Bevilacqua, 1586). See also the recent English translation: Peggy Osborn, trans., *Discourse to Lady Lavinia, His Daughter,* edited, with an introduction, by Peggy Osborn (Chicago: University of Chicago Press, 2003). For a rich account of music education among early modern Italian elites, see Lorenzetti, *Musica e identità.*

44. Giovanni Camillo Maffei recommended both forms of practice in his well-known letter about singing, first published in *Delle lettere del Signor Gio. Camillo Maffei da Solofra, libri due . . . v'è un discorso e della voce e del modo d'apparare di cantar di garganta* (Naples, 1562), and reprinted in Nanie Bridgman, "Giovanni Camillo Maffei et sa lettre sur le chant," *Revue de musicologie* 38 (1956): 3–34.

45. Guasco, *Ragionamenti ad Lavinia sua figliola,* fol. 14v, as translated in Osborn, *Discourse to Lady Lavinia,* 66.

46. On the concept of investing in a girl's skills to create an "intangible dowry" in lieu of one raised from the transfer of property, see Nino Tamassia, *La famiglia italiana nei secoli XV e XVI* (Milan: Sandron, 1911).

47. Guasco, *Ragionamenti ad Lavinia sua figliola,* fol. 18r, as translated in Osborn, *Discourse to Lady Lavinia,*72–73.

48. Letter of Angelo Grillo to Giulio, written from Subiaco in 1601, first published in Angelo Grillo, *Lettere dell'Illustrissimo et Eccellentissimo Sig. Abbate D. Angelo Grillo Monaco Cassinentense, raccolte dall'Illustro et Eccellentissimo Sig. Ottavio Menini* (Venice: Ciotti, 1602), and reprinted in Elio Durante and Anna Martellotti, *Don Angelo Grillo O.S.B. alias Livio Celiano: Poeta per musica del secolo decimosesto,* Archivium Musicum, Collana di studi E (Florence: Studio per edizioni scelte, 1989), 452–453.

49. Giulio Caccini, *Le nuove musiche* (Florence: Marescotti, 1601–1602). H. Wiley Hitchcock's modern edition of this volume was published in the series Recent Researches in the Music of the Baroque Era (Madison, WI: A-R Editions, 1970).

50. This translation is by Margaret Murata, as published in *Strunk's Source Readings in Music History,* vol. 4, *The Baroque Era,* ed. Margaret Murata (New York: Norton, 1998), 100.

51. This narrative of the Medici's consolidation of the granducato is based mainly on Furio Diaz, *Il Granducato di Toscana—I Medici* (Turin: Utet, 1987). See also Elena Fasano Guarini, ed., *Il Principato Mediceo*, vol. 3 of *Storia della civiltà toscana* (Florence: Le Monnier, 2003).

52. On Ferdinand's policies regarding musicians on his household staff, see Kirkendale, *Court Musicians*, esp. chap. 1, 33–58, and Warren Kirkendale, *Emilio de' Cavalieri, "Gentilhuomo Romano:" His Life and Letters, His Role as Superintendent of All the Arts at the Medici Court, and His Musical Compositions* (Florence: Olschki, 2001), esp. chap. 4, 85–120.

53. See Giulio Caccini, preface to *Le nuove musiche*, as translated in Murata, *Baroque Era*, 102–103.

54. On the perceived qualities of high voices in early modern Italy, see Maffei as printed in Bridgman, "Giovanni Camillo Maffei," 17; Girolamo Mei's letter of 8 May 1572 to Vincenzo Galilei, as translated and printed in Claude Palisca, *The Florentine Camerata: Documentary Studies and Translations* (New Haven: Yale University Press, 1989), 58; Giovanni De' Bardi's "Discorso sopra la musica antica e'l cantar bene," addressed to Giulio Caccini, as translated and printed in ibid., 108–109; and Gioseffo Zarlino, *Le istitutione harmoniche* (Venice: 1558), pt. 3, chap. 58, p. 281. Each author assumed that the soprano voice was produced by a man, either a falsettist or a castrato. Indeed, the word *soprano* is a masculine noun in Italian, referring in the sixteenth and seventeenth centuries only to a vocal register or to the men and boys who sang in that register. Women who sang were called *donne*. For two quite different explorations of the early modern fetish for singing in the soprano register, see Giuseppe Gerbino, "The Quest for the Soprano Voice: *Castrati* in Renaissance Italy," *Studi musicali* 33 (2004): 303–358; Bonnie Gordon, *Monteverdi's Unruly Women: The Power of Song in Early Modern Italy* (Cambridge: Cambridge University Press, 2005).

55. According to both Mei's and Maffei's entirely androcentric categorizations, the tenor voice was neither high nor low but mediated between these registers. Thus, it was the voice of reason and balance.

56. Francesco Sansovino, *L'Edificio del corpo humano nel qual brevemente si descrivono le qualità del corpo del huomo e le potentie dell'anima* (Venice: Comin da Trino Monferrato, 1550), vol. 2, fol. 24r, described the diaphragm's two functions thus.

57. The contemporary scholar-singers Sally Sanford and Julianne Baird agree that there is a natural speed for gorgheggiando. Baird likens the speed and feeling of the technique to those produced by a light giggle in her interview with Bernard D. Sherman in *Inside Early Music: Conversations with Performers* (New York: Oxford University Press, 1997), 231. I am grateful to Sally Sanford for several conversations and one singing lesson on the subject of gorgheggiando. The technique continues to be a prized part of Italian vocality, cultivated along with improvised dramatic singing in *ottava rima* in the folk genre of music drama known as *maggio*, in the Lucchese Alps. I am grateful to Linda Barwick and Allan Marett for introducing me to a maggio performance in the summer of 1996. See Barwick, *Gestualità e musica di un Maggio garfagnino* (Lucca: n.p., 1994).

58. See Zarlino, *Le istitutione harmoniche*.

59. For a fuller discussion of these ideas, see Gordon, *Monteverdi's Unruly Women*, 10–46.

60. See Sansovino, *L'Edificio del corpo humano*, vol.. 1, n.p., under the heading "la voce."

61. This discussion is based primarily on Laqueur, *Making Sex,* chap. 2.

62. Laqueur, ibid., 36, cites the ancient evidence for believing that women who sang and danced professionally were likely to experience menstrual dysfunction because the physical exertion so heated their bodies that they had no need to release excess fluids.

63. Vincenzo Galilei described the romanesca thus in his *Primo libro della prattica del contrapunto,* compiled between 1588 and 1591. For more on the romanesca, see chapter 7.

64. Peri's *L'Euridice* is generally considered the earliest "opera" for which a score survives. The matter of when the first opera was composed and by whom has always been highly contested. For the main points of the debates then and now see Nino Pirrotta, *Music and Theatre from Poliziano to Monteverdi* (Cambridge: Cambridge University Press, 1982); Tim Carter, *Jacopo Peri (1561–1633): His Life and Works* (New York: Garland, 1989); Tim Carter, "'Non occorre nominare tanti musici': Private Patronage and Public Ceremony in Late Sixteenth-Century Florence," *I Tatti Studies* 4 (1991): 89–104; and Gary Tomlinson, *Metaphysical Song* (Princeton: Princeton University Press, 1999). See also Tim Carter, "Rediscovering *Il rapimento di Cefalo,*" *Journal of Seventeenth Century Music* 9 (2003), http://www.sscm-jscm.press.uiuc-edu/v9/no1/carter.html.

65. Michelangelo Buonarroti, *Descrizione delle felicissime nozze della cristianissima maestà di Madama Maria Medici Regina di Francia e di Navarra* (Florence, 1600), fol. 21.

66. The musica segreta was the private ensemble of the duchess of Ferrara. It consisted of several highly accomplished women and, often but not always, several men. See Anthony Newcomb, *The Madrigal at Ferrara* (Princeton: Princeton University Press, 1980); Nina Treadwell, "Restaging the Siren: Musical Women in the Performance of Sixteenth-Century Italian Theatre," PhD diss., University of Southern California, 2000; and Richard Wistreich, *Courtier, Warrior, Singer: Giulio Cesare Brancaccio and the Performance of Identity in Late Renaissance Italy* (Aldershot: Ashgate, 2007).

67. These performances were all mentioned in the diary of politically significant events in the life of the court kept by Cesare Tinghi. The first two volumes of Tinghi's diary, covering the years 1600–1621, are now at I-Fn, MS Gino Capponi 261, volumes 1 and 2; the third volume, kept by another Tinghi after Cesare's death and covering the years 1622–1646, is at I-Fas, Miscellanea Medicea 11. As many music scholars know, the diary was the basis for Angelo Solerti's pioneering documentary history of performance culture at the Medici court, *Musica, ballo e drammatica alla corte Medicea dal 1600 al 1637* (Florence: Bemporad, 1905).

CHAPTER 2

1. I-Fas, MdP 4729, fol. 118 is Marie's letter. I-Fas, MdP 4728, p. 185, is Henri's; it is cited in Warren Kirkendale, *The Court Musicians in Florence during the Principate of the Medici* (Florence: Olschki, 1993), 148. Kirkendale's narrative at 148–150 is by far the most detailed and accurate to date.

2. I-Fas, Carte Strozziane I, vol. 30, fol. 6, cited in Kirkendale, *Court Musicians,* 149. The annual salary paid the Caccini family by the granducato was 192 scudi.

3. I-Fas, MdP 2920, letter of Flaminio Boni to unknown official, 9 October 1604.

4. I-FcasaB, A.B. 44, no. 438, letter of Giulio Caccini to Michelangelo Buonarroti, 11 November 1604, from Lyon. Tertian fever was an often life-threatening form of malaria characterized by chills followed by a fever spike every third day. Two forms were known:

in the mild form, if the chills and fever failed to return on the fifth day the patient was considered cured; in the severe form chills and fever returned constantly on a three-day cycle, though they became gradually less severe. Since the Caccini moved on after five days in Milan, it seems likely that Francesca had the mild form. Nonetheless, she had contracted a chronic disease that she and her family would have believed was caused by an excess of black bile, possibly leading to the cold and dry temperament of a melancholic and therefore also, by causing humoral dryness, possibly affecting the flexibility of her voice. On the forms of malaria as they were understood in the early modern period, see A. C. Celso, *Della medicina traditionale* (Florence: A. di Lungo, 1985), 122–123; A. Celli, *Malaria e colonizzazione nell'agro Romano dai più antichi tempi ai giorni nostri* (Florence: Vallecchi, 1927).

5. I-FcasaB, A.B. 44, no. 438, letter of Giulio Caccini to Michelangelo Buonarroti, 11 November 1604.

6. On the Caccini family's lodging, see I-Fas, MdP 4617a, fol. 369r, letter of Bacio Giovannino to Belisario Vinta, 25 December 1604. Concini had reported the gift he gave on their arrival directly to the grand duchess in his letter of 6 December, now at I-Fas, MdP 4748, letter of 6 December 1604.

7. I-Rasc, F.O. 1st ser., 114a, no. 73, letter of Giulio Caccini to Virginio Orsini, 16 January 1605. The letter, along with a French translation, is published entirely in Horace Boyer, "Giulio Caccini à la cour d'Henri IV (1604–05) d'après des lettres inédites," *Revue musicale* 7, no. 11 (1926): 244–245. Excerpts from the letter in Italian are printed in Kirkendale, *Court Musicians*, 149–150.

8. The letter of 16 January 1605 from Giulio Caccini to Virginio Orsini reports on the family's new fashion and on the women's response to kissing. Concini's letter, at I-Fas, MdP 4748, fol. 78, 2 March 1605, clarified that a total of two hundred scudi had passed through his household to the Caccini.

9. Letter of 16 January 1605 from Giulio Caccini to Orsini.

10. I-Fas, MdP 4617a, fol. 369r, letter of Bacio Giovannino to Belisario Vinta, 25 December 1604.

11. I-Fas, MdP 4748, letter of Concino Concini to Belisario Vinta, 7 December 1604.

12. I-Rasc, F.O., 1st ser., 114a, no. 99, letter of Giulio Caccini to Virginio Orsini, 1 March 1605.

13. I-Fas, MdP 921, fol. 642, letter of Giulio Caccini to Ferdinando I, 19 February 1605; MdP 921, fol. 643, letter of Giulio Caccini to Belisario Vinta, 19 February 1605; and MdP 4617a, fol. 398r, letter of Bacio Giovannino to Belisario Vinta, 20 February 1605.

14. I-Fas, MdP 5417a, letter of 4 March 1605, Bacio Giovannini to Belisario Vinta, explained that though Concini had offered Giulio a thousand-scudi dowry for Settimia, the king had meant to offer only five hundred scudi. In the same letter Giovannini reported that it had been Concini who had opened the subject of a position as a painter for his oldest son Pompeo. The offer for Pompeo was reported by Concini, I-Fas, MdP 4748, letter of 2 March 1605 to Belisario Vinta, and by Giulio, I-Rasc, F.O., 1st ser., 114a, no. 99, letter of 1 March 1605 to Virginio Orsini. In that letter Giulio reported the Duchesse de Guise's offer for Settimia and his reply cagily protecting some prior arrangement he had made with Virginio Orsini.

15. I-Rasc, F.O., 1st ser., 114a, no. 99, letter of 1 March 1605 from Giulio Caccini to Virginio Orsini.

16. I-Fas, MdP 921, fol. 642, letter of 19 February 1605 from Giulio Caccini to Grand Duke Ferdinando I.

17. I-Fas, MdP 5417a, n.p., letter of Bacio Giovannino to Belisario Vinta, 4 March 1605.

18. Ibid.

19. I-Rasc, F.O., 1st ser., 114a, no. 99, letter of Giulio Caccini to Virginio Orsini, 1 March 1605.

20. Ibid.

21. Richard Schechner, *Between Theater and Anthropology* (Philadelphia: University of Pennsylvania Press, 1985).

22. French singing technique required constant air pressure, speed, and volume (compared to the Italian preference for constantly changing pressure, speed, and volume), and it emphasized the nuanced delivery of consonants (compared to the Italian emphasis on nuanced delivery of vowels). See Sally Sanford, "A Comparison of French and Italian Singing in the Seventeenth Century," *Journal of Seventeenth-Century Music* 1 (1995), http://sscm-jscm.press.uiuc.edu/v1/no1/sanford.html.

23. Marie de' Medici's recommendation, dated 29 April 1605, is found at I-Fas, MdP 4729, fol. 153; Henri's, dated 4 May 1605, is found at I-Fas, MdP 4728, fol. 65. Concino Concini reported the Caccini's departure somewhat defensively in a dispatch to the grand duke dated 7 May 1605, at I-Fas, MdP 4748, fols. 16–17, describing the whole family as "persone furbacci"—crafty or money-grubbing people—in the postscript to another letter written that day, found at fol. 21. I-Fas, MdP 4617a, fol. 433–434, letter of Concini to Vinta, 7 May 1605, lists the purses given the Caccini, attributing the amounts to Concini's good efforts and noting that the consistently ungrateful Giulio had complained that the three hundred scudi that Pompeo received should, by rights, have been given to him.

24. I-Fas, MdP 4858, fol. 186 contains Marcello Acciolti's letter of 6 June 1605 alerting the Tuscan resident at Turin that Giulio and his "brigata" would arrive at the court of Savoy the next day or the day after that. On 25 June 1605 Lelio Tolomei, the Tuscan resident at Modena, wrote Florence to say that Giulio "and his company" had left there after a satisfying eight-day sojourn and probably would be in Florence by the following Wednesday. His letter is found at I-Fas, MdP 2920, letter of 25 June 1605.

25. I-Fas, MdP 2920, letter of Flaminio Boni to an unnamed official, 9 October 1604, described Princess Giulia, "donna di rarissimo intelletto," as having especially enjoyed sitting in with the Caccini ensemble when they made music for the Este court in Modena on the way to Paris. In I-Fas, MdP 4617a, a long, unsigned insert after fol. 426v explores the possibility of marrying the Princess of Modena to the Duc de Guise, and compares his declarations of love to the apparently more passionate ones of the Duc de Nemours. Princess Giulia d'Este never married.

26. I-Fas, MdP 5990, fol. 207, letter of Virginia Medici d'Este to "Madama," i.e., Grand Duchess Christine, 18 November 1605.

27. I-Rasc, F.O. 1st ser., 115/1, no. 133, letter of Giulio Caccini to Virginio Orsini, 7 January 1607. Excerpts of this letter were published by Boyer, "Giulio Caccini à la cour d'Henri IV," 305. It is discussed by James Chater in "Musical Patronage in Rome at the Turn of the Seventeenth Century: The Case of Cardinal Montalto," *Studi musicali* 16 (1987): 179–227, at 183 (where he mistakenly assigns it a date of January 1606; when writing from Florence, the Caccini always dated their letters in the Florentine style,

beginning a new year on 25 March). Kirkendale, *Court Musicians*, 151, reprints about half the letter. John Walter Hill transcribes and translates a smaller excerpt in *Roman Monody, Cantata, and Opera from the Circles around Cardinal Montalto* (Oxford: Clarendon, 1997), 1:48 and n. 152.

28. On the Montalto circle, see Hill, *Roman Monody*.

29. To put Montalto's annual income in context, it was nearly one thousand times Giulio Caccini's known annual income.

30. I borrow the argument about these performers' work, and the quoted passage, from Hill, *Roman Monody*, 53

31. I-FEas, Archivio Bentivoglio, Mazzo 9–55, fol. 621r, letter of Cesare Marotta to Enzo Bentivoglio, 12 November 1610. The letter is printed in Hill, *Roman Monody*, appendix A, letter 32, p. 311–312, but the translation here is mine.

32. For allowing a pregnant woman to be represented as moving about in public space in his Carnival 1619 entertainment *La fiera*, Buonarroti incurred the wrath and censorship of Grand Duchess Christine. His defense—that there could be no one at court who had not seen a pregnant woman—entirely failed to address what she considered an offense against womanhood. See I-FcasaB, A.B. 39, fols. 102r–106v, draft letter of Buonarroti to Francesco dell'Antella, 14 February, 1618/19. Janie Cole, "Michelangelo Buonarroti il giovane' (1568–1647): A Musician's Poet in Seicento Florence." PhD diss., Royal Holloway College, University of London, 2000, 97–104 gives the best account of *La fiera*.

33. A woman known for her beauty, graciousness, and excellence in both poetry and music, Flavia Peretti ne' Orsini had passed most of her child-bearing years in Florence, her household constantly intertwined with the similar household of her aunt by marriage, Grand Duchess Christine. On the continuity of their households in Florence in the 1590s, see I-Fas, Carte Strozziane I, filza 5 (book of maestro di casa Giovanni del Maestro), fol. 15v, for 1595, where the *dame* and *donne* supported by the Medici payroll are listed not by name but by person served: "6 donne della Duchessa di Bracciano," "7 del S. Don Virginio," and so on. Virginio and his wife had left Florence for Rome on 27 November 1605 with six of their seven sons. The seventh was left behind with his tutor, and their three daughters were left to be educated at the Monastero della Concezione (also known as the Monastero Nuovo). All four children left in Florence were described in contemporary documents as being raised "as if they were children of the grand duke." See I-Fas, Manoscritti 131, fol. 467, for one instance of this turn of phrase.

34. I-Rasc, F.O., 1st ser., 115/1, no. 133, letter of Giulio Caccini to Virginio Orsini, 7 January 1607.

35. I-Rasc, F.O., 1st ser., 114a, no. 99, letter of Giulio Caccini to Virginio Orsini, 1 March 1605.

36. Possibly he had already discussed placing Francesca with Margherita della Somaglia ne' Peretti. Although no documents support this hypothesis, a prior agreement with the Montalto would explain Giulio's hesitant response to the French monarchs' interest in his girls.

37. The letter to Orsini is at I-Rasc, F.O., 1st ser., 116/4, no. 732, 5 March 1607. That to the grand duchess is at I-Fas, MdP 5992, fol. 359, letter of 5 March 1607.

38. I-Rasc, F.O., 1st ser., 116/4, no. 732, letter of Giulio Caccini to Virginio Orsini, 5 March 1607.

39. I-Fas, MdP 5992, fol. 359, letter of Giulio Caccini to Christine, 5 March 1607.

40. I-FcasaB, A.B. 81, fol. 302r–v preserves the draft of a letter Buonarroti intended to attach to the draft of an official description of that carnival's principal entertainment, the barriera *La stiava,* for which Francesca had composed the music. The first half of this letter draft, up to the passage quoted above, is printed in Hill, *Roman Monody,* appendix A, no. 17, p. 305. Hill describes the letter as addressed to Grand Duke Ferdinando, but the manuscript clearly heads the draft "A Madama." "Madama" was the term used at court to refer to Grand Duchess Christine and only her. For the rest of the draft letter, see below and note 58.

41. Tinghi's brief account is at I-Fn, MS Gino Capponi 261, I, fol. 173; it is reprinted in Solerti, 38. The word "stiava" is a Tuscan variant of "schiava," meaning female slave. A *barriera* staged small-scale chivalric battles between opposing squads of costumed "knights" who were separated by a barricade erected across the performance space. Each squad consisted of four, eight, or sixteen patrician boys and men, opulently costumed in distinctive colors, and each was "led" in battle by one of the Medici princes. See Maria Alberti, "Le 'barriere' di Cosimo II granduca di Toscana," in *Musica in torneo nell'Italia del Seicento,* ed. Paolo Fabbri (Lucca: Libreria Musicale Italiana, LIM Editrice, 1999), 81–96. I-FcasaB, A.B. 81, fol. 270r; the heading of Buonarroti's draft invenzione and text refers to *La stiava* as a barriera, although the Grand Duchess's secretary Curtio Picchena referred to it in several of his letters as a *sbarra.* An invenzione sketches the character types, plot, stage action, and often ideas for costumes and sets, very like a story board for a film.

42. The surviving documentary evidence about *La stiava* includes letters and drafts of letters among Buonarroti, Giulio Caccini, and Christine's secretaries about production details; a copy of the draft invenzione and poetic text Buonarroti had sent for his patron's approval, I-FcasaB, A.B. 81, fols. 270–273r; the draft of a letter to Christine that accompanied the invenzione, fol. 274r–v; a draft description, fols. 275r–277r; a second draft letter addessed "Madama" accompanying that draft, fol. 277r–v; a plan for the combat action, fol. 278r–v; and, finally, a fair copy of the description indicating that Christine wanted to send it to her father the duke of Lorraine ("volle mandarla al S.r Duca di Lorena suo Padre"), fols. 279–282r. A second autograph of the script is at I-FcasaB, A.B. 84, fols. 160r–162r, headed "per il principe a requisizione di Madama intorno a un abbatimento fattosi da lui, e da alcuni paggi, che si conversi in un ballo." A marginal note reads "Principibus placuisse viris sed ultima laus est. Horat. Lib. P.o et r ep. 17." See also Janie Cole, "Michelangelo Buonarroti il giovane' (1568–1647): A Musician's Poet in Seicento Florence," PhD diss., Royal Holloway College, University of London, 2000, 87–91.

43. I-FcasaB, A. B. 51, no. 1432, letter of Curtio Picchena to Buonarroti, 29 January 1607. The rejected scenario was based on a well-known story from Livy's *Ab Urbe condita* in which three Roman brothers, the Horatii, fight the Curiatii, three brothers from the rival city Alba Longa, to the death. Confronted at the end of the battle by his grieving sister Camilla, who had been engaged to one of the Curiatii, the lone surviving Horatius killed her. Condemned to death for her murder, he saved himself by appealing directly to the people of Rome. We cannot know how Buonarroti planned to adapt the tale, but it does seem more than a little violent for a Carnival show.

44. I-FcasaB, A.B. 51, no. 1433, letter of Picchena to Buonarroti, 5 February 1607.

45. I-Fas, MdP 5992, fol. 307, letter of Buonarroti to "Serenissima Madama," i.e., Grand Duchess Christine, 5 February 1607. A draft of the letter is at I-FcasaB, A.B. 81,

fol. 274r, at the end of what seems to be a full first draft of the invenzione, action, and text of *La stiava*, written in two hands on two kinds of paper. It is clear that the Caccini daughter whom Buonarroti mentioned was Francesca from a letter she wrote asking for a copy of the text. Her letter is at I-FcasaB, A.B. 44, no. 454, letter of 21 June 1626. See appendix B.

46. I-FcasaB, A.B. 44, no. 439, letter of Giulio Caccini to Buonarroti in Pisa, 18 February 1607. Giulio's letter implies that Francesca had composed *La stiava*'s music because her father was ill, a notion conspicuously absent from Buonarroti's communications. It is easy to imagine that each man wrote a partial truth, inflected according to momentary agendas, Giulio needing to assert paternal control over the work done by his daughter, Buonarroti wanting to promote Francesca's usefulness to the grand duchess.

47. Pompeo was in the cast of Gonzaga's commedia in musica, scheduled for performance on Thursday, 22 February. He was eventually in the cast as a last-minute substitute for the leading role in *La stiava*, presumably singing falsetto against his father's usual aesthetic preference because of the castrato Giovannino's indisposition. The original cast is indicated in the second draft of the invenzione at I-FcasaB A.B. 81, fol. 270r.

48. In the discussion of *La stiava* below I use the words "onstage" and "offstage" to mark the boundary of representation. But it is important to acknowledge that *La stiava* was enacted not on a stage but on a dance floor prepared in the Medici's palace at Pisa. The show was conceived (like many Medicean Carnival entertainments) as a theatrical interruption in an evening of social dancing.

49. I-FcasaB, A.B. 81, fols. 270–273r contains the whole invenzione and script.

50. I-FcasaB, A.B. 51, no. 1434, letter of Picchena to Buonarroti, 6 February 1607. As usual at the Medici court, the music for dancing was to have been composed before the words, for use in dance rehearsals.

51. I-FcasaB, A.B. 81, fol. 275r.

52. The plan for combat given at I-FcasaB, A.B. 81, fol. 278r–v indicates that Cosimo and his brother Don Francesco led the opposing teams.

53. On princes' claims to authorship of their servants' and courtiers' intellectual labor, see Mario Biagioli, *Galileo, Courtier: The Practice of Science in the Culture of Absolutism* (Chicago: University of Chicago Press, 1993), 52–53.

54. On Ferdinando's illness and the epistolary evidence of Christine's de facto regency, see chapter 3.

55. I-FcasaB, A.B. 81, fol. 280r–v.

56. Ibid., fol. 280v.

57. Ibid., fol. 271r–v: "O servitù soave / O carcer dolce, e giogo non indegno / [v] … Cristiana io miro, entro'l cui nobil seno / Virtù Real vera pietà si serra, / Ond'io sper'anco un giorno / Lieta'mpera ritorno / Lacrimata Regina all'India terra."

58. Ibid., fol. 277r–v, draft letter of Buonarroti marked "A Madama," dated 6 March 1607: "A Madama. … Conforme a che V.A. comanda ho cercato destramente di intendere da M.o Giulio Romano come sia passato sino a ora il negozio della Cecchina sua figliuola intorno all'andare a servire Il. Ill.mo Cardinale Montalto."

59. Ibid.: "e ne ho ritratto solo che egli stesso ne voleva scrivere a V.A. come io credo che ora mai abbia fatto. E volendo intendere del medesimo dal Sig.r Piero Guicciardini ho trovato che era in villa si che presi risoluzione di parlarne al Sig.re Gualterrotto Giucciardini zio del Sig.r Abbate Rucellai / [v] e da lui ho assai apertamente inteso che il negozio tra l'una parte e l'altra era al presente assai raffreddato di modo a tal, che io feci

fermo conseguenza che non ci facessero bisogno ~~molti offici~~ in potersi valer ~~liberamente~~ della ~~Cecchina~~ fanciulla liberamente senza ~~punto~~ nuove diligenze che possa ~~apparir generarsene~~ apparir ~~violenza resistenza~~ alcuna resistenza noiosa altrui ~~la qual fanciulla del favore che V.S.~~" The part of this letter that reports on the dissolution of Giulio's contract with Montalto is quoted in Hill, *Roman Monody*, appendix A, no 17, p. 305; Hill's transcription stops at the word "raffreddato," omitting the point of the story for both writer and reader.

60. I-Fas, Riccardi 283 is Giovanni Lami's inventory of the Riccardi archive as it existed in the middle of the eighteenth century, including this item: "Scritta di Parentado della Sig.ra Francesca Caccini di Roma, e Gio: Batt.a di Piero Signorini Malaspina, fatto dal Sig.re Riccardo Riccardi d'ordine di Madama Christine di Lorena Gran Duchessa di Toscana." The item, filed as number 6 under the year 1607, cross-references an item titled "Signorini Malaspina = Sig.re Gio Batt.a. Per una promessa fattagli dal Sig.re Riccardo Riccardi," also filed as number 6 for 1607. That item, in turn, is cross-referenced to "Signorini = Gio. Batt.a Musico di Corte. Per una promessa fattagli dal Sig.re Riccardo Riccardi = Sue Consequenze," filed under 1638 as number 10. I-Fas, Riccardi 490, "Spoglio dei Processi Antichi," has a slightly different description, dated 1 November 1741 and indicating that the documents were in Armadio I, the second shelf, at inventory number 43–46. When the Riccardi papers became part of the Archivio di Stato di Firenze in the nineteenth century, they were reorganized and assimilated into the Manelli-Galilei-Riccardi collection. This collection's organization renders Lami's punctilious index to Riccardi's papers useless. On the unfulfilled dowry promises, see chapter 12. For Lami's acccount, see his *Amplissimi viri Richardi Romuli Richardi Patrici Florentini Vita* (Florence, 1748), 229–230.

61. I-F, Archivio Arcivescovile, Libro di Matrimonii, Santa Maria Maggiore: "A di 4 [novem]bre 1607, Francesca figliuola del Sig.r Giulio Caccini Parrocchia di S. Maria Maggiore, doppo le tre solite denunzie secondo la forma del Concilio Tridentino contrasse matrimonio per verba de' presenti, in casa di suo padre, con il Sig.r Giovanbattista Signorini della Parrocchia di Santa Maria Novella, dal quale hebbe l'annello matrimoniale; Testimonii a questo furono Il Sig.r Rustico Piccardini, et il Sig.r Ricardo Ricardi." The marriage was listed in civic records on 11 November 1607. See I-Fas, Manoscritti 551, Repertorio Generale dei matrimoni della città di Firenze, 1564–1620, vol. 1, fol. 356v. According to Edward Muir, *Ritual in Early Modern Europe* (Cambridge: Cambridge University Press, 1997). 34, the location of the ceremony in Giulio's home rather than in a church was the norm in Florence.

62. I-Fas, Monte di Pietà. 1381, Campioni di Depositi Condizionati, opening 387. The Monte di Pietà was Florence's oldest dowry bank.

63. I-Fas, Notarile Moderno, Protocolli 2171 (Atti di Noferi Maccanti, 1607), item no. 36, fols. 26v–27v. I am grateful to Gino Corti for help in transcribing and translating this document and the cluster of other documents to which it refers.

64. I-Fn, MS II.____.105, fol. 84v, Signorini's horoscope, lists this birthdate. According to Kirkendale, *Court Musicians*, 285, Signorini first appeared on the roll of the grand duke's paid musicians on 12 May 1590, at a monthly salary of six scudi. His salary rose to seven scudi monthly on 10 July 1599, to nine on 1 October 1602, to eleven in 1603, and finally to thirteen on 1 January 1605. He would continue to be paid thirteen scudi monthly until his death in December 1626. This summary of his career is based on ibid., 285–287.

65. I-Fas, MdP 5986, letter of Enea Vaini to "Madama," i.e., Christine, 27 September 1603.

66. Ibid.

67. I-Rasc, F.O., 1a Serie, 160, no. 132, letter of Jacopo Cicognini to Virginio Orsini, 2 April 1616, fol. 2: "et Venere la potrebbe rappresentare la S.ra Fran.ca et il S.r Giovanni Battista fu la parte d'Adone poiché il Signorini ha bellissimo aspetto."

68. I-Fas, Depositeria Generale, Parte Antica 389, no 756: "Madonna Francesca di Giulio Romano, et moglie di Giovanni Battista Signorini allievo del Franciosino Musico con provisione di scudi 10 il mese ch'alli 15 di novembre come per rescritto di S.A.S."

CHAPTER 3

1. Cristoforo Bronzini, *Della dignità e nobiltà delle donne*, I-Fn, Magliabecchiana (hereafter Magl.) VIII. 1525/1, 65–66.

2. The exchange also describes with perfect precision the two families, biological and padronal, that produced Caccini's career.

3. This description of Christine's living circumstances is based largely on material cited in Tim Carter, *Jacopo Peri (1561–1633): His Life and Works* (New York: Garland, 1989), and on her papers in I-Fas. These are listed in the bibliography. I-Fas, Carte Strozziane I, filza 51, fol. 4v, describes the entire Medici household as inventoried by Giovanni del Maestro by 5 August 1590. Christine was served by four matrons and twelve dame, three of whom were from France. Princesses Marie and Leonora were served by four women, apparently neither dame nor donne because their surnames are not mentioned. Twenty-one others, including three female dwarves, a male dwarf, and "la Margherita che canta," served the princesses collectively. On fol. 15v del Maestro provided a similar list of dame and donne from 1595, adding five unnamed donne of the duchess of Bracciano, Flavia Peretti ne' Orsini. Del Maestro's inventory is cited in Carter, *Jacopo Peri*, 21 n. 60. In the early 1590s the princesses were served artistically by former members of Grand Duke Francesco's disbanded concerto delle donne, including Francesca's mother Lucia. Laura Guidiccione ne' Lucchesini, living amid the women's court for most of the decade, composed texts and possibly music for several maschere and balletti that the women produced among themselves. It is entirely possible that Christine's decision to be an "extraordinary benefactrix" to Francesca was partly based on vivid, even affectionate memories of her mother Lucia Gagnolandi from these early years in Florence. The "women's court" was a heterosocial community that Christine could command by virtue of superior social rank, whereas the official court of the granducato over which Ferdinando I presided was a male homosocial community. This division matches precisely *La stiava*'s representation of the social world.

4. The most detailed biography of Christine is found in Gaetano Pieraccini, *La stirpe dei Medici di Cagaggiolo* (Florence: Vallecchi, 1947), 317–335.

5. This very brief summary of the interests involved in Christine's marriage to Ferdinando is drawn from Jacopo Riguccio Galluzi, *Istoria del Granducato di Toscana sotto il governo della casa Medici* (Florence: per Gaetano Cambiagi Stampatore Granducale, 1781), 5:14–48.

6. An *intermedio* was a display of musical, balletic, and scenic virtuosity performed between the acts of a spoken play. On the literally spectacular marriage celebrations, see

Aby Warburg's essay "I costumi teatrali per gli Intermezzi del 1589: I disegni di Bernardo Buontalenti e il 'Libro di conti' di Emilio de' Cavalieri," in *Gesammelte Schriften*, ed. Gertrud Bing (Leipzig: Teubner, 1932), 259–300, 394–441; Daniel P. Walker, ed., *Musique des intermèdes de la Pellegrina* (Paris: Editions du Centre national de la recherche scientifique, 1963); James Saslow, *The Medici Wedding of 1589* (New Haven: Yale University Press, 1996); and Nina Treadwell, *Music, Wonder and the Mystery of the State* (Bloomington: Indiana University Press, 2008).

7. Galluzi, *Istoria*, 18–22.

8. Cosimo I was born in 1590; Eleonora in 1591; Caterina in 1593; Francesco in 1594; Carlo in 1596; Filippo in 1598; Lorenzo in 1599; Maria Maddalena in 1600; and Claudia in 1604. Christine miscarried in January 1595. For a sharply negative account of Christine's physical and mental health, including a discussion of her pregnancies, see Pieraccini, *La stirpe dei Medici*.

9. Bronzini, *Della dignità*, I-Fn, Magl. VIII. 1519/1, fol. 255: "posciaché se si riguarda la maestà del volto, et dei portamenti suoi, si dirà esser nata ad imperare, et commandare."

10. This biographical sketch is based primarily on Estella Galasso Calderara, *La Granduchessa Maria Maddalena d'Austria* (Genoa: Sagep Editrice, 1985). Bronzini's biography of Magdalena is at I-Fn, Magl. VIII. 1514, 177–213.

11. Galluzzi, *Istoria*, 6:200–270, traces the history of the de jure regency Christine and Maria Magdalena shared. At 6:385–422 he dismisses the whole period from the death of Ferdinando I to 1637—the period of Christine's regency—as a time of languor, declining creative energy, and bad management. Because his was the founding text for the history of the granducato, Galluzzi's view pervades almost all the historiography since, including that produced by music and art historians. Although Furio Diaz' *Il Granducato di Toscana: I Medici* (Turin: Utet, 1976) reframed the history of the granducato in post-Enlightenment terms, Diaz was not concerned with reevaluating the possible contributions of any Medicean women to the political health or longevity of the Tuscan state. For the era from 1600 to roughly 1635, which he sees as the reigns of Ferdinando I, Cosimo II, and the young Ferdinando II, see especially Diaz, pt. 3, "La Toscana nell'età della controriforma e dell'egemonia spagnola," 231–464.

12. I-Fas, MdP 1325, fol. 187, letter from Christine to Curtio Picchena, 2 November 1604.

13. Ibid., fol. 189, letter from Christine to Picchena, 7 November 1604.

14. Christine was also careful to note that she had no spiritual need to visit these shrines—that is, no sin for which she needed to atone.

15. I-Rasc, F.O., 2d ser., 309, no. 80, undated minute.

16. I-Las, Anziani della Libertà, Ambasciatori Toscani, Filza 601, as quoted by Amadeo Pellegrini, *Relazioni inedite di ambasciatori Lucchesi alle corti di Firenze, Genova, Milano, Modena, Parma, Torino (Sec. XVI–XVII)* (Lucca: A. Pelicci, 1901), 126.

17. I-Fas, MdP 1325, 215ff. is a set of letters in Benedetto Barchetti's hand from 1607, all addressed simply to "Picchena," ordering the grand duke's response to memos from the Ruota and the Depositeria. All are signed by Christine. I-Fas, MdP 1326, no. 339, an undated dispatch from Picchena to Vinta, filed between two letters signed by Picchena and dated 15 July 1608, declares, "Tutto lo spaccio che V.S. mi mandò hiersera, arrivò à hora che ognuno andava al letto, et questa mattina mentre che Madama si vestiva ha sentito tutte le lettere che V.S. m'ha scritto." Picchena's dispatch goes on to dispose of

various matters according to Christine's will, specifying that Ferdinando was indisposed because he was purging. But Picchena's dispatches for all of June and early July had commented that the grand duke was indisposed, seldom hearing any but the most important letters, those from Spain. Among the issues before Christine that day was the dispute over details of Fulvia Salviati's marriage to Bartolomeo dal Monte; on that dispute, see below.

18. For example, in a dispatch of 14 October 1614 the Modenese resident diplomat Manfredo Malaspina complained about the two-hour evening conversation that the special envoy Fabio Scotti had with Christine, "[G]uessing that it was a negotiation Your Highness wanted to carry out without my input, and that it was a sign of your diffidence toward me . . . moved by my usual concern for reputation, not only did I feel myself gravely troubled by people murmuring about me, but I also set out to learn the subject of the negotiation." See I-MOas, Ambasciatori. Firenze. Busta 45, 1611–1615, fasc. 5.

19. I-Fas, MdP 1341, letter of Andrea Cioli to Orazio della Rena, 23 February 1609, comments on the good relations between the women. I-Fas, MdP 303, letter of 30 May 1611 from Belisario Vinta to Orso d'Elci, fol. 140v, notes that Christine constantly sought to please her daughter-in-law; on fol. 141r, he notes that "wife, husband, mother, sons and daughters get along so well, with such mutual love and agreement and tranquility, that one could not desire more."

20. See, e.g., I-MOas, Ambasciatori. Firenze. Busta 45, fasc. 2, letter of 15 March 1611 from Manfredo Malaspina, which asks the Duke of Modena to write a letter to "Madama the grand duchess such that my uncle (Piero Cambio) can obtain his desire"— appointment to the Magistracy of the Forty-Eight.

21. Malaspina tells the story in I-MOas, Ambasciatori. Firenze. Busta 45, fasc. 3, letter of 3 January 1611/12.

22. Records of the testimony and verdict in Ottieri's trial in Florence are at I-Fas, Otto di guardia e balia, principato, 2793. A number of witnesses repeated the claims about Suora Maria Vittoria's virtuosity. Some of the trial materials are printed in Kirkendale, *Court Musicians*, 314–316. Voluminous records of the trials of Frescobaldi and her two accomplices, all sentenced to life imprisonment by being walled up in their cells, are at I-Rasv, Sacra Congregatione Vescovi e Regolari. Sezione Monache. Positiones. 1620, busta D-M. Their various petitions for release into normal cloistered life can be found in the same fondo for subsequent years. For instance, the busta for 1632 includes a petition by Frescobaldi to be released. Her petition was denied. The busta for 1635 includes a memo from the nuns at San Giuseppe, where she had been transferred, objecting to a reprieve granted by the Pope that allowed her to have voice and vote in their chapter. Frescobaldi seems to have been incorrigible, for she was still causing uproars for her scoffing refusal to accept monastic discipline as late as 1644.

23. I-Rasv, Sacra Congregatione dei Vescovi e Regolari. Sezione Monache. Positiones. 1620, D-M, letter of 10 August 1620 from the investigating archbishop of Candia to the congregation's chair, Cardinal Sauli. In the end, Ottieri was sentenced to life imprisonment in the tower at Volterra; the state seized his property.

24. I-MOas, Ambasciatori, Firenze, busta 47, fasc. 1, dispatch of Paolo Boiardi, 18 November 1619, comments that Cosimo stood near a little bed placed in his audience room. Boiardi's dispatch of 28 February 1620, in the same busta and fascicle, notes the grand duke's attendance at a comedy played in his bedroom.

25. Ibid., dispatch of Paolo Boiardi, 7 July 1620.

26. Cosimo II's will and establishment of a regency council are summarized in Galluzzi, *Istoria*, 6:195–200, and Galasso-Calderara, 93–94. Its main points can also be found in Boiardi's report as the Modenese ambassador, I-MOas, Ambasciatori. Firenze, busta 47, fasc. 4, dispatch dated 13 March 1621, and in I-Fas, Manoscritti 132, fol. 609. The regency council consisted of the veteran diplomat Orso Pannocchieschi-d'Elci (1569–1636); the head of the Tuscan militia, Giovan Francesco del Monte (dates unknown); Marchese Fabrizio Colloredo (1576–1646); and the archbishop of Pisa, Giuliano de' Medici di Castellina (1599–1636). Curtio Picchena (1554–1626) and Lorenzo Usimbardi (1547–1636) were appointed secretaries to the regents, with career secretaries Andrea Cioli (1573–1641) and Ottaviano Lotti (fl. after 1611) as backup appointments. For more on the regency, see chapter 9.

27. I-Las, Anziani al tempo della Libertà. Ambasciatori. Firenze. Filza 609, dispatch of 29 October 1626, as published in Pellegrini, *Relazione inedita di ambasciatori Lucchese*, 158–159.

28. Ibid., Filza 610, 1628, as quoted in Pellegrini, *Relazione inedita di ambasciatori Lucchese*, 169 and 178, comment on Christine's continued importance to state decisions, despite "the chilling of her blood by the advanced age of 69, and [being] beset by many pains" (178).

29. Two kinds of collections of letters in the Mediceo del Principato fondo at Florence's Archivio di Stato document the lives of the women's court—letters to and from the princesses themselves, and letters to and from the secretaries assigned to the princesses. Both kinds of collections are easily accessed by means of a published inventory. Roughly 70 percent of the princesses' correspondents were men, whereas the Medici princes hardly ever had women correspondents outside their immediate biological families. Thus the correspondence reflects the heterosociality of the Medici women's world and the homosociality of the Medici men's world. The use of letters to understand the dynamics of a community largely sustained by daily oral communications requires great caution. Preserved written records are likely to emphasize exchanges that seemed, at the time they were written, to require documentation—for example, an exchange of which one party or the other imagined he or she might someday need proof. Furthermore, because the vast majority of princesses' letters were dictated to male secretaries, they were unlikely to transgress gender norms. Even if they did, genuinely transgressive letters were unlikely to be preserved by archivists serving a family that styled itself as embodying the Tuscan state. I am grateful to Deanna Shemek and Bruce Edelstein for thoughtful conversations about the problems of reading past secretarial mediation to decipher the worlds to which elite women's letters refer.

30. See Galasso-Calderara, 72–74, on Magdalena's correspondence. Galasso-Calderara cites I-Fas, MdP 6083 as an especially good source of letters of this type.

31. I-Fas, MdP 6006, fol. 159, letter of Donato dell'Antella to Christine, 2 May 1614, includes a geneaological table showing the relation to Corsini, Ulivieri, Carducci, and Cambi banking interests of court attorney Taddeo Orselli's prospective bride, Aloysia di Piero Corsini. Antella's research also revealed that Aloysia's family would pay an enviable dowry of four thousand scudi. An undated letter from Orselli to Christine at fol. 189 thanks her effusively for granting him permission to marry Aloysia.

32. I-Fas, MdP 5966, fol. 86, letter of the archbishop of Siena to Christine, 7 December 1602, asked her to act as "tutrice" (female guardian) of the onestà of Siena's women

by preventing them from having to see and hear obscene things in comedies performed in the city's public squares.

33. Letters from the groom's adoptive father and the Tuscan secretaries who were managing the negotiation for Christine accompany a copy of the marriage contract in I-Fas, MdP5998 (unfoliated volume), dated 27 and 28 February 1609/10. Christine had issued orders to Donato dell'Antella about this marriage as early as mid-July 1608; the orders are included in Curtio Picchena's dispatch to Belisario Vinta at I-Fas, MdP 1326, no. 339, an undated dispatch filed between two letters in Picchena's hand dated 15 July 1608.

34. The clause guaranteeing that Christine would choose the time of these ceremonies may point toward the series of elite weddings celebrated more or less privately by the women's court, weddings for which Francesca Caccini among others provided theatrical music. See chapter 4.

35. I-Fas, MdP 1716, letter of Dimurgo Lambardi to Andrea Cioli, 28 Feburary 1622. The daughter of Tuscany's first secretary from 1587 to 1613, Belisario Vinta, Tommasa had been married to the wealthy Sienese Sinolfo Ottieri, the marriage fully approved if not actually brokered by the grand duchess. She was without a husband in 1622 because of Christine's energetic prosecution of her husband for the scandal at the Monastero di Santa Verdiana described above.

36. I-Fas, MdP 1716, letter of Cioli to Lambardi, 4 March 1622.

37. I-Fas, MdP 1716, letter of Lambardi to Cioli, 6 March 1622. Vinta remained unmarried and childless, in service as a dama to one or another of the Medici princesses until her death. On her infertility and longevity, see I-Fn, MS II.____.105, Orosocopi diversi.

38. I-Fas, MdP 120, no. 263, letter of Christine to Gio. Batt. Malvazzi, 13 January 1629, and the letter to which she replied, no. 264, 2 January 1629.

39. I-Fas, MdP 120, no. 414, letter of Archduchess Maria Magdalena to Lucrezia Seta, 6 June 1628.

40. I-Fas, MdP 6371 [unfoliated], letter of Leonora Orsina Sforza to Magdalena, 24 May 1616.

41. I-Fas, MdP 120, no. 382, letter of Magdalena to the Auditore di Siena, 26 November 1628.

42. I-Fas, MdP 120. The draft of a letter from Magdalena to her sister-in-law Caterina de' Medici (widowed duchess of Mantua and official governor of Siena) on the verso specifies that Magdalena has acted on Ippolita's behalf "not only because her goodness merits it, as does the good service she has given, but also out of respect for Your Highness, whom I am always happy to be able to serve." Another draft of a letter from Magdalena to Caterina at no. 389 threatens Bolgerhini with imprisonment, adding, "I believe it will be necessary, because I hear from every source that he has no sense."

43. Dowry abuses were subject to the judgment of the Ruota civile (civil court) or, if children were involved, the Magistrato dei pupille (magistrate of orphans). On the organization and history of these two agencies of the Florentine judiciary, see R. Burr Litchfield, *Emergence of a Bureaucracy: The Florentine Patricians, 1530–1790* (Princeton: Princeton University Press, 1986). On their specific relation to women and children, see Giulia Calvi, *Il contratto morale: Madri e figli nella Toscana moderna* (Bari: Laterza, 1994).

44. I-Fas, MdP 1696, fol. 665, memo of 22 April 1609/10. See Kirkendale's discussion of this incident in *Court Musicians*, 340–341. Giulio, Francesca, and Settimia Caccini all wrote imploring Virginio Orsini to intercede with Christine to get the dowry paid;

their letters, dated 6 March 1609/1610, are at I-Rasc, F.O., 1st ser., 119/2, nos. 184, 185, and 186 respectively.

45. I-Fas, MdP 6012, [unfoliated,] letter of Lavinia Saracinelli to Christine, 25 April 1625, urges her to intercede for the restitution of her sister-in-law's dowry. MdP 5971, fol. 415 is a letter from Cardinal Crescentio of Orvieto to Christine, 5 January 1527, pressing the same case.

46. I-Fas, MdP 6005, fol. 210, letter of Francesco Aioruioli to Christine, 24 August 1613.

47. I-Fas, MdP 5986 [unfoliated], letter of Vittoria Ardinghelli to Christine, 16 May 1603.

48. I-Fas, MdP 6009, fol. 57, letter of Laura di Centi to Christine, 13 March 1619/20.

49. I am grateful to Deanna Shemek for this felicitous phrase, as well as for several clarifying conversations about the social and sexual dynamics of women's courts.

50. Given that about twenty-five years later the widowed Orsini would enter a convent, where her "goodness" was notable enough for her to have been declared venerable in the eyes of the church, it seems likely that the girl's claim was genuine. Records of her beatification are at I-Rasv, Carte Borghese 29 (Documenti pertinenti al processo di Beatificazione di Camilla Orsini Borghese), two bundles of papers wrapped in ribbon and still sealed with wax.

51. I-Fas, MdP 6108, fol. 813v, letter of Curtio Picchena to Caterina de' Medici ne' Gonzaga, 24 May 1619.

52. I-Fas, MdP6029, [unfoliated], letter of Christine to Camilla Orsini, 12 July 1619.

53. I-Fas, MdP 6009, fol. 174, letter of Camilla Orsini ne' Borghese, princess of Sulmona, to Christine, 20 July 1619.

54. Gayle Rubin, "The Traffic in Women: Notes on the 'Political Economy' of Sex," in *Feminism and History*, ed. Joan Wallach Scott, 105–151 (Oxford: Oxford University Press, 1995).

55. Irigaray's essays concerning the exchange of women, "Women on the Market" and "Commodities among Themselves" fill chaps. 8 and 9, respectively, of her *This Sex Which Is Not One*, trans Catherine Porter (Ithaca: Cornell University Press, 1985; originally published Paris: Editions de Minuit, 1977).

56. For readings of *La liberazione*'s representations of the women's court, see chapters 9 and 10.

57. I-Fas, MdP6009, fol. 187, letter of Camilla Orsini ne' Borghese to Christine, 10 August 1619. I-Fas, MdP 6009, fol. 211, letter of Camilla to Christine, 6 September 1618, thanks her for arranging the girl's admission to La Concezione.

58. In seventeenth-century Italy, female monastic communities were called *monasteri*, and monastic communities for men were often called *conventi*. I have used the Italian *monastero* and the English word convent interchangeably, against the good advice of historian Katherine Gill.

59. Convenient summaries of the council's policy to reform female monastic life can be found in Robert Kendrick, *Celestial Sirens: Nuns and Their Music in Early Modern Milan* (Oxford: Clarendon, 1997); Craig Monson, *Disembodied Voices: Music and Culture in an Early Modern Italian Convent* (Berkeley: University of California Press, 1995); Colleen Reardon, *Holy Concord within Sacred Walls* (Oxford: Clarendon, 2002).

60. One especially vivid description of the traffic in and out of such a community can be found in Anton Maria Reconesi's 1640 exhortation to the community at La Crocetta.

Excerpts were published in Gerardo Antegnati, *Vicende e tempi di Suor Domenica del paradiso* (Siena: Cantagalli, 1983). On La Crocetta, see chapter 12.

61. I-Rasv, Sacra Congregatione dei Vescovi e Regolari. Sezione Monache. Positiones. Busta 1615, F-G, no. 12.

62. Ibid.

63. I-Rasv, Sacra Congregatione dei Vescovi e Regolari. Sezione Monache. Positiones. Busta 1615, F-G, no. 11, dated March 1615. The abbess in question is identifiable as Cybo by the license dated 5 June 1615 granting her as abbess permission to consecrate six gentlewomen, item 10 in the packet. Item 7 is a petition on behalf of D. Giovanna Medici, daughter of D. Pietro Medici, to enter Le Murate, where her two older sisters already lived, seconded by "Madama la Gran Duchessa da chi vien desiderata tal grazia."

64. I-Rasv, Sacra Congregatione dei Vescovi e Regolari. Sezione Monache. Positiones. Busta 1615, F-G, no. 4, letter of Christine to the Sacra Congregatione, dated 20 July 1615.

65. I-Rasv, Sacra Congregatione dei Vescovi e Regolari. Positiones. 1617, D-F, no. 9, letter of the sisters of Le Murate to Pope Paul V, dated 1 February 1617.

66. Ibid.

67. I-Rasv, Sacra Congregatione dei Vescovi e Regolari. Positiones. 1623, C-F, packet titled "Murate" after item 14, petition dated 8 October 1620.

68. Ibid.

69. Ibid.

70. Ibid.

71. Ibid.

72. Ibid., separate item headed "Ad instanza dell'Altezze Serenissime di Toscana": "Illustrissimi et Reverendissimi Sig.ri."

73. The relationship that Bronzini implies existed between Christine and Francesca is reminiscent of the twentieth-century Italian feminist practice known as *affidamento.* Complementary to the practice known in North America as "consciousness-raising," affidamento involved creating couples of women, usually as different from each other as possible in age, class, profession, and so on, who committed to struggle candidly toward understanding their differences. The relationship was meant to be empowering to both parties, teaching both to give voice to their experience fearlessly. On affidamento, see Paola Bono and Sandra Kemp, eds., *Italian Feminist Thought* (Oxford: Blackwell, 1991); and Luisa Muraro, *L'ordine simbolico della madre* (Rome: Editioni Riuniti, 1991). Although from a North American perspective there is a decided lesbian valence to the practice, affidamento does not seem necessarily to evoke that valence among Italians.

CHAPTER 4

1. Caccini's hiring at ten scudi per month is recorded at I-Fas, Depositeria Generale Parte Antica 389, no. 756. In 1612 her salary was raised to twelve scudi monthly to compensate her for teaching two of three named female pupils; the raise is noted at I-Fas, Deposteria Generale Parte Antica, 389, no. 1099. Both I-Fas, Depositeria Generale Parte Antica 389, no. 1241, and I-Fas, Manoscritti 321, fol. 412 record her salary as having been raised to twenty scudi monthly on 17 December 1614. Caccini's salary seems to have remained at that level through 1626, except for 1617, when it was recorded in I-Fas, Manoscritti 321, fol. 434, as having dipped to eighteen scudi monthly.

2. On the parts that Caccini sang in 1608 court entertainments and her performance

on the theorbo, see Tim Carter, "Music for a Florentine Wedding in 1608," *Acta musico-logica* 55 (1983): 89–107. On her other instrumental competences, see Bronzini, I-Fn. Magl. VIII. 1525/1, p. 54. Claudio Monteverdi described her performances, including all instruments but the harp, in 1610, I-MNas, Autogr. 6, fol. 108v, published in Claudio Monteverdi, *Lettere, dediche e prefazioni*, ed. Domenico de' Paoli (Rome: De Sanctis, 1973), 52. The letter is quoted in Warren Kirkendale, *The Court Musicians in Florence during the Principate of the Medici* (Florence: Olschki, 1993), 312 and n. 652. I-Fas, MdP 3883, fol. 494 is a letter dated 5 April 1624 from Vincenzo Salviati to Curtio Picchena about a harp that Christine had ordered made for Francesca at Rome.

3. Bronzini seems to use the word "maniera" to mean mode, although John Florio's 1611 English-Italian dictionary translates the word as "manner, fashion, style, guise." I have chosen not to translate the word as mode, to allow the possibility that Bronzini meant something more than a way of organizing music's pitches, some styles of perform-ing these modes that might never have been captured in language.

4. Cristoforo Bronzini, *Della dignità e nobiltà delle donne*, I-Fn, Magl. VIII. 1525/1, 56–60. See appendix C for the Italian text.

5. Bronzini, *Della dignità*, I-Fn, Magl. VIII. 1525/1, 49–50.

6. Ibid., I-Fn. Magl. VIII. 1525/1, 38–39. Bronzini only mentioned Vittoria Archilei in passing, on p. 78, as "once so rare and celebrated in singing, resident now in our city for more than thirty years."

7. Ibid., I-Fn, Magl. VIII. 1519/1, 22, interprets the myth of Amphion's musical building of Thebes thus: "il che altro non significa se non che egli con la sua prudenza e soavissima eloquenza, potè condurre gli huomini di quella religione che habitavano spersi per i campi e per le selve ad abitare civilmente in una medesima città."

8. For a complete list of Francesca's known performances, see appendix A. Table A1 lists her performances in staged entertainment, table A2 her performances as a chamber musician, and table A3 her performances for the court's annual, semi-public concerts for Holy Week.

9. See appendix A, table A4 for Francesca's known theatrical compositions.

10. See her letter of 13 February 1618 to Buonarroti, at I-FcasaB, A.B. 63, fol. 129v, in appendix B.

11. See her letter of 18 December 1614 to Buonarroti, at I-FcasaB, A.B. 44, no. 441, in appendix B. Tinghi lists no entertainment by Buonarroti that season, but it seems possible that he had at first been assigned the *Ballo delle zigare*, with words attributed to Ferdinando Saracinelli, that was performed in the Salone delle Commedie of Palazzo Pitti on 24 February 1615 for the marriage of Magdalena's dama Sofia "Todesca" to "Cav.re Castiglione, provveditore di Livorno." On 16 January 1614/15, Francesca wrote asking Buonarroti to join Saracinelli for a meeting in her home that evening, "so that everyone can be together, both poet and musician, and to be with me in the final resolution of what has to be changed." The letter is found at I-FcasaB, A.B. 44, no. 443, and in appendix B. Tinghi lists Lisabetta Giraldi, another dama of Magdalena's, as one of the six dancers. With the four singers that he mentions, the cast numbered ten women. Sofia and Lisa-betta were both to dance in the penultimate number of *La liberazione di Ruggiero* in 1625.

12. I-FcasaB, A.B. 44, no. 441, letter of 18 December 1614. See appendix B.

13. See her letter of 27 December 1614 to Buonarroti, at I-FcasaB, A.B. 44, no. 442, in appendix B.

14. I-FcasaB, A.B. 44, no. 441, letter of 18 December 1614.

15. I-FcasaB, A.B. 44, no. 441, letter of 27 December 1614 to Buonarotti.

16. Buonarroti's papers include an undated adaptation of Berni's satire and an original comic scenario with singing and dancing, written for "le donne di Giulio Romano." Both cast people known to have been in Giulio's household in 1604: Giulio, his wife, his son Pompeo, his daughters "la Cecchina" and Settimia, and his pupil Livia Schieggia, as well as "Niccolò castrato" and one Giovanni Battista, who might be either Giulio's second son or the man Francesca would marry. The Berni adaptation is at I-FcasaB, A.B. 84, fols. 391v–394v, and specifies that the prologue will be delivered by "Beco, cioè dalla Cecchina di Giulio." The original scenario is at I-FcasaB, A.B. 86, fols. 78r–79v. On Berni, see Giampieri Giampiero, *Francesco Berni* (Fucuchio [(Florence]: Edizione dell'Erba, 1997). A modern edition of *La Catrina* is found in *Opere di Francesco Berni* (Milan: G. Daelli, 1864), pt. 2, 19–50.

17. I-FcasaB, A.B. 44, no. 442, letter of 27 December 1614 to Buonarroti.

18. Francesca referred to herself as "without my *compagnia*" in a letter to Andrea Cioli, 19 March 1631. See appendix B for the letter and chapter 11 for a fuller discussion.

19. The phrase "do themselves honor" is from Francesca's letter of 27 December 1614.

20. In a letter of 23 February 1618, Francesca reported to Buonarroti that she had been asked to compare his still-unfinished comedy *La fiera* to *Il passatempo,* performed at Carnival in 1614. See I-FcasaB, A.B. 44, no. 448, fol. 1r, and appendix B. She replied diplomatically that they were nothing alike. Years later, a slyly negative comment about Andrea Salvadori's *Iole ed Ercole* caused the cancellation of the performance. See chapter 5.

21. Ibid. The letter is fully translated in chapter 6.

22. The then-childless Francesca thus earned 25 percent more than the household wage of sixteen scudi paid to her father, who was responsible for ten children. When the stipend paid to Francesca's husband is factored in, her household earned more than twice what her father's had earned.

23. Francesca complained about the decision, and the weak justification for it, in a letter to Orsini dated either 18 or 28 April 1614. The letter is poorly preserved at I-Rasc, F.O., 1st ser., 127/1, no. 664, and transcribed in appendix B. I-Rasc, F.O., 1st ser., 162/1, no. 167 is a letter from Paolo Giordano Orsini to his father, dated 15 April 1614, explaining the official reason: Francesca was to perform at a postpartum celebration when the pregnant Magdalena delivered that summer. Magdalena bore her next child in October 1614.

24. The cardinal's retinue is listed at I-Fas, Carte Strozziane I, fasc. 13, fols. 137–150v. The document was first cited in Tim Carter, *Jacopo Peri, 1561–1633: His Life and Works* (New York: Garland, 1989), 80, n. 25.

25. Tinghi reported the distribution of "bruno," mourning cloth for the servants to wear in response to Francesco's death, on 23 May 1614. See I-Fn, MS Gino Capponi 261, vol. I, fol. 573r; fols. 582r–584v describe his funeral.

26. Tinghi first reports Cosimo's illness on 3 September 1614 at I-Fn, MS Gino Capponi 261, vol. I, fol. 593v. Cosimo was "listening to music and instrumental playing" on 2 December and "listening to sung music" on 4 December. See ibid., fol. 609r. According to Galluzzi, Cosimo made his first will in 1615. See Jacopo Riguccio Galluzzi, *Istoria del granducato di Toscana sotto il governo della casa Medici* (Florence: Nella stamperia di R. del-Vivo, 1781), 6:195.

27. The orders for *La fiera* are found at I-FcasaB, A.B. 93, fol. 65r–v. Girolamo Guicciardini was then superintendent of buildings, Giulio Parigi was the court architect, Vincenzo Giugni was the *guardaroba,* and Giovanni del Turco was the superintendent

of music. The poet Jacopo Cicognini and the painter Cosimo Lotti were assigned to do whatever Buonarroti asked regarding the acting and the distribution of parts.

28. That had been the case in 1600, when Giulio composed the parts of Ottaviano Rinuccini's *L'Euridice* that would be performed by members of his studio, while Jacopo Peri composed the rest.

29. I-FcasaB, A.B. 45, no. 665 is Christine's letter of 26 December 1613. Buonarroti's attribution of the whole of *Il passatempo* is known from his draft reply, scribbled on the back of I-FcasaB, A.B. 45, no. 660, a letter about something completely different written by Donato Corsi, dated 14 December 1613. I-FcasaB, A.B. 50, no. 1255 is a letter of Domenico Montaguto to Buonarroti dated 26 February 1613/14, listing Cosimo II's gifts to the women who participated in a recent comedy, presumably *Il passatempo*, including "un paio di orecchini con perli per la S.ra Cecchina, un centiglio da capello per quella donna che fece la contadina nella commedia moglie del mainardi, quindici scudi di moneta per la figliuola di Pippo Sciameroni pittore."

30. These attributes of la Tancia's character are established in her first appearance onstage, act 1, scene 4, a song scene in which she first sings only to herself, then sings full voice. Although she means still to be singing to herself, she is overheard by Pietro.

31. The song is in act 2, scene 5, fol. 265r in the manuscript copy of the play found in I-FcasaB, A.B. 61, fasc. 3. This text is not present in the published versions. It is the one excerpt from *La Tancia* that Francesca preserved in print, as the crazy-quilt *aria sopra la romanesca* "La pastorella mia" in her *Primo libro*.

32. I-FCasaB, A.B. 43, no. 424: "faccia che io possa vedere se siano di agevolezza tale che io potessi farle capire a questi giovani . . . essendo agevoli come mi pare ricordare crederci."

33. I-Ru, MS 279, fols. 61r–68. On the provenance and other contents of the manuscript, see John Walter Hill, *Roman Monody, Cantata, and Opera from the Circles around Cardinal Montalto* (Oxford: Clarendon, 1997).

34. Monteverdi gendered these styles in an exactly opposite way in *Tirsi e Clori*. I am grateful to Tim Carter for pointing this out to me.

35. In a letter to Buonarroti dated 18 December 1614, Francesca reported singing bits from the show for the grand duchess, prompting her to praise Buonarroti for exactly this sort of mastery. See I-FCasaB, A.B. 44, no. 441.

36. On the politics of *La fiera*, see Nancy Canepa, "The 'Piazza' Motif and Encyclopedism in Tomaso Garzoni's *La piazza universale* (1585) and Michelangelo Buonarroti il Giovane's *La fiera* (1619)," *Canadian Journal of Italian Studies* 20 (1997): 171–192; Claudio Varese, "Ideologia, letteratura e teatro nella *Fiera* di Michelangelo Buonarroti il giovane," *Biblioteca di storia Toscana moderna e contemporanea: Studi e Documenti 26; Il Firenze e la Toscana dei Medici nell'europeo del 500* (Florence: Olschki, 1983), 585–610; and the edition with introduction by Uberto Limentani, *Michelangelo Buonarroti il giovane: La Fiera; Redazione originaria, 1619* (Florence: Olschki, 1984).

37. Francesca's letter of 25 January 1618/19 suggests that "Arcangela might better compose the aria introducing the final ballo than I." See appendix B. The *intermedi* of the syphilitics and of the wanderers, with their music, were performed in Pesaro for Carnival in 1622. See I-FcasaB, A.B. 47, no. 913, letter of Francesco Folchi, 22 January 1622, requesting them, and no. 914, letter of 6 February 1622, thanking Buonarroti for sending them. Letters from Domenico Filicai to Buonarroti in 1624 and 1625 suggest that both *Il passatempo* and *La fiera* had been read with pleasure by members of the

Barberini family during that period. See I-FcasaB, A.B. 46, no. 675, letter of 30 March 1624, no. 676, letter of 13 September 1624, and no. 678, letter of 4 January 1625. In 1631 Tommaso Salviati wrote to say that Taddeo and Cardinal Francesco Barberini had read both plays again with pleasure and expressed his own opinion that it would be good, in that calamitous time, to have them produced again, with singing. See I-FcasaB, A.B. 53, no. 1663, letter of 4 January 1631, and no. 1675, letter of 4 May 1631. In 1637 Cardinal Barberini's secretary Federigo Ubaldini wrote suggesting the possibility that *La fiera* might be performed for the following Carnival; see I-FcasaB, A.B. 55, no. 2003, letter of 26 December 1637. A series of letters from 12 March to 24 September 1639 from Carlo Strozzi discusses yet another reading Cardinal Barberini has given to *La fiera*, ending in a commitment to help Buonarroti publish it; these letters are found at I-FcasaB, A.B. 54, nos. 1925–1933.

38. A draft of Buonarroti's defense of *La fiera* is found at I-FcasaB, A.B. 39, fols. 102–106, letter of 14 February 1618 to Francesco dell'Antella.

39. I quote from the title page of Tinghi's diary, written 22 July 1600. See I-Fn, MS Gino Capponi 261, vol. I, fol. 1r.

40. Tinghi fails to mention the "offices" for 1626, and by 1627 the widowed Francesca was negotiating her withdrawal from service.

41. When the court spent the winter in Pisa, the church was San Nicolà; when it was in Florence, the church was Santa Felicita.

42. Tinghi, MS Gino Capponi 261, vol. 1, 384, mentions the crowds. Although Tinghi's descriptions imply that the offices were sung at the end of the day, he occasionally describes them as "mattutino" rather than either Vespers or Compline.

43. This account is based on Tinghi, MS Gino Capponi 261, vol. II, fol. 133; Bronzini, *Della dignità . . . giornata terza* (Florence: Pignoni, 1622), 70; and a letter that Curtio Picchena wrote to Caterina de' Medici, the Duchess of Mantua, on 10 April 1618. Picchena's letter is found at I-Fas, MdP 6108, fol. 977r–v.

44. Bronzini, *Della dignità . . . giornata terza*. Bronzini's completely gynocentric account omits mention of Don Lorenzo and the other adult men.

45. Ibid., stanzas 11 and 12: "Or la volubil voce in arco tende, / Or la vibra, or la sparge, ora l'unisce, / Or l'allunga, or l'annoda, ora la fende, / Or l'assottiglia, e inalza, or la smarrisca, / Ora la tempra grave, e bassa rende, / Or l'innaspa, e l'inaspra, or l'addolcisce, / Segnando a tempo i musicali viaggi, / Or con trilli, or con groppi, or con passaggi. // Tal'or per false note il volo affretta, / E volontaria tempera durezze, / Ma mentre offender par, via più diletta / Scoprendo più l'armoniche dolcezze; / Tal a l'amor, amata Dama alletta / Gli amanti più con sdegnosette asprezze; / Così col dolce il medico l'amaro/ Mischia ad arte, e il Pittor l'oscur col chiaro." I am grateful to the soprano Emily Van Evera for lending what she called her "knowledge in the larynx" to my translation in an email of 26 May 2005 and a telephone conversation of 28 May 2005. As Tim Carter and Elizabeth Randall Upton have both reminded me, Santi's poem is obviously influenced by Guarini's "Mentre vaga angioletta," especially well-known among musicians because of Monteverdi's setting.

46. Ibid., stanza 15: "Veduto havresti intento ogn'uditore / Mentre il canto durò, non batter ciglio / Bramoso, ch'à quel giorno eterni l'hore / Fermando il carro di Latona il figlio / E queste poi le melodie canore / Applauso far con placido bisbiglio; / Rimanendo ciascun da sé diviso / Col corpo in terra, e l'alma in Paradiso."

47. Some of the documents relating to this sojourn in Rome were published and analyzed by Anna Maria Crinò, "Virtuose di canto e poeti a Roma e a Firenze nella prima metà del Seicento," *Studi secentesche* 1 (1960): 175–193. See also Kirkendale, *Court Musicians*, 321–322.

48. For a complete list of Francesca's performances in Rome that season, see appendix A, table A2.

49. I-FCasaB, A.B. 48, no. 1037 is Guiducci's letter, which specifies that she sang the "stanzas on Saint Cordula" by Salvadori and would have sung more poetry of Buonarroti's if he had been crafty or ambitious enough to send some with her. Kirkendale, *Court Musicians*, 322, quotes from the letter. See also his notes 703 and 704.

50. I-Fas, MdP 3645, letter of Antimo Galli to Dimurgo Lambardi, 25 November 1623. A partial text of the letter is published in Crinò, "Virtuose di canto e poeti," 180.

51. Galli to Lombardi, 25 November 1623, gives the date of her appearance among the Umoristi. On the Accademia degli Umoristi, see Michel Maylender, *Storia delle Accademie dell'Italia* (Bologna: Lincinio Cappelli, 1930), 5:370–384. In the 1620s the academy met at the home of Paolo Mancini; it was among the few academies that admitted women to its meetings. In the 1620s its members included Giovanni Savelli, Alessandro Tassoni, Francesco Bracciolini, and Adriana Basile's brother Giovanni Battista.

52. Materdona included a sestina and three sonnets to Francesca that seem to refer to her 1623–1624 Roman sojourn in *Dalle Rime di Gianfrancesco Maria Materdona: Parte Seconda* (Venice: Vangelista Denchino, 1629), 62–66. A copy exists at I-Rvat with the placement designation Ferraioli Stampati 7071.

53. Materdona, *Dalle Rime*, 62–64: "(1) Donna, e che dissi donna! / Forse ch'io te devea / Musa appellar più tosto, o semidea! / Angela, o dea? / No'l sò, nè sò se stia / Ne la terra, o nel ciel l'anima mia. (2) Non sò se'l mondo nostro / È sù l'empireo asceo / O se nel nostro il mondo empireo è sceso: / Così mi hà reso / Ebro un canto, ebro un suono, / che non sò chi tu sei, nè dove io sono. (3) Vaga man, dotta bocca / Ove in bel misto accorde / L'aure canore e le sonore corde, / Pende concorde / Da i labbri, e da le dita / L'orecchio, e l'occhio, e l'anima è rapita. (4) Nè più culte potevi / Rime cantar di quelle, / Che già scrisse il marin, felici, e belle, / Nè potean elle, / Pompea di nostra estate, / Da più maestra lingua esser cantate. (5) Ma perche canti estinto / Il gentil giovinetto? Mancava ne l'ADON forse soggetto / D'alto diletto, / Di gioia, e gioco, e riso, / Che vuoi cantare il bello Adone ucciso? (6) Sì sì, t'intendo, è un'arte / Da scoprir valor franco: Canti un trafitto, e lacerato fianco, / Per mostrar anco, Che sai ne' tuoi concenti / Dolce la morte far, dolci i lamenti. (7) Non havria morso Adone / La fier cinghiali se udiva / Pria le tue voci: o l'amorosa diva, / Qualhor languiva / Sù l'estinto, a i tuoi canti / Temprato havrebbe il duol, frenati i pianti. (8) O havrian lor corso i cieli / Fermo a quel dolce immenso, / E'l mostro havria perduto il moto, e'l senso / O almeno i' penso, / Che'l vago Adon già morto, / A sì gran melodia saria risorto. (9) Godi pur, bello spento, / Siati pur morte grata, / Pur che sia da costei sempre cantata. / Bocca spietata / Ti fè di vita privo, / Bocca dotta, e gentil ti rende hor vivo."

54. The image of a woman's erudite mouth is, of course, open to double entendre.

55. It seems possible that in her choice of stanzas to sing for Marino, Francesca had intentionally evoked a comparison to Orpheus, whose last song before dying in Ovid's *Metamorphoses* told Adonis' tale. Adonis' death is recounted in book 10, lines 709–799, Orpheus' in book 11, lines 1–261.

56. Materdona, *Dalle Rime*, 65: "Per la medesima, mentre il Tevere cominciando ad innondar Roma, era gionto alla casa di lei." The quatrains read: "Queste, cui teme il cor, cui l'occhio vede / Uscite fuor del cristallino letto, / Acque latine, ò quel ruine al tetto, / Minacciar di Francesca il mondo crede. // Deh non sia chi paventi, ov'ella hà fede / Vien frettoloso il Tebro a trar diletto / Dal suo bel canto, e sotto altero aspetto / Corre a baciarle humilmente il piede." According to I-Rvat, Urb. Lat. 1094, Avvisi di Roma, high water flooded via Giulia and the Campo de' Fiori on 23 December 1623.

57. Ibid. At 65, the terzets read: "Tracia possanza altri ammirar poteo / Tosca virtute hor l'età nostra ammira, / E sà donna rifar quant'huomo già feo. // Ma differenti in ciò: con la sua lira / Affrenò il moto, e'l corso a i fiumi Orfeo, / E costei col suo plettro a sè gli tira."

58. Ibid., 66: "Per la medesima. In arrivando a Fiorenza, patria di lei": "Pace a voi, Toschi campi: a voi mi mena / Amor: dal vostro ciel, piagge feconde, / Vaga Angioletta uscì, che in larga vena / Scioglendo il canto, alta dolcezza infonde. / Pace a te, nobil Arno; ambe le sponde / Di smeraldo rivesti, e d'or l'arena; / Poichè da le tue chiare, e limpid'onde / L'unica al mondo forse alma Sirena. // Nacque dal vostro FIOR frutto, ond'hor nasce / A noi gioia, a lei fama, e voi decoro, / Frutto, che'l cor non sazia, e sempre il pasce. // Deh mirare il bel nido a me si lasce; / Ch'io possa, se reliquie havri di loro, / Baciar la culla, e adorar le fasce."

59. For a quick summary of these figures' relation to Florentine self-fashioning, see Mary Bergstein, "Marian Politics in Quattrocento Florence: The Renewed Dedication of Santa Maria del Fiore in 1412," *Renaissance Quarterly* 44 (1991): 673–719.

60. The phrase both used was "in voce." I am grateful to Mauro Calcagno for reminding me that in early modern Italy knowledge communicated "in voce" was the most privileged.

61. Bronzini, I-Fn, Magl. VIII. 1525/1, 126. The speaker is Vittoria, the hostess.

62. The mastery of details was an important value, as Giulio had noted in *Le nuove musiche* (1602): "In the profession of singer . . . not only are the details useful, but everything taken together makes it better." See Murata, *Source Readings*, 102.

Chapter 5

1. I mean for the chapter title to play on the title of the first song in Francesca's *Primo libro delle musiche*, "Chi è costei . . . (Who is she)?" and on the distinction that the philosopher Adriana Cavarero draws between knowing what a person is (her subject position) and who she is (her uniqueness as an "existent") in *Relating Narratives: Storytelling and Selfhood*, trans. Paul A. Kottman (London: Routledge, 2000), first published as *Tu che mi guardi, tu che mi racconti* (Milan: Feltrinelli, 1997).

2. When he wrote his two wills, dated 1612 and 1617, Giulio described himself as living in a house he owned at the Croce al Trebbio, bought from Guido Gagnolandi. I-Fr, Ricc. 2303, no. 4, fol. 250 describes property belonging to the Collegio del Gesù Pellegrino, including a house next to property belonging to Giulio's heirs in the via degli Asini at the Croce al Trebbio. See Warren Kirkendale, *The Court Musicians in Florence during the Principate of the Medici* (Florence: Olschki, 1993), 164–166 for excerpts of Caccini's wills and codicils and notes 294–295 for their locations. On the location of the via Sebastiano property, see chapter 1, note 20.

3. Florentine law required that dowries be invested in easily liquidated assets so that

the dowry could be restituted in the event that a marriage failed; investment in real estate was the most common way of meeting this requirement. On early modern dowry practices in Florence, the locus classicus is Christiane Klapisch-Zuber, "The 'Cruel Mother': Maternity, Widowhood, and Dowry in Florence in the Fourteenth and Fifteenth Centuries," in *Women, Family, and Ritual in Renaissance Italy,* trans. Lydia Cochrane (Chicago: University of Chicago Press, 1985). Via Valfonda now runs along the northwest side of Florence's principal railway station. The houses the Caccini-Signorini occupied were probably destroyed by the time of the station's construction. According to the sale documents, the Caccini-Signorini property was bounded by the street, by property still owned by the parcel's seller, Benedetto di Francesco Landi, property belonging to the builder Lorenzo di Vincenzo Cavalcanti, and property belonging to the monastery of Santa Maria Novella. The sale document is at I-Fas, Notarile moderno, Protocolli 10609–10622, Atti di Niccolò Minacci, vol. 10611, fols. 62r–64v. Documents establishing financial good faith and the conditions of sale are in the same volume, fols. 18r–v, fols. 22r–23r, and 23v. I am grateful to Professor Gino Corti for helping me transcribe and understand these documents. A document from the late 1620s describing the property of Riccardo Riccardi's heirs indicates that property belonging to "Signora Francesca di Giulio Caccini" bordered the Riccardi gardens on their easternmost end and adjoined the property of Casini and Mochi. See I-Fas, Manelli-Galilei-Riccardi 357, "Bene della prima primogenitura visitati confinati et ricontrati col primo inventario . . . per adempimento del testamento del Signor Riccardo Ricardi."

4. This description of the property is taken from I-Fas, Manelli-Galilei-Riccardi 357, "Bene della prima primogenitura," In the eighteenth century Riccardi's library became the core collection of the Biblioteca Riccardiana, now located on via Ginori.

5. See, e.g., her own hastily written note to Buonarroti asking him to come to a meeting in her home with one of the court's superintendents of music, Ferdinando Saracinelli, on 16 January 1614/15, at I-FcasaB, A.B. 44, no. 443, in appendix B.

6. Signorini's will is at I-Fas, Notarile moderno. Protocolli 13734–13737. Atti di Paolo Lapi. Testamento del 23 dicembre 1626, G. B. Signorini, fols. 31r–34r. See chapter 11.

7. I-Fas, Decima Granducale 3597 (Campione Santa Croce. Gonfalone Ruote), no. 28, fol. 33 describes the property and records the tax that Signorini owed on the property at the time his name changed to include the suffix "Malaspina." I am grateful to Paola Peruzzi of the Archivio di Stato di Firenze for helping me locate and understand all the documents in the Decima Granducale that are relevant to this property.

8. The documents related to this sale are at I-Fas Notarile moderno, Atti di Tommaso Mati. Protocolli 11740, no. 46, fol. 63r–v; and ibid., Protocolli 111742, no. 59, fols. 93v–94v; no. 60, fols. 94v–98; and no. 61, fols. 98r–100r. A career diplomat, Pandolfini (1594–1655) was Tuscany's ambassador to Milan from 1626 to 1634; he was often away during this period as a renter. The 1632 census is at I-Fn, MS Palat. E.B. 15.2.xx.

9. It seems likely that this Guido Gagnolandi was related to the one from whom Giulio Caccini had bought his property at Croce al Trebbio and that both were related to Francesca's mother, Lucia Gagnolandi. So far, however, I have found no firm evidence of these relationships.

10. A summary inventory of Mochi's estate is at I-Fas, Magistrato dei Pupille. Principato. 2726, unnumbered document dated 25 February 1638/39.

11. For more on Belli see Kirkendale, *Court Musicians*, 355–359; for Sciamerone, see ibid., 359. The two were paid a monthly household stipend of sixteen scudi from the Depositeria Generale; Sciamerone was paid an additional four scudi monthly from another source. By contrast, Francesca alone was paid twenty scudi monthly, and her husband was paid between thirteen and twenty scudi monthly.

12. The inventory of Belli's estate is at I-Fas, Magistrato di Vedove e Pupille. Principato. 785, no. 65.

13. Giulio left Francesca his "istrumento di tasti dipinto a mano da Cigoli" in the last codicil to his will, dated 6 December 1618. See I-Fas, Notarile moderno, Protocolli 5611–5618. Andrea Marii. Testamento di 6 dicembre 1618, fol. 93v. For the instruments Signorini had on consignment, see I-Fas, Guardaroba medicea 391, ins. 5, fol. 490. The inventory, conducted when the position of *guardaroba della musica* passed from Antonio Naldi detto il Bardella to Lorenzo Allegri in 1621, is the subject of Mario Fabbri, "La collezione medicea degli strumenti musicali in due sconosciuti inventari del primo Seicento," *Note d'archivio per la storia musicale*, n.s. 1 (1983): 51–62. On the sordellina, see Maurizio Tacrini, Giovanni Farris, and John Henry van der Meers, eds., *Giovanni Lorenzo Baldano: Libro per scriver l'intavolatura per sonare sopra le sordelline (Savona, 1600); Facsimile del manoscritto e studi introduttivi* (Savona: Editrice Liguria, 1995).

14. In the 1620s the couple had at least one servant, named Tommaso, who occasionally picked up the monthly pay of one or both, as the paymaster noted in the book now kept at I-Fas, Depositeria General Antica 1522, fol. 97.

15. For more on Signorini's fiscal negligence, see chapter 11. On the value of otium, see Brian Vickers, "Leisure and Idleness in the Renaissance: The Ambivalence of Otium," *Renaissance Studies* 4, no. 1 (1990): 1–37, and 4, no. 2 (1990): 107–154.

16. Bronzini, *Della dignità e nobiltà delle donne*, I-Fn, Magl. VIII. 1525/1, 66–67. See appendix C.

17. I-Rasc, F.O., 1st ser., 126, no. 858, letter of Francesca Caccini to Virginio Orsini, 11 May 1613, is the cover letter for two madrigals that Francesca had promised to send Orsini "per quelle Signore" in her chattier letter of 4 May 1613, I-Rasc, F.O., 1st ser., 124/2, no. 233. See appendix B for the full texts of these letters. I-Fas, MdP 6108, fol. 1036, letter of Curtio Picchena to Caterina de' Medici, credits Francesca with having composed three intermedii for his daughter, twelve girls, and seven little girls to perform in his home. The performance was repeated in the rooms of the Medici princesses at Cosimo II's request, as described by Tinghi at I-Fn, MS Gino Capponi 261, vol. II, fol. 238r. Francesca is known to have passed time with Picchena's daughter, the painter Caterina Buondelmonte, earlier, entertaining Caterina in daily conversation when she stayed at Galileo Galilei's home at Bellosguardo in May 1619. See I-Fn, Galileiana, Gal. 15, fols. 8r–9r, copy of a letter of Galileo Galilei to Curtio Picchena, 26 May 1619. Neri Alberi's request for canzonette, forwarded through Buonarroti, is at I-FcasaB, A.B. 95, fol. 174, letter of 2 July 1626. Twenty days later he acknowledged receipt of the music, in a letter at I-FcasaB, A.B. 95, fol. 158. Neither letter refers to payment.

18. John Walter Hill, "La monodia in Toscana: Nuovi appunti sui manoscritti" (forthcoming). I am grateful to Professor Hill for sharing a pre-publication copy of his work. The "Barbera manuscript" is I-Fc, CF83. It includes, on p. 112, an anonymous setting of "S'io men vò, morirò," a text set by Francesca for which no other concordance is known.

19. I-Rasc, F.O., 1st ser., 126/2, no. 300, letter of Giulio Caccini to Virginio Orsini, 6 September 1614, printed in part in Kirkendale, *Court Musicians*, 314.

20. I-Rasc. F.O., 1st ser., 125/1, no. 164, letter of Francesca Caccini Signorini to Virginio Orsini, 22 March 1613/14. See appendix B.

21. I-FcasaB, A.B. 44, no. 446, letter of Francesca Caccini Signorini to Buonarroti, 26 May 1617. See appendix B.

22. I-Fas, MdP 1427, fols. 77r–78r, letter of Francesca Caccini Raffaelli to Andrea Cioli, 19 March 1631. See appendix B for the full text and chapter 11 for fuller analysis of this letter.

23. Antonio Brunelli, *Prima parte delli fioretti spirituali a 1.2.3. quattro e cinque voci per concertare nell'organo* (Venice: Bartolomeo Magni, 1626), preface, as translated and quoted in Tim Carter, "Printing the 'New Music,'" in *Music and the Cultures of Print*, ed. Kate van Orden (New York: Garland, 2000), 8.

24. The payments for teaching are at I-Fas, Depositaria General Antica 389, no. 1099, and are cited in Kirkendale, *Court Musicians*, 349. The same payment order assigns Domenico Poggi as much to teach one of the three girls mentioned as Francesca was paid to teach two. There is indirect evidence that Francesca had some kind of pedagogical relationship to the princely children during this period because she clearly coached and accompanied musical performances by Princesses Margherita and Anna and by Princes Giovan Carlo and Leopoldo. On the possibility that she taught Princess Anna and her niece Vittoria della Rovere in the Monastero della Crocetta in the 1630s, see chapter 12. She would not have been the first prominent musician to teach the Medici children, however: I-Fas, MdP 1371, letter of Jacopo Peri to Andrea Cioli, 29 January 1618, asserts that Peri had taught singing to the daughters of Cosimo I.

25. I-Fas, MdP 1716, letter of Ferdinando Saracinelli to an unnamed court official, 11 February 1622/23. Like her teacher, Emilia eventually served the court as a theatrical singer and improvising chamber musician and perhaps as a composer. I-FcasaB, A.B. no. 773, letter of Giovanni del Ricco to Buonarroti, 2 December 1629, is a letter Ricco wrote on behalf of his wife Emilia Grazi reporting that Christine had brought her to La Crocetta especially to sing his spiritual songs, having heard them praised by Selvaggia de' Medici. For more about Grazi, see Kirkendale, *Court Musicians*, 349–50.

26. I-Rasc, F.O., 1st ser., 126/1, no. 67, letter of Francesca Caccini Signorini to Virginio Orsini, 26 December 1614. See appendix B.

27. I-Fas, MdP 1427, fol. 77r–78r, letter of Francesca Caccini Raffaelli to Andrea Cioli, 19 March 1631. See appendix B.

28. I-Fas, MdP 1426, insert 1, letter of Francesca Caccini Signorini [Malespina] to Andrea Cioli, 25 March 1619. The feast of the Annunciation-Incarnation, 25 March, marked the new year in Florence and was therefore a holiday. Given that the feast celebrates a woman's obedience to the command brought by a higher authority's messenger, it was an ironic date for Francesca to decline orders from the granducato.

29. The commission Francesca declined may have been for Rinuccini's semidramatic *Versi sacri*, performed in Maria Magdalena's private chapel at Compline on 2 April. According to Jacopo Cicognini's description, the performance featured a chorus of angels and "the best singers in Florence," each representing different saints. For the description and text, see Angelo Solerti, *Gli albori della melodrama* (Milan: Sandron, 1904–1905), 2:336–345. Francesca's husband Giovanni Battista Signorini added the suffix Malespina to his name in 1619, the year he agreed to pay Florence's general tax, the Decima Granducale, as a head tax rather than as property tax. The suffix suggests that he was related to the noble family Signorini-Malespina. No other evidence supports this possibility.

30. Among the many things she may have taught her pupils was the reinforcing lesson that women could exercise such power every day.

31. See Kelley Harness, *Echoes of Women's Voice: Music, Art and Female Patronage in Early Modern Florence* (Chicago: University of Chicago Press, 2006), 85–88 and Documents 3.3 to 3.9, 100–109. At 80–99 Harness thoroughly covers the background, content, and political allegory of *La regina Sant'Orsola*.

32. I-Fas, MdP 111, fol. 182r–v, letter of Ferdinando Saracinelli to Maria Magdalena, 23 October 1624, as translated in Harness, *Echoes of Women's Voice*, 100.

33. I-Fas, MdP 111, fol. 180r, minute of Magdalena to Saracinelli, 26 October 1624, as translated in Harness, *Echoes of Women's Voice*, 101.

34. I-Fas, MdP 1703, letter of Ferdinando Saracinelli to an unknown recipient, 26 November 1624. See Harness, *Echoes of Women's Voice*, 103, for a slightly different translation. Francesca's rage at Salvadori was also noted in a letter that Cardinal Carlo de' Medici wrote to Magdalena on 28 November 1624, at I-Fas, MdP 3883, fol. 693–694.

35. I-Fas, MdP 1703, letter of Saracinelli to an unknown recipient, 26 November 1624. See Harness, *Echoes of Women's Voice*, 103, for a slightly different translation.

36. Saracinelli quotes Francesca's accusation in his letter of 26 November 1624, cited in note 36. He describes Maria Botti's impertinence as unsurpassed in a letter of 27 November 1624 at I-Fas, MdP 1703. See Harness, *Echoes of Women's Voice*, 105 for a translation of this letter.

37. I-Fas, MdP 1703, letter of Ferdinando Saracinelli to an unknown recipient, 27 November 1624, as translated in Harness, *Echoes of Women's Voice*, 106.

38. I-Fas, MdP 1716, letter of Saracinelli to an unknown recipient, 11 February 1622/23.

39. I-Fas, MdP 1703, letter of Saracinelli to an unknown recipient, 28 November 1624, as translated in Harness, *Echoes of Women's Voice*, 108.

40. I-Fr, MS 2270, 287r–290r. Cavalcante's father owned land adjacent to the Caccini-Signorini, so he may have known Francesca personally. The manuscript contains several other prose narratives, including a misogynist account of Caterina Picchena ne' Buondelmonte's transgressive middle life. For the most widely read modern interpretation of the Cavalcante narrative, see Alessandro Ademollo, *La bell'Adriana ed altre virtuose del suo tempo alla corte di Mantova* (Città di Castello: Lapi, 1888). The full Italian text is reprinted in Kirkendale, *Court Musicians*, 325–326.

41. Salvadori had presumably based his libretto at least in part on Ovid's account of Hercules as seen through the eyes of his wife Deianira in the ninth letter of the *Heroides*.

42. On the effeminacy of men who surrounded themselves with women, as perceived in the Classical imagination, see David M. Halperin, *How to Do the History of Homosexuality* (Chicago: University of Chicago Press, 2003), chap. 3, "Historicizing the Subject of Desire," 81–103.

43. For Bronzini's fantasy about the muses as musical servants of sovereign women, see chapter 3.

CHAPTER 6

1. For the book as evidence of her importance as a composer, see Severo Bonini, *Prima parte de discorsi regole so[p]ra la musica*, I-Fr, Ricc. 2218, fol. 85v; Cristoforo Bronzini,

Della dignità e nobiltà delle donne, I-Fn, Magl. VIII. 1525/1, 55. See appendix C. For the book as evidence of her performances, see Gary Tomlinson's introduction to the facsimile printed in *Italian Secular Song,* vol. 1, *Florence* (New York: Garland, 1985), xv.

2. Ellen Rosand, "'Senza necessità di autore': Printed Singing Lessons in Seventeenth-Century Italy," *Atti del XIV Congresso della Società Internazionale di Musicologia: Bologna 1987* (Turin: Edizione di Torino, 1990), 2:214–224.

3. This concept was introduced in Sandra Gilbert and Susan Gubar, *The Madwoman in the Attic* (New Haven: Yale University Press, 1979).

4. See John Walter Hill, "Training a Singer for *Musica Recitativa* in Early Seventeenth-Century Italy: The Case of Baldassare," in *Musicologica Humana: Studies in Honor of Warren and Ursula Kirkendale* (Florence: Olschki, 1994), 345–357; Rosand, "Senza ncessità di autore."

5. Pietro della Valle, "Della musica dell'età nostra, che non è punto inferiore, anzi è migliore di quella dell'età passata," in *De' trattati di musica di Gio. Batista Doni,* ed. Anton Francesco Gori, 2:249–264 (Florence, 1763). See Warren Kirkendale, *The Court Musicians in Florence during the Principate of the Medici* (Florence: Olschki, 1993), 329, for the Italian text and Margaret Murata, ed., *Strunk's Source Readings in Music History,* vol. 4, *The Baroque Era* (New York: Norton, 1998), 37–43, for a full translation.

6. Bronzini, *Della dignità,* p. 68. See appendix C.

7. F-Pn, Cons. Rés. 24, marked "ex libris du prince M. A. Borghese"; I-MOe, Mus. D. 39, marked as being from the library of "Prince Alex. Card.le Esten," that is, Cardinal Alessandro d'Este (1568–1624); and I-Fn, Musica antica 23, possibly the copy known to have been in the library of D. Antonio de' Medici. Each has been trimmed a bit differently over the centuries, but they have approximately the same measurements.

8. The guitar-playing, pleasure-loving Carlo de' Medici, 1595–1666, was Christine's third son. After his brother Don Francesco died in 1614, Carlo became the likely Medici cardinal. Pope Paolo V elevated him on 2 December 1615 and gave Carlo his *beretta* and the deaconry of his father's church, Santa Maria in Domnica on 18 May 1616. Because Cosimo II's will at the time named Carlo co-regent with Magdalena in the event of his death, many in Florence assumed in 1618 that Carlo would be the next ruler of Tuscany. The day before he died, however, Cosimo changed his will to name Christine co-regent.

9. I mean to evoke *Vogue's* historical associations with fashion, constructed femininity, and, in its covers and photographic aesthetic, the modernist avant-garde.

10. For a partial and speculative answer to this question based on platonic number theory, see Suzanne G. Cusick, "This Music Which Is Not One: Inaudible Order and Representation of the Feminine in Francesca Caccini's *Primo libro della musiche* (1618)," in *Early Modern Women* 2 (2007): 127–162.

11. Bonini, *Prima parte de discorsi regole* fols. 85–86.

12. Bronzini, *Della dignità,* 55–56. See appendix C.

13. Ibid., 66–69. See appendix C.

14. Ibid., 69. See appendix C. This remark also suggests that the fatigue that sent Francesca to bed in late March 1619 was more serious than her letter implied. For letters by Francesca that implied illness that winter, see I-FcasaB, A.B. 44, no. 447, letter to Michelangelo Buonarroti, 25 January 1619, in which she suggests that Arcangiola Palladini should sing her parts in *La fiera;* and I-Fas, MdP 1426, insert 1, letter to Andrea Cioli, 25 March 1619, in which she declines to compose, teach, and perform with her pupils a seventy-line text by Ottavio Rinuccini. Both letters are printed in appendix B.

15. The passage in quotation marks, referring to the canonic tradition of Italian poetry that Francesca chose not to set, is from Virginia Woolf's acerbic characterization of her epoch's institutional elites in *Three Guineas* (New York: Harcourt Brace, 1938), 62.

16. Tim Carter has argued that no singer-composer would have been well served by publishing music that could be taken as somehow transcribing his or her performances. It was, instead, in their interest to sustain an aura of unrepresentability around their virtuosity. He notes that "if the virtuoso art of the 'new music' could be captured fully on the printed page, it would be a feeble art indeed." See Carter, "Printing the New Music," in *Music and the Cultures of Print*, ed. Kate van Orden, 3–37 (New York: Garland, 2000); the passage quoted is at 28.

17. The conventional view is implied by Nino Pirrotta's classic description of the three musicians' tangle at the beginning of "Early Opera and Aria," chapter 6 of his *Music and Theatre from Poliziano to Monteverdi* (Cambridge: Cambridge University Press, 1982), 237–254. In his equally classic formulation of the scramble for authorship, Tim Carter affirms Pirrotta's view that Ferdinando I meant to squelch a three-way rivalry that reflected badly on his famiglia; see Carter, "'Non occorre nominare tanti musici: Private Patronage and Public Ceremony in Late Sixteenth-Century Florence," *I Tatti Studies* 4 (1991): 89–104.

18. In 1602 Tinghi acknowledged Giulio Caccini as the composer of *L'Euridice*, performed in December for Cardinals del Monte and Montalto. See I-Fn, MS Gino Capponi 261, vol. 1, fol. 42v, entry for 5 December 1602. It would be ten years before he named another composer, one "Lorenzo Todesco," who composed a madrigal on the tune of a ballo from the previous Carnival, to words by Ferdinando Saracinelli. See I-Fn, MS Gino Capponi 261, vol. 1, fol. 409v.

19. Mario Biagioli, *Galileo, Courtier: The Practice of Science in the Culture of Absolutism* (Chicago: University of Chicago Press, 1993), 52–53.

20. Tinghi cites the following specific composers: Marco da Gagliano, the "Balletto di Montanine," performed at the end of a Carnival joust in 1614/15, I-Fn, MS Gino Capponi, vol. 1, fol. 551r; "Pompeo, organista del duomo," Jacopo Peri, and Lorenzo Todesco, for various parts of the balletto *l'Imperiale* danced by pages on 9 February 1614/15 for the baptism of the grand duke's third child and second son, Gian Carlo, vol. 1, fol. 552r; Jacopo Peri (inaccurately), for the music for Buonarroti's Carnival-night entertainment that year, *Il passatempo*, vol. 1, fol. 557r; Lorenzino del Liuto (Lorenzo Allegri) and Jacopo Peri for the "aria" (instrumental music) and "musica" (vocal music) for the ballo known as *L'Iride*, performed on 4 February 1615, vol. 1, fol. 646r and v, respectively; Francesca, for all of the music for the *Ballo delle zingare* performed on 24 February 1615 for the marriage of lady-in-waiting Sofia "todesca" to Cav.re Castiglioni, vol. 1, fol. 650v; Marco da Gagliano, for the *Ballo delle donne turche*, performed for the Thursday before Carnival, 1615, vol. 1, fol. 653; Jacopo Peri, Paolo Grazii, Giovanni Battista Signorini, and music superintendent Giovanni del Turco, for the horseback ballet *Guerra d'amore*, performed in Piazza Santa Croce on 11 February 1616, vol. 2, fol. 24v; Jacopo Peri and Lorenzo Allegri, for music for a ballo performed on 16 February 1616, vol. 2, fol. 25; Peri and "Paolo Francesino" [probably Paolo Grazi], for music for the *Guerra di bellezze*, performed on 16 October 1616 in Piazza Santa Croce, vol. 2, fol. 62v; Marco da Gagliano, for *La liberazione di Tirreno*, performed on 6 February 1617 in the Sala della Galleria, vol. 2, fol. 92; Alessandro Covoni, for the music sung by "gentiluomini fiorentini" from three carriages

beneath the window of Grand Duke Cosimo on 1 May 1618, vol. 2, fol. 139; Francesca, for the music for Buonarroti's Carnival comedy *La fiera*, performed in the "sala grande delle commedie di galleria" on 11 February 1619, vol. 2, fol. 188v; Marco da Gagliano and Jacopo Peri, for Salvadori's *Lo sposalizio di Medoro et Angelica*, "cantata tutta in musica" on 25 September 1619 to celebrate the election of Emperor Ferdinand (brother of Archduchess Maria Magdalena d'Austria), vol. 2, fol. 232r; and Francesca, for a "pastoralina" performed by the Medici children for their ailing father on 22 July 1620, vol. 2, fol. 259. Cosimo died on 28 February 1621.

21. Pignoni's investors were Giovanni del Turco, Ludovico Arrighetti, and Cosimo del Sera (whose investment passed through the hands of Giovanni Battista da Gagliano). The composers whose music he published in his first year were Antonio Brunelli, Giulio Caccini, Marco da Gagliano, Giovanni del Turco, Raffaello Rontani, and the neophyte Domenico Visconti, a protégé of Gagliano's. On the complicated history of the Marescotti-Pignoni firm see Tim Carter, "Music-Printing in Late Sixteenth- and Early Seventeenth-Century Florence: Giorgio Marescotti, Cristoforo Marescotti and Zanobi Pignoni," *Early Music History* 9 (1990): 27–72.

22. One reader has suggested a third impetus, the possibility that by February 1618 Giulio Caccini was terminally ill. Although he died in December of that year and Francesca was concerned about his failure to answer her letters in February, there is no evidence that Giulio was then perceived to be dying.

23. The overarching conceit of Bronzini's treatise was that it documented conversations held in the gardens of the Medici palace on twenty-four days in July. The penultimate leaf of Bronzini's first printed volume, published by Zanobi Pignoni in December 1622, reproduces the pertinent permissions. Cosimo Minerbetti, archdeacon of Florence, read and approved the text of the first six days by 10 April 1618. At the request of Florence's inquisitor, the sixth day was reviewed and approved again by Canon and Apostolic Protonotary Francesco Maria Gualterotti by 30 April 1619. A note at the end of the manuscript volume for the final day, I-Fn, Magl. VIII.1531, indicates that the copying began on 6 April 1619 and ended on 28 April 1619. Final approval to print came only in April 1621 from Bacio Bandinelli (a court paymaster) and Niccolò dell'Antella (a member of Maria Magdalena's Regency Council) and in May 1621 from Piero Niccolini, Vicar of Florence. Magdalena had formally assumed her regency on 10 March 1621.

24. The Florence copy may have been one of the two listed on p. 61 of the undated inventory of Don Antonio de' Medici's library, now at I-Fas, MdP 5132a. Francesca may have first known Alessandro d'Este (1568–1624) when she taught Giulia d'Este to sing in the French style in 1605. She apparently sustained a relationship with that family, for as late as 1639 she dared to ask Duke Francesco to intervene on her behalf in a legal matter. Their exchange is known indirectly from a letter the judge hearing her lawsuit, Lodovico Zuccoli, sent the duke on 19 May 1639, in the Raffaelli file of I-MOas Cancelleria Ducale particolari 1150 [Rebion-Ragazzoni]. In 1617 Marc'Antonio Borghese married Camilla Orsini, one of Virginio Orsini's daughters, whom Caccini visited on their father's behalf in the Monastero della Concezione in Florence, and for whom she composed madrigals. See appendix B for Francesca's letters about these relationships.

25. I-Fas, MdP 5269a, an unfoliated, unsigned letter to Curtio Cioli in Pisa, marked "Ad instantia della S.ra Fran.ca Caccini," on the reverse of a letter to Card.le Capponi of Bologna, 4 August 1618, appoints Calestani to the post. I-Fas, MdP 1377, unfoliated,

letter of Francesca Caccini Signorini to Andrea Cioli, 19 September 1618, refers to an unnamed young man on whose behalf she has petitioned Cioli to help obtaining permissions. Pignoni's name is written across the top of her letter in another hand. Francesca had known Falconieri since they both had served the household of Cardinal Carlo de' Medici in Rome during the latter's installation in 1616. Falconieri published his *Quinto libro delle musiche à una, due e tre voci* with Pignoni in 1619, dedicating his work to a third member of the Cardinal's household in 1616, Niccolo Berardi, who is listed as among the "gentilhuomini" qualified to join the cardinal at table in I-Fas, MdP 3882, p. 546; see appendix B. The letter asking Angelica Badii ne' Cioli for an appointment is at I-Fas, MdP1377, unfoliated, letter of Francesca Caccini Signorini, 11 August 1618; see appendix B.

26. I-FcasaB, A.B. 44, no. 448, letter of Francesca Caccini Signorini to Buonarroti, dated 23 February 1618. See appendix B.

27. Ibid.

28. Ibid., postcript.

29. See Harold Bloom, *The Anxiety of Influence* (New York: Oxford University Press, 1973).

30. Gilbert and Gubar, *Madwoman in the Attic*, articulates the notion of "anxiety of authorship" most sharply in chapter 2, "The Infection in the Sentence."

31. The fragments in quotation marks paraphrase the sentence in ibid., 48–49, in which they define "anxiety of authorship": "Thus the 'anxiety of influence' that a male poet experiences is felt by a female poet as an even more primary 'anxiety of authorship'—a radical fear that she cannot create, that because she can never become a 'precursor' the act of writing will isolate or destroy her."

32. Gilbert and Gubar, in ibid., 49, argue that women who find their voices do so "by actively seeking a female precursor who proves by example that a revolt against patriarchal literary authority is possible." In the less agonistic formulation of Luisa Muraro, *L'ordine simbolico della madre* (Rome: Editori Riuniti, 1991), women who find their voices are imagined to do so by finding authorization in the symbolic authority of another woman, usually an older one. Christine de Lorraine may have been such a symbolic authority for Francesca Caccini.

33. Buonarroti had written Giulio's dedication letter to Lorenzo Salviati in *Le nuove musiche;* his autograph is at I-FcasaB, A.B. 40, no. 187. A second letter, above which "per un musico per dedicazione che egli fa a un signore di alcuni suoi madrigali nel darli alla stampa, parmi ricordar che fusse Marco da Gagliano al S.r Conte Cosimo della Gherardesca," is at I-FcasaB, A.B. 40, no. 174. Both documents are cited in Kirkendale, *Court Musicians*, 144, n. 186. Kirkendale notes that the dedication text does not match any known printed collections of Gagliano's music. Piero Benedetti dedicated a collection of musiche to Cosimo della Gherardesca in 1611. I have not seen this collection.

34. On these negotiations, see chapter 2.

35. Giulio's letter to Buonarroti is at I-FcasaB, A.B. 44, no. 440, dated 24 February 1606/07.

36. I-Fas, MdP 1370, letter of Giulio Caccini to Andrea Cioli, 3 March 1617/18.

37. The codicil is at I-Fas, Notarile moderno, Protocolli 5618, fol. 93r–v, codicil dated 6 December 1618, reported in Kirkendale, *Court Musicians*, 165–166.

CHAPTER 7

1. For detailed readings of these songs, see Suzanne G. Cusick, "'Who is this woman?': Self-Presentation, *Imitatio Vergine* and Compositional Voice in Francesca Caccini's *Primo libro delle musiche* (1618)," *Il saggiatore musicale* 5 (1998): 5–42.

2. The touchstone texts on courtly subjectivity as performance are Norbert Elias, *The Court Society*, trans. Edward Jephecott (New York: Pantheon, 1983) and Steven Greenblatt, *Renaissance Self-Fashioning: More to Shakespeare* (Chicago: University of Chicago Press, 1980).

3. My reading follows the order of songs in the book, from front to back. Readers should note that this is not the order in which songs are listed in the table of contents.

4. "Ardo infelice, e palesar non tento."

5. For the song's full text and a translation by Massimo Ossi, see Ronald J. Alexander and Richard Savino, eds., *Francesca Caccini's Il primo libro delle musiche of 1618: A modern critical edition of the secular monodies* (Bloomington: Indiana University Press, 2004), 9–10; their edition of the song is at 27–37. A seventeenth-century copy of the poem can be found at I-Fn, MS Palatino 251, fols. 256–258; a parody of the first stanza, followed by a second stanza not set by Caccini, is found in I-Fr, Ricc. 1131, fol. 50. Both manuscripts attribute the stanzas to Andrea Salvadori.

6. On the recitative soliloquy as a genre of emotionally unified narrative explored introspectively by a serious character, eventually associated with mad scenes, scenes of lament, or narratives of catastrophe in a woman's poetic voice, see Margaret Murata, "The Recitative Soliloquy," *Journal of the American Musicological Society* 32 (1979): 45–73. Murata considers Salvadori the first poet to have developed the recitative soliloquy.

7. The gender of both lover and beloved are unknowable in the first stanza; by the second it becomes clear that the beloved is female, inviting the heteronormative interpretation that the speaker is a man so feminized by his sexual desire that, uncharacteristically for early modern love poetry, he cannot even speak it. By the fifth stanza, the speaker is identified as a "new Clizia," that is, as like the female sea nymph transformed into a sunflower to punish her illicit love for Apollo. For more about Clizia, see below.

8. On the story of Clizia, see Ovid, *Metamorphoses*, trans. Rolfe Humphries (Bloomington: Indiana University Press, 1955), bk. 4, lines 206, 234–237, 256–270. In the seventeenth century the lamenting Clizia was a common subject of paintings, most notably those by Rubens. His workshop's *Clizia Grieving*, painted in the 1630s for Torre de la Parada, El Pardo, Spain, was long catalogued as *Ariadne Abandoned*. For more about this painting, and a chronological list of representations of Clizia, see Jane Davidson Reid, ed., *The Oxford Guide to Classical Mythology in the Arts, 1300–1900* (Oxford: Oxford University Press, 1993), 1:306–308.

9. I hesitate to raise to the possibility that Francesca could have referred to a modal system that was already obsolete in her time. But the fact is that, however antiquated the practice seems, a passaggio articulating the characteristic range (ambitus) of one of the modes discussed in sixteenth-century counterpoint manuals is present in almost every song of her *Primo libro*. Usually it is the final passaggio of a stanza or song, seeming to function as an affirmation of the way one should interpret the relation between a song's final and its range.

10. Some readers may find it useful to think of the b-natural as shifting the overall sound world from what we now call minor to major, and, simultaneously, shifting from the world of flats to a world of naturals and perhaps sharps.

11. Readers who are unfamiliar with systems and modes will nonetheless notice the disappearance of b-naturals after m. 26, followed by a gradual drop in register. The passaggio that fills m. 34 perfectly articulates the characteristic range of the Hypodorian from d′ to d″, encircling the g′ between them as a point of rest. All the passaggi, in fact, follow the instrumentalist's practice of articulating an octave species that reinforces the point of harmonic cadence: in effect, then, the voice and the hands struggle out of the mode and out of the system in a complementary if ultimately failed partnership. Good introductions to the modes as Francesca would have known them and to the affects each was understood to have evoked are Bernard Meier, *The Modes of Classical Polyphony*, trans. Ellen S. Beebe (New York: Broude Bros., 1988) and Frans Wiering, *The Language of the Modes* (New York: Routledge, 2001). For more about the interaction of mode and system, see Eric Chafe, *Monteverdi's Tonal Language* (New York: Norton, 1992). For a provocative reading of mode as a medium for the performance of subjectivity, see Susan McClary, *Modal Subjectivities: Self-Fashioning in the Italian Madrigal* (Berkeley: University of California Press, 2004).

12. The handwritten direction reads "va cantata allegramente, allargando la battuta."

13. On the relation of breath to body heat, sexual desire, and even sexual identity as conceived in Francesca's time, see chapter 1.

14. These are songs 4 through 8 of the collection. All five texts can be found among the papers of Michelangelo Buonarroti. Four appear in a manuscript *laudario* that he wrote and compiled, I-FcasaB, A.B. 82, fols. 355–408, where they are linked to particular occasions for prayer. The same four also appear in a miscellany of Buonarroti's poetry, much of it poesia per musica, at I-FcasaB, A.B. 84. "Maria, dolce Maria" is at I-FcasaB, A.B. 82, fol. 378, marked as a prayer to the Virgin, and at A.B. 84, fol. 207; "Nel cammino aspro" is at I-FcasaB, A.B. 82, fol. 380v, marked as a prayer to the Florentine saint Giovanni Gualberto, founder of the Vallombrosan order, and at A.B. 84, fol. 207v; "Pietà, mercede, aita" is at I-FcasaB, A.B. 82, 376v, indicated for the Day of the Dead, and at A.B. 84, fol. 206v; "Ferma, Signore, arresta" is at I-FcasaB, A.B. 82, fol. 376r, also indicated for the Day of the Dead, and at A.B. 84, fol. 206v. The fifth, "Ecco, ch'io verso il sangue," appears in a miscellany principally devoted to poetry by Buonarroti's contemporaries, shortly after poems definitively attributed to Andrea Salvadori; it is at I-FcasaB, A.B. 95, fol. 504.

15. The words "io canto" come in the middle of the poem's extravagantly long first sentence: "Maria, sweet Maria / name so gentle / that pronouncing you enraptures the heart, / Sacred and holy name / that enflames my heart with celestial love, / Maria, never as long as I sing / can my tongue / a happier word / pull from my breast than to say [to say], Maria." It would be possible to interpret the passaggio on "io canto" as a mere madrigalism or as a response that translates the poem's performance of desire's deferral into musical performativity.

16. The text translates the Improperia, part of the liturgy for Good Friday. Giving voice to Christ's reproaches from the Cross, the Improperia is sung between the lessons of the day and the veneration of the Cross. As traditionally performed, the reproaching refrain is first sung antiphonally between the two sides of the choir; thereafter the verses are sung antiphonally by soloists on each side, and the reproaching refrain by the whole choir. Giovanni Battista da Gagliano published a setting of the same translation for soloist and five-voice ensemble in his *Varie musiche: Libro Primo* (Venice: Alessandro Vincenti, 1623), published in facsimile in Gary Tomlinson, ed., *Italian Secular Song, 1606–1636*, vol.

1, *Florence* (New York: Garland, 1986). For a fuller description of the Good Friday service, see John Harper, *The Forms and Orders of Western Liturgy from the Tenth to the Eighteenth Century* (Oxford: Clarendon, 1991), 145.

17. On women's spiritual identification with Christ, including identification with his suffering, in pre- and early modern Europe, one classic text is Carolyn Bynum, *Jesus as Mother: Studies in the Spirituality of the High Middle Ages* (Berkeley: University of California Press, 1982). On musical suffering, see Bruce Holsinger, *Music, Body and Desire in Medieval Culture* (Palo Alto: Stanford University Press, 2001). The early seventeenth-century Florentine saint Maria Maddalena de' Pazzi (1566–1607) was well known for raptures in which she both spoke and sang as if in the voice of the crucified Christ. Some of her raptures, written down by the teams of nuns assigned to transcribe them, are published in Maria Maddalena de' Pazzi, *Le parole dell'estasi*, ed. Giovanni Pozzi (Milan: Adelphi Edizioni, 1984).

18. "Deh, chi già mai potrà, Vergine bella / cantar tua lode a tua grandezza equale? / Sei Regina del Ciel, sposa novella / In te discende, e fass'Iddio mortale. / Deh, solo il pianto sia la mia favella / Il silenzio la tromba alta immortale / Cosi puote umil cor lodare à pieno / Chi congiunge la terr'al ciel sereno" (Alas, who could ever, beautiful Virgin / Sing praises equal to your greatness? / You are Queen of Heaven, a new bride / In you God descends and makes Himself mortal. / Alas, [let] weeping be my story, / Silence my lofty, immortal trumpet / Thus could a humble heart fully praise / She who joins earth to the blue heaven).

19. Seventeenth-century users of the book would have known that "Ecco, ch'io verso il sangue" was a translation of the Improperia and would have understood that the Improperia is followed liturgically by Thomas Aquinas's hymn of praise to Christ's victory over death, the Pange Lingua. Thus, "Deh, chi già mai potrà" responds inappropriately to "Ecco," replacing masculine praise of a masculine deity with affectively feminized praise of the queen of heaven.

20. For a sense of the secondary literature that treats the romanesca as an aria (not as only an ostinato bass or only a melodic formula), see Georg Predota, "Towards a Reconsideration of the Romanesca: Francesca Caccini's *Primo libro delle musiche* and Contemporary Monodic Settings in the First Quarter of the Seventeenth Century," *Recercare* 5 (1993): 87–113; L. F. Tagliavini, "Metrica e ritmica nei 'modi di cantare ottavi,'" in *Forme e vicende: Per Giovanni Pozzi*, ed. O. Besomi, G. Giamella, A. Martini, and G. Pedrojetta, 239–267 (Padua: Antenore, 1989); John Walter Hill, *Roman Monody, Cantata and Opera from the Circles around Cardinal Montalto* (Oxford: Clarendon, 1997), 203–204; and Claude Palisca, "Vincenzo Galilei and Some Links between 'Pseudo-Monody' and Monody," *Musical Quarterly* 46 (1960), 344–360. One instance of secondary literature that treats the romanesca primarily as an ostinato bass is David Gagne, "Monteverdi's *Ohimè dov'è il mio ben* and the Romanesca," *Music Forum* 6 (1987), 61–91, which focuses on the best-known example.

21. Sigismondo d'India, Antonio Cifra, and Stefano Landi all included several romanescas in song collections published between 1617 and 1619, and all treat the romanesca primarily as a bass line.

22. Vincenzo Galilei characterized the romanesca as excitable in his treatise on counterpoint. In a discussion of the intrinsic sounds of the ancient modes, he advised readers seeking an analogy in their own experience to compare the *concitato* sound of the roman-

esca to the *quiete* sound of the *passamezzo*." See I-Fn, MSS Galileiani 1, fasc. 2, [Vincenzo Galilei, "Primo libro della prattica del contrapunto (1588–1591)"], fol. 47v.

23. "Nube gentil, che di lucente velo / Cuopri'l re della gloria, odi il tuo vanto. / Tu rendi raggi al sole il sole al cielo, / E degli angeli fai più dolce'il canto. / Ahi, che te non produsse il caldo il gielo / ma i concenti sospir l'amaro pianto / Di quei che rimirar nel lieto giorno / fare il re delle stelle al ciel ritorno." (Gentle cloud, that with a shining veil / covers the king of glory, hear your praise. / You return rays to the sun, [and] the sun to heaven / and you make the angels' song more sweet. / Alas, neither heat nor cold produced you / but the conceits, sighs, bitter weeping / of those who saw on that happy day / the king of stars returned to heaven.) The heading in Francesca's book, "Aria sopra la romanesca," implies that the pattern will be treated very freely. On "Nube gentil" in relation to Giulio's only published romanesca, "Torna, deh torna," in *Le nuove musiche e nuova maniera di scriverle*, 1614, see Predota, "Towards a Reconsideration of the Romanesca."

24. The text appears unattributed in a manuscript of poesia per musica at I-Fr, Mor 309. See Alexander and Savino, *Francesca Caccini's Il primo libro*, 11, for an English translation by Massimo Ossi, and 38–44 for a modern edition of the duet.

25. Severo Bonini, *Discorsi e regole sovra la musica et il contrappunto*, I-Fr, MS 2218, fol. 87: "fu tanta gradita che non è stato casa, la quale, avendo cembali e tiorbe in casa, non avesse il lamento di quella." The lament is from Monteverdi's *tragedia in musica* for the 1608 marriage of Margaret of Savoy to Ferdinando Gonzaga, Duke of Mantua. On the 1608 festivities, see Anne MacNeil, *Music and Women of the Commedia dell'Arte in the Late Sixteenth Century* (Oxford: Oxford University Press, 2003), chap. 4; Tim Carter, *Monteverdi's Dramatic Music* (Oxford: Oxford University Press, 2002). On Arianna's lament in particular see Nicholas Routley, "Arianna Thrice Betrayed" (Armidale, New South Wales: University of New England Press, 1998); Suzanne G. Cusick, "'There was not one lady who failed to shed a tear': Arianna's Lament and the Construction of Modern Womanhood," *Early Music* 22 (1994): 21–41; Irving Godt, "I casi di Arianna," *Rivista italiana di musicologia* 29 (1994): 315–359; Eric Chafe, *Monteverdi's Tonal Language* (New York: Norton, 1992); Gary Tomlinson, "Madrigal, Monody and Monteverdi's *via naturale alla imitatione*," *Journal of the American Musicological Society* 34 (1981): 60–108; Peter Westergard, "Toward a 12-Tone Polyphony," in *Perspectives on Contemporary Music Theory*, ed. Benjamin Boretz and Edward T. Cone, 239–41 (New York: Norton, 1972). On laments in general, see Wendy Heller, *Emblems of Eloquence: Opera and Women's Voices in Seventeenth-Century Venice* (Berkeley: University of California Press, 2004); Leofranc Holfred-Stevens, "'Her eyes became two spouts': Classical Antecedents of Renaissance Laments," *Early Music* 27 (1999): 379–394; Tim Carter, "Lamenting Ariadne?" *Early Music* 27 (1999): 395–405; Anne MacNeil, "Weeping at the Water's Edge," *Early Music* 27 (1999): 406–418; Jeanice Brooks, "Catherine de Médicis, *nouvelle Artémise*: Women's Laments and the Virtue of Grief," *Early Music* 27 (1999): 419–436; Jane Bowers, "Women's Lamenting Traditions around the World: A Survey and Some Significant Questions," *Women and Music* 2 (1998): 125–146; Susan McClary, "Excess and Frame," in *Feminine Endings: Music, Gender and Sexuality*, 80–111 (Minneapolis: University of Minnesota Press, 1991); Ellen Rosand, "The Descending Tetrachord: An Emblem of Lament," *Musical Quarterly* 55 (1979): 346–359.

26. The full text of "Lasciatemi qui solo," with Massimo Ossi's translation, is in Alexander and Savino, *Francesca Caccini's Il primo libro*, 11–12. On the concept of the work of

pain as especially delegated to women in contemporary Mediterranean folk cultures, see Tullia Magrini, "Women's 'Work of Pain' in Christian Mediterranean Europe," *Music and Anthropology* 3 (1998), http://www.musicandanthropology.unibo.spett.it.

27. Francesca's setting of these stanzas of *settenari* as a strophic aria rather than a recitative soliloquy followed convention.

28. Monteverdi and Caccini alike might have been referring to a set of musical gestures in oral culture that would recognizably identify a song as a lament: whereas Monteverdi chose to use it as the starting point for his construction of Arianna's abandonment to her own disorderly feelings, Caccini chose to use it as a framing device. The notion would lend support to Tim Carter's speculation that Virginia Andreini, the singing actress brought in to play Arianna as a last-minute replacement for Caterina Martinelli in 1608, had contributed ideas for her own song scene from her long experience in commedia dell'arte. See Tim Carter, *Monteverdi's Musical Theatre* (New Haven: Yale University Press, 2002), 210–211; and Emily Wilbourne, "La Florinda: The Performance of Virginia Ramponi Andreini," PhD diss., New York University, 2008.

29. See chapter 1.

30. Magrini, "Women's 'Work of Pain' in Christian Mediterranean Europe."

31. On this function of the lament, see MacNeil, "Weeping at the Water's Edge."

32. Buonarroti's Christmas canzonetta is at I-FcasaB, A.B. 82, fol. 357, and at A.B. 84, fol. 185v.

33. The secular poem is at I-FcasaB, A.B. 84, fol. 213v. Its last stanza reads "Voglio in quel volto angelico sereno / e'n quel candido seno / L'alma spirar tra i fior di paradiso / Tra i fior e le viole / Venite, andiam. Pastore, ecco'l mio sole."

34. In the Paris copy, the words "sopra la Romanesca" appear between "Aria" and "Prima Parte," crossed out in ink. These words are hidden by a paste-over in the Modena and Florence copies.

35. On deictics, see Mauro Calcagno, "'Imitar con canto chi parla': Monteverdi and the Creation of a Language for Musical Theater," *Journal of the American Musicological Society* 55 (2002): 383–431.

36. It is the first song of the so-called Balletto della cortesia, with which the long night's entertainment ended. The text, with an English translation by Massimo Ossi, can be found in Alexander and Savino, *Francesca Caccini's* Il primo libro, 12. For more about *Il passatempo*, see chapter 4. In the context of Francesca's *Primo libro*, the fictional emergence of this woman from the sea could seem to respond to the call for a woman—the Virgin—to rise from her grave with which "Giunto è'l dì" has ended. It could also have evoked the local myth of Florence's "discovery" by foreigners amazed by the Arno's flowering banks, a myth best known through its representation by Botticelli in *The Birth of Venus*.

37. The text, with an English translation by Massimo Ossi, can be found in Alexander and Savino, *Francesca Caccini's* Il primo libro, 12. It appears in one of several manuscript versions of *La Tancia* gathered at I-FcasaB, A.B. 61, in fasc. 3, fol. 265r. "La pastorella mia" was replaced in later versions by verses in which Pietro, even more improbably, likens himself to Orpheus. For more about *La Tancia*, see chapter 4.

38. The transposition to durus was presumably part of the joke on Sannazaro's text, given the frequency with which madrigalists set texts about hard-hearted lovers to durus harmonies. Pietro has chosen the wrong system to describe a pliant girl, if a possibly right mode to characterize her as wifely.

39. See I-FcasaB, A.B. 61, fasc. 3, fols. 265r–266r.

40. A version of the text appears as the second stanza of two beginning "S'io fui sempre fedele Amor tu'l sai," marked "per romanesca" in Buonarroti's miscellany of his own poesia per musica, I-FcasaB, A.B. 84, fol. 195v. Although no textual gestures allow identification of the poetic speaker's gender, the clearly marked femininity of the beloved suggests the heteronormative inference that the song's poetic voice is that of a man. The text, with an English translation by Massimo Ossi, can be found in Alexander and Savino, *Francesca Caccini's* Il primo libro, 13.

41. On the explicit if heavy-handed interpretations of Arianna's abandonment that circulated at the turn of the seventeenth century, especially in connection with Giovanni dell'Anguillara's very popular translations, see Cusick, "'There was not one woman.'"

42. Ottavio Rinuccini, *L'Arianna* (1608), lines 860–862, as printed in Angelo Solerti, *Gli albori del melodramma* (Milan, 1904; Hildesheim: Olm, 1969), 178: "Mirate di che duol n'han fatto erede / L'amor mio, la mie fede e l'altrui inganno / Così va chi tropp'ama e troppo crede." An unornamented version of Francesca's setting was published in Fabio Costantini's collection *Ghirlandetta amorosa, arie, madrigali e sonetti, di diversi eccellentissimi autori, a uno, a due, a tre & a quattro . . . Opera settima. Libro primo* (Orvieto: M. A. Fei et R. Ruuli, 1621), 10–11. Francesca's setting in *Primo libro* of the anonymous parody was published barely a month after a version for solo voice and Spanish guitar was included in Giovanni Stefani's anthology *Affetti amorosi canzonette ad una voce sola poste in musica da diversi con le parte del basso, & le lettere dell'alfabetto per la chittarra alla spagnole raccoloto da Giov. Stefani con tre arie siciliane, et due vilanelle spagnolo* (Venice: G. Vincenti, 1618); Stefani's dedication to Giuseppe Scadinari is dated 20 July 1618. Her setting shares with Stefani's the general tonal design, moving from g for the opening phrase through F to a cadence on C at the end of the second line of each stanza. Stefani's and Francesca's settings share remarkably similar melodic contours for the second phrase and the refrain. Possibly both allude to a common source in oral tradition, an aria for singing these verses that circulated among courtiers who improvised the singing of canzonette to guitar accompaniment.

In 1619, Francesca's protegé Andrea Falconieri included a setting of "Dove io credea" on pp. 4–6 of his *Il quinto libro delle musiche à una, due e tre voci di Andrea Falconieri Napolitano* (Florence: Zanobi Pignoni, 1619), a publication that Francesca's interventions with Andrea Cioli may have faciliated. See chapter 6. "Dove io credea" was also published as a poetic text with guitar chords in Remigio Romano's *Seconda raccolta di canzonette musicali: Bellissime per cantare, et suonare, sopra arie moderne* (Vicenza: Salvadori, 1620). Neither Falconieri's setting nor that published by Romano resembles Francesca's or Stefani's. On Falconieri's relationships with Medicean musicians, see Dinko Fabris, *Andrea Falconieri* (Rome: Torre d'Orfeo, 1987). On Romano's anthologies of poetry for improvised vocal performance, see Silke Leopold, "Remigio Romano's Collection of Lyrics for Music," *Proceedings of the Royal Musicological Association* 110 (1983): 45–61.

43. (1) "Where I believed my hopes to be true / There I found my trust most damaged: / So it goes for one who loves and trusts too much. (2) A sincere heart that loves with trust / In the end sees itself betrayed, without hope: / So it goes . . . (3) My love, my trust, and another's lie / Have made me heir to infinite sorrow: / So it goes . . . (4) Alas, I now realize and dare to see / That the untrustworthy cannot make promises: / So it goes . . . " (my translation).

44. Brooks, "Catherine de Médicis."

CHAPTER 8

1. Bronzini, I-Fn, Magl. VIII. 1527/1, 45, characterizes Arianna thus. Francesca, who studied astrology and "the occult sciences," according to Bronzini, was born under the sign of Virgo. According to Bronzini's astrological musings on the Medici family, Virgo was also the constellation that ruled Astrea, to whom he likened Christine de Lorraine. See I-Fn, Magl. VIII. 1527/1, 43.

2. Many scholars have written about seventeenth-century efforts thus to rehabilitate music. See, e.g., Tim Carter, "'In Love's Harmonious Consort'? Penelope and the Interpretation of 'Il ritorno d'Ulisse in patria,'" *Cambridge Opera Journal* 5 (1993): 1–16; Massimo Ossi, *Divining the Oracle: Monteverdi's Seconda Prattica* (Chicago: University of Chicago Press, 2003); and Margaret Murata, "Image and Eloquence: Secular Song," in *The Cambridge History of Seventeenth-Century Music*, ed. Tim Carter and John Butt, 378–425 (Cambridge: Cambridge University Press, 2005).

3. The heading paraphrases Bronzini, who used the phrase "il tacito parlar della mano" for the expressive powers of Lucrezia Urbani, the wife of Domenico Visconti and, like her husband, a musical servant of Don Antonio de'Medici. See I-Fn, Magl. VIII. 1525/1, 107.

4. For a facsimile of the motet, see Gary Tomlinson, ed., *Italian Secular Song, 1606–1636* (New York: Garland, 1986), 1:245–247.

5. All but one of these texts is liturgical, but they are not presented in liturgical order. Rather, as in the first half of the book, they seem to be distinguished by textual genre. "Laudate Dominum" is the final psalm of Lauds. "Haec dies" is an antiphon; proper for Lauds on Easter, it can function as a substitute for the hymn, chapter, and response of Compline in Eastertide. "Regina caeli laetare" is the Marian antiphon for Eastertide, sung at the end of Compline. "Adorate dominum omnes angelis eum" combines a respond for Epiphany that can be used as an antiphon in the second nocturne of Matins on that day with Psalm 97:4, the third antiphon of the third nocturne of Matins for Christmas. "Te lucis ante terminum" is the hymn for Compline, and "Jesu corona virginum" is the hymn for Second Vespers in the Common Office of Virgins. The association of three of these texts with Compline and two others with Lauds suggests that they may have been useful for the dame and donne who are known to have sung these offices privately for the Medici family in their palace chapel. See chapter 4.

6. A quick reference for the usual cadence points for various modes can be found in Bernhard Meier, *The Modes of Classical Polyphony*, trans. Ellen S. Beebe (New York: Broude Brothers, 1988), 109.

7. Many readers will know that it was common for early seventeenth-century musicians to develop ideas in ways that were self-consciously analogous to the figures of classical rhetoric. "Laudate Dominum," "Haec dies," "Adorate Dominum," and "Beate Sebastiane" all seem to me to develop ideas by means of various forms of *anaphora*—figures of repetition. In the first two motets, the ideas seem to originate in voiced language, whereas in the second two, the ideas originate in the instrumental part. For a text about the musical use of rhetorical figures in Francesca's time, see Johann Burmeister, *Musical Poetics (1606)*, translated with introduction and notes by Benito Rivera (New Haven: Yale University Press, 1993).

8. The antiphon's text is Psalm 118:24. For a facsimile score, see Tomlinson, *Italian Secular Song*, 1:248–249.

9. I am grateful to Emily Van Evera for describing these alleluias as a "breathing puzzle" in a telephone conversation in April 2002.

10. The antiphon is sung at the end of Compline between Easter and Pentecost; as a prayer it substitutes for the Angelus during the same season. For a slightly different reading of "Regina caeli laetare," see Suzanne G. Cusick, "'Who is this woman?': Self-Presentation, *Imitatio Virginis,* and Compositional Voice in Francesca Caccini's *Primo Libro delle Musiche* (1618)," *Il saggiatore musicale* 5 (1998): 5–42. A facsimile of the score is in Tomlinson, *Italian Secular Song,* 1:250–251.

11. It was conventional to set the word "alleluia" to a single phrase that repeated, like a refrain, but each of Francesca's alleluia phrases is different from the others.

12. . The text "Regina caeli laetare" traditionally inspired highly structured musical settings. It was common for all the alleluias to be sung to the same phrase, which, when repeated, produced a form that John Bettley has likened to the rondo. See his "'L'ultimo Hora canonica del giorno': Music for the Office of Compline in Northern Italy in the Second Half of the Sixteenth Century," *Music and Letters* 74 (1993): 163–214, especially 183 on "Regina caeli."

13. For discussion of "Chi è costei?" and "Maria, dolce Maria," see chapter 7.

14. On Saint Sebastian see Jacobus de Voragine, *The Golden Legend,* trans. William Granger Ryan (Princeton: Princeton University Press, 1993), 97–101; his healing of the mute Zoë is mentioned on 99. It may be significant that Giulio Caccini's principal teaching site was located in via Sebastiane, now via Gino Capponi.

15. In "Adorate" the latter are written as if in recitative style, but all can be performed as triple meter. For a facsimile score of "Adorate" see Tomlinson, *Italian Secular Song,* 1:252–253; for "Beate Sebastiane" see ibid., 1:254–255.

16. See Katherine Rowe, "'God's handy work': Divine Complicity and the Anatomist's Touch," in *The Body in Parts: Fantasies of Corporeality in Early Modern Europe,* ed. David Hillman and Carla Mazzio (New York: Routledge, 1997), 285–309. I have quoted a passage on p. 287.

17. The score of "Te lucis" is in Tomlinson, *Italian Secular Song,* 1:256–257; "Jesu corona virginum" is at 1:258–260. Semantic meaning is not entirely ignored. For example, in "Te lucis," at the words "noxium phantasmata" (nocturnal phantasms), ornaments that produce a syncopation emphasize and enact semantic meaning. See ibid., 1:256, fifth system.

18. In the last day described in his massive work Bronzini compares the complementarity of husband and wife in marriage to the complementarity of elements in music: "come si fa nella Musica, et negli stromenti, con diverse voce e corde unite si facesses' un Armonia dolce." See I-Fn. Magl. VIII. 1532, 31. In *Divining the Oracle,* Massimo Ossi argues that Monteverdi, too, worked with some elements of canzonette—notably strophic form and the convention of instrumental ritornellos between stanzas—to rehabilitate music from its supposed subservience to language. I mean to complement his insights about the development of musical modernity by showing that Francesca worked toward the same end by focusing on different elements and that her immediate circle would have attributed a different significance to that rehabilitation.

19. The first stanza is certainly by Michelangelo Buonarroti; see I-FcasaB, A.B. 84, fol. 214r, a version in which later verses differ substantially from the text Francesca set. See Alexander and Savino, *Francesca Caccini's* Il primo libro delle musiche of 1618*: A Mod-*

ern Critical Edition of the Secular Monodies (Bloomington: Indiana University Press, 2004), 14 for the text with English translation by Massimo Ossi, and 68–69 for the score.

20. In this and subsequent representations of these songs' accents, I transcribe the accents produced by Francesca's musical setting. In many cases, these are different from the normative scansion implied by poetic meter alone, and they result in distinctive ways to read the poem in song.

21. Such songs, called variously canzonette, villanelle alla napolitana, and arie villanelle, had circulated widely in manuscripts and printed books since the 1580s. They are now believed to have been arrangements for bourgeois or courtly performance of a solo repertoire like the one in which Scipione della Palla had trained the young Giulio Caccini. Chiabrera's metrical and conceptual reforms, which were firmly based in humanistic erudition about Classical poetic practice, had ensured the new canzonette's contributions to the Medicean cultural program. Furthermore, the new genre inevitably had strongly accented meters, so it would easily accompany and accommodate dancing. Thus, it was a medium that, in spite of the relative frivolity of its subject matter, could seem to to realize fully the aesthetic intentions of the Florentine humanists who hoped to revive the ideal of *melodia* (song or music)—the perfect union of word, tone, and gesture that Plato was believed to have prescribed for a well-ordered state in the *Republic* and the *Laws*. On the history of the canzonetta see, among other sources, Claude Palisca, "Aria Types in the Earliest Operas," *Journal of Seventeenth Century Music* 9, no. 1 (2003): http:www .sscm-jscm.org/jscm/v9/no1/Palisca.html; Concetta Assenza, *La canzonetta dal 1570 al 1615*, Quaderni de Musica/Realta 34 (Lucca: Libreria Musicale Italiana, 1997); James Haar, "Ariosto and Canzonetta: Rhythm as a Stylistic Determinant in the Madrigals of Giaches de Wert," *Yearbook of the Alamire Foundation* 3 (1999): 89–120; Nina Treadwell, "The 'chitarra spagnola' and Italian Monody, 1589 to circa 1650," master's thesis, University of Southern California, 1995; Robert Holzer, "'Sono d'altro garbo . . . Le canzonette che si cantono oggi': Pietro Della Valle on Music and Modernity in the Seventeenth Century," *Studi musicali* 21, no. 2 (1992): 253–305; Concetta Assenza, "La trasmissione dei testi poetici per canzonetta negli ultimi decenni del secolo XVI," *Rivista italiana di musicologia* 26, no. 2 (1991): 205–240. The record of Michelangelo Caccini's baptism on 3 August 1598, with Tomaso Strinati standing in for his godfather, "Gabriello Chiabrera Savonese" is at I-Fd, Battesimi Maschi, 1596–1597, fol. 120v.

22. Maria Rosa Moretti believes that the Signorini stayed in Brignole's Villa Albaro in San Nazaro, outside the city, where Chiabrera, Ansaldo Cebà, and Bernardo Castelli held irregular meetings of their Accademia degli Addormentati, meetings that always focused on discussion of the new poetry and that sometimes included women. See Maria Rosa Moretti, *Musica e costume a Genova tra Cinquecento e Seicento* (Genoa: Francesco Pirelli Editore, 1992), 66. Both Chiabrera and Francesca wrote letters to Michelangelo Buonarroti about their time together in 1617. Chiabrera noted that "here she is taken for marvelous . . . and she is everywhere honored," and Francesca reported that the three frequently toasted their mutual friend Buonarroti. Chiabrera's letter of 26 May 1617 is at I-FcasaB, A.B. 44, no. 527; Francesca's, written the same day, is at I-FcasaB, A.B. 44, no. 446. Both are reprinted in appendix B.

23. For the text of "Il Geri," see Marcello Turci, ed., *Opere di Gabriello Chiabrera e lirici non marinisti del Seicento* (Turin: Utet, 1970), 570–583. On the relation of Chiabrera's poetics to meter and Petrarchan love, see the essays in Fulvio Bianchi and Paolo Russo,

eds., *La scelta della misura: Gabriello Chiabrera; L'altro fuoco del barocco italiano*. Atti di convegno di studi su Gabriello Chiabrera nel 350° anniversario della morte. Savona, 3–6 November 1988 (Genoa: Costa & Nolan, 1993), especially Giorgio Bertone, "Appunti per una ricerca metriologica su Chiabrera," 321–341; Paolo Fabbri, "Metro letterario e metro musicale nella pagine di un critico di Chiabrera: il 'discorso delle ragioni del numero del verso italiano' di Ludovico Zuccolo," 342–351; Antonio Vassali, "Chiabrera, la musica e i musicisti: le rime amorose," 353–369; and Paolo Russo, "Chiabrera e l'ambiente musicale romano," 370–376.

24. Chiabrera, "Il Geri," in Turci, *Opere di Gabriello Chiabrera*, 573.

25. Ibid., 576–580.

26. I-FcasaB, A.B. 62 includes five fascicles, the first four of which contain more or less complete versions of *Il passatempo*. "Che desia di saper che cosa è amor" is at fasc. 1, fol. 3v; fasc. 2, p. 3; fasc. 3, fol. 3r; and fasc. 4, fol. 136. For the text with English translation by Massimo Ossi, see Alexander and Savino, *Francesca Caccini's* Il primo libro, 15; the score is at 70.

27. The text, unattributed, is in I-Fn, MS Palatino, 251, fol. 329. A modern edition of the text with English translation by Massimo Ossi is found in Alexander and Savino, *Francesca Caccini's* Il primo libro, 15–16; the score is at 71.

28. "Che t'ho fatt'io?" might also have reminded a singer or listener at the Medici court of the comic egloga "Tirsi et Filli" from *Il passatempo*, in which Buonarroti used the contrast between long and short lines to satirize the gender conventions that kept these would-be pastoral lovers apart. See chapter 4.

29. Not necessarily understood as heterosexual in a culture where sodomy had been so widely practiced a century earlier that fully half the men of Florence had been arrested for it, the amorous couple in this case could easily represent the usual adult-adolescent pair of Mediterranean sodomy. As Michael Rocke has shown, the couple was sharply gendered, the "passive" partner being understood to be almost womanishly disempowered. See Michael Rocke, *Forbidden Friendships: Homosexuality and Male Culture in Renaissance Florence* (New York: Oxford University Press, 1996).

30. For the text with an English translation by Massimo Ossi, see Alexander and Savino, *Francesca Caccini's* Il primo libro, 13–14; the score is at 64–67.

31. For the text with an English translation by Massimo Ossi, see Alexander and Savino, *Francesca Caccini's* Il primo libro, 16–17; the score is at 72–73.

32. On early modern notions of mutual orgasm as constituting the ideal sexual encounter because it was a requirement for fertilization, see Constance Jordan, *Renaissance Feminism* (Ithaca: Cornell University Press, 1990); Thomas Laqueur, *Making Sex: Body and Gender from the Greeks to Freud* (Cambridge: Harvard University Press, 1992); and Roy Porter and Mikalàs Teich, eds., *Sexual Knowledge, Sexual Science* (Cambridge: Cambridge University Press, 1994).

33. Tronco lines end on accented syllables and piano lines end on unaccented ones. Tronchi can end either on an accented vowel or on a consonant because a word's final vowel has been omitted: the latter is characteristic of late sixteenth- and early seventeenth-century poetry, especially that of Chiabrera. Readers familiar with English and French versification, or indeed with a now-obsolete usage in music theory, may be tempted to think of these as "masculine" and "feminine" endings, respectively. It is possible that Francesca thought of them in this way because these terms are used to describe French poetry in Italian metrics manuals. Given her familiarity with French poetry and

song, the likely influence of the Francophile Chiabrera on her thinking about canzonettas, and her obvious intention to flatter the French-born grand duchess elsewhere in the *Primo libro*, Francesca may have meant to evoke sexual differences in the metrical problem posed by this duet's text.

34. For the text with an English translation by Massimo Ossi, see Alexander and Savino, *Francesca Caccini's* Il primo libro, 17; the score is at 74–75.

35. A smoother way of translating the poem that removes its deliberate syntactical contortion would be "If a lover believes he can swear fealty to the court of love without losing himself and pouring forth pain, then he does not know the law by which Love governs and rules his servants."

36. For the text with an English translation by Massino Ossi, see Alexander and Savino, *Francesca Caccini's* Il primo libro, 18; the score is at 76.

37. For the text with and English translation by Massimo Ossi, see Alexander and Savino, *Francesca Caccini's* Il primo libro, 18–19; the score is at 77. An anonymous setting of this text is on fol. 23r of I-Fn, Magl.xix.24.

38. The text was set as a trio by Monteverdi in Claudio Monteverdi, *Scherzi musicali cioè arie et madrigali in stil recitativo con una ciaccona a 1. e 2. voci* (Venice: Gardano, 1632), no. 17, and as a duet in Claudio Saracini, *Le musiche* (Venice, 1614), 8, also in Tomlinson, *Italian Secular Song,* 2:100. Another version attributed to Caccini, I-Fn, Magl. XIX. 66, fol. 156, bears no significant resemblance to this one.

39. Given the way Francesca had implicitly gendered accent-by-ornamentation and metrical accents in the duet "S'io men vò," the balance in this case might also be a gendered one.

40. Sexual candor was certainly not unknown among the court's women. I-Fas, MdP 6110 contains a set of letters from Christine to Caterina de'Medici that include ample advice about ways to attract her husband, become pregnant, and so on.

CHAPTER 9

1. My account of *La liberazione's* first performance is based on Tinghi, I-Fas, Miscellanea Medicea 11. Fol. 109v describes the show itself; fol. 110r describes the seating of the guests.

2. Tinghi describes the dedication and renaming of Villa Imperiale on 24 May 1624 at I-Fas, Miscellanea Medicea 11, fols. 42–43, briefly cited in Solerti, *Musica, ballo e drammatica alla Corte medicea dal 1600 al 1637: Notizie tratte da un diario con appendice di testi inediti e rari.* Bibliotheca musica Bononiensis (Bologna: Forni, 1989), 172. After dinner on the previous evening, Francesca Caccini and "the two princesses" had visited Villa Imperiale to sing for the "granduchessa madre" and the visiting Duke of Mantua. A stone inscription read "Augustis nomen consecuta—Futura e magnae Duces Etruriae—Vestro ocio deliciisque aeternum inservat" (Taking its name from august Austrians, [let this villa] always serve future grand duchesses of Tuscany as a place of delightful leisure). See Fiammetta Faini and Anna Maria Punti, *La villa Mediceo Lorense del Poggio Imperiale* (Florence: "Lo Studiolo" Amici dei Musei Fiorentini, 1995), 8. The stone bearing the inscription is now conserved in the Opificio delle Pietre Dure in Florence.

3. No account mentions where the male guests sat or stood or who escorted them to their places.

4. According to the account of Cesare Molza, the ambassador from Modena, Christine

observed these events incognito, seated behind a curtain. See I-MOas, Ambasciatori. Firenze. Busta 53, fasc. 18.

5. By convention, if Francesca composed the music she would also have chosen the performers from among her pupils and protégées and rehearsed the singers and the instrumentalists, but no documents survive to confirm that *La liberazione*'s preparation followed convention. Given that she had recently been embroiled in a bitter dispute about the casting and composition of *La regina Sant'Orsola* in which her ability to serve the archduchess well had been compromised, it is possible that Francesca was assigned sole authority over *La liberazione* to relieve her tension. But it is also possible that the dispute with Marco and Giovanni Battista da Gagliano and Jacopo Peri erupted because they envied her this commission.

6. According to Tinghi, Magdalena heard five rehearsals of the new production of *La regina Sant'Orsola* between November 1624 and its performance on 28 January 1625; she heard four rehearsals of the barriera performed on 10 February 1625, *La precedenza delle dame.* See I-Fas, Miscellanea Medicea 11, fols. 89v–103r.

7. Five printed copies of the score, published by Pietro Cecconcelli in 1625, survive. They are at the British Library in London, the Bibliothèque Nationale in Paris, the Biblioteca Casanatense and the library of the Conservatorio Santa Cecilia in Rome, and at the Biblioteca Nazionale Marciana in Venice. Alfonso Parigi's engravings of his father's stage drawings are bound into the copies at the Casanatense and the Biblioteca Nazionale Marciana. Copies of Saracinelli's libretto are relatively abundant; they appear at the Biblioteca Marucelliana in Florence and the New York Public Library, among other locations. The score, stage drawings, and libretto were published in facsimile in 1998 with an introduction by Alessandro Magini (Florence: Studio per edizioni scelte, 1998). Copies of Parigi's engravings can also be found in Florence in the Galleria degli Uffizi, Gabinetto dei disegni e stampe, Stampe sciolte numbers 2303, 2304, 2305, 2306, and Uffizi 95789 N.A. To date I have found no information about the work's casting or costs.

8. Tinghi gives a moving account of his death, followed by an account of the autopsy at I-Fn, MS Gino Capponi, vol. 2, fols. 312ff. See also Jacopo Galuzzi, *Istoria del granducato di Toscana sotto il governo della casa Medici* (Florence: Nella stamperia di R. del-Vivo, 1781), 6:192, for an account that evaluates Cosimo's reign.

9. For a detailed account of the regency's installation and of the codicil, see the dispatches of the Modenese ambassador Paolo Emilio Boiardi at I-MOas, Ambasciatori. Firenze. Busta 47, fasc. 4, dispatches dated 2 March and 13 March 1621. The story about the codicil is repeated in I-Fas, Manoscritti 132, fol. 609.

10. I-MOas, Ambasciatori. Firenze, Busta 46, fasc. 3, Relazione del Cav. Ippolito Tassoni, dated December 1612, described Magdalena in terms that emphasize affect more than the substance he attributed to Christine. Fascicle 4 contains Giuseppe Fontanelli's dispatch of 20 June 1613, which again reports a substantive conversation with Christine about the Garfagnana war, contrasting her with Magdalena, "who listened laughingly, and whose words were all formulas of courtesy."

11. I-Fas, Acquisti e Doni 242, inserto 2, letters of Christine de Lorraine to Count Orso d'Elci from 1608 to 1618, letter of 24 August 1610.

12. I-Fas, Acquisti e Doni 242, inserto 2, letters of Christine de Lorraine to Count Orso d'Elci from 1608 to 1618, letter of 25 August 1611.

13. I-Fas, MdP 303, letter from Belisario Vinta to Orso d'Elci dated 30 May 1611, fol. 140v.

14. I-Fas, MdP 303, letter of Vinta to d'Elci, 30 May 1611, fols. 140v–141r. Vinta's view of Christine and Magdalena as bound by mutual affection was to be echoed in Bronzini's biographical sketch of Magdalena in the manuscript of *Della dignità e nobiltà delle donne,* I-Fn, Magl. VIII. 1514, fols. 177–211. Estella Galasso Calderara echoed Galluzzi's view of their relationship as consistently antagonistic in her biography of Magdalena, *La Granduchessa Maria Magdalena d'Austria: Un amazzone tedesca nella Firenze medicea del '600* (Genoa: Sagep Editrice, 1985). See, e.g., p. 89, where she recounts as typical one especially barbed exchange concerning Tuscany's military aid to the empire.

15. A report questioning Magdalena's fertility because of adolescent menstrual anomalies attributed to "too much heat and fieriness" is at I-Fas, MdP 6068, fol. 184r. The letter is cited in Galasso Calderara, *Granduchessa Maria Magdalena,* 31.

16. Magdalena's children were Maria Christine (1609–1632), who lived in the Monastero della Concezione; Ferdinando II (1610–1670), who succeeded his father as grand duke; Giovan Carlo (1611–1663), a cardinal; Margherita (1612–1679), who eventually married Odoardo Farnese, Duke of Parma; Mattias (1613–1667), a soldier and eventually governor of Siena; Francesco (1614–1634); Anna (1616–1676), who married Archduke Ferdinando Karl of Austria; and Leopold (1617–1675), a cardinal and the founder of the Accademia del Cimento, Europe's first modern scientific academy.

17. On Magdalena's disdain for makeup, see Galasso Calderara, *Granduchessa Maria Magdalena,* 77 and n. 21, which cites I-Fas, MdP 6071, letter of 6 November 1616. For one comment on her interest in receiving schmalz from Austria, see her letter to her sister-in-law Caterina de' Medici, I-Fas, MdP 6108, fols. 28–29.

18. Bronzini, *Della dignità,* vol. 3, 54–76. I-Fn, Magl. VIII. 1514, fols. 177–211 is a draft that includes corrections made at the court's request before it went to press.

19. I-Fn, Magl. VIII. 1514, fols. 182–183.

20. I-Fn, Magl. VIII. 1514, fol. 183. A race of female warriors believed to have lived in eastern Turkey, near the Black Sea, Amazons were said to have had their right breasts removed to facilitate archery and spear-throwing.

21. Cristoforo Bronzini, *Della dignità e nobiltà delle donne* (Florence: Zanobi Pignoni, 1622–1632) and I-Fn, Magl. VIII. 1513–1538.

22. On Isabella, see Donna Cardamone Jackson, "Isabella de' Medici, Duchess of Bracciano: A Portrait of Self-Affirmation," in *Music, Gender and Sexuality in Early Modern Europe,* ed. Todd Borgerding, 1–25 (London: Routledge, 2000); Caroline Murphy, *Murder of a Medici Princess* (Oxford: Oxford University Press, 2008).

23. Tinghi notes at least one exception: on 1 May 1618, Cosimo II, Carlo, Don Lorenzo, and Magdalena dined at the Villa Baroncelli, as it was then called. See I-Fn, MS Gino Capponi 261, vol. 1, fol. 139, and Solerti, *Musica, ballo e drammatica,* 130.

24. Faini and Puntri, *La villa Mediceo Lorense,* 7.

25. On the extensive rebuilding project, see Kelley Harness, *"Amazzoni di Dio:* Florentine Musical Spectacle under Maria Maddalena d'Austria and Cristina di Lorena (1620–30)," PhD diss., University of Illinois, 1996; Ornella Panichi, *Villa di Poggio Imperiale: Lavori di Restauro e di Riordinamento, 1972–75* (Florence: Editrice Edan, n.d.); Matteo Marangoni, *La Villa del Poggio Imperiale* (Florence: Fratelli Alinari, n.d.); Ornella Panici, "Due Stanze della Villa del Poggio Imperiale," *Antichità viva* 12, no. 5 (1973): 32–43; and Faini and Puntri, *La villa Mediceo Lorense.* Galasso Calderara, *Granduchessa Maria Magdalena,* 87, points out the utility of the rebuilding as a public works project

during the economic crisis of the 1620s. Harness's report on p. 88 of *Amazzoni di Dio* that Magdalena purchased the villa in 1622 is contradicted by most other sources.

26. Two of these are reproduced in Kelley Harness, *Echoes of Women's Voices: Music, Art, and Female Patronage in Early Modern Florence* (Chicago: University of Chicago Press, 2006), as figures 2.1 and 2.2. Harness's excellent monograph provides the first comprehensive view of artistic patronage during the regency of the 1620s.

27. Bronzini's account of Magdalena as closely supervising the preparation of court spectacles is supported by the evidence of her involvement with Cicognini's *Il martirio di Sant'Agata* and Salvadori's *La regina Sant'Orsola*. See Harness, *Echoes*, especially chap. 3, "Amazons of God," 62–99. In this, too, she differed from Christine, who preferred to engage with the representational themes of court entertainments but not with their rehearsals.

28. I-Fn, Magl. VIII. 1514, 183.

29. For a differently situated account of the *Guerra di bellezza* in relation to the chivalric ethos promoted during Cosimo II's reign, see Kelley Harness, "Hapsburgs, Heretics, and Horses: Equestrian Ballets and Other Staged Battles in Florence during the First Decade of the Thirty Years' War," in *L'arme e gli amori: Ariosto, Tasso and Guarini in Late Renaissance Florence*, vol. 2, *Dynasty, Court and Imagery*, ed. Massimiliano Rossi and Fiorella Gioffredi Superbi, 255–283. Acts of an International Conference, Florence, Villa I Tatti, 27–29 June 2001 (Florence: Olschki, 2003).

30. See I-Fn, Magl. VIII. 1514, fols. 184–186 for his entire description. The passage I have paraphrased is on fol. 185.

31. I-Fn, Magl. VIII. 1514, fols. 186–187.

32. I-Fn, Magl. VIII. 1514, fols. 188–189.

33. Plato, *The Laws*, trans. R. G. Bury, Loeb Classical Library (London: Heinemann's Sons, 1926), 1:93.

34. See Thomas M. Greene, "Labyrinth Dances in the French and English Renaissance," *Renaissance Quarterly* 54 (2001): 1403–1466; Mark Franko, *Dance as Text: Ideologies of the Baroque Body* (Cambridge: Cambridge University Press, 1993), esp. "Prologue: Constructing the Baroque Body," 1–14, and chapter 2, "Ut vox corpus, 1581," 32–51.

35. The choice of genre may also have evoked a matrilineal Medici identity, given that as a girl Christine de Lorraine had danced at her grandmother Catherine de' Medici's court in the *Balet comique de la Royne*, which, like *La liberazione*, focused on the purging of a Circe-like figure from the stage.

36. The prologues to *La regina Sant'Orsola* and *La liberazione* represent Władisław as a military hero, but these claims seem to have been overblown. See Harness, *Echoes*, 161–162, nn. 44–47.

37. The diplomatic sources for this claim are I-MOas, Cancelleria Ducale, Ambasciatore. Firenze, busta 53, fasc. 18, dispatches of Cesare Molza from December 1624 to February 1625, and I-Las, Anziani al tempo della libertà 642, letters from Florence between 1 January 1622 to 12 October 1630, written by Vincenzo Buonvisi. See also I-Fas, MdP 3518, for instructions charging the Tuscan ambassador in Rome, Francesco Niccolini, to enlist Pope Urban VIII's participation. Niccolini's reports to the regency's foreign secretary, Curtio Picchena, are in I-Fas, MdP 3340. See also Jacopo Galuzzi, *Istoria del Granducato di Toscana sotto il governo della Casa Medici* (Capolago: n.p., 1842), 5:240–45; Furio Diaz, *Il Granducato di Toscana: I Medici* (Turin: Utet, 1976), 363–70.

38. The betrothal never took place. In 1628, Margherita de' Medici married Odoardo Farnese, Duke of Parma, to whom she had long been promised.

39. The second half of the season apparently had been postponed from late 1624. On 8 November 1624, Andrea Cioli wrote to Tuscany's resident ambassador in Rome, Ippolito Buondelmonte, "Many feste are being prepared for the honor and pleasure of the Prince of Poland; but because they cannot be finished so quickly, the Archduchess would like that, instead of coming here right away, His Highness take the possibly more comfortable route through Romagna, to go to Loreto and Rome, and then to pass Carnival here in Florence." Cioli's letter is at I-Fas, MdP 111, fol. 198. Archduke Karl died in Spain. News of his death reached Florence on 15 January 1625, putting an apparent end to Magdalena's diplomatic initiative.

40. For a detailed reading of *Sant'Orsola*, see Harness, *Echoes*, 79–99.

41. Ibid., 83 and document 3.1 allude to the Modenese ambassador Cesare Molza's report that the court had spent twenty-four thousand scudi on *Sant'Orsola*.

42. Tinghi mentions the performance in I-Fas, Miscellanea Medicea 11, fol. 103r. The libretto is published in Andrea Salvadori, *Poesie* (Rome: n.p., 1668), 1:422–531.

43. Salvadori, *Poesie*, vol. 1 (between 422 and 531): "Ch'ogni anima gentile / Ogni petto più fiero / a beltà femminile / doni di se l'impero."

44. Elena Fumagalli, Massimiliano Rossi, and Riccardo Spinelli have shown that the Medici were fascinated with *Orlando* and with Tasso's *La Gerusalemme liberata*, especially because Christine imagined herself to be descended from Goffredo Buttiglione. See their catalogue and essay collection *L'arme e gli amori: La poesia di Ariosto, Tasso e Guarini nell'arte fiorentina del Seicento* (Florence: Sillabe, 2001). Several court spectacles had derived their themes from one or the other of these romances, including *La disfida di Mandricardo*, a joust performed on 6 February 1614, with a concluding balletto composed by Marco da Gagliano; intermedi by Andrea Salvadori titled *La liberazione di Tirreno*, performed on 6 February 1617 to music by Gagliano and Jacopo Peri; Salvadori's *Lo sposalizio di Medoro et Angelica*, "rappresentato in musica" by Gagliano and Peri on 23 and 25 November 1619 to celebrate the election of Magdalena's brother Ferdinando as emperor; and Salvadori's *Le fonti d'Ardenna: Festa d'arme e di ballo*, with music by Gagliano, performed on 3 February 1623 in the Gherardesco family's palace for the visit of Henri II Bourbon, prince of Condé.

45. The account below is drawn from the Polish visitor Jagodynski's published description of the 1625 scene, *Apparatus z scenami abo Ksztalt rzezy teatrowych*, as translated by Matteo Glinski in *La prima stagione lirica italiana all'estero (1628)*, Quaderni dell'Accademia Chigiana 4 (Siena: Ticci Editore Libraio, 1943), 65, n. 1. On the figure of Neptune in Medicean symbolism, see Janet Cox-Rearick, *Dynasty and Destiny in Medici Art: Pontormo, Leo X and the Two Cosimos* (Princeton: Princeton University Press, 1984). Other Medicean entertainments that used this trope include Ottaviano Rinuccini's *La mascherata di ninfe di Senna*, performed in 1611 for the marriage of Arnea [Renee] de Lorraine to the Conte d'Umena, Duca Sforza; and Andrea Salvadori *La regina Sant'Orsola*.

46. Saracinelli's libretto is available as part of a facsimile edition of the score with an introduction by Alessandro Magini, published in Florence by the Società per edizioni scelti in 1998. Hereafter I refer to the libretto as "Saracinelli," followed by line numbers. This passage is Saracinelli, lines 63–90.

47. Saracinelli, lines 91–186, constitutes the scene with Alcina. Lines 187–260 constitute the entertainment that her minions stage for Ruggiero after Alcina's departure. As Kelley Harness has shown in detail, Saracinelli developed the lovers debate between Ruggiero and Alcina not from Ariosto's poem but from canto 16, stanzas 17–26 of Torquato Tasso's *Gerusalemme liberata*. See Harness, *Echoes*, 153–162.

48. Saracinelli, lines 261–313, constitutes the exchange between Ruggiero and Melissa-as-Atlante.

49. Saracinelli, lines 314–364, constitutes their scene with the plants.

50. Sarcinelli, lines 365–458, constitutes the scene in which Alcina learns of Ruggiero's liberation and decides to take action. Lines 395–420 and 424–441 constitute the messenger's account. She describes herself as hidden among the branches, hearing all, at lines 436–437: "Io, che tra rami ascosa / Non veduta da loro, il tutto udia."

51. Saracinelli, lines 441–455, reveals Alcina's resolve. She signals her intent to use song and tears as means of persuasion at lines 450–452: "E con soavi note, / E con l'umide gote / Ammollirò l'insuperbito core."

52. Saracinelli, lines 459–494, constitutes Alcina's direct confrontation with Ruggiero.

53. Saracinelli, lines 495–515, constitutes Alcina's grieving with her damigelle. Lines 523–569 contain her increasingly enraged exchange with Ruggiero and Melissa. As she begins the speech "Qual temerario core" at line 569, the stage is engulfed in flames that persist until her exit at line 632.

54. Saracinelli, lines 633–654, constitutes Melissa's final soliloquy, in which she commands the plants to be free. Although according to the libretto only liberated dame danced at first, the rubrics on p. 67 of the printed score indicate at the end of Melissa's speech: "Qui viene il ballo di otto dame della Serenissima Arciduchessa con otto cavalieri principali, e fanno un ballo nobilissimo."

55. Saracinelli, lines 655–685, constitutes this final dramatic exchange before the libretto devolves into texts for dance songs. Two of these, "A diletti, a gioire," which appears at the end of the ballo for liberated dame and cavalieri, and "Tosche del sol più belle," which appears at the end of the balletto a cavallo, were printed in Caccini's score. The other two, "Chi racchiude l'Amore nel petto," intended for the first half of the balletto a cavallo, and "Se l'huom, che nacque al cielo, ha pene in terra," to which Melissa made her triumphant entrance amid the dancers on horseback, were not published as music; no settings of these texts are known to survive in manuscript.

56. The details of the way indoor dancing elided with the final outdoor number are from Jagodynski's account as it appears in Glinski, *La prima stagione lirica italiana.* "Queste, nell'ultima scena, sparirono anche'esse par dare luogo ad una vasta piazza. E subito si fecero vedere 24 cavalieri che, desiderosi di fare un balletto di cavalli, si recarono in una piazza ancora più vasa dove noi utili ammirammo finchè arrivò Melissa, trascinata dai centauri—e questo fu l'epilogo dello spettacolo."

57. On the importance of centaurs in Medicean symbolism, see Cox-Rearick, *Dynasty and Destiny.*

58. This connection is strongest in Jagodynski's description, as translated in Glinski, *La prima stagione lirica italiana:* "Il terzo quadro rappresentava Alcina che nel suo furore cambiava il mare in vampe di fuoco, dopodiche, trasmutatasi in un orribile mostro, essa scompariva." Tinghi does not attribute the fire to any character's agency, nor do the Modenese and Lucchese ambassadors.

59. For the purpose of this description, I have counted only lines that occur prior to the beginning of the second balletto, because it is impossible to know how many of the ensuing stanzas of dance songs might have been sung in performance. According to Harness the libretto has 733 lines, which makes it only about 60 lines shorter than Rinuccini's *L'Euridice.*

60. Harness shows that Saracinelli developed both the idea and some of the imagery for Alcina's complaint from Tasso's construction of the similar character Armida in canto 16 of *Gerusalemme liberata*. See Harness, *Echoes*, 156. He had no clear poetic model for the messenger scene, although it has obvious resonances with Dafne's well-known soliloquy "Per quel vago boschetto," in Jacopo Peri and Ottaviano Rinuccini's *L'Euridice*, lines 191–223, and with the better-known scene of the Messagera in Claudio Monteverdi and Alessandro Striggio's *L'Orfeo*, beginning "Ahi, caso acerbo."

61. Contemporary accounts imply that she appeared as one or the other onstage.

62. They could also easily be understood as a butch-femme couple, and, by extension, as together constituting the feminist subject that Sue-Ellen Case imagined as possible if butch and femme were internalized into a single sensibility. See Sue-Ellen Case, "Toward a Butch-Femme Aesthetic," in *Making a Spectacle: Feminist Essays on Contemporary Women's Theatre*, edited Lynda Hart, 282–299 (Ann Arbor: University of Michigan Press, 1989).

63. The most significant primary sources concerning female homoeroticism in early modern Italy are Ambroise Paré, *Monstres et prodigues* (Paris: n.p., 1573); Agnolo Firenzuola, *Prose* (Florence: Giunta, 1548); Pierre de Bourdeille, Seigneur de Brantôme, *Oeuvres: Tome 3e et 4e Contenant des Vies des Dames Galantes* (London: Aux Depens du Libraire, 1779); and Leo Africanus (Giovanni Leone), *History and Description of Africa, and of the Notable Things Therein Contained: Done into English in the Year 1600, by John Pory, and Now Edited with an Introduction and Notes by Dr. Robert Brown* (London: n.p., 1896). See also Thomas Laqueur, *Making Sex: Body and Gender from the Greeks to Freud* (Cambridge: Harvard University Press, 1990); Katherine Park, "The Rediscovery of the Clitoris," in *The Body in Parts: Fantasies of Corporeality in Early Modern Europe*, ed. David Hillman and Carla Mazzio, 171–194 (New York: Routledge, 1997); and Valerie Traub, *The Renaissance of Lesbianism in Early Modern Europe* (Cambridge: Cambridge University Press, 2002).

64. Pierre de Bourdeille, Seigneur de Brantôme, *Les dames galantes*, ed. Maurice Rat (Paris: Editions Garnier Freres, 1967), 119–128, passim; on 123 he comments that such intimacy could be an apprenticeship for heterosexuality, and on 129 he notes that men could be cuckolded by wives who became emotionally involved with their women partners.

65. For a reading of *Orlando furioso*'s representations of Africans, see Delphia Robinson Eboigbe, "The Depiction of the Negro African in Three Old French Chansons de Geste and Two Renaissance Epico-Chivalric Poems," PhD diss., Indiana University, 1983, 21–331. See also T. F. Earle and K. J. P. Lowe, eds., *Black Africans in Renaissance Europe* (Cambridge: Cambridge University Press, 2005).

66. Leo Africanus, *History and Description of Africa*, 2:458.

67. A rich literature about early modern projections of the sexuality of donne con donne onto African women has sprung from Patricia Parker's classic "Fantasies of 'Race' and 'Gender': Africa, *Othello* and Bringing to Light," in *Women, 'Race' and Writing in the Early Modern Period*, ed. Margo Hendricks and Patricia Parker, 84–100 (New York: Routledge, 1994).

68. On early modern notions of gender as a dominant-submissive binary regardless of the sex of the partners, see Anne MacNeil, *Music and Women of the Commedia dell'Arte* (Oxford: Oxford University Press, 2003), chap. 3; Michael Rocke, *Forbidden Friendships: Homosexuality and Male Culture in Renaissance Florence* (Oxford: Oxford University Press, 1996).

Chapter 10

1. For a more linear, narrative-based reading, see Suzanne G. Cusick, "Of Women, Music and Power: A Model from *Seicento* Florence," in *Musicology and Difference: Gender and Sexuality in Music Scholarship,* ed. Ruth Solie, 281–304 (Berkeley: University of California Press, 1993). Kelley Harness offers a different interpretation in *Echoes of Women's Voices: Music, Art, and Female Patronage in Early Modern Florence* (Chicago: University of Chicago Press, 2006), 152–162. Reading through both the Ariosto source and Saracinelli's borrowings from Tasso's *Gerusalemme liberata,* she hears *La liberazione* as aimed at motivating Magdalena's nephew Prince Władisław of Poland to eschew his tolerance of Protestants and join her Catholic League.

2. I was emboldened to acknowledge this by Carolyn Abbate's essay "Music—Drastic or Gnostic?" *Critical Inquiry* 30/3 (Summer 2004): 505–536.

3. Gary Tomlinson, "The Historian, the Performer, and Authentic Meaning in Music," in *Authenticity and Early Music,* ed. Nicholas Kenyon, 115–136 (Oxford: Oxford University Press, 1988). Although Tomlinson's position has been maligned by postmodern scholars of various stripes, I have found that thus reconstructing my sensibility enabled me to hear, see, and understand things about *La liberazione* that I could not have imagined had I listened or looked only at the notes in the published score as they compared with the notes of other composers active in her time.

4. For a summary of the ideas about music in Bronzini's text, see Suzanne G. Cusick, "Francesca among Women: A *Seicento* Gynocentric View," in *Musical Voices of Early Modern Women: Many-Headed Melodies,* ed., Thomasin LaMay, 425–443 (Aldershot: Ashgate, 2004).

5. The performances given in mid-May 1999 were produced by Alain Clement, artistic director of MuBarOp in Fribourg, Switzerland, in collaboration with the FrauenMusik-Forum. Gabriel Garrido was musical director, leading the Choeur d'Opera Orlando Fribourg, and his own Ensemble Elyma. Emanuela Galli played Alcina, Alicia Burgos played Melissa, and Furio Zanasi played Ruggiero. Ruth Orthmann was the stage director. I am grateful to M. Clement and to the production's dramaturg, Marc-Joachim Wasmer, for allowing me to work with a copy of the recording made for broadcast on Radio Suisse Romande, Espace 2 and DRS2, 5 June 1999. Many of the same musicians recorded *La liberazione* for broadcast on Radio France 5 in the spring of 2002.

6. Schechner's ideas about performance as creating a subjunctive mode of experience are most fully elaborated in *Between Theater and Anthropology* (Philadelphia: University of Pennsylvania Press, 1985), chap. 2, "Restoration of Behavior," 35–116.

7. Saracinelli's libretto is available as part of a facsimile edition of the score with an introduction by Alessandro Magini, published in Florence by the Studio per edizioni scelti in 1998. Hereafter I refer to the libretto as "Saracinelli," followed by line numbers, in this case Saracinelli, lines 314–316: "Ruggiero de danni asprissimi / di queste piante flebile / Deh senti al cor pieta" (Ruggiero, the most bitter injuries / Of these plaintive plants / Oh! Hear in your heart, and have pity).

8. The scene is at pp. 37–43 in the facsimile score published in Florence by the Studio per edizioni scelte in 1998. Hereafter, I refer to this score as SPES, followed by page numbers.

9. One thinks of Monteverdi's romanesca "Ohimè, dov'è il mio ben" and perhaps even more of the heroic but failed struggle against constraint that is enacted by the later *Lamento della Ninfa.*

10. I am grateful to Kevin Phelps for the wonderful phrase "modified rapture," as for much else.

11. See Torquato Tasso, "Discorso delle virtù femminile e donnesca," in *Rime e prose* (Venice: Giulio Vassalini, 1583). Lucretia Marinelli, in *La nobiltà et l'eccellenza delle donne, co' diffetti e mancamenti degli uomini* (Venice, 1601), 128–130, critiqued Tasso's elitist view and argued that women of all social ranks are capable of masculine virtù. Marinelli's treatise was well known at Maria Magdalena's court, and her ideas may well have informed courtly women's reception of *La liberazione*.

12. For the scene with Ruggiero, Alcina, and the damigelle in her garden, see SPES, 16–23.

13. For Alcina's leave-taking, see SPES, 23–24. In lines 168–179 of the libretto, she promises him, "You will have a thousand delights: / here lovely birds / fill the fields, / here nymphs, and shepherds / hear from happy cupids, / swans and sirens / sweet songs that could / put [even] Argus to sleep." See SPES, 28–30 for the shepherd's song. Its ritornello was probably played by a three-piped *sordellina* of the sort that Francesca's husband had on consignment from the Medici Guardaroba.

14. See SPES, 31–34.

15. Constructed to channel, confuse, and thereby entrap the desires of listeners of 1625, Francesca's siren song "Chi nel fior di giovinezza" has apparently enchanted others, for an excerpt was included in a manuscript of arias and cantatas compiled at Rome in the 1630s and now housed at I-Vnm, MS IV, 740.

16. Simone Fornari, *Delle espositione sopra l'Orlando furioso, parte seconda* (Florence, 1550), 43: "la violentia et forza che sopra gli amanti usa cotal femina . . . per Alcina si puo intender l'ambitione, e la cupidità di dominare popoli e terre."

17. I am grateful to Bonnie Gordon for the conversation that first made me understand this scene as an outrageous performance of vocality as sex and to Margaret McFadden for the burst of laughter with which she greeted the idea—showing me a joke in the show that I had long missed.

18. On the origins and conventions of the recitative soliloquy, see Margaret Murata, "The Recitative Soliloquy," *Journal of the American Musicological Society* 32/1 (1979): 45–73.

19. Alcina's announcement of her intentions is at lines 447–52. Her damigella sets up the complaint scene at lines lines 457–58: "Or vedrem quanto puote/ Con dolce lagrimar beltà divina."

20. Murata, "Recitative Soliloquy," makes the point that the lament was one of the most common forms of recitative soliloquy. On the early modern lament's ritual importance in marking transitions from one state of being to another, see Anne MacNeil, "Weeping at the Water's Edge," *Early Music* 27 (1999): 406–18; Anne MacNeil, "The Politics of Description," in *Music and Women of the Commedia dell'Arte in the Late Sixteenth Century*, 127–162 (Oxford: Oxford University Press, 2003).

21. SPES, 53–54.

22. On tonal desire as sexual agency, see Susan McClary, "Constructions of Gender in Monteverdi's Dramatic Music," *Cambridge Opera Journal* 1 (1989): 203–23, reprinted as chapter 2 of McClary, *Feminine Endings: Music, Gender, Sexuality* (Minneapolis: University of Minnesota, 1991), 35–52. I thank David E. Cohen for a conversation that helped clarify my thinking about the construction of tonal desire throughout this scene.

23. SPES, 55–56.

24. SPES, 56–57.

25. Arguably the bursting of the stage into flames snapped that spell, lest it actually overwhelm the audience. Certainly, the display of scenic meraviglia could have returned the audience to a condition of appreciating the show's sheer entertainment value. The fire, seemingly ignited by Alcina's and her damigelle's song, consumes the stage world that was made of Ruggiero's gynophobic fantasies.

26. The scenes are in the following order: the siren's song; Ruggiero's liberation; the scene of enchanted plants; Ruggiero's liberation recounted among women; and Alcina's complaint.

27. Saracinelli, lines 436–37: "Io, che tra rami ascosa / Non veduta da loro, il tutto udia."

28. SPES 34–36.

29. I am grateful to Kelley Harness for first drawing my attention to the cadence-filled quality of Melissa's recitative.

30. In Düdingen, Alicia Burgos played this scene wearing a false beard made of household cotton batting, ensuring that the audience would take her performance of masculine magic as a joke.

31. See McClary, *Feminine Endings*, 39–44, for the classic interpretation of this scene in relation to gender and sexuality.

32. SPES, 48.

33. SPES, 49.

34. The catastrophe of Euridice's death was announced by a female messenger whose voice intruded dissonantly on a sound world dominated by men's voices in both Jacopo Peri's and Giulio Caccini's settings of Rinuccini's *L'Euridice*, which appeared in 1600, and in Claudio Monteverdi's 1607 setting of Alessandro Striggio's *L'Orfeo*. As much a stock scene type as the lament was to be the for next half-century, it was one of many common bits from which early modern musical spectacles could be quickly constructed. Louise Clubb coined the word "theatregram" for such bits. See Louise Clubb, *Italian Drama in Shakespeare's Time* (New Haven: Yale University Press, 1989).

35. I am well aware how dangerous it would be to set too much store on any opera's tonal plan. Yet because early modern tunings made each tonal area acoustically and affectively distinctive in a way that post-Enlightenment equal temperament obscures, it seems reasonable to consider the tonal relations inscribed in a published score as evidence of the composer's acoustical intentions.

36. The liberating soliloquy is in lines 267–294; the last line before the concluding balletti is 685. Kelley Harness first pointed out Melissa's centrality to the libretto in her dissertation "*Amazzoni di Dio:* Florentine Musical Spectacle under Maria Magdalena d'Austria and Cristina di Lorena (1620–30)," PhD diss., University of Illinois, 1996.

37. Melissa's opening soliloquy is at SPES, 14–16, and is lines 63–90 of the libretto. Her closing soliloquy is at SPES, 66–67, and occupies lines 633–654 of the libretto.

38. Melissa's speech is found at lines 339–344 of a total of 685 lines.

39. The scene is at SPES, 67–69, and lines 655–685 in the libretto.

40. Bronzini, *Della dignità e nobiltà delle donne* (Florence: Pignoni, 1622), signature A3v–A4, as translated in Constance Jordan, *Renaissance Feminism* (Ithaca: Cornell University Press, 1990), 268.

41. See chapter 5.

42. Anne MacNeil has shown how detailed versus expansive perspectives were gendered in early modern Italy. See MacNeil, *Music and Women of the Commedia dell'Arte* (Oxford: Oxford University Press, 2003), 95–99.

43. Bronzini, I-Fn, Magl. VIII. 1525/1, 57–58. See appendix C.

CHAPTER 11

1. On the intermedi by Andrea Salvadori for the marriage of Claudia de' Medici and Archduke Leopold, which were written for an unnamed pastoral, see Tim Carter, *Jacopo Peri, 1561–1633: His Life and Works* (New York: Garland, 1989) 96–99 and passim. In n. 64 Carter cites I-Fas, Manoscritti 133, fol. 314–316, and Angelo Solerti, *Musica, ballo e drammatica alla Corte medicea dal 1600 al 1637* (Florence: Bemporad, 1905), 185–186, as sources for his brief remarks. Carter's n. 68 identifies I-Fn, MS II.iv.22, fols. 170–183 as the source of at least one intermedio, "L'arme d'Achille nell'isola degl'eroi," in which Francesca may have been cast as "La Discordia." On *La Giuditta*, written by Salvadori with music (now lost) attributed to Marco da Gagliano, see the extended discussion in Kelley Harness, *Echoes of Women's Voices: Music, Art, and Female Patronage in Early Modern Florence* (Chicago: University of Chicago Press, 2006), 216–269.

2. Władisław's letters are at I-Fas, MdP 4292, fol. 560, letters of 2 July 1626. Magdalena's replies are not known to have survived.

3. Signorini's death date is noted on his horoscope, at I-Fn, MS II.__.105, fol. 84v. I-Fas, Ufficiali poi Magistrato della Grascia 105, Libro dei Morti 1626–69, records his burial in Santa Maria Novella on 30 December 1626.

4. I-Fas, Notarile Moderno 13734–37 (Paolo Lapi), Testament of 23 December 1626, G. B. Signorini, fol. 32v.

5. Ibid., fols. 32v–33r.

6. Ibid., fol. 32r.

7. Ibid., fol. 33r.

8. Ibid., fol. 34r. In a deposition taken at Sinolfo Ottieri's trial in 1621, Signorini had claimed that his net worth was four thousand scudi. It is possible that he meant to claim property that his will acknowledges as Francesca's property. For the deposition see I-Fas, Otto di guardia e balia, Principato. 2793, fol. 27r–v, testimony given on 24 March 1620/21.

9. On gender in marriage, see Christiane Klapisch-Zuber, "The 'Cruel Mother': Maternity, Widowhood, and Dowry in Florence in the Fourteenth and Fifteenth Centuries," in *Women, Family and Ritual in Renaissance Italy*, 117–119 (Chicago: University of Chicago Press, 1985). According to Klapisch, Florentine family law conceived of households as established and enriched by men; the women of a household were thought of as passing through. Although Signorini's rhetorical framing clearly referred to this norm, the fact that his household was described as having been built almost entirely with his wife's resources reversed the frame.

10. I-Fas, Notarile Moderno 13734–37 (Paolo Lapi), Testament 23 December 1626, G. B. Signorini, fol. 32r provides for Signorini's burial site, leaving the organization and expenses of the funeral to Francesca's discretion. His burial notice is at I-Faa, in Parocchia Santa Maria Novella, Registro de Morti dal 1556 al 1668, fol. 38.

11. This description of burial and funeral practices is based largely on Sharon Strocchia, *Death and Ritual in Renaissance Florence* (Baltimore: Johns Hopkins University Press,

1992). Strocchia (50) points out that the presence of a deceased person's name in the ministry's records simply indicates that the body was prepared by the beccamorti, whose work was jointly supervised by the doctors' guild, the spicer's guild, and the Magistrato della Grascia, the ministry of grain, which managed the city's food supply. Note 69 specifies that the beccamorti continued to be regulated by the grascia during the reign of the Medici. Note 70 explains that in the fifteenth century the fee for washing, shaving, and dressing the corpse was two lire, and the beccamorti charged ten soldi each for keeping vigil over the body, for carrying the corpse into the main room of the house, and for preparing the bier. On the Libri dei Morti, see G. Parenti, "Fonti per lo studio della demografia fiorentina: I libri dei morti," *Genus* 6–8 (1943–49): 281–301.

12. Women in her family, friends, or servants would have been dispatched to acquire these items.

13. Given Caccini's and Signorini's shared profession, the group of women mourners is likely to have included many highly skilled singers. Besides Caccini herself, her stepmother Margherita, her stepsister Dianora, and possibly her sister Settimia and her cousin Paola, women singers whom one can imagine to have participated include Vittoria Archilei, Angelica Sciamerone, Emilia Grazi, Maria Botti, one or both of the Parigi sisters, and any number of Francesca's pupils.

14. The Ordre de Saint Michel was a chivalric order founded in 1469 by Louis XI of France as a kind of honor guard of thirty-six noblemen sworn to defend the French king. After 1560 the limit on the number of members was lifted, and appointments to the order were distributed to retainers of noble and of common birth, at the urging of powerful courtiers. According to his horoscope, Signorini was inducted into the order in Rome in 1623, probably at the urging of Christine. There is no evidence that Signorini belonged to the musician's guild, although as an instrumentalist he probably did.

15. After publication of the 1614 *Rituale Romanum*, requiem masses were obligatory parts of the burial ceremony. See Strocchia, *Death and Ritual*, 232–233.

16. The classic description of Florentine traditions concerning widowhood remains Christiane Klapisch-Zuber's "The 'Cruel Mother.'" See also Isabelle Chabot, "Lineage strategies and the control of widows in Renaissance Florence," in *Widowhood in Medieval and Early Modern Europe*, ed. Sandra Cavallo and Lyndan Warmer, 127–144 (Harlow, Essex, UK: Longman, 1999), especially 132 on the *tornata*, a black-clad widow's ritual procession back to her birth family's home to announce her readiness for remarriage. For the ritual elements, see Chabot, "'La sposa in nero': Le ritualizazzione del lutto delle vedove fiorentine (sec. XIV–XV)," *Quaderni storici* 86 (1994): 443–445. On the longevity of these traditions, see the essays gathered in Giulia Calvi and Isabelle Chabot, eds., *Le richezze delle donne: Diritti patrimoniali e poteri familiari (XII–XIX sec)* (Turin: Rosenberg & Sellier, 1998). For a sophisticated history of the role of the *madre-tutrice*—the widow-guardian—as it was created by the seventeenth-century rulings of Florence's Magistrato dei Pupilli, see Giulia Calvi, *Il contratto morale: Madri e figli nella Toscana moderna* (Rome: Laterza, 1994).

17. On the generally accepted age limits of a woman's remarriageability, see Klapisch-Zuber, "The 'Cruel Mother,'" 120, and Calvi, *Il Contratto morale*, 128.

18. I-FcasaB, A.B. 44, no. 455, letter of 1 January 1627. See appendix B.

19. Given that only eighteen months earlier Francesca had humiliated her older brother Giovanni Battista by exposing his callous treatment of their widowed stepmother

and her undowered daughter, he seems likely to have been quite unsympathetic to her concerns. See chapter 12, note 37 for details of this incident.

20. I-FCasaB, A.B. 44, no. 456, letter of 13 January 1626/27. See appendix B.

21. On Margherita's frequently postponed marriage to Farnese, see Harness, *Echoes*, 162–166.

22. Widowhood by itself did not bar women from making or teaching music at the Medici court. For at least eight years after her husband's death in 1612, Vittoria Archilei continued to sing during Holy Week and to lead the private performances of the arch-duchess's dame in Magdalena's private chapel at Pitti. Although she seems not to have sung after 1620, Archilei remained among the *provvisionati* until the reform of the court's staff in 1641; she died sometime after 1644, the date of her will. Angelica Sciamerone remained on the court's payroll for eleven years after her husband Domenico Belli's death, although she is not known to have sung again. For both women's performances, see Tin-ghi, I-Fn, MS Gino Capponi 261, II and Solerti, *Musica, ballo*. For the 1641 reform, see Frederick Hammond, "Musicians at the Medici Court in the Mid-Seventeenth Century," *Analecta musicologica* 14 (1974): 151–179, based on his reading of I-Fas, Guardaroba Mediceo 644 (1590–1669); Warren Kirkendale, *The Court Musicians in Florence during the Principate of the Medici* (Florence: Olschki, 1993), 35–57, passim.

23. The date of Francesca's marriage to Raffaelli is recorded at Lucca, Archivio della Parrocchia di San Frediano, Liber Matrimonii 1618–1636 (vol. 123), p. 50. It was wit-nessed by Raffaello Mansi and Santucco Santucci. The archive notes that the customary banns had been waived at the pleasure of Lucca's bishop. I-Las, Gabella dei Contratti e delle Doti, 166 (1628), opening 5, lists Raffaelli's payment of tax on Francesca's dowry of sixteen hundred scudi, the value of the homes on via Valfonda, on 3 January 1628.

24. I-Fas, MdP 2828, insert 1, letter of Orazio Tuccarelli to Dimurgo Lambardi, 28 July 1627. I-Fas, MdP 120, nos. 234 and 235 identify Tuccarelli as a "long-standing servant and minister of this Most Serene House." I-Fas, MdP 119, fol. 250, letter of 23 February 1627, indicates that he was involved in negotiating the release from prison of Tommaso Raffaelli's nephew, a Cavaliere di Santo Stefano. Dimurgo Lambardi was a priest who served as Christine's secretary in the 1620s. The papers he collected during that era teem with documents relating to the regents' management of women's remar-riages and convent placements, many of them framed in terms of the imminent end of the regency.

25. I-Fas, MdP 2828, insert 1, letter of Orazio Tuccarelli to Dimurgo Lambardi, 13 August 1627

26. Ibid., letter of Orazio Tuccarelli to Dimurgo Lambardi, 15 September 1627.

27. I-Las, MSS 22, 3:109; the first record of Antonio del Tornaio dates from 1443.

28. Rita Mazzei, *La società lucchese del Seicento* (Lucca: Maria Pacini Fazzi, 1977), 39–40. The Raffaelli are listed among Lucca's noble families in I-Las, Libro di corredo alle arte della Signoria 83, Libro delle Famiglie Nobili della Repubblica di Lucca e loro Stemmi formato l'anno 1628 per decreto dell'eccellentissimo consiglio di gennaro detto anno, 170.

29. I-Lbg, MS 900, fols. 69–70 provide these figures concerning comparative net worth.

30. On Raffaelli's association with Lucchesini's academy and his own subsequent importance to academic life in Lucca, see Angelo Bertacchi, *Storia dell'accademie lucchese*

(Lucca, 1881), fol. 1, 154–157; Luigi Nerici, *Storia della musica in Lucca* (Lucca: Tipografia Giusti, 1879), 326. On Lucchesini's and Guidiccione's importance to artistic life among the women who lived with Christine in the 1590s, see Angelo Solerti, "Laura Guidiccione Lucchesini ed Emilio d'Cavalieri: I primi tentativi del melodramma," *Rivista musicale italiana* 9 (1902): 797–829.

31. Bernardino Baroni, *Famiglie lucchese*, I-Las, Bibl MSS 127, vol. 4, fols. 136r–v, cites a series of notarial documents relative to the inheritances that Tommaso Raffaelli received from his father and his uncle Giufredo. Giufredo left possession of his villa at Monsaquilici to the heirs of Antonio Raffaelli, Alessandro and Tommaso. Giufredo died in 1597. According to I-Las, Notari 2492, fols. 183r–250r, containing a set of contracts that Francesca made with her late husband's farmers in June 1630, the villa was surrounded by those of the Buonvisi, Burlamacchi, Franciotti, and Santini families.

32. Adriano Banchieri, *Lettere armoniche* (Bologna: Girolamo Mascheroni, 1628), 66, letter "Al Sig. Thomaso Raffaelli. Lucca. Di Ringratiamento." The presence of Girolamo Raffaelli in his uncle's household is recognized in Tommaso's will, I-Las Notari 188, fols. 822r–834v.

33. See I-Las, Libro di corredo alle arte della Signoria, 83, the so-called "libro d'oro" cited above, n. 28, and Mazzei, *La società lucchese*, chapter 5.

34. Banchieri, *Lettere armoniche*. The surviving accounts of Vincenzo Buonvisi's household are at I-Las, Archivio Buonvisi, ser. 1, vol. 79, at the end of a file of dictated letters dated 1610–1639 kept by the administrator of his never-married daughter Caterina's finances. Buonvisi had been Lucca's special envoy to Florence on several occasions, including a visit during Carnival in 1625, when he was in the audience for *La liberazione di Ruggiero*.

35. I-FEas, Archivio Bentivoglio, Lettere Sciolte, 210, fol. 382, letter of Antonio Goretti to Enzo Bentivoglio, from Parma, 29 October 1627. In a letter dated 2 November, Goretti elaborated that Settimia Caccini would not succeed in the role under consideration because when she sang listeners could not understand her words. Goretti thought it imperative to have Francesca sing the part, despite having heard that she and her sister were "mortal enemies." Both letters are published in Dinko Fabris, *Mecenati e Musici* (Lucca: Libreria Musicale Italiana, 1999) as document 849, p. 412, and document 856, p. 415. I am grateful to Professor Fabris for drawing them to my attention. Excerpts from the second letter also appear in Irene Mamczarz, *Le Théâtre Farnese de Parme et le drame musical italien, 1618–1732* (Florence: Olschki, 1988), 463, n. 4, and in Maria Grazia Borazzo, *Musica, scenotecnica, illusione nel grande apparato farnesiano del 1628 a Parma* (Tesi di laurea, Università di Parma, 1981), 182–183. I am grateful to Tim Carter, Andrew Dell'Antonio, and Kelley Harness for drawing my attention to these sources.

36. I-Lbg, MS 383, Manuale dell'Accademia delli Oscuri, fols. 39r–72v provides an intermittent narrative of the production's history, as reported to the membership by the committee charged with Carnival entertainments. The intermedi by Lelio Altogradi, which were to be based on the fable of Esione, were interpolated into a tragicomedy titled *Alissa*.

37. Ibid., fol. 53r, minutes of 9 March 1628. The minutes of 7 September 1628, on fols. 69v–70r, report the recommendation of a three-man committee concerned with publication of the intermedi. Still basking in the glow of their 1628 success, on 1 January 1629 the Oscuri voted to perform a "heroic work" for that year's Carnival, one that would, however, use only members of the academy in the cast. See fol. 72r–v.

38. I-Las, Notari 188, fols. 822r–834v comprises the testament of Tommaso Raffaelli, dated 24 February 1630, and three codicils (one dated 7 April and two dated 13 April). On the collapse of the Buonvisi, see Mazzei, *La società lucchese,* and I-Fas, MdP 2828, insert 1, letter of Federigo Tuccarelli to an unnamed secretary, 13 April 1630, describing the sale of the family's antiquities collection in the streets.

39. I-Las, Notari 188, fol. 824r. In legal terms Tommaso need have done no more than mention Francesca, her dowry, and the terms of her statutory usufruct—just as their shared friend and benefactor Vincenzo Buonvisi was to do when he dictated his will in 1650. I-Las, Archivio Buonvisi, ser. 1, 40, fols. 185–189, contains a copy of Vincenzo Buonvisi's will, dated 26 August 1650. Buonvisi did not name his widow the executrix of his estate.

40. Raffaelli's concern to protect his widow-executrix' authority as if it were his own pervades his will. The specific authority to evict persons who did not behave well toward her is at I-Las, Notari 188, fol. 825r.

41. Ibid., fol. 827v.

42. Ibid., fol. 825r–v authorizes Francesca to give Margherita Signorini up to two hundred scudi from his estate as her legacy, if Francesca should "judge that said Signora Margherita needs it in some occasion."

43. The contracts that survive are at I-Las, Notari 2492, fols. 183r–250r. They may not represent the whole of Raffaelli's estate, but they indicate the kind of property that was its income-producing core. Executed at Monsanquilici on 4 June 1630 under the watchful eye of Vincenzo Buonvisi, they involve forty-seven parcels of land in the foothills bounded by Fondagno, Pescaglia, and Gelli. One was foreclosed as the result of a tenant's insolvency, and the rest were rented to eight different farmers for periods ranging from one to five years. The farmers worked the land and mills for the Raffaelli estate and in turn received a relatively small proportion of their labors' fruits. The estate, however, received annually a minimum of 170 bushels of chestnut flour destined for sale at market, plus half the oil and wine of almost every farmer's harvest, along with firewood, hemp, and dry grain delivered directly to Francesca's household. Francesca's sale of the two houses on via Valfonda was managed by Piermaria di Agniolo di Jacopo Trucchi, a Florentine notary acting as her *procuratore* (agent) under authority notarized in Lucca by Piermaria di Lelio Bandinelli on 20 July 1630. She sold both properties to Dianora di Girolamo Capponi, a Florentine noblewoman who was the wife of Ulivieri di Vincenzo Falconieri. The sale and related documents are at I-Fas, Notarile Moderno, Atti di Tommaso Mati, Protocolli 11740, no. 46, fol. 63r–v, a *mandatum* of the Ufficiali dei Pupilli e Adulti dated 13 March 1628 liquidating the assets of an annuity worth fifteen hundred scudi that Dianora's brother Piero Capponi had left her; Notarile Moderno, Atti di Tommaso Mati 11742, no. 59, fols. 93v–94v is a mandatum dated 13 August 1630 by which Dianora appointed her husband to act as her agent in the purchase of property from Francesca Caccini; Notarile Moderno 11742, no. 60, fols. 94v–98v is the bill of sale for the larger house dated 16 August 1630; and Notarile Moderno 11742, no. 61, fols. 98r–100r is the bill of sale for the smaller house, also dated 16 August 1630. I am grateful to Doctor Paola Peruzzi at the Archivio di Stato di Firenze for helping me track these documents and to Professor Gino Corti for helping me to transcribe and interpret them.

44. On the dowry arrangements that Giulio made in April 1588, see chap. 1, n. 5.

45. I-Fas, MdP 1427, fol. 77r–78r, letter of Francesca Caccini Raffaelli to Andrea Cioli, 19 March 1631. See appendix B.

46. She alludes to the epidemic of plague that beset central Italy, including Florence and Lucca, from the summer of 1630 through the winter of 1633/34.

47. Although Francesca would claim to act on her daughter's behalf in a 1639 lawsuit, there is no documentary evidence that she ever accepted the legal guardianship about which she had sought Buonarroti's advice in January 1627.

48. In this, Francesca was in step with the general feeling that Giulia Calvi documents and explores in *Il contratto morale*.

49. As the child of Princess Claudia's brief marriage to Federico della Rovere, Vittoria embodied Christine's hope of recovering the Medici's ancient claim to Urbino for greater Tuscany. To further Tuscany's claim, at the age of three Vittoria was betrothed to her fifteen-year-old cousin Ferdinando II de' Medici. Thereafter the little girl was known as the "granduchessa," although she did not legally take on the role of grand duchess until her marriage to Ferdinando in 1637.

50. I-Fas, MdP 121, fol. 278, letter of Andrea Cioli to Francesca Caccini Raffaelli, 24 May 1631.

51. Ibid., fol. 279, letter of Francesca Caccini Raffaelli to Andrea Cioli, 26 May 1631.

52. I-Lbg, MA 1095, fols. 55–91v contains one citizen's meticulous diary of the plague at Lucca. The narrative below is based on this diary.

53. Ibid., fol.90r.

54. Archivio del Monastero di Santa Croce, detto La Crocetta, armadio B, cassetta C, a loose vellum *breve* dated 22 June 1633, links the two licenze into a single document. Parts of the brief, translated into Italian, are cited in Gerardo Antignani, *Vicende e tempi di Suor Domenica del Paradiso* (Siena: Cantagalli, 1983), 252. I am grateful to Professor Gino Corti and the late Stefano Corsi for their help in understanding the document and to Kelley Harness for first alerting me to its existence. The *breve* explains what Grand Duchess Christine's two secretaries, Ugo Cacciotti and Perseo Falconieri, so urgently awaited, in their patron's name, in the post from Rome on 21 and 22 June. For their exchange see I-Fas, MdP1453, unfoliated, letter of 22 June 1633 from Ugo Cacciotti, with a signed annotation by Falconieri written between the letter's body and Cacciotti's signature.

55. Princess Maria Maddalena (1600–1633) had lived with six servants in special apartments built adjacent to La Crocetta since 1619. Her widowed sister Princess Claudia (1604–1648) lived there with her daughter Vittoria della Rovere from 1623 until her remarriage to Archduke Leopold of Austria in 1626. As the only Medici princess left at court when her sister Margherita married Odoardo Farnese in 1628, Cosimo II's youngest daughter Princess Anna began to frequent La Crocetta to enjoy the companionship of "the other two princesses," her aunt and her niece, at least as early as September of that year. See I-Fas, MdP 120, nos. 360, 372, and 375, letters from Dimurgo Lambardi and Maria Magdalena discussing the specific terms for Anna's licenze, which Tuscany's ambassadors to Rome were commanded to negotiate with church officials.

I-Fas, MdP 1453 includes a number of memos about the salaries and living arrangements of secular women who served this formidable women's court, including Isabella Tassoni, Caterina Lucchesi, Maddalena Angioli, Caterina Vannori, Caterina Parigi, and Margherita Papino, under the direction of Maddalena Strozzi ne' Salviati (d. 1634) and later of Ortenzia Guadagni ne' Salviati. A memo at I-Fas, MdP 1453, no. 734 notes that the duchess of Guise and her daughters had been granted a licenza to enter and leave La Crocetta twenty times per year beginning on 23 February 1635, so long as they did not do so during Lent. For more on the community at La Crocetta, see chapter 12.

56. A will disposing of the property of one Francesco Forte is at I-Fas, Notarile Moderno, Protocolli 11727–11759, testament of Francesco Forte, 20 September 1634, fols. 27v–30v. He left the title to his house on Borgo Pinti to his mother Clemenza in the hope that his widow Lucrezia and son Tommaso might live with her there, while ceding property on the via del Moro to his mother as restitution of her dowry. His grandson Francesco, son of Tommaso, matriculated in the Arte della Lana (a guild) on 16 March 1635 and collected the rent that the court's paymaster, Vincenzo Vespucci, paid on Francesca's behalf semiannually. Francesco the younger's matriculation is at I-Fas, Arte della Lana 22, fol. 200. His signature on a receipt for six months' worth of Francesca Caccini Raffaelli's rent in 1637 is at I-Fas, Depositeria Generale Antica 1034, Filze de Recapiti, 1637, no. 30. A legal judgment against Francesca in 1639 describes her as then living in Borgo Pinti. See I-Fas, Ruota Civile 869, fol. 99r for the address. See also chapter 12.

CHAPTER 12

1. Francesca and her family lived in Borgo Pinti, their rent paid by the court. On Christine's continued involvement in public policy discussions in the 1630s, see chapter 3.

2. See Kelley Harness, *Echoes of Women's Voices: Music, Art, and Female Patronage in Early Modern Florence* (Chicago: University of Chicago Press, 2006). Chapters 7 and 8 of her book present by far the most comprehensive treatment in English of the founding, decoration, and musical life of the community. Princess Maria Maddalena de' Medici, born in 1600 with an unspecified disability to Ferdinando I and Christine, is not to be confused with her aunt, the Archduchess Maria Magdalena d'Austria, who died while traveling to Austria in the autumn of 1630.

3. The building permit granted by church authorities was copied as part of the petition for a similar project at the Monastero della Concezione to accommodate Princess Maria Christiana's entry there in 1623; it is found at I-Rasv, Sacra Congregatione dei Vescovi e Regolari. Positiones 1623, C–F. Giulio Parigi described La Crocetta's palace in a letter of 10 July 1624, now at I-Faa, Filze di Cancelleria, no. 11. The purchase of property for the palace is described at I-Fn, II.III.499, insert 18. Guidelines for its construction are at I-Rasv, Sacra Congregatione dei Vescovi e Regolari, VR Reg. Regularium 13 (1619), 291r–291v, letter of Cardinal Gallo to the Archbishop of Florence, 24 August 1619, and a copy of that letter at I-Fas, Miscellanea Medicea 5, insert 1, 7r–7v. The latter is published as document 8.a in Harness, *Echoes*. Maria Maddalena's household is described in I-Fas, Miscellanea Medicea 5, insert 1, 108r, letter of Andrea Cioli to Benedetto Barchetti, 14 December 1627, and I-Rasv, Sacra Congregatione dei Vescovi e Regolari. Positiones 1622, B-G, no. 6, letter of the archbishop of Florence. Her life at La Crocetta, including her date of death, is summarized in I-F, Archivio del Monastero di Santa Croce, detto La Crocetta, Armadio B, Nota delli oblighi che h[a] il nostro Monastero et altri con noi . . . dal 1602 final al 1759, fol. 5r.

4. I-F, Archivio del Monastero di Santa Croce, detto La Crocetta, Armadio B, Nota delli Oblighi, fol. 5r records Princess Claudia's entry on 13 January 1623/24 and departure on 7 March 1625/26 and Princess Anna's arrival on 8 January 1628/29. Armadio B, Cassetta C contains cover letters and breve signed and sealed by Pope Urban VIII specifying the conditions under which Claudia and two dame could leave during Carnival in 1624, 1625, and 1626, or at other times when Claudia wished to spend the night with

her mother. In all cases, the women could leave only if accompanied by Christine or by Archduchess Maria Magdalena. I-Fas, MdP 120, nos. 360, 372, and 375 are letters of Dimurgo Lambardi to Archduchess Maria Magdalena discussing the terms of Anna's licenze. The licenze permitting others to enter and leave at will are too numerous to cite. One dated 13 February 1629 allowing Christine both free access and authority to introduce teachers and serving companions to the princesses is at I-F, Archivio del Monastero di Santa Croce, detto La Crocetta, Armadio B, Cassetta C. A memo at I-Fas, MdP 1453, no. 734 grants the duchess of Guise and her daughters access to La Crocetta twenty times per year, beginning 23 February 1635, so long as they did not visit during Lent.

5. I-F, Archivio del Monastero di Santa Croce, detto La Crocetta, Armadio B, Nota delli oblighi, fol. 5v records the departure of Vittoria della Rovere and Princess Anna on 28 November 1636. Ibid., fol. 6r records the inspection and sealing of the passageway by Archbishop Piero Niccolini on 21 October 1637, the feast of Saint Ursula. The passageway was destroyed the following day on the orders of Ferdinando II.

6. Florence, Archivio del Monastero di Santa Croce, detto La Crocetta, Armadio B, Anton Maria Riconesi, *Alle molto Reverende Priora e Monache del Venerabile Munisterio della Croce di Firenze volgarmente chiamato della Crocetta*, especially fols. 15v–17r (hereafter Riconesi). Part of Riconesi's text was published in Gerardo Antignani, *Vicende e tempi di Suor Domenica del Paradiso* (Siena: Cantagalli, 1983).

7. Riconesi, fol. 16v.

8. Riconesi, fol. 15v.

9. See Giulia Calvi, *Histories of a Plague Year*, trans. Dario Biocca and Bryant T. Ragan Jr. (Berkeley: University of California Press, 1989; originally published as *Storie di un anno di peste*, Milan: Bompiani, 1984), especially pt. 2, "The Universe of Symbols," 197–254.

10. For a detailed account, see Harness, *Echoes*, chap. 7, esp. 224–248.

11. Ibid., 292–312, describes three such performances: one on 8 February 1622, vividly described by Curtio Picchena in a letter at I-Fas, MdP 6108, fol. 1026r; a dialogue titled *Anima e corpo* performed on 22 November 1623, described by Tinghi at I-Fas, Miscellanea Medicea 11, 3v and by Angelo Solerti, *Musica, ballo e drammatica alla Corte medicea dal 1600 al 1637* (Florence: Bemporad, 1905), 170 that may be the one attributed to Domenica del Paradiso in I-Fr, Ricc 2633, 157v–160r or the one in a collection of *laude* once owned by Princess Anna's servant Lucia, I-Fn, Magl. VII. 432, 5v–17v; and Jacopo Cicognini's *Il martirio di Santa Caterina*, performed on 27 November 1625.

12. I-Fas, MdP 5183, 474r, letter of Princess Maria Maddalena to Cardinal Carlo de' Medici, 15 October 1623, notes that the princess took advantage of the presence of "Signora Francesca, who sings" to write a letter that Francesca presumably carried to the cardinal in Rome. On Francesca's service to his household in 1623–1624, see chapter 4. The letter is cited in Harness, *Echoes*, 296, n. 47. An annotation to the manuscript prologue of Cicognini's *Il martirio de Santa Caterina* says, "[H]ere a solo voice would need to sing, as Signora Francesca knows." The manuscript was discovered at I-Fr, Ricc 3470, 325r–429r by Silvia Castello, who discusses it in "La drammaturgia di Iacopo Cicognini," Tesi di laurea, Storia dello spettacolo, Università degli studi di Firenze, Facoltà di lettere e filosofia, 1988–1989. I am grateful to Kelley Harness for bringing this material to my attention and to Doctor Castello for her generous conversations with me.

13. I-Fas, Depositeria General Antica 1561, "Salariati di Serenissima Vittoria, 1635," opening 36, lists payments made to Francesca Raffaelli from 1 September 1635 through all of 1636, including her receipt of a full year's salary in advance on Christmas Day,

1635. I-Fas, MdP 6043, fol. 147, minute of Ugo Cacciotti to Vincenzo Vespucci (Vittoria's paymaster), 3 April 1635, ordered these ongoing payments transferred to Vespucci's books from those of Lorenzo Veneri. I-Fas, Depositeria Generale Antica 1034, no. 182 is a memo of Ferdinando II to Cosimo Sera (his principal treasurer), 27 February 1636/37, ordering that "all the court and service of Madama . . . our Grandmother, who is in heaven, be punctually paid the provision and salary they enjoyed during her life." An attached list specifying those to be paid names "Francesca Raffaelli musica" alongside her usual monthly stipend of eighteen scudi.

14. I-Fas, MdP 6043, fol. 1, letter of Christine to Princess Maria Maddalena, 4 May 1633.

15. I-Fas, MdP 6042, fol. 30, minute of Christine to Camilla Orsini ne' Borghese, 24 November 1635, includes this observation about the princesses's response to Costanza della Porta. I-Fas, MdP 6044, fol. 185, minute of Christine to Camilla, 31 May 1635, includes a postscript asking Orsini to allow della Porta to teach the "little daughter of Francesca Raffaelli, who learns exquisitely, . . . how to play the harp." I-Fas, MdP 6017, letter of Camilla to Christine, 16 June 1635, grants permission for her servant to teach Margherita.

16. I-FcasaB, A.B. 52, no. 1545, letter of Francesca Raffaelli to Buonarroti, 25 May 1636, notes, "[S]ome nuns have asked me urgently for certain canzonette spirituali that you have written on the same meter as certain Mantuan canzonette." For the details of Francesca's licenza, see chapter 11.

17. I-Fas, MdP 6043, fol. 1, letter of Christine to Princess Maria Maddalena, 4 May 1633.

18. I-Fas, MdP 6026, letter from Christine to Claudia de' Medici, archduchess of Styria, 25 February 1634/35, notes that Vittoria and Anna "played the major parts" in two comedies performed at Castello for Carnival. The same volume includes two letters of Ugo Cacciotti dated 16 February 1634/35 that refer to comedies: one asks an unnamed recipient to invite the Duchess of Lorraine to Castello for a comedy the next day; the other asks Lorenzo Poltri to tell prince Leopoldo that his sister Anna cannot reply to his letter because she is "extremely busy with a comedy in which she must play tomorrow." I-Fas, MdP 1454, letter of 7 February 1634/35, is a memo of Marco Papi about the costumes for a comedy of "fisherfolk and coquettes."

19. Tim Carter first discovered the six of these letters that survive among Buonarroti's papers, I-FcasaB, A.B. 44, nos. 460–465. I am grateful to Professor Carter for bringing them to my attention. The other three letters, consisting of Buonarroti's replies to Cacciotti, are in I-Fas, MdP 1454, letters of 5 February, 7 February, and 8 February 1634/35.

20. I-FcasaB, A.B. 44, no. 460, letter of Cacciotti to Buonarroti, 4 February 1634/35.

21. I-FcasaB, A.B. 44, no. 461, letter of Cacciotti to Buonarroti, 6 February 1634/35.

22. I-FcasaB, A.B. 44, no. 460, letter of Cacciotti to Buonarroti, 4 February 1634/35.

23. I-Fas, MdP 1454, letter of Buonarroti to Cacciotti, 6 February 1634/35, suggests the costumes and comments on Francesca's age. I-Fas, MdP 1454, letter of Buonarroti to Cacciotti, 8 February 1634/35, suggests that the girls hold bunches of flowers or branches in their hands as a way to hide their scripts.

24. I-FcasaB, A.B. 44, no. 462, letter of Cacciotti to Buonarroti, 7 February 1634/35, notes Francesca's plan for the singing. I-FcasaB, A.B. no. 464, letter of Cacciotti to Buonarroti, 10 February 1634/35, alludes to Buonarroti's suggestion of cembali, which may have come in a now-lost letter or in conversation.

25. I-FcasaB, A.B. 44, no. 465, letter of Cacciotti to Buonarroti, 12 February 1634/35.

26. For Francesca's interventions of behalf of the three musicians, see chapter 6. Her effort to enlist Galileo Galilei's support for her cousin is noted at I-Fn, Galileiana, Gal, 19 (Div. 2a-P1, t. 9), no. 39, letter of Don Orazio Morandi to Galileo Galilei, 2 May 1626.

27. I-Fas, MdP 1717, unnumbered letter of Francesca Signorini Malaspina to Curtio Picchena, 25 March 1624, refers to the favor she had received from their highnesses--an order to the directors of the Arte delle Lana forbidding her stepmother's and stepsister's eviction from their home in property that her brother Giovanni Battista had inherited from Giulio in via Sebastiani, now via Gino Capponi. Francesca's letter is printed in appendix B. I-Fas, Decima Granducale 896 (Suppliche detta 24) no. 96, is a petition signed by Andrea Cioli on 28 April 1630 asking that she be liberated from a tax debt because of her years of service.

28. I-FcasaB, A.B. 52, no. 1543, letter of Francesca Raffaeli to Michelangelo Buonarroti, 14 December 1634, asks for canzonette that she could use "for my girl," and no. 1545, letter of 25 May 1636, asks for canzonette for "some nuns." See appendix B.

29. I-FcasaB, A.B. 52, no. 1543, explains the circumstances that prevented Francesca from inviting Soldani to visit. I-FcasaB, A.B. no. 1547, letter of 10 July 1637, explains that she wanted either to retrieve an instrument of hers from the prince or sell it to him. Leopoldo's possession of her instrument suggests that Caccini may have taught him instrumental performance in the 1630s.

30. I-FcasaB, A.B. no. 1544, letter of 14 September 1635, and no. 1546, letter of 14 December 1636, respectively. Described as living at number 27 on a street behind Santissima Annunziata, Maddalena Quoreli may have been the widowed mother of the apothecary Lorenzo Quoreli to whom Giovanni Battista Caccini, Francesca's brother, had secretly sublet their father Giulio's former house in 1624. The Quoreli had threatened to evict Francesca's stepmother and stepsister if they did not pay a surcharge on their customary rent, precipitating the appeal described above in note 27.

31. I-Fas, MdP 1453, letter of Perseo Falconcini to Ugo Cacciotti, 12 January 1635/36.

32. I-Fas, Ufficiali, poi Magistrato della Grascia 195 (Libro dei Morti 1626–1669), "Margherita della Scala, vedova moglie fu di Giulio Caccini, sepolta in San Michele Visdomini 7 February 1635/36." Her death is also registered among those for February 1635/36 in I-Fas, Arte Medici e Speziale 258.

33. The codicil is at I-Fas, Notarile Moderno, Protocollo 5618, fol. 93r–v, codicil dated 6 December 1618. It is discussed in Warren Kirkendale, *The Court Musicians in Florence during the Principate of the Medici* (Florence: Olschki, 1993), 165–166. See chapter 6.

34. I-Fas, Arte della Lana, 448, consisting of a packet of unnumbered documents, includes the order that Picchena sent the directors of the Arte delle Lana on 2 April 1624, granting Margherita Caccini's petition for the sake of "the long and good service Giulio Caccini gave their highnesses." According to the accounts written by the director of the Arte della Lana, Paolo Rucellai, at the time of his death Giulio Caccini had had a "livello," or lifetime lease, on one house "behind SS. Annunziata" belonging to the Arte della Lana on which he paid thirty-five fiorini annually, and he had rented another for thirty-three fiorini. As his heir, Giovanni Battista Caccini, though he lived in neither house, had held onto both properties, renting the smaller one in part to his stepmother and in part to the apothecary Lorenzo Quoreli. Unable to keep up his payment to the Arte, however, Caccini had given up his lease on that smaller house, which the Arte della Lana had, on 10 February 1623/24, rented in its entirety to Quoreli and his mother for three years

scheduled to begin the following 1 May. Quoreli, claiming that he needed all of the space, was unwilling to continue renting half the house to the Caccini women. Giovanni Battista Caccini, meanwhile, claimed that he had offered his stepmother comfortable rooms in the larger house, but she refused to move. See I-Fas, Arte della Lana 448, unnumbered petition immediately after petition dated 18 May 1623. An anonymous account in the same packet of documents accuses Giovanni Battista of deliberately trying to oust his stepmother and sister, who were blind in one eye and "storpiata" (crippled), respectively. The rather piteous details about the Caccini women exactly match details included in an undated letter from Margherita Caccini to Buonarroti, now at I-FcasaB, A.B. 44, no. 457, asking him to intercede with "Buonuomini di San Martino for the grace to give me a bushel of grain . . . because once I pay the taxes and the rent . . . I have nothing left for the month."

35. I-Fas, MdP 1454, letter of Francesca Caccini Raffaelli to Ortensia Salviati, 9 February 1635/36. See appendix B.

36. Ibid.

37. I-Fas, MdP 1454, letter of Francesca Caccini Raffaelli to Ugo Cacciotti, 11 February 1636. Dianora's death record implies that she lived in her brother's property, if not necessarily in his household, for the rest of her life. See I-Fas, Ufficiali poi Magistrato della Grascia 195, Libro dei Morti 1626–1669: "[28] February 1642/43, Dianora figliuola di Giulio Caccini Romano sepolta in San Michele Visdomini."

38. I-Fas, MdP 1453, letter of Perseo Falconcini to Ugo Cacciotti, 12 January 1635/36, comments, "I use my wits to conform always to the pleasure of her highness, who I know feels affection for Signora Caccini, and esteems and honors her virtù."

39. I-Rasv, Fondo Borghese, ser. III, 14A, p. 181, letter of Christine de Lorraine to Camilla Orsini ne' Borghese, 26 July 1636.

40. I-Fas, MdP 6026, minute of an unsigned letter from Christine's household at Castello to Claudia de' Medici, archduchess of Styria, in Innsbruck, 9 December 1636.

41. I-Fas, Manoscritti 135, fol. 184r–v, gives an account of Christine's death just after midnight on 20 December and her burial in San Lorenzo on 22 December. Ibid., fols. 185r–194v, is a copy of her will. According to a notice on fol. 196r, the friars of Santissima Annunziata held a memorial service for her on 3 February 1636/37.

42. See Mario Biagioli, *Galileo, Courtier* (Chicago: University of Chicago Press, 1993), 35, quoting Geoffrey Parker, *Philip II* (London: Hutchinson, 1979), 170. Likened by Biagioli to the game Monopoly, Barros's The Courtier's Philosophy was published in Madrid in 1587.

43. I-Fas, MdP 1453, letter of Giovanni Bontemps to Ortensia Salviati, 10 December 1636, reports that "Margherita Signorini is vested by Madama for San Giovanni and Christmas, and when Francesca Raffaelli her mother wanted to give her the clothing she petitioned Madama, [who] was pleased to pay her twenty-four scudi from her treasury . . . and secretary Cacciotti will send the memo to Madama's treasurer there, and thus the money will be quickly paid."

44. I-Fas, MdP 1454, letter of Francesca Raffaelli to Ugo Cacciotti, 19 December 1636, urges Cacciotti to obtain Madama's signature. See appendix B.

45. I-Fas, MdP 1453, letter from Girolamo Bufalini to Cacciotti, dated only "Capodanno," announces the review, along with the distribution of mourning clothes to the staff and his receipt of an order to pay Christine's staff their December stipends. I-Fas, MdP 1453, letter of Lorenzo Polti to Andrea Cioli, 12 January 1636/37, alludes to his

having "penetrated Signora Francesca's intentions" in connection to the staff review that Cioli headed.

46. These events included Giovanni Carlo Coppola's *Le nozze degli dei*, "rappresentata in musica" composed by five unnamed Florentine composers and staged in the courtyard of the Pitti Palace on 8 July 1637 with Prince Giovan Carlo and Settimia and Paola Caccini in the cast, and a "festa a cavallo" to a text by Ferdinando Saracinelli titled *Armida e l'Amor pudico*, performed in the Boboli garden behind Pitti. See Robert Weaver and Norma Weaver, *A Chronology of Music in the Florentine Theater, 1590–1750* (Detroit: Information Coordinators, 1978), 113; Cesare Molinari, *Le nozze degli dei* (Rome: Bulzoni, 1968); and Sara Mamone, *Dei, semidei, uomini* (Rome: Bulzoni, 2003). To date there is no evidence that Francesca contributed music to either event.

47. I-Fas, MdP 6026, minute of Vittoria della Rovere to Prince Giovan Carlo, dictated to Ugo Cacciotti on 27 January 1637.

48. I-Fas, MdP 6026, undated minute of "Cav.re Usimbardi" to Prince Giovan Carlo, dictated to Ugo Cacciotti.

49. I-Fas, MdP 1427, Particolari F à Cioli, fols. 77r–78r, letter of Francesca Caccini, 19 March 1631. See appendix B and chapter 11.

50. I-Las, Offizio sopra Vedove e Pupille 328, fol. 135 (act of 19 January 1637); 329, fol. 22 (act of 15 July 1637); 331, fol. 58r–v (memos dated 23 February to 20 June 1638); I-Las, Archivio Notarile, Protocolli di Jacopo Motroni, 2383–2424, 1640, fols. 244v–245v and 502v–503v, contain documents pertaining to Francesca's ongoing management of the Raffaelli property.

51. I-Fas, Ruota Civile 869, fols. 83r–86v; fol. 98r–v; fols. 277r–278r–v. I am grateful to Professor Gino Corti for helping me transcribe these documents and to Professors Corti, Thomas Kuehn, and Anne Jacobsen Schutte for helping me imagine their meaning and immediate historical circumstances.

52. I-Fas, Ruota Civile 869, fol. 83v.

53. Paolo Malanima, *I Riccardi di Firenze: Una famiglia e un patrimonio nella toscana dei Medici*, Biblioteca di storia toscana moderna e contemporanea, Studi e documenti, 15 (Florence: Olschki, 1977), 162. I am grateful to Professor Malanima for counseling me by telephone about the use of the complex and disorganized Riccardi family archive as it is preserved in Florence's Archivio di Stato, as well as for his comments on Francesca's case.

54. It is maddening that, although Giovanni Lami's 1741 inventory of the Riccardi archive named the exact location of Riccardi's dowry promise and Francesca's marriage contract, neither document has yet been found in the dramatically reorganized and, to date, poorly indexed Riccardi archive as it exists in Florence's Archivio di Stato. Lami's inventory is at I-Fas, Manelli-Galilei-Riccardi, Riccardi 490. See Lami's account of the case in his biography of Riccardi, *Amplissimi viri Richardi Romuli Richardi Patrici Florentini Vita* (Florence, 1748), 229. Lami describes Francesca as a "comoedam" (theater person), suggesting that this woman who refused to let her daughter sing on stage, and whom court records portray as mainly a chamber musician, was intelligible to an eighteenth-century reader as a stage performer.

55. I-Fas, Ruota Civile 869, fols. 83r–86v, is the official record of this part of the case.

56. Ibid., fol. 98r–v.

57. As was customary for the Ruota Civile, the judge who presided at Francesca's trial was a foreigner, the Modenese Ludovico Zuccoli, who wrote to Duke Francesco d'Este

telling him not to expect a copy of his ruling until late August. Zuccoli's letter of 19 May 1639 is at I-MOas, Cancelleria Ducale, Particolari 1150 [Rebion-Raggazzoni], "Raffaelli." His letter of 29 May 1639 is at I-MOas, Ambasciatore. Firenze, busta 63, letter of Ludovico Zuccoli.

58. I-Fas, MdP 146 [minute di Ferdinando II], no. 132: "Benservita 8 mag. 1641. Havendoci Francesca Caccini Raffaelli lungamente servito di Musica con estraord.ia n.ra satisfazione et con particolare fama del suo singolare valore in quella professione, habbiamo voluto con publico assegno del merito suo con questa Casa, dichiarando espressem.te come facciamo, che ella vive nella nostra protezione, acciò resti tuttavia più fruttuosamente segnalata la virtù sua del possesso delle maggiore prerogative, et onori che attualm.te godono i miei più accetti più degni et più stimati servitori. In fede di che saranno questo nostre lettere patente firmato di nostra mano, imponendolo nostre sigille, et contrassegne dal infrascritto Segretario di Stato."

59. I-Rasc, F.O., 1st ser., 186/3, no. 405, Francesca Caccini Raffaelli to Paolo Giordano Orsini, 18 June 1641. See appendix B.

60. A file copy of Orsini's reply is at I-Rasc, F.O., 1st ser., 310/2, no. 411. See appendix B.

61. By February 1645, young Tommaso's legal guardian was Raffaello Mansi, whom Tommaso Raffaelli had named guardian in the event that Francesca was unable to continue. Mansi, the father of thirteen children, petitioned Lucca's Offizio sopra Vedove e Pupilli to be liberated from his obligation; his petition was granted on 30 March 1645. Mansi's petition, various supporting documents, and the judgment are at I-Las, Archivio Mansi, 30, Processi 1636–86, no. 7, fols. 1–10, "Processo e sentenza che contiene la liberazione della tutela dello spettabile Raffaello Mansi, di Tommaso Raffaelli, dato questo dì 30 marzo 1645."

62. I-Lcr, Archivio Arcivescovile, LVII. Mortuorum A e B.. 1595–1651 [San Piero Maggiore], fol. 135r: "Die 21 Augusti 1646. Francisca Jo: Romani de contrata S Concordij de Par.a S. Petri Maioris in communione S.M. Eccle anima Deo reddidit, cuius die 22 sepultum fuir in Eccle. Utdr di Pontetetto de n.ra licentia in scriptis: mihi Greg. o Gregorij Curato confessa die 20 sacratissimoq viatico refecta die supras.ta et sacri olei unctione roborata. P. R. Dnu Curatu Pontetitecti de nocte die d.a." This is the only death record for someone named Francesca in the urban parishes of seventeenth-century Lucca that could even remotely refer to Francesca Caccini, and the possibility seems to me quite remote. Still, the enormous fame (or notoriety) of the Caccini in Florence seems not to have reached the notarial or clerical classes in Lucca, for Francesca's and Giulio Caccini's names are mangled in the documents referring to her 1627 marriage to Raffaelli. Although the prominence of the Raffaelli family suggests that any deaths in that family would be accurately recorded, because she was a foreigner and a widow, Francesca's name could have been mangled yet again.

63. I-Fas, MdP 1427, Particolari F à Cioli, fols. 77r–78r, letter of Francesca Caccini, 19 March 1631. See appendix B.

64. I-Fas, Corporazioni Religiose Soppresse (Francese) 96 (S. Girolamo sulla costa), vol. 31, Entrate et Uscite, p. 11, lists the first payment to the community for Margherita's board. An otherwise unidentified Cavaliere Cesi paid nine scudi of 7 lire each on 16 November 1640. Cesi made similar payments on 17 February 1640/41 (fol. 14) and 11 July 1641 (fol. 18). Possibly this Cavaliere Cesi was the same man who was then a paymaster of the Medici's Depositeria Generale.

65. The deposit is noted in I-Fas, Monte di Pietà 1409, fol. 595, and in I-Fas, Corporazioni Religiose Soppresse (Francese) 96, vol. 91 (Liber H), with the anomalous gender of Margherita's parent mentioned in both places. I have not been able to identify anyone named Francesco Signiorini Malespina as ever having existed in seventeenth-century Florence; none can be traced in the usual genealogical sources, namely, I-Fas, Raccolta Sebregondi; I-Fn, Poligrafo Gargani; I-Fn, Necrologia Fiorentino Cirri.

66. The promised dowry of 400 scudi was transferred from the Monte di Pietà to the Monastero di San Girolamo sulla costa on Saturday, 11 October 1642. See I-Fas, Monte di Pietà 1409, fol. 595; I-Fas, Monte di Pietà 1410, p. 262; I-Fas, Corporazioni Religiose Soppresse (Francese) 96, vol. 91, Liber I, p. 595. All three notations affirm that Margherita Signorini had professed on the thirtieth of the previous month, that is, September. A payment to the "Padri di Ognissanti" of 10 scudi listed in I-Fas, Corporazione Religiose Soppresse (Francese) 96, vol. 13, p. 15, indicates that there had been a *sacra* in the community on that day, in addition to the regular celebration of the feast of Saint Jerome.

67. The identity of Suor Placida Maria as Margherita Signorini is established in I-Fas, Corporazioni Religiose Soppresse (Francese) 96, vol. 13, fols. 175v–177v, a document dated 1 May 1652 that granted certain privileges to Margherita Bucetti, who wanted to live at San Girolamo as a secular person. All members of the community signed the agreement, using their names and their secular surnames. Other distinguished members of Margherita's monastic community included Maddalena Broumans, the orphaned daughter of Francesca's musical colleague Arcangiola Palladini, who entered San Girolamo on 18 June 1632, according to Liber H, cited above; the musically gifted niece of Galileo, Olimpia Landucci, who entered the community on 11 September 1640, whose dowry payments are also recorded in Liber H; and the playwright Maria Clemente Ruote.

68. Severo Bonini, *Prima Parte de Discorse Regole Sora* [sic] *la Musica,* I-Fr, Ricc. 2218, fols. 85v–86r.

69. On Ruoti's plays, see Elissa B. Weaver, *Convent Theatre in Early Modern Italy: Spiritual Fun and Learning for Women* (Cambridge: Cambridge University Press, 2002), chap. 5.

70. See I-Faa, Inquisizione 11, fol. 236.

71. Margherita received ten lire every April and August from 1642 until May 1654, when she began to receive seventy lire annually in addition. See I-Fas, Corporazioni Religiose Soppresse (Francese) 96, vol. 32, p. 28v. Vol. 13, fol. 180r in ibid. notes that on the same date she was relieved of the community's work obligation because "la detta e di poca sanita" (the aforementioned is in ill health), provided that she pay twenty scudi annually for the privilege. She became maestra to Lavinia Studilla and Olimpia Landucci in the 1660s (ibid., vol. 13, fol. 196v) and to Margherita Vittoria Bartolini and Cintia Galoppini in 1672 (ibid., vol. 14, pp. 90 and 82, respectively); as manager of the foresteria in 1662–1663 (ibid., vol. 14, pp. 99, 118), and again in 1668 (ibid., vol. 14, p. 40); as sacristan in 1674 (ibid., vol. 14, p. 102) and 1675 (ibid., vol. 15, fol. 11v); and as maestra di sala in 1683 and 1684 (ibid., vol. 34, pp. 75, 79). She died at the age of sixty-eight and was buried on 1 May 1690 (ibid., vol. 17, p. 47).

72. I-Fas, MdP 6251C, lists payments on 6 March and 18 August 1682 to Suor Placida Maria Signorini Malaspina for Lucchese figurines, and on 5 May 1682 for embroidery that she had evidently done herself. I am grateful to the art historian Eve Straussman-Pflanzer for bringing these payments to my attention.

73. I-Lcr, Archivio Arcivescovile, Battesimi: "Maria Francesca del Signor Tommaso del già Signor Tommaso Raffaelli e della Signora Elisabetta Gianpauli sua moglie, parrochia di San Piero Maggiore, fù batt.a a 15 settembre 1656 fu Compadre Signor Settimio Diceironi et Commadre la Signora Felice moglie del Signore Benedetto Santini." Tommaso Raffaelli had married his cousin Girolamo Raffaelli's widow, Elisabetta Nicolai Giampauli on 18 November 1655. Both their dispensation to marry and the marriage itself are recorded in the *Liber Matrimonij dal 1615 al 1670* of San Piero Maggiore in Lucca on fol. 381.

74. I-Fas, Corporazione Religiose Soppressi (Francese) 96, vol. 32, Entrata e Uscita 1651–1663, fol., 138r, lists the first support payment of 20 scudi for Signora Maria Francesca Raffaelli on 30 November 1663. Ibid., vol. 33, Entrata e Uscita 1663–1674, lists payments for the girl's support on fols. 6r (24 May 1664), 11r (30 November 1664), 17r (29 May 1665), 24r (12 January 1665/6), 32r (17 November 1666), 45r (27 December 1667, without her surname), 54r (28 December 1668, without her surname), and 62r (23 November 1669).

75. Ibid., vol. 33, Entrata e Uscita, fol. 79v, specifies a payment for the support of Maria Francesca Raffaelli of 46 scudi, 13 soldi, and 4 denari paid on 2 July 1671 by Bartolomeo Corsini, "Tesauriere della Serenissima Gran Duchessa Vittoria." I-Fas, MdP 6241, a record of payment orders (*mandati*) from Vittoria's accounts, provides cross-references for several payments to the community of San Girolamo on behalf of Maria Francesca Raffaelli. On 22 November 1669, the grand duchess paid the same amount, 46.13.4, to San Girolamo "per il servo della Maria Francesca Raffaelli," that is, to be set aside for the young Francesca. The last payment, dated 24 August 1671, specifies that the payment of 6 scudi of 4 lire each, 13 soldi and 4 denari, was "paid to the nuns of San Girolamo . . . for every installment on the board of Maria Francesca Raffaelli." I-Fas, MdP 6251b, Filze dell'Entrata e Uscita, notes that Vittoria paid 1,200 scudi as a dowry to Giovanni Battista Bucetti when he married her former dama Francesca Raffaelli on 7 October 1677. Bucetti's receipt is dated 20 October 1677. I am grateful to Eve Straussman-Pflanzer for details of Raffaelli-Bucetti's dowry.

76. In a letter dated 11 February 1688 to Francesco Redi, Maria Selvaggia described being escorted to a commedia by "La Signora Bucetta" and commented that "the grand duchess, particularly honoring her for her grace, could not dispense her favors better or more justly, [this woman] being the most witty and gracious dama that I have ever known." The letter is quoted in Domenco Moreni's annotations to *Lettere di Benedetto Menzini e del Senatore Vincenzio da Filicaia a Francesco Redi* (Florence: Nella Stamperia Magheri, 1828), now at I-Fr, Ricc. S.Q.7.9/1.

77. On the death date and burial place of Francesca Raffaelli the younger, see I-Fn, Necrologia Fiorentino Cirri, vol. 15, p. 336. I will forever be grateful for the jocular dare with which Jean Grundy Fanelli prompted me to look for her name in this source. Maria Francesca Raffaelli's will is at I-Fas, Notarile Moderno, Protocolli 22960–32967 (Atti di Pitro Perier), testament of 13 March 1717, fols. 79–82r, with a codicil dated 11 September 1718 at fol. 91. The codicil revoked small legacies to the daughters of her servants and to Sister Regina Maria Lucchesini in San girolamo sulla costa.

Selected Bibliography

MANUSCRIPT AND ARCHIVAL SOURCES

I-F, Archivio del Monastero di Santa Croce, detto la Crocetta
 Armadio A, Libro di partiti (1513–18th c.)
 Armadio B
  Cassetta C, letters and papal breve regarding Medici princesses at La Crocetta,
   1624–1633
  Nota delli oblighi che h[a] il nostro Monasterio et altri con noi . . . dal 1602 fino al
   1769
  Anton Maria Riconesi, Alle molto Reverende Priora e Monache del Venerabile
   Munisterio della Croce di Firenze volgarmente chiamato della Crocetta
I-Faa
 Cause civile, C.D. 219, 1–4; 220–1–6
 Filze di Cancelleria, 11, 18
 Inquisizione, 10, 11, 34
 Parocchia Santa Maria Maggiore, Libro di Matrimonii
 Parocchia Santa Maria Novella, Registro di Morti
 Visitazione, V.P.D. 21.4 (La Crocetta); V.P.D. 21.14 (Le Murate)
I-Fas
 Acquisti e Doni 242, insert 2
 Arte della Lana, vols. 22, 448
 Arte Medici e Speziale 258
 Carte Strozziane I, vols. 5, 13, 30, 51
 Corporazioni Religiose Soppresse (Francese) 96 (S. Girolamo sulla costa)
  vols. 13–17, 31–34, 91 (Liber H and Liber I), 96, 111
 Decima Granducale
  63, Partiti 1631

221, Filze di Partiti 1631

896 (Suppliche detta 24) nos. 96, 489

2012, Gonfalone Nicchio

2390, Arroti Santa Croce 1627, no. 16

3235, no. 217

3596, Campione. Ruote. 1618

3597 (Campione S. Croce, Gonfalone Ruote), no. 28

Depositeria General Antica 73, 306, 389, 395, 601, 649, 650, 668, 795, 995, 1002, 1013, 1014, 1034, 1522, 1561

Guardaroba Medicea 390–391, 401, 405bis, 406, 410, 420–421, 423, 714

Magistrato dei pupilli. Principato 785, 2659, 2660, 2717, 2718, 2726

Manelli-Galilei-Riccardi

Manelli-Galilei-Riccardi 345, 352, 357, 360, 362

Riccardi 75, 80–82, 85, 88, 89, 92, 95, 117, 281, 283, 335, 338, 488, 490

Manoscritti 131–33, 135, 321, 581

Mediceo del Principato 66, 80–92, 111, 116–117, 119–122, 125–126, 136–140, 144–146, 154, 163, 303, 844, 921, 927–928, 970–973, 980, 994, 1003–1004, 1016, 1220, 1325–1326, 1330, 1340–1341, 1370–1371, 1377, 1392, 1426–1429, 1449, 1453–1454, 1688, 1692, 1695–1705, 1713–1717, 1737, 2641, 2828–2829, 2915, 2920, 2925, 2944, 2948, 2960, 3127, 3143, 3322–3323, 3325, 3331, 3339–3340, 3502, 3518, 3642, 3645, 3882–3883, 4292, 4617a, 4728–4729, 4732, 4741, 4748, 4852–4853, 4858–4859, 4860, 5131, 5132a, 5183, 5269a, 5269b, 5348, 5395, 5417a, 5501, 5505, 5948, 5950–5955, 5957, 5962, 5965–5971, 5980, 5986–5987, 5990–5998, 6002, 6005–6007, 6009, 6011–6013, 6015–6017, 6020–6021, 6025–6026, 6028–6032, 6036–6037, 6042–6044, 6068, 6069–6071, 6074, 6080, 6083–6085, 6087, 6091–6093, 6095–6098, 6100–6102, 6103–6104, 6108, 6110, 6149, 6152, 6170, 6241, 6251c, 6371, 6424

Miscellanea Medicea 5 (insert 1), 9, 11 (Tinghi III), 92 (insert 6), 142, 264 (inserts 20H, 44), 357

Monte di Pietà 1381 [Campioni di Depositi Condizionati, opening 387], 1409–1410

Notarile moderno

Protocolli 1993, Atti di Lorenzo Muti, 1588

Protocolli 2171, Atti di Noferi Maccanti, 1607, no. 36

Protocolli 5503, Andrea Andreini, Testamento di 26 dicembre 1612

Protocolli 5611–5618, Andrea Marii, Testamento

Protocolli 10609–10622, Atti di Niccolò Minacci, vol. 10611

Protocolli 11727–11759, Atti di Tommaso Mati (including 11740, no. 46; 11742, nos. 59–61

Protocolli 13734–13737, Atti di Paolo Lapi. Testamento del 23 dicembre 1626, G. B. Signorini

Protocolli 18942–18956, Atti di Lorenzo Gorgigiani. Testamento di Giovanni Bucetti, 30 September 1713

Protocolli 22960–32967, Atti di Pitro Perier. Testamento di Maria Francesca Raffaelli Bucetti, 13 March 1717

Otto di guardia e balia. Principato. 2793

Raccolta Sebregondi 1171 (Caccini di Roma), 4936 (Signorini dalla Docia)

Ruota civile 869, 2302

Ufficiali, poi Magistrato della Grascia 105, 194, 195

I-Fc, CF 83

I-FcasaB (Casa Buonarroti), Archivio Buonarroti

 39, nos. 102–106

 40, nos. 174, 187

 43, no. 424

 44, nos. 438–443, 446–448, 454–457, 460–465, 527

 45, nos. 660, 665

 46, nos. 675–678, 773

 47, nos. 913–914

 48, no. 1037

 51, nos. 1432–1434

 52, nos. 1543–1547

 53, nos. 1663, 1675

 54, nos. 1925–1933

 55, no. 2003

 61–63, 81–82, 84, 86, 93, 95, 464, 1544, 1546–1547

I-Fd, Battesimi Femmine 1587–1622: Battesimi Maschi, 1579, 1588–1606

I-FEas, Archivio Bentivoglio, Lettere Sciolte, 210, Mazzo 9–55

I-Fgu, Gabinetto dei disegni e stampe, Stampe sciolte numbers 2303–2306, 95789 N.A.

I-Fn

 II.III. 499, insert 18

 Galileiana

  Gal.1, fasc. 2 (Vincenzo Galilei, "Primo libro della prattica del contrapunto, 1588–1591)

  Gal. 15, f. 8r–9r (letter of Galileo Galileo to Curtio Picchena, 26 May 1619)

  Gal. 19, Div. 2a-P1, t. 9, no. 39 (letter of Orazio Morandi to Galileo Galilei, 2 May 1626)

 Magliabecchiana (abbreviated in notes as Magl.)

  VII. 432

  VIII. 1513–1538

  XIX. 24–25

  XIX. 66

  XXVI. 133, 135 (Gab.T. 5 Notif. 1594/95), 139

 MS II.____.102–108, Orosocopi diversi

 MS II.iv.22

 MS Gino Capponi 261, vols. I–II (Tinghi I and Tinghi II)

 MS Palatino

  251

  E.B. 15.2.xx

 Necrologia Fiorentino Cirri

 Poligrafo Gargani

I-Fr, Mor. 309, MS 2270

 Ricc. 1131

 Ricc. 2218 (Severo Bonini, Prima Parte de Discorse Regole Sopra la Musica)

Ricc. 2302, no. 4,

Ricc. 2633

Ricc. 3470

Ricc. S.Q.7.9/1

I-Las

Anziani al tempo della libertà, 642, Ambasciatori Toscani, filza 601, 609, 610

Archivio Buonvisi, 1st ser., vols. 40, 79

Archivio Mansi 30, Processi 1636–1686, no. 7

Archivio notarile, Protocolli di Jacopo Motroni, 2383–2424, 1640

Bibl MS 127, vol. IV—Bernardino Baroni, Famiglie Lucchese

Gabella dei Contratti e delle Doti 166 (1628)

Libro di corredo alle arte della Signoria 83, Libbro delle Famiglie Nobili della
        Repubblica di Lucca e loro Stemmi formato l'anno 1628 per decreto
        dell'eccellentissimo consiglio di gennaro detto anno

MS 22, vol. 3, p. 109

Notari 188, 2492

Offizio sopra vedove e pupille 328, 329, 331

I-Lbg

MS 383, Manuale dell'Accademia delli Oscuri

MS 900

MS 1095

I-Lcr, Battesimi

LVII. Mortuorum A e B. 1595–1651 [San Piero Maggiore]

Liber Matrimonij dal 1615 al 1670 [San Piero Maggiore]

I-Lucca, Archivio della Parrocchia di San Frediano, Liber Matrimonii 1618–1636
        (vol. 123)

I-MAa, Autogr. 6

I-MNas, Archivio Gonzaga, busta 1132

I-MOas

Ambasciatore. Firenze, Buste 35, 45–48, 53, 59, 60–62, 63

Cancelleria Ducale, Particolari 1150 [Rebion-Raggazoni], "Raffaelli"

I-Rasc

Fondo Orsini

1st ser., 114a, nos. 73, 99; 115/1, no. 133; 116/4, no. 732; 119/2, nos. 184–186;
        124/2, no. 233; 125/1, no. 164; 126, no. 858; 126/1, no. 67; 126/2, no. 300;
        127/1, no. 664; 159/1, no. 187; 159/2, nos. 303, 322–323, 379, 520, 586; 159/3,
        nos. 435, 437, 476, 528; 159/4, no. 681; 160, no. 132; 162/1, no. 167; 186/3, no.
        405; 310/2, no. 411

2d ser., 309, no. 80

I-Rasv

Carte Borghese 29 (Documenti pertinenti al processo di Beatificazione di Camilla
        Orsini)

Fondo Borghese, 3d ser., 14A

Sacra Congregatione dei Vescovi e Regolari. Sezione Monache. Positiones. 1615–1645
        (for the letter F)

VR Reg. Regularium 13 (1619)

I-Ru, MS 279
I-Rvat, Urb. lat. 1093
I-Vnm, MS IV, 7

Printed Sources

Abbate, Carolyn. "Music—Drastic or Gnostic?" *Critical Inquiry* 30, no. 3 (2004): 505–536.

Ademollo, Alessandro. *La bell'Adriana ed altre virtuose del suo tempo alla corte di Mantova.* Città di Castello: S. Lapi, 1888.

Africanus, Leo. *History and Description of Africa and of the Notable Things Therein Contained. Done into English in the Year 1600 by John Pory and Now Edited with an Introduction and Notes by Dr. Robert Brown.* London: Hakluyt Society, 1896.

Alberti, Leon Battista. *The Family in Renaissance Florence.* Edited by R. N. Watkins. Long Grove, IL: Waveland, 2004.

Alberti, Maria. "Le 'barriere' di Cosimo II granduca di Toscana." In *Musica in torneo nell'Italia del Seicento,* edited by Paolo Fabbri, 81–96. Lucca: Libreria Musicale Italiana, 1999.

Alexander, Ronald, and Richard Savino. *Francesca Caccini's* Il primo libro delle musiche of 1618: *A Modern Critical Edition of the Secular Monodies.* Bloomington: Indiana University Press, 2004.

Allen, Michael J. B. *Nuptial Arithmetic: Marsilio Ficino's Commentary on the Fatal Number in Book VIII of Plato's* Republic. Berkeley: University of California Press, 1994.

Allen, Prudence. *The Concept of Woman.* Vol. 2, *The Early Humanist Reformation, 1250– 1500.* Grand Rapids: Eidmann, 2002.

Annibaldi, Claudio. "Towards a Theory of Musical Patronage in the Renaissance and Baroque: The Perspective from Anthropology and Semiotics." *Recercare* 10 (1998): 173–182.

Antignani, Gerardo. *Vicende e tempi di Suor Domenica del paradiso.* Siena: Cantagalli, 1983.

Assenza, Concetta. "Arioso and Canzonetta: Rhythm as a Stylistic Determinant in the Madrigals of Giaches de Wert." *Yearbook of the Alamire Foundation* 3 (1999): 89–120.

———. *La canzonetta dal 1570 al 1615.* Quaderni de Musica/Realta 34. Lucca: Libreria Musicale Italiana, 1997.

———. "La trasmissione dei testi poetici per canzonetta negli ultimi decenni del secolo XVI." *Rivista italiana di musicologia* 26, no. 2 (1991): 205–240.

Baldano, Giovanni Lorenzo. *Libro per scriver l'intavolatura per sonare sopra le sordelline (Savona, 1600): Facsimile del manoscritto e studi introduttivi.* Edited by M. Tacrini, Giovanni Farris, and John Henry van der Meer. Savona: Editrice Liguria, 1995.

Banchieri, Adriano. *Lettere armoniche.* Bologna: Girolamo Mascheroni, 1628.

Barwick, Linda, and Joanne Page. *Gestualità e musica di un Maggio garfagnino: Il Maggio* I paladini di Francia *(attribuito a Giuseppe Grandini) secondo la rappresentazione della compagnia di Gorfigliano (LU) a Gragnanella (LU).* Lucca: Centro Tradizioni Popolari della Provincia di Lucca, 1994.

Belli, Domenico. *Il primo libro dell'arie a una e due voci.* Venice: R. Amadini, 1616.

Bergstein, Mary. "Marian Politics in Quattrocento Florence: The Renewed Dedication of Santa Maria del Fiore in 1412." *Renaissance Quarterly* 44 (1991): 673–719.

Berner, Stuart. "Florentine Society in the Late Sixteenth and Early Seventeenth Centuries." *Studies in the Renaissance* 18 (1971): 203–246.

Bertacchi, Angelo. *Storia dell'Accademie Lucchese.* Lucca: Tipografia Giusti, 1881.

Bettley, John. "'L'ultimo Hora canonica del giorno': Music for the Office of Compline in Northern Italy in the Second Half of the Sixteenth Century." *Music and Letters* 74 (1993): 163–214.

———. "The Office of Holy Week at St. Mark's, Venice, in the Late 16th Century, and the Musical Contributions of Giovanni Croce." *Early Music* 22, no. 1 (1994): 45–60.

Biagioli, Mario. *Galileo, Courtier: The Practice of Science in the Culture of Absolutism.* Chicago: University of Chicago Press, 1993.

Bianchi, Fulvio, and Paolo Russo, eds. *La scelta della misura: Gabriello Chiabrera; L'altro fuoco del barocco italiano.* Atti di convegno di studi su Gabriello Chiabrera nel 350° anniversario della morte, Savona, 3–6 November 1988. Genoa: Costa & Nolan, 1993.

Bloom, Harold. *The Anxiety of Influence.* New York: Oxford University Press, 1973.

Bono, Paola, and Sandra Kemp. *Italian Feminist Thought.* Oxford: Blackwell, 1991.

Borazzo, Maria Grazia. "Musica scenotecnica illusione nel grande apparato farnesiano del 1628 a Parma." Tesi di Laurea, University of Parma, 1981–1982.

Bowers, Jane. "Women's Lamenting Traditions around the World: A Survey and Some Significant Questions." *Women and Music* 2 (1998): 125–146.

Boyer, Horace. "Giulio Caccini à la cour d'Henri IV 1604–05 d'après des lettres inedites." *Revue musicale* 7, no. 11 (1926): 244–245.

Brantôme, Pierre de Bourdeille, seigneur de. "Vies des Dames Galantes." In *Oeuvres.* London. Aux dépens du Libraire, 1779.

Bridgman, Nanie. "Giovanni Camillo Maffei et sa lettre sur le chant." *Revue de musicologie* 38 (1956): 3–34.

Bronzini, Cristoforo. *Della dignità e nobiltà delle donne.* Florence: Zanobi Pignoni, 1622–32.

Brooks, Jeanice. "Catherine de Médicis, *nouvelle Artémise:* Women's Laments and the Virtue of Grief." *Early Music* 27, no. 3 (1999): 419–436.

———. *Courtly Song in Late Sixteenth-Century France.* Chicago: University of Chicago Press, 2000.

Brown, Howard Mayer. 1981. "The Geography of Florentine Monody: Caccini at Home and Abroad." *Early Music* 9 (1981): 147–168.

Buonarroti, Michelangelo. *Descrizione delle felicissime nozze della cristianissima maestà di Madama Maria Medici Regina di Francia e di Navarra.* Florence: Giorgio Marescotti, 1600.

———. *La Fiera (1619).* Edited by U. Limentani. Florence: Olschki, 1984.

———. *La Tancia.* La letteratura italiana: Storia e testi 39. Edited by Luigi Fasso. Milan: Riccardo Ricciardi, 1956.

Burmeister, Johann. *Musical Poetics (1606).* Edited by B. Rivera. New Haven: Yale University Press, 1993.

Butler, Judith. *Bodies That Matter.* New York: Routledge, 1993.

———. *Gender Trouble: Feminism and the Subversion of Identity.* New York: Routledge, 1991.

Bynum, Carolyn. *Jesus as Mother: Studies in the Spirituality of the High Middle Ages.* Berkeley: University of California Press, 1982.

Caccini, Francesca. *Il primo libro delle musiche.* Florence: Zanobi Pignoni, 1618.

———. *La liberazione di Ruggiero dall'isola d'Alcina.* Florence: Pietro Cecconcelli, 1625.

———. *La liberazione di Ruggiero dall'isola d'Alcina.* Facsimile with introduction by Alessandro Magini. Florence: Studio per edizioni scelte, 1998.

Caccini, Giulio. *Le nuove musiche.* Florence: Giorgio Marescotti, 1601/2.

———. *Le Nuove Musiche (1602).* Edited by H. W. Hitchcock. Madison, WI: A-R Editions, 1970.

———. *Nuove musiche e nuove maniere di scriverle.* Florence: Zanobi Pignoni, 1614.

Calcagno, Mauro. "'Imitar con canto chi parla': Monteverdi and the Creation of a Language for Musical Theater," *Journal of the American Musicological Society* 55 (2002: 383–431.

Calestani, Vincenzo. *Madrigali et arie per sonare et cantarse nel chitarrone leuto o clavicembalo a una e due voci.* Venice: G. Vincenti, 1617.

Calvi, Giulia. *Il contratto morale: Madri e figli nella Toscana moderna.* Rome: Laterza, 1994.

———. *Histories of a Plague Year: The Social and the Imaginary in Baroque Florence.* Translated by Dario Biocca and Bryant T. Ragan Jr., with a foreword by Randolph Starn. Berkeley: University of California Press, 1989.

Calvi, Giulia, and Isabelle Chabot, eds. *Le richezze delle donne: Diritti patrimoniali e poteri familiari XII–XIX sec.* Turin: Rosenberg & Sellier, 1998.

Canepa, Nancy. "The 'Piazza' Motif and Encyclopedism in Tommaso Garzoni's *La piazza universale* 1585 and Michelangelo Buonarroti il Giovane's *La fiera* 1619." *Canadian Journal of Italian Studies* 20 (1997): 171–192.

Canova-Green, Marie-Claude, and Francesca Chiarelli. *The Influence of Italian Entertainments on Sixteenth- and Seventeenth-Century Music Theatre in France, Savoy and England.* Studies in History and Interpretation of Music, 68. Lewiston, NY: Edwin Mellen, 2000.

Carandini, Silvia. *Teatro e spettacolo nel Seicento.* Rome: Laterza, 1997.

Cardamone-Jackson, Donna G. "Isabella de' Medici, Duchess of Bracciano: A Portrait of Self-Affirmation." In *Music, Gender and Sexuality in Early Modern Europe*, edited by T. Borgerding, 1–25. London: Routledge, 2000.

Carter, Tim. "'An air new and grateful to the ear': The Concept of Aria in Late Renaissance and Early Baroque Italy." *Music Analysis* 12, no. 2 (1993): 127–145.

———. *Jacopo Peri, 1561–1633: His Life and Works.* New York: Garland, 1989.

———. "Lamenting Ariadne?" *Early Music* 27 (1999): 395–405.

———. *Monteverdi's Musical Theatre.* New Haven: Yale University Press, 2002.

———. "Music for a Florentine Wedding of 1608." *Acta Musicologica* 55, no. 1 (1983): 89–107.

———. "Music-Printing in Late Sixteenth- and Early Seventeenth-Century Florence: Giorgio Marescotti, Cristofano Marescotti and Zanobi Pignoni." *Early Music History* 9 (1990): 27–72.

———. "Non occorre nominare tanti musici: Private Patronage and Public Ceremony in Late Sixteenth Century Florence." In *I Tatti Studies: Essays in the Renaissance* 4, 89–104. Aldershot: Ashgate, 1991.

———. "Printing the 'New Music.'" In *Music and the Cultures of Print*, edited by Kate van Orden, 3–37. New York: Garland, 2002.

Case, Sue-Ellen. "Toward a Butch-Femme Aesthetic." In *Making a Spectacle: Feminist Essays on Contemporary Women's Theatre*, edited by L. Hart, 282–299. Ann Arbor: University of Michigan Press, 1989.

Castello, Silvia. "La drammaturgia di Iacopo Cicognini." Tesi di laurea, University of Florence, 1988–89.

Castiglione, Baldassare. *Il libro del cortegiano*. Florence: Eredi di Filippo Giunta, 1528.

Cavarero, Adriana. *For More Than One Voice: Toward a Philosphy of Vocal Expression*. Translated with an introduction by Paul A. Kottman. Stanford: Stanford University Press, 2005.

———.*Nonostante Platone: Figure femminili nella filosofia antica*. Rome: Editori riuniti, 1990.

———. *Relating Narratives: Storytelling and Selfhood*. Translated by Paul A. Kottman. London: Routledge, 2000.

———. *Stately Bodies: Literature, Philosophy and the Question of Gender*. Translated by Robert de Lucca and Deanna Shemek. Ann Arbor: University of Michigan Press, 2002.

Celli, Angelo. *Malaria e colonizzazione nell'agro Romano dai più antichi tempi ai giorni nostri*. Florence: Valecchi, 1927.

Celso, Aulo Cornelio. *Della medicina: Libri otto*. Translated by Angel Del Lungo. Edited by Dino Pieraccioni. Florence: Sansoni, 1990.

Chabot, Isabelle. "Lineage Strategies and the Control of Widows in Renaissance Florence." In *Widowhood in Medieval and Early Modern Europe*, edited by Sandra Cavallo and Lyndan Warmer, 127–144. Harlow, Essex: Longman, 1999.

———. "'La sposa in nero': Le ritualizazzione del lutto delle vedove fiorentine sec. XIV–XV." *Quaderni storici* 86 (1994): 443–445.

Chafe, Eric. *Monteverdi's Tonal Language*. New York: Schirmer, 1992.

Chater, James. "Musical Patronage in Rome at the Turn of the Seventeenth Century: The Case of Cardinal Montalto." *Studi Musicali* 16, no. 2 (1987): 179–227.

Chiabrera, Gabriello. *Delle opere*. Venice: Geremia, 1730.

———. *Opere di Gabriello Chiabrera e lirici non marinisti del Seicento*. Turin: Utet, 1970.

Chiavarra, Elissa Novi. "Ideologia e comportamenti familiari nel predicatori Italiani tra Cinquecento e Settecento: Tematiche e Modelli." *Rivista storica italiana* 100, no. 3 (1988): 679–723.

Chilesotti, Oscar. "*La liberazione di Ruggiero dall'isola d'Alcina* di Francesca Caccini." *Gazzetta musicale di Milano* 51 (1896): 32.

Clubb, Louise. *Italian Drama in Shakespeare's Time*. New Haven: Yale University Press, 1989.

Cole, Janie. "Michelangelo Buonarroti il giovane' (1568–1647): A Musician's Poet in Seicento Florence." PhD diss., Royal Holloway College, University of London, 2000.

———. *A Muse of Music in Early Baroque Florence: The Poetry of Michelangelo Buonarroti il Giovane*. Florence: Olschki, 2007.

Conti Odorisio, Ginevra. *Donne e società nel Seicento*. Rome: Bulzoni, 1979.

Costantini, Fabio. *Ghirlandetta amorosa arie madrigali e sonetti di diversi eccellentissimi autori a uno a due a tre et a quattro . . . Opera settima*. Vol. 1. Orvieto: M.A. Fei et R. Ruuli, 1621.

Cox, Virginia. *Women's Writing in Italy, 1400–1650*. Baltimore: Johns Hopkins University Press, 2008.

Cox-Rearick, Janet. *Dynasty and Destiny in Medici Art: Pontormo, Leo X and the Two Cosimos*. Princeton: Princeton University Press, 1984.

Crinò, Anna Maria. "Virtuose di canto e poeti a Roma e a Firenze nella prima metà del Seicento." *Studi secentesche* 1 (1960):175–193.

Cusick, Suzanne. "Feminist Theory, Music Theory and the Mind/Body Problem." *Perspectives of New Music* 34 (1993): 8–27.

———. "Francesca among Women: A *Seicento* Gynecentric View.'" In *Musical Voices of Early Modern Women: Many-Headed Melodies*, edited by Thomasin LaMay, 425–445. Burlington, VT: Ashgate, 2005.

———. "Francesca Caccini: Questioni per una biografia tra gender e musicologia," *Teatro e storia*, Anno xxi, no. 28 (2007): 339–351.

———. "Of Women, Music, and Power: A Model from Seicento Florence." In *Musicology and Difference: Gender and Sexuality in Music Scholarship*, edited by Ruth Solie, 281–304, Berkeley: University of California Press, 1993.

———. "'There was not one lady who failed to shed a tear': Arianna's Lament and the Construction of Modern Womanhood." *Early Music* 22, no. 1 (1994): 21–41.

———. "This Music Which Is Not One: Inaudible Order and Representation of the Feminine in Francesca Caccini's *Primo libro delle musiche* (1618)." *Early Modern Woman* 2 (2007): 127–162.

———. "'Who is this woman . . . ?' Self-Presentation, *Imitatio Virginis* and Compositional Voice in Francesca Caccini's Primo Libro of 1618." *Il Saggiatore musicale* 5, no 1 (1998): 5–41.

de la Fage, Adrian. "La prima compositrice di opera in musica, e la sua opera." *Gazzetta musicale di Milano* 6, no. 45 (1847): 354–355.

della Robbia, Enrica Viviani. *La figlia di Galileo: Lettere raccolte, con introduzione*. Florence: Sansoni, 1942.

———. *Nei monasteri fiorentini*. Florence: Sansoni, 1946.

della Valle, Pietro. "Della musica dell'età nostra che non è punto inferiore anzi è migliore di quella dell'età passata." In *De' trattati di musica di Gio. Batista Doni*. Florence: A. F. Gori and G. B. Passeri, 1763.

de'Pazzi, Maria Maddalena. *Le parole dell'estasi*. Edited by G. Pozzi. Milan: Adelphi, 1984.

de Voragine, Jacobus. *The Golden Legend: Readings on the Saints*. Translated by W. G. Ryan. Princeton: Princeton University Press, 1993.

Diaz, Furio. *Il Granducato di Toscana: I Medici*. Vol. 3, *La Toscana nell'età della controriforma e dell'egemonia spagnola*. Turin: Utet, 1976.

Diotima. *Il pensiero della differenza sessuale*. Milan: La Tartaruga, 1991.

Dolce, Ludovico. *L'istituzione delle donne*. Venice: Gabriel Giolito de Ferrari, 1545.

Du Plessis, Rachel Blau. *Writing Beyond the Ending*. Bloomington: Indiana University Press 1985.

Durante, Elio, and Anna Martellotti. *Cronistoria del Concerto delle Dame principalissime di Marghertia Gonzaga d'Este: Prima ristampa con una aggiunta.* Florence: Studio per edizioni scelte, 1999.

———. *Don Angelo Grillo O.S.B. alias Livio Celiano: Poeta per musica del secolo decimosesto*, Archivium Musicum: Collana di studi. Florence: Studio per edizioni scelte, 1989.

Earle, T. F., and Katherine J. P. Lowe. *Black Africans in Renaissance Europe*. Cambridge: Cambridge University Press, 2005.

Eboigbe, Delphia Robinson. "The Depiction of the Negro African in Three Old French Chansons de Geste and Two Renaissance Epico-Chivalric Poems." PhD diss., Indiana University, Bloomington, 1983.

Elias, Norbert. *The Court Society.* Translated by E. Jephecott. New York: Pantheon, 1983.

Fabbri, Mario. "La collezione medicea degli strumenti musicali in due sconosciuti inventari del primo Seicento." *Note d'archivio per la storia musicale,.n.s.,* 1 (1983): 51–62.

Fabbri, Paolo, and Angelo Pompilio, eds. *Il corago, o vero alcune osservazioni per metter bene in scene le composizioni drammatiche.* Florence: Olschki, 1983.

Fabris, Dinko. *Andrea Falconieri Napoletano: Un liutista-compositore del Seicento.* Rome: Torre d'Orfeo, 1987.

———. *Mecenati e musici: Documenti sul patronato artistico dei Bentivoglio di Ferrara nell'epoca di Monteverdi (1585–1645).* Lucca: Libreria musicale italiana, 1999.

Faini, Fiammetta, and Anna Maria Punti. *La villa Mediceo Lorense del Poggio Imperiale.* Florence: "Lo Studiolo" Amici dei Musei Fiorentini, 1995.

Falconieri, Andrea. *Il quinto libro delle musiche a una, due e tre voci di Andrea Falconieri Napolitano.* Florence: Zanobi Pignoni, 1619.

Ferrante, Lucia, Maura Palazzi, and Gianna Pomata. *Ragnatele di rapporti: Patronage e reti di relazione nella storia delle donne.* Turin: Rosenberg & Sellier, 1988.

Firenzuola, Agnolo. *On the Beauty of Women.* Translated and edited by Konrad Eisenbichler and Jacqueline Murray. Philadelphia: University of Pennsylvia Press, 1992.

———. *Prose.* Florence: Giunta, 1548.

Fornari, Simone. *Delle espositione sopra l'Orlando furioso.* Vol. 2. Florence: Lorenzo Torrentino, 1550.

"Francesca Caccini, la Cecchina." *Revue et gazette musicale de Paris* 4 (1837): 37–44.

Franko, Mark. *Dance as Text: Ideologies of the Baroque Body.* Cambridge: Cambridge University Press, 1993.

Fumagalli, Elena, Massimiliano Rossi, and Riccardo Spinelli, eds. *L'arme e gli amori: La poesia di Ariosto, Tasso e Guarini nell'arte fiorentina del Seicento.* Florence: Sillabe, 2001.

Gagliano, Giovanni Battista. *Varie musiche: Libro Primo* (Alessandro Vincenti, 1623). In *Italian Secular Song, 1606–1636,* edited by G. Tomlinson. New York: Garland, 1986.

Gagliano, Marco. *La Flora.* Florence: Zanobi Pignoni, 1628.

———. *Musiche a una, due e tre voci.* Venice: R. Amadino, 1615.

Gagne, David. "Monteverdi's 'Ohimè dov'è il mio ben' and the Romanesca." *Music Forum* 6 (1987): 61–91.

Galasso-Calderara, Estella. *La Granduchessa Maria Maddalena d'Austria: Un amazzone tedesca nella Firenze medicea del '600.* Genova: Sagep, 1985.

Galluzzi, Jacopo Riguccio. *Istoria del granducato di Toscana sotto il governo della casa Medici.* Florence: Nella stamperia di R. del Vivo, 1781.

Garbero Zorzi, Elvira, and Mario Sperenzi. *Teatro e spettacolo nella Firenze dei Medici: Modelli dei luoghi teatrali.* Florence: Olschki, 2001.

Gerbino, Giuseppe. "The Quest for the Soprano Voice: Castrati in Renaissance Italy." *Studi Musicali* 33 (2004): 303–358.

Giazotti, Remo. *Le due patrie di Giulio Romano.* Florence: Olschki, 1984.

Gilbert, Sandra, and Susan Gubar. *The Madwoman in the Attic.* New Haven: Yale University Press, 1979.

Glinski, Matteo. *La prima stagione lirica italiana all'estero 1628.* Quaderni dell'Accademia Chigiana 4. Siena: Ticci Editore Libraio, 1943.

Godt, Irving. "I casi di Arianna." *Rivista italiana di musicologia* 29 (1994): 315–359.

Gordon, Bonnie. *Monteverdi's Unruly Women: The Power of Song in Early Modern Italy.* Cambridge: Cambridge University Press, 2005.

Greenblatt, Stephen. *Renaissance Self-Fashioning: From More to Shakespeare.* Chicago: University of Chicago Press, 1980.

Greene, Thomas. "Labyrinth Dances in the French and English Renaissance." *Renaissance Quarterly* 54 (2001): 1403–1466.

Grillo, Angelo. *Lettere dell'Illustrissimo et Eccellentissimo Sig. Abbate D. Angelo Grillo Monaco Cassinentense raccolte dall'Illustro et Eccellentissimo Sig. Ottavio Menini.* Venice: Giovanni Battista Ciotti, 1602.

Guarini, Elena Fasano, ed. *Il Principato Mediceo.* Vol. 3, *Storia della civiltà toscana.* Florence: Le Monnier, 2003.

Guasco, Annibale. *Discourse to Lady Lavinia, His Daughter: Concerning the Manner in Which She Should Conduct Herself When Going to Court as Lady-in-Waiting to the Most Serene Infanta, Lady Caterina, Duchess of Savoy.* Edited by P. Osborn. Chicago: University of Chicago Press, 2003.

———. *Ragionamenti ad Lavinia sua figliola della maniera di governarsi in corte.* Turin: Eredi del Bevilacqua, 1586.

Halperin, David M. *How to Do the History of Homosexuality.* Chicago: University of Chicago, Press 2002.

Hammond, Frederick. "Musicians at the Medici Court in the Mid-Seventeenth Century." *Analecta musicologica* 14 (1974): 151–179.

Harness, Kelley. "Amazzoni di Dio: Florentine Musical Spectacle under Maria Maddalena d'Austria and Cristina di Lorena 1620–30." PhD diss., University of Illinois, 1996.

———. *Echoes of Women's Voices: Music, Art, and Female Patronage in Early Modern Florence.* Chicago: University of Chicago Press, 2006.

———. "*La Flora* and the End of Female Rule in Tuscany." *Journal of the American Musicological Society* 5 (1998): 437–476.

———. "Hapsburgs, Heretics and Horses: Equestrian Ballets and Other Staged Battles in Florence during the First Decade of the Thirty Years' War." In *L' arme e gli amori: Ariosto, Tasso and Guarini in Late Renaissance Florence.* Acts of an International Conference, Florence, Villa I Tatti, 27–29 June 2001. vol. 2, *Dynasty, Court and Imagery,* edited by Elena Fumagalli, Massimiliano Rossi, and Riccardo Spinelli, 255–283. Florence: Olschki, 2003.

Harper, John. *The Forms and Orders of Western Liturgy from the Tenth to the Eighteenth Century.* Oxford: Clarendon, 1991.

Harris, Barbara. "Women and Politics in Early Tudor England." *Historical Journal* 33 (1990): 259–281.

Heilbrun, Carolyn. *Writing a Woman's Life.* New York: Ballantine, 1989.

Heller, Wendy. "Chastity, Heroism, and Allure: Women in Opera of Seventeenth-Century Venice." PhD diss., Brandeis University, 1995.

———. *Emblems of Eloquence: Opera and Women's Voices in Seventeenth-Century Venice.* Berkeley: University of California Press, 2004.

Hill, John Walter. *La monodia in Toscana nuovi appunti sui manoscritti.* Forthcoming.

———. *Roman Monody, Cantata, and Opera from the Circles around Cardinal Montalto.* 2 vols. Oxford: Clarendon, 1997.

————. "Training a Singer for 'Musica Recitativa' in Early Seventeenth-Century Italy: The Case of Baldassare." In *Musicologia Humana: Studies in Honor of Warren and Ursula Kirkendale*, 345–357. Florence: Olschki, 1994.

Holford-Strevens, Leofranc. "'Her eyes become two spouts': Classical Antecedents of Renaissance Laments." *Early Music* 27 (1999): 379–393.

Holsinger, Bruce. *Music, Body and Desire in Medieval Culture.* Palo Alto: Stanford University Press, 2001.

Holzer, Robert. "'Sono d'altro garbo . . . Le canzonette che si cantano oggi': Pietro Della Valle on Music and Modernity in the Seventeenth Century." *Studi Musicali* 21 (1992): 253–306.

Imbert, Gaetano. *La vita fiorentina nel Seicento, secondo memorie sincrone: 1644–1670.* Florence: Bemporad, 1906.

Irigaray, Luce. "Women on the Market" and "Commodities among Themselves." In *This Sex Which Is Not One*, 170–191, 192–197. Ithaca: Cornell University Press, 1985.

Jenkins, Chadwick. "*Ridotta alla perfettione:* Metaphysics and History in the Music-Theoretical Writing of Giovanni Maria Artusi." PhD diss., Columbia University, 2007.

Jones, Ann Rosalind. *The Currency of Eros: Women's Love Lyric in Europe, 1540–1620.* Bloomington: Indiana University Press, 1990.

Jordan, Constance. *Renaissance Feminism: Literary Texts and Political Models.* Ithaca: Cornell University Press, 1990.

Kelso, Ruth. *The Doctrine of the Renaissance Lady.* Urbana: University of Illinois Press, 1956.

Kendrick, Robert L. *Celestial Sirens: Nuns and Their Music in Early Modern Milan.* Oxford Monographs on Music. Oxford: Oxford University Press, 1996.

Kirkendale, Warren. *The Court Musicians in Florence during the Principate of the Medici: With a Reconstruction of the Artistic Establishment.* Florence: Olschki, 1993.

————. *Emilio de' Cavalieri, Gentilhuomo Romano: His Life and Letters; His Role as Superintendent of All the Arts at the Medici Court and His Musical Compositions.* Florence: Olschki, 2001.

Klapisch-Zuber, Christiane. *Women, Family and Ritual in Renaissance Italy.* Translated by L. Cochrane. Chicago: University of Chicago Press, 1985.

Lami, Giovanni. *Amplissimi viri Richardi Romuli patrici florentini Vita in qua alia multa ad historiam florentinam spectantia e re nata tractantur.* Florence: Typographio ad Plateam Sanctae Crucis, 1748.

Laqueur, Thomas. *Making Sex: The Body and Gender from the Greeks to Freud.* Cambridge: Cambridge University Press, 1990.

Lenz, Maria Ludovica. *Donne e Madonne: L'educazione femminile nel primo Rinascimento italiano.* Turin: Loescher Editore, 1982.

Leopold, Silke. "Remigio Romano's Collection of Lyrics for Music." *Proceedings of the Royal Musical Association* 110 (1983): 45–61.

Litchfield, R. Burr. *Emergence of a Bureaucracy: The Florentine Patricians, 1530–1790.* Princeton: Princeton University Press, 1986.

Lorenzetti, Stefano. *Musica e identità nobiliare nell'Italia del Rinascimento: Educazione mentalità immaginario.* Florence: Olschki, 2003.

Lozzi, Carlo. "La musica e specialmente il melodramma alla corte medicea." *Rivista musicale italiana* 9 (1902): 297–338.

MacLean, Ian. *The Renaissance Notion of Woman.* Cambridge Monographs in the History of Medicine. Cambridge: Cambridge University Press, 1980.

MacNeil, Anne. *Music and Women of the Commedia dell'Arte in the Late Sixteenth Century.* New York: Oxford University Press, 2002.

———. "Weeping at the Water's Edge." *Early Music* 27, no. 3 (1999): 406–417.

Maffei, Camillo. *Delle lettere del Signor Gio. Camillo Maffei da Solofra libri due . . . v'è un discorso della voce e del modo d'apparare di cantar di garganta.* Naples: Raimondo Amato, 1562.

Maggi, Armando. *Uttering the Word: The Mystical Performances of Maria Maddalena de'Pazzi, a Renaissance Visionary.* Albany: SUNY Press, 1998.

Magini, Alessandro. "I Conti Bardi di Vernio." In *Neoplatonismo, musica, letteratura nel Rinascimento: I Bardi di Vernio e L'Accademia della Crusca: Atti del convegno internazionale di studi, Firenze-Vernio, 25–26 settembre 1998,* edited by Piero Gargiulo, Alessandro Magini, and Stéphane Toussaint, 195–249. Prato: Tipografia Cav. Alfredo Rindi, 2000.

Magrini, Tullia. "Women's 'Work of Pain' in Christian Mediterranean Europe." *Music and Anthropology* 3 (1998). http://www.levi.provincia.venezia.it/ma/index/number3/magrini/magro.htm.

Malanima, Paolo. *I Riccardi di Firenze: Una famiglia e un patrimonio nella toscana dei Medici.* Biblioteca di storia toscana moderna e contemporanea 15. Florence: Olschki, 1977.

———. "L'economia dei nobili a Firenze nei secoli xvii e xviii." *Società e storia* 14 (1991): 829–848.

Mamczarz, Irene. *Le Théâtre Farnese de Parme et le drame musical italien, 1618–1732.* Florence: Olschki, 1988.

Mamone, Sara. *Dèi, semidei, uomini: Lo spettacolo a Firenze tra neoplatonismo e realtà borghese (XV–XVII secolo).* Rome: Bulzoni, 2003.

Marangoni, Matteo. *La Villa del Poggio Imperiale.* Florence: Fratelli Alinari, n.d.

Marinelli, Lucretia. *The Nobility and Excellence of Women.* Edited and translated by Anne Dunhill; introduction by Letizia Panizza. Chicago: University of Chicago Press, 1999.

———. *La nobiltà et l'eccellenza delle donne co' diffetti e mancamenti degli uomini.* Venice: G. B. Ciotti, 1601.

Masera, Maria G. "Alcune lettere inedite di Francesca Caccini." *Rassegna musicale* 13 (1940): 173–182.

———. *Michelangelo Buonarroti il giovane.* Turin: Tipografia Vincenzo Bona, 1941.

———. "Una musicista fiorentina del Seicento: Francesca Caccini." *Rassegna musicale* 14 (1941): 181–207.

———. "Una musicista fiorentina del Seicento: Francesca Caccini." *Rassegna musicale* 15 (1942): 249–266.

Materdona, Gianfrancesco Maia. *Rime di Gianfrancesco Maria Materdona: Distinte in tre parti.* Vol. 2. Venice: Vangelista Deuchino, 1629.

Maylender, Michel. "Accademia degli Umoristi—Roma." In *Storia della Accademie d'Italia,* 5:370–384 Bologna: Lincinio Cappelli, 1930.

Mazzei, Rita. "Lucca e Firenze: I Lucchese Cavalieri di Santo Stefano in età Medicea." *Archivio storico italiano* 157 (1999): 269–283.

———. *La società Lucchese del Seicento.* Lucca: Maria Pacini Fazzi, 1977.

McClary, Susan. *Feminine Endings: Music, Gender and Sexuality.* Minneapolis: University of Minnesota Press, 1991.

———. *Modal Subjectivities: Self-Fashioning in the Italian Madrigal.* Berkeley: University of California Press, 2004.

———. "The Transition from Modal to Tonal Organization in the Works of Monteverdi." PhD diss., Harvard University, 1977.

McGee, Timothy. "Pompeo Caccini and 'Euridice': New Biographical Notes." *Renaissance and Reformation* 26 (1990): 81–99.

Meier, Bernhard. *The Modes of Classical Polyphony.* Translated by E. Beebe. New York: Broude Brothers, 1988.

Molinari, Cesare. *Le nozze degli Dei.* Rome: Bulzoni, 1968.

Monson, Craig. *Disembodied Voices: Music and Culture in an Early Modern Italian Convent.* Berkeley: University of California Press, 1995.

Monteverdi, Claudio. *Lettere dediche e prefazioni.* Edited by Domenico de Paoli. Rome: De Sanctis, 1973.

———. *Scherzi musicali cioè arie et madrigali in stil recitativo con una ciaccona a 1. e 2. voci.* Venice: Gardano, 1632,

Moreni, Domenico. *Lettere di Benedetto Menzini e del senatore Vincenzio da Filicaia a Francesco Redi.* Florence; Nella Stamperia Magheri, 1828.

Moretti, Maria Rosa. *Musica e costume a Genova trà Cinquecento e Seicento.* Genoa: Francesco Pirelli, 1992.

Muir, Edward. *Ritual in Early Modern Europe.* Cambridge: Cambridge University Press, 1997.

Muraro, Luisa. *L'ordine simbolico della madre.* Rome: Editori Riuniti, 1991.

Murata, Margaret. "Image and Eloquence: Secular Song," in *The Cambridge History of Seventeenth-Century Music,* ed. Tim Carter and John Butt, 378–425. Cambridge: Cambridge University Press, 2005.

———. "The Recitative Soliloquy." *Journal of the American Musicological Society* 32, no. 1 (1979): 45–73.

———. *Source Readings in Music History.* Vol. 4, *The Baroque Era.* Edited by L. Treitler. New York: Norton, 1998.

Murphy, Caroline. "Lavinia Fontana and 'le dame della città': Understanding Female Artistic Patronage in Late Sixteenth-Century Bologna." *Renaissance Studies* 10 (1996): 190–208.

———. *Murder of a Medici Princess.* Oxford: Oxford University Press, 2008.

Nerici, Luigi. *Storia della musica in Lucca.* Lucca: Tipografia Giusti, 1879.

Newcomb, Anthony. *The Madrigal at Ferrara.* Princeton: Princeton University Press, 1980.

Nogarola, Isotta. *Complete Writings.* Edited by Margaret L. King and Diana Robin. Chicago: University of Chicago Press, 2004.

Ossi, Massimo. *Divining the Oracle: Monteverdi's Seconda Prattica.* Chicago: University of Chicago Press, 2003.

Ovid [Publio Ovidio Nasone]. *Metamorphoses.* Translated by R. Humphries. Bloomington: Indiana University Press, 1955.

Palisca, Claude. "Aria Types in the Earliest Operas." *Journal of Seventeenth Century Music* 9, no. 1 (2003). http:www.sscm-jscm.org/jscm/v9/no1/Palisca.html.

———. *The Florentine Camerata: Documentary Studies and Translations.* New Haven: Yale University Press, 1989.

———. "Vincenzo Galilei and Some Links between 'Pseudo-Monody' and Monody." *Musical Quarterly* 46 (1960): 344–360.

Panichi, Ornella. "Due Stanze della Villa del Poggio Imperiale." *Antichità viva* 12, no. 5 (1973): 32–43.

———. *Villa di Poggio Imperiale: Lavori di Restauro e di Riordinamento, 1972–75.* Florence: Edan, 1973.

Paré, Ambroise. *Monstres et prodigues.* Paris, 1573.

Parenti, Giuseppe. "Fonti per lo studio della demografia fiorentina. I libri dei morti." *Genus* 6–8 (1943–49): 281–301.

Park, Katherine. "The Rediscovery of the Clitoris." In *The Body in Parts: Fantasies of Corporeality in Early Modern Europe,* edited by Carla Mazzio and David Hillman, 171–193. London: Routledge, 1997.

Parker, Geoffrey. *Philip II.* London: Hutchinson, 1994.

Parker, Patricia. "Fantasies of 'Race' and 'Gender': Africa, Othello and Bringing to Light." In *Women, "Race" and Writing in the Early Modern Period,* edited by Margo Hendricks and Patricia Parker, 84–100. London: Routledge, 1994.

Patrizi, Francesco. *L'amorosa filosofia.* Edited by J. C. Nelson. Florence: Le Monnier, 1963.

Pellegrini, Amedeo. *Relazioni inedite di ambasciatori Lucchesi alle corti di Firenze, Genova, Milano, Modena, Parma, Torino, Sec. XVI–XVII.* Lucca: A. Pellicci, 1902.

Pieraccini, Gaetano. *La Stirpe de Medici di Cafaggiolo.* Vol. 2, Florence: Vallecchi, 1947.

Pirrotta, Nino. "Early Opera and Aria." In *Music and Theatre from Poliziano to Monteverdi,* edited by N. P. and E. Povoledo. Cambridge: Cambridge University Press, 1982.

Plato. *The Laws.* Translated by R. G. Bury. Loeb Classical Library, 9–10. New York: Putnam and Sons, 1926.

Porter, Roy, and Mikalàs Teich, eds. *Sexual Knowledge, Sexual Science.* Cambridge: Cambridge University Press, 1994.

Predota, Georg. "Towards a Reconsideration of the Romanesca: Francesca Caccini's *Primo libro delle musiche* and Contemporary Monodic Settings in the First Quarter of the Seventeenth Century." *Recercare* 5 (1993): 87–113.

Raney, Carolyn. "Francesca Caccini, Musician to the Medici, and Her *Primo Libro* (1618)." PhD diss., New York University School of Education, 1971.

Razzi, Serafino. *Sermoni per le più solenne così domeniche come feste de' santi.* Florence: Bartolomeo Sermartelli, 1575.

Reardon, Colleen. *Holy Concord within Sacred Walls: Nuns and Music in Siena, 1575–1700.* New York: Oxford University Press, 2002.

Reid, Jane Davidson, ed. *The Oxford Guide to Classical Mythology in the Arts, 1300–1900.* Vol. 1. Oxford: Oxford University Press, 1993.

Richa, Giuseppe. *Notizie istoriche delle chiese fiorentine devise ne' suoi quartieri.* Rome: N.p., 1754–62.

Roach, Joseph. *Cities of the Dead: Circum-Atlantic Performance.* New York: Columbia University Press, 1996.

Rocke, Michael. *Forbidden Friendships: Homosexuality and Male Culture in Renaissance Florence.* New York: Oxford University Press, 1996.

Romano, Remigio. *Seconda raccolta di canzonette musicali: Bellissime per cantare, et suonare, sopra arie moderne.* Vicenza: Salvadori, 1620.

Rosand, Ellen. "The Descending Tetrachord: An Emblem of Lament." *Musical Quarterly* 55 (1979): 346–359.

———. "'Senza necessità del canto dell'autore': Printed Singing Lessons in Seventeenth-Century Italy." In *Atti del XIV congresso della Societa Internazionale di Musicologia, Bologna, 1987: Trasmissione e recezione delle forme di cultura musicale*, edited by A. Pompilio, 214–224 Turin: Edizioni di Torino, 1990.

Routley, Nicholas. *Arianna Thrice Betrayed*. Armidale, New South Wales: University of New England Press, 1998.

Rowe, Katherine. "'God's handy work': Divine Complicity and the Anatomist's Touch." In *The Body in Parts: Fantasies of Corporeality in Early Modern Europe*, edited by Carla Mazzio and David Hillman, 285–309. London: Routledge, 1997.

Rubin, Gayle. "The Traffic in Women: Notes on the 'Political Economy' of Sex." In *Feminism and History*, edited by J. W. Scott, 105–151. Oxford: Oxford University Press, 1996.

Salvadori, Andrea. *Le poesie del sig. Andrea Salvadori fra le quali contengonsi unite insieme tutte quelle, che furono divisamente impresse in diverse stampe vivente l'autore, e l'altre non piu divulgate*. Rome: Michele Ercole, 1668.

Sanford, Sally. "A Comparison of French and Italian Singing in the 17th Century." *Journal of Seventeenth Century Music* 1 (1995). http://www.sscm.harvard.edu/jscm.

———. "Seventeenth- and Eighteenth-Century Vocal Style and Technique." D.M.A. diss., Stanford University, 1979.

Sansovino, Francesco. *L'Edificio del corpo humano nel qual brevemente si descrivono le qualità del corpo del huomo e le potentie dell'anima*. Vol. 2. Venice: Comin da Trino Monferrato, 1550.

Saracinelli, Ferdinando. *La liberazione di Ruggiero dall'isola d'Alcina*. Florence: Pietro Cecconcelli, 1625.

Saracini, Claudio. *Le musiche*. Venetia: Giacomo Vincenti, 1614.

Saslow, James. *The Medici Wedding of 1589*. New Haven: Yale University Press, 1996.

Schechner, Richard. *Between Theater and Anthropology*. Philadelphia: University of Pennsylvania Press, 1985.

Scott, Joan Wallach. "Gender, a Useful Category of Historical Analysis." In *Feminism and History*, edited by Joan Wallach Scott, 152–180. New York: Oxford University Press, 1996.

Sherman, Bernard D. *Inside Early Music: Conversations with Performers*. New York: Oxford University Press, 1997.

Silbert, Doris. "Francesca Caccini, called La Cecchina." *Musical Quarterly* 32 (1946): 50–62.

Solerti, Angelo. *Gli albori del melodramma (Milano, 1904)*. Hildesheim: Georg Olms, 1969.

———. "Laura Guidiccioni Lucchesini ed Emilio d'Cavalieri: I primi tentativi del melodramma." *Rivista musicale italiana* 9 (1902): 797–829.

———. *Musica, ballo e drammatica alla Corte medicea dal 1600 al 1637: Notizie tratte da un diario con appendice di testi inediti e rari*. Bibliotheca musica Bononiensis. Bologna: A. Forni, 1989; reprint, Florence, 1905.

Stefani, Giovanni. *Affetti amorosi canzonette ad una voce sola poste in musica da diversi con le parte del basso, & le lettere dell'alfabeto per la chittarra alla spagnole raccolto da Giov. Stefani con tre arie siciliane, et due vilanelle spagnolo*. Venice: Giacomo Vincenti, 1618.

Strocchia, Sharon. *Death and Ritual in Renaissance Florence*. Baltimore: Johns Hopkins University Press, 1992.

Tagliavini, Luigi F. "Metrica e ritmica nei 'modi di cantare ottavi.'" In *Forme e vicende, Per Giovanni Pozzi*, edited by Ottavio Besomi, 239–267 Padua: Antenore, 1988.

Tamassia, Nino. *La famiglia italiana nei secoli XV e XVI*. Rome: Multigrafica, 1971.

Tasso, Torquato. "Dialogo delle virtù donnesche." In *Dialoghi*, edited by G. Baffetti. Milan: Rizzoli, 1998.

———.*Tasso's Dialogues: A Selection with the Discourse on the Art of the Dialogue*. Translated with introduction and notes by Carnes Lord and Dain A. Trafton. Berkeley: University of California Press, 1982.

Tomlinson, Gary. "The Historian, the Performer and Authentic Meaning in Music." In *Authenticity and Early Music*, edited by N. Kenyon, 115–136. Oxford: Oxford University Press, 1988.

———. *Italian Secular Song, 1606–1636*. Vols. 1–2. New York: Garland, 1986.

———. "Madrigal, Monody and Monteverdi's via naturale alla immitatione." *Journal of the American Musicological Society* 34 (1981): 60–108.

———. *Metaphysical Song*. Princeton: Princeton University Press, 1999.

Totaro, Pina. *Donne, filosofia e cultura nel Seicento*. Rome: Consiglio nazionale delle ricerche, 1999.

Traub, Valerie. *The Renaissance of Lesbianism in Early Modern Europe*. Cambridge: Cambridge University Press, 2002.

Treadwell, Nina. "The 'Chitarra Spagnuola' and Italian Monody, 1589–c. 1650." Master's thesis, University of Southern California, 1995.

———. *Music and Wonder at the Medici Court: The 1589 Interlude for "La pellegrina."* Bloomington: Indiana University Press, 2008.

———. "Restaging the Siren: Musical Women in the Performance of Sixteenth-Century Italian Theatre." PhD diss., University of Southern California, 2000.

Turci, Marcello, ed. *Opere di Gabriello Chiabrera e lirici non marinisti del Seicento*. Turin: Utet, 1970.

Varese, Claudio. "Ideologia, letteratura e teatro nella *Fiera* di Michelangelo Buonarroti il giovane." In *Firenze e la Toscana dei Medici nell'europeo del '500*, 585–610. Florence: Olschki, 1983.

Vickers, Brian. "Leisure and Idleness in the Renaissance: The Ambivalence of Otium." *Renaissance Studies* 4, no. 1 (1990): 1–37.

Walker, Daniel P., ed. *Musique des intermèdes de la Pellegrina*. Paris: Editions du Centre national de la recherche scientifique, 1963.

Warburg, Aby. "I costumi teatrali per gli Intermezzi del 1589: I disegni di Bernardo Buontalenti e il 'Libro di conti' di Emilio de' Cavalieri." In *Gesammelte Schriften*, edited by G. Bing, 259–300, 394–441. Leipzig: Teubner, 1932.

Weaver, Elissa B. *Convent Theatre in Early Modern Italy: Spiritual Fun and Learning for Women*. Cambridge: Cambridge University Press, 2002.

Weaver, Robert Lamar. *A Chronology of Music in the Florentine Theater 1590–1750: Operas, Prologues, Finales, Intermezzos, and Plays with Incidental Music*. Detroit: Information Coordinators, 1978.

Westergard, Peter. "Toward a 12-Tone Polyphony: Perspectives on Contemporary Music Theory." In *Perspectives on Contemporary Music Theory*, edited by Benjamin Boretz and Edward. T. Cone. New York: Norton, 1972.

Wiering, Frans. *The Language of the Modes*. New York: Routledge, 2001.

Wilbourne, Emily. "La Florinda: The Performance of Virginia Ramponi Andreini," PhD diss., New York University, 2008.

Wistreich, Richard. *Courtier, Warrior, Singer: Giulio Cesare Brancaccio and the Performance of Identity in Late Renaissance Italy*. Aldershot: Ashgate, 2007.

Woolf, Virginia. *A Room of One's Own*. London: Harcourt Brace and World, 1929.

———. *Three Guineas*. New York: Harcourt Brace, 1938.

Yates, Frances. *Astrea: The Imperial Theme in the Sixteenth Century*. London: Routledge and Kegan Paul, 1975.

Zannini, G. Ludovico Masetti. *Motivi storici dell'educazione femminile (1500–1650)*. Naples: M. D'Auria, 1982.

Zarlino, Gioseffo. *Le istitutione harmoniche*. Venetia: Pietro da Fino, 1558.

Index

Note: page numbers in italics refer to illustrations or musical examples; a t following a page number indicates a table.